PROPHECY

THE CHILDREN OF THE WHITE LIONS
VOLUME II

R.T. KAELIN

ISBN-13: 978-0-615-67885-6

Book Design by Donna Overall
donnaoverall@bellsouth.net

Cover Design by R. T. Kaelin
Cover Art by Donna Overall

Terrene
Press
Columbus, Ohio
www.terrene.info

"R.T. teaches a master class in world-building. Rich in characters and details, he pulls you through a breathtaking tale that surpasses good versus evil."
— *Jean Rabe, USA Today bestselling author*

"R.T. Kaelin is one of those few new authors who understand both the importance of immersing the reader in the story and how to accomplish it. From the first word, he grabs you and holds you captive throughout. I enjoyed reading *Progeny* and look forward to more books from R.T. Kaelin."
— *Maxwell Alexander Drake, Author of Genesis of Oblivion Saga*

"After an exciting adventure getting to know the characters and backgrounds of our promising heroes in *Progeny*, R.T. Kaelin does a phenomenal job developing these young heroes into the warriors they must become in *Prophecy*, the second installation of the White Lions series. This is a refreshingly beautiful coming-of-age story of courage, hope, and young love; something the fantasy genre has lacked in recent years."
— *T.L. Gray, Author of The Arcainian series*

"Overall, I would favorably compare his writing with Brandon Sanderson, Scott Lynch, (early) Robert Jordan and even a bit of David Eddings flavor mixed in."
— *LuxuryReading.com*

"R.T. Kaelin has done it again. Beautifully rich characters combine with an entrancing plot in a compelling dance certain to allure current and new fans of the White Lion series."
—*Mandy O'Brien, Living Peacefully with Children*

"I found the author carefully planned out the topography, the language, the poetry, the events and the battles just like Tolkien did and I think that is partly why I loved the book so much."
— *Family Literacy and You*

ACKNOWLEDGEMENTS

First and foremost, I must thank my wife for putting up with me and this unexpected dream. You are a wonderful woman, wife, and mother. To my children, Nikalys and Kennedy, who helped inspire me to write in the first place: thank you and I love you.

To Mom, Donna, Diane, Caleb, Nate, Jean, Chris, Jim, Dani, Charlotte, Mike, Lee, Caroline, Jessica, Talita, Kenneth, Simon, Rose, T.L., and Uriah: thank you for your help, support, and guidance. I cannot tell you how much I appreciate it.

CONTENTS

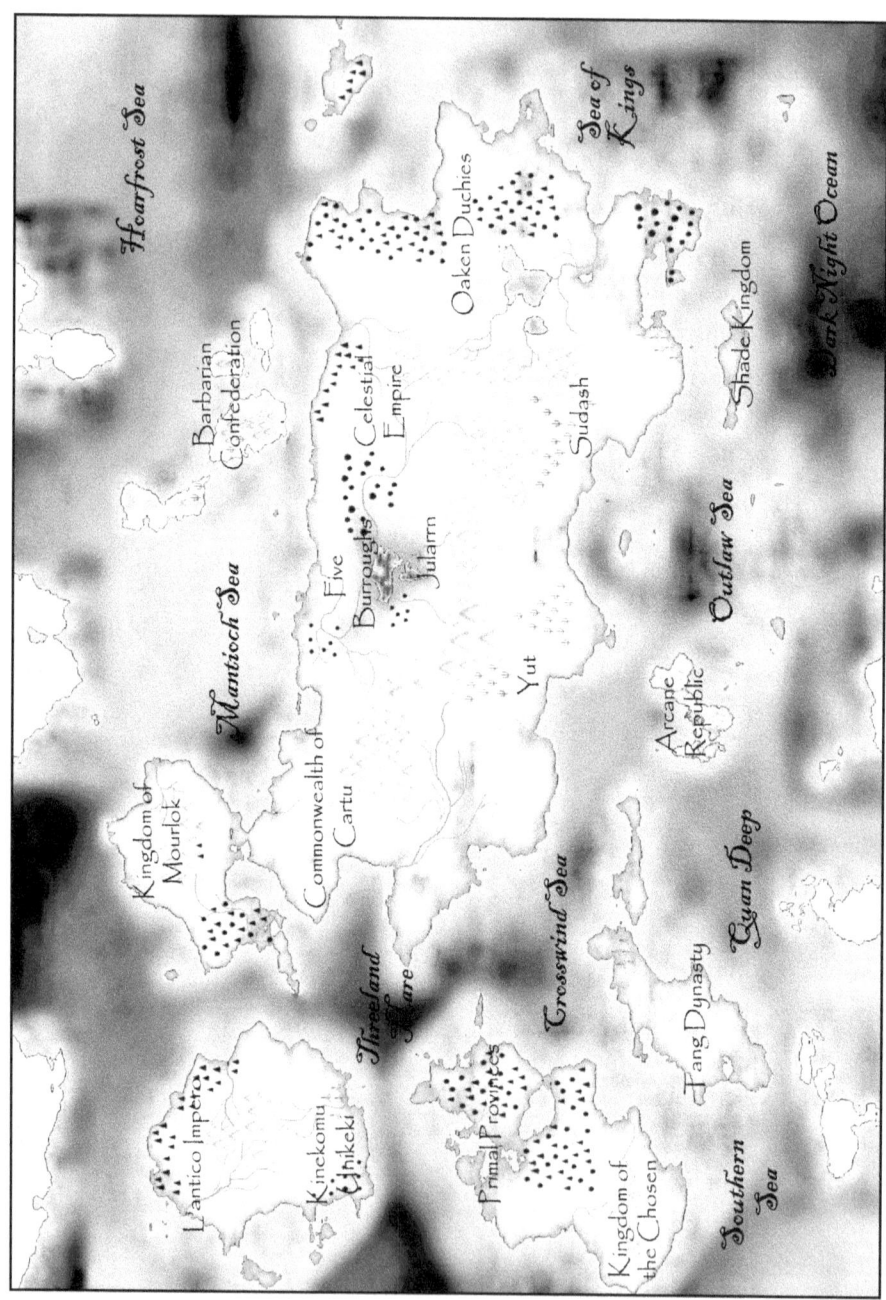

TERRENE

The roar of the Lions will drive back the spawn,
And the lines of men, strong once again, will be redrawn.
Yet that which drives man's soul will fray at the seams,
While the strength of the Lions will fade as do last night's dreams.

Torn apart by deceit and distrust,
One will perish and One will be lost.
One will leave, while Another will stay.
And Two shall find each Other one day.
Against his will, one must fight,
While it falls upon the Half-man to unite.

Chaos will rise again, unraveling what has been made,
With Strife, Pain, and Deception in tow, lending aid.
Hidden, then found,
Willingly come around,
The Progeny must rise to lead the fight,
Along with new and old, seek to make it right.

– As recorded by High Priest en'Sul, First of Indrida
   3rd day of the Turn of Lamoth, 4639

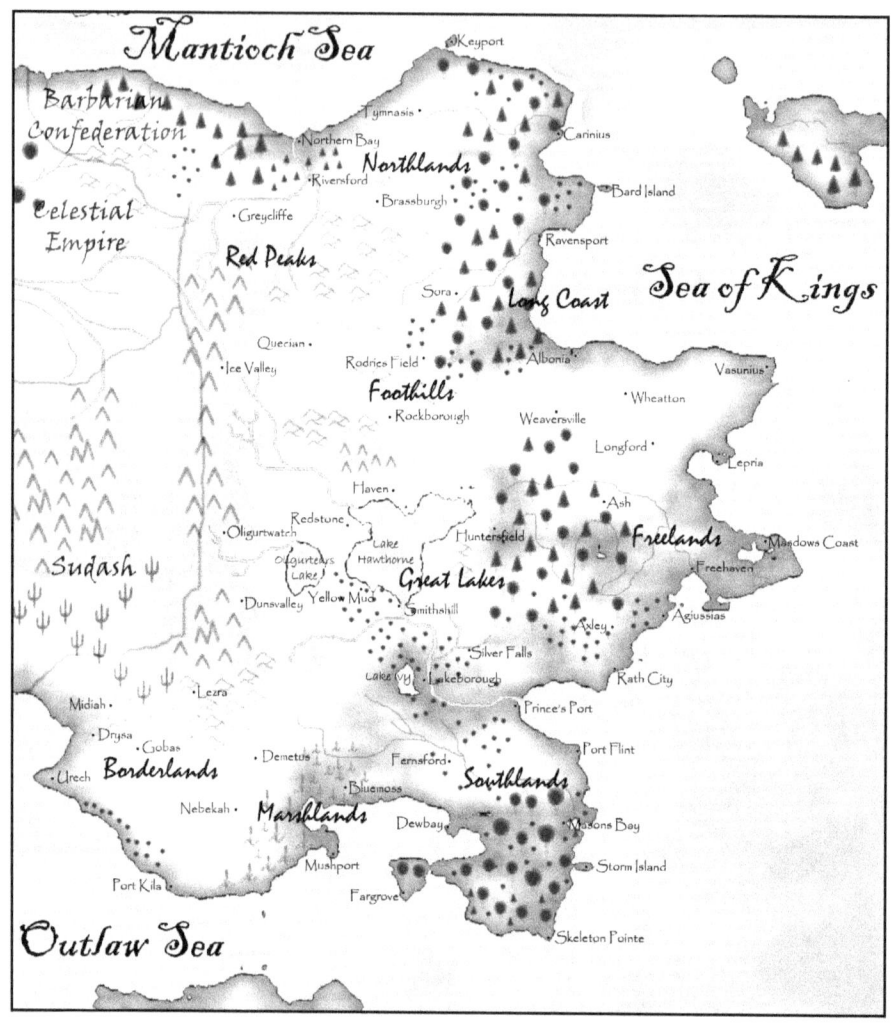

THE OAKEN DUCHIES

PROLOGUE

5ᵗʰ of the Turn of Roden, 4751

Tandyr stared at the tiny village on the far side of the wooden bridge. A weary sigh worn from the ages slipped from his lips.

Mountain peaks towered over the settlement of Nentnay, the jagged, slate gray rock a stark backdrop to the lush, green valley in which he stood. Snowmelt from the white-capped range fed the river that rushed under the bridge, tumbling over the smooth rocks and filling the air with a vibrant, almost happy, gurgling sound. Silver fish the length of his hand stubbornly attempted to swim upstream, leaping into the air before falling back to the water to be swept away by the current. Birds warbled in the evergreen branches.

The idyllic setting had no effect on Tandyr. He eyed the village, a frown on his wide lips, consumed with tired skepticism. He noted the need to have a talk with Jhaell, his new researcher at Immylla. The saeljul preceptor had insisted repeatedly that his research pointed to one of the stones being in or near this village. Tandyr had had his doubts, even after reading Jhaell's purported proof: a scrawled inscription in the back of an old Cartusian book about farming.

"This cannot possibly be the right place."

Nentnay could not have been more out of the way. He had trekked for three days from Tutetup—the nearest town of any note—stumbling over the rocky, winding trail that ran along the river. What he sought should never have been left to rot in such obscurity.

He took a long, deep breath of mountain air and exhaled.

"Well, I am here now."

He stepped onto the bridge, his sandaled feet scuffing the damp boards. Built of planks cut from the spruce pines that dominated the region's thick forest, the bridge was coated with some sort of resin that had turned the grain a deep, crimson red. Tandyr found the color garish and out of place. This area of southern Cartu was mostly a palette of greens, stony grays, and fertile browns.

As Tandyr stepped from the bridge and onto the road that ran into Nentnay, he lifted the hem of his black robe several inches. His feet squished as he walked and the cold slime of mud slipped between his toes. He regretted not purchasing those boots from the street hawker in Tutetup.

The sun was fighting its way through the canopy of rain clouds left over from a mid-morning shower, but was losing its battle. The damp air of the valley was chillier than recent days, but most definitely welcome. Three days ago, he had been roasting in the plains of Yut.

Colossal, moss-covered boulders rose from a low-lying blanket of mist, looking like hunks of potatoes floating atop a thick stew. Carefree, happy voices drifted through the haze. Somewhere ahead of him, a chicken clucked.

The longhouses of Nentnay were built using the great, round pine trunks, stained the same crimson red as the bridge. At both ends of each structure two logs protruded high into the air, crossing one another and continuing for another ten feet, their sharp angles reminiscent of the sheer mountains to the north. Smoke curled from the tops of stone chimneys, drifting upward to become one with the foggy mist. The smell of charred wood smoke filled the air, swirling with the fresh, clean aroma of spruce sap.

As Nentnay was so near the border, the skin tones of the men and women were mixed, ranging from the dark, nutty brown common to most Yutians to the paler skin of southern Cartusians. Nearly everyone he saw had thick, brown or black hair, making his own long, whitish-blonde hair—pulled together and bound by three cords—decidedly out of place. As were his elongated arms, fingers, and facial features. He suspected he was the first saeljul any of these people had seen. The inquisitive, silent looks he received as he strode past the first buildings confirmed it for him.

Several dozen paces into the village, he halted. The happy chatter he had heard earlier on his way into Nentnay was gone. The only sounds in the village were the rush of the river and the songbirds' chirping.

Standing before one of the longhouses on his right were three men and a boy, all dressed in stitched leather tunics and breeches.

"Excuse me. I was wondering if you might assist me with something?"

All four stared at him, mute.

After a moment, Tandyr lifted an eyebrow and raised his voice a bit. "I said, I was wondering if you—"

"Are you an ijul?" asked the boy suddenly. The question was spoken in Argot, the accent clipped and short.

The man closest to the child reached out to put his hand on the boy's shoulder. He whispered to him, quiet enough that the sound of the river washed away his words. Tandyr's gaze shifted between the pair. Their tan skin was of similar tone and their thick, wavy black hair was nearly identical.

Turning, he approached who he reasoned were father and son. The other men standing with them both took a few, quick, unconscious steps backwards. One bumped into the wall of the longhouse.

Tandyr offered the boy a slight smile and asked gently, "Do I look like an ijul to you?"

The boy nodded once.

"Yes."

"Ah…" murmured Tandyr. "And have you ever seen an ijul?"

Shaking his head, the boy said, "No."

"Then how would you know what one looks like?"

"Batta tells us stories."

"Does he?" asked Tandyr. "And what do ijul in…Batta's stories look like?"

"Hair that shines as bright as the sun, arms that flow like a river reed blowing in a soft breeze, and the quiet grace of a snow leopard."

Tandyr smiled at the flowery description.

"Batta sounds like a good storyteller."

"He is," replied the boy. "He knows a lot of them on account he's so—"

"Menet!" interjected the boy's father. "That is enough." Glaring at his son, the man muttered, "Go inside with your mothers, please."

"But I—"

"Now, Menet!"

Tandyr lifted his gaze to the father. The man's tone was curiously terse.

Menet scowled at his father as he mumbled, "Yes, Father." He scampered to the entrance of the longhouse, lifted some sort of tanned animal skin hanging from the entryway, and disappeared inside the darkened interior.

Tandyr returned his attention to the three men. The two against the wall had withdrawn further and were now sweating, an unusual fact due to the slight chill in the air. Menet's father showed a touch more steel, holding Tandyr's gaze without flinching.

"You," said Tandyr, nodding at the father. "What is your name?"

The man hesitated a moment before answering.

"I am called Dese."

"Greetings, Dese," said Tandyr. "I have been seeking some unusual…things for quite some time now. I have reason to believe one might be here."

Dese remained motionless and quiet, the defiant glint in his eye irritating Tandyr. Eventually, the man spoke with a frown.

"We are a simple people, wanderer. Unless you consider hide, fish, or pine-wood 'unusual,' I fear your journey has been in vain. Perhaps you should look elsewhere."

The inquisitive cluck of a chicken pulled Tandyr's attention to the longhouse's corner. A single brown-feathered fowl emerged from the side of the building, strutting, its head bobbing as it walked.

Looking back to the man, Tandyr said, "I find your words to be less than hospitable, Dese."

Dese's face hardened.

"Hospitality is for friends and neighbors, ijul. You are neither."

Tandyr regarded the man, studying him. He was brave. Brainless, but brave.

"Ah," muttered Tandyr. "I see." His gaze flicked to the pair of men standing behind Dese. "Are these your friends, Dese?"

Dese crossed his arms over his chest, the colored beads hanging from strings draping along the sleeves clicking softly against one another.

"They are my brothers."

Tandyr studied the two men. One had dark skin and a bald pate, while the other had light skin and long, light brown hair held that fell past his shoulders.

"Truly?" said Tandyr with honest surprise. "They look nothing like you."

"We share the same father," replied Dese. "We are house brothers."

Tandyr expected some sort of explanation would be forthcoming, yet Dese offered none. The Cartusian's reticence was starting to irritate him. As he stood there, waiting, the chicken wandered between him and three villagers, pecking at the ground as it searched for a stray seed or grub.

"Which of your 'house brothers' do you care for more, Dese?"

The man stiffened.

"Pardon?"

"It is a simple question," said Tandyr, an edge to his voice now. Nodding to the pair of men, he asked plainly, "Which is your favorite?"

The man's expression shifted, his worry deepening.

"Why do you ask?"

Tandyr glared at the man.

"Answer my question, man."

Dese's eyebrows drew together.

"Who are you, ijul?"

Tandyr was trying to keep calm, but this mortal was not making it easy.

"Choose, Dese." He peered between the two men against the wall. "Or I will choose for you."

The man stared at Tandyr for a long, quiet moment. The chicken at their feet clucked softly.

Tandyr's eyes narrowed. Lowering his voice, he said, "Surely you are wondering: choose them for what?"

Reaching for the bright white Strands of Air, Tandyr knit a quick pattern and directed the Weave around the chicken. The fowl squawked in alarm as it was suddenly held in place, prevented from continuing its leisurely search for grubs or whatever it was chickens ate.

Tandyr lifted his gaze to the three men and found the trio staring at the fowl with wide eyes. He allowed himself a tiny smile.

He glanced around the village once, wondering if he might encounter resistance. He severely doubted any competent Air mage would languish here, but over the years, he had learned to be careful. When he did not spot even a flicker of recognition in anyone's eyes, Tandyr looked back down and tightened the Weave.

Instantly, the chicken's clucking morphed into sharp shrieks of pain, slicing through the misty solitude of the mountain valley. Other villagers stared in shock as the bird thrashed helplessly, screeching as Tandyr's pulsating white Weave slowly constricted around its body. Men and women rushed from longhouses and onto the muddy road, drawn by the chicken's cries. He took his time, hoping to draw the entire village out.

As the street filled, the brown-feathered fowl stopped squawking, no longer able to draw breath. At that point, Tandyr squeezed the Weave tight, eliciting a series of moist, crunching pops. The chicken's yellow-beaked head lolled to one side and Tandyr released the Weave, letting the bird fall limply to the ground.

Dese, his brothers, and the citizens of Nentnay stared at the dead bird in wide-eyed silence. The boy, Menet, was peering out from behind the leather skin covering of the entryway, his eyes locked on Tandyr rather than the bird. A dark-skinned woman stood behind him, hovering protectively.

Raising his voice so everyone could hear, Tandyr said, "If you answer my questions, nothing else needs to die today."

If he could avoid killing anyone, he would do so. Stories spread when strange ijuli marched into villages, indiscriminately killing people. Chickens, less so.

"Now, I'm looking for a stone." Lifting his hand, he extended his long, thin thumb and said, "It is supposedly the size of one's—" He stopped when he noticed Dese's gaze shift, flicking to something behind him. Turning around quickly, he spotted a figure shuffling towards him, feet scuffling in the muddy road.

Tandyr's already wide eyes grew round.

The individual that was approaching was tall and incredibly thin, more so than even a malnourished ijul. Lightweight linen robes hung from his bony frame like too-dry stringmoss drooping from a willow tree. Skin as thin as scraped parchment covered his hands and skull, stretched so tight that it seemed that any sudden movement might split it open. His head was bald, his lips so slender they were nearly absent. Vibrant blue eyes perched over a pair of dual vertical slits where most had a nose.

Clean, unadulterated excitement flooded Tandyr's veins. He had finally found one of them.

The aicenai moved deliberately, padding ever closer to Tandyr. Halting a dozen paces away, he fixed Tandyr with a sharp, intelligent stare and sighed. The long, weary breath sounded eons old itself.

Tandyr tilted his head, observing, "You sound tired."

"I am," replied the aicenai. His voice reminded Tandyr of a faint breeze rustling through a field of tall grass "Very...*very* tired."

With a respectful incline of his head, Tandyr said, "The years have been hard on you, have they not?"

The parchment-like skin around the aicenai's eyes crinkled. "Your concern is as false as it is unnecessary." Each word was spoken with a drawn out deliberateness. "My plight does not matter to you."

Tandyr shrugged, saying, "Believe what you must." He paused a moment, half expecting the figure to disappear at any moment. "What are you called?"

"Batta Badukralda."

Tandyr glanced over his shoulder, back to where the boy stood in the long-house entryway.

"You are young Menet's storyteller, then, are you?"

Batta ignored the question entirely, his bright eyes locked on Tandyr, legitimate confusion etched in the lines of his face. Leaning forward as if trying to see inside of Tandyr, he asked, "Which of the nine are you?"

Tandyr smiled.

"Surely you know that your talent will not work on me."

Batta nodded slowly.

"I am aware. That is why I am asking the question. *Which* of the nine are you?"

The question gave Tandyr a moment's pause.

"What do you mean? Which of the nine what?"

The ancient aicenai shook his head.

"Do not patronize me. I know what you are, what is housed in that saeljul's form."

Curious, Tandyr took a number of steps closer to Batta.

"How could you?"

Time—and many mistakes—had taught Tandyr it was best he keep his identities, both of them, a closely guarded secret. Only a handful of individuals throughout all of Terrene knew who he truly was.

Batta held his ground against Tandyr's slow advance and, in a voice wheezing like a late-Harvest wind, said, "We discovered what the Suštinata was."

"Did you?" asked Tandyr.

The aicenai nodded, his eyes narrowing.

"It was only a matter of time before your kind came looking for it."

Tandyr could not hold back the grin that sought to spread wide over his face. His mortal heartbeat quickened even as he tried to temper his excitement. He needed to keep control of his emotions, else his true nature might escape. He took a deep, steadying breath.

"So one of them is here, then?"

With a slow nod, Batta said, "It is."

Tandyr's heart pounded harder, accompanied by a sudden surge of suspicion. This was too good to be true. Halting in the street, he stared hard at Batta.

"What game do you play with me, aicenai?"

Batta shook his head.

"I play no game."

Tandyr did not believe him.

"You know what the Suštinata is?"

"I do," muttered Batta. "I have for nearly nine hundred years."

Cocking a surprised eyebrow, Tandyr asked, "Why did you not fulfill your promise?"

"It was best the stone remain lost."

"You broke your oath."

A flicker of grimace touched Batta's thin lips.

"Regrettable, but necessary."

Lifting his gaze to the sprawling pine forest, the towering Yaubno Mountains to the north, and the rustic longhouses, Tandyr asked, "Why here?"

Sadness trickled briefly over Batta's wizened face. "When the others perished, I continued our charge for a time. However, I grew weary of hiding." Looking around at the forest and mountains, he said, "We had studied in this valley long ago, and it pleased me. So, I came back." His gaze drifted to the villagers behind Tandyr. "The people here are kind and quiet."

Tandyr was almost disappointed. He had expected that when he found one of the stones, it would be protected by a thousand mages or the army of three nations.

"How long have you been here?"

Batta shrugged.

"I have lost count of the years. A few hundred or so."

Tandyr's eyes grew wide. His search had been underway for eons. To discover that one of the Suštinata had been sitting in one place for so long, unprotected, was terribly frustrating.

"Where is it?"

Batta lifted a bony arm and pointed down the street, further into town. Swiveling his head, Tandyr spotted four wooden poles in the middle of the street, arranged around a gray stone pedestal. Four more logs rose from the posts at an angle, meeting at a point and providing the frame for a roof that was not there. Unlike the red, treated wood in the rest of the village, these poles were gray. Years of weather had leached any color from the wood.

"The shrine?" muttered Tandyr.

In small villages like Nentnay, worship to the entire pantheon of Gods and Goddesses was done in a single shrine like the one in the street. Only cities had temples.

"The stone is there," answered Batta. "I assure you."

In disbelief, Tandyr asked, "You left it out in the open?"

Batta shook his head, a slight smile gracing his lips.

"No, that would be unwise."

Tandyr glared at him, confused.

"What do you mean?"

"It is inside the box."

Tandyr looked back to the shrine and, for the first time, noticed a small black box resting atop the stone pedestal. He was so close.

"You are going to simply give it to me?"

"I am."

After countless years of frustration, innumerable dead ends, and dozens of failed attempts to find the Suštinata, finding one like this was terribly anticlimactic.

Tandyr stared at Batta and shook his head. Something was not right here.

"You truly have no intention of stopping me?"

"I am but a scholar and a simple mage," replied Batta. "I was the least talented of the Daputa Devet. How can *I* ever hope to stand against one of the Cabal?"

A number of nearby villagers drew in quick breaths.

Tandyr pressed his lips together and strode closer to the ancient figure, glaring at him as the villagers' quiet murmuring rippled outward through the street.

"You fool. I have to kill them, now."

Batta inclined his head sadly.

"As I expected."

The villagers' murmuring was growing louder by the moment, more agitated.

Glowering at the aicenai, he muttered, "You know far less than you think, Batta. I had no intention of hurting anyone today."

Batta's eyes widened a fraction, an unusual display of surprise for an aicenai, as Tandyr began to reach for a massive number of Strands of Air.

Shaking his head, the God of Chaos said, "But now...now I must. Rumors cannot spread." He glanced up into the air, knitting the Strands together. "You might be interested to know that this is the *first* stone we have found, Batta."

The aicenai's wise, ancient eyes opened wide.

"No..."

"Oh, yes," said Tandyr. "These people were fated to live long lives, Batta. Menet's great-grandchildren would have been long dead at the rate we are going."

Batta's gaze shot beyond Tandyr to rest upon the souls he had doomed.

As Tandyr pulled the Strands into a large and complex pattern, he kept a careful eye on the old figure, waiting for some sort of retaliation. When none came, none at all, he smiled. This was going to be easy.

Looping one brilliant white Strand after another, twisting them into a massive, globed pattern, he said, "I had thought Nelnora brilliant for entrusting your kind with the stones."

A steady wind began to blow through boughs of the spruce forest. His robes fluttered in the new breeze. The low-lying mist in the village began to swirl and twist. The villagers stared around them, wide-eyed.

Raising his voice to be heard over the creaking trees, Tandyr said, "Yet, every plan has a flaw. And you, Batta, are this one's."

The aicenai dropped his head and stared at the ground.

Tandyr finished the Weave, held onto the completed pattern for a moment, and stared at the aicenai.

"Give Maeana my regards."

With that, Tandyr expanded the Weave in all directions, quickly encompassing the entire village. The wind surged, whipping furiously through Nentnay as every last breath of air was sucked from inside the Weave and thrust outside the crisscrossing pattern. Tandyr ensured he kept a single pocket of air around him.

Breath was ripped from the aicenai's lungs as Batta begin to silently choke. His eyes bulged outward as if someone was poking them from inside his head. Disgusted by the sight, Tandyr turned to leave Batta to die and walked away.

Scanning the village, he watched one doomed soul after another succumb to suffocation. Some tried to run, but only made it a few steps before collapsing to the ground. Dese rushed to Menet and tried to pick him up, but the pair tumbled to the ground in the doorway of the red longhouse. Dese's 'house brothers' slumped against the red logs, grasping their necks. People's mouths were open as if they were screaming, but Tandyr did not hear a single cry. Other than the sound of his own measured breaths, the world was utterly silent around him.

Villagers who managed to reach the edge of the Weave found themselves prevented from escaping. Tandyr watched one young woman pound weakly on the Weave itself, her face twisted in confusion and agony as she stared at a lone, orange butterfly fluttering over a patch of violet flowers only paces from where she lay.

Tandyr turned his gaze to the pedestal, away from the dying villagers. He had no interest in savoring their deaths. He was the God of Chaos, not the God of Misery.

Stepping between the two front wood poles of the shrine, he stood over the black box and studied it carefully. A stray beam of sunlight poked through the clouds, lighting up the street and the shrine. The lacquer on the box glistened in the light.

For a few moments, he simply stared at the box, hesitant to open the lid. Perhaps Batta had been lying to him. Perhaps there was nothing in the box at all.

Frowning, he muttered, "Staring at it will not change what's inside…"

Reaching out a tentative hand, he touched the box. It was well crafted, made of ordinary hardwood. As far as Tandyr could see, there were no markings on it at all. No carvings, no inlays, nothing.

Suddenly, he got the sense that someone was watching.

Withdrawing his hand, he scanned the buildings and terrain around him. Dozens of bodies filled Nentnay, none of them moving. Wondering if a villager or two had been outside the scope of his Weave, he studied the trees and fields outside the white pattern. He saw nothing.

Dismissing his feeling as simple paranoia, he released the Weave surrounding the village, while keeping the protective padding around him. The air outside rushed to fill the void, triggering a crack of thunder so loud that it rattled the box on the pedestal. As the rumble echoed through the valley and off the stark mountainsides, Tandyr dropped the last of the Weave and turned his full attention back to the box.

With his heart thudding in his chest, he reached out again, gripped the lid gently, and tilted it back.

An unexpected surge of effervescent, throbbing silver Strands of Soul exploded around him, filling the village street and sky. Startled, he shut his eyes tight and pulled back his hand. The lid dropped shut and the Strands disappeared.

He stared at the box, wide-eyed. A quiet curse slipped from his lips.

"Beelvra…"

He stared into the sky and around the village, searching for any glimmer of silver. There was nothing. Looking back to the box, a few additional stunned moments passed before a slow, triumphant smile spread over his face. He reached out to touch the lid again, steeling himself before he opened it.

"Finally, we can begin."

CHAPTER 1: EBEL

16ᵗʰ of the Turn of Rintira, 4999

The late afternoon sun hung low in the sky, bright and intense. Silas squinted against the glare, his right hand shading his eyes, his left gripping the handle of his buckler shield. A warm, arid breeze drifted idly from the west, rustling the dry grass of the hills and carrying with it the musky scent of unwashed dog. Winter was near, but that meant little in the Borderlands.

Silas shook his head as he stared west, down the street leading from Ebel. He was having a difficult time believing what he saw. The creature in the middle of the uneven dirt road was straight from either a playman's tale or a child's nightmare. Silas had yet to make up his mind which.

He marked the crest of the demon-man's head a few inches short of seven feet, discounting the four thick, ridge horns that sprang from its head, spiraling a foot into the air. Shaggy black hair hung loose to its shoulders, wild and unkempt. Its skin, probably once dark like a Borderlander's, reminded Silas of stained leather, but with an unusual reddish tint to it. Were it not for the horns and the leathery skin, the figure standing at Ebel's edge could have simply been a man. An enormous, muscled man clad in black armor and carrying a wicked blade, but a man nonetheless.

Silas had never believed the tales murmured in refugee camps. The stories were too wild, mad claims told by wide-eyed men and women. Horrible, twisted creatures of the Nine Hells were leading the Sudashian invasion, true demons. Yet, as he stood in the village center, he could no longer deny the truth. That was a demon-man. And the endless rows of mongrels standing behind him, hunched over and waiting, were his charges.

An anxious, hushed voice cut the nervous quiet of Ebel's center.

"What are they waiting for?"

Silas glanced over at the man who had spoken. Like every soul here, he had dark skin, wiry black hair, and eyes that were wide and unblinking.

A man standing next to the first whispered, "Perhaps they aren't going to attack? They could decide to just go around us?"

Silas shook his head ever so slightly, a tiny frown on his face. The man was dreaming.

Glancing to his left, he eyed Corporal Lurus. The afternoon sun shone bright on the Dust Man's bald, scarred pate. Mismatched patches of skin—dark and light brown, some even an odd pink color—covered the right side of the soldier's head and neck, old burns healed as best they could. A small, dark hole sat where his right ear should be, like a tiny cave entrance on a jagged cliff side. Like Silas, the corporal wore a brown tabard, trimmed with light tan ribbing, and emblazoned with a tan kite shield stitched across the right breast. He held no shield, however. Corporal Lurus never did. His maimed right hand prevented him from doing so.

Silas expected the corporal to say something encouraging. The men here were clearly frightened and needed something on which to tie their hopes. Yet for a long, drawn-out moment, the corporal merely gnawed on his lip, a grim expression etched his face as he gazed at the demon and the mongrels behind it. Just when Silas thought he might remain silent, Corporal Lurus turned to the pair of frightened villagers and spoke, his voice firm and hard.

"They *will* attack. To think otherwise is foolish."

Both villagers dropped their heads and stared at the dirt.

Silas eyed their dejected posture for a moment before saying, "Eyes up and to the west, men."

As one, the pair lifted their eyes and stared west, their expressions still fearful.

Frowning, Silas ordered, "Look brave. Give them a reason to reconsider."

The villagers drew themselves tall, threw back their shoulders, and glared at the invaders, setting their jaws.

Silas nodded once.

"Good."

He looked to the west as well and caught the corporal staring at him, the only eyebrow the man had—his left—cocked. The look on his face was plain. Corporal Lurus had lost hope weeks ago and had been slowly stomping out the tiny ember of it to which Silas still clung.

With a frown and a sigh, Silas turned away and stared at the demon-man again, his gaze tracing the edge of the oddly curved sword at the spawn's side. Silas wondered if the demon might attempt to take Ebel by himself. Only ninety-six men stood here, ninety-four of which had never lifted a blade against another soul. The mongrels could take a nap if they liked. In fact, some might be doing so right now. Half the creatures were lying on the ground, waiting.

Leaning to his left and keeping his voice low, he muttered, "What are they doing?"

The corporal shrugged his shoulders.

"Waiting."

"For what?"

The corporal sighed.

"I have no idea, Silas."

Silas nodded in the direction of the demon and asked, "Think he likes our wall?"

Corporal Lurus' mouth twitched upwards a fraction.

"He's probably wondering why we bothered building it."

A crude, four-foot wall stretched north and south across the street. Broken chairs, tables, stretched-hide doors, clay pots, and any other object that they had scrounged from the village had been stacked together to block the main road. It and two hundred paces were all that separated them from the Sudashians.

Finally, the demon-man moved, swiveling his massive torso around to speak to the mongrel lines. One of the creatures—draped in brown fur with a white muzzle—loped forward on all fours, stopped at the demon's side, and rose to stand on hind legs. Once mostly upright—the mongrel still hunched over slightly—the beast stood a full foot shorter than the demon. White splotches of fur covered its chest and forearms, matching the white of his snout. Its ears remained pointed and alert, twitching as the demon-man spoke to it. For the first time, Silas noticed it had hands, not paws as he had expected.

The men in Ebel watched the conversation in silence, unable to hear anything being said. After a few exchanges, the demon-man lifted his arm and pointed straight to where Silas and the corporal stood at the center of the line. The mongrel turned its head and stared.

Frowning, Silas mumbled, "Uh-oh."

Corporal Lurus remained silent.

The demon said one last thing to the mongrel, pivoted in place, and marched back through the ranks of the beasts behind him. The brown and white mongrel remained in the street, staring into the village.

Keeping his eyes on the mongrel, Silas muttered, "Blast the Gods, it's ugly."

"Wonder what it thinks of you?" mused the corporal.

A quiet, dry chuckle slipped from Silas. Ensuring his voice was low enough so that none of the villagers could hear, he said, "I've never actually seen one before. Have you?"

Corporal Lurus shook his head.

"No, Silas…I have not."

These villagers believed the Dust Men to be seasoned veterans. Corporal Lurus certainly looked the part. However, neither of them had ever lifted a blade against another living soul outside of drills.

With his gaze locked on the mongrel, Silas murmured, "It looks like a hairy man with a dog's head."

The corporal grunted, "Huh. I would have said prairie wolf."

"Does it matter?" grumbled Silas. "Look at those blasted jaws! They could rip out a man's throat in one—"

"Silas!"

He turned quickly to look at the corporal and found the man glaring at him and wearing a disappointed frown. Corporal Lurus' gaze danced to the villagers and Silas' followed. The two men from before were staring at him with wide eyes.

Pressing his lips together, Silas dropped his head and made a show of inspecting the leather straps on his shield back, upset with himself. He knew better.

As Silas shifted his feet, kicking the dirt, Corporal Lurus called to the men, "You two! Take these men—" he pointed to the two other closest villagers "—and do a quick walk around the barrier's perimeter. If you see anything odd, report it immediately."

Silas glanced up as the four men hurried away quickly, striding to the north. The nearest citizen of Ebel now stood two-dozen-feet away, his face taut and drawn. Silas ran his gaze along the long line of villagers. Worry was threatening to bloom into outright panic. He sighed and turned back to the corporal.

"I'm sorry. They don't need to hear that."

"No, Silas, they do not," answered the soldier firmly. "We cannot have them running to Freehaven the moment the first mongrel charges."

Silas nodded.

"I understand, Corporal."

"And stop calling me that," muttered the corporal. "'Rhohn' is fine. We're not in the army any longer."

"I know," said Silas. He glanced to the line of villagers. "But they think we are. And that helps them."

The corporal eyed the men briefly before shrugging his shoulders.

"Hells. In that case, call me 'Captain Lurus.'"

The corners of Silas' mouth curled up slightly.

"Yes, Captain."

Corporal Lurus' eyes narrowed.

"I was jesting."

"I know." Looking over, eying the man who was both his friend and his commander, Silas asked, "So…what do we do now?"

Corporal Lurus sighed, reached up, and ran a hand over his head. Two weeks' worth of growth covered the left side of the man's face and head where hair still grew.

"The only thing we can. Wait. They will come eventually. My guess is just after sunset."

Silas glanced up at the late afternoon sun and frowned. Dusk was near.

"What makes you say that?"

The corporal shrugged his shoulders.

"I heard mongrels prefer to hunt at night."

Silas could not help but chuckle softly, saying, "I heard day."

Corporal Lurus frowned, the left side of his lips turning down a fraction further then the right.

"Wondrous. We are fighting an enemy about which we know nothing."

"Oh, I don't know about that," muttered Silas. "I know plenty about mongrels and demons. Granted, it's all from playmen's tales and rumors."

The corporal grunted, "Not helpful."

"No," said Silas. "I suppose it's not."

Corporal Lurus stared west again, as did Silas. The lone brown and white mongrel still stood in the road, staring into the center of Ebel, directly at the pair of Dust Men.

"What do you think that one is doing?" asked Silas.

"Another question to which I have no answer."

Silas locked eyes with the creature and tried to hold the beast's gaze, not wanting to show the uncertainty and fear bubbling deep within him. After a few thudding heartbeats, however, he dropped his stare. All he could think about was the animal's teeth ripping into his flesh. He looked back up quickly, and found the mongrel glaring at the corporal now. For a long moment, beast and man glowered at one another.

"I don't think he likes you, Rhohn," muttered Silas.

"I like him less."

With a quick toss of its muzzle, the mongrel dropped to all fours, turned, and loped back to the lines. The corporal turned to Silas immediately.

"I want you to check on the line to the south. I'll take north."

Silas nodded, saying, "Yes, Corporal." He started to turn.

"And Silas?"

Stopping, Silas looked back and said, "Yes?"

"Be careful what you say. I don't want anyone to think they will survive this."

Silas peered at his friend and frowned.

"Men fight better when they have hope."

"It's a false hope you're giving them."

Silas shrugged, saying, "Perhaps. But false hope is better than no hope."

Corporal Lurus shook his head.

"No, Silas, it's not. Their fates—our fates—are what they are. Do not spend the last hours of your life deluding yourself and others."

Silas held the corporal's gaze for a long moment before shaking his head and turning away to stride south. He had taken two steps when Corporal Lurus called out softly.

"Scared men fight harder than hopeful ones, Silas."

Silas did not stop or respond. As he walked toward the first few men, he stared westward, eyeing the rows and rows of mongrels. If the corporal was right, if scared men truly were better fighters, then the ninety-four villagers in Ebel were going to be the toughest force the invaders had met yet.

CHAPTER 2: MONGREL

Rhohn Lurus' life had not been an easy one.

Life was a struggle in the Borderlands, filled with dust, dirt, and infinite horizons of chest-high, dried-out, brown grass. He grew up in Dashti, a village not dissimilar to Ebel, with his mother, father, and the Lurus family's herd of goats. In his eighth year, a grass fire had swept through the region, swift and without warning. The Lurus' home caught fire in the middle of a one-moon night, trapping the family inside. His father managed to pull son and wife free, but Rhohn's mother was already dead. Rhohn suffered severe burns over the right half of his face and torso.

He healed as best he could. Life went on. He and his father rebuilt their home and continued to herd goats. When Rhohn was sixteen, a terrible illness struck the village, sending his father to Maeana's hall along with half of Dashti.

Rhohn buried his father in the morning, sold the herd for a pittance at midday, and left Dashti in the afternoon, wanting to be free of a place so full of tragedy and bad memories.

He traveled to Gobas, the capital of the Borderlands, strode straight to the Dust Man training grounds, and signed his name on the army rolls. The sergeant, unable to take his eyes from Rhohn's burn scars, had never even asked his age.

Rhohn enjoyed the life of a soldier. The constant direction was welcome, providing a sense of order and structure for him when life seemed random and callously chaotic. He spent a full two years in Gobas, training and working as a city guard before he was assigned to an outpost on the northwestern edge of the Borderlands.

Fort Jorodas was one of dozens spread along the long border with Sudash. The Dust Men stationed at the outposts were the first line of defense against raids by the oligurts, razorfiends, or mongrels residing to the west. The Sudashians had been quiet for over two decades before Rhohn arrived, but none expected it to last forever. Border skirmishes had been the rule for generations.

He spent four uneventful years at Fort Jorodas, riding routine patrols through the dusty hills or training in the fort's yard. During his third Winter there, he was promoted to the rank of corporal. Despite his earlier hardships, he felt blessed. He had found his place, his purpose. He was content.

However, like peace in the Borderlands, his reprieve from hard times would not last. Greya, the Goddess of Fate, seemed determined to make him suffer.

A year ago, disturbing reports began to arrive via dispatches from the southern posts. A great host of Sudashians had amassed along the border in numbers impossible to believe. Tens of thousands of oligurts, razorfiends, and mongrels were heading east, marching together as one enormous army. For well over a turn, Rhohn refused to accept the tales, as did most of the Dust Men at the garrison. The disparate races of Sudash loathed one another, resulting in constant war between them. Their fractured existence kept the Borderlands safe more than the Dust Men.

Yet, as the dispatches from nearby posts slowed to a trickle, Rhohn came to accept the rumors were true. Soon, every corner of Fort Jorodas was alive with anxious whispering. Only three hundred Dust Men were garrisoned within the old earth and stone stronghold. Should even a fraction of the attacking army come their way, Fort Jorodas would fall. Quickly.

He and the other soldiers expected a directive from Gobas to fall back, gather with other Dust Men, and form a more formidable force. However, weeks passed without a single missive arriving from the east. Then, the reports from the other outposts stopped altogether.

The Sudashian army, however, did not.

One morning, scouts returned from a patrol to report a thousand oligurts in a nearby valley, heading for Fort Jorodas. They would arrive within the day. Both Rhohn and his sergeant pled with their lieutenant to abandon the post and head east. Yet the man, proud and stubborn-as-stone, refused, insisting that Gobas and Duke Vanson surely had a plan.

Rhohn's sergeant showed infinitely more wisdom than the lieutenant did and ordered four men east to carry word of Fort Jorodas' inevitable fall. That evening, Rhohn and three other men—Silas included—had ridden from the gates of the doomed stronghold. He loathed leaving his fellow soldiers behind, but he had ridden hard nonetheless, hoping the message he carried could make a difference in the grander fight.

They arrived in dusty Midiah three days later and found a town in disarray. Reports about the massive invasion ran rampant. The populace was terrified.

Rhohn shared the fate of Fort Jorodas with the Dust Man captain there and was dismayed to learn that he, too, had not heard from Gobas. The words 'Duke Vanson' were used mostly as a curse by those in Midiah. Despite lacking the authorization to do so, the captain wisely ordered the town's populace to flee east. Most complied, although a handful of naysayers stayed behind, insisting the Sudashian invasion was a playman's fantasy. Rhohn could only assume they were now dead.

For a full turn, the four Dust Men from Fort Jorodas traveled east with the ever-growing exodus, collecting people and soldiers at every settlement. Food was scarce, hope even more so.

Rumors drifted through the migration, whispers that a resistance force was fighting the Sudashians. Of the four Jorodas' men, only Rhohn and Silas turned to join the fight. For three weeks, they traveled against a tide of humanity, seeking the Borderlands' resistance. They found none.

Three days ago, the pair had come across Ebel, an unremarkable village nestled among three grassy hills. Most of the villagers had fled a week before, but ninety-four men had stayed behind, foolishly determined to defend their homes. Rhohn pleaded with them to leave or at least come and join the resistance—if any such existed—but they refused.

Rhohn was ready to ride away and leave, but Silas wanted to stay. After leaving their fellow soldiers in Fort Jorodas, Silas could not bring himself to leave these villagers to die alone. Tired, hungry, and despondent, Rhohn gave in to Silas' impassioned argument. Ebel was as good a place to die as any.

For the past three days, Rhohn and Silas had developed and implemented a plan for a very meager defense. Silas seemed certain that only a small force would come to Ebel, and was set on trying to defeat them. Rhohn simply wanted to kill was many of the invaders as possible before passing on.

Shortly after midday today, the invaders had crested the western horizon and had reached Ebel by early afternoon. Silas had remained quiet for a long time, staring at the hundreds upon hundreds of mongrels. It seemed Rhohn's plan was the only one with any chance of succeeding.

By now, Mu's orb had dipped behind the western horizon, abandoning the few wispy clouds in the sky and plunging Ebel's valley into dusk. Dozens of torches, already lit, were planted in the ground behind the piled fortification of chairs and tables. Within the hour, their flickering flames would be the only source of light in the area as both moons would not rise until midnight. Rhohn doubted he would see them.

Silas stood beside him, sword in one hand and bronze shield in the other. The men of Ebel stretched before him, staring anxiously to the west. Each held whatever meager, improvised weaponry he had been able to scrounge up or cobble together. Mostly, Rhohn saw sharpened sticks, worn shovels, and a few poorly crafted spears. He and Silas were the only two men armed properly.

The enemy still stood two hundred paces away, peering down the open length of road, eerily quiet. To this point, the men of Ebel had managed to match their silence, the only sound being the gentle whisper of the wind rustling the grass.

Rhohn's eyes narrowed, spotting movement at the rear of the mongrels. The horned head of the demon-man strode quickly through the ranks and, upon reaching the front, emerged from parted lines. Grabbing the neck scruff of the nearest mongrel, he continued forward, dragging the beast along with him as he trudged closer. His curved sword rested on his right shoulder the way Rhohn might carry the pole to a water tote. After fifty paces, the demon stopped in the street, released the mongrel, and said something to it. The black-furred beast stood at his side, unmoving.

The demon-man studied the men of Ebel for a moment before calling out, "Do you truly think you can stand against me?" His voice, deeper than distant thunder, reverberated with a strange, thudding power that Rhohn felt in his chest as much as he heard.

A quiet moment passed before Silas shouted, "We do not fear you, demon!"

Rhohn shook his head and sighed. Silas' words were as empty as the grass and dried-mud buildings around them.

The demon's crimson blood eyes locked onto Silas, burning hot.

"I doubt that was wise," muttered Rhohn.

"You doubt?" murmured Silas. "I'm quite sure it wasn't."

After a moment, the demon broke his gaze off and ran it along the line of villagers while bellowing, "I give you two choices today! The first: I send my pack in and they rip your throat from your neck while you watch."

Silas whispered, "That sounds undesirable."

Rhohn ignored him, keeping all his attention on the spawn before them.

The demon took two steps back from the mongrel and exclaimed, "The second: come forward now and I will end you swiftly!" He lifted the giant sword from his shoulder, whipped the blade around, and cleanly severed the mongrel's head from its shoulders. The body collapsed to the dirt as the head rolled a few paces down the road, bouncing closer to the center of Ebel.

Silas drew a sharp breath.

"Gods protect us…"

Rhohn shifted his gaze to watch the men, slightly concerned that some might take the demon's offer of a quick death. If one broke, they all might, leaving him no hope of killing even a single Sudashian. After a few, tense moments, a grim smile slowly spread over his lips. None of the men budged. They were fools for staying here, but they were brave fools.

When nobody stepped forward, the demon captain spun around and headed back to his army, leaving the mongrel's corpse lying in the road.

Rhohn glanced over at his friend.

"Now, Silas."

His fellow Dust Man quickly sheathed his sword, ripped a nearby torch from the ground, and jogged forward. Two sets of men rushed to lift a pair of tables and stretched-hide doors from the barrier, creating a small opening through which Silas squeezed.

The sudden activity drew the demon's attention back to the fortifications. Halting his return to the mongrels, the spawn twisted around and watched Silas sprint down the road. He eyed the Dust Man much as Rhohn might an ant scurrying about the ground.

Ten paces past the fortifications, Silas leaped over a shallow ditch and continued ten more before stopping in the road. He lowered the burning head of his torch to the second trench and, with a soft whoosh, flames spread outward along the channel dug clear across the road, from one earthen building to another. Silas ran back toward the barrier, leapt over the first ditch, paused long enough to light the trench, and then sprinted through the opening in the wall. The villagers quickly replaced the stacks of ruined chairs and tables, sealing the gap in moments.

Rhohn muttered mockingly, "That ought to stop them…"

During his first night in Ebel, Silas had noticed the torches in the village burned longer and brighter than was typical. When he asked why, one of the villagers showed the soldiers a pit full of a sticky, black substance oozing from the ground. The man explained the people of Ebel had dipped their torches into the muck for generations. When Silas had suggested they dig trenches and fill them with sludge, Rhohn had agreed, indifferent to the plan. It at least gave the villagers something to do while they waited to die.

Silas returned to Rhohn's side, jammed the butt of his the torch back into the dirt, and asked, "Do you think it will slow them down?"

"Not at all."

The flames were only three feet tall. Glancing at the powerful rear legs of the mongrels, Rhohn expected they could easily clear the fire. Or, if the demon cared to, simply wait until it burned out.

The demon-man eyed the flames a moment longer before turning and marching back to the mongrel lines. A premature cheer arose from the men of the village, apparently thinking they had gained a small measure of victory. Rhohn remained quiet, letting the cheer go on longer than it deserved. He supposed the villagers deserved one last happy moment.

Rhohn turned to study the northern and southern roads into Ebel, ensuring the men there had lit the trenches covering those narrow ways. From what they could tell, the mongrel force lay solely to the west, yet he could not discount an attack from the flanks. Although, with the overwhelming numbers the Sudashians had, he doubted the demon-man would bother. There was no need for subtlety or strategy today. One, mad charge should take care of them.

Rhohn looked west again to find the demon standing at the head of the mongrel ranks, staring at Ebel. The spawn of the Nine Hells turned his horned head and said something to the beast beside him. Immediately, the mongrel tilted its head back and howled, the haunting cry setting the hair on the back of Rhohn's neck on end and filling the evening air.

Rhohn tensed, squeezing the hilt of his drawn sword, and shouted, "Ready yourselves!"

The men lifted their makeshift weapons in silence. Rhohn took in a few quick, steadying breaths, and wondered how many mongrels he could kill. He hoped at least one.

The howl rose in pitch, echoing about the three hills of Ebel.

Rhohn bit down hard and crouched into a defensive position, glaring at the Sudashian mongrels.

The mongrel's howl continued a moment longer before abruptly cutting off. Without looking over, Rhohn whispered, "Kill as many as you can, Silas."

"That was the plan," muttered Silas.

Rhohn nodded.

"That's a good plan."

Fate, apparently, disagreed.

The demon and mongrels did not move. They stood still and silent, glaring down the street at the Borderlands men. After several anxious, much-too-quiet moments, Rhohn relaxed and rose from his crouch. Something was not right here. Silas felt it, too.

"Rhohn?"

A scowl on his face, Rhohn muttered, "I know."

He turned his gaze to the earthen buildings lining the northern and southern sides of the street, scanning every shadow, studying. Suddenly, a cry of alarm rang out to his right.

"Corporal!"

He swiveled his head to stare north and spotted one of the villagers pointing behind them to the east. Rhohn spun quickly, dirt crunching under his boot heels, and caught a flicker of movement dash past an open doorway. Its hunched shape marked the obvious: it was not a man of Ebel. Rhohn pressed his lips together.

"Hells!"

Glancing back west, Rhohn saw the wall of mongrels still in place, still unmoving. The demon-man's eyes were locked on Rhohn, watching, waiting.

"How did it get into the town?" asked Silas.

Rhohn shook his head.

"It doesn't matter."

"What do we do?"

Chewing on his lip and thinking, Rhohn muttered, "Give me a moment…"

"Why aren't they just—"

"Blast it, Silas! Give me a moment!"

His friend shut his mouth and frowned, glaring at Rhohn.

He stared back to the demon, wondering what the monster was doing. The spawn could send a quarter of his force and kill every man here in mere moments. Yet he had not.

"Why?"

He did not mean for the word to slip from his lips, but it did. Silas chose to answer him.

"He's playing with us," muttered the footman.

Rhohn glanced over.

"Pardon?"

"You know how lions play with their prey once they are assured the kill?" asked Silas. He nodded at the horned monster. "He's the lion. We're his prey."

"Why would he do that?"

Silas raised his eyebrows.

"Are you asking me to explain what a demon of the Nine Hells is thinking?"

Rhohn shook his head and stared west, back to the spawn and his small army. "Sorry. Foolish question."

After a moment, he swiveled his head back to the building where he had seen the mongrel. The men of Ebel were murmuring worriedly now, staring back and forth between the massive, visible force to the west and the hidden unknown to the east. Rhohn needed to do something before full panic set in.

Keeping his voice low, Silas asked, "Do you want me to go back there?"

"Alone?" asked Rhohn. "You have no idea how many are inside."

Silas nodded to the line of men and muttered, "You need to do something. They're going to break."

Rhohn glared at the building, his frown deepening. He wished the mongrels had simply attacked already. Sighing, he looked to the line of men and called softly, "Jebedeh!"

A skinny man holding a shovel turned around. Rhohn waved a hand.

"Come here."

Jebedeh immediately hurried to where Rhohn and Silas stood. With wide eyes, the man said, "Yes, Corporal?"

Rhohn stared hard at the man and said, "Stand here." He pointed to his own boots. "Right *here*, do you understand?"

Jebedeh nodded emphatically.

"Yes, Corporal."

Rhohn leaned closer to the man and whispered, "The moment—the *absolute moment*—any of them—" he nodded at the mongrels and demon "—move, I want you to scream as if someone jammed a dagger in your gut. Am I clear?"

The man was clearly terrified, yet managed to respond with another, almost confident, "Yes, Corporal."

Rhohn nodded once, saying firmly, "Good." Looking to Silas, he ordered, "You're with me." Without a moment's hesitation, he began to stride toward the darkened entryway of the occupied building. Silas hurried beside him.

Like every other building in Ebel, the single story structure was made from piled earth and dried mud, reinforced with beams of weak bulboa wood. It was thirty feet, wall to wall, with a single doorway and three small, uneven holes for windows. The actual stretched-hide door was gone, a part of the makeshift barrier in the street.

"How should we handle this?" muttered Silas.

Rhohn had no idea. This situation had not been covered during his Dust Man training.

"First, we see what we are dealing with."

Silas stared at his face, frowning.

"You don't know what to do, do you?"

Rhohn pressed his lips together and shook his head.

"I'm accepting suggestions if you have any."

Silas remained quiet, his sword and shield held at the ready. Rhohn frowned.

"Wondrous…"

When they were twenty paces from the building, Rhohn held up his right hand to indicate they should halt. Due to his burns, Rhohn used his left hand to hold his sword and did not carry a shield. It was hard to grip the handle with only two fingers and a thumb.

"Stay here."

Silas looked over, surprised.

"Are you going in?"

Rhohn shook his head.

"Not yet. I just want to see what we're dealing with here."

Silas eyed the darkened doorway and whispered, "Be wary."

Nodding, Rhohn crept toward the two windows on the left, thinking he could get a glimpse of what awaited them inside the house. He kept his steps slow and measured, constantly glancing between the windows and open doorway. Sweat dripped from his brow, running into his eyes.

He stopped an arm's length from the earthen wall and peered through the windows. A deep, disappointed frown spread over his lips. He could barely see anything. The gloom of dusk had laden the building's interior with dark, murky shadows. Frustrated, he backpedaled, quietly and quickly, retreating to where Silas waited.

"It's too dark. I can't see a thing in there."

Silas murmured, "Shall I charge in there blind and start swinging?"

A quick look over told Rhohn that Silas was only half-jesting.

"Stay here while I get a torch."

Silas nodded.

"I suppose that is a better idea."

Rhohn turned, took a step back to the fortifications, and stopped. Staring at Silas, he muttered, "Don't do anything brainless, Silas. Wait for me."

With his gaze locked on the dark doorway, Silas nodded.

"Of course."

Rhohn turned and trotted back to the line of men, sliding his thin-bladed sword into his scabbard as he hurried. Stopping beside Jebedeh, he ripped a torch from the ground and stared past the flaming trenches down the road. The Sudashi-ans had still not moved. The demon's red eyes were fixed on Rhohn, a wicked grin on his face.

Glancing at his impromptu deputy, Rhohn asked, "Anything?"

"No, Corporal," replied Jebedeh. The man did not take his eyes off the mon-grels. "Rest assured, I will scream when something happens."

Rhohn did not doubt it.

"I'll be right back."

The man nodded.

"Hurry."

Rhohn turned from the mongrels, faced east, and froze. The area in front of the building was empty. Silas was gone.

He turned quickly back to the line of men, about to ask if anyone had seen what happened, but he found the villagers wholly focused on the threat to the west. None were looking back to the occupied building. He shut his opened mouth, afraid to provoke a panic if they knew one of their two true soldiers had vanished. A scowl on his face, he hurried back to the building, switching the torch to his maimed hand, and drawing his blade.

Upon reaching where he had left Silas, he lowered the torch to illuminate the ground and studied the area, but the hard-packed dirt was impervious to any sort of tracks.

"Blast it, Silas…you didn't—"

He cut off as he lifted his eyes to the darkened doorway. His heart lodged in his throat as he spotted two glowing, yellow eyes staring at him from the shadows inside, flickering with the reflected light from his torch. As he gaped, something arched from the darkened doorway and landed on the ground with a dull metal clang. A Dust Man's blade skidded across the dirt, coming to rest a half-dozen paces from Rhohn.

A boiling hot anger surged through Rhohn and he charged the doorway, rais-ing sword and torch as he ran. The glowing eyes shifted quickly, disappearing into the gloom. Rhohn was in the midst of crossing the threshold when he realized what a foolish thing he was doing. He skidded to a stop in an instant, but it was too late. He was already inside.

Something struck him hard in the back, shoving him to the ground. He dropped the torch and sword as he crashed hard to the dirt, arms and legs splayed out. An instant later, something large and heavy leapt on his back—sending breath from his lungs—and grabbed his wrists, pinning them to the ground. The musty odor of dog washed over him as a breath a thick, wet voice growled softly into his good ear.

"Do *not* move, smooth-face!"

Rhohn ignored the directive and tried to toss his attacker off, but the beast held tight.

"Hold still!" barked the mongrel. "Or end up like him!"

Rhohn ceased his struggle for a moment and scanned the room. His dropped torch was a few paces away, still alight and illuminating the empty interior. Like the door, the furniture was part of the wall outside.

Silas lay against the back wall, slumped over and unmoving, his eyes wide open and frozen in stunned terror. The front of his tabard was stained dark with blood and his throat a mushy, pulpy mess of mangled flesh.

Rhohn's fury surged, thrice as intense as before. He began to thrash about again.

"Get off me!"

The mongrel was incredibly strong, however, and held tight. Rhohn was not going anywhere.

"Stop struggling!" growled the mongrel. "We don't have much time!"

Through his rage, Rhohn realized the mongrel was speaking Argot, the common tongue. He did not know they could do so. The wet, warm breath on his neck returned.

"If you listen to me, you will live through the day!"

Rhohn arrested his struggling for a moment, unsure he heard the beast correctly. He tried to twist his head around to see the mongrel, but could not see much more than the animal's fur-covered forearms and disturbingly man-like hands.

"*What* did you say?"

"If you want to live, smooth-face, you will be quiet and listen to what I have to say."

Rhohn blinked. This did not make any sense.

"Why haven't you killed me?"

A low growl emanated from the beast.

"I still will if you do not be quiet! I have an offer for you."

His confusion deepening, Rhohn muttered, "An offer? What are—"

"Quiet!" barked the mongrel. "I need you to carry a message for me. Far to the east. Say yes, and live. Say no, and die. Decide quickly."

"Why in the Nine Hells would I help you!?"

The beast tightened its grip on Rhohn's wrists and gave an exasperated growl.

"Because, if you do, we can be gone from your lands!"

Wincing from the pressure on his back and arms, Rhohn hissed, "You want to leave?"

"Yes!" snapped the mongrel.

"Then go!" hissed Rhohn. "Leave!"

"We cannot!"

"Why not?!"

The mongrel barked, "I do *not* have time to explain. The others are waiting for my signal. Make your choice, smooth-face!"

Rhohn lay in the dirt, a mongrel on his back and his fellow soldier dead in the corner. This situation did not favor him in the slightest. In a growl that nearly mimicked the mongrel's, he said, "If you get off me, I will listen."

Surprisingly, the mongrel immediately released his wrists and stood, alleviating the pressure on his back. As Rhohn scrambled to his feet, he whipped his head around, scanning the dirt for his sword.

"Looking for this?"

Whirling around, Rhohn found the mongrel standing a half-dozen paces away, glaring at him with alert, yellow eyes, the same brown and white beast that had stood in the road earlier, glaring at him. The mongrel's typically white muzzle was red with Silas' blood. Sharp canine teeth jutted down from its top jaw, pressing down on his black lips.

Rhohn's gaze shot to the beast's right hand. The mongrel held his sword, its tip pointed at the ground.

"Give me that."

The fur around the mongrel's eyes twitched.

"No."

The beast tossed the sword behind him. Rhohn watched helplessly as the blade skidded through the dirt.

"You said you would listen, smooth-face."

"I lied," snapped Rhohn.

A low, angry growl arose from the beast's throat as it said, "You *must* listen, smooth-face." Its eyes widened a fraction. "*Please.*" The pleading note in its voice was entirely unexpected.

Before Rhohn could respond, a sharp yelp from outside pulled the mongrel's attention to the windows. An impatient puff of air escaped from its nose.

"I must signal to the others. Do *not* raise an alarm. Do *not* run to fight. Do not do *anything* but stand and listen."

"If you think I'm—"

"Silence!"

Ignoring the beast, Rhohn raised his voice and said, "I am not—"

The mongrel cut him off with a sharp, threatening growl. Scampering forward, its eyes flashing wide, it barked, "Are you fool? Listen to what I am offering you! This is a chance to end this war!"

Rhohn glared at the mongrel, unable to make sense of any of this. With less defiance than before, he said, "But the villagers—"

"Are going to die!" snapped the mongrel. "Today's battle is already lost! Why are you still fighting it?!"

Rhohn frowned. The mongrel had a point.

Another sharp, quick yelp echoed outside. The mongrel's black nostrils twitched.

"The time to choose is now, smooth-face."

Rhohn stared long and hard into mongrel's eyes. The beast could have easily killed him when he first rushed in—and still could right now—yet Rhohn was still breathing. There had to be a reason.

Eyeing the mongrel, he muttered, "What do you offer?"

The beast huffed once.

"Hope, smooth-face. The only hope your kind has. Are you interested or not?"

Cursing himself for what he was about to do, knowing that he was sentencing the ninety-four men of Ebel to die—horribly, painfully, and very alone—Rhohn gave a short nod.

"I'll listen."

The mongrel tilted back his head immediately, and let out a deep, ear-piercing howl. Rhohn winced and resisted covering his ears. As soon as the beast went silent, dozens of howls answered back. Jebedeh began shouting.

"Corporal! Corporal! They're charging!"

As Rhohn glanced to the doorway, the mongrel stepped closer to him, growling lowly, "They are already dead."

Grinding his teeth together, Rhohn demanded, "Talk, mongrel."

The beast sneered, his thin black lips stretching against sharp, yellowed teeth.

"Do not insult me! I am kur-surus!"

Rhohn forced himself to hold the mongrel's intense glare, neither understanding how he had insulted the animal nor caring much if he had. The two stared one another down as the howls outside grew louder and men's panicked screams bloomed into shouts of fear.

The mongrel tossed its muzzle, huffing in exasperation, "We don't have time for this, man." Pointing over Rhohn's shoulder, it said, "Go there and sit down."

Rhohn looked back to the far back corner.

"Why?"

"Blestem argel!" barked the mongrel. "Just do as I ask!"

As Rhohn reluctantly shuffled to the corner, the mongrel strode to Silas' body and rubbed its hands on the soldier's bloody neck. Rhohn collapsed to the dirt, glaring at the mongrel while trying to shut out the screaming outside. The beast returned to Rhohn, squatted down, and stretched out its hands.

"Hold still. It must look real."

Instantly understanding what the mongrel was doing, Rhohn allowed the beast to cover him in Silas' blood, letting it smear his friend's gore on his face, neck, and chest. Throughout, the cries of the villagers turned from cries of terror to shrieks of pain. Rhohn shut his eyes, praying their deaths were swift. This was not how he had wanted this to happen.

After a moment, he reopened his eyes, stared at the mongrel, and asked, "What happens when the others come to eat me? This won't fool them."

A short series of puffs and snorts burst from the mongrel's snout. It almost sounded like laughter.

"You must have us confused with grayskins, smooth-face. Kur-surus do not eat men."

"That's not what I heard."

"Then you have heard wrong," growled the mongrel. It shifted its yellow-eyed gaze to his face as it applied the last of the blood in silence. Sitting back on his haunches, the beast studied Rhohn, and growled, "You were in a fire, yes?"

Rhohn nodded.

"As a boy."

"And you survived," said the mongrel gruffly. "That is good." The beast paused, leaned in closer, and growled, "Now, remember every word I say."

The mongrel proceeded to recite an unusual message, one given to it by a woman. Little of the missive made sense to the Dust Man, yet he listened intently, baffled and intrigued. The beast repeated it twice more, by which time Rhohn had it memorized. Once he recited it back, the mongrel nodded its approval and stood.

"After my pack is gone, head to the territory you call the Southlands and find a place named Storm Island."

"The Southlands?" exclaimed Rhohn. "How am I to get there?"

"That is your problem, smooth-face," snapped the mongrel. "When you get there, you are to ask whoever you see for Miriel Syncent. The people you must give the message to will find you."

Confused, Rhohn said, "Did you not just say the message was from her?" The name sounded familiar, but he could not mark why.

A great cacophony of howls arose from outside. The mongrel swiveled around to face the door.

"The battle is over."

The screams from the men had ceased. Ninety-four souls were on their way to visit Maeana. Rhohn's gaze slipped over to where Silas lay slumped against the wall and he frowned. Ninety-five souls.

The mongrel allowed him a lone breath to mourn their passing.

"Lie down, smooth-face, and face the wall. Baaldòk will be here soon. No matter what, hold still, and pretend you are as dead as your pack-mate."

Without waiting to see if he complied, the mongrel scampered to the door-way, stomping his bare paw on the torch along the way, extinguishing the flame. The room dipped into blackness.

Rhohn briefly considered retrieving his sword, but as it was on the far wall, it seemed a bad idea. Frowning, he lay down on the dirt floor, facing away from the door, and listened to the howls. Shortly thereafter, the mongrels were rushing about town, barking and yipping in what Rhohn could only assume was the mongrel tongue.

Suddenly, a deep voice bellowed, "Okollu!" The echo of power reverberating in the words made it impossible to deny to whom it belonged.

"Yes, tas-vilku?"

The response came from the doorway and matched the voice of the brown and white mongrel. However, all brazenness was gone from the beast's tone. The mongrel almost sounded meek.

Heavy footsteps approached, stopping just outside the entryway. Oddly enough, the aroma of wildflowers drifted though the dark and abandoned building.

"The Dust Men are dead?"

"Yes," replied Okollu.

"Were they any trouble?"

"No, tas-vilku," growled the mongrel respectfully. "They were not."

"What was the delay with the second one?"

"The first man died too quickly. I took my time with the second."

"Good, Okollu. *Very* good," replied Baaldòk, a smile in his voice. "Move aside. I wish to see."

There was a moment of hesitation prior to the mongrels' response.

"Yes, tas-vilku."

Rhohn heard the scuffling of the mongrel's paws on dirt, followed by heavy footsteps crossing the threshold and entering the building. Wondering how the massive demon could fit through the door, he held his breath and prayed the demon could not hear the incessant thudding of his heart.

Baaldòk chortled softly.

"Vicious, Okollu. Especially this one…"

"He was the first."

"I see why he perished so swiftly."

Remembering Silas' ripped-open throat, some of Rhohn's original rage returned, quickly bubbling back to the surface.

Baaldòk shuffled a few steps closer to Rhohn, his boots grinding the dirt floor.

"And the one in the corner?"

Rhohn's lungs were beginning to burn.

"He fought," growled Okollu. "And he lost."

The demon grunted wordlessly. His boots scuffled again, signaling the spawn was on the move and leaving the building. Okollu followed, the mongrel's paws padding softly. The moment the pair were outside, Rhohn exhaled and drew in a long, silent breath of sweet air. The scent of wildflowers was thrice as strong now, heady and intoxicating.

Baaldòk continued walking after he exited, relaying a list of instructions as he went.

"Check to see if they have food stores hidden, then burn anything that…"

The commotion of the mongrels rushing about Ebel swallowed the rest of his words.

Rhohn remained in place, listening carefully should anything else step through the door. A short time later, he smelled smoke. Soon, the air was thick with it. For a horrific moment or two, he was a boy again, lying in the Lurus home as it burned. He shoved away the memories, focusing on his current nightmare.

Risking a bit of movement, Rhohn draped the collar of his shirt over his mouth and nose, doing his best to keep from coughing. He remained there as Ebel burned, waiting anxiously for the mongrels to leave, all the while searing Okollu's strange message into his memory.

> *Indrida's prophecy is upon us. The Eternal Anarchist is a saeljul who goes by the name Tandyr. The Borderlands have fallen, the Marshlands are next. Vanson and Everett are in his palm for reasons I still do not understand. Time grows short. The Shadow Manes must rise.*

CHAPTER 3: ADVISOR

Chalchalu's Day of Leisure, 4999

The smoke from the Yutian incense made Kenders' head swim.

Sitting cross-legged on a faded-green reed mat in the dim, cold room, she stared at the items on the floor, arranged equidistant between her and her teacher.

Three tan incense sticks jutted up from a bulbous, cream-colored pottery bowl, one end jammed into white sand, the others lit and glowing orange. Wisps of smoke curled upward, filling the air with a thick, musky sweetness. Two shallow ebonwood saucers sat next to the bowl, one on either side. The plate to her left held a puddle of water, while a fist-sized chunk of limestone sat atop the other. She had yet to discern the purpose of the water or the stone.

She reached up to brush a few stray strands of blonde hair from her eyes and shifted her gaze to the figure sitting across from her. Khin, also on a mat and cross-legged, had his eyes closed and white, bony hands folded in his lap. His clasped, interlocked fingers reminded her of a rabbit's sun-bleached ribcage she had once found along the shores of Lake Hawthorne. The rest of Khin was just as thin and skeletal. In private moments, Kenders had jested with her brothers that she thought Khin might shatter into a hundred pieces if he tripped and fell.

His pale skin stretched tight over his frail frame, thin and nearly translucent. A web of blackish-blue veins crisscrossed his bald head and face, reminding her of the maps stored in the enclave's library. Most of his features were like her own, except where she expected a nose, he had only a pair of vertical slits. His eyelids were shut now, but she knew that beneath them lived two bright cerulean eyes, alive and sharp.

A turn ago, the day they had arrived at the enclave, Broedi had led her and her brothers up to this very room in the western tower. He opened the door, stepped into the room first, and asked the trio to follow him. When the three siblings entered, they stood, mouths agape, staring at the lone figure in the stone room.

Playmen's tales told of the aicenai, a race that had walked Terrene eons before the Locking, their lives dedicated to study and knowledge. Blessed with extraordinary long life, aicenai were nonetheless a doomed people, rumored to be incapable of having children.

Once Broedi introduced the trio, he explained that Khin was to be Kenders' primary teacher at the enclave. The aicenai could touch Fire, Water, Air, Stone, and Soul, making him one of the most powerful mages the Shadow Manes had. At first, the prospect of studying under Khin had seemed exciting, but a full turn of instruction with him, had tempered her enthusiasm dramatically.

Kenders pressed her lips together and sighed inwardly. Khin had not moved in hours. She did not know how he could stand it. Her own legs were cold and stiff from the lack of movement.

Exasperated, she let her gaze drift throughout the rest of the square room, anxious to stare at anything else other than her teacher and the confounding saucers.

Two oak chairs sat squared against the wall to her right, taunting her. She did not understand why Khin even had chairs in his room. He never sat in them, nor allowed her to sit in one, either. A plain round-topped, four-legged table stood in the far corner of the room, the resting place for a pewter water pitcher and two wooden cups. Other than the two glass-covered, rectangular openings near the wooden rafters, the room's gray, stone-block walls were completely bare. She did not understand how Khin lived here.

Khin's robes rustled as he shifted ever so slightly.

Kenders quickly looked back to her teacher, thinking he might finally begin today's lesson. She waited, staring at Khin, silently urging him to do or say something, anything at all.

He did not, however. He remained perfectly still and quiet.

As she sat there grinding her teeth, a tiny, chilled shiver ran up her spine, through her shoulders, and along her arms. Despite choosing her heaviest wool dress this morning, she was still cold. The stone beneath her mat had been leaching heat from her body all morning.

The chilly weather of Storm Island was new to her. The coldest night of the year in Yellow Mud was never as chilly as it was outside right now, and it was not even truly Winter yet. As much as she disliked the cold, her teacher relished it. At times, she would spot Khin standing atop the battlements, his nonsensically thin white robes whipping in the chill wind.

Khin had given her one instruction when she arrived this morning: "Remain silent." She swallowed her question as to why her quiet was necessary and followed the directive. The one thing she had learned without doubt during her lessons was that to ask Khin anything was pointless. The aicenai made Broedi look like the village gossip.

During her first few lessons, she had pelted the aicenai with dozens of questions about magic, the Strands, and different Weaves. Khin politely turned every one aside. When she shared her frustration with Broedi, the hillman gave her one of his slight smiles and rumbled a single word.

Patience.

Sitting in the tiny, cold room, Kenders frowned. She and patience did not mix.

Khin was supposed to be teaching her how to better control her ability. He was supposed to be an expert in weaving the Strands. He was supposed to teach her new patterns. What he was doing instead, was wasting her time.

Her bitterness slipped out in the form of a tiny, frustrated sigh.

Khin's wispy voice followed a moment later, startling her.

"Stone fibríaal first. Then Air. Begin."

A soft crackling filled her head and chest as the aicenai immediately reached for the Strands. Pushing back a quick flash of panic, she tried to recall the correct patterns, but the heady sweetness of the incense, her cold and stiff muscles, and her irritation with Khin all interfered with her concentration.

Khin's intricate pattern of loops and curls was half-complete already, hovering in the air above the incense, a mix of heavy, dark brown Strands of Stone and the sparkling silver of Soul. Her eyes went wide. The speed with which he worked the Strands never ceased to astonish her. She had taken half a breath and was already far behind.

Reaching out for her own Strands of Stone and Soul, Kenders began to work the strings of magical energy, knitting her own Weave. She shot a furtive glance towards Khin's pattern to compare hers to his, and was surprised to see that while their designs were comparable, his had far fewer Strands of Stone.

He abruptly directed his Weave to the limestone in the saucer, surprising her. A soft crack filled the room as the chunk of stone split in half, morphed into a vaguely humanoid shape no bigger than her fist, and stood on two rocky legs. Dust and pebbles fell from the fibríaal's new joints.

Kenders pressed her lips together, angry with herself. His Weave had been different because he used the limestone with the magic. Despite staring at the hunk of rock for hours, it had never occurred to her to do that. Finishing her Weave a moment later, a tiny stone fibríaal appeared from nowhere to stand beside Khin's creature. The other half of limestone remained unused in the saucer.

Kenders moved on to the second pattern, glanced up, and found Khin nearly done with his, interlocking white and silver Strands, wispier and less rigid than the first Weave.

She could still beat her teacher, but only by resorting to using her gift from Gaena, the Goddess of Magic. She could simply will the air fibríaal into existence if she wished, but knew that would defeat the point of the exercise, earn a rebuke from Khin, and make her want to take a nap all at once. She was here to learn how to weave the Strands the correct way.

A cool breeze rushed through the room, flaring the glowing tips of the incense sticks and announcing the arrival of Khin's air fibríaal. The diminutive, whistling twister of air was invisible to the naked eye, yet Kenders could clearly see the white and silver pattern swirling beside the pair of stone fibríaals.

With a frustrated sigh, she finished her own Weave and sat, glaring at the four motionless fibríaals. Before she could stop herself, a whispered curse escaped from her lips.

"Hells."

Speaking softly, drawing each word out, Khin said, "An understandable senti-ment, but ineloquently conveyed." It took twice as long for him to say something as it did anyone else. He sat as still as a marble statue, his ice blue eyes studying her. Knowing how this went, she simply held his stare and waited for him to speak.

Ten, agonizingly long and silent minutes passed as the two stared at one an-other through the wisps of incense smoke. The near-constant wind outside surged and waned, an atonal harmony filing the room as each new gust worked to find every minuscule seam between the windows and stone.

Kenders held Khin's stare, gnawing on the inside of her lip. She was moments from snapping when the aicenai finally stirred.

"You are learning some patience," murmured Khin. "Even though it is only surface deep." He spoke so softly, the whistling of the wind almost drowned him out. "You are a lidded pot of boiling water."

Kenders did her best not to react to his perfectly accurate assessment.

"You may go, now."

Her eyes went wide.

"Pardon?"

"You may go," said Khin slowly. "Today's lesson is over."

"That's it?" exclaimed Kenders. "You made me sit here for hours!"

"How observant of you to notice."

Her irritation flared into determined anger. Glaring at the aicenai, she de-manded, "Give me another chance!"

"No."

"No?" repeated Kenders. "You can't give me one chance and then shove me out the door!"

Khin's gaze locked onto hers, his blue eyes burning both cold and hot like the Winter sun. The aicenai might be ancient, but time had not dimmed the intensity of his stare.

"How many chances will the God of Chaos give you?"

The question acted like a punch to the gut would to breath, knocking the indignant irritation from her in an instant. She dropped her eyes and stared at her reed mat. Khin had made his point.

"You have great power," whispered Khin. "*Incredible* power. More than ev-eryone here at the enclave combined. More than every mage I have known." He paused, a short one for him, before adding, "Yet you lack discipline, concentration, patience."

Kenders continued to stare at her mat and did not respond.

After a quiet moment, Khin asked, "Why did you not unravel my Weaves?"

Kenders looked up quickly.

"I…I did not think I was allowed to do that."

"Allowed?" inquired Khin. He shook his head. "Will the God of Chaos agree to a set of rules when he or she faces you? Will you determine what is allowed and what is not beforehand?"

"I…"

She trailed off, having no idea what she was going to say. She wanted to argue but could not refute a single word Khin had spoken. Sighing, she dropped her head again, her frustration returning in an instant. Khin spent more time playing with her mind than he did teaching her about the Strands.

Only three turns ago, her mornings were spent helping her mother make the midday meal, or going with her brothers to help their father in the olive groves or vineyards. They were not spent sitting with an aicenai mage, preparing to help lead the charge against the evil Gods of the Cabal.

She had no idea how she was supposed to do any of this.

"Doubt yourself for but a moment," whispered Khin. "And the Cabal will destroy you."

Khin's uncanny ability to gauge her thoughts only irritated her further.

Lifting her gaze, she lied, saying firmly, "I do *not* doubt myself."

Khin studied her for a long moment before a tired sigh escaped his thin lips. He closed his razor thin eyelids and murmured, "Go now. I must meditate. I suggest you do the same."

Kenders quickly uncrossed her legs and stood, ignoring the protests of her stiff muscles. Turning around, she strode to the only door, grasped the rope handle, and pulled hard. Fresh, cold air smacked her in the face, whipping her hair and dress back, into the room.

Behind her, Khin said, "Leave the door open, please. It is warm in here."

She sighed, wondering yet again if the aicenai was coldblooded. Releasing the rope handle, she took a bracing breath and stepped from the room, moving past the old statue of a soldier that seemed to stand guard beside Khin's door.

The stiff wind blowing off the sea buffeted her as she hurried along the stone walkway. She did not dare look over the wall's edges, knowing that even a quick glance would make her dizzy. The keep sat perched atop a tall bluff overlooking the Sea of Kings, the ocean whipped white by the late Harvest wind. The sound of waves crashing against the shore rushed from below, triggering visions of the jagged black rocks that jutted from the cliff's base. Even after spending an entire turn here, the smell of the air, salty and somehow thick, remained odd to her nose.

Halfway across the battlements, her eyes started to water from the stinging wind. Twisting her head so it did not blow into her eyes, she briefly glimpsed the tops of the forest to the west before her long hair whipped forward. Reaching up, she held it from her face, wishing she had braided it this morning. Able to see again, she spotted the last leaves of the year still clinging to bare branches. Two weeks ago, the trees had been a stunning mixture of reds, yellows, and oranges, but the interminable wind had robbed them of their beauty.

She broke into a quick trot, rushing ahead to reach the northwest tower where the stairwell offered cover. As she reached the door, a muted clanging of metal striking metal pulled her attention to the courtyard below her. Dozens of men filled the open space, doing whatever soldiers did. Most of the time, Kenders was still with Khin when morning drills concluded.

Bursting into the tower, she slammed the door shut behind her and breathed a sigh of relief. She hurried down the torch-lit stairwell to the ground floor and navigated the halls, intent on heading to the courtyard. As she swept through the passageways, she passed a dozen or so of the castle's residents, all of whom greeted her warmly.

Reaching a set of ebonwood doors, Kenders took a deep breath, readying herself for the wind again, and shoved the right-hand door. She took a step outside and stopped, surprised to find the air calm.

Canvas tents on the far side of the yard were still taking a beating from the gusts, but where she stood, the air was as still as a Summer day in Yellow Mud. Sensing a slight crackling, she tilted her head back and spotted a dim net of faint, white Strands stretching across half of the courtyard. A quiet word of surprised awe slipped from her.

"Huh."

She would have noticed the Weave earlier, but with the number of mages at Storm Island, she had grown accustomed to the soft, constant hum and crackling of people weaving.

She glanced around the courtyard, curious who was responsible for the simple yet elegant Weave. Almost immediately, her eyes settled on a tall, barrel-chested, redheaded individual standing off to the side, watching the practicing soldiers. The man caught her eye, lifted a hand, and waved. Kenders smiled and returned the friendly gesture. She pointed upward, silently asking if he was holding the wind back. A wide smile spread over his face and he nodded.

"Gamin," muttered Kenders. "I should have known."

Meeting the head of the mages when they first arrived at Storm Island had been a pleasant, bittersweet experience for Kenders and her brothers. While he was a stranger to them, Gamin and his brother, Sevan, had been close friends with Thaddeus and Marie Isaac, her parents in all but blood. Since arriving, the three Isaac children had spent more than a few evenings with Gamin, enjoying the man's stories about their parents when they were younger, stories Thaddeus and Marie had kept from them. Gamin swore that Sevan told them all better, but his older brother was away, somewhere in the Commonwealth of Cartu, seeking support—monetary and magical—for the Shadow Manes.

At least eighty men were scattered about the center of the yard, practicing with their swords, sparring in groups of two or three. Five high-backed wooden benches lined the southwestern wall of the courtyard, all of them empty except for one. A lone, sandy-haired young man wearing a light gray tunic and dark gray pants reclined, resting comfortably, his right, black-leather-booted leg crossed over his left knee.

She set off across the courtyard, aiming for Nikalys. As she neared, it struck her how different he was from a few turns past. He was only weeks past his eighteenth yearday—a small celebration had been held for him here at the enclave—but recent events had more to do with his entrance into manhood than any date on the calendar.

Nikalys did not look up as she approached, his gaze locked on two soldiers dueling. His eyes danced about as he actively watched the pair, but they were the only part of him exerting any effort.

Kenders collapsed to the bench beside Nikalys. She glanced at her brother, trying to catch his eye. He ignored her, keeping his gaze focused on the swordwork.

"Can't you rest a moment?"

"I stop when they do," responded Nikalys, nodding to the courtyard. "Wil's been working with a man from the Marshlands for a couple of weeks. He's trying to teach Sergeant Trell the style now. Look at the swords they're using."

Kenders looked and noticed that instead of normal longswords, the men were using shorter blades, their edges curved on one side and ending in a hooked tip.

Nikalys explained, "There are certain things you can do with a sword like that that you can't with a straight—"

"Nik?" interrupted Kenders firmly. "I don't care about swords."

He glanced over at her for a moment before returning his gaze back to the duel.

"So…you're done early."

Kenders shrugged her shoulders and ran her fingers through her hair, trying to untangle the knots caused by the wind.

"And?"

He looked over briefly again.

"What happened?"

Yanking at a knot, she said, "Not much. When I got there, Khin told me to sit down and be quiet. So I did. I sat. I was quiet." She paused before adding, "For the entire blasted morning." Sarcasm dripped from every word. "It was a wondrous time. I learned so much."

"Why did he have you do that?" asked Nikalys, his eyes still on the soldiers.

"I have no idea," grumbled Kenders.

Wrinkling his nose, Nikalys said, "Try not to take this the wrong way, sis… but you reek."

Kenders eyed her brother.

"Pardon?"

Without looking over, he pointed at her dress.

"You smell like that herb shop in Claw."

Kenders lifted an arm and sniffed her sleeve. The musky-sweet smell of Yutian incense lingered. Perhaps she should go stand on the battlements for a while and let the wind strip the scent from her.

"So, after sitting there for hours, all of a sudden, he whispers—" she changed her voice, trying to mimic the aicenai's breathless tone. "'—Stone fibríaal first. Then Air. Begin.'" She shook her head, a frown on her lips. "He expected me to Weave instantly. No warning—nothing! With the incense, the cold, and the blasted waiting, I swear, it was almost as if he were purposely trying to…distract…"

She trailed off as the true point of today's lesson dawned on her. She sat quiet for a long moment before muttering, "He did that all on purpose, didn't he?" Turning to her brother, she found him wearing a small grin.

"Khin does everything on purpose."

She drew in a deep breath, held it a moment, and then exhaled. "I wish Gamin was my teacher."

She glanced over to where the tall redheaded mage stood, arms crossed, idly watching practice. Grunts of exertion and the clang of swords filled the yard.

"Or that Broedi and Nundle were still here. I think I learned more from them in that one afternoon on the hilltop than I have in four weeks here."

"You are lucky to have Khin," counseled Nikalys. "He has more experience than Broedi, Gamin, and Nundle put together. Try to learn what you can from him."

Kenders frowned and did not respond. Nikalys was right. And that only further irritated her.

After a few moments, Kenders spoke.

"At least I didn't cheat today."

Raising his eyebrows, Nikalys said, "See? You *are* learning."

Every mage in the history of Terrene other than her blood mother, Eliza Kap, needed to know the pattern of a particular Weave in order to craft it. Kenders, however, could simply envision the result, and the correct Weave would pop into existence, fully complete. Unfortunately, the physical and mental drain required to use the Strands in such a manner made it a highly inadvisable approach for any feat of significant magnitude. In the short time since discovering her ability, she had passed out multiple times when she overextended herself, remaining unconscious up to a day. Broedi warned her that such foolishness could even result in death.

Wil and Sergeant Trell paused in their duel, dropping the tips of their curved swords for a moment to catch their breath. The older sergeant turned to glance at Nikalys on the bench and, upon seeing Kenders, gave a friendly smile and nod. The younger soldier did the same, although his smile had a nervous twitch to it.

Nikalys whispered, "Wil is saying hello." There was an unmistakable teasing note in his tone. "You should be polite and wave back."

Kenders lashed out with her left hand, intending to smack Nikalys in the chest. Before she was anywhere near him, he caught her arm. One instant, he had been sitting comfortably, totally at ease with arms crossed. The next, he was gently gripping her arm.

"Too slow."

As Kenders had inherited her gift from their blood mother, Nikalys possessed the same extraordinary skills as their blood father, Aryn Atticus. Besides incredible speed and strength, he could observe any type of martial activity and execute it himself perfectly, without practice. In the lone turn here, he had become an expert in three different styles of swordwork, spear and staff fighting, and certain kinds of hand-to-hand combat, simply by sitting on this bench and watching.

Glaring at him, she said, "Let go, Nik."

He smiled and released her arm.

"What's the matter, Kenders? Does Wil not catch your eye? The young women in Claw have taken a liking to him."

With a roll of her eyes, Kenders huffed, "They are just excited to have sixty new young men show up." She shook her head firmly. "I do *not* have eyes for Wil." Unwillingly, her gaze flicked to another pair of men on the far side of the courtyard.

One of the men was her brother in all but blood. A younger version of his father, Jak had thick, curly black hair, a sturdy build, and strong arms. As of late, he had been attempting to grow a beard to match the fashion of the Southlands. It was not going well.

The other man garnered most of her attention. His dark skin and close-cropped, pitch-black hair made him stand out from the other soldiers in the yard. While he was a few inches shorter than Jak and of slighter build, he was not letting his larger opponent intimidate him.

Nikalys leaned over and whispered, "Zecus is looking handsome today, don't you think?"

Pretending to ignore the comment, Kenders sighed and leaned back. She reached out her left arm as if to rest it on the bench back, slipped it behind Nikalys' head, and smacked the back of his neck.

"Ouch!"

Nikalys glared at her, his teasing grin gone. He reached up and rubbed where she had slapped him.

"Blast it! That hurt!"

Smiling contentedly, Kenders said, "Tougher to stop when you can't see it coming, isn't it?"

As he glared at her, and she grinned at him, a voice called out, "I think you've finally met your match, son."

Brother and sister looked up as one to find Sergeant Trell striding toward them, the unusual, curved sword with hooked tip still gripped in his hand. Steam rose from the man's sweaty brow, drifting away in the cold air. A glance to where he had been practicing with Wil revealed the young swordsman walking among the other pairs, observing and offering tips. Wil was a natural with the sword.

Still rubbing his neck, Nikalys said, "It would seem that is the case, Sergeant."

Kenders sighed.

"Oh, please, Nik. I barely hit you."

Nodding to the bench, Sergeant Trell asked, "Do you mind if I sit down? I'm a touch weary."

Nikalys gestured to the open bench beside him.

"Please. Sit."

The soldier collapsed on the bench and let out a long sigh.

Pointing to the Marshland sword, Nikalys said, "You looked good out there with that."

Sergeant Trell eyed Nikalys, smiled, and said, "You, son, are quite kind. And a liar."

Nikalys shook his head quickly.

"No, truly, Sergeant. You are one of the better swordsmen here. Sentinels and Manes included."

Laying his sword against the bench seat, Sergeant Trell said, "Most of these men are fifteen years younger than me. They're quicker, faster—" he gave another tired sigh as he mopped his brow "—and they have much more endurance."

Kenders leaned forward to look past Nikalys.

"But you have years of experience they cannot claim. They are lucky to have you to learn from."

Nikalys turned his head to stare at her, one eyebrow cocked.

"My, but that sounds familiar…"

She blinked, confused by his words and tone. After a moment, she realized that her counsel to the sergeant was effectively the same as what Nikalys had offered her regarding Khin's value as a teacher. Her eyes narrowed.

"Don't puff your feathers too much, Nik. You might get a few plucked."

Nikalys nodded and ducked his head, trying to keep his amused grin to himself.

"Yes, Kenders."

Sergeant Trell glanced between brother and sister a few times before his gaze settled on Kenders.

"Might this have something to do with your lessons?"

With a resigned sigh, Kenders said, "Perhaps…"

He raised a single eyebrow and nodded, saying, "I have spent a few late nights in the commons with Khin, speaking on all manner of subjects. Nikalys is right. Learn what you can from him. He is a walking library. More so than Nundle, even." A tiny frown touched his lips. "And he is an incredible knuckles player."

Kenders looked up, surprised.

"Khin plays placards? He gambles with you?"

The quality did not fit the quiet, reserved teacher.

A soft chuckle slipped from the sergeant.

"More like he steals from me. I have won only two or three hands against him. And those I think he let me win because he felt pity for me."

Kenders tried to envision her teacher sitting in the darkened commons, huddled over a table, playing knuckles with the sergeant. She had an easier time imagining a school of fish flying in the sky.

Nikalys nodded his chin in the direction of the soldiers and said to the sergeant, "Jak's getting better. He's much more fluid than even a week ago."

Sergeant Trell shifted his gaze to where Jak and Zecus were practicing and nodded, saying, "He's a fast learner." Smiling, he glanced at Nikalys. "Excluding you, he's our quickest study."

Kenders eyed her brother sparring with Zecus. Even to her unpracticed eye, it was plain to see he had improved much over the past turn. Zecus, however, appeared to be no better than when they had arrived at Storm Island.

She asked, "And Zecus?"

As the question slipped from her lips, Jak pressed an attack against the Borderlander. It was all Zecus could do to turn aside each blow while backpedalling quickly, kicking up gravel.

Frowning, she turned to Sergeant Trell to wait for his evaluation.

The sergeant shared a quick look with Nikalys before saying diplomatically, "Learning the blade is a difficult task and Zecus is a hard worker. If he keeps at it, someday he will be able to turn aside most simple attacks."

Kenders was disappointed. She wished the sergeant was wrong, but knew he was not.

Sergeant Trell sat forward and said, "Now, give the man a staff or spear, and he's one of the best here. And with a properly weighted dagger, he can hit an acorn from twenty-five paces away."

Kenders gave Sergeant Trell a quick, grateful smile. The man had a gift for reading people.

"That's kind of you to say, Sergeant."

The three sat quietly, watching the men duel and enjoying the crisp day. Without the wind, she did not mind the nippy air as much. Kenders took a moment to enjoy the quiet and stared out at the courtyard, watching the men to whom she owed her life.

Two hundred Shadow Manes, most of them soldiers, had stumbled upon the Progeny at Shorn Rise, and helped them to repel the last of Jhaell Myrr's attack. After taking a night to dispose of the oligurt and razorfiend corpses, their troop continued to Storm Island. Over a week later, they reached the small land bridge that led to the enclave. Apparently, the island was not a true island, at least not all of the time. Tidal shifts covered the strip of land four times every turn. Broedi said it had something to do with the phases of Terrene's two moons.

After crossing the muddy land bridge, their party passed through an oak forest, leaving the towering ebonwood trees of the mainland. The leaves of the oaks were just beginning to change at the time, turning the landscape a myriad of reds, oranges, and bright yellows.

A half day later, they emerged from the forest and were greeted by a long, dark, flat line that filled the eastern horizon. Kenders, her siblings, all of the Red Sentinels, and the two farm girls they had rescued from bandits—Sabine and her younger sister, Helene—openly gaped at the vast Sea of Kings. None of them had ever seen the ocean.

Broedi called back for everyone to remain calm, they were about to ride through the protective veil hiding the enclave. Moments later, a stone castle suddenly appeared on the cliff's edge, a village larger than Yellow Mud sitting outside its walls.

They rode through the small town of Claw, gathering a large following as people rushed from their homes and shops to stare. Upon reaching the courtyard of the castle, over five hundred individuals trailed them. Men and women made up most of the crowd, but Kenders spotted a number of hillmen as well, easily recognizable as they stood a full foot above the tallest man in the crowd. Much to Nundle's disappointment, there were no tombles.

Once the crowd quieted, the baroness in charge of the enclave, Lady Vivienne, made a short speech, warning that the time for which they had been preparing was at hand. The God of Chaos was on the move in the Borderlands. The time was near for the Manes to reveal themselves to the duchies and lead the fight to stop the Cabal. Facing Nikalys and Kenders, she announced that the Progeny had returned.

The courtyard erupted into loud, raucous cheering.

Even now, a full turn later, she swore she could hear the joyous roars echoing about the courtyard. It had terrified her seeing how much faith these people put into her and Nikalys. It still did today, more so, perhaps.

When Nikalys suddenly spoke, breaking the silence, Kenders started. She had been lost in the memory.

"Can't say I've ever seen him out of the castle."

Glancing up, she saw Nikalys eyeing the far side of the courtyard.

Following his gaze, Kenders spotted a skinny man hurrying across the gravel, his thin blond hair whipping wildly in the wind. He was dressed in a simple blue tunic, tan breeches, and leather sandals. Kenders recognized him immediately as Lady Vivienne's attendant.

"He must be freezing," said Sergeant Trell.

Sure enough, the man gripped his arms about himself, trying to stave back the biting cold of the wind.

Kenders wondered aloud, "Why is he out of Lady Vivienne's offices?"

Nobody hazarded a guess. The three of them sat, quiet and motionless, watching as the man broke into a hurried, flailing run. He was quite anxious to reach the calmer air on this side of the Weave.

Nikalys uttered, "Sergeant, I'll bet you a copper ducat he trips and falls."

"Accepted," replied the soldier with a smile.

The aide passed through the magical barrier and stopped. He rubbed his eyes and went about fixing his mussed hair before heading into the soldiers' midst.

"You owe me a copper, son."

Nikalys shrugged and grinned.

"So I do…"

The attendant angled straight to where Jak and Zecus sat, taking a rest from their practice. He stopped before the pair and started to speak to them. Jak and Zecus stayed seated, arms draped over their legs, and stared up at the man curiously.

"I wonder what he wants with them," mused Kenders.

The man appeared most interested in speaking with Zecus, but Jak continued to interject himself, much to the aide's apparent frustration.

Sergeant Trell sighed and said, "Excuse me, but I'm going to see what this is about. The commander does not like it when Lady Vivienne interrupts our drills."

He rose from the bench and strode toward Jak, Zecus, and the aide. When he arrived, the aide threw his arms up in the air and began talking to the sergeant directly, gesturing at the Borderlander.

Keeping her eyes on the exchange, Kenders asked, "Have you noticed Lady Vivienne asserting herself since Broedi left?"

"Impossible not to," muttered Nikalys. He did not sound pleased.

Kenders had expected that Broedi, as the lone White Lion currently with the Manes, would be in charge here at the enclave. However, it seemed authority rested mostly with Lady Vivienne, the Baroness of Argolles. She deferred to Broedi publically but now that the hillman was on his way to the Celestial Empire with Nundle, Lady Vivienne governed the enclave as though it were a part of her barony.

After a few minutes of discussion, the aide turned toward the direction from which he came and began to walk. Zecus stood, gathered his things, and, after a pat on the back from Sergeant Trell, followed the man across the yard.

Kenders glanced at Nikalys.

"What does he—what does *she* want with Zecus?"

Nikalys shook his head, replying, "I don't know…" He sounded as bewildered as she felt.

As Zecus strode across the courtyard, he glanced over to where Nikalys and Kenders sat. His eyes locked with hers and he gave her a quick smile. Her heart skipped a beat.

His smile widened a bit as he turned and broke into a jog, chasing after the aide. As she watched him go, she realized she had not even smiled back.

"Zecus is a good man, Kenders. You could do a great deal worse than him, but you won't do much better."

She looked at her brother to find him staring at her with a kind, if measured, expression. She was surprised. Her brothers had always been a tad overprotective with her when it came to boys. Once, when she had confided in them that she liked a particular young man in Yellow Mud, they had carried the boy to Lake Hawthorne and tossed him in.

Unsure what to say in response, she kept quiet and turned back in time to see Zecus disappear through a set of tall ebonwood doors.

Nikalys asked gently, "Have you spoken with him at all?"

Kenders shook her head quickly.

"Oh, Gods, no."

The thought terrified her.

"You should," said Nikalys.

Kenders huffed and said, "Why? With whatever is coming, I doubt I'll have time for…" She trailed off and dropped her head to stare at her dress, unsure how to end her thought. "I won't have time for him."

She felt Nikalys' silent gaze on her but did not look up until she heard the scuffle of boots on gravel. Lifting her chin, she spotted Sergeant Trell returning to the bench with Jak in tow. Neither man looked happy. As they neared, Jak's voice emerged from the clanging of swords echoing through the yard.

"—she can't just make decisions without at least telling us her reasons. Without Broedi here, we never know what is happening." Looking up, Jak gestured at Nikalys and Kenders. "They're the Progeny, right? They should know what's going on."

Nikalys sat forward and asked, "And what *is* going on?"

Jak and the sergeant halted a few paces from the bench. Now that her eldest brother was closer, she could see the patches of dark whiskers wandering down from his sideburns and coating his chin, but leaving his cheeks bare. It looked the same as it had two weeks past.

With a deep frown on his face, Jak said, "That parchment weasel saunters up to us and says"—he shifted to mimic the proper, clipped tone of the aide—"'The Lady Vivienne requires your presence at once, Mr. Alsher. Please bathe and dress appropriately before attending to her.'"

Kenders asked, "What does she want with him?"

The baroness had paid no attention to the Borderlander since arriving at the enclave.

Jak shrugged and said, "I asked, of course, but the man refused to answer any of my questions. He just kept saying, 'The baroness requires him, that is all you need to know,' over and over. Gods, she is so blasted arrogant!"

The first time they had met Lady Vivienne, she had made a rather insensitive comment about the sacrifice their parents had made to raise them. Jak carried a grudge still.

Staring across the courtyard to the doors, he said, "Zecus had no idea what was happening, but is—of course—too polite to tell the 'Lady' what she can do with her *request*." With a nod at Sergeant Trell, Jak added, "The aide would not even tell Sergeant Trell."

Kenders glanced at the quiet soldier. He had yet to say a word since returning and was staring blankly at the stone wall behind her, a frown on his face. Something was bothering him.

"Sergeant?"

He pressed his lips together and peered down at her.

"Tomorrow is the first of the Turn of Luraana."

It was a statement, not a question, almost as if he were thinking aloud. He was right, of course, today was Chalchalu's Day of Leisure—a small feast was planned for later in the commons to honor the God of Wealth—meaning tomorrow was the first of a new turn.

"And that means what?" prompted Jak.

Sergeant Trell turned his head to stare at Jak.

"How would you like to go to Freehaven?"

Jak's eyes widened.

"Pardon?"

"Freehaven, son," said Sergeant Trell. "Would you like to go?"

Jak blinked once and replied, "Um…sure, I suppose…wait, what?" His earlier irritation was gone, replaced now by open confusion.

"The baroness wishes to take Zecus with her to Freehaven tomorrow," said Sergeant Trell with confidence. "And I intend to convince her that you and I should go along."

Nikalys lifted a hand and stated the obvious.

"Pardon me, but the capital is hundreds of miles from here. It would take a few turns to get there overland. Weeks, still, if she goes by sea."

A natural harbor rested at the bottom of the bluffs large enough for a pair of ships to find protection from the strong squalls that gave the island its name. One ship resided there currently, however, although no one at sea could see it. The Weave protecting the enclave extended to the harbor, making it appear to be a treacherous group of sharp rocks jutting from the sea.

Sergeant Trell nodded, agreeing with Nikalys' assessment.

"Yes, it would. However, she does not intend to travel by horse or ship."

Kenders understood in an instant.

"A port?"

Sergeant Trell glanced at her and nodded.

"I believe so."

Shaking her head, Kenders said, "But she can't. We have no Void mages here."

Nundle could touch Void, but he was gone. Moreover, he had never been to Freehaven, so he could not Weave a port to the location anyway.

Sergeant Trell said, "True, but that will not be an issue." The man was wholly confident.

With a quizzical tilt of her head, Kenders asked, "What aren't you telling us?"

The soldier looked at them apologetically and said, "Broedi shared a few things with me before he left. He made me promise to keep silent until necessary."

Jak tilted his head back and stared into the uniformly gray sky. "He's not even here and he's keeping secrets from us." Dropping his head, he asked, "Care to share, Sergeant?"

"I would not be a very good keeper of secrets if I told you, now would I?" said Sergeant Trell with a smile. "Suffice it to say that he has everyone's best interests in mind."

"Can you at least tell us why Lady Vivienne wants to go to Freehaven?" asked Nikalys.

Sergeant Trell paused a moment, shrugged his shoulders, and said, "I suppose so. On the first of every turn, citizens of the duchies are allowed to bring petitions directly before the First Council. Broedi confided in me that Lady Vivienne would most likely attend."

"But why take Zecus?" asked Kenders.

The sergeant glanced at her and frowned.

"Sorry, but Broedi asked me to keep *that* part quiet."

Kenders said stubbornly, "Fine. Keep your secrets. But, I'm going, too."

Nikalys, Jak, and Sergeant Trell all spoke simultaneously, saying firmly, "No."

Peering from face to face, she asked, "Why not?"

"The city has too many eyes," answered the sergeant. "It is much too dangerous for you." He glanced at Nikalys. "To be clear, that goes for you, too."

Nikalys nodded, adding, "I figured as much, Sergeant." He looked at Kenders.

"Surely the God of Chaos knows about Jhaell's failure now. We don't know where he has more agents. The enclave is the only safe place for you and me now."

Kenders frowned. They were right.

Looking to Sergeant Trell, she asked, "Why does Jak get to go, then?"

The sergeant said, "Since you cannot go, Broedi suggested I take Jak to be your eyes and ears. He does not trust that Lady Vivienne would tell you everything."

With a light chuckle, Jak said, "*Broedi* is worried about too many secrets? That's a show."

Sergeant Trell shrugged.

"I am the messenger, Jak. That is all."

Nikalys stood from the bench and stretched, saying, "Ketus with you, Sergeant. You still must convince Lady Vivienne to allow you to come."

"True," replied Sergeant Trell. "But, again, that will not be a problem."

"Another one of Broedi's secrets?" asked Kenders.

Sergeant Trell raised his eyebrows and gave the trio a sly, silent smile. Turning to face Jak, he said, "Drills are over for you today. Go get cleaned up and wait in your room. I'm going to speak to the baroness now." Facing Kenders and Nikalys, he gave a short, polite nod. "Good memories behind." Spinning on his heel, he strode purposefully toward the dual doors where Zecus had disappeared.

Jak watched the soldier for a few moments before glancing at his siblings and saying, "If you will excuse me, I must go take a bath." He turned and headed toward the doors Kenders had used to come to the courtyard.

Nikalys called after him, "I want stories, Jak!"

Their brother lifted an arm in the air and waved without turning around.

Nikalys chuckled and began striding off to where the soldiers were still practicing.

Staring after him, Kenders asked, "Where are you going?"

Pointing to the Manes and Sentinels, he said, "I saw a new thrust used by Wil that I want to try." He glanced over his shoulder. "I'll see you in the commons for midday meal."

As Kenders watched her brothers walk in opposite directions, she suddenly felt very alone, sitting on the bench all by herself.

CHAPTER 4: CHAMBER

1ˢᵗ of the Turn of Luraana, 4999

The stiff, upturned collar itched Jak's neck something fierce.

He reached up, stuck a finger between neck and shirt, and began to scratch incessantly. A moment later, he felt Lady Vivienne's eyes on him, glaring. Turning his head slightly, he glanced past Sergeant Trell and confirmed the baroness was indeed staring, silently urging him to quit. The sergeant was looking at him as well, amused by Jak's persistent battle with his court finery. Giving one last diffident scratch, Jak pulled his finger from the collar and grasped his hands together, plopping them in his lap. A heavy sigh slipped from him as he stared about the cavernous council chamber.

He and the others sat in the balcony of the horseshoe-shaped room, perched twenty feet above the tan and white marble floor below. A great dome swept overhead, its peak another eighty feet high. A colorful mural covered the ceiling, filled with scenes of ancient battles and portraits of rulers who were long dead. Jak was mostly interested in how the artists ever managed to paint the ceiling.

Dropping his gaze, Jak peered over the oaken railing to the floor below. To his left, a long, wooden table waited at the head of the chamber with ten ornately carved chairs lining one side. Each seat was arranged to face the open floor and the fourteen bare benches to his right. Jak was sure there were fourteen. He had counted them five times.

Dozens of clerks and other servants hustled about the floor, intent on performing one task or another. It reminded Jak of watching ants scurry about an anthill. Occasionally, one clerk would halt another and hand over a parchment or scroll. Then the pair would look it over together for a while, speaking in hushed tones. Jak briefly wondered what was they were doing or discussing before realizing he did not much care.

Lifting his gaze, he scanned the balcony level. Black marble columns alternated with large, arched windows open to the outside. A pleasant breeze drifted into the chamber, carrying with it the warm, moist smell of the salty sea. The distant calls of some sort of bird floated in on the wind, mingling with the low hum of quiet conversation and soft rustling of clothes.

The finery worn by council attendees was astonishing. Jak had never seen such elegance and expense. Women's dresses were elaborate concoctions of soft, muted colors with large, puffy shoulders and tapered arms. The attire worn by men also favored fashion over function, resulting in such horrid things as stiff, incredibly restrictive collars that choked their wearers.

Jak reached up again, planning to give his neck a satisfying scratch when Zecus leaned over and whispered, "The baroness is watching."

Shooting a quick glance past Sergeant Trell, he found Lady Vivienne indeed glaring at him, almost daring him to pick at his collar.

Jak dropped his hand, shifted in his seat, and turned away from the noblewoman. Keeping his voice low, he muttered in exasperation, "Why do we have to wear these blasted things anyway?"

A small smile crept over Zecus' face.

"A snake does not worry about boots."

Jak stared at his friend, confused.

"Say again?"

"Words from my father," replied Zecus. "It means 'worry about what is important,' I doubt your collar is worthy of your ire."

Jak frowned. Zecus was right.

"Am I permitted to worry about why we are here?"

Zecus nodded, muttering, "I am."

Lady Vivienne had yet to reveal the purpose of their visit to the First Council proceedings despite persistent questioning by Jak, both last night and this morning. The baroness had ignored every inquiry made.

Eyeing Zecus, Jak asked, "You are *sure* you don't know why she wanted you here?"

The Borderlander hesitated briefly before replying.

"I do not believe so."

Jak stared closely at his friend, curious at the choice of words.

"That's not a 'no.'"

Zecus gave him a sidelong look before shaking his head.

"I do not wish to give voice to a hope that may be false."

Physically and mentally shrugging, Jak let the issue drop. He tilted his head back, closed his eyes, and waited for something to happen. As he sat there, a tiny smile of wonder graced his lips. He, Jak Isaac of Yellow Mud, was in the Oaken Duchies' capital, sitting in the Council House, surrounded by nobles. A disbelieving chuckle slipped from his lips.

Yesterday morning, after washing away the sweat and grime from morning drills, he returned to his room. When they had arrived at the enclave, the Shadow Manes had given Nikalys and Kenders private rooms in a tower as some sort of honor. Nikalys insisted that Jak remain nearby, so he had received a room on the same floor as his brother.

Later in the afternoon, the baroness summoned him to her offices and announced he was going to Freehaven. Jak was surprised Sergeant Trell had succeeded in convincing the noblewoman to allow him to come. Lady Vivienne had proven she was a person who preferred to give orders rather than take them.

With no explanation of what was happening, the baroness pulled a large, metal key from the folds of her dress, faced the rear wall of her office, and dragged the key vertically along the stone, top to bottom. Upon reaching the floor, the wall appeared to flutter as if made from canvas rather than stone.

A moment later, the baroness implausibly stepped into the wall. Jak stared at the inky void with wide-eyed trepidation. Kenders had explained the concept of a port to him, but seeing one this close had been disconcerting.

Sergeant Trell had gone next, followed by Zecus. Jak was the last to step through, entirely unsure what he should expect. One moment he was in Lady Vivienne's cold and dark office at the enclave, the next he was in a warm, richly furnished room, squinting against the bright sunlight streaming through garden window. Plush couches and cushioned chairs filled the room, a massive, four-post bed against the far wall.

Glancing behind him, he found a different stone wall, one crafted of smooth white stone with gray specks. The strange, dark line delineating the port entrance hovered on its surface.

Lady Vivienne swept him aside and draped the palm of her hand over the obsidian globe on the key's bow. The white stone wall solidified in an instant. Apparently, they were in Freehaven. The baroness had Southern Arms guards escort them to their room after issuing a stern warning to not touch anything. They were to be ready at dawn the next day.

As the soldiers escorted the new arrivals through the structure, navigating a confusing series of hallways, they occasionally passed an arched window which allowed Jak to steal a quick glance outside. Much to his disappointment, all he could see were the sides of other buildings or a lush garden full of flowering bushes.

The trio spent the entire evening alone in a well-appointed room with a view of a stone wall. Four Southern Arms stood outside their door, refusing to speak with them or let them leave. Jak felt more prisoner than guest. Had Sergeant Trell not seemed so calm about the situation, Jak would have been quite concerned.

This morning, they awoke to find three sets of court clothes provided for them along with a simple morningmeal of bread, cheese, and a tart fruit juice. After eating, Jak attempted to dress. It was a struggle. Sergeant Trell needed to show Zecus and Jak which buttons attached to which loops, which flaps went to the correct buckles. Afterwards, the guards ushered the trio to an enclosed courtyard where a covered carriage awaited them on a pebbled path.

Lady Vivienne was already waiting for them in the cab, an impatient expression etched on her face. Once they had settled, she ordered the door shut and drew the curtains. Jak bit his tongue, upset. He had hoped to glimpse a bit of Freehaven on the way to the Council Hall. Instead, he was forced to listen to the bustling city rush by and try to imagine everything that he was missing.

Upon arriving at the Council Hall, they disembarked in yet another sheltered yard. Lady Vivienne led them through a side entrance of the chambers, giving them explicit instructions to remain silent once inside. Jak had the impression that Lady Vivienne would have liked to toss a blanket over their heads if propriety would allow it.

Fortunately, no one stopped them on their way up to the balcony. In fact, most people seemed to give the baroness a wide berth. Lady Vivienne led them directly to their seats in the front row, and had forced them to wait in near-silence ever since.

Jak sighed, opened his eyes, and dropped his head. His gaze noticed two new arrivals sitting across from him, on the opposite side of the balcony.

With surprise, he muttered, "Huh."

Two small female figures—no more than three feet tall—sat together, each wearing identical, deep-purple robes and talking in hushed tones to each other. While both had rich, auburn hair, one wore it free and unbound while the other had hers tied into two long braids. They almost looked like sisters.

Tapping Zecus' leg, Jak nodded in the direction of the pair.

"Look."

Zecus peered at them, lifted an eyebrow, and said, "Tombles? Here?"

Jak nodded.

"I'd give good coin to have Nundle here. I have a feeling he would be quite excited."

Zecus chuckled softly, saying, "And water is wet…"

Jak smiled and scanned the balcony, spotting a handful of other souls that were odd to his eye. Three ijuli sat together on the far side of the room, their tan skin and black hair marking them as tijuli. Jak frowned. Their light, loose robes looked quite comfortable.

"Why do they get to—?"

"Hush!" interrupted Lady Vivienne in a whispered voice. "Keep your tongue or wait outside!"

Jak glared at the baroness, his annoyance flaring again, and demanded, "When is this going to start anyway?"

As though his question were the cue, a door opened behind the long oak table. A pale man wearing a white tunic and crisp, black breeches emerged and strode forward, moving to stand at the center of the table. He waited as the attendants below hurried to stand against the walls of the chamber. The multitude of people in the balcony began to quiet, the buzz of conversation fading quickly.

Jak muttered, "Thank the Gods."

He felt Lady Vivienne glaring at him, but he did not care.

Once the room was quiet, the man called out, speaking crisply, snapping off each word.

"Citizens of the Oaken Duchies, ambassadors, and honored guests, I present the First Council."

His words echoed throughout the chamber.

"Representing the Northlands Duchy, I present to you Duke Anders' prime minister, Lord Hader, Baron of Carinius!"

Stepping forth from the door behind the table marched a man in black leather armor trimmed in gold cloth ribbing. He carried a pole upon which a black pennant hung, the gold and white image sewn upon the flag obscured by the cloth's folds.

Jak stared, confused. The man looked more soldier than baron.

Sergeant Trell leaned over and whispered, "An honor guard of the Black Watchers, the baron comes next."

Jak glanced over and nodded, grateful for the explanation.

The guard marched to the center of the table, turned sharply to the left, and strode to stand behind the chair at the far end of the table. He lowered the pole until it rested at a gentle angle, unfurling the black flag to reveal an emblem of a white teardrop-shaped shield with a golden tower at its center.

Two other men strode from the doorway, heading directly for the chair where the Black Watcher guard stood. The first was thin and balding, wearing a muted gold tunic, black pants, and black leather boots. The man following him wore garb matching the announcer and carried a leather binder under his arm.

The first man reached the chair, pulled it back from the table, and sat down. Immediately, the man behind him laid the binder upon the table and opened it. Jak assumed the man sitting down was Lord Hader, the Baron of Carinius.

Although the First Council was meant for the sovereigns of the ten duchies, rare was the occasion when a duke or duchess attended. Typically, a minister acted on their behalf, handling most mundane matters that never required approval of their sovereign.

The redheaded announcer called out again.

"Representing the Foothills Duchy, I present to you Duke Eli's prime minister: Lord Lucius, Baron of Vale!"

Another soldier stepped from the door, dressed in a slate gray and white uniform and carrying a wooden pole with a white flag draped down. The soldier marched to the center of the table and turned right, walking closer to where Jak sat.

Jak's stomach sunk as he realized they were going to have to wait for all ten ministers to be announced. Zecus caught his eye and frowned. The same thought had crossed his mind.

Everyone in the chambers waited—some more patiently than others—as each representative's name, title, and lands were announced before the noble took his or her place at the table. When the fifth member of the Council was announced, Jak sat up and paid attention.

"Representing the Great Lakes Duchy, I present to you Duke Everett's prime minister: Lord Treswell, the Baron of Deartfield!"

A Red Sentinel stepped from the doorway, wearing a fancier, more elaborate version of the armor with which Jak was familiar. A quick glance at Sergeant Trell revealed a tense man, muscles twitching in his jaw.

Jak empathized with the sergeant. He had dedicated his entire life to the Sentinels, only to discover that his liege lord, Duke Everett, was conspiring with the evil Gods of the Cabal. To what ends, no one knew, but the betrayal Sergeant Trell felt was clear to see.

Once the honor guard took his place, a tall, skinny man with immaculately combed black hair strode forth to take his place under the red and black pennant of the Great Lakes Duchy.

As the baron walked to his seat, Sergeant Trell muttered, "There's something wrong with that man."

Jak braced for another withering stare from Lady Vivienne warning them to remain quiet, but instead, she murmured a soft, almost agreeable response.

"Yes, Sergeant, there is."

Surprised, Jak turned to find the baroness with a thoughtful frown on her face. The next announcement pulled Jak's attention below a moment later.

"Representing the Borderlands' Duchy, I present to you Duke Vanson's prime minister,: Lord Tilas, the Baron of Ethemer!"

Zecus shifted in his seat, sitting up taller.

The honor guard that stepped from the doorway was wearing a dress uniform of muted browns and tans. From what Zecus had described to Jak about the dry and dusty region, he thought the colors were entirely appropriate.

Leaning close to Zecus, Jak asked softly, "Do you know who Lord Tilas is?"

Zecus shook his head, his dark brown eyes following the path of the baron to his seat beside Baron Treswell. Lord Tilas was dark-skinned like Zecus, but his head was shaved clean.

Zecus whispered, "Ethemer is in the southeast, bordering the Marshlands, I believe. Very far from home."

Jak sat as patiently as he could as the next pair was announced, a Lady Jonda representing the Red Peaks and Lord Osvanni for the Colonial Duchy. He was more interested in the different colored banners and soldiers than the nobles themselves.

Once Lord Osvanni took his seat, the announcer drew himself up an inch or two taller and called out, "Lords and Ladies, citizens of the Oaken Duchies, ambassadors and guests, please rise."

A soft murmuring of surprise rippled through the crowd. Jak caught a few snippets of whispered exchanges over the rustling of a few hundred people all standing at once.

"—rumors are true, then. I did not—"

"—remember when four attended?"

"—of this is quite interesting."

Not understanding why he must stand, he did nonetheless, along with everyone in the balcony. He shot an inquisitive look at Sergeant Trell and Lady Vivienne, but neither met his gaze. When he glanced at Zecus, the Borderlander shrugged his shoulders as he rose from the bench.

When the chamber was once again quiet, the man below resumed his announcing duties.

"I present to you the Duchess Adnil, the Lady of Nova Litora and sovereign ruler of the Long Coast Duchy!"

Jak suddenly understood why they were standing. Four sovereigns were here.

Two men dressed in maroon uniforms trimmed with silver, exited the door and marched to an open chair, one carrying the flag of the Long Coast Duchy, the other empty-handed. Once the guards were in place, Duchess Adnil entered the chamber.

The noblewoman was a short woman, perhaps only a few inches over five feet, with soft, blond hair cut short and held in place by a thin, golden band encircling her head. Jak guessed the duchess was in her late fifties, but could not be sure from where he sat. She hurried to her chair and sat quickly, fussing with her long, maroon dress, trying to arrange it just so. Jak got the distinct impression that the duchess found the pomp surrounding the introductions as tedious as he did. And for that reason alone, he liked her.

Duke Rholeb of the Marshlands entered next, a short and wide man with luxurious shoulder-length, gray hair. Matching the Duchess Adnil's no-nonsense attitude, he marched straight to his chair and sat beneath the green and white pennant of his duchy. As he settled in his seat, he gave a quick nod to the Duchess Adnil. It was so slight, Jak was sure most in the room had missed it.

"Allies," whispered Sergeant Trell.

Jak turned to stare at the soldier and found Lady Vivienne doing the same. Sergeant Trell had an incredible gift for being able to read people. If he believed the duke and duchess were allies, it was so.

Duchess Aleece of the Southlands, a stunningly beautiful woman in her late twenties, entered next. Her sleek brunette hair hung straight to the middle of her back, kept clear of her face by a blue silk headband. The dress she wore was a rich, deep Southlands blue trimmed with gold, snug above the waist but loose below, draping freely to the floor. She moved with the utmost grace, gliding silently across the marble floor.

Her gaze shot upwards as she walked, scanning the crowd in the balcony on the side of the chamber where Jak sat. For a moment, it seemed as if she were staring straight at Jak. A slight smile touched her lips.

Forgetting she was a noblewoman, let alone a duchess, Jak smiled wide, returning the grin as he would if any pretty young woman eyed him.

Ever so slightly, the duchess' eyes shifted. Now she was staring at him. Jak's smile turned into grimace.

"Oh, Hells."

The smile had not been for him.

Jak's neck and cheeks felt flushed and warm. Dropping his smile and his gaze, he stared at his shiny new leather dress boots while wondering why he had reacted in such a way. His heart belonged to another. As he stared downward, paying undue attention to the shiny bronze buckles that ran up the sides, he wondered at whom the duchess had been smiling. Whoever it was, he or she sat nearby.

The tenth and final member, Duke Kyle of the Freelands, stepped into the chamber next wearing a light blue vest over a puffy-sleeved white shirt. He was a pale man, well-fed and round, and his blue clothes combined with his white skin reminded Jak of a cloud-filled Spring sky. Once the duke took his seat, the herald instructed the crowd to return to their seats. With that, the man exited the chamber, closing the door as he left.

Jak was immensely relieved the proceedings were finally starting.

With a short, firm nod of his head, Duke Kyle cleared his throat before calling, "Thank you for coming today!" Amazingly, his voice carried through the cavernous room. "I see that we have higher attendance than normal and as I do not like to shout, I ask you to remain quiet!"

The duke scanned the balcony as he spoke.

"I expect most of you are here due to the reports that we would have some very important members attending. For once, it seems the rumormongers have earned their trade." Looking to his left, he said, "I would like to formally welcome Duke Rholeb, Duchess Aleece—" he turned right "—and Duchess Adnil to Freehaven and today's council. Thank you for coming."

Duke Kyle paused as the three leaders of the Duchies acknowledged his greeting with respectful nods and smiles.

"As one who attends every meeting, I would like to offer my assistance to any of you should you have questions regarding procedure or the like."

A soft, intense whisper from Jak's right caught him off guard.

"Of course you attend every meeting. You live in the blasted city, you pompous fool."

As one, Zecus, Jak and Sergeant Trell turned to stare at Lady Vivienne. If she felt their stares, she did not acknowledge them.

Jak exchanged a quick look with the sergeant, raising a lone eyebrow, and stared back to the table below just as Duke Kyle resumed speaking.

"Before we hear this turn's petitions, there is one issue outstanding from our last meeting. Baroness Vivienne of Argolles, the representative from the Southlands, motioned to delay a response to one particular petition."

Again, Jak and Zecus turned to peer at Lady Vivienne. She, in turn, continued to ignore their stares. Broedi had not been jesting when he said the Shadow Manes had powerful members. Lady Vivienne apparently sat on the First Council. Sergeant Trell kept his eyes forward, showing no reaction to the revelation which Jak assumed meant the soldier already knew. He eyed the sergeant, both impressed by the man's ability to keep such wondrous information a secret and perturbed that he had done so.

Jak's curiosity was cut short as Duke Kyle's booming voice filled the chamber again.

"Procedure dictates that the member who motioned for delay must call for resumption. Duchess Aleece, as the baroness is your minister, the decision to resume the petition is yours to make. Do you wish to do so?"

In a clear, mellow tone that easily cut through the large room, Duchess Aleece responded, "I do."

Jak suddenly made sense of the duchess' earlier smile. It was directed at the baroness.

"So be it," called Duke Kyle. "Please bring the petitioners in."

At the opposite end of the chamber—to Jak's far right—two attendants opened a set of double oaken doors, loosing a ragged, metal clatter that resonated through the room. Two dark-skinned men strode into the room, dressed in tan shirts and breeches with braided leather sandals strapped to their feet. One of the men was tall and thin, walking a step ahead of his companion, a shorter, fatter man. Both individuals had close-cropped, black beards and hair with thick, white bands wrapped around their heads. Jak marked them immediately as Borderlanders.

Zecus drew in a sharp breath and hissed, "Bless the Gods."

The intensity of his friend's reaction caused Jak to turn and stare at Zecus. The young man's eyes were as wide as gold ducats and locked on the men walking across the marble floor below.

Alarmed, Jak whispered, "Zecus? What's—"

A strong hand tightly gripped his right leg, causing Jak to wince sharply and halt his question. Looking down to his right knee, he found Sergeant Trell's white-knuckled left hand grasping him. He glanced up to the sergeant's face and found the soldier's intense gaze on his face. He gave a quick, sharp shake of his head and spoke in a low, hushed tone.

"Let things play out. Remain quiet."

Lady Vivienne was staring hard at him as well, her sharp green eyes silently pleading he comply. Had the baroness alone asked, Jak would have demanded to know what was going on right now. Yet as the request had come from Sergeant Trell, he swallowed his question and nodded.

Sergeant Trell released his leg and Jak stole a quick look back at Zecus. His friend was still staring wide-eyed at the pair of Borderlanders on the chamber floor. Frowning, Jak looked down as well.

The men stopped twenty paces from the council table and waited in silence. The thin man appeared calm and relaxed considering the situation while the larger man was actively bouncing on the balls of feet.

Duke Kyle leaned forward and called, "Please state your names for the record, citizens."

The taller man bowed slightly, and said, "My name is Joshmuel Alsher and he is Boah Rasus. We are of the village Drysa. My pleasure is to meet you in peace today, great Lord."

Now Jak's eyes went wide. He whipped his head to his left to gape at an unresponsive Zecus.

"That's your—"

Again, Jak felt Sergeant Trell's hand grip his leg, thrice as strong this time. Jak winced and shut his mouth. The sergeant wanted him to remain quiet.

Turning to stare at the soldier, Jak tried to make sense of things. If Lady Vivienne had been the one to postpone this petition, she had known about Joshmuel for well over a full turn. And if Lady Vivienne knew, then so did Broedi, as did Sergeant Trell.

Jak's eyes narrowed as he glared to his right. Sergeant Trell should have told them that Zecus' own father had been sitting in Freehaven for a full turn.

Sergeant Trell stared back, an expression of true regret on his face. He even appeared slightly ashamed. Jak shook his head and gave a disappointed sigh. He was getting tired of all the secrets everyone around him was keeping.

Duke Kyle called out, "And for the record, as well as the benefit of those that were not here last turn, Joshmuel Alsher of Drysa, can you please restate your petition for the council?"

Joshmuel bowed, saying, "Yes, great Lord." He took a breath, composing himself, and then began speaking, his voice loud, clear, and touched with the same strange accent that Zecus himself exhibited.

"For generations upon generations, we on the western edge of the Borderlands have lived with the constant threat that oligurts, mongrels, and razorfiends might raid our lands and homes. Years would pass without any sign of the Sudashians, but eventually some chieftain or pack leader would crave glory and conquest and raid the duchy. Villages burned, people died, and the duke would respond, sending the Dust Men forth to repel the invaders."

From the measured and deliberate way he spoke, it was apparent this was a rehearsed speech.

"Our ancestors would honor the dead by rebuilding the villages, refusing to allow the tribes of Sudash to chase us from our lands. Of course, the raiders would come again. So, we would rebuild. And the raiders would come again. Such is the life of a Borderlander."

Joshmuel paused and drew a long breath.

"A year ago, however, the cycle changed. Men, women, and families who lived closer to the border than we—" he indicated himself and Boah "—began to come east. Raiders had come again. Only now, there were thousands of oligurts, mongrels, razorfiends, and even men all banded together. They fought as one." He paused and eyed the table of nobles. "My Lords and Ladies, such cooperation is unheard of. Sudashian infighting has been the one thing that has kept us in the west safe. If the fell races unite, the Borderlands fall."

Jak pulled his eyes away from Joshmuel and glanced at Lord Tilas, the Borderlands' representative. The man sat as still as a carved marble statue.

Joshmuel continued his tale, saying clearly, "There has been almost no pushback from our soldiers. The Dust Men are absent. People have been left to defend their homes without the help of the duke's army. Chaos rules the west."

Jak bit his lip. Joshmuel's choice of words was more accurate than he knew.

"So, great Lords and Ladies, Boah and I traveled to Freehaven, hoping to petition the First Council to lend aid to the Borderlands." He paused again, spared a quick glance at his compatriot—who nodded firmly—and then added, somewhat reluctantly, "In addition to our previous request, we now also ask the council to seek answers to the poor response by the Dust Men." Joshmuel bowed at the waist. "That is all, great Lord."

Joshmuel's last word had barely tumbled from his lips when the Borderlands' baron sat forward, looked in Duke Kyle's direction, and asked, "My Lord, may I speak?" After a curt nod from the duke, Lord Tilas shifted his gaze on the pair of men before the council.

"As I said last turn when these…*men*—" the word was said with an audible sneer "—came before us, I have no idea about what they speak. There are no 'invaders' from Sudash marching through the Borderlands. I again contend that these men are mad."

The baron's words stunned Jak. Shooting a questioning look to his left, Jak found Zecus equally astonished, if not more so. Zecus had seen the invasion firsthand, having been captured by oligurts and razorfiends deep within Borderland territory.

From beneath the green and white banner of the Marshlands, Duke Rholeb spoke up.

"Baron Tilas, I respectfully disagree with your 'assessment' of the situation."

While the duke's tone was polite on its surface, an undercurrent of strained fury bubbled beneath it.

Turning to face the Marshlands' sovereign, Lord Tilas said, "I'm sorry you feel as such, my Lord, but I would know the affairs of the Borderlands infinitely better than you, would I not? I assure you, there is no danger from Sudash."

The baron's disrespectful tone prompted a low, whispered buzz to ripple through the balcony.

Glaring at Lord Tilas, Duke Rholeb growled, "I have nineteen thousand Borderlands' refugees sitting outside of my capital, begging for food, that say otherwise, Tilas!"

Lord Tilas sat back in his chair and said with brazen smugness, "Might they not be your own citizens? Perhaps they finally gave up trying to survive in that swampland you call a duchy and have decided to simply beg for handouts instead."

The blatant, open affront triggered more mumbles of disapproval amongst the crowd. Jak knew little about expected etiquette between nobles, but he was quite confident that it was bad form for a baron to insult one of the ten sovereigns publicly.

Duke Rholeb brought his left hand down hard atop the wooden table, sending a sharp crack that echoed through the chamber.

"Blast you, Tilas! What in the Nine Hells is going on?!"

"Gentlemen!" exclaimed Duke Kyle. "Please! Try to keep a sense of decorum here!"

Duke Rholeb continued to stare daggers at a grinning, haughty Lord Tilas.

After a moment, Duke Kyle turned to the Marshlander and said, "Now, Rholeb—if Lord Tilas says there is no trouble, we are honor-bound to believe him. He is Duke Vanson's representative and speaks for him."

With an upraised hand, the Great Lakes member of the council, Lord Treswell, said timidly, "My Lord, if I may add something?"

Jak was especially curious to hear what Duke Everett's representative had to say.

Once Duke Kyle nodded, Lord Treswell said, "Might I point out that were there any such invasion, Duke Vanson would have surely requested aid of Duke Everett. However, to date, no such requests have been made."

Jak frowned. The baron had spent more care wording his statement than a one-eyed, half-blind woman would threading a needle.

The soft, melodic voice of Duchess Aleece suddenly cut through chamber.

"I agree with Lord Treswell."

Noticeably wary, Lord Treswell nodded his head, appearing surprised to have elicited the agreement of the duchess. Lord Tilas nodded as well, staring at the duchess as if he were a hunter wandering the woods, trying to remember where he had placed his own snare.

After a moment, Lord Tilas said, "You do, my Lady?"

The duchess nodded, saying, "Oh, yes. Quite so. Everett could never answer a request for aid if none were sent forth." Her tone shifted, turning harder suddenly. "Which I can only conclude means Vanson has sent none." Turning to stare directly at Lord Tilas, Duchess Aleece said pointedly, "Tell me something, Tilas. Why has Vanson not replied to any of the messages sent to him by Rholeb or me? We've been more than polite in our requests for clarification regarding the refugees."

Jak sensed a trap being set.

Turning her stare on Joshmuel and Boah, the duchess added, "Also, it puzzles me why two Borderlanders would travel so far to beg for help if none were needed. You claim they are mad, Tilas. I think they look perfectly sound. Which means—if we are to believe your words—that they are lying."

Lord Tilas shook his head vigorously, saying, "Lying or mad, my Lady, what difference—"

Swiveling her head, the duchess glared hard at the Borderlands baron.

"I was *not* finished speaking, Tilas!"

Lord Tilas closed his mouth, his eyebrows drawing together.

Duchess Aleece held her gaze on the baron, daring the man to respond. When he wisely remained quiet, she turned away, sweeping her gaze around the entire balcony. Jak had the sudden impression he was watching a playman's show. Whatever was happening here was as much for the observers as it was for the council.

The duchess, her eyes scanning the room, called, "Ample evidence of a mass exodus from the Borderlands abounds despite Lord Tilas' feckless denials! What could possibly cause so many people flee their homes?!" Pausing for effect, she sat forward, rested her elbows on the table, and asked, "A better question, yet, is why Lord Tilas would make claims that seem utterly contrary to the truth?"

Her words caused another uproar amongst the crowded gallery, louder this time. Duke Kyle began to shout through the din, trying to quiet the chamber.

As the crowd buzzed, Jak turned to Sergeant Trell and muttered, "What is going on?"

"It would seem the duchess is within a thread of charging Lord Tilas of lying." Gesturing around the balcony, he said, "Based on their reaction, it would seem that is a rather serious accusation."

Leaning forward, Zecus said vehemently, "But he *is* lying! I saw the oligurts and razorfiends there myself!" The passion in Zecus' tone startled Jak. The Borderlander was normally a quiet, reserved man.

Sergeant Trell nodded and fixed a hard glare on Zecus.

"Yes, but nobody here knows what you saw. As it stands, it's the word of two simple petitioners against a baron."

Jak thought Sergeant Trell's formal acknowledgement of Zecus' father to be odd. The soldier certainly knew who Joshmuel was.

Duke Kyle, after demanding silence for a full minute, finally achieved it by threatening to clear the balcony. As none in attendance wanted to miss whatever might happen next, they quickly quieted. A scowl on his face, the duke swiveled his substantial girth about his chair to face the Southlands' duchess. The overweight man's forehead had a light sheen on it.

"Aleece, might you wish to withdraw your words? It sounded as if you were claiming that a member of this council is intentionally deceiving us."

Duchess Aleece gave a polite inclination of her head and said, "I am quite sorry, Kyle. I should have been clearer with my words."

The duke relaxed some, evidently anticipating an apology. Jak had the feeling he was not going to hear one.

The duchess leaned forward, eyed the balcony again, and said in a raised voice, "I did not mean to insinuate that Lord Tilas is lying. Rather, I am stating with *absolute conviction* that he is!" Glaring down the table, she added, "Along with Lord Treswell!"

The Great Lakes' baron sat straighter, shooting a worried glance at Lord Tilas. The crowd's whispers and murmurings forced Duchess Aleece to raise her voice.

"Moreover, I have cause to believe they are both acting under direct orders of Vanson and Everett!"

The spectators in the balcony began to cry out, prompting Duke Kyle to pound on the table, again demanding silence. As the nobleman shouted for quiet, Jak carefully watched the council table. The two Barons from the Great Lakes and Borderlands shared multiple, quick glances. Jak thought they looked guilty. A quick sequence glance—pleased and content—shot between Duke Rholeb and Duchess Aleece.

Jak's eyebrows drew together. Peering around the gallery of spectators, he muttered with quiet wonder, "They planned this…" He looked to Sergeant Trell. "This was all a show, wasn't it?"

The soldier leaned over and said softly, "Theatre and politics are two sides of the same ducat, Jak." He dropped his voice to a whisper. "Try to remain silent for a little while longer. I think I finally understand what Lady Vivienne has planned."

Jak stole a quick look at the baroness. She was staring past him, straight at Zecus, a cold, calculating glint in her eyes. It took all of Jak's confidence in the sergeant to reluctantly mutter, "Fine."

This time, Duke Kyle needed twice as long to quiet the crowd. Once he did, he bellowed, "Might I remind all of you that you are here at the pleasure of the council? I will not tolerate such outbursts from anyone, regardless of stature or class! If it happens again, I shall order the balcony purged!" Pausing to let his instructions sink in, he turned to face a very calm Duchess Aleece and said, "The accusations you have leveled, my Lady, are beyond severe. I pray to Tirnu you can substantiate them."

Before she could answer Duke Kyle's question, Duchess Adnil of the Long Coast interrupted.

"Pardon, Kyle. But I would like to give Lords Tilas and Treswell an opportunity to respond first. Before we hear of evidence, should any exist."

Duke Kyle hesitated briefly before saying, "Fine." He set his gaze to the pair of barons. "Have you anything to say in response to the duchess's statement?"

Chairs creaked as every council member twisted in their seats and stared at the two barons. Every pair of eyes in the balcony also shifted to the men.

After a few tense, deathly-silent moments, Lord Tilas stood from his chair. Staring directly at Duchess Aleece, he said in a voice dripping with acid, "With all respect due to you, my Lady, I assert your accusation is wholly without cause." He peered down at Lord Treswell expectantly.

The baron of the Great Lakes glanced up to meet his stare, frowned, and offered weakly, "I stand with Lord Tilas, my Lady." He looked as if he might get ill. "Your words are without merit…"

With a firm nod, Lord Tilas pulled his gaze from the baron and stared up to the balcony, exclaiming, "Duke Vanson is an honorable man! He will be both saddened and offended by your statement, Duchess Aleece." He stared hard at the noblewoman. "You understand it is my duty to inform him of what has transpired here."

Duchess Aleece nodded, saying calmly, "Oh, I was hoping you would. Please, tell him *exactly* what I said, Tilas. Word for word. In fact, if you like, I can have a scribe write them down for you if you do not trust your memory."

Lord Tilas stood straight as a rod, glowering hard at the duchess as she pressed on, a hard edge to her voice.

"As you will be corresponding with Vanson, might I ask a favor of you? Since the man will not respond to me or Rholeb, add the following question to your missive: 'What were you promised?'"

Lord Tilas stiffened but remained silent.

Lady Jonda, the elderly baroness of Yar, leaned forward and asked, "Pardon me, my Lady, but what do you mean by that?"

Duchess Aleece raised her eyes to the crowd, paused for effect, and then called, "If one of the ten sovereigns has betrayed us all to conspire with Sudash, I would simply like to know what was promised in return!"

A hushed gasp rippled through the balcony, but was quickly cut off after a sharp glare from Duke Kyle. Jak was in awe of the duchess. She was fearless. Or mad.

Finally finding his voice, Lord Tilas shouted, "How dare you! Being duchess does not give you the right to impugn the honor of my liege! You have yet put forth any evidence of this supposed treachery. It is Duke Rholeb's word against mine and that of Baron Treswell. And I swear upon the Gods and Goddesses themselves, there is nothing to fear in the Borderlands!" Pointing a finger at the duke of the Marshlands, a near-unhinged Lord Tilas shouted, "I ask Duke Rholeb for proof of his claims! I am wondering if he perhaps mistook a trade caravan for his perceived 'nineteen thousand refugees' in Demetus! Perhaps the duke is growing addled in his old age?"

Jak's eyes widened.

"Oh, my…"

Duke Rholeb sat straight, his face turning bright red. Jak expected him to leap up and punch the baron, but after a moment—and a few harsh, direct glares from Duchesses Aleece and Adnil—he crossed his arms and remained seated.

Looking over at Sergeant Trell, Jak asked in a whisper, "All three are in on this, yes?"

Sergeant Trell replied softly, "Good eyes, Jak."

"Quiet!" hissed Lady Vivienne. "Both of you!"

Frowning, Jak eyed the noblewoman and was surprised to find that she was not looking at him or the sergeant, but rather staring in Zecus' direction, a tiny, content smile resting over her lips. Confused, Jak turned to his friend. The man was seething, his eyes burning, his hands clasped into fists, his lips pressed so tight they were white.

Jak glanced back to Lady Vivienne, eyes narrowed, but the baroness had already returned her attention below. After a moment, Jak did as well.

Lord Tilas was still staring at Duke Rholeb, a confused look upon his face. It seemed he had expected a fiery response from the sovereign and did not know what to do now.

After letting the man drift in the wind for a few moments longer, Duchess Aleece said calmly, "To be clear, Lord Tilas, this is not a case of your word against that of Rholeb's." Gesturing to where Joshmuel and Boah still stood before the table—both men appeared quite uncomfortable by this point—she continued, "We have two men here before us, citizens of your duchy, claiming their home is under siege. Why would they say such a thing?"

Lord Tilas' gaze turned to the pair, hate simmering in his eyes. "Are you going to take the word of two goat-herders"—the baron sneered—"over my own? A lord of the land? I am a *baron*! They are nothing!"

Jak glanced over at Zecus just in time to watch the dam holding back his friend's emotions break. Zecus launched himself from his seat, stood tall, and began to yell.

"I have seen the Sudashian camps! I have smelled the roasting flesh of their victims! I have been beaten by oligurts and watched razorfiends slice through men like a sword through water! I have stood, face to face, with a demon of the Nine Hells!"

Jak did not have to look about the chamber to know that every pair of eyes was focused on Zecus. Lord Tilas stared upward, utterly baffled by the outburst. Zecus glared back with a fervent, passionate loathing.

"Baron or not, *Lord* Tilas. You are a *liar*!"

Zecus' words echoed through the chamber, fading quickly, and leaving the room feeling empty and oddly quiet. A lone call from a seagull outside made its way through an open window.

All at once, everyone in the council chamber began to talk and shout. Duke Kyle started yelling and gesturing about, directing guards throughout the room to usher people from the balcony. He pointed up to the balcony, his glare locked on Zecus.

Standing up, Jak leaned close to his friend and said, "Well, you certainly kicked the beehive."

Zecus turned to stare at him, his eyes still burning.

"Pardon?"

A lopsided grin on his face, Jak said, "I think that was exactly what she wanted."

The intense heat drained from Zecus' eyes, replaced by an equal amount of confusion.

"She?"

Jak nodded to the table below. Duchess Aleece was staring up at Jak and his companions, a satisfied smile on her face.

Zecus muttered, "I do not understand."

Jak sat back down and tugged Zecus' arm, encouraging his friend to do the same.

"Have a seat, Zecus. I expect we'll be here a while."

CHAPTER 5: DREAMS

Kenders placed a hand on the oaken door, paused a moment, and said a silent prayer the hinges would not creak as normal. Her plea would go unanswered.

She pushed gently, wincing as a long, drawn-out screech filled the mages' hall, announcing her arrival to those gathered in the room. The soft glow of candles and mage lights greeted her, along with half the faces in the room as people stared at the intrusion, looking up from their work or twisting about on their benches.

Meeting the gaze of a few nearby mages, she frowned and said softly, "So sorry."

Her apology was brushed aside with quiet, almost reverent whispers of "No trouble, Progeny" or "Welcome, Progeny." Their politeness threatened to turn her frown into a scowl. She could sing as loudly as she could, interrupting everyone's studies, and the mages here would still smile and tell her it was no bother. It was unnatural.

She stepped into the long hall and shut the door behind her, sending an encore of creaking through the chamber. Once the door softly thudded closed, she breathed a sigh of relief and studied the room, hoping Gamin was here.

Thick ebonwood rafters crisscrossed overhead, each one as thick as a well-fed man's torso. Two dozen dark wooden tables filled the hall, half of them occupied by mages in the midst of researching, practicing, or reading. Books and parchments lay strewn about the tabletops, illuminated by candles or simple Weaves of Charge or Fire hovering overhead the mages who could touch those particular Strands. The soft undercurrent of magic filled the hall, crackling inside of her. As always, she was reminded of the sensation of crumbling straw.

The room was quiet and still, making the sudden movement at the far end of the hall that much more noticeable. Sabine sat at one of the long tables, waving her arm and smiling. Gamin sat beside her, back to Kenders, his red hair glistening in the light of candles and Weaves. He twisted around, met her gaze, and motioned for Kenders to come down to where they sat.

A tiny, satisfied grin touched Kenders' lips.

"Perfect…"

She turned left and moved along the wall, scooting about the perimeter of the room, tying to be as inconspicuous as possible. Yet as she walked along the windowless walls, passing the twin hearths, she felt the eyes of every mage on her. She had been here for over a turn and still people stared.

Upon reaching the opposite end of the hall, she scooted over to where Sabine and Gamin rested on a bench. As she approached, Sabine glanced up and lifted a finger to her lips, motioning for her to be quiet. Kenders raised an eyebrow in silent inquiry, prompting Sabine to point to the back right corner of the room. Looking over, Kenders spotted two figures sitting at a small oak table. One of the pair was Marick, a young mage skilled in Fire and Water, while the other was a raven-haired girl no older than four or five years old. A fat, yellow beeswax candle sat on the tabletop between them, glowing from within. The little girl was staring at Marick intently, listening to whatever the young man was saying and nodding. Helene was in the midst of one of her lessons.

Sabine and Gamin sat together on one bench, facing Helene while watching from afar. Kenders smiled at them both as she sat next to Gamin. Adjusting her dress, she peered around the barrel-chested mage and whispered to Sabine, "How's she doing?"

Sabine shook her head and murmured, "You are asking the wrong person. Every so often, I feel a flicker of orange and blue, but…" She trailed off and shrugged her shoulders. The frustration in her friend's tone was clear.

Kenders nodded, sympathizing with Sabine. While Helene showed great talent with Water, Fire, Stone, and Soul, Sabine herself could only barely sense Fire and Water. Both sisters had started taking lessons upon arriving at the enclave, but Sabine's talent was so meager that after two weeks and no improvement, she had said she wished to quit trying. Gamin had not talked her out of it.

Keeping his eyes on Helene, the large mage murmured, "She is making good progress recognizing the proper way to reach for Fire." He nodded approvingly. "Which, considering her age and inexperience, I am more than happy with."

"That's good," said Kenders softly.

Gamin nodded, whispering, "Very. Strands of Fire are wild and perhaps the most difficult to control. All it takes is one mistake and…" He trailed off, leaving the rest to their imagination.

Kenders was intimately familiar with the untamed nature of Fire. During the journey to the enclave, Broedi had attempted to teach her some simple Weaves of pure Fire. Were it not for the giant hillman around to fix her errors, she would have set the Southlands' prairie aflame more than a few times.

Feeling a tiny flicker of orange, Kenders glanced over to the table and watched a single Strand of Fire pop into existence, wrap itself into a simple knot, and then disappear into the candle. The flame dancing upon the wick surged, briefly flaring thrice as tall and bright before returning to normal. Helene stared at the candle and smiled.

"Her or him?" whispered Kenders.

"Marick," answered Gamin. "Helene is only permitted to pull forth Fire Strands. Until she has complete control, Weaves are forbidden to her. I do *not* want mistakes."

Kenders nodded, murmuring, "Good idea."

The trio had watched in hushed quiet for a few moments when Gamin turned to peer at Kenders, his eyes searching her face.

"If I am not mistaken, this would be the second day in a row you are done with your lessons early."

Kenders frowned, a weary sigh sneaking from her lips before she could halt it.

"You are *not* mistaken."

Sabine leaned forward to look over, her long black hair brushing the tabletop. She reached up to tuck it behind her ear, a teasing yet kind smile on her lips.

"And what did you do wrong this time?"

Kenders shook her head defiantly and whispered, "Nothing. Nothing at all."

A bemused chuckle slipped from Gamin.

"Were that the case, you would not be here."

Frowning, Kenders said, "I speak true, Gamin. I did exactly what Khin told me to do."

"What was today's lesson?" asked the mage.

"To light a candle."

Gamin's brow drew together.

"And?"

With an exasperated wave of her hand, Kenders whispered, "That's it."

Gamin was quiet a moment.

"That's it? You lit a candle?"

Sighing softly, Kenders said, "That's it."

"Hells," murmured Sabine. "*I* can do that."

Confusion on his face and in his voice, Gamin asked, "To be clear, Khin had you do the same Weave, over and over again? All morning?"

Kenders shook her head, murmuring, "No. I worked on a *single* Weave. One. Blasted. Pattern." She turned to stare at them both, adding firmly, "For hours." It had been an incredibly long and tedious exercise.

Nodding, Gamin said, "Ah, now, I see." His blue eyes studied her, glinting with reflected candlelight. "From your tone and posture, it would seem you did not grasp the lesson's goal."

Kenders' eyebrows lifted high and to a peak. "Oh, I grasped it just fine. I am to learn patience." Frowning, she muttered, "Patience, patience, and more blasted patience." A quiet moment passed as she sat, reliving the frustration she had felt sitting in Khin's chilly tower room.

Sabine broke the silence, whispering, "Sounds like you need more practice."

Kenders looked over to find an amused grin on Sabine's face.

"Yes, well…"

Another burst of orange crackling pulled Kenders' attention back to the table in the corner in time for her to watch a tiny Strand of Fire twist into a knot, sending the candle flaring again. Kenders' frown deepened. Such a simple Weave took less than a heartbeat to complete, yet she had been forced to draw out hers all morning.

"Why are you here, Kenders?" asked Gamin, the tone of his voice both inquisitive and probing.

Looking over, she found the mage staring at her with knowing eyes. Starting slowly, Kenders said, "Well, I was thinking that since *you* are the head of the mages here, perhaps I might convince you to alter my lessons."

Gamin's eyes narrowed.

"Alter them how?"

Kenders gave the man a weak smile.

"I'd prefer it if you were to teach me instead—"

"No," interjected Gamin quickly, shaking his head. "Absolutely not."

"But if you—"

"*No*, Kenders," whispered Gamin, his tone firm. "Broedi wished for you to study with Khin, and I wholly agree with him, especially after observing you for the past few weeks. You *must* learn—if I may use your phrasing—'patience, patience, and more blasted patience.'"

Kenders had expected this would be the way of things, but she had needed to try anyway. A defeated sigh slipped from her lips and her shoulders slumped.

"Fine."

She turned away from Gamin and stared over to Helene, almost envying the little girl. She looked as if she were enjoying her lessons, staring intently at the candle's flame, a tiny smile on her face. The smile disappeared as Helene's lips parted and she yawned. For the first time, Kenders noticed how tired she looked.

A door leading to another of the castle's hallways opened—quietly, Kenders noted with a frown. A nearly seven-foot-tall female figure, built like Broedi, but with narrower shoulders and slimmer legs, moved through the entryway. Auburn hair hung loose to her shoulders but for a single bunch tied in a topknot and bound with a band of turquoise beads. She strode straight to their table, moving to block their view of Helene and Marick, and stopped.

Meeting Kenders' gaze first, she inclined her head and rumbled, "Good morning, Progeny."

Kenders forced herself to smile and barely succeeded.

"Good morning, Chandrid."

There were a handful of the hillmen race here at the enclave, but Chandrid was the only female. After Kenders and her brothers had first met her, the siblings had huddled together later that evening, wondering as to the proper way to refer to her. Hillman did not seem appropriate. By the end of the conversation, the best they had come up with was 'hillwoman.' They had inquired with Broedi if he thought the term acceptable, and had received a slight, bemused smile and nod in return.

Chandrid exchanged a quick and quiet greeting with Sabine before shifting her gaze to Gamin and saying, "Commander Aiden has need of you in the courtyard."

Gamin sighed and asked, "Does he now? I don't suppose he said why?" His tone indicated he already knew the answer.

"No, sir, he did not," replied Chandrid. "But it is terribly windy outside right now, and…" A small lopsided grin spread over the hillwoman's lips. "Well, sir. The commander looked cold."

"Well, we can't have that, now can we?" asked Gamin with a smile. Glancing between Kenders and Sabine, he added, "Pardon me." He placed his hands on the tabletop, pushed himself up, and stepped free of the bench. "Good memories behind to you both."

After Sabine and Kenders said farewell, the two mages exited the room leaving the two friends alone. The pair sat in silence for a while, watching Helene practice with Marick. At one point, Helene glanced over, saw Kenders, and offered a smile.

Kenders grinned and waved. As Helene waved back, she yawned again.

"She looks exhausted," whispered Kenders.

When her friend did not respond immediately, Kenders looked over to find Sabine staring at Helene, a frown marring her pretty features. For the first time, Kenders noticed puffy bags under Sabine's eyes.

"Is everything alright with you, Sabine?"

The elder Moiléne sister sighed, shook her head, and muttered, "It's just…" She trailed off. Something was bothering her.

Concerned, Kenders scooted down the bench, closer to her friend.

"What is it?"

On the journey south to Storm Island, Helene had exhibited a few traits that had caused them all worry. While in Fernsford, she had steadfastly insisted that someone was trailing them. While true, her claim was wholly unexpected as everyone had been careful to keep that worrisome detail from the young girl. When they pressed her as to how she knew such a thing, she got upset and nearly used the Strands without intent. Since then, Broedi had watched the girl carefully, but with him gone now, more than a few folks at the enclave, Kenders included, shared the task of observing the girl's behavior.

Sabine reluctantly looked over and said, "You remember the dreams I told you about?"

A furrow of bewilderment split Kenders forehead.

"Pardon?"

"One night, on the way here, I told you about Helene's dreams, the ones—"

Kenders nodded quickly, interrupting Sabine, saying, "Yes, yes. Of course." Her confused surprise had more to do with the question's subject than any lack of recall. She remembered the conversation clearly. During one of their evening talks around the campfire, Sabine had confided in Kenders that bad dreams had plagued Helene her entire life.

Sabine was quiet a moment, an anxious frown on her face, before she muttered, "Well, they've been worse the past two weeks. She wakes up three, four times a night now."

"You said it's sometimes worse than others."

With her gaze locked on her little sister, Sabine gave a tiny shake of her head and whispered, "It's different this time, Kenders. Much different."

Kenders eyebrows drew together.

"Why?"

Sabine remained quiet and motionless for a long moment, her stare never leaving the table in the corner. Eventually, she drew in a deep breath, exhaled, and turned to Kenders.

"I want to tell you. Truly, I do. But I do *not* want this to get back to Broedi. Or Gamin. Or anyone with the Manes."

Kenders frowned inwardly.

"Why?"

Sabine pressed her lips together and shook her head.

"Because they might make us leave."

Kenders eyes narrowed.

"I doubt that very much, Sabine. Nobody would make you leave here."

Sabine gave her a dry smile and said, "And the barncat promised not to eat the mouse."

Worried in more ways than one, Kenders reached out a hand and placed it on Sabine's.

"Please, Sabine. You can tell me."

"I will," said Sabine. Turning to meet Kenders' beseeching gaze with a hard-eyed stare, she added, "I will if you promise not to tell *anyone*."

Kenders frowned. Sabine was putting her in a difficult position.

"Well…"

Sabine pressed her lips together, shook her head, and said, "Never mind. Forget I said anything."

"Now, hold a moment," said Kenders quickly. "You did not give me a chance to answer."

Her friend eyed her doubtfully.

"And what is your answer?"

Kenders hesitated. If she was going to give her word, she wanted to be sure that she could keep it. Besides her brothers, Sabine was the closest friend she had since leaving Yellow Mud. Deciding that she owed Sabine, she gave a quick nod.

"I promise."

Sabine's eyes narrowed, a chilly glint in her glare. When it came to Helene, she was fiercely protective.

"I will hold you to that."

"I would be surprised if you did not," whispered Kenders.

Sabine held her gaze a moment longer before looking across the room, back to Helene. In a small and quiet voice, she said, "She started to tell me what her dreams are about."

Kenders cocked an eyebrow.

"I thought she never told you."

Sabine shook her head.

"She never has. I even stopped asking."

After waiting a moment for Sabine to continue, Kenders prompted gently, "So?"

"It's the same dream," whispered Sabine. "Every time, she says. She's with me—just the two of us—hiding in a dark room, crouched behind some tables. She hears screaming and thunder outside. Then, suddenly, we aren't alone anymore. Someone steps from the shadows, and…" Her eyebrows drew together as she shot a worried glance at Kenders. "And it kills me with 'a ball of fire,' according to Helene."

A shiver ran up Kenders' spine as Sabine looked back to Helene. After a moment, she sighed and continued softly.

"Then, there's fire everywhere, and the person takes Helene and 'runs into the black.' Those are her exact words. 'Runs into the black.'"

"It's the same dream?" asked Kenders. "Every time?"

Sabine nodded, saying, "For a while now, yes. Ever since Shorn Rise."

"What were they before that?"

Sabine shrugged and whispered with a touch of exasperation, "I don't know, Kenders. She still won't tell me those." She frowned. "I'm hoping she doesn't remember them."

Patting Sabine's hand, Kenders said soothingly, "Hey, Sabine, it's fine."

Sabine pulled her hand back, shook her head firmly, and said, "Fine?" She was agitated, yet managed to keep her voice low. "How is this 'fine?' Every night, my sister has a dream—or four—where I die!"

Kenders did not know what to say or do. She sat still, trying to understand what Sabine must be going through, what both sisters must be going through. Knowing her friend, Sabine's worry had nothing to do with her own fate. She was concerned for Helene's well-being, her state of mind. Kenders tried to imagine living her life where every night, she had to watch her brothers die. She did not linger on the thought long. It was too upsetting.

"The person in the dream," whispered Kenders. "The one who…" She trailed off, not wanting to give voice to the act. "Who is it she sees?"

Sabine shook her head.

"All she's told me is 'long, white hair.' Other than that, she refuses to talk. And I don't press her."

"I don't understand," murmured Kenders. "Why, after never wanting to talk about the dreams, why is she talking now?"

Sabine sighed and said, "Now, *that* I can answer." She paused and turned to stare at Kenders. "The night we arrived here, Helene was hungry and Broedi pointed me in the direction of the commons. The moment we stepped into the room, Helene grabs my leg and begs me to pick her up." Sabine's eyes were wide. "She was *terrified*, Kenders, shaking in my arms. It took me quite a while to calm her down enough to where she would tell me why."

Afraid she knew the answer already, Kenders nonetheless muttered, "Why?"

Leaning closer, Sabine whispered, "Sitting in my lap, she stares up, tears in her eyes, and says, "'This is where you die, Sabine. Please don't die.'"

Kenders stared at her friend, unsure what to say and ashamed that the only thought running through her head was that she needed to break her promise. Broedi had to know about this. Shoving aside her burgeoning sense of betrayal, she said comfortingly, "Sabine, it's just a dream."

A quiet, dry chuckle burst from Sabine's lips.

"Just a dream?"

Shaking her head, she hissed, "Hells, Kenders!" She motioned around her. "Look at where we're sitting. Look at what's happened! What *is* happening! This is not 'just a dream!'"

"But—"

"Keep the sweet, Kenders. I see nothing but sour here. Nothing! Everyone here has a purpose. You, Nikalys, Jak, Broedi, Nundle, *everyone*. Hells, apparently even Zecus considering he's off in Freehaven doing Gods knows what. But me and Helene? What about us? What is our purpose? Why are we here?"

Kenders opened her mouth to respond, but Sabine was not truly looking for an answer. The young beauty continued whispering, unabated.

"I had accepted that our fate, our father's fate, was a cruel twist of Greya's will. By the time we reached the enclave, I was actually grateful you found us. But then, the *very day* we show up, Helene recognizes the room where I die from her *blasted* dream? This is not a rude word or look that I can easily brush aside!"

Kenders stared blankly at Sabine, her lips shut tight. Not much rattled the young woman, but this business with the dreams certainly did. The sisters' mother had passed to Maeana's hall giving birth to Helene and bandits had murdered their father less than two turns ago. Sabine was all Helene had left. Kenders could see the idea of leaving Helene alone worried her greatly.

Kenders had yet to think of something to say when Helene's happy voice suddenly cut through the hall, startling both young women and most of the room.

"Sabine!"

Glancing up, Kenders saw Helene running toward their table, a wide grin on her face. Marick was trailing her with an amused expression on his.

Sabine managed to shove aside her distress, turned to Helene, and said in a hushed voice, "Helene! Quiet voice, please!"

The little girl climbed atop the bench opposite the girls, clambered over the table—earning another quiet rebuke from Sabine—and plopped herself between Kenders and Sabine. Looking up to Kenders, Helene said in an exaggerated whisper, "Hi, Kenders!"

Kenders peered at Helene. She had a difficult time associating the ominous dream with the smiling little girl.

"Hello, Helene," murmured Kenders. "How did your lesson go?"

Helene turned to Marick as the mage arrived at the table.

"Did I do good?"

Marick's amusement bloomed into a full smile as he nodded and said, "Yes, Helene. You did well." He shifted his gaze to Sabine. "You have a very talented sister."

Sabine nodded and managed a thin smile in return.

"Thank you, Marick. Is she done for the day, then?"

"I prefer my students to be able to concentrate fully," replied the young mage. "She has been yawning all morning, and just now, she announced that she was hungry. So…yes, we're done for the day."

Helene turned to peer up at Sabine.

"Can I have a sweet cake?"

Nodding, Sabine said, "Yes, but you need to eat something else before you get a sweet cake."

"No carrots," declared Helene. "They're mushy."

Kenders could not help but smile a bit. Even Sabine seemed a touch amused. Melancholy moods did not last long around Helene.

Sabine glanced up to Marick and asked, "See you tomorrow morning, then?"

"Right after morningmeal, please," answered the mage. Turning his gaze to Helene, he added, "Enjoy the rest of your day. Rest if you can, Helene. I need you alert and paying attention."

Helene did not respond as she was too busy playing with a bow on Kenders' dress.

Marick shifted his gaze to Kenders.

"Good memories behind, Progeny."

Wishing the man would simply call her by her name, Kenders smiled politely and said, "Good day, Marick."

As the young mage turned and began to stride from the table, Sabine and Helene rose from the bench. Helene tugged on Kenders' dress and said, "Come with us, Kenders."

Kenders shot a look at Sabine. The elder Moiléne sister needed someone to talk to now, preferably, about anything other than dreams.

Smiling at Helene, Kenders nodded and said, "Of course, dear. To the commons." She reached out and took Helene's hand. Giving her a little wink, she whispered, "I feel like a sweet cake or two myself."

Helene's face lit up and the three girls strode to the door in the mages' hall.

CHAPTER 6: PERFORMANCE

Zecus stood next to his father on the chamber floor, head down, eyes staring at the white marble floor streaked with flecks of gold and tan. He could not bring himself to meet his father's gaze.

Turns upon turns had passed since Joshmuel had left his family in Demetus and while part of Zecus was happy to see him, the dominant emotion felt was shame. He dreaded the inevitable questions that were sure to come.

Zecus, where are your mother, sisters, and brother?

Zecus, why did you leave them alone?

Zecus, what were you thinking?

A tiny sigh slipped from his lips. He did not know how to answer any of them.

For well over a full turn after his father left, Zecus had remained with his mother and siblings, trying to eke out a life in the strange, wet land. However, as more and more refugees poured into the Marshland's capital, paying work disappeared, the cost of food rose quickly, and the Alsher family resorted to begging.

Prideful and angry, Zecus left his family in Demetus and returned to the Borderlands, hoping he could help fight back the invading Sudashian horde. The Goddess Greya, the Cold Twister of Fate, had other plans for him.

A series of improbable events had delivered him to the Southlands where he met the Progeny and the White Lion, Broedi. Zecus had joined their ranks, seizing upon the chance that he might have found the ones who would ultimately drive the Sudashians from his home.

While he was proud of every action he had taken since leaving Demetus, nothing could erase the shame he felt over the decision that had set him on his path. Soon, he would have to explain to his father what he had done.

For the moment, however, he had other things to worry about. Besides his father and Boah, Jak, Sergeant Trell, and Lady Vivienne stood with him in the empty chamber hall, strung out in a line before the long council table. The vast room felt cavernously bare. The balcony above was empty now.

During their march to the lower floor, Lady Vivienne had given them two simple instructions. One, no one was to speak unless asked a direct question by the council, and, two, none of them were to say anything about the Progeny, White Lions, or Indrida's prophecy.

The nobles at the council table had been carefully eyeing the four new arrivals since they had emerged from the rear doors. Most held their gaze on Zecus alone.

A moment or two after the quartet stopped beside a baffled Joshmuel and Boah, Duke Kyle leaned forward and demanded, "Vivienne, would you care to explain who in the Nine Hells this young man is? And why he interrupted—" He cut off and turned to glare to Zecus. "Why did you interrupt today's proceedings in such a manner?! I should toss you in the stockade for what you've done! The rumors you have started already!"

Lady Vivienne, standing rod-straight, her hands clasped tightly before her, said crisply, "They are *not* rumors, my Lord."

Duke Kyle rolled his eyes and sat back in his chair. "I have as much use for accusations without proof as I do for a boat in the desert."

Zecus glared at the Freelands' duke, biting his tongue. He wondered if the pile of four-hundred charred oligurt and razorfiend corpses atop Shorn Rise would be proof enough for this man.

"Absence of proof does not invalidate our claims, my Lord," replied Lady Vivienne curtly.

Lord Tilas sat forward, resting his elbows on the long, oaken table.

"And repeating something a thousand times somehow validates it, Lady Vivienne? I swear upon my honor and my holdings: there is no threat from Sudash! The Borderlands are perfectly safe."

Boah let a low, disbelieving huff of air slip, earning him a sharp glare from the table and Lady Vivienne. Zecus was surprised that the boisterous man had kept quiet this long.

After a moment, Duke Rholeb turned to Lord Tilas and asked, "Would you have an objection to me sending a detachment of Reed Men over the border, then? Simply so we can confirm your claims?"

Lord Tilas eyed the duke and shot back, "Please do so, my Lord, if you would like to be the one to start a war. Duke Vanson has instructed me to say that should even a single green and white set foot in the Borderlands, he will consider it an act of aggression."

Duke Rholeb huffed, sat back hard in his chair, and crossed his arms.

"Why am I not surprised?"

Duke Kyle sat forward and said hurriedly, "Let us not be hasty, Baron Tilas. There is no need to level idle threats."

The baron said firmly, "Threats are not idle if one intends to follow through with them, my Lord."

Zecus knew little of Oaken Duchies history, but he was certain open warfare between the sovereigns had not occurred in centuries.

Duchess Aleece interjected herself, asking in a tranquil, even tone, "How long will you continue with your lies, Tilas? Sooner or later, we will discover what Vanson is hiding."

With a grim, haughty smile, Lord Tilas replied, "Your words carry as much water as a bucket with a dozen holes."

The duchess eyed the baron carefully, showing no reaction to the man's rudeness. Others did not share such calm, however.

Lady Jonda, the representative of the Red Peaks Duchy, sat forward and said with clear exasperation, "This is getting us nowhere!" The elderly, white-haired woman shook her head, saying, "Vivienne and Tilas have walked down this road before, and it went nowhere. I'll be blasted if I will listen to this again. The *only* thing I care to hear right now, is an explanation as to who he—" she jabbed a finger at Zecus "—is and what he was shouting about in the balcony." The woman's blue eyes bored into Zecus. "Young man, say your piece."

Chairs creaked and clothes rustled as every set of eyes in the room turned to gaze at Zecus. He felt his father's eyes on him, staring with more curiosity than any other person in the room.

Zecus stared at the nobles' faces in silence. He had no idea where to begin.

"So *now* you wish to remain quiet?" asked Duke Kyle, eyebrow raised. "You have our attention, Borderlander. Speak if you will."

Zecus took a deep breath and, deciding to start with something simple, said in a strong, clear voice, "My name is Zecus Alsher of the village Drysa." He stopped there, expecting the revelation to prompt some questions. Sure enough, Duke Kyle sat taller immediately, his gaze flicking to Zecus' father.

"Alsher? From Drysa? You are related to the petitioner, then?"

Zecus nodded.

"Yes, my Lord. He is my father."

Lord Tilas clapped his hands together and exclaimed, "Hah!" He spun to face Duke Kyle. "You want proof, my Lord? I offer this as proof of a conspiracy against me and Duke Vanson!" Glaring back at Zecus and Joshmuel, he sneered, "Father and son, both of them liars!"

Boah took a step forward, but stopped when Joshmuel reached out and grabbed his arm. Holding tightly to Boah's wrist, Zecus' father responded quickly, yet calmly, saying "My Lords and Ladies, this morning was the first time I have seen my son in many turns. I am as stunned as everyone here by his presence and his claims." Peering directly at Zecus, he continued, "Truthfully, I would venture no one is more surprised." The look of concern and worry on his father's face tore at Zecus' heart.

Taking advantage of the quiet moment, Boah ripped free of Joshmuel's grip, stepped forward, and called out, "Joshmuel is telling the truth! The last time we saw Zecus, he was in Demetus." Zecus' father reached his hand back out in an attempt to restrain Boah, but the brazen Borderlander yanked his arm away. Jabbing a finger at Lord Tilas, Boah barked, "Joshmuel and Zecus might be the most honest men I have ever known. I will *not* stand by while they are called liars, especially by a smug lout of a baron!"

Zecus grimaced.

Leaping from his chair, Lord Tilas rested his hand on the tabletop, leaned forward, and snapped, "Show me respect, you brainless goat-herder, else I will slice your—" Lord Treswell reached out quickly and grabbed Lord Tilas' arm, interrupting him. The baron ceased his threat and stood motionless, his rage held in check yet still clearly simmering. After a moment, he took his seat and folded his hands, resting them on the table. His knuckles were white.

Duke Rholeb, resplendent in his green and white tunic, slid forward to the edge of his chair, his eyes on Zecus. "Young man, I'd be interested in hearing how you came to be in Demetus. Perhaps you could share that with us how you came to my capital?" Glancing at Lord Tilas, he added sharply, "As well its condition when you were there?"

With a respectful nod, Zecus replied, "Yes, my Lord. Our family was one of the first to head west, to leave the Borderlands." He glanced at Joshmuel. "Father recognized the threat long before anyone in Drysa. I disagreed with him wanting to run, but now I realize it was the correct choice."

Joshmuel gave him a small, kind smile.

After a short pause, Zecus faced Duke Rholeb and continued, "When we arrived in your city, my Lord, Father and Boah left, leaving me with my mother, two sisters, and brother. At first, I found your city to be tolerable."

A flicker of a smile crossed the duke's face.

Realizing he had insulted Duke Rholeb's seat of his duchy, Zecus quickly added, "What I mean to say is that it was a good city, but…it was a strange land for us."

Duke Rholeb gave a brief nod, indicating his understanding. "I take no offense, young man. I find the dust of the Borderlands 'tolerable' as well."

"Of course, my Lord."

"So," said the duke. "You arrived in my 'tolerable' city. Then what?"

"We found a small room at an inn and stayed there for a short time. I found work and some coin as a day laborer, doing whatever people would pay me to do. Mother and Tiliah looked for work, but we were…out of place. Neither had skills worthy of the city. Jezra and Jerem were simply too young."

"The little coin we had or made disappeared quickly, along with paying work as more people came from the west. Within weeks, a hunk of bread that had cost two coppers suddenly cost three silver. And it had maggots. In order to eat, we left the inn and moved outside of the city walls to live in the camps. We slept on the ground, without a roof. It was a hard life, my Lord."

Zecus paused and hazarded a glance at his father. The man looked heartbroken to hear of his family's suffering.

With a quiet, burning intensity, Duke Rholeb said, "I am very sorry for your hardship, young man. Please know that I did what I could to help your countrymen." He shot a hard glare at Lord Tilas. "But we were simply *not* prepared for thousands to arrive at our walls."

The baron stared straight ahead, refusing to meet the duke's gaze.

Duchess Aleece said, "Where is your family, Zecus? Did you leave them in Demetus?"

Zecus winced inwardly at the question and nodded, saying, "I did, my Lady."

Duchess Adnil, the sovereign of the Long Coast, lifted an eyebrow and asked, "You left them behind? Why?"

"I was angry, my Lady," replied Zecus. "Angry about what had happened to my family. Angry at what had happened to my home." He paused, took a deep breath, ashamed for what he was about to say. "And I was angry at my father for leaving on what I believed to be a fool's errand. I wanted to *stand* against whatever the evil was. I did not want to run away." He dropped his head to stare at his absurdly shiny boots. "So, I went home to fight."

A heavy sort of quiet filled the room briefly before Lord Tilas, in a voice absent any sympathy, asked mockingly, "And at what point in your sad tale were you supposedly captured by the mythical oligurts roaming the Borderlands? Or would you like to retract your claim and save yourself a week in the stockade?"

Zecus' shame fled in an instant. Snapping his head up, he glared at the baron, his eyes hot.

"You want the *whole* tale? You shall have it, my Lord."

Zecus relayed everything that happened once leaving Demetus. His journey home to find Drysa nearly deserted, his search for the rumored resistance, how they had found him instead, and the attack by Sudashians mere hours later. How he was knocked cold by the glancing blow of an oligurt's club, woke up in a dark tent, and carried through an encampment filled with countless oligurts and razorfiends. He included every detail he could to legitimize his story. The pennants flying over the tents. The earthen burrows of the razorfiends. The rotten-sweet smell of men roasting over bonfires.

He took careful time to describe the Sudashians' leader, a demon-man with horns, blood red eyes, and the unusual scent of wildflowers that wafted from the monster. He told them about the saeljul mage interrupting his interrogation to speak with the demon and the fight that fortuitously broke out a short while later. The demon-man rushed out to put an end to it, at which point the saeljul mage called forth a magical black doorway that he stepped through, disappearing from the tent. Zecus could still remember the desperation he had felt.

"My feet were bound, yet I hopped across the tent, and leapt straight through the flap. I could not know what lay on the other side, but I was willing to take a chance. It was better than what faced me if I remained."

He glanced along the table to find every lord and lady staring intently at him. Whether or not they believed him, they certainly were intrigued by his tale.

"One moment, I was in the demon's pavilion, the next I crashed into a wooden beam and collapsed in a pile of straw. I—"

"Enough!" bellowed Lord Tilas. Everyone in the room turned to stare at the wide-eyed baron. "This man is wasting all of our time! Demon-men? Mages with magical doorways to—"

"Quiet!" shouted Duchess Aleece. Her eyes burning as she glared at the man, she said, "*Baron* Tilas, you will hold your tongue until Zecus is finished with his tale else I will see to it that you are the one visiting the stockades for a few days!"

The man stared daggers at the duchess but kept his mouth shut regardless. When it was clear he was going to comply with her order, Duchess Aleece looked back to Zecus.

"Continue, young man."

Before Zecus could do so, however, Lady Vivienne stepped forward and said, "Actually, my Lady, I might be better able to explain what happened next. It seems the blow to his head was severe enough that he was knocked unconscious. One of my servants found him—bound and injured—in the stables of my estates in Argolles. He was brought to the servants' quarters where he slept for days on end. Once he awoke and recounted his story, my steward sent a dispatch to me here in Freehaven that included this seemingly outrageous story. It only arrived the day before last turn's public petitioning and was the reason I requested the hold when I heard their tale."

She turned and nodded toward Zecus' father and Boah.

"Their shared name and similar claims seemed implausible. So, I sent for the young man to come to Freehaven as soon as he was able to travel, escorted by my personal guard. They arrived this morning at my city villa as I was preparing to come here today."

Zecus, along with Jak and Sergeant Trell, gaped at the baroness. Lady Vivienne was lying outright, every word an utter falsehood. Ignoring their stares, the noblewoman pressed on with her yarn.

"I had no time to warn Duchess Aleece, even though she most certainly should have had this information before today's public hearing. Had the timing been better, perhaps we all could have avoided today's embarrassment. I apologize to the First Council for my part in the young man's outburst."

The baroness delivered the account with such conviction, that had Zecus not lived a different path, he would have believed every word. He was beyond impressed. Her story explained his presence in the Southlands without revealing anything of the Progeny, the Shadow Manes, or the prophecy of Indrida.

A few quiet moments passed before Duchess Adnil offered, "That is quite a tale." Her eyes locked on Zecus. "Disturbing, if it's true." Her concern sounded genuine.

Sitting back in his chair, Lord Tilas crossed his arms and asked, "Are you finished, young man?" He shot a quick frown at Duchess Aleece.

Zecus nodded.

"I am."

"Good," said Lord Tilas with a nod. "An excellent story, I admit. Were we at festival, and you a playman, I would award you first prize, but, honestly…oligurts? Razorfiends? Demons? The level of preposterousness is obscene. Not to mention the unsanctioned magic, by an ijul no less! Truly?! You expect us to believe this tale?!"

A voice, nasal and thin, wafted through the chamber.

"I do."

Zecus' eyes flicked to Lord Lucius, an olive-skinned man with shaggy, black hair and bushy mustache. The representative of the Foothills Duchy sat forward, leaning his elbow on the table.

"The detail in his story is too rich to be false."

"Cook the stew long enough and even the toughest meat will be tender," retorted Lord Tilas. "He's had turns to concoct his tale!"

Lord Lucius shook his head, his eyes on Zecus, studying him as one would an onion, peeling back the layers one-by-one, looking for any hint of rottenness. After a moment or two, the baron said, "He spoke with such passion earlier. And just now, when he spoke of the Sudashians' camp…" He trailed off, sat back in his chair with a heavy sigh, and said, "I am sorry, Tilas, but I believe him. Fully."

"As do I," agreed Lord Osvanni, the representative of the Colonial Duchy. He turned to glare at Lord Tilas. "Which means I *don't* believe you, Tilas."

Zecus scanned the rest of the council, hoping to find more support. Duchess Aleece and Duchess Adnil both appeared quite pleased with the announcements made by the two barons. A quick glance at Duke Rholeb confirmed that he, too, seemed quite satisfied. Duke Kyle, however, looked very nervous, a thin sheen of sweat clearly visible on his brow.

The Freeland's duke reached up to wipe his forehead and asked, "Hader? Jonda? What say you?"

The black-and-gold-clad Baron Hader waved a dismissive hand.

"I will take the word of a nobleman over that of any citizen. I am tired of wasting time on this. Borderlands issues affect the Northlands not."

Zecus frowned.

"And you baroness?" asked Duke Kyle, turning to stare at the Red Peaks' representative.

Lady Jonda sat still for a long moment, her hand caressing her chin as she stared hard at Zecus. After a few moments, she said, "I do not know, my Lord. I was inclined to believe Tilas before, but I am not so sure now. Talk of demons is of particular concern to the Red Peaks."

"Oh, please," snapped Lord Tilas. "I would bet coin they only added that falsehood to sway you, Jonda!" The man sounded desperate.

With a shrug of her shoulders, Lady Jonda conceded, "Perhaps, but the risk is too substantial to dismiss outright."

Tossing his hands up in frustration, Lord Tilas exclaimed, "This is madness!"

Duke Kyle gently suggested, "Perhaps Vanson would consider an investigation into the claims? A small joint force by a few of—"

Lord Tilas slammed the table with his fist, sending a rattling boom throughout the chamber.

"No! He will not accept such an intrusion! You have no right! Our lands are as sovereign as yours!"

"Are you afraid of what might be found?" asked Duchess Aleece innocently.

Lord Tilas glared at her, stewing like a covered pot resting over a roaring fire.

"Let me be *perfectly* clear: should a single soldier of *any* duchy—any!—cross into the Borderlands, Duke Vanson will declare war on the offending lord or lady!"

He immediately shifted his gaze to a visibly uncomfortable Lord Treswell. The pair's eyes met for only a moment before the Great Lake's representative sighed and said reluctantly, "I have been instructed by Duke Everett that should there be such a conflict, then he will side with Duke Vanson."

Zecus shot a quick glance to Jak and Sergeant Trell, both of whom were from the Great Lakes Duchy. The pair wore bitter, angry expressions.

Other than the muffled sounds of a bustling city outside, the council chamber was deathly silent.

Duke Kyle broke the quiet, saying softly, "Such an action would mean civil war, Tilas. Are you sure you are speaking with Vanson's authority?"

"I most assuredly am, my Lord," replied Lord Tilas confidently. "He was incensed to hear of the accusations from last turn. He is prepared to withdraw the Borderlands from the Oaken Duchies if need be." Lord Tilas glared at Lord Treswell, whipping the man with his eyes alone. "I believe Duke Everett has said the same, am I correct, Treswell?"

The baron nodded, muttering, "My liege lord's loyalty lies with his friend and neighbor, Duke Vanson." The words were spoken in a wooden, emotionless manner, as if he were reciting something from memory.

Again, a tense, suffocating quiet swelled within the chamber. Zecus shook his head. The nation was falling apart before his eyes.

Duchess Aleece's clear voice cut through the silence.

"It would seem that we are at an impasse, then. We have two petitioners standing before us, requesting the help of the council. Yet the ruling lord of the duchy in question insists help is not necessary. What to do?"

As if on cue, Duchess Adnil answered, "According to First Council procedure, we must rule on the petition one way or another." Glancing up and down the table, she asked, "What say everyone?"

Duke Kyle nervously interjected, "We cannot provoke a civil war, my Lady."

"I do not think Adnil is suggesting such a thing, Duke Kyle," responded Duchess Aleece.

A furrow appeared in the man's brow, providing a nice channel for the sweat to follow on its way down his nose.

"Then what are you proposing?"

Shifting her gaze to Zecus and the others standing with him, the duchess of the Southlands said, "I believe we have ample evidence that something is happening in the Borderlands. And that Vanson is hiding something."

Lord Tilas immediately spit, "Again, you have no proof but the—"

Swiveling her head to glare at the baron, Duchess Aleece raised her voice, saying firmly and crisply, "Bless the Gods, Tilas! Shut your mouth and let me finish!"

The baron complied with the duchess' order, but sat back in his chair, festering.

After a moment, Duchess Aleece continued, her tone tranquil yet again, saying, "Vanson has every right to refuse entry to whomever he wants. I will not dispute that accord." A smug expression filled Lord Tilas face. "However, the same law also permits any one of us to grant access to the other. Therefore, I propose those of us of like mind reach an agreement."

Almost immediately, Duchess Adnil asked, "What are your terms, Aleece?"

With a nod to the older duchess, the Southlands sovereign responded, "I will open my borders to the armies of anyone who pledges to fight against what I believe is to be a massive Sudashian army—complete with demons who were once men—openly marching through the Borderlands, unchecked and perhaps even aided by Duke Vanson. A second Demonic War could very well be at our threshold, and unlike our predecessors, I hope to be prepared for whatever is coming."

Without pause, Duke Rholeb spoke, saying, "Consider the Marshlands open to the Southlands, Aleece." He glared at Lord Tilas. "I will *not* allow my lands to be overrun by whatever marches east."

In the time it had taken for a dozen heartbeats to pass, two duchies had apparently formed an alliance against two others. Considering the brevity with which it had happened, Zecus suspected that had been the plan all along.

Duke Kyle looked along the table and declared, "There has not been armed conflict between the duchies in centuries. Please, be reasonable!"

"I believe Aleece has been extremely reasonable, Kyle," said Duchess Adnil. "So much so, that I formally pledge my support to you both. The Long Coast Duchy will join with the Marshlands and Southlands."

Duke Kyle stared at Duchess Adnil in shock.

"You cannot be serious, my Lady!"

"Oh, don't look at me like that Kyle," replied Duchess Adnil sharply. "I am not advocating that we attack anyone. I simply am of the opinion that Aleece's wish to be prepared is wise."

"May the Gods save us," muttered Duke Kyle. Sweating even more profusely now, the nobleman patted the excess moisture from his head and glanced up and down the length of the table. "Where do the rest of you stand?"

Both Lord Lucius and Lord Osvanni stated their own personal support for the Duchess Aleece proposal, but professed that any formal decision would have to be made by Duke Eli of the Foothills and Duchess Catherine of the Colonial Duchy. Lord Hader insisted the Northlands would refuse to take sides in the dispute while Lady Jonda said she would need more information before she could recommend anything to Duke Thomas.

Zecus listened in quiet awe, the fate of countless lives resting on these proceedings. History was unfolding before him. Glancing at those on his side of the table, he found that Jak, Boah, and Joshmuel looked as worried as he felt. Both Sergeant Trell and Lady Vivienne were stone-faced, their expressions utterly blank.

Once every noble but the Freelands' duke had voiced his or her intentions, Duchess Adnil asked, "And you, Kyle? What say you? Where do the Freelands fall?" Her tone and frown indicated she already knew what the man's answer was going to be.

Duke Kyle looked ill. With a quick shake of his head, he muttered, "I refuse to commit Freelands soldiers or resources to prepare for war against another duchy." Shooting an uneasy glance between the others at the table, he added, "The Freelands remains neutral in this dispute while I personally pray that sanity will prevail and you all come to your blasted senses."

Zecus frowned. He doubted that would happen. The God of Chaos would not let it.

Lord Tilas rose from his chair and announced formally, "If that is the case, you will all excuse me. I must contact Duke Vanson to warn him of the treachery perpetrated here this morning. Good day, council."

After one last sneering glare toward Zecus and his companions, the baron strode to the doorway behind the council table, grabbed the handle, and yanked hard. He stepped through the exit, letting the oaken door crash against the stone wall, its crack reverberating through the chamber.

Lord Treswell stood and said in a polite, almost embarrassed, tone, "Excuse me, but my duties require me to inform Duke Everett. Good day to you all." With a short bow, he turned and hurried out the door as well.

Once the baron was gone, Duke Kyle said, "I suppose this means council is adjourned. If you will excuse me, I must go speak with my advisors." Looking up to Zecus and the others standing opposite him, he said, "I hope you are pleased with what you have wrought here today."

Zecus glared at the man, irritated. War was coming one way or the other. This was not his fault.

As the duke pushed his bulky figure from the table, stood, and exited the chamber, Zecus heard Lady Vivienne whisper, "You weak-willed, short-sighted fool of—"

The screech of the wooden chair legs scraping against the marble floor swallowed the remainder of her comment as the rest of the First Council stood and left through the back door. Some went alone, others in pairs with their heads tilted close together, whispering. Duchess Aleece glanced in their direction and gave a short nod before turning and leaving with Duchess Adnil by her side.

Lady Vivienne immediately took three quick, dress-swishing steps forward and turned to face them.

"We will now head back to my villa. There you will wait for me while I attend to a number of things. Understood?"

A frustrated Boah crossed his arms.

"I'm not going anywhere until someone explains to me what in the Nine Hells is going on. What just happened here?"

Unconcealed annoyance flashed across Lady Vivienne's angled face. "I do not have time for this." She swept past them, striding toward the double doors at the rear of the chamber. "If you have questions, Boah Rasus, ask the sergeant. Or Jak. They seemed to have figured things out."

Boah glanced over at Sergeant Trell and Jak with a raised eyebrow. With a lopsided grin, Jak inclined his head.

"Hi. I'm Jak. And this stern-looking fellow beside me is Sergeant Trell."

Both Boah and Joshmuel eyed the pair. After a moment, Joshmuel asked, "You are Lady Vivienne's guards, then?"

Shaking his head, Jak said, "Gods, no! I'd rather be a fish in a boat. That was pure show." He turned his eye to the retreating form of Lady Vivienne, striding between the rows of empty benches. "Convincing, wasn't she?"

As bewilderment filled Joshmuel and Boah's faces, Sergeant Trell stepped forward and said, "Gentlemen, you, along with young Zecus, have unwillingly performed the lead roles in the most important play of the last two hundred years of the Oaken Duchies."

Joshmuel lifted an eyebrow.

"Pardon?"

"You have been played," said Sergeant Trell, looking at the three Borderlanders. "All of you. They wished your reactions to be as authentic as possible for some of the council's benefit." Glancing down the hall, toward Lady Vivienne, he raised his voice and called, "Not everyone can tell a lie with such conviction."

Halfway to the doors, Lady Vivienne stopped in her tracks. She spun on her heels, stared directly at Sergeant Trell, and gave him a small, tart smile.

"Judge if you like, Sergeant, I care not. Results matter, not how you achieve them." Her gazed rested on the soldier a moment longer before taking them all in. "Now, please, let us go. Baron Tilas will attempt to gain some measure of revenge for us forcing him to show Vanson's hand sooner than he wished. It would be unwise for any of you to be in the city past this evening."

She had already turned halfway around before Zecus called out.

"My Lady!"

Returning her gaze to him, she asked impatiently, "What is it?"

"Do you mean for all of us to go?"

He glanced at his father and Boah, both of whom were growing increasingly confused by the moment.

"Of course," replied the baroness. "They'd be dead inside a day if they stay here." She spun on her heels and resumed her hurried pace to the double oaken doors.

Joshmuel turned a critical eye toward Zecus.

"Son? What is this all about?"

Zecus stared at his father, unsure where to begin. The longest, most uncomfortable moment of his life slipped past before Sergeant Trell rescued him.

The soldier stepped forward, put an arm around both Joshmuel and Boah, and said, "It would be my pleasure to explain as we go." He began to lead them down the aisle. The two Borderlanders went along without protest. "First, Joshmuel, you should know your son is one of the bravest men I have ever met..." The sergeant's voice trailed off as the three moved to the double doors.

Zecus watched the trio of men move away, grateful that the talk with his father had been postponed, even if only for a short while.

Jak said softly, "Once he knows everything, he'll understand."

Unable to take his gaze from his father's back, Zecus muttered, "I don't know, Jak. I left our family." He eyed his friend and sighed. "How do you expect him to understand that?"

Jak stood silent for a second before murmuring, "I don't know." He offered a tiny smile. "Blame it on the Gods mucking with our lives."

"I don't know if I believe that, Jak."

"Broedi would not have marched off to the Celestial Empire on a hunch, Zecus."

Zecus pressed his lips together. The White Lion was convinced some of the Gods and Goddesses were meddling in mortal affairs, trying to arrange things to their liking. If that were the case, it made Zecus angry.

"I am not a peg upon a radigan board," muttered Zecus. "Nor a placard in a hand of knuckles."

"Today you were," said Jak gently. "Only it was nobles playing you, not the Gods."

Zecus grimaced, his eyes narrowing sharply.

"That is not any better."

Clapping a hand to Zecus' shoulder, Jak said, "Try to see the sweet of it, Zecus. Without what happened here today, the only force ready to stand against the God of Chaos would be the couple hundred men on Storm Island, some mages, and us. Now, we have the support of the Southern Arms, Reed Men, *and* Shore Guard."

Zecus nodded, admitting the outlook for the coming war seemed slightly more hopeful.

"I suppose…"

Jak smacked him hard on the back, saying, "Come on. Let's go before Lady Vivienne leaves without us. Which, she very well might do."

Zecus nodded and the two headed down the aisle. After a few steps, Jak reached up, tugged at his collar, and mumbled, "I can't wait to get these blasted clothes off."

CHAPTER 7: HEART

Nikalys' stomach rumbled. He did his best to ignore it, and concentrate on the words before him, but the emptiness gnawed at him. Lifting his gaze, he stared blankly at the stone wall of his room, wondering what might be in the kitchens to eat. There was only one way to find out.

Gripping the blue canvas cover, he slammed the book shut, sending a muffled whump through his room. He pushed his chair back from the table and stood, shrugging off the wool blanket and letting it fall to the chair. Wriggling his cold toes to loosen them, he extended his arms outward, flexing his muscles and letting out a small exhalation of air. The breath formed a tiny cloud and drifted away from his face. Watching it dissipate, he shook his head in quiet wonder. He had yet to grow accustomed to seeing his own breath.

A waft of cool air whispered past the back of Nikalys' neck. He shivered, cursing the persistent draft in his room. The first two weeks here, he had not minded the breeze, but now that they were on the cusp of Winter, the chill was unwelcome. A particularly strong gust of wind blew, whistling more of its cursed iciness inside his room. He looked up, glared at the glass as if it were the window's fault, and noticed the sky was growing darker. Another storm was on its way.

After stretching, he took a few steps to his bed and picked up his blood father's sword. He moved to the wooden door in the wall opposite the table, affixing the belt and scabbard around his waist. Halfway to the door, he stopped in the middle of the room, turned, and stared at the desk. The book sat there, taunting him.

Nikalys had promised the commander he was going to have the entire tome completed three days ago, along with the author's subsequent volume, but both books had sat on his desk for weeks, dusty and unopened. He had only started reading the first book this morning.

Sighing, he hurried back to the table and retrieved it. Bracing the volume in the crux of his arm, he strode across the room and pulled the door open by the simple rope-ring handle. Stopping in the doorway, he peered over his shoulder, stared at the brightly glowing ball sitting on the desk and clearly enunciated, "Jah marel." The words were ancient aicenai and had taken some practice to get correct.

The light within the magical globe winked out, plunging the room into a gloom fit for dusk. A tiny blur danced before Nikalys' eyes where he had stared directly at the yellow-white light, obscuring the sphere from his vision.

Stepping into the torch-lit hall, Nikalys shut the door behind him, sending a hollow thud echoing down the stone hallway. As he strode toward the stairwell, he approached the only other door in the tower's upper hall. Nikalys eyed Jak's room as he passed, silently wishing his brother was around. Jak was always up for a quick trip to rummage through the larders. He, however, was in Freehaven, most likely having the time of his life.

Upon reaching the stairwell, Nikalys shuffled down the stone steps, his legs limbering up as he went. He slowed at the landing leading to the floor below his and considered going down the hall to Kenders' room but his guilt about needing to read urged him on without her. With a firm resolve, he plowed ahead, determined to get something to eat, sit in front of one of the fires, and read the entire book grasped in his hand.

By the time he reached the ground floor of the stairway, the air seemed balmy compared to his room. As he neared the commons, the halls were no longer empty. He made it a point to look each person he saw in the eye and greet them, challenging himself to remember the names of everyone. It was one of the few tasks on which Commander Aiden had him working that Nikalys did not mind.

Rounding a corner, Nikalys came across a thin, bearded man carrying a lumpy burlap sack. From the way the man was struggling, whatever the bag contained was heavy. As Nikalys met the man's eyes, he smiled, trying to place the man's name with his face. After a moment, he recognized him as a member of the kitchen staff, one of the head cook's helpers.

"Good days ahead, Gregor," said Nikalys.

The man's eyes widened and he stumbled to a halt. With a notably nervous twinge to his voice, Gregor replied, "And good memories behind, Progeny."

Nikalys' friendly grin faltered a bit. He loathed when people called him that.

Despite his unease with the honorific, he did not correct the man. Commander Aiden insisted that Nikalys allow the Shadow Manes to call him 'Progeny' or 'sir' or whatever they wanted, saying "it helps morale, something we will need plenty of in the days to come." Nevertheless, Nikalys did not like being treated as if he were someone important. Even if he was.

The man resumed his walk down the hall, struggling with the large sack.

Nikalys offered, "If you need help with that, Gregor, I could carry it to wherever you are headed." He eyed the bag, knowing he could carry it easily with one arm.

Gregor's eyes widened and he immediately shook his head back and forth.

"Oh, no, sir! Goodness, no! I would not dream of it. They are just potatoes. I brought the wrong type from the pantry for the cooks' stew. I can manage, sir."

Nikalys sighed. The man was fifteen years older than him, and calling him 'sir.'

Stepping aside to give the man room to pass, he said, "Okay, then. Be careful, Gregor. They look heavy."

Gregor nodded as he labored past, grunting, "Yes, sir, I will. Thank you, sir."

Nikalys watched as the man grappled with the burlap sack, wobbling down the hall. After letting out a heavy sigh, he resumed his walk to the kitchen, a slight frown on his face. He knew he was different from everybody else here, yet he wished people did not treat him so. The heart of a simple farmer still beat in his chest.

When he reached the spacious commons, he was relieved to see that nearly all of the long tables and benches sat empty. Still, a handful of tables had groups of two or three people sitting at them who were catching a late midday meal or just enjoying the pleasant warmth of the room. Nikalys smiled as he spotted the three massive hearths, one on each wall other than the one from where he had just marched. A giant fire roared in each stone cavity. The sweet, yeasty smell of something baking filled his nose.

Nikalys had taken a few steps to the back wall to seek out a kitchen worker when a loud, happy shriek ricocheted throughout the stone room, startling him along with most others in the quiet room.

"Nik-lys!"

A smile split his face immediately as he scanned the room, trying to find the origin of the voice. His gaze settled on the corner to his right and his grin widened.

A small girl was clambering over the top of a table, ignoring the protests of the two young women sitting with her. Raven-black hair hung past her shoulders, her dark brown eyes were wide and staring, and a brilliant smile radiated from her slightly plump cheeks. As she scurried over the tabletop, kicking wooden plates as she went, Nikalys' gaze shifted to the other pair at the table.

His sister, sitting on the table's far side, caught his eye and flashed him a smile. Nikalys nodded back a silent greeting, his attention mostly focused on the other woman as she helped the young girl climb over the table while chastising her to behave properly. Upon lowering the child to the ground, she swiveled her head around and stared at Nikalys.

As happened every other time he saw Sabine, his throat caught.

Like the younger girl, the woman had the same intense, deep brown eyes and black hair, longer of course, pulled back and bound, reaching the middle of her back. Unlike her sister, however, her face was sharper, edged with high cheekbones and a perfectly lined nose sitting over flawless, lush lips that were currently parted to reveal a brilliant, flattering smile that shot into Nikalys' soul.

A second shout from the little girl shattered the moment.

"Nik-lys!"

Helene's exclamation was more insistent this time, demanding that he pay attention to her. Shifting to watch the little girl run toward him, he tossed the book he was carrying on a nearby table and dropped to a knee. Extending his arms, he said with a genuine smile, "Come here, Helene!"

The girl launched herself into his outstretched arms and he stood up, cradling her and giving her a hug. With affection matching the cozy warmth of the fire-heated room, he said, "It's good to see you, Helene. I missed you."

Helene wrapped her arms around his neck and squeezed.

"I missed you, too, Nik-lys."

She had yet to learn how to pronounce his name correctly. He loved the way she said it and hoped she would never stop.

Pulling back, Helene stared at him with sparkling eyes.

"Did you know that I can eat five potatoes?"

Nikalys smiled wide at the randomness of the question and gave Helene another hug, patting her back gently.

"I did *not* know that, Helene. I don't think even I can eat that many."

"Sabine told me not to. She said I would get sick." Shaking her head side-to-side vigorously, she added, "But I didn't. I ate all five!"

With that, she shot a proud look over to her sister, claiming victory in a debate that was apparently very important to the four-year-old. Nikalys followed Helene's gaze and locked eyes with Sabine again. His grin faltered a bit.

Helene began tugging at Nikalys' collar. Turning her big brown eyes on him, she begged, "Come sit with us!"

Nikalys hesitated.

"I don't know, Helene. I have reading I should be doing."

His reluctance had nothing to do with the book on the table. For reasons he could not name, something about the young raven-haired beauty at the table gave Nikalys pause.

While traveling though the Southlands, the Isaac siblings and Broedi had interrupted a brigands' attack on the Moiléne farm. They disposed of all but one of the bandits, saving Helene and Sabine from a horrible fate, but were too late to save their father. Upon learning that one brigand was still alive and unconscious, Sabine had slit the man's throat without hesitation.

To this day, the image of her standing over the man, bloody knife in hand, still haunted Nikalys. Despite everything about Sabine that called to Nikalys, the cold callousness she displayed that day repelled him. He felt pushed and pulled at the same time.

Shortly after the Battle of Shorn Rise, he had discovered that Jak harbored feelings for her as well. Ever since, Nikalys avoided Sabine whenever possible. For the most part, his strategy worked. He had managed not to speak with Sabine since everyone said farewell to Broedi and Nundle.

Now, as he stared at the beauty, he tried to think of a way to wriggle free yet again.

Helene pulled his tunic again, pleading, "Please sit with us, Nik-lys?"

Powerless against the adorable four-year-old, Nikalys smiled.

"Sure. I can sit for a little while."

Helene's face lit up with pure joy.

"You can sit with me!"

Nikalys prayed the girl's exuberance would help him get through what was sure to be an uncomfortable few minutes.

Carrying Helene in his arms, he walked to where Kenders and Sabine sat. His sister shot him a quick, sympathetic look as he neared, knowing the quiet turmoil he felt over Sabine. He had made her promise to never say a word to Jak or Sabine and, so far, it seemed as if she had kept her word.

As he approached, Sabine affixed an innocent smile on her face and said politely, "Good days ahead, sir. I do not believe we have met. My name is Sabine Moiléne." While her words—spoken with a lilting, musical tone unique to her—were kind and courteous, she wielded them like a sharply pointed dagger.

Nikalys cringed. He supposed he deserved that.

Stopping beside her bench, he offered, "Good memories, Sabine. I apologize for my absence as of late. I have been very busy."

Sabine cocked an eyebrow.

"Busy? Doing what?"

Nikalys paused a moment before answering, "Training?" Somehow his response came out as a question. He wondered if the excuse sounded as pathetic to her as it did him.

Sabine's other eyebrow joined the first.

"You consider sitting around, watching others practice 'training?'"

He forced a small grin.

"In a manner of speaking, yes. I still have to watch."

Helene pointed to a spot on the bench next to Sabine and demanded, "Nik-lys, you sit here." He wavered for a moment, long enough that he saw that Sabine noticed. The smile on her face twitched, shrinking the tiniest of margins.

With an internal, silent groan, Nikalys lifted one leg over the bench and sat, straddling the bench. Helene settled herself on the bench, trying to sit as Nikalys did, but her tan dress got in the way. She shimmied side-to-side, freeing her legs from the cloth to let them dangle in the air.

Nikalys made a show of adjusting Helene on the bench while trying to think of something to say. He wished more than ever that he had stayed in his chilly room.

Thankfully, Helene broke the awkward silence, saying, "See, Nik-lys? That's my plate. There were six potatoes. Now there is only one."

Glad to have something to focus on besides Sabine, Nikalys stared at the wooden platter as if it were the most interesting thing he had ever seen. Sure enough, there was a single small red potato drenched in a pool of butter and herbs along with two long, untouched carrots.

"What about the carrots, Helene?"

The little girl tilted her head up to stare at him, squishing her face together in an expression that revealed she did not hold a high opinion of the vegetable. Her answer was firm.

"They're mushy."

Nikalys leaned forward and whispered in Helene's ear, "You know, I don't like mushy carrots, either. I'll tell the cook to make them a special way—my way. I'm sure you'll like them."

Helene scrunched up her face, considering his offer, before giving a short nod. "I'll try your way."

Sabine let out a low huff, pretending to be perturbed.

"I've been trying to get her to eat carrots since we got here. You walk in and—poof!—she says she'll eat carrots." There was a friendly, teasing tone to her voice. "Too bad those are the last in the storerooms."

Nikalys was relieved. He hated carrots.

He looked up at Sabine and smiled the first natural grin he had given her in turns. At first, she returned his smile with one of her own, but her expression quickly shifted to one of anxious interest. She stared at him beseechingly, asking a dozen unspoken questions with her eyes alone. As much as he wanted to look away, he could not. Something about Sabine mesmerized him.

Suddenly, Kenders stood up, cutting short the odd interlude. In a firm, decisive tone, she announced, "Helene, as you did such a wonderful job eating your potatoes, perhaps we should venture into the kitchen and see if they have any of those sweet cakes we were talking about earlier."

Nikalys threw his sister a dagger-filled glare. He did not want to be alone with Sabine. Completely ignoring him, Kenders moved to the end of the table and held out her hand.

"Let's go, dear."

Helene freed herself from Nikalys' suddenly tight embrace and was halfway off the bench when she stopped. Peering at her sister, she asked, "Sabine, may I?"

"Yes, Helene. But only one cake." Turning around to face Kenders, Sabine reiterated the point. "Only *one*, Kenders."

Nikalys' sister nodded solemnly.

"Of course, Sabine. Only two."

Helene giggled as she gripped Kenders' hand and the two scurried away to the back of the commons.

They were less than a dozen paces away when Sabine turned back, stared straight at Nikalys, and said, "So, you've certainly been going out of your way to be everywhere I'm not. Care to share why?"

Nikalys blinked twice. Sabine did not waste any time. He opened his mouth, thinking he was going to protest, but not having any idea how he possibly could. She was right. He sat that way, gaping for a moment before pressing his lips shut.

No lie would be believable, and the true reason—that he and Jak both had feelings for her—was not something he wished to discuss.

Wholly misinterpreting his hesitation, Sabine said in crisp, clipped tone, "Fine. If you won't talk, I'll find somewhere else to be."

She put her hands on the table and began to stand up. Before he could stop himself, Nikalys reached out and placed his right hand on top of hers. He was surprised how soft her skin was.

"Don't go," he said.

Sabine halted, holding her half-standing position, and glanced at his hand on hers. As soon as she did, he pulled it back, embarrassed that he had been so presumptuous. She sat back down on the bench, her dark blue dress rustling quietly. Once seated, she folded her arms on the table and turned her gaze on him, eyebrow cocked. She waited with an expectant expression, her long, silky black hair framing her perfect face. She was going to make him speak first.

Nikalys took a deep breath, exhaled and tried to say something, anything.

"I..."

The single syllable hung in the air. He had no idea what to say.

Frustrated, he dropped his chin to his chest and stared at his hands, resting on the wooden bench. A flash of reflected firelight near his left hip caught his attention. His gaze flicked to regard the silver band encircling the white stone carving of the lion's head pommel on his sword. He stared at the lion's head, mouth permanently open in an eternal, silent roar, reminding him of his purpose, his duty.

Clenching his jaw, he looked up to meet Sabine's eyes. Whatever expression he wore caused her to flinch.

"First, I apologize for my behavior. Suffice it to say, were you to hazard a guess as to why I have been avoiding you, there is a good chance you would be correct."

That was as close as he was going to get in admitting he had feelings for her.

The corners of her lips turned upward even though she stared at him with wary eyes. More was to come and she knew it. Something she would not want to hear.

Plunging ahead, he said softly, "Whatever is happening in the Borderlands right now is only the beginning. Things will get worse, Sabine. Much worse. I don't know how exactly, but I doubt Indrida offers prophecies about easy fights."

Her face darkened. She knew it, too. Nikalys continued, ensuring no one besides her could hear his gloomy assessment.

"You see how Lady Vivienne carries herself. She's on constant edge. Commander Aiden, too. He hides it better than most, but he's worried. And there were times before Broedi left where he would stand on the battlements, staring at nothing for hours."

Sabine gave a short nod of her head and muttered, "I saw."

Nikalys sighed and said, "There are thousands upon thousands of oligurts, razorfiends, mongrels, and demons out there. *Demons,* Sabine! All marching this way as we sit here and eat sweet cakes. For reasons we do not even understand!" His eyes flashed wide. "We have less than *three hundred* soldiers here!"

He muted his passion as best he could, afraid that others in the room might hear him. It would not do to have any member of the Shadow Manes here doubting their odds, no matter how low they were.

Taking a deep breath, he continued in a calmer tone, saying softly, "Which is why I must remain completely focused on the task at hand."

Sabine held his gaze and shot back firmly, "That does not mean you need to avoid me, Nikalys. I want to help."

He smiled thinly.

"I know you do, Sabine. You outshine nearly everyone when it comes to courage. It is one of the things I admire most about you."

Her face lit up at the compliment, which, in turn, made Nikalys wince inwardly. He did not want to be eliciting that sort of reaction.

Frowning, he said sternly, "I promise to do everything in my power to keep you and your sister safe." He paused, not wanting to say the next set of words. "But in order to do so, any feelings I have for you need to remain that. Only feelings. *Nothing* can happen between us."

"But—"

With a firm shake of his head, he said, "No! That is the way of things. All sour, no sweet. I'm sorry."

She closed her mouth, swallowing whatever she was going to say, biting her lip.

He eyed her a long moment, wondering if he dare ask what was lingering at the back of his mind. Knowing that he might regret it, he pressed ahead anyway, asking softly, "Besides, do you not have eyes for another?"

Her eyes widened.

"What…?"

She trailed off and turned to glare to where Kenders and Helene stood at the back of the commons, speaking with two kitchen workers.

Guessing what she was thinking, he said, "Kenders did not spoil your secret, Sabine. I have seen the way he looks at you."

She turned back to stare at him but remained quiet.

"Jak is a good man," said Nikalys. "The best. Through everything that has happened, he has stood by my side."

A look of fondness flashed across Sabine's face, confirming his fears. He was surprised how much it hurt to see it. Nevertheless, he peered into her brown eyes, no longer hesitant to hold her gaze. She, however, dropped her head, unable to meet his stare.

With a deep, reluctant sigh, he murmured, "I suppose that is why I decided that he can have you."

Sabine's head shot up with the speed of an arrow loosed from a bow, eyes wide. "Pardon?"

Her voice was as hot as a new blade when pulled from the forge. The pleading look in her eyes was gone, replaced with a fierce, burning anger.

"You've decided that Jak *'can have me?'*"

Nikalys froze, realizing his mistake. Before he could stammer out an apology, Sabine exploded upward and stepped over the bench. She glared at him with the same expression Nikalys had seen the day he met her, right before she sliced the unconscious bandit's neck: anger, hurt, bewilderment, and determination all swirling together, highlighted with a strange cool-headedness that Sabine exuded in times of distress.

In a surprisingly even tone, Sabine spit out, "You are the Progeny, yes, and I can't imagine how heavy the weight you carry is. Of course, how could I? You never blasted talk to me!"

She gestured around wildly, waving both hands in air to indicate the commons. He was sure the few Shadow Manes in the room were watching even if they were pretending not to.

"I know what everyone here is expecting from you. You've been given an impossible task. 'The Progeny must rise to lead the fight' and all of that." She jabbed a finger toward him, snapping, "But that blasted prophecy *does not* give you the right to make decisions about who can 'have me!'"

Nikalys sat motionless, afraid to move. All he could do was nod, stunned mute.

Shaking her head, Sabine muttered, "You are an absolute lout, Nikalys Isaac. An absolute lout!"

She spun around and headed to the back of the room where Kenders and Helene stood. Nikalys watched her go, briefly wondering if he should go after her.

He did not.

Sabine reached Kenders and Helene, who had apparently succeeded in securing a sweet cake from the kitchen. After a brief exchange with Kenders, Sabine scooped up Helene and began to walk back in the direction of Nikalys, heading for the exit. She weaved through the maze of tables, ensuring she did not pass him as she left. Helene peered at him and smiled wide, her face smeared with the sweet, brown spice of the cake she still had clasped in her hand. With her free hand, she waved at Nikalys until the pair passed through the open archway. Nikalys smiled and waved back, but both were half-hearted.

He sat, staring at the doorway.

"Hells."

A few moments later, Kenders' voice echoed through the hall.

"What did you say to her?"

Pulling his eyes from the empty archway, he found Kenders striding up the aisle of tables, heading straight for him. She looked almost as angry as Sabine had been. Rolling his eyes, he stood from the table and started to walk, intent upon retrieving his book before leaving. He did not feel like discussing any of this with his sister.

Kenders did not intend to let him escape, though. With a stubborn insistence he had heard countless times while growing up, she exclaimed, "Nikalys!"

He stopped in his tracks, the soles of his boots scuffing against the rock floor. If he did not face her now, she would follow him wherever he went. He decided to let her yell at him and get it over with. He sighed, turned around, and peered at his sister.

"What, sis?"

There was strange hopelessness in his voice that he did not expect to hear.

The moment she saw his face, her quick pace slowed and the anger in her eyes drained away. In a kind, sympathetic voice, she said softly, "Oh, Nik. I'm so sorry." His sister knew him better than he did himself at times.

For a long moment, neither sibling said a word.

Finally, he mumbled, "I said something I shouldn't have, sis. That's all." After a resigned sigh, he rationalized, "It's probably for the better, though. She's angry and hurt now, but in time, she'll realize I was—"

Interrupting, Kenders said, "She has feelings for you, Nik. Saying something brainless won't change that."

Nikalys peered at his sister, frowned, and asked, "And she has feelings for Jak, too, doesn't she?"

Kenders did not respond, her face suspiciously void of any expression. Taking her non-reaction as confirmation, Nikalys let out a short, humorless chuckle.

"Right, then."

Taking a moment to compose himself, Nikalys continued, "It's better for everyone if we keep things simple, right? It makes the most sense, doesn't it?"

He had turned and taken a few strides towards where his book waited for him when Kenders called gently, "The head cannot tell the heart how to feel, Nik."

Nikalys' step faltered at his sister's words, but he did not stop. Picking up the thick volume, he headed for the commons' entryway. His cold, drafty room now seemed like a much more hospitable place to read.

CHAPTER 8: AID

Nathan sat in an oversized, cushioned chair, comfortable but not relaxed, his gaze locked on Zecus and Joshmuel across the room. Father and son were perched on two tall stools, leaning forward, resting their elbows on a round-top table, and talking. Two silver goblets of sweet wine sat untouched between them. One of five arched windows that looked over the well-tended garden below framed the pair. For Zecus' sake, Nathan prayed things were going well.

Joshmuel appeared to be handling the discussion well. The elder Alsher had displayed signs of worry, but Nathan had yet to detect any anger in the man's demeanor. Nathan was impressed. A certain strength must run through the Alsher blood.

Nathan went to draw in a deep breath as a precursor to a sigh, but grimaced at the first waft of air. The perfume of the garden's flowers was overpowering, so much so it was giving him a headache. He closed his eyes and rubbed his temples, frowning, almost missing the malodorous soldiers' barracks back in Smithshill.

The ride back from the Council House had been a quiet, somber experience, full of murmured explanations for Joshmuel and Boah's benefit. Lady Vivienne allowed him and Jak to do most of the talking while she sat in thoughtful silence and they did their best to convey everything that had happened.

The attack on Yellow Mud.

Broedi and the White Lions.

Indrida's prophecy.

The Progeny.

The Battle of Shorn Rise against oligurts and razorfiends.

The Shadow Manes.

Throughout most of the tale, the two Borderlanders gaped at them as if they were mad. Had Nathan not lived much of it, he would have felt the same, he supposed. However, once Zecus swore it all true, the pair seemed to accept the grand tale.

Upon reaching Lady Vivienne's villa, she led them to her personal room—the same one in which they had arrived via the port—and left the five men alone, informing them that she would be back later. As the door was still closing, Zecus turned to his father and asked to speak with him. The pair had retreated to the stools by the window and not moved since.

The remaining three men had settled into a trio of cushioned chairs beneath a large painting of a grand, nameless city. Water canals meandered through the buildings instead of streets, covered with countless, colorful rafts of people. To pass the time, they chatted about the painting, wondering aloud at its location and discussing the perceived difficulties of having waterways instead of roads.

A servant arrived a short time later, carrying five wine goblets on a silver platter. Jak and Boah accepted theirs readily, smiles on their faces, and sampled the
drink immediately. While Nathan had taken his cup, he had yet to take a single sip.
The events of the First Council weighed on his mind.

Jak was in the midst of detailing the Battle of Shorn Rise for Boah, when the
sole oaken door to the room opened, swinging inward, and groaning on its hinges.
Four soldiers entered the room, two dressed in the blue and gold of the Southern
Arms and two wearing the maroon and silver of the Long Coast Duchy's Shore
Guard. The men took up positions on both sides of the doors, standing as straight
as the spears they carried.

Duchess Aleece swept into the room a moment later, followed by Duchess
Adnil and Lady Vivienne, all three still wearing the formal dresses they had on
during the First Council.

Jak turned his head, and upon seeing the two duchesses, attempted to leap
to his feet. Sunk deep into his chair's cushions, he threw his weight forward and
thrust himself up, losing his grip on his goblet in the process. The half-full cup flew
from his hand and landed a couple of paces from the chair, splattering red wine all
over the polished white marble and clanging as it bounced away. As he scrambled
forward to gather up the rogue cup, he tripped over his feet and fell to the ground,
sliding into the newly spilled puddle of wine.

Had two sovereigns not been in the room, Nathan was confident everyone
would be laughing heartily at the clumsy display. Perhaps even the somber Alsher
pair. Boah managed to restrain his delight, letting his mirth expand to a wide grin,
but no further. Nathan allowed himself a small smile only.

As the duchesses dismissed their respective honor guards, Nathan rose from
his own chair—with extra care—and placed his goblet on the marble table that rest
between them. Keeping one eye on the three noblewomen as they walked toward
the trio of men, Nathan leaned over and muttered, "Do you need help?"

Jak gave him a sharp look.

"I'm fine."

As the young man pushed himself from the floor, his cheeks redder than the
wine on the floor and tunic, Nathan turned to face the noblewomen.

When he had been standing on the chamber floor before the First Council,
Nathan had judged Duchess Aleece to be one of the most attractive women that he
had ever laid eyes on. Upon seeing her a second time, he amended his earlier assessment. All other women paled in comparison.

Long, glistening, sandy brown hair draped past her shoulders, perfectly framing her face. Her skin was without blemish, the only marks being two dimples
summoned forth by the broad smile she wore. She appeared as amused by Jak's fall

as Boah was. Duchess Adnil—quietly chuckling to herself—seemed to be enjoying the accident as well. Only Lady Vivienne wore a disapproving look. Nathan wondered if the baroness knew how to smile.

Looking over, Nathan saw that Zecus and Joshmuel had left their private table before the garden window and were coming to stand with them. Both men's eyes had a haunted look to them, sad and worried at the same time. As they neared, Joshmuel reached up and gently patted his son's back. Nathan's opinion of the Alsher patriarch rose even higher.

Their dresses rustling, the three noblewomen stopped before the men. Duchess Adnil fixed her stare on Jak and asked, "Are you hurt, young man?" She had stopped chuckling, but still wore an amused smile.

"Ah, no. I'm fine, thank you."

"Good to hear," replied Duchess Adnil. With a twinkle to her eye, she added, "I wish I could get that kind of response every time I entered a room. It would make my days so much more enjoyable."

Jak's cheeks and neck turned an even deeper shade of red. Facing the baroness, he said apologetically, "Lady Vivienne, I'm sorry for the mess I made." Holding up the goblet that he had successfully retrieved, he added, "And for this." The cup had a few flattened dents on the lip and base from bouncing on the hard marble floor. "I'll pay for it. Somehow."

Nathan wondered where Jak thought he could get the ducats. The goblet looked expensive.

Duchess Aleece said, "Nonsense, Jak. You will do no such thing."

Jak looked to the duchess.

"You know my name?"

"Of course," replied the noblewoman. "Vivienne has been keeping me apprised of everything. If I am not mistaken, your martial training is progressing well, yes? I have heard you have quite the mind for tactics, as well."

Jak stood, mouth open, speechless.

Turning her gaze to Zecus, the duchess said, "You as well, Zecus Alsher—although I hear the spear and staff suit you better."

Zecus managed better than Jak, offering a small bow and a gracious, if slightly befuddled, "Thank you, my Lady."

Nathan took a small step forward and said, "Excuse me, my Lady, but neither know of your involvement with the Manes." The confused stares of Jak and Zecus now turned on him. Ignoring them for the moment, he glanced at Lady Vivienne. "I was unsure if you wished them to know yet."

Duchess Aleece shifted her gaze to Nathan. For the first time, Nathan noticed the duchess' soft, hazel eyes. They were stunning.

"And you must be the Red Sentinel sergeant, then? Nathan Trell?"

She gave him a friendly smile, completely disarming him. Forced to swallow a lump that had inexplicably appeared in his throat, he inclined his head and responded, "I am, my Lady."

The duchess' smile widened.

"Commander Aiden has had nothing but high praise for you, Master Sergeant. Thank you for all you have sacrificed. Your mettle and conviction astound me."

Nathan's neck felt warm.

"Thank you, my Lady. You are too kind."

Jak muttered, "Hold a moment." He glanced at Duchess Aleece. "If she knows about the Shadow Manes, does that mean she knows about...uh..." He trailed off, unsure what he should or should not say.

With slight smile, Duchess Aleece said, "Your brother and sister? Broedi? The White Lions? Oh yes, Jak. Most definitely, I do. I was a member of the Manes long before I ever sat in the Sovereign's Chair."

Jak and Zecus were dumbfounded, Boah and Joshmuel only slightly less so. Perhaps the older Borderlanders had experienced enough shock for one day. A hint of a grin rested upon Duchess Aleece's face. Apparently, she found their bafflement mildly amusing.

Jak glared at Nathan.

"You knew?"

With a quiet sigh an apologetic shrug, Nathan said, "I did. Broedi told me before he left."

"And you didn't tell us?"

"I promised not to," said Nathan. "I am sorry, Jak. Truly."

Joshmuel shook his head, murmuring, "All of this is very confusing to me."

Boah added with a lopsided grin, "I'm glad I'm not the only one." Holding up his goblet, his smile widened as he said, "I thought perhaps this wine was stronger than it tasted."

With a smile, Duchess Aleece conceded, "Explanations are owed to you all, I suppose."

Eyeing the noblewoman, Nathan asked politely, "May I do so, my Lady? I feel obligated to explain my silence to Jak and Zecus. While I understood the need for it, I am not proud of my part in the deception."

Her deep, hazel eyes shifted to him, swallowing him. She gave him a tiny smile and said, "I shall add honorable to the long list of your admirable traits." She waved her hand toward the other men. "Please share what you will."

Turning to address the young men, Nathan said, "Before he left, Broedi warned me of what might come to pass today. At the time, the plans were still under discussion but—" he glanced at the baroness "—Lady Vivienne convinced him that should today's show become necessary, it would be best if Zecus remain ignorant of his role."

Nathan turned to the frowning Borderlander and said, "He hated to deceive you, Zecus—as did I—but we agreed with the baroness. And after seeing what transpired in the chamber, I can see there was merit to the choice. I am, however, sorry for my role in your deception. You as well, Jak. I could not tell you, Nikalys, or Kenders for fear one of you would slip. Or, tell Zecus outright."

Jak frowned, saying, "Which is exactly what I would have done had I known." Shaking his head, he eyed the noblewomen and asked, "Was all the deceit necessary?"

"Perhaps not," said Duchess Aleece. "But it was the most effective means by which to accomplish our goals. We now have a public alliance of three duchies, possibly five if things go well with Eli and Catherine. And, we managed to do so without revealing anything about the prophecy, the Progeny, or the White Lions." A smile crossed her lips. "Even Rholeb is unaware of what is truly happening. He believes Vanson is behind everything."

Duchess Adnil added, "And do not forget the power of the whispered word." She shifted her sharp-eyed gaze to Zecus. "Your outburst in the balcony was perfectly dramatic, young man. By now, half of Freehaven has heard what you saw in that demon's camp. Within weeks, all of the Freelands will be talking about the invasion. By Year's End, Duke Kyle will have no choice but to join us."

"What about the other duchies?" asked Jak. "It will take turns to deliver messages and get responses."

A sly smile on her face, Duchess Adnil said, "Actually, it won't."

Cocking an eyebrow, Jak asked, "Do you have horses that can fly, my Lady? Because I don't see how you could reach the Foothills in under two turns. And the Colonial Duchy? How long does it take to sail there?"

Duchess Aleece, somewhat reluctantly, answered, "You have touched upon a rather closely guarded secret amongst the First Council, Jak." She glanced at the Long Coast duchess. "Should I?"

With a short huff, Duchess Adnil said, "You're hesitant about sharing this? Considering to whom we're speaking, I believe we can share." Turning to face the waiting men, the older woman said, "When the First Council outlawed magic two and a half centuries ago a provision—one that was never publicly disclosed, of course—was written into the law. Simply put, the ten sovereigns are exempt."

Nathan raised his eyebrows in surprise.

Duchess Adnil continued, "While all mages were removed from the courts, a number of the more useful magical artifices remained, many of which we continue to employ to this day. Some allow for much more efficient communication than that by horse or ship. Council business would be nigh impossible without it."

Duchess Aleece said, "Lady Vivienne will be happy to explain much of this to you, but it will have to wait until later."

The frown upon the baroness' lips indicated that she was not pleased by the prospect of having to explain anything to anyone.

Duchess Aleece nodded at the wall and said, "For the moment, we must get going. Storm Island awaits."

Nathan turned a surprised eye toward the duchess.

"You are going back with us?" asked Jak. "Both of you?"

Duchess Aleece nodded, saying, "Yes, but only for a few hours. I have been quite anxious to meet your brother and sister."

Addressing Duchess Adnil, Nathan said politely, "Pardon me, my Lady, for all that Broedi shared with me, he never mentioned you as a member of the Manes."

"Because I am not," replied Duchess Adnil. "Until Aleece approached me a few weeks ago, I had no idea of their existence. Or of the growing threat in the Borderlands."

Glowering at Duchess Aleece, Jak said, "The Cabal is intent on finding and killing my brother and sister. I think it'd be best if you don't go around telling people about them."

Lady Vivienne sucked in a quick, furious breath and glared at Jak. Nathan frowned. One did not go giving orders to a duchess.

The ruler of the Southlands held Jak's gaze, silently studying the black-haired young man, her expression blank and unreadable.

A long, quiet moment passed. Surprisingly, Duchess Adnil broke the tense silence.

"Young man, Aleece spent her childhood with me, growing up at court in Albonia. She is as much family to me as your foster brother and sister are to you. I am more than capable of keeping her secrets."

Jak gave an almost imperceptible nod.

"Oh, well. I suppose that is fine, then."

With a calm, kind voice, Duchess Aleece said, "Jak, I admire your devotion to your brother and sister. And, I know that your words come from a place of good intentions." She paused for moment and, with hands clasped in front of her, took two, quick steps toward Jak. In an instant, her eyes grew hard and her voice sharp. "But if you were to *ever* address me in that manner in public, I would have you arrested on the spot, tossed in the stockade, and flogged in the nearest town square." Raising her voice, she snapped off each word, crisply and clearly, "My position *demands* respect. A leader cannot lead without it, do you understand that?"

Jak wilted like a fresh flower tossed in a blacksmith's forge. With a tiny, contrite nod, he said softly, "Yes, my Lady."

Tempering her tone slightly, the duchess added, "I am glad. Because soon, many will be looking to you for guidance."

Jak looked up.

"Me?"

Duchess Aleece nodded.

"You are the sibling of the Progeny, whether in blood or not. As this war grows—and it will—your responsibility will grow as well. And I request—nay, I demand—that you rise to the challenge. You are *not* an olive farmer anymore, Jak. Stop acting like one."

Nathan noticed a slight grin of approval on Duchess Adnil's lips.

A visibly chastised Jak said, "I am sorry, my Lady. I spoke hastily and without thought. I am unfamiliar with being in the presence of nobility."

Duchess Aleece smiled warmly. The firm authoritativeness melted away so quickly and completely, Nathan was not sure if it had ever been there in the first place.

"I am no different from you, Jak. I worry, hope, love, and cry. Yet, when I am performing my role as 'Duchess Aleece, Sovereign of the Southlands,' I expect all of the respect my position deserves. The rest of the time, I prefer to be treated like any other person."

Nathan's opinion of Duchess Aleece continued to rise. She was everything a ruler should be.

Duchess Adnil stepped forward, patted Duchess Aleece on the back, and promptly said, "Now that the lesson in etiquette is over, can we continue on? I truly have but a few hours before my advisors come looking for me."

"Of course, Aunt Adnil," replied Duchess Aleece. Turning to Lady Vivienne, she said, "The key, please?"

Lady Vivienne reached into a fold of her dress, pulled out the unusual key she had used to open the port at Storm Island, and handed it over to Duchess Aleece's outstretched hand. The duchess strode to the back wall—her grand, Southlands-blue dress swishing as she walked—and dragged the key along the stone, opening a rippling black rift. Turning back to face the group assembled in the room, she said with a glint in her eye, "Let's go see the Progeny, shall we?"

Without waiting for an answer, she wheeled around and stepped through the port. One after another, they walked into the inky blackness suspended between two flaps of the wall. As Nathan strode to the wall, a small smile touched his lips. He wondered what Nikalys and Kenders would think when they came face to face with two sovereigns of the Oaken Duchies.

CHAPTER 9: KUR-SURUS

8ᵗʰ of the Turn of Luraana, 4999

Battles were chaos distilled.

The low thudding of the grayskins' war chants rumbled in Okollu's chest as much as it beat against his eardrums. The blade-men's incessant shrieking and clicking was thrice as bad, each shrill call feeling like a bladed quill digging into his skull. He cursed both races as he ran. Their racket was making it difficult for his pack to hear his directions.

Okollu sprinted, along with the rest of the Drept pack, through the dry, grassy plains and toward the great stone walls of Gobas. Great, jagged gaps in the sand-colored ramparts awaited him and his pack mates, holes caused by the flying rocks tossed by the grayskins and their cursed nedabiks. Men stood atop the walls; more smooth-faces would die today.

Thick, black smoke filled the air, making each gasping breath that Okollu drew a torturous one. Much of the city ahead of him was on fire, caused by the grayskins sending bolts of lightning beyond the walls. Okollu was relieved that part of the assault was over. Thunder made the pack skittish.

He stared at the towering walls as he rushed through the grass, a low, angry growl slipping from his throat. The Drept should not be here. This was not their fight.

Baaldòk's voice bellowed over the other din of battle.

"Through the breach!"

Okollu looked over his shoulder to see the false tas-vilku of the Drept pointing to one of the gaps with his oversized sword. The red-skinned diavol ran with the pack, sprinting faster than any creature with two legs should move.

Loping on all fours, Okollu turned to study the indicated hole in the wall. The gap was narrow and well-defended still. Men stood atop the intact sections on either side, armed with the stringed weapons that launched the sharp, pointed sticks. An open charge through the walls meant more Drept would die today.

Baaldòk shouted, "Okollu! The breach!"

The diavol wanted him, needed him to relay the order. The pack was spread out over the plains and the battle's cacophony drowned out even Baaldòk's echoing voice.

Okollu hesitated a moment as he considered giving a different order, wondering what would happen if he called for a retreat instead. He delayed long enough that Baaldòk reiterated his demand, roaring, "Okollu! Now!"

He wanted nothing more than to turn and rip the demon's throat open. Yet he maintained control. He could not take the demon alone.

"Okollu!" screamed Baaldòk.

Okollu waited a moment longer before tossing his head back and loosing a long howl, adjusting pitch and tone to convey Baaldòk's orders to the rest of the pack. When he was done, he snapped off the cry and shut his jaw, smacking his teeth together with enough force to snap the leg bone of a boar. Okollu, along with hundreds of the Drept pack, shifted directions and aimed for the breach.

As the pack turned, new kur-surus moved to run at his side. Grrash, an all gray female, sprinted on his left. Rargol, a brown-furred male with black markings on his muzzle, was on his right. Both were good hunters, Grrash was one of the best the Drept pack had.

Staring ahead to the walls, he watched as one of the giant machines perched atop a tower loosed a ball of flame from its cup. The sphere soared through the air, tumbling and dripping fire as it flew. Okollu eyed the ball carefully, trying to gauge where it might land. His two hearts began to pound even harder than they had been as he realized the globe would land in the midst of the Drept.

Okollu tilted his head back and began to howl a warning to his pack when Baaldòk cried out, "Do not stop! Straight ahead!"

Snapping his jaw shut, Okollu whipped his head around to glare at the diavol. Baaldòk's disregard for the pack was maddening. Facing forward, he stared into the blue sky and watched the ball of flame hurtling straight for him. A long trail of white smoke trailed the sphere.

Okollu did not want to die today. He could not die today. With his death, hope for the Drept would perish as well.

Moments before the fire crashed to the ground, Okollu dragged his right paw through the grass, pretending to trip and stumble. As he tumbled to the ground, he reached out and grabbed Grrash—she was closer than Rargol—wrapping his fingers around the bone where leg met hind paw. As the two fell to the ground, sliding through grass and dirt, Okollu heard the sizzle of the flames and felt a flash of heat.

Fire, dust, and chunks of dirt exploded a dozen paces ahead of Okollu and Grrash. A dozen kur-surus yipped and howled in pain. Okollu lifted his head and saw several of his pack mates on fire. Rargol—running by his side only moments ago—lay dead a dozen paces away. His body was bloody, charred, and absent its head. Okollu would not have even known it was Rargol were it not for the brown and black fur.

As dust and dirt rained down on Okollu, he heard Baaldòk roar, "Keep going! Take the walls!"

Drept rushed past Okollu and Grrash, dashing around the crater in the ground and ignoring their dead pack mates. Grrash whipped her head around and glared at Okollu, her yellow eyes wide an angry. Kicking her leg, she growled, "Let go of me!"

The moment Okollu released her paw, she jumped to all fours and began to sprint straight for the breach. If this were any other fight, Okollu would admire her bravery. Yet it was not courage driving Grrash forward.

"Get up!" shouted Baaldòk. The diavol grabbed Okollu by the scruff, hoisted him from the ground, and shoved him toward the walls. "Get into the city!" His blood-red eyes danced with the reflected flames of the burning bodies and grass. "Now!"

Swallowing his hatred like a hunk of rotten meat, Okollu growled, "Yes, tas-vilku."

Baaldòk began to run toward Gobas and Okollu followed, wondering what the point of attacking this place was. Utter destruction seemed to be the only goal here. It made no sense.

Soon, the pointed sticks of the men began to rain down on the Drept, striking down even more of his pack. A low, constant growl hovered in Okollu's throat as he ran. He hated this war.

CHAPTER 10: CABAL

10ᵗʰ of the Turn of Luraana, 4999

Raela was bored.

With a sigh, she shifted her body, assuming a new position in the richly cushioned chair in which she sat. She peered around the dark, cavernous room, searching out anything that might hold her interest while she waited.

Darkened torches lined both sides of the long room, cold and extinguished for two days now. The only light in the room streamed through a cracked-open door to Raela's immediate right. Beyond lay a caved-in hallway, pummeled by one of the massive boulders hurled during the assault. The light quickly diffused only a few paces in, however, leaving most of the chamber gloomy and gray.

Raela could have lit the torches to brighten the hall, but there was no need to do so. The mortal body she currently inhabited had no issue with seeing in low light.

Her gaze settled on the one thing with any color in the drab hall. A ten-foot wide, lush red rug ran the length of the long room, leading from her chair, down four, wide steps, and all the way to a pair of towering doors on the opposite wall. Polished sandstone floor spread out on both sides of the runner.

With an exasperated sigh, she let her head fall backward, making a soft thud as the cushion softened the blow against the wooden back.

"Where are they?"

As she absently eyed the wide beams of hardwood crisscrossing one another, supporting the domed, stone roof overhead, the acrid scent of charred wood filled her nose. The wind had shifted, bringing fresh smoke into the room. Raela let her head fall to the side, staring out the broken door. The faint screams of the unfortunate souls still alive were snaking their way into the chamber.

"—him alone. Take me instead! Please—"

"—swear to you, I will do whatever you—"

"—High Host! Protect me from these foul—"

Raela shook her head, a frown on her lips.

What was happening outside was artless. Inflicting such blatant misery on others was heavy-handed and inelegant. Great things could be achieved without conflict and pain. It took time and careful planning, but the fruits of subtle chicanery were infinitely sweeter.

Raela was musing on the manner in which she would have gone about things when the sound of ripping fabric filled the empty hall. Glancing to the center of the room, she spotted the telltale fluttering flaps of reality.

"It is about time…"

Sitting up a bit taller, she adjusted her gauzy dress and checked that her hair—light brown and perfectly straight—was in place. Content, she faced the port just as a dark-skinned man emerged from the rip in midair. Bald, with dark brown eyes sunk in deep sockets, a wide, globular nose, and lips that seemed too thick for his face, the man was not by any means pleasing to the eye. A richly adorned, deep purple tunic draped below his waist, loose black breeches hung over the tops of leather boots.

As soon as he was through the port, he stopped short, and let out a quick, whispered curse.

"Blast!"

Raela began to chuckle lightly, the lilting sound wafting about the chamber. The man's head swiveled around, searching for the source.

"Raela? Is that you?"

"Were you expecting someone else?" asked Raela.

Squinting about the shrouded room, he asked, "Why are you sitting in the dark?"

"Is it dark? I had not noticed."

The man's eyes finally locked onto her, narrowing in an instant. He was still straining against the gloom, but he was able to see her. Drawing himself up, he ordered, "Get out of my chair!"

Raela raised an eyebrow, mildly surprised.

"My, my, Vanson. Your chair?"

Someone had become a little too comfortable in the role he was playing.

The man whom mortals knew as Duke Vanson, the sovereign ruler of the Borderlands, released his hold on the port—sending a soft pop through the hall—and began striding toward her, arms to his side with fists clenched.

"The Sovereign's Chair is still mine, Raela."

She eyed the man, choosing not to respond. There was no point. The moment Vanson opened his ears, he would lose interest in her.

He was halfway to her when he stopped suddenly and tilted his head to the half-open doorway. His lips curled up into a cruel smile. Raela rolled her eyes and let out a short, annoyed sigh. He was so predictable.

His gaze on the cracked door, Vanson asked softly, "Do you hear that?"

"It's hard not to," muttered Raela.

He took a few steps toward the ruined hall, drawn by the sounds of distress as a nightmoth is to a candle, his eyes wide and alight with excitement.

"Is it not glorious?"

Raela shook her head in disgust, muttering, "Not the word I would have used." She hoped the others would arrive soon.

Vanson's gaze flicked to her.

"Do you think I have time to go down to—?"

An abrupt, metal clang cut his question short. Raela stared to the far end of the hall as the left side of the tall doors cracked open a few feet, letting a second, long shaft of light into the dark room. A tall, lithe figure dressed in flowing robes passed before the backdrop of light, entering the hall and plunging back into the shadows. The individual's elongated arms and legs removed any doubt as to who had just arrived, as did the cool, calm voice that leapt across the hall.

"Not now, Vanson. Perhaps you can indulge later."

The quiet curse that slipped from Vanson's lips prompted a slight smile on Raela's. Was it anyone else, she might have wondered how the figure striding though the dark now had heard Vanson's question through the thick, wooden doors. However, as Tandyr was in the body of a saeljul, there was no mystery. Ijulan hearing was superb.

Remaining seated in the Sovereign's Chair, Raela called, "Nice of you to show. I was beginning to think I had the wrong ruined city."

"I have been busy," Tandyr replied dryly. "I apologize for my tardiness." He was close enough now that Raela could see his long blond hair was pulled back, tightly bound.

Vanson asked, "Did your beasts truly have to ruin everything, Tandyr?" He was glancing around the room, peering at the destruction, a frown on his face. "This seems excessive."

The saeljul reached where Vanson stood and, without breaking stride, said, "I fail to see why it matters."

Vanson glared at Tandyr as he passed.

"My hall was glorious!"

Without looking back, the ijul replied, "Your assessment of what is 'glorious' is much different from mine, Vanson. You have been trapped here too long."

Vanson continued to stare at Tandyr's back, but remained quiet. The saeljul stopped at the stairs that lead to the Sovereign's Chair and eyed Raela.

"Greetings, Raela."

She nodded.

"Hello, Tandyr."

She wondered which of them trusted the other less.

As the two eyed each other silently, Vanson moved from the center of the red rug to approach where Tandyr stood, tripped on an overturned urn, and stumbled forward.

"Blast it!"

He steadied himself and looked around the room. Raela felt the soft, faint crackling of the Strands as reddish-orange strings of energy danced dimly before her eyes. Fire was not one of her strengths, but she could still sense it. The two dozen torches still bolted to the walls lit up simultaneously, flooding the room with enough light that Raela was forced to squint against the sudden brightness. Tandyr shut his eyes briefly, as well.

A satisfied Vanson mumbled, "That's better."

Vanson moved forward to stand beside Tandyr, all the while studying the disheveled room and shaking his head in obvious disgust.

"We can begin," announced Tandyr. "It will only be the three of us today."

Vanson muttered, "Good." He sounded relieved.

Raela agreed with the sentiment, happy the fourth member of their group was not attending. While Vanson's infatuation with misery disgusted her, Cardin's behavior made her ill.

Addressing them both, Tandyr said, "To start with, I wish to report that nearly the entire Borderlands west of Gobas has been secured and the Dust Men rendered useless, while our army has suffered only minimal losses." He glanced at the duke of the Borderlands. "Thank you, Vanson."

The God of Strife waved his hand in a dismissive gesture and let out a disappointed sigh.

"I wish I could have been here for the actual attack on Gobas. It would have been glorious to watch."

Raela shook her head, pointing out, "The confusion caused by your absence made the city that much easier to take."

Tandyr nodded. "I agree." Looking to Vanson, he added firmly, "And so did you beforehand. Raela should not have needed to remind you of that."

A day before the attack, she had visited Vanson, ensuring that the God was going to leave as planned. It was a good thing she had. Vanson had seemed content to sit and watch the city fall around him, reveling in the collective misery of the populace.

Shrugging, Vanson said, "It is difficult to suppress my nature."

The muscles in Tandyr's face tightened.

"If I can do it, you certainly should be able to."

"I did," snapped Vanson. "For thirty years, I sat in that blasted chair—" he jabbed a finger toward Raela "—fighting what I am meant to do." His head swiveled to face the cracked door and the faint screams wafting through it. "I simply felt I was owed some enjoyment after so long." The bald duke alternated his gaze between them both, a wicked smile spreading over his lips. "Perhaps you two can provide me a taste of what I missed."

Raela recognized the look on his face and did not like what it portended.

"What happened?"

"Something that I am sure neither of you will like. Something that *you*, dear Raela, caused."

Raela sat a little straighter, suddenly tense. Her eyes narrowed.

"Me?"

"Had you not rushed me to leave, perhaps I might not have made such a terrible error."

His delaying was distressing her, which was exactly what he wanted of course.

"I have no patience for your games. Speak."

A soft chuckle slipped from Vanson as his smile widened. Raela glared at the man, digging her fingernails into her thighs, trying hard not to show her irritation. Tandyr, on the other hand, managed to remain surprisingly calm. Expressionless, he swiveled his head to stare at Vanson, his long blond hair—pulled taut and constrained with three black cords—draped over his right shoulder.

Raela marveled at Tandyr's tranquility. She had known him in his previous forms, most recently the divina Norasim, and he had never been able to remain as at peace as he appeared now.

After a few seconds of quiet staring, Tandyr spoke, his tone even and calm.

"What sort of 'error?'"

The former duke met the saeljul's composed stare with a disappointed frown, evidently displeased he had been unable to upset Tandyr.

"When I left the castle, I brought a number of loyalists along with me. After moving through the port I had opened a few miles north of the city, I sent them away with instructions to meet me at a prearranged location while I attempted find a decent place to observe the battle."

"Hold," muttered Raela. "You opened a port in the middle of your lands? That was brainless. What if someone had seen you step from a port?"

The longer people believed Vanson was nothing more than the weak, ineffective Duke of the Borderlands, the better.

Vanson shook his head, saying, "I may have a few short-comings in your eyes, but being witless is not one of them. I scouted a small gully three turns ago and have had men guarding it since. Trust me, it was empty when I arrived."

"Then what was your error?" asked Raela.

"Well," muttered Vanson. "As this city is built on what I am convinced is the flattest land in all of Terrene, short of marching with the unwashed masses of the Sudashians, I would never be able to find a suitable vantage point to watch Gobas fall."

Raela glared at him.

"Which explains why I found you standing in the Dust Men's tower."

Vanson shrugged and said, "It was as—"

"The mistake, please." interjected Tandyr. "What was the mistake?"

The duke's gaze flicked to the ijul. For a brief moment, undeniable trepidation filled his expression. Raela steeled herself. If Vanson was ashamed or afraid, this was bad indeed.

"Before I sent my loyalists from here, I gave them a number of documents and valuables to carry for me. I made the mistake of putting everything together, and handing it to a rather feckless baron to carry. When I eventually arrived at the camp, I discovered that four men had waylaid him—"

Raela sat upright, fully alert. Her voice was tight with accusation, she snapped, "You didn't!"

Tandyr held up a hand, motioning for her to remain quiet. "Allow him to finish, please."

Raela glared at Vanson, but remained silent for the moment. Slipping her hand beneath the folds of her own thin robes, she felt for the small pouch strapped around her waist. Pressing it against her right hip, she felt the oblong, finger-length stone contained within the purse. She never let hers out of sight.

Vanson's gaze shifted between Tandyr and Raela, he was hesitant to continue. After clearing his throat, he said, "The bandits—Marshlanders by all accounts— took the baron's coin and valuables."

"And what was with those valuables?" asked Tandyr.

Vanson paused a moment.

"Ah…Suštinata na pori."

Raela pushed herself from the Sovereign's Chair and advanced on the sovereign, her bare feet brushing through the thick, red rug as she demanded, "Does that body you inhabit have an illness of the head?!" She halted at the bottom of the wide steps, mere paces from the pair. "Perhaps I should strike you down right now and force you to find another mortal to infect with your stupidity!"

Vanson tensed, his eyes wide and alert. He was waiting for some signal that she was reaching for the Strands. She would never be so predictable. The poisoned dart she had hidden in the broach hanging from her dress would kill him within four breaths.

Vanson said in a hushed tone, "You wouldn't dare. You need me."

"Do we?" she shot back. "Your role is complete, is it not?" She jabbed a finger at the half-open door nearby. "Gobas has fallen and the Borderlands are in our hands. Tens of thousands of refugees have already flooded into the Marshlands with more crossing the border every day. Duke Rholeb's ability to form any sort of effective resistance diminishes with each Borderlander that shows up at his gates. The Marshlands will fall even faster than this forsaken land!"

The God of Strife's expression hardened.

"Duke Everett and I can—"

Waving a hand in the air, Raela interjected, "You can do *nothing*! Everett will do whatever he is told to do. By Tandyr or by me! He's a simpleton, a shield to protect us from the north. You've served your purpose. You are a duke without a duchy!"

Vanson shot back, "I am a *God*!"

A derisive laugh leapt from her lips.

"Fine. You're a God. In present company, that means little. What you are is a fool! No! You are worse than a fool." Taking a swift step forward, she peered up into his eyes and whispered with thick, hot vehemence, "Even the biggest fool in all of Terrene would not have lost one of the Suštinata!"

For just a moment, shame filled Vanson's eyes. It was fleeting, but Raela had seen it. With a final, derisive snort of revulsion, she stepped backward.

"Idiot."

She glanced at Tandyr to see what he thought of Vanson's momentous gaffe and found the ijul standing extraordinarily still, hands clasped together at his waist as he stared at the ground.

Raela shook her head.

"Blast it, Tandyr! If this doesn't get you upset, what will?"

A few moments later, Tandyr asked softly, "You have more to share, do you not, Vanson?"

Raela glared at Vanson.

"There's more? What else did you do? Report our plans to the High Host?"

Withering under the combined intensity of her burning stare and Tandyr's eminently cool one, Vanson uttered, "I admit to the gravity of my error. However, you have made one yourself."

Her eyes narrowed.

"What does that mean?"

"Duke Rholeb is indeed beset by the exodus of refugees. And if he were the only one we had to worry about, we could feel secure about the situation." He paused and licked his lips. "Unfortunately, that is not the case."

Raela shook her head, muttering, "I enjoy riddles as much as I do your company at the moment. Speak clearly."

The unexpected sound of soft laughter drifted through the empty hall. Surprised, she turned to stare at Tandyr and found the saeljul still staring at the ground while shaking his head, a slight smile on his lips.

Confused, Raela asked, "What about this is humorous?"

Tandyr sighed and said with mirthful resignation, "It was only a matter of time, I suppose."

"What are you talking about?" asked Raela. "What was only a matter of time?"

Baffled as well, Vanson stared at Tandyr and asked, "Do you know what happened with the First Council? How could you? We haven't spoken in—"

"I know *nothing* for a fact," snapped Tandyr. His mirth vanished as quickly as it appeared. "However, your mediocre attempt at being cryptic is as transparent as a pane of newly spun glass." The saeljul walked away from them and headed up the stairs.

Raela watched him for a moment before asking, "I don't suppose you'd like to share?"

Upon reaching the Sovereign's Chair, Tandyr faced Raela and Vanson, sat down, and pressed his back into the chair's cushions, letting out a soft sigh of approval.

"This is a nice chair, Vanson. I can see why you grew used to it."

Speaking with a quiet intensity, Raela said, "One of you had better tell me what has happened."

Tandyr's eyes flicked up sharply and stared at her, saying, "You know, for one who preaches the efficacy of a good lie paired with quiet restraint, you exhibit a stunning lack of patience." The flickering torchlight lent a maniacal quality to the saeljul's eyes. Of all the Cabal, Tandyr was the most dangerous. The others were predictable. Tandyr was not. Behind his current façade of calm and control bubbled a cauldron of anarchy.

Shifting his gaze to the former duke, Tandyr asked, "Duke Rholeb no longer defends his lands alone, does he?" It was more statement than question.

Vanson frowned.

"No, he does not."

Raela shut her eyes and sighed.

"Tandyr, you swore that would not happen."

"I was wrong," answered the ijul plainly. "Shall we quit because of that?"

Opening her eyes, Raela shook her head and muttered, "No." Looking over to Vanson, she asked, "How did that happen?"

"How it happened does not matter now," said Tandyr. "I am more interested in who is aiding him." Staring at Vanson with his ice blue eyes, he demanded, "What has Lord Tilas reported?"

"The Southlands and Long Coast have pledged their support—and armies—for the Marshlands."

"Why?" asked Raela. "On what are they basing their decision?"

With a frown, Vanson's said, "Apparently a handful of Borderlanders made a rather convincing case before the First Council. Duchess Aleece claims that I am deceiving everyone, that I am hiding the invasion."

Tandyr shrugged.

"Then they are not fools. What do the others say?"

"Two other duchies are leaning toward offering assistance as well," replied Vanson. "The remaining three have remained neutral so far."

Shaking her head in disbelief, Raela said, "So the Marshlands will be defended by the armies of *three* duchies—perhaps more?"

Vanson shook his head, replying quickly, "Yes, but it will take time for them to move their forces into place, especially the Long Coast. Besides, we have mages.

They don't. They would need to have an absolutely overwhelming number of soldiers to stand against us. And they simply don't have that."

Tandyr said, "Now it is you who is making assumptions."

The duke looked back up the stairs.

"What do you mean?"

The ijul stared at him, frowning.

"You are forgetting a very important force in all of this."

Raela, guessing to whom Tandyr was referring, said, "The Progeny?"

Tandyr nodded, his frown deepening.

"You still believe they exist?" huffed Vanson.

"Fool," muttered Raela. "When has Indrida ever been wrong?"

Vanson glared at her and snapped, "If we subscribe to the infallibility of her
words, why are we even bothering with this undertaking?"

Raela shook her head, unable to answer him. She asked herself that same question at least once a day.

Tandyr raised his voice, saying clearly, "Indrida's prophecies are *not* without
flaw. I promise you that."

Raela turned to stare at the saeljul curiously. He spoke with confidence.

"You know something, don't you?"

The ijul lowered his voice to just above a whisper and said, "There is no need
to debate the Progeny's existence any longer. There are two of them. A boy and girl,
not yet in their twentieth year."

A quiet moment filled the hall.

Raela asked, "How can you be sure?"

Tandyr lifted his gaze from the floor to meet her stare.

"Cadrin has made some recent progress with the prisoner."

Vanson took an angry step forward, demanding, "Why are we only finding
out about this now? You should have told us this earlier!"

"Do you understand the meaning of the word 'recent?'" asked Tandyr coldly.
"I only received notice a few days ago. The Progeny exist. What we do not know—
cannot know—is whether they are aware of this new alliance in the Marshlands
and have any interest in aiding them."

"And here I was thinking you were omnipotent," murmured Vanson.

"And I thought you were competent," replied the saeljul.

Not interested in any sort of squabble, Raela asked, "So what do we do now?"

Tandyr looked to her, his expression one of utmost determination.

"We retrieve Vanson's lost Suštinata and continue as planned."

Crossing her arms over her chest, Raela asked, "And how do we find the lost
Suštinata?" She glanced over at Vanson. "And, to be clear, I mean the one *you* lost.
Not the others."

The former duke of the Borderlands glared at her in perfect silence.

Tandyr asked, "Did you kill the baron who was robbed?"

Vanson shook his head, replying, "No. He's alive." A wicked smile spread over his face. "I've been enjoying his agony as he awaits his fate."

Raela shook her head, disgusted.

With a faint smile and nod, Tandyr rose from the Sovereign's Chair.

"Good. I have an idea, then."

Drifting down the stairs of the dais, he passed Vanson and Raela.

"Retrieve him and meet me in the soldiers' practice yard in one hour."

Her brow drawn together, Raela asked, "Where are you going?"

Already a dozen steps down the red rug, Tandyr halted, turned to face them, and said, "To visit the mongrels." With a slight smile, he spun around and resumed his walk toward the double doors.

Raela stared after him a moment before glancing at Vanson curiously.

The duke shrugged his shoulders and mumbled, "Don't ask me..."

He walked off, leaving Raela staring at both Gods' backs. Sighing, she shook her head and followed them to the doors.

CHAPTER 11: PRISONER

12th of the Turn of Luraana, 4999

A low, heavy thudding rumbled across the rolling prairie.

Rhohn immediately crouched low to the ground, dropping his head below the shafts of the tall, dry grass. He held perfectly still, peering through the thin stalks of grass swaying in the breeze, staring toward the dirt road, and listening to the distant reverberation. A worried grimace spread over his face as he realized the sound did not belong to horses.

"Blast it."

A few days ago, he had spotted a patrol of oligurts on the prairie's horizon, riding atop their ugly part-boar, part-wolf mounts. Luckily, he noticed them first, giving him plenty of time to hide in the grass. The rumbling he heard now could very well belong to those beasts.

Rhohn scowled, noting the way the prairie grass bent with the wind. The gentle breeze was surely carrying his weeks-without-a-wash scent toward the dirt road that rested almost a hundred paces away.

He cursed his error. He was growing lax.

Frowning, he studied his surroundings. Having left the steeper hills behind days ago, the slopes here were gradual and sweeping, a transitional area of land caught between foothills and plains. The hills might be smaller, but the terrain's rise and fall still played tricks with sounds. Rhohn could not tell from where the rumbling was coming.

He turned his gaze back to the west, following the road's winding path to where it wrapped behind a hill. Rhohn tried to recall the land's layout on the other side of the rise, but could not. He had just marched over that knoll, yet all he could remember was the constant, never-ending, brown grass and a few, random bulboa trees.

Rhohn sighed. He could not think straight. He needed food and clean water.

As he scanned the land for any sort of movement, he noticed a small plume of smoke on the eastern horizon, a grayish-white line meandering upward to where it disappeared against a backdrop of gray clouds.

Rhohn's eyes narrowed.

"Hold a moment."

Tilting his head back, he stared at the overcast heavens just as another deep, drawn-out rumble rolled over the hills and plains.

He shut his eyes.

"You are a fool, Rhohn Lurus."

Standing tall, he turned around and eyed the southwestern sky. Thunderclouds filled the horizon, bulky and clumped together to form a towering dark gray wall. A muted flash of distant lightning briefly lit up the clouds. Rhohn cocked his lone eyebrow, surprised.

Outside of the Winter turns, rain in the Borderlands was a rare event. He tried to recall what day it was, but after a few moments, he realized he had no idea even what turn it was. Perhaps it was Winter.

Shaking his head, he sighed, "I was hiding from a rain storm."

At least his water problem would be solved for a time. Once the storm reached him, he could fill his scavenged waterskin with puddled rainwater before the rock-hard land softened and eventually absorbed every drop. Content that he would not die of thirst, Rhohn swiveled to stare back to the eastern horizon and the plume of smoke.

"Fools."

If refugees had built the fire, they were not very bright. The smoke curl was visible for miles, the scent of charred wood perhaps even further downwind. If the fire belonged to a camp of Sudashians, Rhohn wanted nothing to do with it.

He turned to the southeast, intent on making his way around the fire, took several steps, and then stopped. The day was warm—every day was warm in the Borderlands—meaning the fire's only purpose could be for cooking something. The thought of meat roasting over flame set off a grumbling in Rhohn's stomach.

Food had been incredibly difficult to come by on his journey. The few abandoned, burned-out villages he had come across had been raided, picked clean by the invaders.

He stood there for a long moment, a slight frown on his face. If they were refugees, perhaps he could beg a bite or two from them. He knew he was mad for even considering approaching the fire, but, in the end, his hunger overruled caution and common sense.

Turning north, he hurried to the dirt road, crossed it, and scampered back into the cover of the dry grass, planning to circle the fire and approach from downwind. If they were Sudashians, he would surely smell their rankness on the air.

The wind picked up as he walked north, shifting from gentle, sweeping gusts into a steady, driving blow. By the time he reached the far side of where the plume had been he was no longer able to see the smoke. The strong wind wiped any trace of it from the sky. He could smell charred wood, though, along with the undeniable aroma of roasting meat.

Crouching low and securing his sword against his body to prevent it from rattling, he began to creep up a slight slope, his boots crunching on the dry ground with each careful step. Strong wind gusts pressed large swaths of the prairie down, sporadically exposing Rhohn's bent form. The clouds were closer now, the flashes of lightning brighter, and the thunder louder. The day was as dim as if it were past dusk.

Believing himself near the fire, Rhohn dropped to the ground and wriggled along, bits of broken grass shafts slipping down his shirt and pants. He sent a short, silent plea to Lamoth, praying no poisonous ran-ras snakes were nearby. He had spotted two sunning themselves on a boulder yesterday, but hoped they were an aberration. The venom of a ran-ras was like fire in the veins, paralyzing a man within minutes and killing him within the hour.

A flash of lightning lit the prairie bright as the air boomed loud enough that Rhohn swore his bones rattled. Moments later, a quick, steady rain began to fall, quickly soaking him. Grateful for the additional cover the rain provided, he continued shimmying along the ground until he caught a voice drifting along with the wind.

"—tied up good. I don't want nothing blowing—"

The wind shifted and the voice disappeared.

From tone alone, Rhohn judged the gruff and rough voice as belonging to an older man. A moment later, a second deep voice responded to the first. Unfortunately, the wind and thunder obscured the words. Remaining motionless and silent, Rhohn strained, listening while the rain turned the top layer of the dry and dusty Borderlands dirt into a filmy mud. After a time of hearing nothing but the clamor of the storm, he resumed his careful approach, sliding through grass and muck.

A shift in the wind parted the grass ahead of Rhohn for a moment, allowing him a quick glimpse into a camp. Four saddle-less horses were picketed to the ground, heads down, hindquarters into the wind. To the right of the horses, two dirty tents struggled to stand, flapping in the gale. A charred area in a stretch of flattened grass was all that was left of the fire. Rhohn frowned. He did not see any meat.

Looking back to the horse, his frown shifted into a wary grimace. Four mounts most likely meant four people, at least two of them men.

To the left of the horses, a small four-wheeled cart rested, its open, uncovered bed holding a few dirty cloth sacks in the back. Sticks rose from the four corners of the cart, topped with red and yellow pennants whipping in the wind. Rhohn's eyes locked on the flags.

"Traders? Here?"

The wind's direction changed again, and his view of the camp vanished as the grass stood tall. Rhohn lay in the mud, wondering why peddlers would still be here. Most of the Borderlands were abandoned. No one was left to buy anything.

He inched closer to the camp on his stomach, wanting to get a better look at whatever was in the exposed cart. Perhaps he could find something of value that he could sell if he ever found a village with people in it again. Peering through the driving rain, he studied the open wagon. Cloth sacks and bags of varying sizes littered the cart, their tops bunched together and tied off with a length of rope. As

Rhohn reached up to wipe rainwater from his eyes, he stopped—hand frozen in midair—and stared.

One of the bags had moved.

Moving his hand over his brow to hold back the rain, Rhohn squinted, wondering if a wayward raindrop in his eye had fooled him into thinking that he had seen movement.

The tan cloth bag moved again. Rhohn's eyes narrowed. He wondered exactly what these traders were peddling.

"What in the…?"

As he watched, the sack scooted to the back of the wagon's edge, tumbled over, and fell, landing hard on the ground. Moments later, the flap of the tent closest to the cart opened. A short, slightly overweight man emerged and stepped into the rain. His skin was pale, unlike a Borderlander, as was the long, stringy dark hair hanging from under a wide-brimmed hat. His left hand pressed the hat tight on his head, holding it against the wind, while his right grasped a style of sword Rhohn had not seen since his days in Gobas. Its blade started skinny at the hilt, widening as it swept upwards in a curved line before ending in a hooked point. Without a doubt, these men were Marshlanders.

The man glared in the direction of the cart and began to stride toward where the large bag had fallen. Upon reaching the cart, he stopped and stared at the sack on the ground, his back to Rhohn. After a few moments, the man—still holding his hat on his head with his left hand—tossed his sword on the back of the cart, the muffled clang of metal striking wood loud enough to be heard over the blowing wind and rain.

With his now-free hand, the man bent over and struggled with the sack, finally hoisting it from the ground. When he released the muddy canvas, the large sack remained upright. Without a doubt, there was a person inside.

Rhohn's hissed, "Blasted slavers."

He had first heard the slaving rumors when he and Silas were in Midiah. Men were supposedly roaming the countryside, kidnapping refugees and stealing them away for sale. At the time, Rhohn had discounted the whisperings, believing the chaotic exodus east responsible for missing friends and family members. Apparently, he had been wrong.

He watched the man struggle with the person in the bag, trying to force them back onto the cart. The captive fought back, however, wiggling and thrashing, trying to pull away.

A white-hot flame of anger flared inside of Rhohn. He was on his feet, sword drawn, and ten quick paces away from his hiding spot before he realized what he was doing and stopped in his tracks. This was a bad idea.

He had no way of knowing for sure how many men were in the tents, nor how skilled they might be with a blade. Rhohn was sure that he could handle the single slaver, but three or four would quickly overwhelm him.

He stood in the driving rain, fifty paces from the man's back. His gaze flicked to the two tents. For the moment, the flaps remained shut. Digging his boots into the new mud, Rhohn began to backpedal. Slavers or not, this was not his business. The message he carried was infinitely more important than this one person's fate.

He had nearly managed to make it back to the prairie's cover when the slaver, frustrated with the captive's struggling, reached back with his free hand and struck the sack hard. A woman's sharp cry of pain pierced the storm's roar.

Rhohn halted in place, glaring at the coward's back. He clamped his jaw together, grinding his teeth and tried to swallow his anger. He could attempt to save this one woman, or—assuming Okollu was not mad—he could go and end a war.

The woman in the sack continued to struggle, undeterred by the blow.

The slaver bellowed, "Hold still!" reached back, and pummeled the woman a second time, doubling her over. Along with eliciting another shout of pain from the woman, the slaver's blow destroyed Rhohn's restraint.

The Dust Man strode toward the cart, squeezing the hilt of his sword with his left hand, ensuring he had a secure hold. Mud had made the leather handle slippery. Trying to clean the muck from the grip, he ran the two fingers of his right hand down the hilt and flung the collected mud to the ground.

As he neared, he heard the stocky slaver threaten the woman again.

"Blast it! Hold still or I'll hit you again!"

Rhohn scowled. That would not happen.

The woman's captor gave up trying to corral her with one hand, released the grip he had on his hat, and reached out to grab the sack with both arms. Moments after letting go of his hat, an ill-timed gust of wind ripped it free. The man reached up quickly, but the hat sailed away, straight toward Rhohn. The slaver whipped around to follow its flight, spotted Rhohn, and froze.

Twenty-five paces still separated them.

Rhohn began to sprint, bringing up his sword into a ready position. The slaver reached behind him, his right arm flailing wildly as he searched the cart bed for his sword. His eyes, as round as copper ducats, remained locked on Rhohn.

The woman, still struggling in the sack, barreled into the man, sending them both slamming to the ground. The slaver rolled on the ground, preparing to leap up just as Rhohn reached the pair. Laying the flat side of his thin blade against the man's neck, Rhohn pressed the steel into the man's pale skin and spoke, just loud enough for the man to hear.

"Do not move. Do not speak. In fact, do nothing at all. Understand?"

Drops of rain fell on the sword and flowed down the length of the blade, rinsing away any remaining mud.

Close up, the slaver was even more absurd looking than he had appeared from afar. He had an impossibly large overbite, to the point where his lower lip was nearly hidden by the yellowed buckteeth jutting from his upper palate. Now without his hat, Rhohn discovered that the front of the man's head was completely bald. The long, stringy brown hair started at the temples and only lined the sides and back of his head.

Angry, defiant eyes stared up at Rhohn before flicking to the sword.

"You are a Dust Man."

Rhohn was surprised the man had been able to discern that fact from sword alone. Before leaving Ebel, Rhohn had discarded the brown soldier's uniform—he did not want to wear Silas' blood—and replaced it with unsoiled clothing from the dead villagers.

Rhohn pressed the thin blade deeper into the man's flesh, stopping just short of the point where he would draw blood.

"I did say 'do not speak,' did I not?"

The man pressed his lips together, at least as much as he could with his overbite interfering.

Rhohn risked a quick glance toward the sack. The woman had not moved or made a sound since crashing into the ground. Keeping the sword pressed against the man's neck, he circled closer to the sack and crouched low.

He whispered, "Are you alright?"

There was a long pause before the woman spoke.

"Well, I'm tied up and stuffed in a bag. Other than that, I'm fine. Who in the Nine Hells are you?"

The defiance in the woman's voice was surprising. He had expected fear or despondency. While he admired her spirit, he wished she would keep her voice lower. He was about to request that she soften her tone when a man's voice yelled out from the tents.

"Nimar!"

Rhohn's head snapped up.

The flap on the closest tent opened, pushed outward from the inside. A man's head poked from the tent.

"Just knock her out and—"

The Marshlander cut off, his gaze dancing over Rhohn and the man—apparently named Nimar—sprawled in the mud. An instant later, he disappeared back into the tent, shouting, "Father! Golt! Get up!"

Rhohn needed to get out of here quickly.

The sound of mud sloshing drew his attention back to Nimar just as the man swept one of his boots into Rhohn's ankle. From his crouched position, Rhohn lost his balance, tilted to the right, and fell to the ground, landing in the muck and grass. He pushed himself back up with his right arm, ensuring he held tightly to his sword with his left. Nimar had already scampered to his knees, and was driving a dagger down toward Rhohn's lower right leg.

Wondering from where the dagger had come, Rhohn whipped his sword around, hacking at Nimar's wrist before the blade could reach his calf. His riposte was weak, but strong enough that the sharp blade slipped past Nimar's flesh and grated across bone.

The Marshlander cried out and dropped the dagger to the ground, reaching up with his uninjured hand to cover his maimed right wrist. The slaver collapsed to the ground, cradling his injury and cursing loudly. Blood dripped to the ground, mixing with mud and rain.

A fury-ridden cry pulled Rhohn's attention back to the tents.

"Blast you!"

The second man was running toward him, a twin to Nimar's sword clasped in his right hand. Oddly enough, the blade was not the only thing the same. The man had the same overbite, bald head, and stringy hair. Beyond the charging man, two new faces were peering out from the second tent.

"Hells…"

As Rhohn scurried to rise, his right foot kicked something hard. Peering down, he saw Nimar's knife resting in the mud. Laying his sword on the ground, Rhohn reached out to grip the dagger's mucky handle, hopped to his feet and, with a quick, underhand flip, tossed the dagger at Nimar's twin. For once in Rhohn's life, Ketus was with him as the blade caught the man square in the chest.

The slaver's angry charge abruptly morphed into a clumsy stumble. His eyes went wide as he dropped his chin to chest, staring down at the dagger's handle. He dropped his sword to the grass and, after a few more lumbering steps, collapsed face first to the ground.

An angry, wordless roar arose from behind him. Wheeling around, he saw Nimar struggling to stand, his eyes fixed on the man Rhohn had just killed. After a moment, his furious glare shifted to Rhohn.

"I'll kill you!"

The slaver moved toward the cart and his sword, still cradling his injured wrist. Rhohn bent down, retrieved his sword, and leapt forward, hamstringing the man's left leg. His blade slid easy, smooth, and deep through the man's breeches and pale skin. Nimar collapsed to the ground, loosing another cry. Should the slaver live past today, he would have a difficult time walking the rest of his life.

Discounting Nimar a second time, Rhohn turned around and stared back at the tents, waiting for the other two men to emerge. When neither did immediately, he eyed Nimar, rolling around in the mud, screaming like a wounded banshee and then looked to the four horses. Sheathing his sword, he knelt beside the woman in the sack, picked her up, and slung her over his right shoulder. At once, the woman began kicking her legs.

"Stop that!" hissed Rhohn.

"What are you doing?!" exclaimed the woman. "Put me down!"

"Hold still! I'm trying to free you!"

The woman stopped struggling.

Rhohn eyed the second tent. The flap remained shut, the men inside.

Hurrying to the side of the cart, he inspected the sacks to see if any others might contain people but they were all too small. Having already wasted too much time, he reached out, grabbed the nearest burlap sack, and jammed it in his belt, praying it held something valuable he could sell. Turning around, he jogged to where the four horses waited, heads down, all the while keeping an eye on the second tent.

Rhohn moved to the healthiest looking mount, a mare who was either dark brown or black. Her wet skin and the gloom of the storm hid the horse's true colorings. He hefted the woman from his shoulder and dumped her on the mare, draping her body over the horse's back.

"Don't move."

Pulling his sword free again, he slashed the picket rope tied to a stake in the ground. Grabbing the rope, he moved to the other three horses and sliced their ties. He went to smack one of the horses' hindquarters with the flat side of his sword when the beast let out a sharp whinny and reared, tossing its head violently.

Rhohn backpedaled quickly and spotted an arrow with three hawk feathers sticking from the horse's rear. Staring back to the tents, he found the two men from the second tent outside now, holding bows and in the midst of nocking their next arrows.

Sheathing his sword, he spun around, bounced on the balls of his feet once, and launched himself onto the mare, inadvertently kicking the woman in the process and prompting an indignant shout of pain. Reaching over the woman, Rhohn wrapped his two fingers and thumb of his right hand through the horse's long mane, and used his left to grip the sack with the woman in it. He kicked his heels into the sides of the horse.

"Get on!"

The horse broke into a trot that quickly turned into a gallop, bolting straight ahead, running in whatever direction it was facing. Rhohn did not care where they headed now as long as it was away from the slavers' camp.

Suddenly, something hard struck his right calf.

He drew in a quick, hissing breath, and glanced down. A wooden shaft stuck out from his leg, just above where his boot stopped. Almost immediately, his lower leg began to burn and throb. It felt like someone had jammed a smoldering ember into it.

Leaning low over the horse's neck, he looked back at camp. Through the rain, he saw the two men had lowered their bows and were hurrying toward their fallen companions. Two of their horses were wandering away from the camp, the third was trotting in a ragged circle, whinnying in obvious pain.

"Are they following us?" called the woman.

"Not right now!"

"Good," said the woman. Her voice grew louder as she demanded, "Then let me out of here!"

Rhohn glanced down at the sack before him.

"Are you mad?! I'm not stopping now! You're going to have to wait until we have some distance between us and them!"

The woman remained quiet, apparently accepting his reasoning.

Looking up at the sky, he found the front edge of the storm and judged that they were heading south. He decided to continue in that direction until he could no longer see the camp behind him. The storm looked like it would rage a while longer, which, for now, was a blessing. If the slavers tried to follow, the hard rain would help obscure Rhohn's trail.

His heart slowed as he rode and began beating at a more normal pace. Glancing back to the sack on the rear of the horse, he could not help but frown. All he had wanted was a bite or two to eat. Instead, he had her.

Rhohn shook his head, faced forward, and let out a long, weary sigh.

"Wondrous."

CHAPTER 12: TOMBLES

Nundle blinked again.

"How is any of this possible?"

Sitting on his small chestnut horse beneath the boughs of an old oak tree, Nundle stared at the lush, hatch-patterned fields in the valley below. Based on the scene before him, he would have sworn that he was home in the Five Boroughs, overlooking a tomble farming community.

Gently rolling landscape of rich, muddy browns and vibrant, lush greens.

Tidy rows of crops forming perfect lines through the tilled fields.

Short, railed fences with -rock piles serving as posts surrounding the fields.

Winding paths that wove a regular web through the growing grounds.

Dozens of tombles roaming the fields and trails, carrying tools or leading beasts of burden pulling wooden carts laden with equipment and leg-dangling tombles.

"I cannot believe this," muttered a wholly astonished Nundle. He pulled his wide-brimmed cloth hat from his head and ran his fingers through his wild red hair. "I mean…I believe it, of course, because it's right there…but…" He trailed off, going silent.

"This is a first," rumbled a deep voice.

Nundle turned to his left. Broedi was watching him, mild amusement on his face. Even though Broedi was standing on his own two feet, and Nundle was on the back of his horse, the tomble was forced to tilt his head up slightly to meet the hillman's gaze.

The White Lion was a full seven feet tall with shaggy, golden-brown hair, deep brown eyes, and skin the color of a lightly roasted almond. A leather bag draped over his shoulder, its thick strap crossing his massive chest. Turquoise and ebony stones dangled from the leather string used to tie the bag shut.

"I have never seen you at a loss for words, Nundle."

Facing the fields below again, Nundle shook his head, mumbling, "In my seventy years, I have never heard of a tomble settlement outside of the Five Boroughs." With a wondering wave toward the pastoral scene below, he added, "Yet, there one is." Pointing northeast, he insisted, "And *that*, Broedi, *that* is a tomble village if I've ever seen one."

On the far sides of the fields, dozens of squat buildings made of stone and wood sat clumped together, each topped with a tidy, straw roof. Either a creek or small gulley separated the fields from the town.

The pair stared in silence for a time before Broedi broke the quiet, rumbling in a deep baritone, "You know, during the Demonic War, this entire region was an endless battlefield." His gaze drifted to stare at the northern horizon. "The sky was dirty with the smoke of the burning homes and towns. The air smelled… unpleasant."

Nundle had a tough time imagining such a desolate scene considering the green, fertile land below and sunny blue sky above.

Pulling his gaze back to the lush fields below, the hillman shook his head as if to rid the image from his memory. In a less-haunted tone, he said, "No Foothill citizen wanted this land after the war. To thank the tombles who helped us fight Norasim, Duke Calich offered it to them. They leapt at the offer. "

Shaking his head, Nundle muttered, "Tombles do *not* fight, Broedi. It's not in our nature."

Broedi's brown-eyed gaze returned to Nundle.

"Atop Shorn Rise, you fought when you had to, did you not?"

"That was different. We had no choice. We either fought or we died."

Raising a single eyebrow, Broedi said solemnly, "That is the case for one side in every war."

Nundle sighed and turned away from Broedi, mumbling, "Perhaps." His eyes fixed on the vaguely homelike vista, he asked, "Are you sure we don't have time to stay? Just a day?"

The hillman shook his head and said firmly, "No, we do not. We discussed this."

The tomble sighed, disappointed. It was worth asking one last time.

"I know, but—"

"No. It will take us over two turns to reach the Seat of Nelnora from here— perhaps longer depending on the weather in the Red Peaks." With a slight frown, he added, "I only agreed to come this way to let you see that the villages do indeed exist. Remember your promise."

Nundle let out a wistful sigh and nodded.

Just over a turn ago, the pair had left the enclave and ported to Huntersfield, a large village on the western edge of the Stunted Forest. One of the mages at the enclave—the very Magistrate Ulius that Nundle had tricked into bringing him to the Oaken Duchies in the first place—had crafted the Void and Air Weave to bring them to the border of the Freeland Duchy. Apparently, the Arcane Republic bureaucrat was a member of the Shadow Manes.

Shortly after arriving at the enclave, Nundle had been on his way to find something to eat when a port opened in the middle of the castle's courtyard and the magistrate stepped out. Both had been rather shocked to see one another. After an amused Broedi explained the situation to them both—Nundle apologized profusely to the magistrate—the longleg had set to teaching him the Weave for a port. Every evening for three weeks, the magistrate would secretly return from his offices in the City of the Strands and guide Nundle as the tomble attempted to master the intricate pattern.

The moment the magistrate was confident in Nundle's ability to get the pattern correct, Broedi announced his desire to begin their journey the next day. The hillman was anxious to speak with the Goddess Nelnora in order to ask a number of questions about recent events. Nundle was along to provide a quick return to the enclave.

Their journey west started in Huntersfield as it was the closest to the Celestial Empire that Magistrate Ulius had ever been. From day one of their travels, Nundle begged Broedi to take a route that would bring them near the tomble villages. A reluctant Broedi had agreed, only if Nundle promised that they would not stop. At the time, he had readily accepted the condition.

However, now that he was here, staring at the vista below, he wanted nothing more than to stop and investigate the village. Perhaps he could find braised lamb leg, mint jam, and a side of spiced turnip. His stomach gurgled at the thought of the roots. He had not had a properly spiced turnip since leaving Deepwell. A wave of homesickness swept over him.

"Broedi?" mumbled Nundle absentmindedly. "Did you ever return home? After the war?" When there was no response for a few breaths, Nundle glanced at Broedi and was surprised to find the hillman's face taut, the muscles in his jaw and neck rippling. "I'm sorry. I didn't mean to upset you."

Broedi did not meet his gaze, instead keeping his eyes on the fields of crops. After a few moments, the hillman visibly relaxed and his expression softened. He drew in a deep breath and let it out, slow and steady.

"I know. It is still a painful memory that I—"

He cut off in mid-sentence, His eyes narrowed abruptly, focusing on something in the green valley below. The hillman took an instinctual, quick step forward as if to get a better look and drew in a sharp, soft breath of surprise.

"It cannot be."

Turning to look in the same direction as Broedi, Nundle scanned the valley for what had elicited such a stunned response. Nundle, however, saw nothing out of the ordinary, other than a tomble village in the middle of the Oaken Duchies, of course.

"What is it? What do you see?"

For a long moment, Broedi remained as still and silent as a marble statue. Finally, he crossed his thick arms over his massive chest, a pensive expression resting upon his face. He spoke, his voice not much louder than the oak leaves rustling overhead in the light breeze.

"You know more than most about the White Lions, little one. What can you tell me about Nelnora's champion?"

The question took Nundle by surprise. It was an odd thing to ask now.

With a shrug, Nundle replied, "Surprisingly little." He paused, trying to recall anything he had read about Nelnora's White Lion. "His name was Tobias. And he was a mage of some sort. Known as the Eye of Nelnora, yes?"

Broedi nodded.

"A name that was well-earned."

Nundle tried to bring to mind any other details, but could not. He had recited the sum of his knowledge and admitted so, saying, "Truthfully, the few books I have read on the White Lions barely touched on Nelnora's champion. Much more attention was given to Aryn and Eliza. You, too. The authors often discounted his contributions."

With a slight frown, Broedi said, "Then they were fools. Without Tobias, the battle against Norasim would have been much longer. Years longer."

"Truly?" replied Nundle, surprised. "Why was he so important?"

"Tobias would have visions of sorts. Often, he would be able to share with us the enemy's movements as they happened."

Nundle's eyebrows lifted.

"That would be incredibly useful, I would think."

"Oh, it was," replied Broedi "But it came with a terrible cost. He had no control over what he saw. Or when he saw it. Seemingly random and always unbidden, the glimpses would sometimes take him at the most inopportune moments."

A sympathetic sigh escaped from the hillman.

"There are many horrors that take place throughout Terrene. And more often than he would have liked, Tobias was forced to watch them as they occurred. After a time, he stopped sharing what he saw unless it was important to our goal. As the years went on, he grew to loathe his gift. He even went to ask Nelnora to take it from him. She refused to see him."

Nundle muttered, "That sounds awful."

"It was," rumbled Broedi. "Tobias was a good soul. A good friend. It pained me to watch him suffer. The final pebble to topple the pile was the scourging of the Carinius coast. Thousands died and we could not discover how or why. That time, Tobias was angry with himself for *not* having a vision of what happened. He blamed himself something fierce. Eliza and I tried to console him, but our words fell on deaf ears. He ignored us completely, standing on that rocky beach for hours, staring at the bodies. We left him there, thinking he needed some time alone."

Broedi paused and sighed.

"And that was the last any of us ever saw of him. He disappeared and never contacted us again. Some of us searched for him for a time, but then magic was outlawed, we were named criminals, and...well, we suddenly had other things to worry about. In the end, most of us ended up losing contact with each other. Aryn,

Eliza, and I remained together, but the others..." He shrugged and went quiet, turning around to stare at the fields below.

Swiveling his own head, Nundle scanned the fields again. The tombles below were all heading in the general direction of the village to the northeast. Their workday must be over.

"Broedi?" muttered Nundle. "I'm a bit confused here."

Broedi lifted his arm, extended a long finger, and pointed below.

"Do you see the lone tomble in the barley field?"

Nundle's gaze followed Broedi's outstretched arm and settled on a single figure, slowly shuffling through the waist-high shafts of grain. His vision was not nearly as good as Broedi's, but he could still see that the tomble had light brown hair, wore simple tan fieldclothes, and was using some sort of farming tool to lean on as he walked. After watching the figure take a number of halting steps, Nundle realized that the individual was using the tool as a cane.

"The fellow with the limp?" asked Nundle, still bewildered.

The figure stopped in mid-step near the edge of the field and remained still.

"Yes," rumbled Broedi softly. "The fellow with the limp."

A few heartbeats later, the tomble finished his half-taken step. He stopped again, shook his head side to side, and turned around in a slow circle, scanning the countryside. As he faced the hill Broedi and Nundle stood upon, he stopped his search and stared straight at them.

Broedi murmured, "I wonder where his cane is. He rarely ever let that thing out of his sight."

Nundle whipped his head around to gawk at Broedi.

"*That* is Tobias?"

Broedi gave a single nod.

"It is."

"One of the White Lions was a tomble?!"

A slight smile touched Broedi's lips.

"He still *is* a tomble."

Nundle stared back down to the fields, mouth agape. The lone tomble had already turned away and was hurrying toward the village at a much quicker pace than before, limping with each scampering step.

In his deep baritone, Broedi rumbled, "That is Tobias Donngord, the Eye of Nelnora."

For the second time since arriving on this hilltop, Nundle was speechless.

Thankfully, Broedi filled the quiet, saying, "He's had the limp ever since he was young. A capable Life mage could have helped him at the time, but we both know how magic is viewed in your home."

Nundle mumbled, "You don't have to tell me."

Magic was not outlawed in the Five Boroughs as it was here in the Oaken Duchies, but mages were still social outcasts, barely a step above criminals. Nundle had kept what he was a secret from nearly everyone back home.

Shaking his head, Nundle asked, "How is it that I've never heard about this? None of the books had anything—" He cut off, turned to glare at Broedi. "Why is it you never mentioned this?!"

Broedi shrugged his shoulders, his eyes still trained on the figure hurrying through the crop fields, and said, "You know more about our history than most everyone else in the duchies. I assumed you knew." He made to start walking down the hill. "Come, we must hurry before—"

"You assumed I knew?" interjected Nundle in disbelief. He was not about to let Broedi brush this aside. "Did you not find it odd that I *never* asked you about it?"

Broedi stopped, turned, and fixed his gaze on Nundle.

"Of course. I found it quite odd. I thought you had merely not gotten around to the topic."

"Had I known about this, it would have been the first thing I would have asked when I met you right after, 'Are you a White Lion?' Hells! A tomble White Lion?! How did that happen?!"

Broedi, ever the visage of patience and calm, cocked a single eyebrow.

"You do not need to shout."

Drawing in a steadying breath and letting it back out, Nundle said, "I am sorry for my outburst. But this all comes as a bit of a shock."

Adjusting the strap to his leather shoulder bag, Broedi turned his gaze to the fields below and rumbled, "Please adjust quickly, little one. Based on Tobias' reaction, he does not seem excited to see me. We must hurry before he disappears again." The hillman strode from the shade of the oaks to the sunny edge of the hill.

Left with no other choice but to follow, Nundle put his heels to his horse and endured a short, jarring trot to catch up to Broedi. He pestered the hillman for details regarding Tobias as the pair hurried down the slope, but Broedi turned all questions aside, insisting that "Tobias' tale is his to tell."

By the time the pair reached the edge of the fields, they were empty of workers, leaving Broedi and Nundle alone to traipse along one of the cart paths.

The barley field to his right was just beginning to yellow, the seeds on the awns of the plants filling the air with a nutty, wheat smell. To his left, red potato plants filled another field, the tiny little white flowers atop the plants fluttering in the warm afternoon breeze. Tomble-sized fences lined their path. For the first time in five years, Nundle did not feel as though he wandered amongst a world of giants.

Turning to look at Broedi walking beside him, he suddenly laughed aloud. The fence barely reached the hillman's thighs. Broedi glanced over, one eyebrow raised.

"What is so funny?"

Nodding to the posts, Nundle said, "You look rather absurd beside that fence."

Broedi looked over at the railings and gave a reluctant smile.

"Yes, I suppose I might seem a bit out of place. Let us hope we do not spend the night. I cannot imagine any inn in Tinfiddle could accommodate me."

"Tinfiddle?"

"The name of this village," answered Broedi. "The other three lie west, farther down the road."

"I see," said Nundle. "So, there *will* be an inn, then?"

An inn meant food as well as a nice bed to sleep in rather than lying on the hard ground another night. Broedi had insisted they avoid towns and villages as they traveled west, which had resulted in every night being spent under the stars and without a proper meal.

"A few, if I recall," rumbled the hillman. "Although I doubt we will have an opportunity to visit any of them." He glanced over. "We are here for other reasons."

With a frown and a sigh, Nundle mumbled, "I know."

One by one, the winding paths merged, growing wider as they did, until Broedi and Nundle were walking on a trail that would fit at least two carts across. Upon cresting the hill, they found themselves on a flat plain, less than a quarter mile from the edge of Tinfiddle. An arched, stone bridge straddled the gulley Nundle had spotted from the hill.

By now, the initial shock of discovering one of the White Lions to be a tomble had passed, leaving behind a strange curiosity.

"Broedi?"

Without looking over, the hillman rumbled, "Yes?"

"You haven't seen Tobias in centuries, correct?"

"Correct."

"He's remained hidden all that time?"

"Again, correct."

Nundle frowned, glanced over, and asked, "And now, while on our way to visit Nelnora, we just *happen* to stumble across him?"

Broedi eyed him for a moment before rumbling, "Do you need any further proof the Celystiela are meddling?"

"No," muttered Nundle, his frown deepening. "No, I do not." A moment later, he added, "Are we nothing more than game pieces to the Gods?"

"It feels that way, does it not?" rumbled the White Lion.

Nundle turned to stare at the hillman.

"I don't much like that feeling."

The hillman shook his head, a stern expression on his face.

"Nor do I."

They continued walking in quiet, up the path, toward Tinfiddle.

A flash of movement drew Nundle's attention to the arched bridge. Two tombles were crossing from the other side and stopped upon the bridge's peak, their gazes locked squarely on Broedi and Nundle. The individual on the left had short, black hair while his companion had hair as red as Nundle's own, but cut much shorter. Both individuals were dressed in plain, matching navy tunics, light tan breeches, and sturdy mud-brown boots.

Nundle whispered to Broedi, "Those almost look like uniforms."

"I believe they are," said Broedi. "Judging by the small clubs at their hips, I would say they are guards of some sort."

Nundle's gaze dropped to the black cudgels hanging from both tombles' belts.

"Why? No one carries a weapon back home."

"This is not the Five Boroughs," rumbled the hillman. "Remember that."

Some of Nundle's earlier excitement evaporated. Broedi was right. No matter how much it felt like it, this was no homecoming.

As they neared, the black-haired tomble lifted his left arm and held his hand up, palm out. In a clear voice, he called, "That's far enough!" The tomble's right hand remained resting on the grip of his club. His redheaded companion was at the ready, too, staring at Broedi and Nundle with suspicious, almost angry eyes. "We'd like it best if you two turned around and headed back the way you came."

Nundle leaned over toward Broedi and, with a touch of confusion, whispered, "We are most definitely *not* in the Five Boroughs. A decent tomble would never be so rude to strangers."

Keeping his voice low as well, Broedi suggested, "Perhaps you should attempt to talk to them."

"Me?" muttered Nundle, peering at the pair on the bridge. "Are you sure?"

Broedi had done all the talking whenever they came across others on their journey west.

"It seems wise," replied Broedi. "Tomble to tomble."

Nundle studied the uniformed pair for a moment before sighing nervously.

"If you think that's best."

"And no Weaves of Will," rumbled Broedi.

Shooting a disappointed look at the White Lion, Nundle asked, "Why not?" Two quick Weaves of Will and they could be past the guards within moments.

"Tobias can sense Will," explained Broedi patiently.

"But he already saw us," pleaded Nundle.

Broedi shook his head.

"*No*, Nundle."

Sighing, Nundle said, "Oh, all right, then. No Weaves. I'll use my wondrous, charming personality on them." Turning back to face the tombles on the bridge, he smiled nervously while shifting in his saddle.

The tomble guards stood on the bridge, staring at Nundle and Broedi in silence. The babbling creek running in the gulley and the light rustle of trees and grass filled the uneasy quiet. Moments passed while Nundle tried to think of an appropriate greeting to use when meeting a community of tombles that should not exist.

"Nundle?" prompted Broedi. "Sooner is better than—"

Nundle blurted loudly, "I don't suppose there's anywhere in town where one could find some spiced turnips?"

The question leapt from his lips before he realized they were moving and he immediately felt the fool. He felt Broedi's eyes on him, staring. Embarrassed, Nundle kept his eyes straight ahead.

The black-haired tomble's eyes narrowed. After exchanging a baffled glance with his companion, he turned back to stare at Nundle.

"Pardon?"

Nundle winced. He did not want to have to repeat himself. After nervously clearing his throat, he said sheepishly, "I… uh…I said, I don't suppose there's anywhere in town where one might find some spiced turnips?"

The tomble cocked his head to the side, deep furrows lining his forehead.

"That's what I thought you said."

After a moment, he swiveled his head around to glance into the town behind him. His hand slipped from the club at his belt. Turning back around, he leaned over to confer with his companion in a hushed whisper.

Taking advantage of the moment, Broedi muttered, "Spiced turnips?"

"Sorry," offered Nundle weakly. "I'm hungry."

Broedi frowned slightly and stared back to the bridge.

"I will speak from now on."

"Wondrous idea. Thank you."

After a few more quick exchanges with his partner, the black-haired tomble stood tall and called, "You aren't merrymakers, are you?"

While Nundle's face scrunched up in confusion, Broedi began to chuckle, a rare occurrence to say the least. The sound reminded Nundle of a cat purring. A very large cat.

Bewildered, Nundle murmured, "What's a merrymaker?"

Broedi ignored his quiet question and called out, "No, friend tomble. We are not."

Nundle asked again, "What is a merrymaker?"

Lowering his voice, Broedi said, "A moment, please, Nundle." Eyeing the tombles on the bridge, he asked, "Why would you ask them such a question?"

The black-haired tomble said, "Because Toby just hobbled down the street, screaming that the merrymakers were coming."

The hillman began to chuckle again.

"Broedi?" muttered Nundle. "What is a—" Cutting off, he turned to the pair on the bridge and called, "What is a 'merrymaker?'"

The tombles stared at him as if he had asked what color the sky was.

Frustrated, Nundle asked, "Will somebody please explain what is going on?"

"They are performers," rumbled Broedi. "From fairs that travel the countryside, stopping near large towns or cities for a week or so at a time. They juggle, perform tricks, tell stories, sing ballads, dance. All for coin. Think playmen, but with more jumping about."

"They are wicked sorts!" shouted the redheaded tomble from the bridge. "They make fools of us, packing us in barrels like apples! Just to make the longlegs laugh!"

The black-haired tomble reached out and grabbed his upset companion's arm. After muttering something to him, he directed the redheaded tomble around and gave him a gentle shove. The admonished tomble strode quickly off the bridge, heading back into town. The remaining individual faced Broedi and Nundle, approached them, and stepped from the bridge onto the path. Stopping a few paces away, he nodded and said, "I am Hanno Mudgup. Good days ahead to you both."

Broedi gave a small bow and said, "And good memories behind, Hanno. I am Broedi. And my friend here is Nundle."

Hanno jabbed a thumb over his shoulder and said, "I apologize for Peldi's outburst. The lofty promises of easy coin and fame lured his youngest sister away the last time a fair was in the area. We haven't seen her in nearly a year. Little love is held for merrymakers here."

Broedi rumbled, "I assure you we are not with a fair."

The tomble looked them over, examining every detail of their person, and said, "Perhaps not, but that does not make you any less strange." Staring up at Broedi, Hanno cocked an eyebrow. "You are the tallest soul I have ever seen." Shifting his gaze to peer at Nundle, he continued, "And you...well, I'm sure you are the first tomble I've ever seen on a horse." Tilting his head, he peered around the sides of the chestnut. "How do you even get up there?"

Nundle gave Hanno a friendly smile and said, "With a great amount of difficulty, I assure you."

"So, which of the Four Towns are you from, Nundle?" asked Hanno. "I usually have a good memory for faces, but I cannot seem to place yours."

Nundle was hesitant to answer, unsure what he should share. He glanced at Broedi and received a reassuring nod. Turning back to Hanno tomble, he said, "Well...I'm not from the Four Towns."

"You're not?"

"No," said Nundle. "I am from Deepwell, a town within the Thimbletoe Principal of the Five Boroughs."

With an unexpected haughty note in his voice, Hanno asked, "Are you now?" A tiny frown of disgust spread over his lips. "I thought Boroughs' tombles were too afraid to step beyond their doorstep."

Taken aback by Hanno's rudeness, Nundle replied tersely, "Now, hold one moment—"

Broedi stepped forward quickly, interjecting, "Pardon me, Hanno, but we're here looking for an old friend." He shot Nundle a quick look, urging him to be quiet. Nundle complied.

Hanno's gaze lingered a moment longer on Nundle before shifting up to the hillman.

"You're here to speak with Toby, then, aren't you?"

"We are," replied Broedi cautiously. "How did you know?"

Hanno stared between Nundle and Broedi, mulling over something. With a deliberate tone, he said, "He's the only tomble here that hails from the Boroughs. I don't see what other old friend you could have here."

"I am curious," began Broedi. "How long has 'Toby' lived here?"

Hanno shrugged his shoulders.

"Oh...thirty years or so."

Broedi's eyebrows lifted a fraction.

"He has lived here for thirty years?"

Hanno eyed the hillman carefully.

"You must be *very* old friends of his if you did not know that."

Nundle hid a tiny smile at the tomble's inadvertently ironic statement.

"Circumstances have prevented us from keeping in touch," said Broedi. "May we pass then, Hanno? It is important we see 'Toby.'"

The tomble was quiet for a few moments before saying, "Fine, you can enter." He tilted his head back to stare up at Broedi. "I'm quite sure I could not stop you even if I wanted."

Broedi nodded graciously, rumbling, "Thank you."

Hanno nodded and turned to face Nundle.

"Might I make a suggestion? Hop off your horse before you come into town. You two will surely draw attention, but less so if you aren't all the way up there. Honestly. A tomble riding a horse? It's absurd."

A few turns ago, Nundle would have agreed with Hanno. Yet lately, he had grown to appreciate the incredible distances that the beasts could cover. Besides, in present company, the horse was indispensable as one of Broedi's strides matched six of Nundle's.

Taking Hanno's advice, Nundle began the process of dismounting. Swiveling his right leg over the back of the horse, he slid on his belly down the side, grasping a pair of metal rings he had a leatherworker in Claw add to his saddle. Hanging in the air for a moment, Nundle dropped nimbly to his feet and turned to grab his horse's reins, ready to go.

Hanno was staring at him with admiration.

"I would have bet you were going to fall and break your neck," said the tomble.

"It is still a concern of my own," admitted Nundle.

Hanno stepped backward, beckoning the pair to follow him, and said, "Come, I'll take you to Toby's home. *And* I'll point out the Joyful Bear." With a wink at Nundle, he added, "The best spiced turnips in the Four Towns." He smiled, spun around, and began walking over the bridge, calling over his shoulder, "Welcome to Tinfiddle!"

Broedi, Nundle, and Nundle's horse followed. The straw-topped buildings of Tinfiddle beckoned.

CHAPTER 13: POUCH

Allowing his stolen horse to slow to a walk, Rhohn swiveled around to check behind them. The long, brown northwestern horizon was clear. Still, there was no sign of pursuit.

The worst of the storm had passed, the rain slowing to a steady trickle. The thunder had changed, no longer sudden claps and crashes, but rather distant booms that rolled over the soaked prairie.

A sudden, sharp bite of pain shot through his calf. Wincing, he stared down at his leg, a deep scowl on his face. He prayed that the arrow was not too deep. Or barbed. More than anything, he hoped it was not barbed.

He glanced at the sack in front of him. The woman had been remarkably patient—and quiet—since leaving the slavers' camp. After one last look to the horizon, Rhohn decided it was safe to stop.

Grabbing a fistful of mane, he gently tugged, hoping the beast understood the intent behind the gesture.

"Hold…hold…"

Whether the mare grasped his meaning or was simply tired from the hard pace Rhohn had set, she stopped.

Instantly, the muffled voice of the woman called, "What's wrong?" She sounded concerned, but not afraid. "Why are we stopping?"

Rhohn said, "I was thinking about letting you out of there."

"Thank the Gods. This is worse than riding in that blasted cart."

Rhohn turned his attention to his right calf, wondering how he might dismount without aggravating the wound. The burning had waned, but the throbbing was worse. He could feel every thudding heartbeat in his leg.

For a short time, he attempted various maneuvers in order to dismount, trying to avoid brushing the arrow against the horse's side. Any pressure exerted along the shaft sent a new burst of pain shooting up his leg. After a particularly bad one, he let out a short, hissing curse of pain.

"Are you alright?" asked the woman. "You sound hurt."

"I have an arrow sticking out of my leg," replied Rhohn tersely. "So, yes, I am hurt."

He tried lifting his right leg over the back of the horse, but stretched his calf muscle in such a way that the burning-ember sensation returned. He drew a sharp breath between clenched teeth, grabbed a fistful of the small burlap sack he had stolen.

"Blast!"

He sat that way for a moment or two, waiting for the agony to subside when the woman spoke up.

"You might want to hurry. If you killed one of them, they will probably come after us. You did kill one, yes? Nimar sounded awfully angry."

Ripping the smaller burlap bag he had tucked in his belt, he tossed it to the ground and said, "I think so."

"You should have killed them all."

"The odds were against me."

"A shame," said the woman. "Now hurry and get me out of here."

Frowning at the woman's demands, Rhohn unbuckled his belt, taking it and the attached sheath and sword off. Leaning over, he dropped it to the ground as carefully as he could.

Lifting his left leg over the mare's neck, he rolled onto his back and slid off the horse, ensuring that he landed on his left foot first. Despite his caution, he still was forced to put weight onto his right, prompting another burst of pain in his right calf. He stood motionless for a few moments, willing it to go away before turning his attention to the woman in the sack.

The top of the bag faced him, bunched together and bound with a length of braided rope. He hobbled over and tried to untie it, but the rain had made the knots difficult to grip and undo. His half a right hand did not help things. Bending over, he retrieved his sword, wincing through the pain the movement caused, and cut through the knot. He opened the sack and peered inside.

All he could see was the top of the woman's head, her short, wiry, black hair, and the back of her neck. Her skin was a touch lighter than Rhohn's own, the color of bulboa bark.

The woman took a deep breath, held it a moment, and then exhaled.

"Bless the Gods, that smells good."

With the bag now opened, Rhohn heard the woman's voice clearly for the first time and was mildly surprised. She sounded younger than he had originally thought.

"Don't suppose you can slip off on your own?" asked Rhohn hopefully. He did not want to try to lift her off with the arrow in his leg.

"Probably not," replied the woman. "My wrists, knees, and ankles are tied together." She tried to lift her head to look up, but in her position, she was unable to do so.

Rhohn sighed.

"Fine. I'll try to lift you off, but I can't put too much weight on my leg. So… if I drop you…well, I drop you. You'll live."

"That looks like it hurts a lot," said the young woman. She might not be able to look up at him, but she had a clear view of the arrow sticking out from his calf. "Get me out of here and I can help you with that."

"That would be wondrous," muttered Rhohn through gritted teeth.

Placing his hands under her shoulders, he began to hop backwards, pulling bag and woman as he went. Three painful hops later, the woman's weight was entirely on one side of the horse. As she began to slide off, Rhohn instinctively placed his right leg on the ground to help slow her fall. The worst jab of pain yet bolted from inside his calf, up behind his right knee, through his buttocks and into his lower right back. He let out a sharp yell, but managed to hold onto the woman as she landed on the wet ground.

The moment she was down safely, Rhohn collapsed, falling forward into the wet, matted brown grass and pounded a balled up fist into the ground. He lay that way for a few moments, catching his breath, and waiting for the pain to subside.

From behind him, the woman said, "Oh, please. You'll be fine. I've seen wounds thrice as worse."

Miffed by her dismissive tone, Rhohn pushed himself up and peered back to find the woman sitting up, the bag having slipped down to her waist. He could not decide if she had reached her Matron's Day or not. She looked both young and old at the same time, no doubt her ordeal had taken a toll on her. The ragged shirt or dress she wore had once been light cream or tan but was now stained, streaked with mud and what looked like old blood. Her face was drawn and dirty, yet an underlying beauty shone through. The richest, darkest brown eyes he had ever seen stared at him, the skin around them crinkled with amusement. Two small dimples dotted her soft cheeks, summoned forth by her disarming smile.

"Nice to finally see your face, too, stranger."

It took Rhohn a moment or two before he could stammer out a response.

"Um, my pleasure is to meet you in peace today, miss."

"And what peace might that be?" asked the girl, skipping the ritual response. "You do know there's a war going on?" Freeing her arms from the bag, she held her bound wrists up and asked, "Could you cut these off, please?"

Nodding, Rhohn said, "Hold a moment."

Wincing, he crawled to where his sword lay in a patch of mud as the girl scooted closer to him. She held out her wrists and he carefully slipped the tip of the sword between her skin and the rope. After a few gentle back and forth movements, the blade sliced through the braid and the ropes fell away. The skin on her wrist was raw. She had been bound for a while.

Pulling the rest of the bag from around her legs, the girl said, "If you'll give me the sword, I'll get my own legs."

Rhohn held out the sword for her to take and, a few moments later, she was free, having severed the ropes binding her knees, then her ankles. Tossing the ropes aside, she stood tall and stretched her high arms over her head, his sword grasped in her right hand.

"Gods! That feels *so* much better."

As she arched her back in another stretch, the lightweight dress she wore, torn and ragged at the knees, clung to her, soaked through from the rain. Rhohn eyed her appreciatively for a moment before staring back to the muddy ground. It was rude to stare. As he peered at the nearby grass, it suddenly occurred to him that she had not stared at him, either, which was strange. Nearly everyone gawked at his deformities.

As he sat there, rain dripping from his forehead and into his eyes, the young woman spoke, a smile in her voice.

"Well, you appear to be a modest soul. That certainly speaks in your favor." She moved closer to him quickly, prompting Rhohn to glance up in time to watch the girl point the tip of his own sword at his chest, mere inches from his heart. Glaring at him, she asked, "Now, who in the Nine Hells are you?" Her friendly tone from moments ago was gone, replaced by a wholly unexpected, hard edge.

Rhohn eyed the sword, a frown on his face. He was a fool for having ever handed the blade to her. After a moment, he stared up to the young woman's face.

"I save you from slavers, got shot while doing it, and you stand here, holding my own sword against me? Your gratitude is overwhelming."

"Nimar said you were a Dust Man. Is that true?"

Rhohn shrugged his shoulders.

"Yes and no."

"And what does that mean?"

"It means I was, but I am no longer. I doubt the Dust Men even exist anymore."

Tilting her head to the side, she asked, "What are you doing out here?" She looked away to scan the landscape. "And where is here? We were headed west before the slavers stuck me in that blasted sack."

Curious, Rhohn asked, "West from where? And where were they taking you?"

The woman's gaze snapped back to him. Still she did not flinch at his scarred appearance.

"I have the sword. Therefore, I ask the questions."

Frowning, Rhohn waved his good hand to the north and said, "Fine. Ask away. But you might want to hurry before they get here."

As he hoped, the woman glanced to the horizon and he attempted to spring up, planning to grab the sword from her. The girl recovered swiftly, however, and pressed the tip of the blade against his stomach.

"Don't do that."

Rhohn glared at her for a long moment before loosing a heavy, dejected sigh and relaxing.

"Fine."

He should have left the woman with the slavers.

Leaving the sword against his gut, the young woman asked, "Now, who are you? And what are you doing out here alone? I'm not letting you up until you explain yourself."

Frowning, Rhohn muttered, "You want my tale? You shall have it."

While sitting in the grass and mud, he told her his name, about his assignment at Fort Jorodas, his journey from there to Midiah, the crumbling backbone of the Dust Men, and his foolish choice to join the non-existent resistance. He told her about the resulting massacre of Ebel, but lied about how he survived, claiming he played dead under the body of two other men. He said nothing about Okollu or the strange message that he was taking to the Southlands. The girl might gut him right now if she learned he was cooperating with a mongrel.

By the time he concluded his story, the girl had pulled back the sword a few inches. She still pointed the tip at Rhohn, but it was no longer jammed into his flesh.

"And what are you doing now?" asked the woman.

"Heading east," replied Rhohn. "Looking for safety." He shrugged. "Or an army to join. There's not much one man can do alone in this war."

Peering intently at him, she asked, "How did you find me?"

"I was hungry and I saw smoke from a fire. I was hoping they were refugees who might share a bite. Instead, I got you."

She stood motionless, staring hard at him with her beautiful brown eyes.

"You found me by *accident*?"

Rhohn stared up into the gray sky and sighed.

"To be clear, I did not 'find' you. To find something, you have to be looking in the first place. I stumbled over you. Call it luck, call it fate, call it 'yesterday's eveningmeal, all anew' for all I care. I mean you no harm, miss. None. All I want from you is my sword back so we can get on that horse and leave before Nimar and the rest show up."

The woman eyed him for another long moment, a tiny frown on her face. Finally, with a short, firm nod, she announced, "Fine." She moved the sword to the side, jammed it into the earth, and released the hilt.

Rhohn cringed. That was no way to treat a sword.

Crouching by his leg, she said, "Now, be a good patient and let me look at that arrow."

Rhohn peered at her, surprised.

"So then you believe me?"

Gripping his leg, she stuck her fingers through the ripped cloth of his breeches and tore it open to expose the wound. Rhohn winced at the sudden movement. Without looking up at him, she replied, "Either I trust you and help get you well, meaning I have a Dust Man by my side as I head east. Or I don't and I'm out here alone." She glanced up to meet his eyes. "I think my odds are better with you than without."

Rhohn admired her sensibility. She acted years older than she looked.

The girl probed the entrance of the wound with her fingers, wiping away the new blood still seeping out. Rhohn grunted in muted pain with each poke. She made no effort to be gentle.

Her gaze focused entirely on the wound, she mumbled, "Try to hold still. I need to check something."

Before he could acknowledge her instruction, the girl gripped the shaft and began to twist it slowly, rotating the arrow in place. Rhohn bit his lip and held in a curse. She only twisted the arrow a fraction before she stopped.

"Good. It's not barbed. I should be able to pull it out."

Rhohn gaped at her, not understanding how she could be positive of that.

"Are you sure? If it is barbed and you—"

He let out a sharp scream as the girl ripped the arrow free of his calf, a flash of white exploding before his eyes. As the white faded, he saw a pointed, non-barbed shaft held before him, red with his own blood. The falling rain was already thinning out the crimson, rinsing it away.

"See?" said the girl. "No barb."

She tossed the arrow aside and ripped away the rest of the cloth around his ruined breeches up to his knee. Using it as a bandage, she began to wrap the material around the hole in his calf.

"This will stop the bleeding as long as you don't run or walk too much on it. But if we're riding the horse, that shouldn't be much of an issue. Oh, and we should keep an eye out for thornroot as we go."

Watching as she expertly bound his calf, he muttered, "Thornroot?"

"Yes, it's a yellowish-green plant, low to the ground—hidden under the grass if you aren't looking for—"

Rhohn interrupted her, saying impatiently, "I know what it is. Why are we looking for it?"

The girl stopped her bandaging, stared up at him, and said, "Because if we don't get some in that hole in your leg, wound-rot will set in, and you'll be dead within a week."

Rhohn held her gaze for a quiet moment before nodding once.

"That's a good reason."

He immediately began scanning the area nearby for any sign of a yellowish-green leaf.

With a firm, final tug, the girl wrapped the cloth inside a previous loop and pulled it tight. She wiped her hands on his breeches and stood, saying, "Come. We'll find some as we go. If Nimar's father has decided to come after us, your screaming like a hungry newborn surely alerted them to where we are."

The girl turned toward the horse and stopped, noticing the small burlap bag that Rhohn had taken.

"Did you take that from the cart?"

"I did," said Rhohn. "I was hoping I might be able to sell it as I move east. Or trade it for food."

"What's in it?"

"I don't know. I haven't looked inside."

She bent over, grabbed the bag, and stood tall.

"Let's see if you grabbed anything useful."

As she started to work on the rope, Rhohn struggled to stand upright. Once he had, he was surprised to find that he could put weight on his right leg. It still hurt, but without the shaft in the muscle, the pain was bearable.

Testing his range of motion, he asked, "How did you know the arrow would come out?"

Struggling with the knot on the bag, she answered, "It spun in your leg. A barbed arrow usually catches on muscle or bone."

Rhohn lifted his gaze to her.

"Usually? And what happens when it doesn't?"

"A lot of screaming."

She glanced up at him and gave a quick, teasing wink before setting back to working on the knotted bag.

Shaking his head, Rhohn moved to pick up his belt and buckled it around his waist. He was a muddy mess, covered in a soupy mixture of wet dirt and grass. With a sigh, he tried to wipe as much of the muck as he could from the blade before sheathing it. He would need to clean it properly as soon as possible before it lost its edge.

A soft, distracted curse from the girl drew his attention.

"This blasted knot is impossible!"

She was still working on the rope and not having much luck with it.

Rhohn scanned the horizon to the north and west. Still no movement. Glancing back to the girl, he asked, "Where'd you learn how to treat arrow wounds…" He trailed off, realizing that they had not exchanged names. "I'm sorry, I don't know your name."

The young woman glanced up from the knot.

"You first."

Following Borderlands custom, Rhohn introduced himself and his heritage.

"I am Rhohn Lurus, son of Ezek and Nebedee Lurus, born of the village Dashti."

He stared at the girl, expecting her to announce her legacy as well. Instead, the girl gave him a small smile and shook her head, amused.

"Truly, Mud Man? Tradition still holds sway over you out here?"

"Dust Man," he corrected her.

Her smile widened and the dimples returned.

"Right now, you look more 'Mud Man' to me. Here, get this open—" she tossed the bag underhand to him "—and I'll tell you my name."

He caught the burlap sack one-handed, and studied the rope. The knots appeared as tight as the others had been so he slid his sword free of its sheath a few inches and ran the rope back and forth along its edge.

The girl stepped closer, watching him, and said, "As to where I learned to treat wounds, I was in Gobas up until the Sudashians attacked. There were plenty of injuries to practice on."

Rhohn's gaze shot up from the bag and fixed on the girl.

"There is fighting at Gobas?"

"No. There *was* fighting at Gobas. Not anymore. The Sudashians took it."

Rhohn could not believe what he was hearing.

"Gobas has fallen?! When?"

"Three days back?" answered the woman. Her eyebrows drew together. "Or was it four?" She was quiet a moment before shrugging her shoulders. "Hells, I don't know exactly."

"But you are sure it fell?"

"Quite, Mud Man. I was there until the day before the battle when Lord Nizeman ordered the city evacuated. I was heading back to Demetus to find my family when Nimar's family kidnapped me."

"Lord Nizeman?" asked Rhohn. "Who's Lord Nizeman?"

The woman gave a careless shrug.

"Some baron from near Gobas. He was in charge at the end."

Rhohn was confused.

"Where was Duke Vanson?"

"That is a wondrous question, Mud Man. No one knew. Rumors said he and half the nobles disappeared the night the Sudashians showed up outside the walls."

Rhohn's eyes opened wide in stunned disbelief.

"He ran?"

"It would certainly seem so," said the young woman. Glancing back to the horizon, she said, "Look, open the bag to see if it's worth keeping so we can start riding. Then you can ask all the questions you wish and I'll do my best to answer them."

Even though a hundred questions burned inside him, Rhohn returned to slicing open the braided twine. She was right. They needed to be on the move.

When the rope finally fell away, he ripped open the bag and looked inside. The aroma of salted, spiced meat rushed to fill his nose, prompting a quick, hungry grumble from his stomach. Peering inside, he found a couple dozen dark strips of dried boar meat. The cloth lining of the burlap bag was coated with a waxy substance that had kept the inside dry.

He was about to report on their luck and findings when he saw a second, smaller drawstring pouch made of a light tan leather partially buried by the strips of meat. Curious, Rhohn reached inside to grab the fist-sized bag. Just before his fingers touched the leather, a sensation of intense, dark foreboding filled him. A crushing, bone-chilling wave of emptiness enveloped him, swallowing him and the world around him. All light was sucked from the sky, turning the plains blacker than a cloudy, one-moon night.

As quickly as the feeling overcame him, it vanished. He pulled his hand back a few inches and stared at the pouch warily.

"What'd you steal, Mud Man?"

Rhohn glanced up at the girl briefly before staring back to the pouch. He reached out with a single finger of his burned hand and prodded at the tan leather.

Nothing happened.

Gripping the pouch, he pulled it free of the meat-filled burlap sack. The leather was soft and supple with golden-thread braiding binding the two halves together. One side of the stitching was ripped at the top and bottom. A leather strip appeared to be missing, one that would allow the purse to be strapped to a belt.

"What is it?" asked the girl. There was a sudden hint of trepidation in her voice.

"A leather pouch," murmured Rhohn. "A nice one, too. This belonged to a merchantman. Or noble."

"What's inside?"

"Let's find out."

Sticking the bag of dried meat under his arm, he undid the drawstring of the leather pouch and turned the small bag upside down, over his left hand. A smooth, black, oblong stone the size of his thumb fell into his palm. He was struck by how heavy the glossy rock was, considering its small size. It seemed heavier in his hand now, than it had been in the pouch. A moment later, he realized it was also incredibly cold.

The girl took a few hesitant steps forward, her gaze locked on the stone. The expression on her face was a mix between bewilderment and outright fear.

In a tiny voice, she said, "Put it away."

Rhohn studied the girl. All of her confidence was gone.

"Why?"

She shook her head.

"I don't know. It's..." She trailed off, eyes fixed on the obsidian stone. A moment later, she glared at Rhohn. "Do it, Mud Man! Put it away!"

He stared down at the smooth rock briefly before slipping it back into the pouch, noting for the first time that the interior was lined with golden-thread. Dropping the leather pouch into the bag of dried boar meat, he looked up to the girl and found her staring toward the horizon, back in the direction where the slavers' camp lay.

A frown on her face, she said, "We really should go. If they aren't coming after me, they'll come after that."

She was right. The pouch alone was worth quite a few gold ducats. He wondered how much the stone could fetch. He almost wished he had left the bag in the cart now.

The girl moved over to the horse, turned to look back at him, and said, "Time to go, Mud Man." Her voice was strained. Clearly, something about the stone had shaken her.

Surveying the area, he retrieved everything that marked their passage. If the slavers did follow, he did not want to make their task easier. By the time he approached the horse, the girl's dark mood had seemingly disappeared.

She looked up as he approached, smiled wide, and said, "I think you should ride in front, Mud Man."

Rhohn cocked his only eyebrow.

"You seem confident you are coming with me."

"I helped you with your leg."

"And I helped you with the slavers."

"How about this?" asked the woman. "If the slavers come back, you deal with them. And if wound-rot sets in on your leg, I deal with that. And I'll tell you all about Gobas if you wish."

Rhohn eyed the young woman, considering her offer.

"You still owe me your name."

"Tiliah," said the girl, flashing her wide, dimpled smile at him. "Oh—I am sorry, Mud Man. You prefer tradition, don't you?" Facing him, she performed a deep, deliberate bow and said in an overly formal tone, "I am Tiliah Alsher, daughter of Joshmuel and Debrah Alsher, of the village Drysa. My pleasure is to meet you in peace today."

"Not one for customs, are you?"

"Customs are for peacetime, Mud Man. They're a waste of time now."

Rhohn nodded, fully agreeing with her point. Tiliah was wiser than her years suggested.

Looking at the horse, she asked, "Will you need help up, Mud Man? Or do you think you can manage on your own?"

Rhohn's eyes narrowed. Without a word, he handed the collected items to Tiliah, placed both hands on the horse's back, bounced on his left leg, and launched himself up, swinging his wounded right leg over the rear of the beast before sitting upright. His calf only hurt a little from the effort.

Looking down to her, he asked, "Will you need help up, Tiliah?"

Tiliah eyed him and smiled.

"I can manage on my own, thank you."

She handed him the bag and other items before walking a dozen paces behind the horse. Hiking her dress to her thighs, she sprinted forward, placed both hands on the mare's rear, and vaulted up, landing behind him. Rhohn was impressed yet again. He had inadvertently gained a companion, but at least she was proving a strong and capable soul.

After taking one last look at the northwestern horizon, Rhohn kicked the sides of the horse firmly, sending the beast into a quick trot eastward to chase the tail end of the storm. Tiliah slipped her arms around him to hold on. After a dozen strides, he turned his head halfway around and said, "Gobas. What happened?"

After a long, drawn-out pause, the young woman spoke, her voice hollow and empty.

"The gates of the Nine Hells opened, Mud Man."

Rhohn let out a long, sad sigh.

"Tell me everything."

CHAPTER 14: PAST

Moving through the tomble village, Broedi felt like an ebonwood tree amongst a field of oak saplings. Most of Tinfiddle's stone houses were a single story, meaning the straw roof peaks and their stone chimneys were but a foot taller than Broedi. From the field carts, the tools resting on walls, the stacks of cut wood for stoves, the buckets and barrels, sacks of feed, everything in Tinfiddle was tomble-sized. Even the beasts of burden were smaller than was typical.

As Hanno led them into the town, they passed three tombles guiding a number of miniature oxen down the street toward a burnt-orange barn. The beasts' shoulders only came up to Broedi's waist yet they still topped the tombles who were driving them to the barn. He supposed the tombles purposely bred them smaller.

As they walked through the tidy, orderly town, Hanno pointed out the more notable locations in Tinfiddle. They passed smithies, tanners, cloth-spinners and other trade shops common to most any duchy town. A three-story building was the Elder's House, where official town business was conducted.

The trio crossed the town green, an open lawn kept manicured by a small herd of belled sheep wandering the grass, munching as they went. Three tall poles stood upright in the middle of the green, spaced thirty paces apart in a straight line. As they walked past, Broedi noted Nundle staring at the poles curiously and wondered why they held the tomble's attention.

Hanno made sure to identify a number of small taverns along their route, ensuring that Nundle paid close attention to the location of the Joyful Bear and the reportedly 'legendary spiced turnips.' Nundle grinned wide, eyeing the inn and its sky-blue sign painted with a caricature of a grinning, white bear.

The residents of Tinfiddle were equal parts friendly and curious. Most everyone offered a polite 'Pleasant afternoon to you' or 'Good days ahead' as they passed while stealing quick, furtive looks afterwards. Broedi returned each greeting he received without paying much attention to them. His mind was focused elsewhere, worried about confronting Tobias. He hoped his old friend would listen.

"Here comes Custodian Belor," said Hanno, pointing down the street.

Broedi glanced ahead to see an older, plumper tomble approaching them, his head absent even a single hair. He wore a brown coat pulled over a brass-buttoned, black vest and white, wide-collared shirt. His pants hung loose, brushing the tops of his leather shoes. The outfit was a few steps above the simple, practical garb most of the tombles wore in Tinfiddle.

Hanno said, "He likes to meet every stranger that visits." With a grin, he added, "And you two qualify as strange."

"At least that's the same," said Nundle. After a questioning look from Broedi, he added, "The custodian heads the town council at the Elder House." He paused, glanced at Hanno, and added guardedly, "At least in Deepwell, he did."

Hanno nodded.

"Here as well, Nundle."

"Hold a moment, Hanno!" called Custodian Belor, hand upraised. "I'd like a word with them."

Hanno slowed to a stop in the middle of the dirt path, forcing Nundle and Broedi to halt behind him. They stood in an intersection of three streets where the main road they had been following split. While they waited for the custodian to approach, Broedi absentmindedly ran his eyes over the stone buildings that lined all three streets.

His gaze fell on the house directly in front of them, a single-story stone building with four round cross-hatched windows. Pale yellow straw, bound with reddish-brown cord, made up the roof and looked like it should be replaced in the next season or two. The faint whiff of mold Broedi caught drifting from the straw confirmed it.

As he eyed the house, something inside of him twitched, Thonda's gift, the 'sixth sense' many animals exhibited.

He studied the building, wondering what had triggered the sensation. As he stared, a dark shadow passed from one of the rounded windows, disappearing from view. Someone was inside. Someone who did not want to be seen.

Broedi sighed and looked away quickly. He would need to be very careful how he played this.

Custodian Belor reached them, stopped, and examined them both for a moment. His eyes lingered on Nundle's chestnut horse, prompting a short shake of his head. With a polite smile, he said, "Welcome to Tinfiddle, strangers. I apologize for the rude greeting at the bridge." The tomble had a particularly wide and squashed nose, as if an invisible hand were pushing it into his face.

"Do not trouble yourself," replied Broedi graciously. "Your response is understandable."

He kept his eyes focused on the custodian before him, but he listened intently in the direction of the house. He could hear quiet breathing inside. Someone was trying to hide.

"Ah! Good, then," answered Custodian Belor, shifting his gaze to Nundle. "You are a long way from home, aren't you, friend?"

"Quite far, sir," replied Nundle respectfully.

Custodian Belor hooked his thumbs into two small pockets in his vest, holding his coat back to the sides as a result, and asked, "You two are here to see Toby, are you?"

Something in the custodian's tone made Thonda's gift twitch again. Keeping his tone even, Broedi replied, "We were in the area, and thought we might stop by and say hello."

Custodian Belor remained quiet, studying Broedi, the smile that was frozen on his face appearing a bit wooden. After a moment, he said, "Hanno, you can go. I will handle things from here."

Hanno nodded and said, "Yes, sir." He gave a friendly nod to Broedi and said to Nundle, "Should you wish to share stories, I'll be at the Joyful Bear later. I'll be sure they have your turnips ready for you."

Nundle smiled wide.

"That would be wondrous, Hanno. I look forward to it."

Throughout the exchange, Broedi eyed the custodian carefully. The tomble was hiding something.

Hanno wished the pair good memories, turned, and headed down the street, glancing over his shoulder a few times as they retreated, visibly curious.

"Well, strangers," announced Custodian Belor. "I am sorry to say that you just missed Toby. I happened to pass him on his way in from the fields and he mentioned he was headed down the road to Rindleview for eveningmeal. He has a weakness for the rabbit and radish stew they serve at one of the inns there."

Broedi crossed his arms and set his feet.

"That is fine. We will wait for him to return."

A soft, muted curse emanated from inside the house.

Custodian Belor's smile remained unchanged.

"Well, if you'd like, I can show you to a place you might get something to eat while you wait. Perhaps we could go to the Joyful Bear now? I will take you there personally." He took a few steps forward and put his arm around Nundle's shoulder, while shooting a nervous look at Nundle's horse. Guiding Nundle around to face the direction they had come, Custodian Belor said, "I would ask you to share your story with me, friend. Peldi told me you were from the Boroughs? Truly?"

Custodian Belor, Nundle, and the horse had made it a dozen tomble-paces down the road before the town's leader paused to turn and stare back at Broedi. He knew the village leader expected him to follow. He did not.

The custodian waved his hand, beckoning to Broedi.

"Come, large friend, I will buy you a cider—or three for one so large. It is the end of last year's batch—one of the best we've had in years!"

Nundle's eyes grew wide in anticipation. Looking to Broedi, he said, "Cider, Broedi! They have cider!"

A number of the town residents hovered nearby, trying to appear as if they were busy doing something when Broedi suspected that they were just being nosey. The custodian's gaze nervously bounced between the gathering crowd, the two strangers, and the house Broedi was confident Tobias was hiding within.

Apprehension slipping into his voice, the custodian implored, "Please! I'll have Grelo bring the food outside and we can eat on the steps." He began to chuckle, but it was an uneasy, forced laugh. "I do not think you will fit inside."

Nundle laughed along, not noticing the custodian's nervousness. His stomach was doing all his thinking at the moment.

As Broedi stared at the custodian and Nundle, he heard an ever so soft "Go away, blast you!" from the building behind him. Turning around, he began to amble to the building, pretending as if he was inspecting the two roads.

"Is Rindleview down one of these paths? Perhaps we could catch Tobias on the road—or meet him at the inn there."

Custodian Belor suddenly rushed forward, dragging a perplexed Nundle and horse along with him.

"That's an excellent idea! I'm sure with your long legs and his…ah, horse—" he shuddered "—you would catch him in no time."

Broedi continued to stare down the road as if he were considering taking such a trip. Instead, he was judging the distance to the red door at the end of the short, paving-stone walkway leading to the building.

Custodian Belor pointed down the right fork and said, "If you follow this road, it will take you out of Tinfiddle, past the wheat and bean fields. Rindleview is a few miles down the road after the fields stop."

Nundle, on the other hand, stood crestfallen, staring down the road lined with the little tomble homes. He sighed and mumbled, "I suppose rabbit and radish stew would be good, too." He did not sound convinced.

Broedi glanced around the street, a frown on his face. The number of curious tombles meandering about the area had increased. There would be an audience for the upcoming show.

In a tone no more expressive than as if he were inquiring about recent weather, Broedi asked, "Nundle, do you recall your lessons with the magistrate? Before we left the island?"

Nundle's demeanor changed instantly. With alert eyes, he peered up at Broedi briefly before shooting a quick glance at the custodian.

"Ah…Do you mean the ones with the—"

"Yes," interrupted Broedi sharply. "Those."

Custodian Belor stared back and forth between the pair, a mixture of worry and confusion merging as one on his face.

Broedi glared at Nundle and said firmly, "Be ready to undo what I cannot."

Nundle's face scrunched up in pure confusion. "What are you—?"

The little tomble cut off as Broedi spun around and, as quick as a mountain lynx, loped to the red door of the stone house. He crouched over as he reached the small door, launching his massive body against it and easily snapping the plank off its hinges. With a sharp crack and explosion of splinters, the door flew across the interior of the stone home, crashing into a small table and chairs. Remaining bent over as he crossed the threshold to avoid striking his head, he moved to the center of the one-room home. He quickly straightened to his full height, the straw thatching of the ceiling scratching the top of his head, and scanned the room.

Other than the overturned chair and tables, the interior was humbly furnished. A small metal stove in the corner with a metal pipe running to the outside, a wooden dresser of drawers, and a tiny bed. Broedi froze as his gaze reached the back left corner.

Tobias Donngord, the White Lion and Eye of Nelnora, a soul Broedi had not seen in two and a half centuries, stood in the shadows, glaring at him. Light brown hair—appearing shades darker in the dimly lit room—hung straight, stopping just above his eyes and covering the tips of his ears. Round, puffy cheeks protruded from his face, making his mouth look abnormally small. He was still wearing the simple, tan clothes from the crop fields, but had discarded the simple tool he had been using as a crutch in favor of a finely carved walking stick instead. Broedi's eyes settled on the carved, white stone lion head on the top of the timeworn wooden staff.

"Blast you and your animal senses!" hissed Tobias. He was angry. Very angry.

Broedi said calmly, "It is good to see you, Tobias." His words were honest. The tomble had been a friend.

The fury in Tobias' face faded a bit, but angry defiance still sparkled in his eyes as he said, "Please, Broedi, just turn around and walk out. Forget I'm here."

Broedi sighed.

"I wish I could, old friend."

Desperate pleading bled into Tobias' voice.

"But I've finally found a place I can be happy."

Hurried footsteps on the stone pathway announced the arrival of Nundle and Custodian Belor. The pair stared through the ruined entryway, surveying the inside and eyeing Broedi as if he were mad. Nundle's gaze shifted to take in Tobias and understanding spread across his face.

"I need you to come with me," Broedi said softly. "I need your help." He knew it was the last thing that Tobias wanted to hear. "Our task is not yet complete."

"No!" growled Tobias, the vehemence returning with renewed force. "I am done with all of that! Let the Gods solve their own blasted problems!"

A soft crackling filled Broedi's chest as bright, white strings of energy danced around him, popping into view. Immediately, they began to draw together to form a pattern. Vast, gaping holes in the middle of the design told Broedi that Tobias was using Strands that he himself could not touch.

Broedi called out, "Stop him, Nundle!"

The sound of ripping cloth filled the house as a five-foot tall seam appeared in the middle of the room, announcing the completion of Tobias' Weave. Reality itself wavered on both sides of the seam, fluttering as if the room were painted on two cloths being teased by a gentle breeze.

Less than ten paces separated Tobias and the port. The tomble began to cross the room, resting on his walking stick with each lurching step.

"Don't try *anything*, Broedi."

Broedi rumbled urgently, "Nundle!"

Tobias was only a step away from the port when it vanished with a soft, muted pop. He halted to stare at the empty space where the port had been.

"How…?" Wheeling to face Broedi, he mumbled with a mystified expression, "You shouldn't have been able to do that. You can't touch—" His eyes narrowed as he shifted his glare to Nundle. "It was you, wasn't it?! How did you learn to do that?"

Squirming under Tobias' intense stare, Nundle mumbled, "Uh…I…"

Broedi said, "Say nothing, Nundle." His soft instruction pulled Tobias' attention back to him. Taking a small step toward Tobias, he said softly, "If you come with us, I will be happy to explain everything."

"No!"

Tobias punctuated his retort by stabbing his walking stick onto the stone floor, sending a sharp crack of wood on stone through the room.

"I will *not* go with you! No more blasted visions! Just leave me alone!"

"I cannot," rumbled the hillman. "I *will* not. This is too important." A deep, heavy sigh slipped from him. "I am sorry, old friend. Truly, I am."

Tobias glared at him for a long moment before dropping his head to stare at the floor, his shoulders slumping. His defiance melted away and he shifted much of his weight onto his walking stick. He looked defeated.

"I knew you were coming," mumbled the tomble. Lifting his eyes upward, he stared at Broedi. "Well, not you specifically. But one of you. The visions started again about a week ago."

"Started again?" rumbled Broedi, confused. "They had stopped?"

Custodian Belor suddenly pushed past Nundle, moving into the center of the room while staring warily from face to face. Settling on the tomble in the corner, he said, "I am sorry, Tobias, but whether you go with them or on your own, you will have to leave now. I will not be able to explain any of this away."

Broedi's gaze shifted to the custodian. He had called Tobias by his true name.

"I understand," muttered Tobias, his voice filled with sadness. Peering at Nundle, he asked, "I suppose you will stop me every time I weave a port, won't you?"

Nundle's gaze flicked to Broedi, looking for guidance. With a small nod,

Broedi indicated that was indeed what he should do. With an apologetic shrug of his shoulders, Nundle said to Tobias, "Uh… yes, sir. I suppose I will. Although, I must say I don't understand why you are intent on running from us. Are you not—"

"Not here, Nundle," warned Broedi softly.

Nundle's mouth hung open for a moment before he shut it, giving a short nod. Broedi could appreciate how difficult it was for Nundle to remain quiet.

After letting out a long, expressive sigh, Tobias said with a touch of bitter sarcasm, "Well, then. Let me gather a few things and we'll be on our merry way." He shuffled to his dresser, using his walking stick to support his crooked right leg as he went, each uneven, hobbling step accompanied by a distinct clack as the stick struck the floor.

As Tobias marched to the corner of the room, Broedi moved beside Nundle— forced to bend over to do so—and whispered, "If he reaches for Void again, stop him. No hesitation. He will try to run."

Nundle stared up at Broedi, baffled. Nonetheless, he nodded. Keeping his voice low, he asked, "What Strands can he touch?"

"Void, Air, and Soul. That is all."

Nundle eyed Tobias warily.

"If he reaches for Soul, I won't know."

"But I will," rumbled the hillman softly. "You are to keep him here, Nundle. I will worry about the rest."

Nodding quickly, Nundle muttered, "Understood."

Still bent over with hands resting on his knees, Broedi eyed the custodian. He had moved just outside the door's threshold and was staring out to the street, a worried expression on his face.

"Custodian Belor? May I speak with you?"

The bald tomble glanced at him, gave a short nod of his head, and stepped further from the door, down the stone pathway. Broedi followed, nearly having to crawl back through the doorway.

A large crowd had gathered on the dirt road and was staring at Tobias' ruined front door. The custodian was standing halfway between the house and the street, his arms crossed over his chest, head tilted back and staring at the sky. Before moving to meet the tomble, Broedi took another look inside the house. Tobias was stuffing clothes and other belongings into a leather satchel while Nundle stood off to the side, watching in silence.

"Be good, Tobias," rumbled Broedi.

Without looking at him, Tobias called, "Gnaw on a chicken bone, Broedi."

The corners of Broedi's lips turned up a fraction. Satisfied for the moment, Broedi turned and took a few steps, stopping beside the custodian. The tomble looked up as he approached, appraising him.

"You are one of them, too, aren't you?" asked Custodian Belor. "The Shapechanger, yes? Thonda's Great Hunter?"

Broedi's heart skipped a beat in quiet surprise. Keeping his expression blank—he had practiced for years at hiding his true thoughts—he answered softly, "I am afraid I do not know of what you speak."

A wry smile crept over the Custodian's lips.

"Tobias said the same thing when I asked him if he were a White Lion."

Broedi glanced up, studying the crowd in the street surrounding Nundle's horse.

"Who else knows?"

The custodian shook his head, saying softly, "No one for sure. A few of the more persistent Four Towns' rumormongers talk and whisper, but few pay heed to their stories." Nodding to Broedi and the shattered doorway, he added, "Although, after today, quite a few more ears will be open, I think."

The fact that every tomble in the crowd was staring wide-eyed at Broedi reinforced the custodian's point.

Broedi murmured, "Yet you know?"

"I do."

Broedi was silent for a long moment before asking, "And how long have you known?"

Custodian Belor shrugged.

"With certainty? About a decade. Although I suspected it the moment Tobias walked into Tinfiddle thirty years ago."

Broedi's eyebrows lifted a fraction.

"And you have kept it a secret?"

The custodian nodded firmly, saying, "Of course. I owed him that." He glanced at the crowd. "We all do. Even if I'm the only one who knows."

Broedi was more than grateful for the custodian's silence.

"Thank you for doing that."

"It was the least I could do for him."

After another moment of quiet, Broedi asked, "How is it that you know who he is?" He glanced at the ever-growing crowd. "Yet no one else does?"

With a heavy sigh, Custodian Belor turned to face Broedi, tilted his head back to stare up at him, and asked, "You know our story, Shapechanger, do you not?"

"I do."

The custodian's gaze shifted beyond the hillman, to the broken doorway of Tobias' home.

"Did you share it with your Boroughs' friend?"

Shaking his head, Broedi said, "Not the whole tale. Only that your ancestors fought in the war."

"That is all?"

Broedi nodded and rumbled softly, "I know Boroughs' culture is complicated. Nundle is a good soul, yet I could not predict how he might react."

"Yes, well…*I* thank you for that," muttered Custodian Belor. His gaze drifted to the tombles in the road. "If your friend knew he might have let the truth slip. They don't know either. None of them do."

Broedi raised an eyebrow, surprised.

"Your heritage remains a secret?"

Custodian Belor swiveled his head to stare at Broedi.

"Against all odds, yes. And with each new generation, it becomes ever easier to do so."

"Would the past matter so much to them?"

The elder tomble pressed his lips together, thinking. After a quiet moment, he said, "I don't know. But I think it would. Many things have changed since we came here, but one thing that has not is the importance of family legacy." His eyes shifted to the doorway. "Tobias tried hard to abolish the custom when he founded the Four Towns, but…Well, he failed."

Broedi took a deep breath, crossed his arms across his chest, and exhaled.

"You still have not answered my question, Custodian. How is it that *you* know the truth? It has been two and half centuries."

With a grim smile, Custodian Belor said, "My grandfather was a very young tomble when the scourging of Carinius happened. Tobias left the Four Towns to investigate and never came back. Grandfather told me stories about him. The great and humble 'Founder of the Towns.'"

He glanced back through the ruined door.

"When I became the Custodian of Tinfiddle, my predecessor shared with me three volumes—an archive of our history. Why we left the Boroughs, why we fought in the war, and why we stayed after it was over. It was disturbing to read. Within the pages, there was a very detailed description of Tobias, along with a drawing of him. When a 'refugee' from the Boroughs showed up thirty years ago and asked to live amongst us, no one but I and the other three towns' custodians had any idea who walked amongst us. Some suspected, of course—the limp and similar name—but no one *ever* challenged him. And myself and the other custodians? We kept our tongue for well over two decades."

"Quite noble of you," noted Broedi. "Yet dangerous. You have been harboring an outlaw."

"I know," muttered the custodian. "But after what he did for our ancestors? For us?" He shook his head. "It was the least we could do. I finally spoke to him about it a decade ago and told him that as long as he did nothing to raise suspicions, he was welcome to stay as long as he liked. I had but one, simple rule. There was to be none of…" He trailed off and gave Broedi an uneasy stare. "None of whatever it was that happened in there."

He frowned, shook his head, and ran a hand over his bald head in consternation.

"Old Toby from the Boroughs was a nice, quiet tomble that kept to himself, helped in the fields as best he could. But after your visit today, the town will be talking. 'Toby' will soon be 'Tobias' to everyone. As much as it pains me to say it, someone is bound to report him now. For his sake, he *cannot* remain here."

A flicker of guilt ran through Broedi. He wished he had not needed to end Tobias' peace.

With a knowing eye, Custodian Belor said, "It seems you have what you came for." His gaze shifted back to the doorway, this time locking on something specific. "I suggest the three of you leave quickly."

Broedi turned to see Tobias exit his home. A clearly nervous Nundle followed him closely. Tobias marched straight to Custodian Belor, cane in hand, and gave a small bow.

"Thank you for everything, Belor. The past thirty years have been the most enjoyable I have ever experienced. I am sorry it had to end this way."

Custodian Belor inclined his head.

"It has been my honor. I will miss our talks. Watch where the road takes you, Tobias Donngord."

"I will," muttered Tobias. "You as well."

The custodian gave a short nod, took a deep breath, and made to turn around. He halted, however, and faced Nundle.

"The next time you are in the Boroughs, I want you to tell everyone you see that we tombles of the Four Towns are as upright as any of them. And ten times braver. Do you understand?"

With a scrunched-up expression of confusion, Nundle nodded his head.

"Uh…yes…I will."

With a satisfied nod, the custodian said, "Good memories behind, travelers." The bald tomble spun and hurried toward the road and the awaiting crowd.

Almost immediately, Tobias asked, "So, Broedi. Just why in the Nine Hells did you ruin my peace?" His voice carried an edge as sharp as a knife blade.

"I promise I will tell you," rumbled Broedi. "As soon as we are free of this place."

Tobias pressed his lips together, sighed, and nodded.

"Fine. Let's go before I start beating you with my stick."

As he made to turn around, Nundle—unable to restrain himself any longer—burst forth with a quick list of whispered questions.

"What is going on here? Shouldn't you be happy to see one another? You're friends, aren't you?" Peering at Tobias, he demanded, "Why did you try to run and why are you hiding here?"

Tobias' expression darkened. Broedi was about to interrupt Nundle when the redheaded tomble wheeled on him.

"And you! Why in the Nine Hells didn't you warn me about any of this? You didn't think you should take a moment to say, 'By the way, Nundle, Tobias can port—he might try to run?'"

Tobias' mood lightened a bit as he eyed Broedi and said, "Still keeping secrets, I see."

Broedi shrugged and gave the tomble a slight smile.

"It is habit."

A shout from the street lifted above the quiet murmuring of the crowd.

"Blast it, Belor! What is going on?"

Broedi, Nundle, and Tobias turned to face the road. Custodian Belor appeared to be having a rather difficult time in answering whatever questions the crowd was asking. Heavy suspicion tainted each glance shot toward Broedi and Nundle.

Frowning slightly, Broedi said, "We should leave quickly, I think."

Nodding, Tobias muttered, "Let's go around back. There's a path that leads out to an alley. We'll be able to reach the road to Rindleview from there." He turned and began to hobble away. Broedi was moments from issuing a warning when the tomble called over his shoulder, "I promise I won't run, Broedi! You've piqued my curiosity as well as ruined my life!"

Broedi closed his mouth and nodded. That was good enough for the moment.

Glancing down to Nundle, Broedi rumbled, "Let us go, little one."

Nundle pointed to the street and asked, "What about my horse?"

His small chestnut still stood in the street, surrounded by the crowd as they peppered Custodian Belor with questions.

Broedi shook his head at Nundle and said, "It would not do to have you face the citizens of Tinfiddle. The Custodian is having a difficult enough time trying to keep them calm."

"But we can't leave him," pleaded Nundle. "All of our things are in the saddlebags."

Broedi rumbled, "Do you have your coin purse?"

Nundle patted a heavy leather sack on his belt.

"Here."

"Then leave him," said Broedi. "We will buy another horse." The truth was, if Broedi's plan worked, there would be little need for purchasing a replacement mount.

Nundle frowned, wavering. Broedi thought he might ignore the warning and march into the crowd anyway.

Tobias called out, "If you two want to get out of town by dark, we had better start now." Standing at the corner of the stone house, he gestured toward his crippled leg. "Remember, Broedi, I walk slowly."

Broedi rumbled, "Come, Nundle. We must go."

With a quiet, melancholy sigh, Nundle muttered, "I was starting to like that horse, too."

Broedi looked down at his friend, slightly amused.

"Enough to give him a name?"

Nundle had refused to name the chestnut, insisting that it was "longleg nonsense to name animals."

"I don't know about that."

The tomble's eyes betrayed him, however. He liked his horse more than he would admit.

A slight smile touched Broedi's lips. Figuring it was impossible to un-spill the spilt wine, Broedi reached out to grasp some green Strands of Life and a few silver Strands of Soul, weaving them together in a unique pattern he had discovered shortly after his time with Thonda.

Nundle's head turned sharply to stare at the pattern forming in the air before Broedi.

"What are you doing?"

Tobias echoed the warning from the corner of the house.

"Broedi…"

Ignoring them both, Broedi reached inside himself, plucked a single, unique Strand—Thonda's Strand as he thought of it—and wove it into the design before him. Directing the small Weave through the air, Broedi watched as it settled over Nundle's horse, melting into the beast's velvety, chestnut skin.

An instant later, he sensed the simplistic mind of the horse. The beast recoiled from the contact at first, tossing his head into the air and loosing a sharp, startled whinny. The tombles surrounding him took a few hurried steps backwards.

Broedi tried to convey a sense of calm.

Peace.

The horse's whicker cut off. Broedi sensed confusion.

I am sorry for the intrusion. But I need you to come here. And try to be gentle to the little ones around you.

Broedi doubted the horse understood his words or thoughts, but, somehow, Thonda's creatures understood the intent behind them.

The chestnut turned to stare at Broedi, the gelding's big brown eyes focusing on the hillman. Broedi's sharp ears caught a short, almost gruff puff of air from the horse. The animal was not overly pleased at being summoned. Nevertheless, the horse took a few hesitant, plodding steps toward the path that led to Tobias' house. The crowd of tombles quickly parted in silence, giving way to let him pass.

By the time the gelding reached Broedi, every tomble within sight was silently staring. Broedi stretched out his arm and let the horse nuzzle the palm of his hand.

Thank you.

The chestnut let out a low nicker in response.

With that, Broedi released the Weave, severing the connection with the horse.

Nundle said with awe, "I did not know you could do that."

Broedi rumbled softly, "I do not like to do so often. It is a horrible intrusion." He regarded his friend and the horse. "But as it is obvious you have grown attached to him, it did not seem right to leave him behind."

Nundle stood tall, the beginning of a protest halting before it could reach his lips. With a simple shrug of his shoulders, he said, "He's a good horse." He reached up to pat the horse's neck, having to stand up on his toes to reach.

"You truly should give him a name."

Nundle shot Broedi a quick look.

"Yes…well…I was thinking about that and—"

"Excuse me," urged Tobias. "This is all very touching and such, but we should leave."

Tobias was leaning against the side of his house, jabbing his cane in the air in the direction of the crowd. Swiveling around to peer at the gathered tombles, Broedi found more than a few openly distrustful expressions. Upon locking eyes with Custodian Belor, it was apparent the village leader was silently pleading for them to go.

"Tobias is correct," muttered Broedi. "We should go."

Nundle glanced at the crowd for a split-second before nodding.

"Right."

He grabbed the reins of his horse and began to walk to where Tobias was waiting.

"I never did get my spiced turnips."

Without another look at the assembled tombles, Broedi followed Nundle, his mind quickly turning to what he was going to say to Tobias.

CHAPTER 15: WOODEATERS

"Another storm is coming."

Rhohn twisted to his left to look over his shoulder, wincing as the horse's backbone dug into his rear. He had not ridden without a saddle in years and had forgotten how uncomfortable it was. Staring back to the northwest, he found a blue sky full of voluminous white clouds.

"I don't see any—"

"Other way, Mud Man," said Tiliah softly.

Swinging around to his right instead, Rhohn peered to the southwest. While the late afternoon sun still shone down on the rolling plains, a wall of gray filled the horizon, clouds heavy with rain. As though it were waiting to be noticed, the first low rumble of thunder reached his ears. Their horse nickered softly.

"Perhaps we should stop for a time?" suggested Tiliah.

"Why?" asked Rhohn, a frown upon his lips. He had only just begun to dry out from the last bout of rain.

"To let the face of the storm pass."

He tried to twist around to meet her stare, but could not.

"We can either stop and get wet, or ride and get wet."

"Yes, well this particular horse you stole shies at loud noises. You won't want to be on her back when the storm arrives, unless you enjoy broken bones."

Another distant peel of thunder rolled over the prairie. Their horse broke into a quick trot for a few steps and tossed her head, letting a puff of air rush from her nostrils. Sighing, Rhohn swiveled his head, studying the grassy terrain around them. A slight rise in the land, topped by a single, apparently dead bulboa tree was a short distance away. Judging it a good vantage point to watch the western horizon, Rhohn nodded toward the hill.

"We stop there."

After a moment's pause, Tiliah asked, "And what of Nimar and his family?"

"We have kept a good pace," answered Rhohn. "Besides, they might not be tracking us."

"Truly?" asked a skeptical Tiliah. "You killed one of them and stole a gem. Do you believe they would let us go so easily?"

Rhohn pressed his lips together, wishing that might be the case, but knowing it was not. Shaking his head, he muttered, "No."

"What? No reassuring words?"

"Why would I do that? I would bet every ducat in the duke's coffers they are trying to find us."

With a soft chuckle, Tiliah said, "At least you are an honest soul."

The pair did not say another word as they approached the tree. The endless fields of chest high grass waved in the wind, rustling quietly. The air was thick and heavy with moisture, hard to breathe, and smelled of wet earth. Rhohn eyed the bulboa tree as they neared. Leaves had not graced its branches for quite some time. It looked like a bony, weathered gray hand clawing its way free of the boundless, tan prairie.

When they stopped atop the hill, Tiliah dismounted, alighting to the ground with ease. After Rhohn handed her the sack of dried meat—which she tossed by the base of the tree trunk—he unbuckled his belt and lowered his sword to her. After lowering it to the ground, Tiliah glanced at his wounded leg.

"Do you need help down?"

Rather than answer her, Rhohn swung his left leg over the mare's neck and slid down, landing hard and wincing as a sharp pain ran up it. Trying to keep his voice clear of discomfort, he muttered, "Not necessary."

Shaking her head, she turned and faced the western horizon.

"It looks clear still."

Rhohn stared westward a moment, confirming her assessment. No horses. No carts. Nothing but grass and a few other random bulboa trees, still with leaves. Content that they were free of immediate danger, Rhohn retrieved his belt and sword, looped the leftover rope around the horse's neck, and led the mare to the tree trunk. As he wrapped the braid around a dry branch, he noticed countless tiny holes in the wood.

Muttering to himself, he said, "Woodeaters."

Behind him, Tiliah said, "Pardon?"

Raising his voice, Rhohn said, "Woodeaters. This tree looks to be infested with them." Buckling belt and sword around his waist, he turned to eye Tiliah's back and asked, "Are you hungry?"

Without turning around, she called back, "Are Summers hot?"

Smiling slightly, he bent down and grabbed the burlap bag. Standing tall, he opened it and was greeted with the spicy saltiness of dried boar. As he reached inside to retrieve a strip, the back of his hand brushed past the nobleman's pouch, instantly triggering an involuntary, cold shiver that rippled up his arm, through his chest, and bounced about the back of his neck. Quickly pulling his hand and the meat free, he peered into the dark bag and stared at the rich leather pouch sitting amongst the boar.

"Is that for me, Mud Man?"

Rhohn glanced up and was surprised to find Tiliah standing beside him. He had not noticed her approach. She eyed him, a curious expression on her face.

"Do you feel ill?"

Rhohn blinked twice, shook his head, and murmured, "No...I..." Trailing off, he stared back to the pouch, his mouth suddenly as dry as a Borderlands Summer.

Suddenly, their horse let out a low, nervous nicker. Rhohn looked up, wondering if he had missed a rumble of thunder. The horse whinnied again, the anxious tone in its call different than before. Rhohn dropped the strip of boar meat back into the bag and slipped his left hand around the pommel of his sword. The leather was tacky, still damp.

His gaze traveled the chest-high grass around them. Beside him, Tiliah held perfectly still, her head swiveling side to side slowly, doing the same. She also recognized the horse's reaction for what it was: fear.

Tiliah whispered, "Do you see anything?"

Rhohn shook his head a fraction and shushed her with a whispered, "Quiet." The wind had picked up with the advent of the storm and was randomly tossing about the grass. Were the air still, he could perhaps sense movement in the prairie. But not today.

The mare nickered again, louder this time, and tossed her head, yanking the rope tight. The bulboa branch audibly cracked.

Rhohn dropped his chin and stared at the ground, wondering if they had stumbled upon a den of ran-ras. The snakes were known to hole up in old, hollowed-out trees. A woodeater-infested bulboa would be a perfect home for a number of the reptiles. His gaze darted about the grass, paying particular attention near the horse's hooves.

Tiliah took a step closer to him.

"What do you—"

"Hush!" hissed Rhohn, still staring about the rise.

Tiliah glared at him and murmured, "Do *not* shush me! What is—" She cut off as, two dozen paces to the east, some sort of creature burst from the prairie, rising a dozen feet above the grass, and soared through the air toward them.

At first, Rhohn though it an animal, but realized quickly that the figure had two arms and legs like a person, only it was much smaller—at least a few feet shorter than him. It had a black, pinched face, and was covered from head to toe with long, sharp quills glistening black and emerald in the sunlight. As the creature reached the apex of its arc, the barbs along both forearms sprang to attention.

Rhohn's eyes went wide. Without doubt, the creature flying toward them was a razorfiend. He had heard frequent descriptions, but this was the first he had ever seen one in person.

The moment Rhohn's gaze locked onto its black, beady eyes, the fiend loosed a series of sharp chitterings and clicks, murdering the soft rustling of the grass and yanking Rhohn from his stupor. The mare began ripping her head back repeatedly, trying to free herself of her bond, its whinnying joining with the fiend's shrieks. Rhohn dropped the sack of meat, reached out with his maimed right hand,

and shoved Tiliah back and away while whipping his Dust Man blade from his scabbard.

Tiliah fell to the ground just as the razorfiend reached Rhohn, the blades along its forearms and hands aiming for his chest. Lashing out with his sword, Rhohn smacked the attack away while stepping to his right. His blade connected squarely with the quills of the fiend, bouncing along them in a series of quick, staccato clacks. Somehow, he managed to deflect the creature's assault and push it aside.

Stumbling through the grass, Rhohn kept his eyes on the fiend as it tumbled to the ground, rolled once, and stopped near the stomping hooves of the panicked horse. He prayed the terrified horse might trample the fiend, but the creature nimbly dodged the hooves. The mare, eyes rolled back and white, gave one last frantic yank of her head, snapped the woodeater-laden branch off the tree, and bolted down the hill, dragging the shattered log behind it.

The fiend righted itself, turned its sharp-eyed gaze to Rhohn, and sneered, "Stazsla mirtinz!" The words were short and clipped, its voice loud and shrill,

Rhohn's heart pounded in his chest, his mouth had a strange, almost metallic taste in it. Fiends were quick, agile, and vicious killers, their quills as hard as steel and sharp as a new-edged blade. While shorter and smaller than most men, they were thrice as deadly. Rhohn knew he was outmatched. He was lucky to have deflected the first attack.

Stealing a quick glimpse at Tiliah, he found the young woman half-sitting up in the grass, her gaze locked on the fiend.

"Tiliah! Run!"

She did not move and Rhohn did not have time to entreaty her to flee a second time as the fiend leapt again, straight for him. Only a dozen feet separated the pair, forcing Rhohn to react quicker than he thought possible, flailing with his sword to block another slashing onslaught. Quill met sword again, sending another strange, muted crack of fiend blade striking metal through the air. Rhohn's arm shuddered. The fiend was small and wiry, but incredibly strong.

Hissing, the fiend attacked again, wildly swinging its left arm. Rhohn dropped his hand and twisted his wrist, barely catching the fiend's longest blade against his hilt's guard. Were he fighting any other creature, Rhohn would have lashed out with his foot to kick it away, but forethought overrode instinct. He would surely impale his leg or foot on the quills covering the fiend's shins and thighs.

Instead, he spun his sword in a tight circle, shoving the bladed arm away, and leapt to his right. Backpedaling as quickly as he could away from the tree and down the slope, he tried to draw the fiend from Tiliah. He stayed close enough not to lose the creature in the dry shafts, but kept enough distance that he could react to the next, inevitable attack. Fifteen hurried paces backward, he lost sight of Tiliah, still crouched on the ground.

"Tiliah! Run!"

The fiend stood to its full height—still shorter than the grass tops—and glared at Rhohn. He forced himself to hold the creature's glare while trying to ignore the throbbing arrow wound in his calf.

The razorfiend began to slink through the grass, like a lion stalking its prey. For the first time, Rhohn noticed the creature wore a pair of short breeches that stopped above its knees and a crisscrossing leather harness on its chest.

The creature clicked a few times before hissing, "You will periszzh, fleszzhling."

Surprised the fiend could speak Argot, Rhohn nonetheless ignored the Sudashian and called out, "Run if you aren't already, Tiliah! Stay low!"

His shout prompted the fiend to stop its advance and stare back in Tiliah's direction. Rhohn immediately halted his retreat.

"Hey! Razorfiend! This way!"

The creature immediately spun around and sneered, "Sizzit clizick!" It crouched low to the ground, its hateful gaze locked on Rhohn's face. With a shrill, chittering shriek, the fiend sprung into the air, shining in the last of the sun, the ominous gray rainstorm wall behind it.

Rhohn dropped to the ground, rolled to his right, and scurried to his knees just as the fiend landed, stabbing its arm-blades into the rain-softened ground. Rhohn thrust his sword forward quickly and managed to slip the point into the yielding, quill-less flesh just below the fiend's rear.

With an ear-clawing shriek of pain, the razorfiend scooted forward, sliding off the sword, and twisting around, its right arm and quills extended. The fiend's blades whistled through the air, cutting through the grass like a new scythe. Rhohn threw himself backward to avoid the wicked swipe, but felt a sharp pain along his right shoulder as the fiend's blade caught him. Wincing in pain, he fell to the ground, losing his sword in the process.

Flipping over, he found the fiend already lording over him, emerald and black quills pointed at his chest, ready to plunge into him. Rhohn frantically, blindly ran his hand along the ground, seeking his blade. He was still searching when the fiend halted suddenly and began to turn around to its right just as Tiliah—her face a visage of rage—popped up behind it, a four-foot branch of bulboa tree in her hands, swinging toward the fiend's head.

"Ahh!"

The wood, as thick as a healthy man's forearm, crashed into the fiend's ear and cheek. A hollow crack and burst of dust filled the air as the woodeater-ridden branch snapped in two, half twirling through the air while the other half remained clasped in Tiliah's hands. The fiend staggered a step from the blow, but did not fall down. The fury on Tiliah's face melted instantly into wide-eyed shock.

Rhohn's hand brushed his sword. Finding the hilt, he grabbed it and, taking advantage of the distraction, hopped up to thrust again at the creature's softer flesh. His blade again met its mark, but was as ineffective as it was the first time, eliciting only another sharp, shrill shriek and a vicious, spinning counter-attack.

Anticipating the response, Rhohn was already moving backward as the fiend's quills sliced through the air. Its back to her again, Tiliah sprinted forward and unleashed a well-aimed kick, right against the fiend's rear, knocking the creature off balance and thrusting it toward Rhohn.

Stepping to the side and dropping to a knee, Rhohn jammed the tip of his blade into the soft dirt and held the hilt high to trip up the stumbling fiend. As the razorfiend fell to the ground, Rhohn was already rising to his feet. Clasping the hilt of his sword with both hands, he screamed and drove the blade down with all the force he could muster, aiming for the bare spot just above the fiend's waist.

The sword point sunk into the creature's back, bounced off something hard inside, and continued on. Rhohn could feel it emerge from the fiend's stomach and impale itself into the Borderlands' earth, stopping a few inches into the ground. A bone-grating shriek burst from the creature. The fiend lashed out with its right arm, forcing Rhohn to jump straight up and over the swipe. Upon landing, he leapt backwards, leaving his blade in place. Blood bubbled from the wound, seeping out around the sword and sullying the emerald quills along its lower back.

Wanting to get closer to retrieve his sword, Rhohn started and stopped three times, but the flailing fiend was too dangerous to get near.

"Just leave it!" called Tiliah.

Glancing at her for only a moment, Rhohn said, "Why?"

She pointed at the fiend.

"It's stuck."

Rhohn looked back to the razorfiend and realized Tiliah was right. He had embedded his sword in the earth so deep that the razorfiend was pinned to the ground like a slaughtered goat against a bleeding rack. The creature attempted to push itself up twice, but stopped both times as the motion only made the wound worse as it slid along the blade. Collapsing to the ground, it futilely tried to reach around and grab the blade.

Rhohn lifted his gaze, searching the grass and wondering if more were near.

"Is it alone?" asked Tiliah. A glance to the young woman revealed her scanning the prairie as well.

"I don't know," muttered Rhohn. "I'm guessing so. I don't think the others would sit around and listen to this." The razorfiend's shrieks, hisses, and clicks rang across the plains. "Even so, we should leave. Now."

Tiliah nodded quickly.

"I agree."

Their horse stood a quarter mile away, its head hung low to the ground.

Guessing the broken bulboa branch had slowed the mare's frenzied escape, Rhohn said a short prayer of thanks to Ketus for the one blessing of luck. Glancing back to the razorfiend as it thrashed about, spitting and screaming, he frowned.

"I can't leave my sword."

Tiliah came to stand beside him, her gaze never leaving the fiend, and said, "I don't think you'll have to. I think it's dying."

As the pair watched, the razorfiend's chittering shrieks grew softer with each passing moment. Its flailing slowed until it was nothing more than random muscle twitches and then stopped completely, the quills along its arms going limp. The soft rustling of the grass in the wind returned, turning the Borderlands' prairie peaceful once again. It was as if the attack had never occurred, an aberration to the plain's tranquility.

When the razorfiend had not moved for a half-dozen heartbeats, Rhohn approached, extended a tentative foot, and gently kicked at the creature's hand. There was no response. Stepping closer, he grabbed his sword's hilt, and tugged upward. It took him four strong pulls to free the blade from the earth and fiend. He immediately stepped back and stared at the dead body.

Tiliah muttered, "What was it doing out here?"

Shrugging his shoulders, Rhohn answered, "I do not know." He paused a moment before adding, "Nor do I much care. It is dead and we are alive."

Tiliah was quiet for a moment before asking, "Your shoulder?"

Rhohn glanced down, pulled aside the slice in his shirt, and found nothing more than a deep scratch.

"Perhaps Ketus felt he owed me after the arrow," said Rhohn. "I'll be fine."

"Are you sure?"

"You are the healer," answered Rhohn. "You tell me."

She made to move toward him, but he pulled away, nodded in the direction of their horse, and said, "Come. We should be on our way quickly. You can attend to the cut once we are moving." He began to move back to the tree in order to retrieve the bag of dried meat.

Tiliah lingered a moment longer, staring at the razorfiend corpse before following.

"Mud Man?"

Without looking back, Rhohn said, "Yes?"

"Do you think there will be more as we go?"

Rhohn found the burlap sack. Some of the meat had fallen out, along with the nobleman's pouch. As he scooped everything back into the sack, he asked, "You prefer honesty, do you not?"

She stopped behind him and spoke in a firm tone, saying, "I do."

Nodding once, he said, "Then, yes. Whether or not it's those, oligurts, or mongrels…" He stood and turned to face her. "I expect more. At some point, we will be near their advance lines. Perhaps we are close now."

Tiliah pressed her lips together. The skin around her eyes twitched. Without a hint of fear, she muttered, "Well, then let's hurry and get past those blasted lines. I don't want to fight any more of those things."

With that, she strode past him, through the grass and toward the horse. Rhohn stared after her, wiping his blade on a handful of grass. After only a few quick swipes, he sheathed it and followed Tiliah, promising himself that he would clean his blade properly later.

CHAPTER 16: EMPIRE

Upon leaving Tinfiddle, Nundle and the White Lions meandered through a series of wheat fields, then bean, before descending a gentle slope and ducking behind a small, rocky ridge. Nundle scanned the wild vegetation around him, sparse and spindly, and concluded that the immediate terrain must be too rocky for cultivation. Slate-gray, striated boulders vastly outnumbered the oak trees. After the lush landscape of the tomble village, such a quick return to a rocky, spottily forested landscape was jarring.

Nundle glanced at the sky and frowned. Mu's orb hovered just above the western horizon, coloring the clouds in the sky a soft red that reminded him of the light burgundy cherries that grew near Alewold. Dusk was quickly approaching. He wondered how much longer they were going to walk before stopping for the evening. Up to this point in his journey with Broedi, camp was already made by this time of day.

Nundle minded his footing as he ambled along, leading his horse behind him. When it had been just Broedi and he, the horse had been necessary. Now that Tobias was with them, that was no longer the case. The White Lion tomble had insisted on traveling on foot, limping along with the aid of his walking stick. Nundle had thrice offered the use of his horse, but Tobias had ignored him every time. In fact, neither he nor Broedi had said a word since leaving Tinfiddle.

Letting out a small sigh, he stared at Tobias' back. He still could not believe what he was seeing.

A tomble White Lion.

The shock and excitement of the discovery still tickled inside.

A perpetually silent Broedi led their group along the path, moving at an absurdly slow pace. For weeks, the hillman had insisted they move quickly, intent upon reaching their destination as soon as possible, yet now he seemed content to crawl as a snail. Eyeing Tobias' bent leg, Nundle frowned. At this rate, they might reach the Celestial Empire sometime next Harvest.

The sun had dropped to the treetops when Tobias peered over his shoulder, locked eyes with Nundle, and abruptly asked, "Getting tired, yet?"

Nundle's heart started to pound. The White Lion, the tomble White Lion, was directly addressing him.

"Me? What? No…no! I'm quite full of energy, sir. I can go as long as you can—longer, I would think, considering your leg."

As Tobias raised a crooked eyebrow at the comment, Nundle's eyes widened.

"Oh, Gods! No! What I meant to say is that I'm not getting tired at all moving this slowly."

Tobias' eyebrow lifted higher, prompting Nundle to protest louder.

"Not that I mind going slow! Because I don't! I certainly understand your need to go slow. Because of your leg and all."

Tobias stopped in the middle of the path and half-turned to face him, his brow furrowing, staring at Nundle as one would at a three-headed sheep.

Nundle dropped his head, his gaze fixing on a random stone in the dirt path. After a few uncomfortable moments, he heard Tobias speak.

"Gods, Broedi. Where did you find him?"

Faint amusement colored his words, giving Nundle hope that he had not taken the unintentional insults too seriously.

"Actually, he found me."

"Did he now?" muttered the tomble in surprise.

Broedi stopped in the path, turned to face the pair, and said, "Only a few turns ago, in fact." Staring intently at Tobias, he added, "He tracked me down shortly after I found the Progeny."

Tobias halted, leaned on his walking stick, and peered up at the hillman.

"You say that as though it's important."

"It is," rumbled the hillman.

"Ah," muttered Tobias. "I see." He paused a moment. "No, I don't. What in the Nine Hells is 'the progeny'?"

Stunned, Nundle blurted out, "They're the Progeny!"

Tobias glanced over his shoulder and said, "Shouting will not help me understand what you are talking about!"

Nundle shut his mouth quickly. Tobias was right. He looked to Broedi and found the hillman with a slight frown on his face.

Broedi rumbled, "I was afraid of this." He stared past Nundle, up the road that lead back toward Tinfiddle. "Can we expect to be left alone for a time?"

With an angry huff, Tobias replied, "After your stunt? Absolutely. You could have marched into town with a dozen heralds carrying the blasted white lion banner and have been less conspicuous."

Broedi raised an eyebrow.

"You are exaggerating."

"Did you truly have to crash through the front door?" demanded Tobias. "That was a nice door. I just painted it last turn."

Broedi moved to the left side of the road, sat on one of the gray granite boulders, and asked, "Had I knocked politely, you would have opened a port to go elsewhere, yes?"

Tobias shrugged.

"Most likely."

"Then you have your answer," replied Broedi, lifting his pack over his head and dropping it to the ground. Crossing his arms over his chest, he stared at Tobias. The White Lion tomble held Broedi's gaze.

Nundle stood in the middle of the wide path, a dozen paces behind Tobias, unsure what to do. His horse took advantage of the pause in travel to wander to the side of the road and begin nibbling on a patch of grass.

After a few long moments of quiet, Nundle asked uneasily, "So, ah, are we stopping here?"

Without taking his eyes from Tobias, Broedi rumbled, "For now, yes."

Nundle nodded and began scanning the forest floor on both sides of the path, offering, "Well, then I'll gather some wood for a fire, perhaps see if there is creek—"

Interrupting him, Broedi rumbled firmly, yet quietly, "Remain here, please."

Nundle peered back to the hillman.

"But it will be dark, soon. We should—"

"Here, Nundle" insisted Broedi.

Tobias said, "He wants you around should I decide to run again."

Nundle glanced to Broedi, looking for confirmation. The hillman nodded.

"Correct."

"Oh," muttered Nundle. "Understood, then." He went quiet and stood at the ready, waiting for any flicker of black or white.

Tobias remained stationary in the middle of the path, leaning on his walking stick. After a few more quiet moments had passed, he said, "Let's go, Broedi. Out with it. Why is our task not yet complete? And explain these Progeny to me. Quickly, please."

"I will tell you everything," rumbled the hillman. "And after I am done, I will ask you to do something for me." He paused a moment before adding confidently, "And you will do it."

A short, haughty laugh burst from Tobias.

"Hah! Will I?"

Broedi regarded Tobias with a steady gaze.

"Most likely."

Tobias took a number of quick, lurching movements toward Broedi, leaning on his walking stick with each hurried step.

"If you think you can get me to just nod and go along with whatever scheme you—"

Nundle was bracing himself for what seemed to be a certain tongue-lashing when Tobias suddenly cut off and halted his advance on Broedi. For a brief moment, Nundle thought the tomble was so irritated that he did not know what to say. After a few heartbeats of silence passed, he realized that was not the case. Curious, he glanced toward Broedi. The hillman was leaning forward, a slight frown on his face. Sitting tall, he raised a hand and waved for Nundle to come closer.

"Nelnora's gift is upon him," replied Broedi. "We might as well get comfortable."

Tugging the reins of his horse, Nundle hurried forward. He moved around to Tobias' front and stared at the White Lion's face. Tobias' eyelids drooped halfway shut and his mouth hung slack.

"He looks dead."

"In one sense, he is," rumbled Broedi. "His soul is elsewhere at the moment."

Nundle continued to stare at Tobias. He almost reached out to shut Tobias' mouth before the tomble started to drool.

"How long will it last?"

Broedi shrugged.

"I do not know. At times, he would fade away for mere moments. Others, he would be gone for an entire morning or afternoon." He frowned and shook his head. "The timing of this vision is rather inopportune, however."

Nundle eyed Tobias and asked, "How does he not fall over?"

"That is a question which none of us ever could answer," rumbled the hillman. "Although, if he remains like that for a time, he will be quite stiff when he returns."

Pushing himself off the rock, Broedi moved to where Tobias stood. He bent down, gently removed the tomble's pack and walking stick, handing both to Nundle. Bending over, the hillman lifted Tobias in his arms, moved to the side of the path, and carefully placed the tomble in a sitting position against the trunk of an ash tree. Once he had seen to Tobias's comfort, Broedi stood tall, but remained hovering over the little tomble.

Still standing in the road, Nundle asked softly, "You count him a true friend, don't you?"

"I do," replied the hillman. "I wish I had not needed to cut short his life in Tinfiddle, but…" He trailed off, allowing a heavy silence to grip the little pathway in the woods.

After a few moments, Nundle said, "I didn't mean to offend him earlier— about his leg."

Broedi returned to the rock, sat, and retrieved his pack from the ground. Reaching inside the leather satchel, he pulled out his long, bone pipe and pouch of smoking-leaf. Glancing up, he said, "Do not worry. I know Tobias well. Words alone do not hurt him. The trials of his past have granted him skin of stone."

"What sort of trials?"

Broedi held Nundle's inquisitive gaze a moment before dropping it to his pipe.

"Is not my tale to tell."

Nundle recognized the tone in Broedi's voice and the look in his eyes. No amount of prodding would get more from him. Frowning, he eyed Tobias, wondering exactly what Broedi meant. He stood there for a time, trying to make sense of everything, alternating staring at Tobias, Broedi, and the dusk sky. Glancing at Tobias' crooked leg, he muttered, "I have a question."

"Then ask it."

Keeping his voice low, Nundle whispered, "How can we expect to reach the Celestial Empire in a reasonable amount of time now? It will be next Summer at the rate he walks."

The corners of Broedi's lips curled up slightly. "We will figure something out." Glancing up from his pipe, he added, "And there is no need to whisper, Nundle. He cannot hear you in that state."

From the base of the ash tree, Tobias said, ""But I can certainly hear you when I'm not."

Nundle spun around to find Tobias alert and looking around, his brow furrowed.

"How did I get here?"

Broedi said, "I did not want you to be uncomfortable."

Glancing up at Broedi, Tobias gave a short nod of thanks. "Ah. Well, that was kind of—" He cut off as his gaze flicked to the pipe in Broedi's hands. His eyes widened a fraction as he asked, "I don't suppose that's some of the Sweetbush cut you favored so much? They never could get the strain quite right here. I think it's the soil."

Broedi shook his head, rumbling, "I am sorry, old friend, but I grew short of Sweetbush a while ago." He held up the pouch. "This is from the Lagis coast and is serviceable."

Tobias cocked an eyebrow and said, "Northlands leaf?"

Nodding, Broedi said, "You are welcome to some if you would like."

Tobias turned to eye Nundle and said, "Well, if your Boroughs' friend would give me back my pack so I can retrieve my pipe, I will take you up on your offer."

Looking down, Nundle realized he was still grasping Tobias' travelling satchel. Dropping the reins to his horse, he hurried over to Tobias and said, "Here you go, sir. I was just holding it for you. I didn't look inside." He paused a moment, wondering why he had said that. "Not that you would think I might. I merely wanted to assure you that I would never do such a thing. To anyone, of course, but especially to someone as important as you, sir. That would be wrong, and I try to do what's right. Well, most of the time, I do. Like when at the Academies, sir. You see—"

Broedi gently interrupted him.

"Nundle?"

Glancing over to the hillman, he frowned and said, "Ah, yes. Sorry about that." He had a tendency to babble when he got excited. He looked back to Tobias. "Sorry."

The White Lion was staring up at him as though Nundle were a touch off.

After a moment, Tobias shook his head, reached up, and took his pack.

"Thank you."

His gaze shifted to Nundle's other hand.

"My stick, too?"

Nundle held the smooth walking stick out quickly.

"Here you go, sir."

Tobias accepted the stick and muttered, "Stop calling me that."

"Yes, s—ah...yes, mister Donngord."

Tobias peered up at Nundle, shook his head again, and began to root about his pack. After a moment, he pulled out a pipe of familiar tomble design, wooden with a deep, sweeping curve and wide oval bowl. After tossing his pack aside, he looked up at Broedi.

"Toss me the leaf, Broedi. And tell me what's going on."

"What did you see in your vision?" asked the hillman.

Tobias glared at Broedi and said, "I'll tell you what I saw after you tell me what is happening. Now, toss me the leaf."

Broedi waited a moment before giving a short nod and softly lobbing the pouch to Tobias.

"Would you like the long version of my tale, or the short?"

Tobias rested his pipe on his lap and began to open the pouch.

"Short if that's possible for you."

Broedi nodded and rumbled, "Did you know that after the Assembly called us to service, Indrida issued a prophecy? One about us?"

Tobias looked up quickly.

"And by us, you mean...?"

"The White Lions."

After a short pause, Tobias frowned and replied, "No. I did not know that."

"At the time, few did. Only she and Nelnora."

Tobias' eyes tightened at the mention of the Goddess of Civilization.

"What were her words?" asked Tobias. "What did it say?"

Broedi looked to Nundle and prompted, "The prophecy if you will."

Nundle's eyebrows rose to a sharp peak as he softly exclaimed, "Me?" This certainly seemed like a discussion for the two White Lions to have.

"If you do not mind," answered Broedi. "I must light my pipe."

Nundle glanced at Tobias to find the tomble staring at him, a doubtful expression fixed upon his face. Swallowing nervously, Nundle cleared his throat and began to recite.

> "The roar of the Lions of the Oak will drive back the spawn,
> And the lines of men, strong once again, will be redrawn.

Yet that which drives men and women will pull at the seams,
And the strength of the Lions will fade as do last night's dreams.

Torn apart by deceit and distrust,
One will perish and One will be lost.
One will leave, while Another will stay.
And Two shall find each Other one day.
Against his will, the cold One will fight,
While it falls upon the Half-man to unite.

Chaos will rise again, unraveling what has been made,
With Strife, Pain, and Deception in tow, lending aid.
Hidden, then found,
Willingly come around,
The Progeny will rise and lead the fight,
And along with new and old, the children seek to make it right."

Tobias listened attentively, his gaze never leaving Nundle's face. Once Nundle finished, Tobias dropped his head, stared at his lap, and remained silent, his pipe still empty and the smoking-leaf pouch half opened.

Nundle looked back to Broedi and found the large hillman smoking his pipe, curls of white smoke drifting up from the small bowl. A sweet and pungent aroma filled the air. Broedi caught Nundle's eye, nodded a silent thank you, and turned his full attention to Tobias. Then, he waited.

Tobias did not speak for a time, visibly mulling over Nundle's recitation.

Nundle did his best to mimic the pair's calm disposition, but found it nerve-wracking to appear as tranquil as they did. He tapped his hands lightly against his thighs, anxious.

Without looking up, Tobias muttered, "Repeat it, please."

Nundle glanced at Broedi, received a nod, and recited Indrida's prophecy again. When he was done, Tobias drew in a long, deep breath, held it a moment, and then exhaled.

"I wonder which of the 'ones' I am."

Nundle burst out, "The 'One who will be lost' is my guess. It makes the most sense according to your history."

Tobias' gaze shifted to regard Nundle, his eyes narrowing sharply.

"What do you know of my history?"

Nundle wilted a bit under the stare of the White Lion, not truly understanding the sharp tone or glare. He shrugged his shoulders, mumbling, "Nothing much." When Tobias did not look away, he added, "Honest."

Frowning, Tobias huffed and dropped his gaze to the pouch of smoking-leaf. Reaching down, he began packing the bowl of his pipe. After a few quiet moments, he glanced up to Broedi and said, "So Norasim is back?"

Broedi pulled the bone pipe from his mouth and exhaled a long plume of white smoke.

"He—or she for all we know—is back. We do not know form or name."

"Wondrous," muttered Tobias. "And these Progeny? Who are they?"

Broedi rumbled softly, "Aryn and Eliza's children."

Tobias nearly dropped the pipe to the ground. Looking up quickly, he gaped at Broedi.

"Pardon?!"

"A lot has happened since we last saw each other, Tobias."

"Aryn and Eliza?" repeated Tobias. "They...they had children?!" He gawked as though Broedi had claimed that White Moon was actually made of cheese.

"Two of them. A boy, who just turned eighteen, and a girl who will complete her seventeenth year shortly."

Bafflement fled from Tobias' face in an instant. He tilted his head to the side, was quiet a moment, and then murmured, "Ah...well, that certainly clears the smoke."

Curious, Nundle asked, "What smoke is that?"

Tobias shot Nundle a sharp glance and asked, "Exactly how does any of this concern a Boroughs bred?"

Broedi rumbled, "Tobias! Your issue with the Boroughs is your own! Nundle played no part and does not deserve to be treated as such. He has been invaluable in the events leading to now, assuming great personal risk in order to help. I would ask that you treat him with the respect he deserves."

Nundle looked back and forth between the pair, bewildered. He had no idea what was happening.

Tobias eyed Nundle with a slight frown for a moment before staring back to the hillman and saying, "Now I want the long version, Broedi. Every last word."

With a slight, satisfied smile, Broedi said, "As you desire."

Broedi told Tobias everything, starting with his time spent traveling Terrene with Aryn Atticus and Eliza Kap. He explained how the three of them encountered the Shadow Manes centuries prior and how another White Lion, Miriel Syncent, had founded the organization shortly after the outlawing of magic in the duchies. He told of the love that blossomed between Aryn and Eliza, the birth of Nikalys and Kenders at Storm Island, and how the Progeny had been hidden away for fifteen years in Yellow Mud to be raised by foster parents.

Tobias listened, clearly fascinated by the tale. Nundle knew the story intimately by now, but Broedi's wonderful storytelling kept his attention throughout.

At one point, he glanced to the sky and was surprised to find that it was past sundown. The sky clung to a bit of leftover daylight, but in a short while, night would reign.

When Broedi recounted the cruel, heartless attack on Yellow Mud only a few turns past, Tobias closed his eyes, shook his head, and interrupted.

In a quiet, sad voice, he asked, "It's starting again, isn't it?"

"It is," replied Broedi solemnly. "And it gets worse. My story is not near complete."

He shared the tale of his time spent with the Isaac siblings. At one point, Broedi turned to Nundle and asked the tomble to share his role in their story. Nundle complied, covering everything from his time as an acolyte at the Strand Academies to his chance meetings with the Red Sentinels in the Southlands of the Oaken Duchies.

By the time they finished the telling of the Battle of Shorn Rise, the sun was a distant memory. Both moons had crested the hills, bathing the path in a soft, bluish-white light providing plenty of illumination to see Tobias' sober expression. The White Lions' pipes had both burnt out long ago, but they both continued to hold onto them, occasionally placing the bits and absentmindedly gnawing on them.

As they started to share the story of their arrival at Storm Island, Tobias held up his hand and announced, "That's enough. I don't need to hear any more."

Nundle protested, "But we haven't told you anything about the enclave. It's—"

Fixing his eyes on Nundle, Tobias interrupted, "It's an ancient stone castle perched atop a steep bluff overlooking the Sea of Kings? With a quaint, little town outside its walls and a giant, open gravel courtyard inside them?"

Broedi and Nundle exchanged a quick glance. Nundle murmured, "Yes, but—"

"And a cozy commons room with three roaring fires," continued Tobias. "Along with a large kitchen staff that—at times—serves roasted Southlands boar, yes? And some sort of spiced sweet cakes seem to be popular."

Nundle was staring at the tomble White Lion, flabbergasted, when something suddenly clicked, like the tumblers in a lock falling into place. His eyes narrowed.

"Your vision was of the enclave, wasn't it?"

"You are a sharp one, Nundle Babblebrook of Deepwell," said Tobias with a thin smile. "And a better—and braver—tomble than I gave you credit. I am sorry for my earlier rudeness. Broedi was right. You did not deserve the treatment."

Nundle nodded quickly, accepting the unexpected apology. He was glad it was dark out, else Tobias might see him blushing from the compliment.

"Thank you, sir."

Tobias' grin twitched a bit, shrinking a fraction.

"But I was not jesting earlier. Don't call me that. And no 'Mister Donngord,' either. Just Tobias. If you 'sir' me one more time, I'll smack you with my walking stick. Understood?"

Nundle nodded quickly.

"I understand."

Broedi rumbled softly, "Be patient, Tobias. Nundle was quite excited to discover a tomble was one of the White Lions."

Tobias twisted to stare up to the hillman and asked, "You did not tell him of me?"

Broedi shook his head and said, "I said nothing, Tobias." He stared hard at the tomble. "*Nothing.*"

"Truly?" asked Tobias in surprise.

"Truly, old friend. Your story is your own."

The White Lion pair stared at one another for a long moment, something silent but understood passing between them.

Tobias gave a quick, single nod and said softly, "Thank you. You did not need to do that."

Nundle could not have felt more lost if he had suddenly appeared in the middle of Freehaven and was asked for directions to the nearest fish market.

"Now, is Nundle correct?" asked Broedi. "Your vision was of the enclave?"

Tobias nodded in the moonlight.

"You tell me. Is my description correct?"

"Disturbingly so," rumbled the hillman. "Miriel's Weave that protects the enclave from prying eyes apparently does not extend to your gift." Leaning forward, he asked, "What exactly did you see?"

Tobias sighed and shifted in place. He had been sitting in once place for a long time.

"Well, I walked through the town, through the open gate, and into the courtyard. Seeing a set of doors, I went through them and followed some people through the hallways—they all seemed to be headed to one place. We entered a large room full of people, eating. I turned to my right and spotted a table in the corner with three men, two young women, and a little girl." Quiet awe slipped into his voice as he said, "Gods, for a brief moment, I swore I was staring at an Eliza years younger than I remembered her."

"Kenders," said Broedi softly. "She is every bit her mother, in temper and in power. You would like her." He paused a moment, then prompted, "The men at the table. Can you describe them?"

"Two young, one older with a black beard. His hair was pulled back in a bunch. One of the young men was clearly Aryn's son. Add some years and weight to his face, and he would be Aryn's twin."

"Nikalys," said Broedi with a slight smile. "He and his father are quite similar, as well."

"From the sullen look on his face," said Tobias. "I do not doubt it."

With a quiet sigh, Broedi mused, "I wonder what is bothering him now."

"If I had to guess," began Tobias, "It had something to do with the striking young longleg at the end of the table. A fair young thing, her hair blacker than a one-moon night."

"Sabine, then," said Broedi softly. "Nikalys has feelings for her."

"Yet pretends he does not," added Nundle. "Although he is fooling no one."

Tobias chuckled softly.

"Well, from the way the young lady was smiling at the strapping, black-haired longleg across from her, she has interest in someone else."

Nundle said uneasily, "Curly black hair? Brown eyes?"

"Yes," replied Tobias.

"And that would be Jak," sighed Broedi.

"The foster brother?" asked Tobias with a raised eyebrow. "Well, that must be awkward."

A slight frown resting upon his lips, Broedi said softly, "It would seem there have been new developments since we left."

Nundle prayed the brothers would be able to focus on the task at hand. Sabine's affections were not important presently.

After a moment, Broedi asked, "What were they all doing?"

Tobias shrugged and said, "Eating and talking from the looks of it. I was going to walk over and listen, but the vision faded before I could." He peered up from the ground. "Broedi, something is bothering me about this. About your tale. About you stumbling over me today. About all of it, truly."

Nundle glanced at Broedi, guessing what Tobias was going to say. The hillman did not meet his gaze, however, keeping his eyes on Tobias.

"What is that?" rumbled the hillman.

Tobias leaned forward, draped his arms over his legs, and said, "It's too perfect." He shook his head. "It's all too blasted perfect."

Broedi nodded, but rather than openly agree, he prodded Tobias, asking, "What do you mean by that?"

Tobias began to list off the long list of coincidences that had brought everyone together. Nundle from the Arcane Republic. Zecus from the Borderlands. The Sentinels to the fort in the Southlands. The Shadow Manes finding them on Shorn Rise. Broedi and Nundle nodded along with each point, silently agreeing.

Once Tobias was done, he stared up and said, "Ketus himself is not so lucky."

"I agree," rumbled Broedi. "And what does that say to you?"

The tomble frowned in the moonlight.

"That some of the Assembly have finally deemed us lowly mortals worthy of their attention again."

"I have come to a similar conclusion," said Broedi. "Which is why Nundle and I are headed to the Seat of Nelnora. I have some questions for her."

"The Seat of Nelnora, huh?" asked Tobias.

Broedi nodded.

"Yes."

The White Lion tomble frowned and let out short sigh. Tilting his head back, he rested it on the rough bark of his tree. A bit of shaggy, brown hair fell before his eyes. He remained in that relaxed position for a short while, sitting quietly and staring up into the night sky, lost in thought. Broedi rested, watching Tobias carefully. They were both so quiet for so long, Nundle wondered if he had time to lie down and take a nap.

Finally—while still peering into the moonlit sky—Tobias said, "She might not see you. Even now."

Nundle was terrified of exactly that. The Gods and Goddesses had ignored Broedi in the past.

"True," rumbled the hillman. "But it is a chance we must take."

Keeping his eyes fixed on the star-littered sky, Tobias muttered, "You were right earlier, you know." A slight smile crossed his lips.

"Was I?" mused Broedi, a coy glint to his eyes.

Tobias' grin widened a bit.

"It gets old, you know? You always being right."

"I am not *always* right," rumbled Broedi. "You forget the tijuli negotiations near Torarik."

Tobias dipped his chin to his chest, chuckled gently, and said "Ah, yes. You were *very* wrong then. I forgot."

Nundle was lost again.

Tobias tapped the side of his pipe against his hand, releasing the cold, spent smoking-leaf ashes from his pipe-bowl. The black residue dispersed and drifted down, reflecting bits of moonlight as they fell. Looking up, he asked, "Now, then, I suppose?"

With a respectful nod, Broedi said, "Please. If you do not mind. No point in wasting more time." The hillman placed his own cold pipe in his satchel, stood from the boulder, and lifted his pack over his shoulder. "Let me help you up."

"Thank you," said Tobias as Broedi outstretched his hand.

Nundle glanced between the two White Lions a few times, blinking and wondering if he had blacked out for a minute and missed something important.

"Are we leaving? *Now?*"

Traveling the night would be dangerous. The road was uneven and the shadows cast by the moon would make their journey treacherous.

Broedi did not answer him and instead moved off to where Nundle's horse had wandered off the path, following the trail of grass into the trunks of the forest.

Suddenly, Nundle felt the crinkling and crackling of the Strands. Staring into the air above the road, he saw white and black Strands pop into existence. In a few moments, the telltale pattern for a port had begun to form.

Panicking, Nundle shouted, "Broedi!" and reached out to pluck at a number of the Strands in the Weave. After ripping only a few Strands free, the entire pattern fell away. Tobias had not even fought him.

In a voice brimming with amusement, Tobias said, "That's rather impressive, Nundle." Looking over to Broedi, he called, "He's a true natural."

"He is even more talented with Will," replied the hillman. He had retrieved Nundle's horse already and was marching back with the chestnut in tow. He did not sound concerned in the least.

Flustered, Nundle said, "Broedi! He tried to port!"

"I know," said the hillman. "This time, let him."

Nundle was not sure he had heard correctly.

"Pardon?!"

Broedi stopped a few paces away and said, "Tobias is taking us to the Seat of Nelnora. Tonight."

Everything suddenly fell into place.

As Tobias had already been to the Seat of Nelnora when he was first granted his abilities by the Assembly two centuries prior, there was no need to travel overland anymore.

"Oh," muttered Nundle. "I had not thought of that." A cautionary thought suddenly crossed Nundle's mind. Eyeing Tobias, he asked, "Are you going to trick us and run away?"

Tobias shook his head and said, "If there's a chance I can stand before Nelnora again, I will happily take it." His eyes grew hard. "You have your questions to ask her, I have one—only one—of my own. Now if you don't mind." He stared up into the air.

Again, Nundle felt the crackling of the Strands and watched the glowing white of Air mix with the black of Void. The sound of fabric ripping filled the night and a seven-foot-tall slit appeared in the middle of the path, the world fluttering like two tent flaps on either side.

Tobias had taken two steps towards the port when Nundle said, "I think I should go first."

Broedi looked at him and, sounding mildly surprised, asked, "Why is that?"

Eyeing the tear in the world, Nundle said, "If Tobias is not being honest with us, and he goes first, he might immediately close the port and then we've lost him. Broedi, if you go first, Tobias might close the port and then I'm left here with no idea where you are. But if *I* go first, and Tobias is trying to trick us, I can at least port myself back here." He glanced at Tobias and added, "Pardon me for not trusting you, but…well, I don't yet."

Broedi and Tobias exchanged a long look before the tomble White Lion shrugged.

"He has a point, you know. Very well thought out."

"True," agreed Broedi. Turning to Nundle, he nodded. "You first, then, Nundle. Then Tobias. I will follow with your horse."

With a short nod, Nundle said, "Good, then." Spinning in place, he took a single step toward the port when it struck him where he was about to go. Stopping, he looked at Tobias and asked, "Where exactly does this lead?"

Tobias said, "The plaza before Nelnora's temple. A simple place, truly. A few plain buildings, nothing like you might expect from a city of a Goddess."

Broedi swiveled his head and peered at Tobias, his face expressionless.

Nodding, Nundle said, "Good enough."

He turned and took a number of confident steps toward the port. Upon reaching the tear, he reached out, grasped the right half of the port's flap, and drew it aside to stare at the nothingness inside. The expected cold, tingling sensation ran up his arm. Taking a deep breath, he put his foot through, felt his boot settle on a hard, flat surface, and stepped through.

It was dusk again, the sky still red from a sun not yet set.

As he looked around him to get his bearings, his mouth fell open.

Grand, majestic buildings of white, polished marble towered over him. Steeples of sparkling crystalline glass rose from the edifices, stretching impossibly high into the sky and reminding Nundle of the great spires in the City of the Strands. Yet rather than the nine colors of the Strands, these twisting, giant helixes were as clear as pure ice, catching the last rays of the setting sun and scattering them about the sprawling plaza within which he stood. Little arcs of tiny rainbows danced everywhere.

"Oh my…"

The words came out as a whispered breath.

Nundle took a few hesitant steps forward, mesmerized by the glorious cityscape surrounding him. He spun in place, finding that he stood at the foot of a vast set of white steps leading up to the most extraordinary structure here. A massive dome of faceted crystal or cut glass rested atop white columns standing guard in an enormous circle. It was as if a giant diamond, sparkling pink and light orange in the sunset, sat perched atop an immense stand, on display for the world.

Gawking, Nundle wondered if Tobias had sent him to the wrong place. There was nothing simple about this place.

A voice behind him muttered in disappointment, "Oh, Hells."

Nundle jumped and whirled around to find Tobias standing next to the port and staring at him.

The tomble said with a small grin, "I was truly hoping to catch your expression when I stepped through." He eyed the colossal buildings, asking, "Impressive, isn't it?" A certain sense of wonderment filled his voice, along with a quiet and surprising hint of bitterness.

Peering back at the dome, Nundle replied, "Most impressive, sir."

With a touch of exasperation, Tobias said, "Nundle. Stop that. Just Tobias."

"Yes, si—I mean, yes, Tobias." Shaking his head in awe, he added, "This place is *amazing*."

"I do not think it has changed since I first saw it," muttered Tobias.

Broedi's deep voice echoed the thought.

"It does look the same."

Nundle glanced back to find the hillman through the port, Nundle's horse trailing him. The little chestnut looked quite out of place in the stark plaza, white buildings, and glass spires. The animal dropped his head to the white stone ground in search for grass and huffed disappointedly.

The chestnut had brought him from Lakeborough, through the open grasslands of the Southlands and to Storm Island. Then from Huntersfield, across the Foothills Duchy, and to the tomble villages. Now, the horse stood at the foot of the stairs leading to the Prime Temple of the Goddess of Nelnora.

"Traveler."

The word slipped from Nundle's mouth.

Broedi eyed him.

"Pardon?"

Nundle grinned and repeated, "Traveler." He pointed to the chestnut. "That's his name."

Broedi glanced at the horse and gave a short nod of approval.

"A good name."

Tobias completely ignored the quick exchange, his gaze dancing along the edges of the plaza.

"Something's wrong here…"

"Do you sense something I cannot?" asked Broedi, looking about the open area. "I see nothing."

"That's the problem. Where are Nelnora's servants? Where are the divina? Every other time I have been here, this plaza was full. Now it is as though—" He cut off, his gaze locking onto something behind Nundle. Broedi, too was staring.

Twisting around, Nundle saw a tall, pale figure in a white tunic, maroon breeches, and a short, cylindrical black hat gliding down the steps. Without a doubt, it was a divina, one of the servant race created by the Gods and Goddesses after the

Locking. While at the Strand Academies, Nundle had studied with a number of divina who had left the service of the Gods.

The divina descending the stairs had white hair with a faint bluish tint flowing from under the black hat, high cheekbones framing his white, iris-less eyes, and a tiny, firm smile on his lips. Stopping three steps from the plaza, he said, "Welcome." His voice echoed as if he spoke from a deep well.

With evident surprise, Tobias said, "Tenerva?"

"It is I," replied the divina, bowing at the waist. He held the position for a moment, and then straightened. "Blessings, Tobias Donngord of Butterfield Crag."

Nundle's eyebrows lifted in surprise. Butterfield Crag was not too far from Deepwell. He wondered how it was he had never heard of the Donngord family.

Shifting slightly to face Broedi, Tenerva repeated the bow and said, "Blessings, Broedikurja Kynsipitka of Vuori Sumun." Turning to face Nundle, he added, "And blessings Nundle Babblebrook of Deepwell."

Nundle gaped at the divina.

"You know who I am?"

Tenerva smiled.

"Certainly. Her Eminence has been watching you for a long time, Nundle Babblebrook."

Nundle was speechless.

Sweeping his arm around, gesturing toward the temple, the divina said, "Please follow me, her Eminence is waiting for you." He began marching up the stairs.

Broedi rumbled, "She is?"

Tenerva stopped, turned around, and said, "She has been expecting you for some time now."

Tobias stepped forward and asked, "Has she now? And just—"

"Please," interjected Tenerva. "*No* questions here. We must get inside as quickly as possible." He looked to Broedi. "But not the horse. Leave it and I will send someone to tend to its needs." He resumed striding noiselessly up the stairs.

Without a moment's hesitation, Tobias followed, an anxious expression etched on his face.

Nundle glanced back to his horse as Broedi dropped the reins and asked, "Will he be okay?"

Broedi eyed him and said, "We are standing in the Seat of Nelnora. I doubt Traveler will come to harm here." Leaning down, he added softly, "Let us do the talking, little one. Unless she asks you a direct question, remain silent. Do you understand?"

The thought that he was about to meet The Watcher of the World already made him uneasy. The suggestion that he might speak to her terrified him.

"For once, you do not need to worry about me opening my mouth."

Broedi gave a short nod.

"Good."

With that, Broedi began to stride after Tenerva and Tobias.

Nundle hesitated and glanced back at his horse. Traveler stared back with his big, brown, orbed eyes. Flashing a nervous smile, Nundle said, "Wish me luck."

Shaking his head, Nundle turned and hurried up the stairs after Broedi, mumbling, "Gods, I'm talking to a horse."

CHAPTER 17: FALLEN

14th of the Turn of Luraana, 4999

From afar, Gobas almost looked like the large, sturdy city it had once been, a citadel of dirty, tan stone rising from the flat, brown prairielands. Yet the blanket of haze that hung low in the sky, hovering over ruined walls and buildings, told a different story. In much of the Borderlands, when a person had passed to Maeana's realm, a death shroud was draped over the body, a thin, gauzy cloth covering the person head to foot. To Tiliah, the layer of smoke over Gobas was the city's death shroud.

Sitting on the back of their shared horse, she peered over Rhohn's shoulder at the ruined, still-smoking capital and wondered how there was anything left that could burn.

The city was two miles away, yet the acrid stench of burning wood and smoldering tar was thick in the air. They had first noticed the foulness at midday and suffered as it grew steadily more potent as they neared the city. As close as they were now, the scent of roasting meat mingled with the smoke. Oligurts were in the city now and—if the tales were to be believed—roasting and eating anything that had once been alive. Anything.

It was madness to be this close to Gobas, but Rhohn had insisted in seeing the capital before they continued east. Tiliah had argued at the absence of wisdom in his decision, but eventually dropped her protests. Rhohn had been determined to come.

Whispering in his ear, Tiliah said gently, "I'm sorry, Mud Man."

Rhohn did not respond. And other than the muscles twitching beneath his scarred cheek and neck, he did not move.

Tiliah leaned back and kept quiet. She did not know the man with whom she was traveling well, but she knew enough to understand that this was hard for him to see. He had spoken fondly of his time in Gobas.

Scanning the plains around her, looking north, south, and west, she searched for any hint of movement. By the grace of Greya, they had yet to see a single Sudashian since their harrowing encounter with the razorfiend two days past. She prayed Ketus would continue to grace them with his luck.

With her arms around Rhohn's midsection, she shifted her weight, trying to move so that the mare's sharp backbone was not digging into her rear. It was a futile attempt and she knew it. Short of finding a saddle or walking, the horse's spine was destined to plague her.

As she moved, her hand grazed the burlap sack resting in Rhohn's lap. She immediately pulled it away and tried to suppress the involuntary shiver that ran through her. In the sack of the dried meat lay the nobleman's pouch. Within the pouch rested the smooth, oblong, black stone. The mere thought of the obsidian jewel triggered a trembling chill deep within her soul for reasons unknown. She loathed the stone. She despised its very existence, even if she could not name why.

In the days since her rescue, she had asked Rhohn numerous times to leave the stone behind, but he refused, insisting they could sell it once free of the war-torn Borderlands. His promise to split with her whatever coin they received for the gem tempered her desire to rip the pouch from him and toss it into the grass. If they could sell it, if she could make it back to Demetus, and if she were able to find her family, her share would help take them away from the misery of the refugee camps.

She closed her eyes and frowned. Countless "ifs" stood between her and a sweet outcome.

Mere days after Zecus had left Demetus all those turns past, Tiliah had followed, determined to track down Zecus and convince him to come back. The well-being of the Alsher family was infinitely more important than her brother's lofty ideals of defending their homeland. It was foolish for him to think he could fight the Sudashians. Zecus was no soldier. Far from it.

For weeks, she traveled alone, backtracking her family's earlier journey east, walking against the wave of people fleeing the invasion. It was a difficult and ultimately fruitless journey. She reached Gobas having never caught her brother on the road. She moved past the gates, into the city, hoping he had delayed a day or two within the capital, and aimlessly wandered the crowded streets.

Hope fled quickly.

Countless people packed Gobas, all huddling inside the walls for protection. She had a better chance finding a puddle of water in Summer. Dejected, she readied herself to continue west, back to their family home in Drysa.

As she was leaving, a large group of battle-weary Dust Men rode into the city. As they trotted past, she thought she heard one of them mention Drysa. She turned and hurried after the men, following them to the Dust Men headquarters. She arrived well after the soldiers had passed through the barracks' gate, leaving her on the outside, looking in. She begged the guard to let her in, but they refused. Frustrated, she stood in place, staring through the gates when three wounded men were carried out and through the streets on flat litters.

Thinking she might get an answer from one of the hurt men, she followed the group to an open pavilion filled with countless injured soldiers and citizens alike. Stunned, she marched up and down the lines of the wounded in a daze. Women and men scurried about the rows of people, trying to aid as best they could, but there were simply too many that needed aid. Without thought, Tiliah volunteered to help, doing whatever was asked of her. Over the course of the next few weeks, she learned how to treat all sorts of grotesque injuries and maladies.

When Lord Nizeman assumed control and ordered Gobas evacuated, Dust Men swept through the streets, forcing everyone capable of walking to leave the city. It had taken two soldiers to drag her from the pavilion as she kicked and screamed, leaving a good number of patients behind. Their faces haunted her dreams. She began to take a deep breath as a precursor to a sigh, but smelled the roasted meat odor again and nearly gagged.

Biting down hard and swallowing the bile in her throat, she shoved the past away. Dwelling on the dead would not help her get back to her family.

Rhohn abruptly broke their shared silence, speaking in a soft, stunned tone.

"I don't understand how this could have happened."

Tiliah pressed her lips together and stared north, away from the city. She had no interest in talking about this again. It was time to move on.

He continued musing aloud, asking, "Where was the defense?"

Tiliah shut her eyes tight. Rhohn had asked that question a dozen times today.

Shaking his head, he muttered, "What in the Nine Hells is Duke Vanson doing?"

Tiliah's patience, already as thin as a light coating of dust, finally gave way.

Her eyes snapped open as she hissed, "Blast it, Mud Man! You can ask that question a thousand times, and I *still* will not be able to give you an answer!"

Rhohn's head turned sideways quickly as if he were about to issue a sharp retort, yet he stopped halfway. He remained motionless for a moment before letting out a long, weary sigh and dropping his chin to his shoulder.

"Then I'll stop asking."

Tiliah stared at the back of his burnt head, black hair covering only the left side of his skull. She sighed softly, her shoulders slumping. Tilting her head forward, she rested it gently on his back, reached up with her right hand, and patted him on the chest.

"I'm sorry, Rhohn. This is hard for you."

The soldier grunted a wordless affirmative and resumed his staring at the ruined city. She allowed him a few additional quiet, reflective moments before patting him again.

"You do know that we aren't safe here, yes?"

He nodded.

"I know."

Sitting tall, pressing against Tiliah in the process, he pulled the makeshift reins fashioned from the leftover rope from her bonds and directed the horse southeast, away from the dying capital of the Borderlands. With a swift kick to the mare's sides, they resumed their journey.

Hoping to change the subject, Tiliah bent over and peered down at Rhohn's right calf.

"How's your leg?"

"Fine," muttered Rhohn.

"The thornroot must be working, then. Does it hurt anymore?"

"I *said* it is fine."

Tiliah nodded and sat upright, deciding to leave him alone. Turning about, she scanned the brown horizon again. Still no movement. She offered a quick prayer to Ketus that their good luck would continue.

CHAPTER 18: HUNT

15ᵗʰ of the Turn of Luraana, 4999

Warm mud squished between Okollu's fingers and paws as he raced through the pre-dawn prairie, each long stride taking him closer to his prey. He tilted his muzzle upward and drew in a deep lungful of air. The scent was stronger.

He let loose a fleeting snarl over his shoulder and slowed his pace to a gentle, loping gait. The four kur-surus trailing him did the same. After a dozen more long strides, Okollu barked out a second short command and stopped. His pack-mates halted a few paces behind and, other than muted huffs from extended exertion, remained silent.

Pushing himself from the ground, Okollu stood upright to get a better look at their pre-dawn surroundings. The hills had grown taller since Saule-acu had rested last evening. The endless grasslands followed the rise and fall of the landscape, broken only by the occasional stubby tree.

Okollu sniffed the air again. The scent of green things drowned his nose. Glancing at the ground by his paws, he frowned at the new shoots sprouting from the dirt. They were troublesome. Their fresh, clean scent combined with the musty and moist earth was making their task difficult.

Lifting his gaze, he spun in a slow circle, scanning the dark horizon. Both Zila-acs and Balts-acu had set already, leaving the sky black and dusted with stars. The lack of light, however, did hamper Okollu in his search. As he faced east, he noticed a slight lightening where land met sky. Saule-acu was awakening. Okollu paused in his search and gave a slight bow, welcoming her return.

He resumed his study of the grasslands, taking short, quick breaths between his panting, filtering through the dozens of scents within each puff of air.

Upon completing his slow spin, returning to the same point on the northwestern horizon from which he started, Okollu let out a disappointed huff. While the scent was undoubtedly stronger, they still had more running to do.

Spinning around, he eyed the four Drept with him. They had remained on all fours and were staring at him, their yellow-irises reflecting what little light there was. In the thick, wet words of the kur-surus tongue, Okollu spoke to his pack mates.

"We will catch our prey before Saule-acu sleeps again."

"Good," growled Grrash. "This hunt grows long." She glanced over her shoulder, back to the east. "We must hurry and return to tas-vilku."

Their growing unease was clear, the urge for them to return to Baaldòk growing ever stronger. It sickened Okollu to see them like this.

Dropping to all fours, he snapped, "Let us go." He turned and began to run again, letting his instincts guide their pursuit and his mind wonder what he and his pack-mates were doing out here.

After taking Gobas five visits of Saule-acu ago, Okollu and his pack had remained outside the walls, awaiting Baaldòk's next order. The tall, regular structures and confined spaces within the city made the Drept—and all kur-surus—skittish. Baaldòk and the other diavoli did not care what their charges did when they were not fighting, so they had left the packs outside.

The respite allowed the Drept—and the other packs—to attend to kur-surus traditions. For two visits of Saule-acu, all kur-surus performed Grif Rol, offering a constant song to aid the souls of those who perished in the assault on their journey to Maeana's open fields. Grayskins or blade-men alike frequently threatened to attack if they would not stop the ceremony, but their diavoli leaders managed to keep such clashes to a minimum.

The day Grif Rol finished, Baaldòk returned to the pack, stomping up to Okollu and ordering him to choose his four best trackers to follow the diavol back into the city. Okollu complied and the five Drept slunk uneasily through the streets and towering buildings. He did not understand how any living soul could live in such a place. Endless walls hid the sky.

Baaldòk led them to a flat field of stone within the city, an open space that stunk of man-sweat, leather, and blood. Okollu was instantly uneasy, the hair on the scruff of his neck standing on end. With each breath, evil filled his snout, coating his tongue and filling his lungs.

A unique group awaited their arrival, two men, a female that was not quite of the smooth-face race, and the hated, yellow-haired, long-lived named Tandyr. The dark-skinned bald man and the female were wrong inside, just as Tandyr was. And while the other man was not twisted as the other trio, he reeked of fear.

The five Drept stopped before the assembled group and waited. Okollu wanted nothing more than to charge Tandyr and rip the long-lived's pale neck wide open. Yet he restrained himself, knowing that he would never reach Tandyr. Others had tried and failed. It would be a foolish attack, one that would doom what was left of the Drept.

Tandyr wanted the kur-surus to retrieve something for him. The terrified man had been assaulted by bandits on a road north of the city and they had stolen something of value. When the long-lived asked if the Drept could track the thieves, Okollu—sensing an opportunity—requested to be shown where the attack had occurred. The group then traveled miles north of the city, eventually stopping in the middle of a dirt road.

The man stammered out what had happened in between repeated, blathering apologies to the bald, dark-skinned smooth-face the others called Vanson. When he was done, Tandyr looked expectantly at the Drept and the five kur-surus converged upon the petrified man. The smooth-face held out a leather strap, stuttering that it was part of a stolen pouch. The Drept sniffed the strap a few times, gathering in its mix of odors, trying to distinguish one from another. Then, they spread out along the road, muzzles pressed to the ground. After a few moments, Grrash barked that she discovered a trail. The other Drept went to confirm it.

Leather from the pouch. Four horses. Old meat. Filthy smooth-faces.

Okollu announced they had a trail. Immediately, the screaming started.

The odor of roasting flesh filled the air and Okollu and the other kur-surus watched as the terrified man shrieked. His skin bubbled, turning from brown to red as he seemed to be cooked from the inside out. Once the man collapsed, Tandyr ordered the five Drept to follow the trail, kill the thieves, and retrieve the stolen pouch. Okollu and his four pack mates left at once, tracking the scent north.

Shortly after they started, the scent changed. The markings of a female smooth-face joined the trail just before it turned west. They ran constantly, hunting when hungry and sleeping when they must. During the last visit of Saule-acu, they came across the third campsite of the thieves. Unlike the first two, they stopped, needing some time to sort out what happened.

Some fighting had occurred. One of the filthy smooth-faces lay dead, his body rotting under the hot, watchful eye of Saule-acu. Another of the thieves had been injured, but was gone now. It was not until Grrash, the best tracker of the group, found the surprising scent of a new man that the scene made some sense. While Okollu recognized the odor instantly, he said nothing. Already concerned, his worry only deepened when he realized the man had moved in the same direction of the thieves and the stolen pouch.

From behind him, a rough voice cut into his thoughts.

Grrash spit out, "I smell blade-men blood." She huffed again. "And rotting flesh."

Okollu sniffed the air. He, too, caught the scent of the fiends along with the putrid aroma of an uncared-for wound. Feeling a flicker of worry, he took a quick, second snort and was relieved that the odor did not belong to the man from the village. That was good. The soldier still lived.

The Dust Man had been the fourth soul to whom Okollu had managed to give the message unbeknownst to Baaldòk or the Drept, but he doubted any of them had survived. Two had been old and feeble, and another emaciated from lack of food. The fact that this particular man still moved east meant he was strong. Per-haps he would succeed in actually carrying the message to its destination. Okollu hoped the trail did not lead to him. If it did, the four Drept with him now would kill the man without hesitation.

Okollu searched the air. The scent of sweaty men, horses, and a rancid wound was potent. For now, he focused on that.

CHAPTER 19: RETURN

The Storm Island weather was still crisp and cool, but for once, the air was blessedly still.

Kenders sat on one of the benches in the courtyard, her head tilted back as she stared at the blue sky, marveling that the sun was actually shining, trying to remember the last time she saw Mu's orb. A few leftover, rogue clouds from last night's squall floated in the cerulean sky, the constant gray that typically dominated the heavens absent for the time.

She closed her eyes, enjoying the warmth on her face, and listened to the sharp, arrhythmic clanging of sword striking sword and the crack of wood against wood.

"A wondrous day, is it not?"

Recognizing the voice, her heart leapt into her throat and her eyes shot open. Dropping her gaze quickly, she swiveled her head in the direction of the voice while trying to blink away the brightness. As she focused on the figure standing beside the bench, her heart slowed to its normal pace. It was not whom she had thought.

Summoning a friendly smile, she nodded and replied, "Yes, sir. It certainly is." When the man lifted a single black eyebrow, she quickly amended, "I mean, 'yes, *Joshmuel.*' It certainly is."

When she had first met Zecus' father, she had repeatedly called him 'sir,' forgetting that—in the custom of the Borderlands—titles were reserved only for people of high honor. In fact, throughout their very first conversation, Joshmuel insisted on calling her the "great hope of all lands." Wanting nothing to do with the silly honorific, Kenders had offered Joshmuel an affable compromise. She would call him by his first name and he would avoid the grandiose titles. To date, both had kept their end of the agreement, although Kenders noticed that Joshmuel still refused to use her name.

The thin Borderlander stood before her, bundled in an impressive amount of clothes, having layered shirts and tunics atop one another to the point where he looked a bit foolish. His ever-present headband was pulled down over the tips of his ears.

Pointing to the bench, he asked, "May I join you?"

"Of course," replied Kenders. "I would welcome the company."

With a small, polite bow, Joshmuel said, "You are most gracious."

He settled to the bench on her right and stared out at the open courtyard. For a short while, the pair sat in a comfortable silence, watching the soldiers work under the direction of Sergeant Trell and Commander Aiden. Half the soldiers practicing were Sentinels, half were original Shadow Manes.

Jak and Zecus were among those sparring and, as usual, they were dueling one another. Although unlike most of the men, they were armed with long, wooden staves rather than swords. As of late, Zecus had forgone bladework whenever permitted and with good reason: he was infinitely better at staves. Jak had been doing his best to fight back the handsome Borderlander all afternoon, but he continued to suffer one defeat after another.

With his eyes still forward, Joshmuel said casually, "I came to watch my son this cold afternoon. What brings you here?"

Kenders blushed. Her reason for coming here was the same.

Trying to sound as nonchalant as she could, she lied, "I wanted to enjoy the sun."

"Ah, yes, of course." There was a smile in his voice even though there was none on his face. Tilting his head up to bask in the warm sunlight, he said, "I was beginning to think Mu's orb did not visit this strange land."

Kenders smiled.

"It rarely does. I am surprised how much I missed it."

Turning to eye her, he asked, "This weather is unusual for you as well, then?"

"Most definitely. The constant clouds, the wind, the rain. Oh! And the cold! Gods, it never got this cold in Yellow Mud. Even in the middle of Winter."

Frowning Joshmuel shook his head and said, "I never imagined the air could chill so."

"Khin insists that it will 'snow' within a turn."

Joshmuel glanced over at her, raised an eyebrow and asked, "Snow?"

With a shrug, Kenders said, "He says it is like rain, but in white flakes that drift down slowly."

Joshmuel's eyes narrowed.

"Surely you are mocking me."

Shaking her head, she smiled faintly.

"I am not. 'Like ten thousand flower petals on the wind,' were his exact words."

Studying her face, Joshmuel suggested, "Perhaps the aicenai is mocking you?"

Kenders let out a humorless chuckle. Turning her gaze back to the practicing soldiers, she said, "Khin would not know how to mock."

Joshmuel also returned to staring out into the courtyard. After a few quiet moments, he mused, "If it is not a tale, I would like to see this 'snow.'"

"Truly?" asked Kenders, mildly surprised. "Why?"

"I have spent my entire life in a dry and brown land," said Joshmuel. "Cold or not, I would like to see 'ten thousand flower petals on the wind.'" He turned to stare at her, the tone of his voice changing as he spoke. "With so little beauty in the Borderlands, we have learned to cherish what little we have when we have it. And do whatever we can to hold onto its magnificence."

Kenders turned to find Joshmuel eyeing her closely. His deep brown eyes were fixed on her, studying, evaluating. There was a definite purpose behind his words.

She asked, "Are we still talking of snow?"

Joshmuel's eyes twinkled as he shook his head.

"No."

Eyes narrowing, she asked, "Then what—"

Interrupting her, Joshmuel asked softly, "What are your intentions for my son?"

Kenders sat up straight.

"Pardon?"

Joshmuel studied her a long moment, his eyes kind and gentle.

"In the Borderlands, tradition is for a woman to voice her feelings for the man she cares for first. Were you aware of that custom?"

Kenders stared at Joshmuel, dumbfounded. That was not how things were done in the Great Lakes. In Yellow Mud, young men must speak to a young woman's father first before any sort of courtship could begin.

After a few moments, she was able to mutter, "Truly?"

Joshmuel's grin widened a fraction.

"Truly."

Kenders looked back across the courtyard to where Zecus and Jak were in the midst of yet another bout, the sudden warmth in her cheeks and neck having nothing to do with the shining sun.

"How did you know that I…uh…have an interest?"

"I did not."

"Then why did you ask?"

"I asked *because* I did not know," said Joshmuel with a smile. "I merely suspected. Your reaction—and words—helped confirm my uncertainty."

He had politely duped her into revealing her feelings, yet she did not care. Other things occupied her mind now. Staring across the practice yard, she asked, "Does he have—?"

Joshmuel held up a hand quickly, interrupting her.

"Please, no. Do not ask me that. I am obligated to answer any question a person of your stature asks. And it is not my place to speak for my son's heart."

Kenders frowned. Joshmuel might refrain from using grand titles for her, but he still saw her as a person worthy of—in her mind—undeserved deference. She stared at the man, tempted to ask the question anyway, yet she refrained. It would have been beyond rude to take advantage of Joshmuel's customs. Instead, she peered back across the open yard, utterly baffled as to what to do about Zecus.

Her worry and confusion must have been clear to see, for Joshmuel leaned forward and whispered, "I will say one thing. When he is in your presence, his smile is wider than I remember it ever being."

A warm sensation of perfect joy burst inside her, filling her chest and bringing a smile to her face. Eyeing Joshmuel, she asked, "Truly?"

The Borderlander nodded and said softly, "I would not speak false of something so important."

She looked back to Zecus just as he advanced on Jak, driving him back with a whirling assault, his staff a blur. Jak backpedaled wildly, an expression of undeniable panic frozen on his face as he frantically deflected the blows.

Staring back to Joshmuel, she said, "Please do not say anything to him. To *anyone.*"

Joshmuel inclined his head, saying, "A request from you earns my silence."

"Thank you," replied Kenders.

Lifting his gaze, he smiled slightly, "Although I would have remained quiet regardless. I do not wish to interfere in my son's life." Joshmuel's eyes narrowed ever so slightly. "Zecus' fate is his own, left to follow its own course."

Kenders eyed the Borderlander curiously, wondering at the man's strange choice of words.

He looked away quickly, stared back to the yard, and asked, "He is improving, is he not?"

Kenders looked back to Zecus and nodded.

"He is getting better."

Joshmuel leaned over and said softly, "Were I two decades younger, I'd be out there myself. Perhaps I could even best him."

Picturing the father and son sparring one another brought a tiny smile to her face. The pair sat in silence for a time before Kenders finally broke the quiet.

"What should I do?"

Joshmuel glanced over, his brow furrowed in confusion.

"Pardon?"

Turning to stare at him, she repeated herself.

"What should I do? About Zecus."

"Ah," muttered Joshmuel. He was quiet a long moment, staring at the ground, apparently thinking. "I will tell you what I have always told my own children when they ask for advice." He lifted his head, locked his brown eyes onto hers and said, "You have good instincts. Follow them, trust yourself, and do what comes natural. Things will work out."

Now it was Kenders' turn to be confused.

"Pardon?"

"I have heard your tale," said Joshmuel. "Numerous times, in fact. While some might mark your actions as rash or thoughtless, it is hard to deny the results. Either you have the luck of Ketus himself or you have incredible instincts. Regardless, keep doing what you are doing. It has served you well so far, yes?"

A rueful grin spread over her lips.

"That is the exact opposite advice that Khin or Broedi would—"

She cut off as a sudden surge of black and white crackled inside her chest and head. The strength of the magic a dozen times greater than the tiny bursts she normally felt at the enclave. She leapt to her feet and scanned the courtyard, using her eyes and whatever the other sense was that allowed her to feel the Strands.

"What is it?" asked Joshmuel in a worried voice.

Running her gaze over the ranks of soldiers, Kenders took a moment to mutter, "Magic." Spotting a bundle of black and white Strands amongst the soldiers, she said, "There it is."

Joshmuel stood from the bench and asked, "What? Where?"

There was no reason to point it out to Joshmuel. He would not be able to see the Weave.

A moment later, the sound of ripping fabric filled the yard. The telltale rippling of a port appeared where the Weave had been, hovering in the middle of the practicing soldiers. Two men in the midst of an intense duel were mere feet away from stepping into the inky void. Remaining calm, Kenders reached for a large number of Strands of Air and quickly knit together a simple pattern Khin had made her practice well over a hundred times. The moment the Weave was complete, she directed it at the port.

A quick, almost solid wall of air rushed outward in all directions from the tear, knocking back at least a dozen soldiers. The men exclaimed in surprise, their sharp shouts of alarm echoing through the yard as they were tossed to the ground. She cringed as they rolled backwards, swords flying. The blast of wind whipped past her a moment later, ruffling her heavy winter dress and unbound hair.

Another rush of muted crackling announced a second Weave, one not of her making. Twenty feet above the port, she spotted a number of white Strands pop into existence, mixing with the dirty brown of Stone. The Air swirled into tight, twisted ropes, fusing with the Stone and fashioning a cage of sorts. As the Weave finished, it slammed down around the port, tossing up gravel into the air. The speed with which the Weave had been completed left no doubt in her mind who was responsible. She glanced over her shoulder and spotted Khin standing on the battlement, staring into the courtyard.

She took a quick look around the courtyard. She and Khin were the only mages here at the moment, although she imagined any mage able to sense Air or Stone was running through the halls now.

Commander Aiden called out, "Surround the port!"

Sergeant Trell followed the order, crying, "Swords drawn! At the ready!"

Jak and Zecus were both running to the front of the men, staves up. Former Red Sentinels and Shadow Mane soldiers alike rushed toward the black rip, forming a loose circle around it and closing in quickly.

Suddenly, a short figure wearing a wide-brimmed hat stepped through the tear. Immediately, everyone in the yard relaxed. Jak and Zecus slowed to a walk. A few soldiers even lowered their blades. A large, relived sigh slipped from Kenders.

"Oh, thank the Gods."

With open astonishment, Joshmuel muttered, "That is the tomble I met in Lakeborough."

Nodding, Kenders said with a tiny smile, "Yes, it is."

Nundle took a few steps forward, away from the port, and halted. He twisted about, gawking at the Weave of Air and Stone entrapping him. Wondering why Khin had not yet dismissed the Weave despite having caged an obvious friend, Kenders peered back to the wall where the aicenai stood, his gaze still fixed on the port. His eyes shifted to her and she felt a short burst of Air. Half a breath later, his light, parchment-thin voice spoke into her ear.

"We know not what else might come through. Remain alert."

Kenders frowned. Khin was right. They should be careful.

She turned her attention back to the port just in time to spot a second tomble stepping through. His hair was light-brown, he was dressed as if he had just come in from the fields, and he used a walking stick to support his right leg.

He stopped a pace from the port and stared about the courtyard with cautious eyes. Nundle said something and waved to the second arrival. The new tomble hobbled over, stood beside Nundle, and appeared to say something in response. Nundle smiled and nodded. They seemed friendly enough. Kenders hoped that was a good sign.

Broedi stepped through the port a moment later, leading Nundle's chestnut horse behind him. Once the horse was safely through, the port shut with a soft pop. Khin's cage winked out of existence a moment later.

"They're back early," murmured Kenders.

Broedi and Nundle could not have reached the Celestial Empire already. Even by Broedi's best estimates, it would take two more turns to reach the nation of the Gods.

Glancing over at Joshmuel, Kenders smiled and asked, "How would you like to meet Broedi?"

Joshmuel's eyes widened at the name.

"The great lion?"

He stared back to the group forming about the three newcomers.

Kenders nodded once and said with a smile, "Come with me."

Knowing that he would surely follow, she hurried across the courtyard to where everyone was gathering. The bulk of the soldiers were already moving away, ordered to fall back by Commander Aiden. When she and Joshmuel reached the group, she found Sergeant Trell, Zecus, Jak, and Commander Aiden all staring at the brown-haired tomble, half of them with mouths hanging open.

Kenders glanced at each of the men, wondering at the reason for their slack-jawed expressions. Nundle peeked out from under his hat, wearing a wide grin on his face. Broedi's lips revealed the typical, slight smile that he wore when he found something amusing.

Stepping up to the group, she asked, "Why are you back so soon?" She shifted her gaze to the new tomble. "And who might you be?"

The brown-haired tomble turned to face her and leaned on his walking stick. As soon as his eyes settled on her, he smiled and shook his head in quiet disbelief.

"Bless the Gods. You look *just* like Eliza."

Kenders froze, her eyes locking onto the tomble's face.

Broedi looked at the little tomble and rumbled, "Tobias, I would like you to meet Kenders Isaac, born to Aryn Atticus and Eliza Kap and reared as daughter by Thaddeus and Marie Isaac."

The tomble nodded politely.

"Good days ahead, Kenders."

Turning to her, Broedi said, "Kenders, I would like you to meet Tobias Donngord, the Eye of Nelnora."

Kenders stared, stunned. She recognized the title instantly. The Eye of Nelnora was one of the White Lions. Yet a tomble stood before her. Her eyes widened as she realized she was gaping like a fool. In a rush, she said, "And good memories behind, sir."

The tomble nodded graciously.

"No 'sir.' Just Tobias."

"Good memories behind, Tobias," corrected Kenders. She paused a moment before adding, "I apologize for my reaction. It's just that, well, I'm a bit surprised."

Nundle spoke up, saying, "There's been a lot of that lately."

Kenders asked, "Where did you find—"

Broedi held up a hand, interrupting her. "We will explain everything, I promise, but I would like to do it only once." Looking around the assembled group, he asked, "Where is Nikalys?"

"Reading, if you can believe it," answered Jak. "I can fetch him if you'd like."

Nodding once, Broedi said, "Good. Bring him to Lady Vivienne's offices immediately."

Jak handed his staff to Zecus, turned, and began jogging to the tower that the three siblings shared.

Broedi announced, "Kenders, Commander, Sergeant, come with me, please."

As he turned to head to a set of doors in the wall, he seemed to spot Joshmuel for the first time. Stopping short, the hillman shifted his gaze to Zecus and then back to the elder Alsher. After a moment, he gave Joshmuel a slight bow and rumbled in his deep baritone.

"My pleasure is to meet you in peace today, sire of Zecus. Welcome to Storm Island."

Joshmuel managed a quick, surprised bow, and replied, "And may peace bless our parting, great lion."

Broedi frowned at the use of the honorific. He had spent weeks trying to break Zecus of the habit. Staring between father and son, he said, "Both of you should come as well. Something has happened to the Borderlands." The foreboding tone of his voice chased away every bit of warmth Kenders felt at seeing Broedi and Nundle again.

Handing the reins of Nundle's horse to a stableman who had run up, the hillman turned and began to stride toward the set of doors. Nundle gave her a sad smile and followed after whispering a quick hello to Joshmuel. Tobias stared at Kenders for another moment, shook his head, and lurched after the group.

Kenders looked at Joshmuel first, then to Zecus. Both wore expressions of deep worry. Her personal concerns from a short time ago seemed suddenly frivolous.

CHAPTER 20: YEARNING

Jak hurried up the chilly stairwell, taking the stone steps two at a time. Upon reaching the top floor, he strode down the cold and drafty hall to the oak door at the passageway's end. Without pausing, he put his hand on Nikalys' door and shoved, sending it flying open, silent on its well-oiled hinges. In the brief moment before the door crashed into the interior wall, Jak spied Nikalys sitting in his chair, slouched over the table. He was either intently reading or asleep. Jak would have bet gold ducats on the latter.

A small, anticipatory smile touched Jak's lips. He would enjoy this.

The oaken door struck the wall inside, sending a resounding crack through the quiet room, loud enough that it even startled Jak.

Nikalys jolted upright in his chair, turned his head quickly, and—a moment later—was standing before Jak, the white Blade of Horum drawn and leveled at Jak's chest.

With his eyes wide and staring at the tip of the sword, Jak muttered nervously, "Ah, Nik?" The shimmering metal shone bright, brighter than it should in the diffused light of the room.

Nikalys lowered his sword and slumped over.

"Gods, Jak! Don't sneak up on me like that!"

Eyebrows raised, Jak said, "Sneak? I could not have made more noise if I were driving a four-horse wagon on the stairs to get here. You should have easily heard me." With a tilt of his head and a friendly smirk, he added, "You weren't asleep at your studies, were you, great Progeny?"

Nikalys peered at Jak and gave him a sheepish smile.

"Would you believe that I was reading?"

Jak grinned wide.

"Would you believe that I have just been named the new king of the duchies?"

Chuckling, Nikalys sheathed the Blade of Horum, eyed Jak, and asked, "What's going on? Had I been asleep—and I'm not saying I was—I was certainly not sleeping long enough for afternoon drills to be over." His eyes narrowed a fraction. "Did something happen?"

Jak gave a cavalier shrug of his shoulders.

"You could say that."

"Oh, just tell me," muttered Nikalys. He nodded back toward his desk. "I have reading I should be doing."

"Don't you mean a nap you could be taking?"

Leveling a steady stare towards Jak, Nikalys asked firmly, "Why are you here, Jak?"

Sensing Nikalys was not in the mood for jesting, without further preamble, Jak announced, "Broedi and Nundle are back."

Nikalys' directness fled immediately, his eyebrows shooting up in clear surprise.

"Already? But they weren't supposed to reach the Seat of Nelnora for…I don't know…at least a few turns still. Did Broedi change his mind?"

With a cryptic smile, Jak said, "No, he did not."

"Then why are they here?"

"They, ah…they came across something unexpected."

Clearly puzzled, Nikalys peered at Jak for a heartbeat or two before asking, "What aren't you telling me?" His tone was oddly demanding and one he would not have used with Jak as recently as last Spring.

Relishing the moment, Jak said, "They found another of the White Lions. He's here with them now, in Lady Vivienne's office."

He was hoping to shock his brother with the revelation, but Nikalys' response was wholly unexpected, simply because there was no reaction at all. His face remained a blank, unreadable mask.

Worried, Jak said, "Nik? Did you hear me? They—"

"He?" interjected Nikalys, a tiny flicker of hope lighting up his eyes.

Confused, Jak stared at his brother a moment before he suddenly realized what Nikalys must be thinking. With his eyes opening wide, he said, "Oh! Gods, no! It's not your…it's not Aryn!" He had almost said father, but could not bring himself to give the designation to the White Lion. As long as Thaddeus remained Nikalys and Kenders' father, he was their brother.

Nikalys' shoulders slumped, the corners of his lips tumbling downward.

"Oh."

"Gods, I'm sorry, Nik. I shouldn't have—"

Jak felt bad. He had wanted to shock his brother, not disappoint him.

Waving his hands in a dismissive gesture, Nikalys said, "Birds have wings." The phrase was one their mother had often used. If a bird slipped from a tree branch, it did not matter much. Birds have wings.

Nikalys eyed the floor, took a quick breath, let it out, and stood tall. "Truthfully, I'm…I'm relieved that it's not him." He peered down at the stone floor and mumbled, "Odd, isn't it?"

Unsure what he should say, Jak chose to remain quiet.

After a moment, Nikalys looked up and sighed.

"Well, who is it, then?"

With a hint of relief the awkward moment had passed, Jak said, "Tobias."

"Tobias?" muttered Nikalys. Shaking his head, he placed his hands on his hips. "The name sounds familiar, I think, but…"

Shrugging his shoulders, Jak said, "I thought the same. But Broedi introduced him as Tobias Donngord, the Eye of Nelnora." He paused a moment before adding with a slight smile, "He's a tomble."

His brother began to chuckle aloud, staring expectantly at Jak, clearly waiting for him to join in the mirth. When Jak did not, Nikalys' smile quickly faded.

"You're not jesting, are you?"

Jak shook his head, saying, "I am not." Holding his hand to his waist, he said, "He's this tall with brown hair, a bent right leg, and carries a cane to help him walk." His smile fluttered a bit wider. "A very tiny cane."

"Truly?"

Nikalys was still skeptical.

Leaning against the open doorframe, Jak crossed his arms and said, "Come see for yourself. Broedi sent me to bring you to Lady Vivienne's offices."

Moving toward the doorway, Nikalys said, "No need to keep everyone waiting." Motioning with a thumb over his shoulder to indicate the open volume on his desk, he added, "I'm finished with that book."

Jak raised an eyebrow.

"Truly?"

Nikalys winked as he passed, a slight smile on his face.

"Yes, Jak. I am finished with it."

Frowning, Jak turned to follow his younger brother into the hallway.

"Did you *read* it, Nik?"

Nikalys glanced over his shoulder, grinned wide, and continued striding down the hall without answering the question.

Shaking his head, Jak pulled the door shut, and hurried after him.

Chapter 21: Windows

As the brothers approached Lady Vivienne's offices, the baroness' aide, sitting at the table beside the double doors, looked up from his papers, made eye contact with them, and motioned for the guards to step aside. Jak nodded at the soldiers as he passed. He had sparred against both a number of times during drills.

Upon entering the spacious room, a wall of welcome, warm air met the brothers. A large fire was roaring in the hearth to Jak's right, easily holding back the day's chill. Jak wished he had a hearth in his room. He was so cold at night that he might as well sleep on the battlements.

Sergeant Trell stood to one side of the fireplace next to Commander Aiden. Both men eyed Jak and Nikalys and gave short nods of greeting which the brothers returned.

Straight across from the double doors, at the rear of the room, Lady Vivienne sat in the red cushioned chair situated behind her large oaken, ebonwood-inlayed desk. Broedi stood to her right—Jak's left—with his arms crossed over his wide chest and deep furrow in his brow. He did not even look up as the Isaac brothers entered the room.

Khin was standing in the back corner, his back pressed against the wall, as far from the fire he could be. Strangely enough, Zecus and his father were here, too, standing in the corner to his immediate left, away from everyone else. Both men wore anxious expressions.

Four chairs were before Lady Vivienne's desk, three of which were occupied. The new White Lion, Tobias, sat in the far left with Nundle next to him. Kenders was in the next chair over, leaving the far right chair open.

Both tombles turned around at the brothers' entrance. Nundle gave Nikalys a small smile paired with a quick wave. Nikalys returned the silent hello with a nod before shifting his full attention to the tomble White Lion. Tobias stared, a lopsided smile resting on his lips as he shook his head in quiet wonderment.

The moment they were through the entryway, the guards outside closed the double doors. As they thudded shut, Jak scanned the room again. Everyone was eerily quiet.

Leaning over to Nikalys, Jak whispered, "Good luck."

Nikalys grunted and headed for the open chair, apparently coming to the same conclusion as Jak: the chair was meant for him alone.

The Progeny.

Jak considered moving to stand with the soldiers, but instead he strode to where Zecus and his father waited. Based on the Alshers' worried expressions, it looked as if they might need some support. Upon reaching the corner, he gave a short nod to the Borderlanders and turned to face the room.

As Nikalys sat in his chair, Nundle leaned forward and whispered a quick introduction to Tobias. Nikalys murmured a polite "Good days ahead" while Tobias completed the greeting, all the while staring intently at Nikalys. The expression on the tomble's face was remarkably identical to the one Broedi had worn those first few nights after finding the Isaacs in the forest. It was as if he were staring at one of the kings of old and not believing a moment of it.

The introductions were barely complete when Lady Vivienne spoke, asking, "May we begin now?" Her tone was clipped and unemotional. "You said there was a need for quick action, Broedi. Yet we sit around, staring at one another. Answers, please."

Everyone turned to stare at the hillman and waited expectantly.

Broedi, however, did not respond. He continued staring at the floor, lost in thought.

Raising her voice, Lady Vivienne prompted, "Broedi?"

The hillman twisted his head to peer at the baroness, rumbling, "Yes?"

"May we begin?"

Broedi looked up and scanned the room. Upon seeing Nikalys and Jak, he nodded and said softly, "Of course."

Jak frowned. Broedi was troubled. He could sense it. For that reason alone, Jak was upset. Broedi never showed trepidation or unease.

After taking a deep breath, the hillman rumbled, "As you can see, we have returned early." His gaze rested on Tobias. "We found more than was expected on our journey."

Tobias cocked an eyebrow, but remained quiet as Broedi launched into a recounting of his and Nundle's journey west, quickly reaching the point where the pair had stumbled upon Tobias strolling about Tinfiddle's fields. He briefly recapped the altercation in Tobias' house and, upon reaching the discussion the trio had shared after leaving Tinfiddle, nodded in the tomble's direction.

"Tobias, tell them of your vision, please."

Everyone in the room turned to listen as Tobias quickly described what he saw as he walked through Claw, the courtyard, and into the commons during eveningmeal. Once returning and listening to Broedi and Nundle's tale, the tomble had opened a port directly to the Seat of Nelnora, delivering all three to the base of the stairs of the Prime Temple of Nelnora.

"It was amazing!"

Jak started at Nundle's excited interruption.

Spinning around in the chair to look at everyone, Nundle said, "The city was unlike anything I had ever seen! White marble and glass towers everywhere! But no people—it was empty. The divina told us they had been ordered away—" His eyes opened wider. "Oh, I forgot! Tenerva! He took us inside the temple to speak with the Goddess, but then made us wait for nearly two days. Can you believe that? Two days in a city of the Celestial Empire?! The food was excellent, though! And they took excellent care of Traveler while we—"

He cut off the moment he caught the disapproving eye of Lady Vivienne, who had been glaring at the tomble throughout his meandering rant. Facing forward in his chair, he dropped his head while offering a mumbled, "Pardon me."

Jak leaned over and whispered to Zecus, "Traveler?"

Zecus shrugged.

"His horse?"

"But he said he'd never—"

"Men," interjected Joshmuel's quiet, somber voice. "Pay attention, please."

Zecus glanced at his father, nodded, and stood straight. Jak mimicked his friend's response, reminded for a moment of similar quiet admonishments from his own father. A flicker of melancholy washed through him, but Broedi's deep voice quickly chased it away as the hillman resumed speaking.

"Nundle has tried to roast the lamb before slaughtering it, but that is essentially what happened. We were kept waiting for two days, during which time we only saw Nelnora's high priest. This morning, he brought us to the center of the temple, straight to the antechamber of Nelnora's viewing room. There, he—"

"Broedi?" interjected Khin in his wispy, drawn-out manner. "You really should explain. Few are as familiar with the temple as you."

Broedi peered at the aicenai and nodded.

"You are right, of course. I forgot."

Jak frowned, worried. He had never heard Broedi utter the phrase, 'I forgot.'

Scanning the faces of the people about the room, the hillman rumbled, "At the center of the temple is a large, circular chamber where Nelnora and her servants keep a close eye on Terrene."

Nikalys asked, "So the Watcher of the World truly watches the world?"

Broedi's eyes narrowed sharply.

"The Celystiela did *not* earn their titles based on playmen's whimsy."

Nikalys did not flinch at Broedi's harsher than normal tone. Keeping his own voice firm, he said, "It was an honest question."

Jak glanced at Zecus with a raised eyebrow. The Borderlander appeared confused as well. Broedi had been as steadfast as a mountain since they had each met him, rarely exhibiting anything other than a quiet and calm confidence. As Broedi continued to glare at Nikalys, Jak's unease grew.

Tobias quickly interjected himself, saying, "Of course it was, young man. Please forgive Broedi's sharp tone. We have not slept well the past few days."

Broedi eyed the tomble, a slight frown on his lips, and quietly admitted, "I am tired."

Jak tensed. The hillman's short and soft acknowledgement said more than a thousand words. Broedi was never tired. Ever. On the journey from Smithshill to the enclave, the hillman had barely slept, keeping constant watch over the siblings. Something was very wrong.

A quiet moment skipped past before Tobias said, "Perhaps I should speak, Broedi? I saw Nelnora first, after all."

Broedi pressed his lips together, let out a long sigh, and took a few steps back. "Please."

Using his walking stick to brace himself, Tobias slid off his chair and turned to face the room, leaving his back to Lady Vivienne. Eyeing Nikalys, he said, "Nelnora indeed watches the world from her chamber, searching for imbalance and disorder. It is her role." Frowning, an acerbic note entered his tone as he muttered, "It is her purpose."

Kenders said softly, "It sounds as if you don't much like her purpose."

Shifting his gaze to her, Tobias said, "Her purpose I respect, dear. It is the Goddess herself I—" He cut off and, with a short wave of a hand as though he were shooing a pest, murmured, "No matter. My personal feelings are not pertinent." Staring about the room, he raised his voice, saying, "As it were, Nelnora would only see us one at a time, and I was asked in first."

Before he could stop himself, Jak asked, "Why?"

Tobias' gaze shifted to regard Jak. Chairs creaked as a number of other people in the room turned their heads as well.

"Why was I first?" asked Tobias.

"No," said Jak with a quick shake of his head. "Why did she only see you one at a time?"

If Tobias was annoyed at the interruption, he did not show it. Nodding his head, he said, "We thought it odd as well and asked Tenerva that exact question." A smirk spread over his lips. "We were told we could either 'accept her Eminence's terms or leave.'"

From beside the hearth, Commander Aiden said, "Not much of an option."

"No, it was not," agreed Tobias. "And as I had been waiting a long time to speak with her, it was not worth negotiating the terms." A curiously indignant edge had slipped into his voice. "So, I marched straight in to the viewing chamber and found the Goddess waiting for me atop the dais in the room's center." His tone turned mocking as he added, "Sunlight streamed through the crystal dome above, shining straight down on her. Very impressive looking, I assure you."

Jak exchanged a quick look with Zecus. The Borderlander appeared to have noticed Tobias' disdain as well.

"Beside her," continued Tobias, "hovering in the air, was a shimmering... 'window' is the best word for what I saw. As Tenerva shut the doors behind me,

Nelnora waved a hand, beckoning me to come closer." He held up his walking stick a few inches and spoke, vinegary resentment seeping into each word. "I'm not a fast walker by any means, but I made sure to take my good time to reach her. After years of keeping me from the barn, it was her turn to till the blasted fields."

Again, Jak glanced at Zecus. This time, even Joshmuel cocked an eyebrow.

"Upon reaching the dais," continued Tobias. "I stared into the window she had woven." His eyes went unfocused as an expression of dismayed wonder spread over his face. Dropping his chin an inch or two, he stared blankly at his empty chair. Jak braced himself. This was going to be bad.

"Ages ago," began Tobias. "When the White Lions' presence was appreciated and not reviled, I had need to visit Gobas. A dispute between two barons had arisen, with both claiming a rare stretch of fertile land in the Borderlands. Duke Caleb— the sovereign at the time—was tired of their bickering and called on the Lions to render a judgment. When the request arrived, Miriel and I were the only ones in Freehaven. We played a hand of knuckles to see who would go and—"

"Hold a moment," interjected Nikalys. "You played placards to decide who would go?"

Tobias shrugged.

"It was as good a way as any."

"Against Ketus' champion?" pressed Nikalys.

Tobias gave a quiet, dry chuckle.

"I always believed I might one day beat Miriel. However, *that* was not to be the day. I lost. Badly if I recall. She had a stocked wagon. Me, a measly two pair."

Shaking his head, the tomble stared about the room.

"The important thing is I was on my way to Gobas. And, as I had never been there before, I was forced to port to Lakeborough and travel overland the rest of the way. Gods, but that was a dreadful trip. Nothing but muck and swampflies for the first half, followed by dust and grass the second."

Jak wondered where Tobias was going with this.

"And as desolate as the Borderlands are—" he glanced to Zecus and Joshmuel "—pardon my insult, when I arrived in Gobas, I was pleasantly surprised. It was a truly wondrous city. Strange, yes, but wondrous. The food took some getting used to, though. The spices used were rather unique."

Jak hid a slight smile. Zecus had said the same thing about Southlands' meals.

"Once I settled the dispute—both barons were pompous and insufferable, so I awarded the land to a family of shepherds instead—I stayed in the city for weeks longer than I had intended. The markets there were astounding. Nothing like the Grand Square in Freehaven, mind you, but wondrous nonetheless. I spent a week wandering about before I reluctantly left and returned to Freehaven."

He paused a moment and frowned.

"I never did make my way back."

Shaking his head, he drew a deep, fortifying breath and said, "The moment I saw the city through Nelnora's window, I recognized it. Only, it was in shambles. Anything wood was either ablaze or already a smoldering ruin. The buildings not already collapsed were severely damaged. Half of the Duke's Hall was a pile of stone and timber. Great, gaping holes split the city's walls, the streets were thick with oligurts, razorfiends, and mongrels. Demon men, too. All of them, tearing the city apart."

Jak stole a quick glance at the two Borderlanders beside him. Both men's expressions were oscillating between sorrow and outright anger.

Commander Aiden muttered, "So they've reached Gobas." The soldier spoke with a hint of sadness, but his words were mostly a statement of fact.

Kenders asked, "What of the people who lived there?"

Tobias peered at her a moment before answering, "Most were dead. Some were not." He frowned before adding, "Yet."

"How many souls lived in Gobas?" asked Nikalys.

Lady Vivienne answered the inquiry, saying softly, "Before all this? Over fifty thousand." Her tone carried none of its usual directness.

"Pardon me, great baroness," said Joshmuel. Everyone turned to look back to the corner. "But when our family moved through, at least twenty thousand of my countrymen were living outside the walls."

Zecus said, "There were even more when I went back."

The room went silent.

Jak shut his eyes. He hoped most of Gobas had fled ahead of the attack.

After a few moments of quiet, Kenders spoke, saying, "We need to help them. Whoever's left."

Opening his eyes, Jak stared at his sister and nodded.

"She's right. Perhaps we could open a port and rescue some?"

The dark look that Tobias and Broedi exchanged was answer enough to their plea, but Commander Aiden gave voice to what Jak was already thinking. In a soft, regretful tone, the soldier said, "A noble thought, but not something we can do."

"Why not?" pressed Kenders.

A few heads turned in surprise when Nikalys was the one who answered.

"When you're trying to win a hand of knuckles, you don't play symbols up."

Jak eyed his younger brother.

"Pardon?"

Swiveling in his chair, Nikalys said, "If we show up to help the people of Gobas, the God of Chaos and the Cabal will know for a fact we—" he glanced briefly at Kenders "—exist. And that there is some sort of force ready to oppose him or her. They might adjust plans accordingly." He shook his head. "We cannot help Gobas."

Jak glanced around the room at the people who typically made the decisions. Broedi. Lady Vivienne. Commander Aiden. All of them wore the same grim look. Sergeant Trell and Tobias, too.

"You're going to let them die?" asked Kenders, her voice rising.

With a firm nod, Broedi rumbled, "Yes."

Jak asked, "What if we send a small—"

"No, Jak," interjected Sergeant Trell. "The risk is heavier than the gain."

Kenders protested, "But the 'gain' is people's lives!" Turning to Nikalys, she said, "Are you truly willing to let them die?!"

Nikalys frowned and looked away, but Kenders was not done.

"Nik! What if it were me there?"

"That's different," muttered Nikalys.

"How?" demanded Kenders.

Broedi answered, rumbling, "You are the Progeny."

Glaring at the hillman, Kenders said, "Fine, then." Jabbing a finger back toward Jak, she asked, "What if Jak were in Gobas, Nik? Would you leave him to die?"

Nikalys shook his head quickly.

"Of course not."

Broedi said firmly, "It would not be up to you, Nikalys." Looking back to Jak, the hillman said, "I am sorry, Jak, but if you were in Gobas at this very moment, you would be on your own. No one's life is worth revealing ourselves to Chaos."

Jak tried not to let the declaration bother him, but it did. Trying to deflect the suddenly charged atmosphere, he muttered, "Good thing I'm not there, then." The jest was ill timed and found only quiet, melancholy stares.

A few moments passed when Zecus demanded, "What happened?" Restrained fury filled his voice. "Gobas was a fortress! How could Duke Vanson not hold it?" Joshmuel reached over and placed a comforting hand on his son's shoulder.

Tobias' gaze shifted back to the Borderlanders and said, "Nelnora does not know. According to her, she has been unable to see Vanson for some time, now. In fact—" his voice took on a heavy, ominous tone "—it has been nearly three decades since she has seen him."

From the back corner, Khin spoke, his airy voice drifting about the offices.

"That is grave."

Peering over toward Khin, Tobias nodded and said, "I agree."

Jak found it odd that Tobias did not seem the least bit surprised by the presence of the aicenai.

Kenders asked, "Why is that grave?"

Looking back to the chairs, Tobias said, "There are a limited number of beings in Terrene able to hide from Nelnora's abilities to look upon them." A weighty sigh slipped from his lips. "None of whom are mortal."

It took Jak—and most of the people in the room—several moments to make sense of the revelation.

Sergeant Trell sighed heavily, Commander Aiden let a whispered curse slip, Lady Vivienne shut her eyes and dropped her chin to her chest, her blonde hair draping before her face. The room was deadly quiet until a log in the fire popped as an air pocket burst.

Kenders spoke first, disbelief dripping from every word.

"Are you suggesting Duke Vanson is one of the Cabal?"

Sergeant Trell said, "It would certainly explain a few things."

"It certainly would," agreed Lady Vivienne.

"Is he the God of Chaos?" asked Nikalys. He sounded as if he already accepted the implausible premise. "Or one of the others? Strife, Pain, or Deception?"

Facing Nikalys, Tobias said, "An excellent question and the first thing I asked Nelnora myself. As to her answer, I will give it to you word for word and suspect you will be as unsatisfied by it as I was: 'I do not know. No one does but him.'"

Jak waited, expecting more. Nothing else came.

Sergeant Trell muttered, "Is that all?"

Tobias shifted his gaze to the soldier.

"Sorry, Sentinel, but that's all I have."

"You know," began Lady Vivienne softly. "Duchess Aleece always suspected something like this." Pressing the tips of her fingers together, she said in a quiet, ponderous voice, "I did not want to believe her."

Jak—along with everyone in the room—stared at the baroness and offered some exclamation of surprise. Unable to help himself, Jak took a step forward and snapped, "I'm sorry. You suspected the Duke of the Borderlands was *of the Cabal*? And you kept it to yourselves?"

The baroness leaned forward to rest her elbows on the desk, settled her cool green eyes on him, and said, "There was no need to share it with you." Her tone was as casual as though she had mentioned that the clouds looked like they had rain in them for tomorrow.

Jak's eyes widened a fraction. Jabbing a finger at Nikalys and Kenders, he exclaimed, "They are the blasted Progeny! Should they not know when it involves, oh, I don't know, the Cabal!"

Lady Vivienne glared at him, pressing her lips together so tightly that they turned white.

Before she could respond, Commander Aiden spoke up, saying, "I agree, my Lady. We all should have been told." His tone was firm yet infinitely more polite than Jak's had been.

Shooting a glance at the older soldier, Jak asked, "You didn't know, either?"

The commander continued glaring at the baroness, clearly upset.

"No. I did not."

"Nor did I," rumbled Broedi.

The hillman's words stunned Jak. He could not believe they would keep such information from a White Lion.

Lady Vivienne held up her hands and said, "Before you all toss me into the sea, I ask you to hold a moment and listen to my precise words. Duchess Aleece *suspected* the duke was of the Cabal. She did *not know*. Years ago, Duke Vanson used to be a reasonable soul and an excellent ruler, which meant his recent irrational and irresponsible behavior was one of three things. He was either suddenly and grossly incompetent, mad as a gray-haired tanner, or—and we thought this highly unlikely for all but the last turn—making illogical, outright cruel decisions because of deliberate, sinister intent."

Broedi continued to glare, apparently dissatisfied with Lady Vivienne's explanation.

"You should have said something to me."

Staring up at the hillman, Lady Vivienne snapped, "When you share all your secrets, Broedi, I will share mine!"

Khin's thin voice drifted through the room again.

"Does your shared acrimony solve some issue of which I am unaware?"

Jak stared into the back corner where the ancient aicenai stood, staring at the rest of the room with his ice-blue eyes.

Having drawn the attention of everyone, Khin said, "Who knew what and when they knew it does not matter now. I care only what must be done next. As should the rest of you." When everyone remained quiet, properly chastised, Khin directed his gaze back to Tobias. "Continue with your tale if you will."

Tobias, a somewhat bemused look on his face, gave one last quick glance between Broedi and the baroness before saying, "Well, there's nothing more to add, truly. Nelnora closed the window, explained that the armies of Sudash were marching east, and told me my time with her was complete. She pointed to the door and told me to send in Nundle." With a quick wave of his hand, he motioned in Nundle's direction and announced, "I'm done. The stage is yours."

As he shuffled to his chair, his walking stick cracking on the stone floor, Nikalys said, "Hold a moment. That's all? After refusing to see you for two-hundred years, she shows you the ruins of Gobas, asks you to leave…and you listened?"

Tobias stopped in his tracks, stared at Nikalys, and said firmly, "At first? No. I asked my questions and said my piece, but she ignored me entirely. All she would say was, 'Send in Nundle, please.' Over and over. Once I tired of talking with myself, I shared a few sharp words with her and I left."

"Truly?" asked Nikalys, his eyes narrowed.

"Are you naming me a liar?" demanded Tobias.

"No, not at—"

"What would you have had me do, young man? Sit down in the chamber and refuse to leave? Would that have helped things?"

Nikalys shook his head.

"I suppose not."

Tobias glared at Nikalys a moment longer, nodded once, and said, "Again, the stage is yours, Nundle." As he moved to his chair and started to climb into it, Nundle hopped from his, spun around and started speaking immediately, clearly excited.

"I was more than surprised when Tobias came out and told me that Nelnora wanted me to come into the chamber. Nevertheless, I went in—terribly nervous. As she was for Tobias, Nelnora waited on the dais for me, but with *three* windows arranged behind her, not just one. Tobias did not tell us about Gobas until later, which is a good thing, I think, else I would have been even more terrified than I was. I probably would have thought she was going to show me something awful. Goodness, what if—"

Kenders gently interrupted the tomble, saying, "Nundle?"

Jak was glad she was the one to stop him. Lady Vivienne's face revealed she was moments away from being more direct.

Kenders prompted, "What did Nelnora show you?"

An embarrassed grin spread over the tomble's face.

"Right. Sorry. Well, I hurried to the dais, up the stairs, and then stood there, waiting for her to say something. But she didn't. She stayed completely silent and simply pointed to the windows. So, I looked."

His face bunched up in confusion.

"In the first, all I could see was a door. A tall, black stone door set in a white granite wall. A round, silver plate was bolted to it, an inscription upon, I think."

"You think?" prompted Sergeant Trell.

Nundle nodded.

"It was not Argot, but the markings looked familiar."

"What were they?" asked Jak.

"And where was the door," added Kenders. "Where did it lead?"

Shrugging his shoulders, Nundle said, "I asked those questions and more, but instead of answering me, Nelnora pointed to the middle window." Again, his brow furrowed in confusion. "In that one, I saw a single flower with purple, pointed petals and a bright yellow center growing in white sand."

Jak glanced around the room, happy to find everyone wearing the same baffled expression he was confident was upon his face.

"Again, I tried to ask what I was seeing, but she ignored me and pointed to the last window. There I saw an old stone statue of a cat of sorts, crumbling and falling apart. It was toppled over on a plaza overgrown with weeds and vines."

Jak's confusion only grew.

Glancing around the room, Nundle said, "After that, she pointed to the doors. I asked about the windows again, but she just stood there, silent. She would not even meet my stare. After a few terribly awkward moments, I left."

Lady Vivienne asked quizzically, "She never said anything to you?"

Nundle glanced back, peering over the top of the oaken desk.

"Not a word, my Lady."

"A door, a flower, and a ruined statue?" mused Sergeant Trell. "What do they mean?"

Nundle shook his head.

"I have no idea, Nathan."

"She is the Watcher of the World," said Nikalys. "They must be places across Terrene, yes?"

Shrugging again, Nundle said, "I thought the same, but where?"

"And why?" added Kenders softly.

"She must have had a point," muttered Commander Aiden.

"The Celystiela always do," rumbled Broedi.

"How does that help anything?" mumbled Kenders.

Most everyone in the room stared at each other, all wearing similar expressions of bewilderment. Khin and Broedi were the only two who remained stoic and composed. The hillman had regained control of himself.

"Well that was a useful trip," muttered Jak sarcastically. He stared at Broedi. "Wasn't the purpose of the two of you going to see Nelnora to get answers? So far, all I hear is new questions."

"They found me," said Tobias.

Jak glanced at the tomble and said, "And I'm glad. But unless you can end this war right this moment all by yourself, I'm more interested in hearing what the Gods plan to do to help us."

A tiny smile touched Tobias' lips as he said, "Excellent point." Turning to Broedi he said, "Your turn, I believe."

As Nundle returned to his chair, Broedi took a few steps forward to reclaim his position beside Lady Vivienne's desk and spoke, saying, "My time with Nelnora was *much* different than that of Tobias or Nundle." His face appeared calm, yet his voice trembled slightly. "She shared a number of things with me, the first of which might come as a surprise to you. It certainly did to me." He paused to glance around the room before announcing, "She claims the Celystiela are *not* meddling in mortal affairs."

Immediately, Jak scoffed, "Impossible."

He was not the only one who let out a quiet exclamation of disbelief.

Waving a hand around the room, Jak said, "Look at us. Look where we all were four turns ago. Nundle in the Arcane Republic, Sergeant Trell a soldier in the duke's army, Joshmuel and Zecus separated—one heading east, one heading west. Yet now we all find ourselves at the secret, hidden enclave headed by a baroness and funded by a *duchess*?" Staring at Broedi, he said, "You yourself said the list of perfect coincidences is too long to be plausible."

Broedi had nodded throughout Jak's short outburst and now said, "Note that I said, '*she claims*,' Jak. I did not believe her then and I do not believe her now. Nelnora will do whatever she must to keep balance. Lie, mislead, even kill. She would help level a city full of innocents if she could secure that neither good nor evil prevailed."

"So you believe she is lying?" asked Jak.

"Will Mu's orb rise tomorrow?" replied Broedi.

"Why would she?" asked Zecus. "To what end? What is her goal?"

"Her goal?" rumbled Broedi. He shook his head. "I do not know. But as to why she might lie, that I *can* answer. Unless an Assembly of seven consents, the laws of the Celystiela prevent them from meddling in the affairs of mortals."

Kenders slid forward in her chair and asked, "What would you call what she was doing with the three of you?"

From the back corner of the room, Khin asked, "Tobias, what did the Goddess say to you?"

The tomble eyed the aicenai carefully and said, "That the Sudashians are moving east."

Nodding, Khin asked, "What else?"

Joshmuel added, "That she cannot see Duke Vanson."

Khin glanced back to the Borderlanders. If he was irritated that Joshmuel answered, he did not show it.

"Correct. What else?"

The assembled stared at one another for a few moments. Jak thought through Tobias' report. He could not think of anything else.

"Nothing," muttered the Lady Vivienne. "She said nothing."

Khin smiled ever so slightly, the thin skin on his face stretching to the point where Jak was afraid it might rip like old, too-dry parchment.

"Exactly."

Nikalys shifted in his seat, eliciting a series of wooden creaks from his chair.

"I don't understand. What's that have to do with anything?"

Jak thought he might know and said so.

"Nelnora never told Tobias to *do* anything. And she simply showed Nundle the three windows. She never said a word to him, never told him what to do either."

"So...what?" asked Commander Aiden. "She goes out of her way to be obtuse simply so she can claim no involvement?"

Lady Vivienne said, "It is an explanation that fits."

Broedi rumbled, "And the same one I arrived at myself. According to Nelnora, the Assembly responsible for the White Lions believes that we should be able to repel this threat from Chaos as we did the last." He paused and stared at Kenders and Nikalys. "Along with your help."

"Are they blasted mad?" asked Kenders. "You had the armies of how many duchies then?"

"Five," answered Tobias.

"And how many mages?"

Broedi sighed and said, "A few thousand."

Kenders said, "And we have what? Thirty?"

Lady Vivienne muttered, "Twenty-eight."

Tobias huffed, "That's all?"

Kenders pressed on, saying, "And you had *eight* White Lions then. Eight!" She looked between Broedi and Tobias. "There are only two of you left."

Lady Vivienne corrected her, saying, "Not true. There are eight White Lions. Only two are here."

With a dismissive wave of her hand, Kenders said, "Fine, but we have no idea where the other six are. You haven't seen Miriel since she founded the Manes, my blood parents have disappeared. That leaves—what—three others unaccounted for?"

Jak frowned. His sister was painting a very discouraging, yet wholly accurate picture.

"That is no longer true," rumbled Broedi. He paused, let out a slow sigh, and said, "I now know where we can find another of the Lions."

Chapter 22: Plan

Nikalys stared at Broedi, surprised by the surge of hope flooding his chest.

"First," rumbled Broedi, shifting his gaze to Kenders and Nikalys. "Let me say that it is neither Aryn nor Eliza."

Nikalys exhaled, curious why he again felt relief at the information. He glanced over at Kenders and found an expression of genuine disappointment on her face. He wondered why he did not feel that way.

Lady Vivienne leaned forward in her chair and asked, "Did Nelnora tell you where?"

"She did."

"Wondrous," exclaimed Jak. "Open a port and go get them. Then we'll be slightly less vastly outnumbered and unprepared."

"Were it that simple," rumbled Broedi patiently.

Jak asked, "And why isn't it?"

"Neither Tobias nor Nundle have ever been to the Primal Provinces," answered the hillman. He turned to look at Lady Vivienne. "And unless I am mistaken, neither has the magistrate."

"No, he has not," said the baroness with a shake of her head. "Halawala is the closest he's been, I believe."

Broedi dropped his head and loosed a quiet sigh of inevitability.

"Which means that the three mages we have who can Weave a port cannot reach our destination."

"I could try," suggested Kenders hopefully.

"No," said Broedi quickly. "We do not know what such an attempt might do to you."

Kenders glared at Broedi and said, "You could at *least* let me try."

"You will do nothing of the sort," rumbled Broedi, his glare intense and firm.

Kenders sat back in her chair and folded her arms.

"Fine."

Nikalys kept an eye on his sister, half expecting her to leap up and try anyway.

Lady Vivienne sat back in her chair and said with dejected sigh, "That leaves but one other option. One that will take longer than I would like."

Broedi nodded and said, "I agree, my Lady, but what choice do we have?"

"None that I can think of," murmured the baroness. Her gaze shot over Nikalys' head to stare in the direction of the hearth. "Commander?"

From behind, Nikalys heard boots scuffling followed by Commander Aiden saying, "I'll head straight to the harbor and tell Captain Scrag to get the Sapphire ready."

Nikalys twisted around in his chair to stare at the soldier, surprised. The Sapphire was the lone ship in the enclave's harbor.

"Thank you, Jules," said Lady Vivienne.

The commander glanced at Sergeant Trell.

"Nathan, you're with me."

Sergeant Trell nodded and the pair immediately moved to the doors at the back of the room. As the oaken doors rattled shut, Jak stared to the baroness' desk and asked, "What is that about?" His brother and the Borderlanders seemed equally confused by the soldiers' sudden exit.

Lady Vivienne answered, "Assuming we cannot create a port, which we cannot, the fastest way to the Primal Provinces is to sail over the Sea of Kings." She glanced at Broedi and asked, "You agree, yes?"

The hillman nodded.

"I do."

The noblewoman nodded and stared around the room, her eyes darting over those still before her.

"The only question that remains is who is going on the voyage."

Kenders stared at Broedi and asked, "Shall I guess? Not me."

Broedi gave her a slight smile.

"I am sorry, but it is best you remain here and continue your studies with Khin."

She gave a short nod and said, "As I thought." She turned a sharp eye to Nikalys. "And if I stay, that means Nikalys goes."

"Correct," rumbled the hillman.

Nikalys shifted his gaze to Broedi.

"Wait—what?"

His stomach instantly felt queasy as his thoughts turned to the rough, white-capped Sea of Kings. Gamin had taken the three siblings out to go fishing on a calm afternoon and Nikalys had loathed every moment of it.

Jak took a few steps forward.

"Can I go?"

Nikalys stared back at his brother, incredulous.

"You *want* to go?"

Kenders spun around and glared at Jak.

"Hold a moment! You got to go to Freehaven!"

"And I saw nothing but her villa—" Jak pointed at Lady Vivienne "—the inside of a stuffy carriage, and the Council Hall."

"You still got to go!" exclaimed Kenders.

Lady Vivienne barked, "That's enough!" Looking from Nikalys to Kenders to Jak, she said, "*This* is why I do not include you in planning discussions. The Borderlands have fallen! More than *seventy-thousand* people perished in Gobas! And you are snipping at one another like children denied a trip to the fair!"

Broedi said softly, "Lady Vivienne, please."

The baroness swiveled her head and stared at Broedi.

"I understand your fondness for them. Truly, I do. But try to be objective. They are immature and unready!"

"It does not matter," rumbled Broedi. "Nikalys and Kenders are the Progeny."

"And perhaps one day they will lead us as Indrida's prophecy says, but right now, they could not lead a baby goose to a pond!"

The baroness' words stung Nikalys like a driving Storm Island rainstorm. He stared at her, wanting to insist she was wrong but knowing she was right.

Broedi took a single, long step forward to tower over the baroness' chair, forcing Lady Vivienne to stare straight up to meet his glowering gaze.

"You were *not* on that ridge, Lady Vivienne!" boomed the hillman, his deep voice filling the room and startling Nikalys with its emotion. "Assault after assault came up that slope and throughout *every* one, those two—" he jabbed a finger in Nikalys and Kenders' direction "—put themselves in great personal peril to keep others safe. *That* is true leadership, my Lady. Not sitting in a warm office, sipping tea at your desk, and holding private councils in order to hear yourself speak!"

Nikalys stared at the hillman with wide eyes. He had never seen Broedi this angry.

Broedi hovered over the baroness, glaring at her. Lady Vivienne sat, head tilted back, meeting his hot stare with an icy gaze of her own.

Uneasy, Nikalys shifted in his chair and glanced around the room. Kenders sat with her mouth open. Nundle had pressed himself down into the seat of his chair as if he were trying to hide in plain sight. Khin stood in the corner, his face impassive as always. Tobias alone was moving, shaking his head, a frown on his face. After a moment he spoke, sarcasm seeping into every word.

"Quite an interesting group you have here."

When neither Broedi nor Lady Vivienne broke off their stare to respond, Tobias continued.

"Perhaps I shall go hide from the world again. I've yet to make it to the southern Yutian coast. I've heard the water is bluer than the sky." Turning to eye Nundle, he asked, "You passed through there, yes? Was it nice?"

Nundle's eyes opened wide.

"Ah...I—"

Broedi interrupted Nundle by growling, "Now is not the time for jesting, Tobias."

The tomble White Lion sat tall in his chair and smacked an open palm on the armrest.

"No! It's not, is it? Nor is it the time for seeing who can stack wood higher, Broedi! Should Chaos see this, I am sure he or she would be elated!" Jabbing his walking stick in the direction of Kenders, he said firmly, "As she pointed out, you are *vastly* outnumbered. Incredibly, impossibly, hopelessly outnumbered! I saw tens of thousands of Sudashians in Gobas! And I doubt that was their full force! Can we perhaps discuss our plan to stop them rather than sit here, trying to bore holes in each other's foreheads with stares alone?"

Lady Vivienne shifted her chilly gaze to Tobias.

"We are not as outnumbered as you might think."

The hard glint in Broedi's glare softened a touch.

"What do you mean by that?"

Staring back up to Broedi, she said, "We have allies now."

Broedi took a step back from Lady Vivienne's chair and paused a moment before asking, "Then your plotting was a success?"

"Plotting?" huffed Lady Vivienne. "Call it what you like, but Duchesses Aleece and Adnil were able to publically announce support for the Marshlands. As we sit here, bickering like two merchants over a copper ducat, twenty thousand of the blue and gold are marching to Demetus."

Nikalys raised his eyebrows. He had learned of the alliance days ago, but this was the first he heard of soldiers on the move.

"Careful planning—or 'plotting,' if you prefer," said the baroness. "Allowed us to also have Duchess Adnil's ships sitting off the Southlands' coast in anticipation of the alliance. Once the official proclamation came, those ships docked in Masons Bay. Thirty-thousand Shore Guard are also marching west, through my barony at this very moment." She leaned closer to Broedi and added, "All of which was done without revealing anything about the Progeny or the Shadow Manes. *That*, White Lion, is what I accomplished by sitting here at my desk, sipping tea."

Broedi held the baroness' gaze and remained quiet. It was difficult to surprise Broedi, yet it seemed Lady Vivienne had done just that.

After a few moments, he spoke in a gentle tone, yielding, "That is infinitely better than I could have hoped for, my Lady." He inclined his head a fraction. "I regret my outburst."

Lady Vivienne nodded her acceptance of the apology and—surprisingly—offered her own version of repentance in exchange.

"I as well, Broedi." She shifted her gaze to Nikalys, Kenders, and Jak. "Yet you spoke more truth than not. Their actions have earned them chances I have been unwilling to grant. In order to rectify that…" She turned her full attention onto Nikalys and asked crisply, "Young man, what are your thoughts on who should go to the Provinces?"

Nikalys froze as every set of eyes in the room suddenly shifted to him.

"Me?"

Lady Vivienne nodded.

"Yes, you. What say you?"

Not once since arriving at the enclave had anyone asked his opinion on any matter of importance. His role was to sit in the training grounds, learn how to fight, and be a symbol of hope.

Struck dumb, he glanced over to his sister. Kenders wore an encouraging smile and, just beyond her, Nundle winked his support. Tobias was eyeing him warily, surely reserving judgment. Turning back to the baroness, Nikalys tried to think of what he might say.

Nothing came to mind.

"Uh…"

The corners of Lady Vivienne's mouth curled downward.

Fighting was easier than this. With a weapon in his hand, there was no thought, only reaction. It was all instinct. Wondering if the same approach would work now, he shut his eyes and emptied his mind, letting his thoughts flow like water in a swollen creek. Dozens of possibilities whipped through his head.

"I know exactly what we should do."

The words had slipped from his lips before he knew he was speaking.

"Do you?" asked Lady Vivienne.

Nikalys prayed that he was not about to make a fool of himself. Opening his eyes, he focused on the baroness and said, "Kenders is right. She should stay here and continue her studies. And I should go."

Lady Vivienne's already existing frown gained a measure of open disappointment.

"That was already something—"

Interrupting her quickly, Nikalys said, "And as much as I'd like Jak to go, he should remain here, too."

Lady Vivienne's eyes narrowed.

"And why is that?"

From behind, Jak spoke up, "Yeah, Nik. Why?"

Swiveling in his chair to look at his brother, Nikalys said, "You should stay here and refine your skills as a soldier. You are becoming a good one, Jak. I can see it, I know Sergeant Trell does. And I'm sure Commander Aiden can as well. Your time would be better spent here rather than sitting on a ship for—"He cut off, turned to Broedi, and asked, "How long is the voyage to the Primal Provinces?"

"Five weeks."

Nikalys' heart sunk.

"Truly?"

Broedi nodded.

"Four if the winds are with us."

"Never mind," said Jak, an easy grin creeping over his face. "Who wants to spend an entire turn on a boat?"

"Not me," murmured Nundle emphatically. The tomble's dislike of ships was well-known.

Nikalys turned to Nundle and said, "Sorry, but you need to come."

The redheaded tomble stared at him with uneasy eyes.

"I do?"

Nodding, Nikalys said, "It might take us over a turn to get there via ship, but you can get us back in a moment."

"So can Tobias," implored Nundle.

"No," said Nikalys. "Tobias should stay here."

Tobias chuckled lightly and fixed his gaze on Nikalys.

"And why is that?"

Nikalys turned to face the tomble and said, "Your visions, for one. If you have one about the God of Chaos' armies, you can't tell anyone if you're in the middle of the ocean."

Tobias jabbed his walking stick in Nikalys' direction.

"Hah! But if I have a vision, I could open a port back here and tell someone if what I saw was important."

"Granted, my knowledge of magic is limited, but for a port to work, you must envision your destination perfectly, yes?"

"Correct," rumbled Broedi.

"And does that work for a ship?" asked Nikalys.

"As long as it's anchored," answered Tobias. A frown slipped over his lips. "Which you cannot do in the Sea of Kings."

"Why?" asked Jak.

"It is much too deep," said Broedi.

Glancing at Tobias' bent right leg, Nikalys asked gently, "And are you a strong swimmer?"

"Only in shallow puddles. You have made your point. I shall stay here."

Kenders shot a curious glance at Nikalys. He detected both mild surprise and a touch of admiration in her eyes. Pretending she was not staring at him, he continued with his impromptu plan.

"And since Tobias cannot go, Broedi must. We need at least one White Lion to convince—" Again, he cut off in mid-sentence. Looking to Broedi, he said, "Hold a moment. You never said who the other White Lion was."

Glancing around the room, Broedi rumbled, "Wren Aembyr has been residing for some time now in one of the great tree cities of the Primal Provinces."

"And which one was he?" asked Jak. "Or is 'Wren' a she?"

"*He* is Lamoth's champion," rumbled Broedi. "Originally from a small tijulan settlement near Albonia in the Long Coast."

"He's an ijul?" asked Kenders.

"No," grumbled Tobias. "He's a blasted lout."

The odd comment drew curious stares from most everyone in the room.

Broedi eyed Tobias, and murmured, "Now is not the time, Tobias."

Tobias glanced at the hillman.

"Am I wrong?"

Pressing his lips together, Broedi rumbled, "No, but now is still not the time." He stared about the room and explained, "Most of us had a strained relationship with Wren. He is not easy to be around."

A derisive laugh slipped from Tobias.

"A rabid badger is easier to be around."

Lady Vivienne leaned forward and asked, "I do not care about your personal feelings. Can he help us?"

As one, Broedi and Tobias answered, "Yes."

"*Will* he help us?"

The pair stared at one another for a long moment before Broedi finally answered, "I believe so."

Shaking his head, Tobias muttered, "You always showed more faith in him than he deserved." Glancing about the room, he added, "Wren does what is best for Wren. For my part, I very much doubt he'll help unless he gains something for himself."

A frown on her face, the baroness asked, "Stopping the Cabal should be enough, should it not?"

Tobias shrugged his shoulders.

"Perhaps it will be."

With a quiet sigh, Lady Vivienne said, "Well, we must at least try." She shifted her gaze back to Nikalys. "Please continue, young man. I wish to hear more of your thoughts." The honest tone of her voice surprised Nikalys.

"Of course, my Lady."

He cleared his mind again, giving himself back over to instinct. The approach was working well to this point.

"A number of the Shadow Manes soldiers should go, as well. Only a small force, though. Perhaps thirty or so. And I'd like Sergeant Trell to come as well."

Lady Vivienne regarded him for a long moment before asking, "Why do you require the sergeant? Are you not to lead us all?"

Nikalys could not tell if the question was honest or a trial of sorts. After a moment, he realized he did not care what it was. His answer would be the same.

"They'll follow me, my Lady, but that does not mean I can lead them. Not yet. The men need someone with experience at their head, something I am sorely lacking. Commander Aiden should stay here, which means Sergeant Trell is the best choice. Moreover, I like the man."

Lady Vivienne peered at him with her cool, green eyes long enough that he felt vaguely uncomfortable. Eventually, she turned to stare up at Broedi and conceded, "You were right. They deserve more of a chance than I have given."

Pride shone from beneath the hillman's stoic expression.

"Yes, my Lady. They do."

Scanning the room, Lady Vivienne asked, "Does anyone have any concerns about Nikalys' plan?"

Startled by her choice of words, Nikalys said, "Plan? No, those were merely my thoughts. There is not much of a plan there."

Lady Vivienne said firmly, "There's more than you think, young man. Details can be looked after, but your reasoning is sound." Looking around the room, she called, "Are there any objections?" When there were none, Lady Vivienne peered up at Broedi.

"Did Nelnora share anything else with you?"

Broedi shook his head once.

"Nothing. Only details on where we can find Wren."

In a rustle of wool and silk, Lady Vivienne stood from her chair and announced, "Then it is settled. Nikalys and Nundle, I suggest that you both go and pack. Captain Scrag will want to sail at high tide." She slipped a parchment from beneath a stack on the corner of her desk, stared at it a moment, and then said, "Which appears to be dawn tomorrow. Be ready."

Looking up, Nikalys asked, "Tomorrow?" That seemed incredibly soon.

"We cannot delay," rumbled Broedi.

Nikalys nodded his understanding.

"No, I suppose not."

Lady Vivienne said, "If there is nothing else, then? I would like to go speak with the commander." Her tone was clear. They were being dismissed.

Nikalys pushed himself from his chair—careful not to catch his scabbard—and began to walk to the double doors, following behind Jak and Kenders. Zecus and Joshmuel exited first with heads close together, whispering.

Broedi's deep voice rumbled from behind, "Nikalys?"

Turning around, Nikalys saw Nundle, Tobias, and Lady Vivienne approaching the door. Broedi and Khin were standing close to one another near the desk. The hillman's gaze was fixed on Nikalys.

"When you leave, close the door behind you."

Lady Vivienne's quick pace faltered. Halting, she looked back to regard the hillman.

"You are staying?"

Eyeing the baroness, Broedi asked politely, "May we use your offices for a few moments, my Lady?"

With strained graciousness, Lady Vivienne replied, "Of course, it is no trouble." She resumed her exit, sweeping past Nikalys, a tight, perturbed expression engraved on her face. Nundle had to nearly jump out of her path to avoid being knocked over.

Tobias stood halfway between the double doors and the baroness' desk. His tone slow and deliberate, he asked, "Would you like me to stay?"

The hillman locked eyes with the tomble and shook his head.

"I only mean to discuss an appropriate set of lessons for Kenders while we are gone. Please take the time to familiarize yourself with the enclave. I am sure Nundle would be happy to show you around."

Tobias held Broedi's gaze for a long enough moment that Nikalys was aware of the fire popping again. Glancing between the two White Lions, Nikalys frowned. Something was off here.

Eventually, the tomble spoke.

"If you think it best."

Tobias hobbled past Nikalys and into the hall. Nundle followed.

Giving the two remaining figures in the offices one last curious look, Nikalys drew the doors closed with a soft thud. Peering down at Nundle and Tobias, he asked, "What was that about?"

Nundle began to speak, "There's some—"

Tobias raised a hand swiftly and nodded at the two guards standing beside the door. Nundle immediately closed his mouth. Motioning for them to follow him, Tobias lurched down the empty, torch-lit hallway. Jak and Kenders were already gone, as were Zecus and Joshmuel.

Upon reaching a crossing of halls, Tobias suddenly stopped and asked, "Why am I leading? I have no idea where I'm going." He looked back to Nundle. "Take us someplace where Broedi's ears can't hear us."

Nundle nodded and stepped past Tobias, choosing a windy, random path through the halls. After a few twists and turns, he stopped in the middle of a dim, unoccupied hallway.

"Is this far enough?"

Tobias nodded.

"Quite."

Nikalys stared between the two tombles, his curiosity burning, and asked, "Why the secrecy?"

After checking up and down the hall to ensure they were alone, Tobias looked at Nikalys and whispered, "Broedi lied."

Nikalys blinked in surprises.

"Pardon? He…he lied? How so?"

Leaning on his walking stick, Tobias said, "He is *not* sharing everything."

"And stones don't float," stated Nikalys flatly. "He always holds things closely."

Nundle shook his head.

"That is not what I mean. His time with Nelnora was much different than ours."

Nodding, Nikalys said impatiently, "Which he said himself. What is the issue?"

Tobias peered up at Nikalys with pensive eyes.

"I was in the chamber for but a handful of minutes."

Nundle added, "My time was even shorter."

Nikalys shrugged his shoulders.

"And?"

Tobias cocked an eyebrow, leaned forward, resting on his walking stick, and said, "Broedi was inside long enough that Tenerva brought us tea." His eyes narrowed. "Twice."

"Why so long?" asked Nikalys, suddenly surprised. "What did they talk about?"

"I asked," said Tobias. "And he begged off answering me."

"Me, too," added Nundle. Tiny flames danced in the tomble's green eyes, reflecting the few torches burning in the hall.

Tobias stared down the hall, back in the direction from which they had come, a deep frown on his face.

"Something happened in that chamber that Broedi is hiding from us."

CHAPTER 23: GOODBYE

16th of the Turn of Luraana, 4999

Sabine reached the top of the stairwell, stopped, and peered down the dark hallway. Two oak doors, both recessed in the stone wall, waited on the left. Three torches in rusted sconces lined the right side of the passageway. She eyed the first door worriedly, half-expecting it to creak open.

She grasped both sides of her dress and lifted gently, ensuring that the hemmed bottom was not touching the stone floor. For at least the tenth time since leaving her room, she considered turning around, hurrying down the stairs, through the halls, and back to the bed she shared with Helene.

She bit her lip and shook her head. Things needed to be said. And tonight was her last chance to say them.

"Hells."

The whispered curse slipped out before she could stop it. It seemed as loud as stone cracking stone to her ears.

Taking a deep breath, she stepped from the wintry stairwell into the hallway. She passed the first door carefully, glancing at it briefly. She lingered for a moment, nearly stretching out an arm to knock. Instead, she turned her head forward and continued until she reached the end of the hall. Turning to face the second door, she stared at the wood grains running through the oak in the dim torchlight. She hesitated.

A light breeze tickled her toes, drifting from under the bottom of the door and chilling her feet. She had worn her house sandals in order to move quietly, which had left her toes icy and exposed.

Taking a deep breath and letting it out, she raised her hand and lightly tapped the door three times with her knuckles, barely making a sound.

Suddenly, a light scuffling of boots on stone echoed from the stairwell back down the hall. She whipped her head, her heart nearly leaping from her chest, and peered down the hall.

The stairwell was brightening. Someone was coming.

Reaching up with her fist clenched tight, she knocked again, louder this time.

She waited, staring down the hall with wide eyes. She was moments from rapping on the door one more time when it blessedly opened. Swiveling her head, she stared up into Nikalys' sleepy yet startled face. A patch of hair on the top of his head stuck out awkwardly.

Rubbing his half-shut eyes, he mumbled groggily, "Sabine?"

Placing her left index finger on his lips, she gently shoved her right hand into his chest, driving him backwards into his room. Nikalys' eyes widened as he backpedaled, but he did not resist. The moment she was inside, Sabine spun around and closed the door quickly, ensuring that wood met stone as gently and quietly as possible. The room plunged into moonlit darkness. Pressing an ear to the door, she listened to see if anyone was reacting to her presence in the hall.

Behind her, Nikalys said, "What is—"

Without turning around, she held up a hand and whispered, "Hush!"

Nikalys obeyed.

For the next minute, Sabine listened as the servant shuffled down the hall, humming a soft tune she did not recognize. From sound alone, she determined the man was replacing the torches. When the footsteps retreated down the hall, back to the stairwell, her shoulders slumped.

"Oh, bless the Gods."

"What was that about?" whispered Nikalys. "Better yet, why are you here?"

Sabine took in a tiny breath and rotated in place. Her eyes had adjusted to the gloomy, almost ethereal room. The shadows were midnight blue or black, every object lit up, a ghostly white.

Nikalys stood a few paces from her, perched in a pool of moonlight streaming through the room's single window. He wore a light-colored, long-sleeved knit shirt and loose fitting, matching pants that draped to cover the tops of his bare feet. He was shuffling from foot to foot, doing an almost impromptu dance. His soles slapped on the chilly, stone floor. She supposed it was to keep warm, but it looked absurd.

"I take it your feet are cold?"

Nikalys grinned and nodded, saying, "Quite." Motioning behind him, he asked, "Do you mind?"

She glanced past him and eyed his bed, his heavy blankets tossed aside. For a moment, she thought he was suggesting something untoward. The shock must have reached her face, for when she looked back at Nikalys his eyes were wide.

He began to quickly stammer in a hushed voice, "Gods, no! I didn't mean… I was just—" Furiously pointing to the floor by the bed, he whispered, "Boots. I meant I want my boots."

She stared back to the bed and saw a pair of leather boots lying on the floor.

"Please, yes, of course."

She was glad it was dark. It would be harder for him to see her blushing.

As he hurried over to his bed, sat down, and began to pull on his boots, Sabine shook her head. This was not how she wanted things to start at all.

Sabine stepped lightly, crossing the small room and inspecting its contents as she went. This was the first time she had been here and she was struck by how bare the room was.

"Where are all of your things?"

Shoving his right foot into the second leather boot with a soft thump, he nodded his head in the direction of the door.

"There. Ready to go to the harbor in the morning."

Sabine turned and spotted a large pile of sacks sitting to the right of the door. It appeared as if he were planning on never coming back.

"Goodness, did you pack your entire life in there?"

She continued to stare at the pile of sacks as if they were terribly interesting, waiting for a response. She could feel his eyes on her.

"Sabine, why are you here?"

She drew in a short, quick breath, fortifying herself, and swiveled back to stare at Nikalys. He was still sitting on the bed, his elbows resting on his knees, a blanket now draped around his shoulders.

Forcing herself to hold his gaze, she said, "Kenders told me you were leaving tomorrow."

He nodded once.

"I am."

A handful of thudding heartbeats passed.

"Were you just going to leave without saying farewell? Helene would be crushed."

A faint smile touched his lips and he dropped his head. "I wanted to stop by and say something this evening, but…" Trailing off, he gripped his hands together and squeezed tight. "I can stop by in the morning before I leave. It'll be early, though. High tide is at dawn."

"That's fine. I'll wake her."

Nikalys nodded.

"Then I'll be there."

"Good."

She smiled as if everything was settled.

A long, awkward silence stretched out, a faint whistling of air the only thing that filled it.

She wondered if she should leave now, as though the entire reason for her visit was a gentle reminder to say goodbye to Helene when it was nothing more than pretense. Instead, she took a few quick steps toward the window and stared outside.

A thin fog coated the world in a translucent haze that glowed in the moonlight. Peering through the mist, she could only make out the tops of a few bare-branched treetops along the bluff. She spotted the remains of a large nest, its twigs and straw still bunched together in a crook between branch and trunk. The faint sounds of waves crashing on the rocky shore drifted through the night.

The scene was serene and peaceful, nothing like the strange, confusing storm of emotions raging inside her. Her chest felt tight.

She shivered, defenseless against the nighttime chill.

"Gods, it's cold up here."

She heard Nikalys rise from the bed and approach. She kept her eyes straight, though, suddenly unsure why she had come. This felt more wrong than right.

He stopped behind her and draped a heavy wool blanket over her shoulders. She wrapped her fingers around the rough fabric, pulled it tight around her, and murmured, "Thank you."

"You're welcome."

His hands lingered on her shoulders for a moment before withdrawing.

Nikalys whispered, "The moons look rather ominous, don't they?"

Sabine nodded silently. Both orbs hung low in the sky, shining through the mist, lustrous halos of faint rainbows surrounding them.

He continued, "When I was little, Mother used to sit with us outside at night. We'd all stare at the sky and she'd point out the constellations, tell us their names."

A wistful smile graced Sabine's lips.

"My mother did the same with me."

The quiet returned.

After a few moments, Nikalys said softly, "I never said anything to Mother, but staring up there, at the moons and stars…I always felt a little uneasy."

"Why?"

"I could not tell you," whispered Nikalys. "Then or now." He paused a moment. When he resumed speaking, his voice had changed. A note of caution had slipped into his tone. "I will never deny the beauty of the night sky, but something about it scares me. I want to turn away as much as I want to stare."

Sabine's eyes narrowed.

"You aren't talking about the sky, are you?"

There was a long pause before he muttered, "No."

Sabine pressed her lips together and, before she lost her nerve, spoke in a firm and quiet tone.

"I have feelings for you."

She continued to stare out the window, mildly upset with herself. She could face a horde of oligurts rushing up a hill, yet a conversation with a man rattled her.

She heard—and felt on the nape of her neck—a heavy sigh.

"Sabine, I—"

"I am going to say what I must, Nikalys. Do not try to shush me."

He drew a breath to respond, paused a moment, and then exhaled.

"Go on, then."

Nodding firmly, Sabine said, "To be clear, Nikalys Isaac, you do not get to tell me how to feel or what I want. Jak is a good man. A very good man."

"Yes, he is, which is why it would be best—"

"Stop right there. If you say 'he can have me' again, you will be sporting a black eye on your voyage."

"I wasn't going—"

"Let me finish!"

A quick, exasperated sigh slipped from Nikalys, yet he remained quiet.

"Now," began Sabine. "For all the wondrous qualities your brother possesses, he lacks one very important one: he is not you." Her voice dropped to whisper. "The day my father died, you were the one who rushed to my rescue, without any thought of your own safety. I will *never* forget what you did for me and Helene that day, Nikalys. *Never.*"

"Jak helped, too."

"But you were the first one down that hill."

"Jak was right behind me."

"Blast it, Nik! Stop it! Stop trying to sell me your brother like he's a charm at a market!" She gave a short shake of her head, took a steadying breath, and continued. "You have feelings for me, do you not?"

She paused for a breath, giving him the chance to deny. He did not.

"And something more than duty—or your concern for Jak's feelings—is holding you back. Am I right?"

She hesitated again, hoping that, this time, he might say something. Yet only silence greeted her plea.

Pressing her lips together, she nodded, and said, "Fine. Hold your tongue." She tried not to be angry, knowing she would regret it, but some heat slipped into her tone. "But think about what I've said while you're gone. I expect you'll have plenty of time to do so starting tomorrow."

She was not expecting Nikalys' response: a soft, bemused chuckle. The quiet laugh washed away her anger and broke her resolve. She could hear his smile and had to see it. Whirling around, she stared up into his eyes, glinting in the moon-light. The slight, lopsided smile she had imagined rested on his lips, kind and gentle. A half-dozen other emotions muddied his amusement, however. Sadness. Guilt. Hope. Happiness. Affection. Worry.

On pure, sudden impulse, Sabine took a step forward, stood on her tiptoes, and kissed him lightly on the cheek. It felt natural to do, up until the moment her lips brushed his skin. Nikalys froze at her touch, flinching ever so slightly. Panic rushed though Sabine and she immediately withdrew.

"I'm sorry. I…I shouldn't have done that."

He stared at her with an honest, stunned expression, seemingly at a loss for words.

Pushing her embarrassment deep inside, she summoned forth a bit of cool calmness and looked him steadily in the eyes. Pretending the past few moments had not occurred, she said in an almost-formal tone, "Please do not forget to say goodbye to Helene in the morning."

After a moment, Nikalys mumbled, "Of...of course."

With a prim, curt nod, Sabine said, "Good." She needed to get out of here. Sweeping past him, she hurried to the door.

"Sabine?"

A flicker of hope dashing through her, she turned around and stared, a tiny smile gracing her lips.

"Yes?"

Nikalys pointed at her.

"You still have my blanket."

Sabine gaped at him for a moment before her eyes narrowed to a pair of thin slits. A single, whispered word slipped from her lips.

"Unbelievable."

With a short huff, she released the blanket and let it drop to the floor. Spinning around, she grabbed the door's rope handle and pulled. She hurried down the hallway and never looked back. As she reached the top of the stairs, she heard a soft rattle as his door closed. She rushed down the stairs quickly, a scowl on her face. She should have stayed in her room.

CHAPTER 24: SLAVERS
17ᵗʰ of the Turn of Luraana, 4999

The cart hit a hole, jostling Nimar sideways, into the side panel. His temple struck the wood with a dull thud, prompting a low, painful moan from his throat. He started to crack his eyelids open, but shut them tight almost immediately. The sky above was ablaze with the light of a thousand bonfires.

He reached out with his left hand, hoping the sudden jolt had not displaced the white crane that had been sitting with him. As he felt about blindly, a tiny shred of sanity fought through the sludge of his mind, reminding him that there was no bird. He was hallucinating again. The wounds he had received from the Dust Man had festered, bringing the expected fever along with it. Lucidity and delusion had been battling for control of his mind and sanity was losing.

A harsh, rough voice, full of reprimand, called out, "Blast it, Golt! Be careful! You're going to break an axle!"

A bad-tempered, scratchy voice replied, "Make up your mind! You want to go fast or slow?"

Nimar recognized that voice as belonging to Golt, which meant the first had been their father.

"Keep that tone with me and I'll cut out your tongue and feed it to you!"

Without doubt, that was their father.

"Why don't we leave the cart here?" asked Golt. "We can take two horses and ride hard after them."

"What about Nimar?" growled his father.

Golt hesitated before saying, "We can come back for him later."

Not trusting his brother and father to come back for him, Nimar tried to protest against his brother's plan, but all that came out was a mumbled moan. His tongue did not want to work.

A distinct creak of wood from the front of the cart resonated over the rhythmic squeaks of the bed. A moment later, Golt announced, "He's awake."

"Of course he is, you muck-feeder. A corpse would awake with the way you're driving."

"We might get to find out if that's so," said Golt. "He don't look too good."

Nimar might have been upset with Golt had he not already come to the same conclusion himself. His death was inevitable. When wound-rot set in, without medicine from a healer, one was dead within days.

He drifted in and out of lucidity for an unknown amount of time, bouncing about the back of the cart, when a sudden, strange howl cut through the air. The cry reminded him of the gray-nosed wolves that roamed the edges of the swamps of his youth, only it was deeper. Much deeper. The wolf's call hung in the air for another heartbeat before cutting off abruptly.

Nimar was about to mark the cry as hallucination when Golt asked, "What in the Nine Hells was that?"

A second howl ripped through the air, deeper than the first and from a different direction. A third howl joined in, quickly followed by a fourth. Then a fifth.

A tiny, wild smile crept over his lips as his fever surged ahead, pushing aside rational thought. Wolves were hunting them, and for some mad reason, that was humorous to him.

"What do we do?!" called Golt. "Hold! Where are you going?!"

In a sharp, frantic panic, his father shouted, "Save yourself!"

Nimar heard the sound of horse's hooves galloping away. Golt cursed and began screaming at the cart horses to run, repeatedly snapping the reins. Nimar began to bounce about the back of the cart as it rattled and creaked with each dip and hole it struck. He started to giggle.

The wolves' cries changed, shifting form long, drawn-out howls to short, quick barks. Golt began blubbering like a scared child.

"Blast the Gods! What are those?!"

His brother sounded terrified. Nimar's wild giggling grew into outright laughing.

A horse's terror-filled whinny cut through the air, followed shortly by a man screaming. The cries belonged to his father and stopped as quickly as they started.

A sharp crack exploded under Nimar. The cart bed smacked into the ground and Nimar slid out the back along with most of the sacks. As he rolled through mud and grass, Nimar heard Golt cursing loudly.

As he came to a rest, Nimar opened his eyes and stared about him. The day was still painfully bright, but he blinked through the glare to spot the wagon bouncing away, its rear axle snapped and wheels dragging. Golt was—somehow—still seated in the driver's bench, screaming as he and the cart rattled over the prairie. Nimar stared at the beasts running alongside the wagon, snapping at the horses' legs and began to laugh hysterically. Wolves were not hunting them. Mongrels were.

One of the horses pulling the cart went down, tripped up by the jaws of an all gray beast. The second horse fell an instant later. The poles attached to the horses' harness jammed into the ground, sending the cart tumbling. Golt went with it, his legs splayed apart as he flew into the air. It was the last time Nimar saw his brother.

Golt's screams filled the barren countryside, turning to cries of pain, before cutting off altogether with a sickening, soft gurgle.

Nimar lay on his side, chortling while waiting to be eaten, and happened to look upon his festering wrist wound. It was a mottled mixture of unhealthy yellows and browns. Some of his flesh even looked black. The stink of the wound-rot filled his nose and he began to retch through his laughter. The sane sliver of his mind was repulsed by his condition. After a torturous period of uncontrollable heaving, Nimar eventually lay still with his eyes closed again, breathing hard.

A soft, wet puff of air nearby prompted him to crack open his eyelids. Five mongrels stood in a line between him and the ruined cart, their mouths wet and red with blood. The perfect blending of man and wolf was unsettling. One of them— all brown with patches of white on its muzzle and arms—stood upright on two pawed-feet, its yellow-eyed gaze locked on Nimar. The mongrel's nose twitched.

In wet, heavily accented Argot, the beast growled, "Where is the leather pouch that this was attached to?" It took a few steps closer to him and crouched down.

Nimar's gaze shifted to a rich-looking piece of leather the mongrel held in a calloused hand. He was as surprised that mongrels had hands as he was by the question and the presence of the strap.

Lucidity reigned for a moment, allowing Nimar to mumble in honest confusion, "Where did you get that?" He swore it belonged to the pouch they had stolen from the nobleman.

The mongrel leaned forward and huffed.

"The pouch! Where is it?"

Nimar choked out, "It's gone. A Dust Man took it."

The beast growled, "You are sure?"

With great effort, Nimar nodded.

"He stole it from us."

A few puffs of wet air escaped from the mongrel's jaws. Spittle dripped to the ground.

"The thief complains of a thief?"

Nimar glared at the monster, irritated that the beast was apparently laughing at him. He tried to reach down to his boot to retrieve his bone-handle dagger, but he was slow and weak. The mongrel's eyes shifted to where Nimar stretched and, reaching down, the monster grabbed the knife first. Nimar dropped his head to the ground in defeat.

"Do what you will, mongrel. End me. Rip my throat out."

The animal's black lips drew back to reveal yellowed teeth as it sneered, "You reek of death, man. I would taste your rot for a season."

It moved suddenly, driving Nimar's dagger into his chest. Oddly, there was no pain, only a strange warming sensation. The beast pulled the dagger free, stood, and walked away with the blade still clasped in its hand, blood dripping to the ground.

Nimar's eyes fluttered shut for the last time.

CHAPTER 25: YEARDAY

18ᵗʰ of the Turn of Luraana, 4999

With each breath that Kenders took of the cold, wet air, the spicy char of oak smoke tickled the back of her throat. If she inhaled too deeply, she might cough. She tilted her head back and stared at the cloud-choked sky, the chilly breeze whipping through the streets of Claw leeching the heat from her body. Tiny droplets of a cold, heavy mist pelted her exposed skin. Kenders silently cursed the weather. Again.

From beside her, Khin's wispy voice interrupted her misery.

"What are your thoughts?"

An exasperated huff escaped her lips. Her thoughts were many.

That she hated this lesson more than all the other ones put together. That Miriel Syncent must have been mad to choose one of the least hospitable places in the duchies for the enclave. That Khin was perhaps the worst teacher anyone could have. That this was—beyond any doubt—the worst yearday of her life.

She did not voice any of that, however, as she turned to stare at the aicenai. With forced calm, she said, "That I should seek out the fibríaal by searching for the imprint his Weave has left."

Khin stood motionless, his eyes closed. After an interminably long pause, his eyelids opened, he turned his head to face her, and he studied her in silence. She gnawed on the inside of her cheek, waiting for some response. She wanted Khin to say something. Anything.

To keep herself from screaming, she looked past Khin and down one of the narrow, gravel-covered streets of Claw, watching the townspeople go about their business. A man with a wheelbarrow full of leaden gray rocks eyed her and Khin as he crossed the alley. Another villager, one cleaning a string of pointy-nosed fish hanging between two posts, shot the pair yet another curious glance. He had been watching them all morning.

Finally, Khin spoke.

"If you spent a fraction of the time thinking about ways to solve this problem as you do ogling the townspeople, you could have been done by now."

Kenders bit her lip hard enough that she tasted blood. With as much respect as she could summon, she said, "I do not understand how I am to complete the task before me."

Khin faced forward and closed his eyes.

"Then we shall stand here until you do. I welcome the breeze."

"What do you expect me to do?"

"Solve the problem," answered Khin. "Preferably before night comes."

Kenders faced forward to stare down the main street and began to think through the situation yet again.

Earlier this morning, Khin had brought her to this very spot in the center of Claw, conjured a tiny fibríaal of pure Fire, and whispered a set of instructions to the creature. Off it had run, startling people as it scampered down the street. A man's small dog had run after the little man of flame as it turned a corner, only to come back yelping moments later, the hair on its nose singed.

Kenders patiently waited for instructions, wondering about her teacher's intent. A long while passed before Khin said softly, "Tell me where the fibríaal is now." She had taken but a single step when Khin stopped her by saying, "Do it from here. You are not to move." As she had stared at him blankly, wondering how she was supposed to do that, he gave her one more instruction "You may ask me a single question. Choose wisely."

At first, she had welcomed the unique challenge. She stood in complete silence, choosing her approach carefully. She thought about sending out a small army of her own tiny fibríaals, each with an order to hunt down Khin's fire man, but dismissed the idea. A dozen creatures of stone, air, lighting, or water running throughout Claw would have caused too much chaos.

Since then, nothing else had come to mind. She had no idea how to track Khin's Weave. Nor had she asked her lone question. She was determined to do this on her own, without the aicenai's help.

Hoping for some random inspiration, she turned her attention to her surroundings and examined the village around her. She and Khin stood in the middle of a narrow street, a tailor's shop before them on their left and a bakery on the right. Unlike most of the stone buildings in Claw, the bakery had a wooden roof rather than a thatched one made of straw. Two large windows were street-side with another in the alley. A single, black ebonwood door stood half-open beneath an overhang of wood that jutted from the roof. Through the right window, Kenders could make out the faint orange glow of the baker's ovens inside. She wondered if the fire fibríaal might have doubled back to hide in the oven. It only took her a moment to dismiss the option. That would be too obvious.

Turning to look at the opposite side of the street, she scanned the tailor's shop. Three windows lined the front, along with a bright crimson door shut tight against the cold. She briefly wondered if the fibríaal was in there before reasoning that a man of fire in a shop full of cloth was an incredibly bad idea. Her teacher was maddening, but not mad.

Standing in the cold, Kenders yet again arrived at what seemed to be the most likely location within Claw for the fibríaal to hide: the forge at the smithy. And, yet again, a quiet sense of melancholy gripped her as she pictured the building in her mind's eye, the place where her parents had lived during their time in Claw.

Shortly after arriving at the enclave, Gamin had offered to take the three Isaac children there. The trio followed the mage through Claw, hearts pounding, and stepped up to the stone building. Gamin explained the situation to the current blacksmith and the man not only graciously let them enter the shop, he stood with Gamin outside, giving the three siblings a few quiet moments alone. Kenders, Nikalys, and Jak had stood in the dim, smoky interior for a long time.

Sighing, she dipped her head and stared at the street's gravel. These bouts of sorrow were coming less frequently, yet they had not lost their sharp edge. And with Nikalys gone, she felt more alone than ever.

Hearing a rustle of cloth to her side, she lifted her head and looked over at her teacher. Khin was staring at her. She was surprised to spot a rare flicker of emotion in his ice-blue eyes. She swore it was sympathy.

She stared at him, confused.

"Why are you—?"

The door to the tailor's shop suddenly rattled opened, startling the quiet solitude of the street. A woman stepped out, wearing a long-sleeved, russet-colored dress with an amber scarf pulled tightly over her head. Underneath her left arm was a white bundle of cloth, rolled up in a cylinder. The woman shut the door behind her, turned to enter the street, and started as she noticed Kenders and Khin.

Kenders wondered how it was possible that she had not noticed them before now. They had been standing there all morning.

The woman stood in place for a moment, the expression on her face making it obvious she knew who they were. Kenders offered a friendly smile and the woman gave an unsure grin in return as she began strolling across the street, toward the bakery. Upon reaching the building, she gently knocked on the half-open door and waited, shooting another furtive glance in Kenders and Khin's direction. After a few moments, it swung inward and a man with wild black hair and a Southlands-style beard filled the empty doorway, a smile spreading across his face.

"Good days ahead, Arlien."

With a short bow, the woman responded, "And good memories behind, Bannick."

Kenders knew she should not eavesdrop, but it was hard not to. The pair stood but fifteen paces away.

"Mild today, isn't it?" asked Bannick, glancing up at the choppy, gray skies.

Kenders assumed the baker was jesting. There was nothing mild about the weather here.

"Always with the sweet, aren't you?" asked Arlien with a smile. Peering out from beneath the bakery's overhang to scan the sky, she added, "A storm is coming, I think."

"One always is."

Arlien pulled the white bundle from under her arm and held it out to the baker.

"We have finished your new aprons."

"Ah, thank you," said Bannick. "I was not expecting them until the end of the week at the earliest." He unfurled one of the aprons, held it up in front of him, and nodded his approval. "These will do nicely. And I shall owe you a favor for early delivery."

"Perhaps I can claim that favor now? I was hoping that you might---oh, never mind. It will be too much trouble."

Rolling up the apron, Bannick said, "Please. Ask your question. I'll be happy to help if I can."

"Well, I know that you have a season's schedule you follow, but, well, Solen's yearday is next week and I thought perhaps you could make him a few loaves of the rosemary and onion bread he likes so much. If you have any rosemary left, that is. I would be happy to pay extra."

Assuming that Solen was Arlien's husband, Kenders smiled. The gesture was a sweet one.

Bannick shook his head and said, "You will do no such thing! I'd be happy to make it for him. Will three loaves do?"

"Oh, that's more than enough!"

As Kenders eyed the woman, her slight smile grew a fraction. One simple question and Arlien got exactly what she had wanted.

A moment later, the grin slipped away, her eyes widened, and a sudden chill swept through her, one that had nothing to do with cold weather. She shut her eyes.

"Hells."

As Arlien thanked Bannick and hurried back across the street, Kenders kept her eyes closed, pretending as though she were deep in a trance. The moment the door to the tailor's shop shut, Kenders let out a heavy sigh, opened her eyes, and stared at Khin's profile. Her lips tightened as she spotted a tiny smile on his face. For the aicenai, it was akin to laughing aloud.

Keeping her voice even and direct, she asked, "Khin, where is the fibríaal?"

"Gone," murmured Khin, turning his head to face her. "After it burnt the dog, I dismissed it. Had you been paying attention as you should have, you would have surely felt it."

Kenders held his gaze, determined not to show any external reaction. Like most of Khin's lessons, this one made her upset. For once, however, he was not the target of her ire. She was mad at herself. Her stubbornness, an admitted flaw of hers, had led to this.

Khin murmured, "Good. You are learning."

Kenders focused on the aicenai, her eyes narrowing. At times, it seemed he knew exactly what she was thinking.

Khin said, "Your expressions are as easy to read as new ink on fresh parchment. That is another thing we will work on. A worthy adversary will anticipate your every move if you are unable to control your thoughts and emotions."

Frowning, Kenders nodded.

"I suppose you're right."

"No. I *am* right. Do not suppose I am."

Some of her irritation shifted back to Khin.

The aicenai eyed her, turned to stare at the bakery, and said, "Wait here. I must retrieve an order."

Nodding, Kenders watched her teacher approach the bakery door and knock with his bony hand. While he waited for the baker and she waited for Khin, she shivered as a gust of wind surged past. Cold and wet, she thought about Nikalys and the others at sea, wondering how they were handling the weather.

Two mornings back, Kenders and Jak had braved a pre-dawn drizzle and went down to the docks to see everyone off. Nikalys was not there when they arrived, much to the vociferous consternation of the Sapphire's captain. Every few moments, the white-haired man would unleash an impressive string of curses about missing the tide, hoping 'the blasted, ground-kissing son of a Lion' might grace them with his presence. The longer they waited, the redder Kenders' cheeks turned. Jak stared at the man with awe in his eyes. A slight smile rested upon Broedi's lips throughout the tirade. From the few exchanges between the captain and the hillman, Kenders reasoned the pair had known one another for some time.

The two-mast ship that awaited her brother seemed overcrowded in Kenders' opinion. Twenty leaden-footed soldiers stood on the deck, staring in wonder at the two dozen sailors nimbly scurrying about, preparing the ship for departure. Along with Sergeant Trell, Kenders spotted a few other familiar faces: the excellent young swordsman, Wil Eadding, and the former Tracker of the Constables, Cero.

Eventually, Nikalys arrived, rushing down the rocky steps etched into the side of the bluff, carrying an impossible number of sacks and satchels. Kenders cringed as she watched him dash down, worrying that he was going to fall on the wet rocks. Whether by the grace of Ketus or Horum's gift, he managed to make it to the dock without tumbling.

Broedi and the others crossed the plank leading from the dock to the Sapphire, leaving the trio of siblings alone on the dock. Even Captain Scrag ceased his screaming briefly, allowing the three some peace for their whispered farewells. Kenders tried—yet again—to give their mother's necklace to Nikalys for his journey, but he insisted that she keep it, saying that at least she would know if he drowned at sea. The jest was a clumsy one and nobody smiled.

Once Nikalys boarded the ship, Captain Scrag wasted no time, calling for the Sapphire to cast off. Jak and Kenders stood alone on the docks, watching the ship drift from the harbor. Once it slipped past the rocky bluff and out of sight, the pair hurried up the stairs, into the enclave, and up to Jak's room. From there, they stared out his window and watched the Sapphire sail away until the blanket of misty rain swallowed the vessel.

Now, as she stood alone in wind-whipped Claw, her chin to chest, a tear of worry rolled down her cheek. She reached up to wipe it away and murmured, "Joyful yearday to me."

Hearing the crunch of footsteps on gravel, she looked up and found Khin approaching her and holding a circular package wrapped in cheesecloth. The aicenai stopped before her and held out the package. Kenders stared blankly at both it and him before realizing he meant for her to take it.

"For me?"

"Yes."

Reaching out, she accepted the package.

"What is it?"

"A gift," replied the aicenai softly.

Kenders eyebrows arched in surprise.

"Truly?"

"That is how your kind celebrates your 'yearday', yes?"

Kenders stared at her teacher, stunned. She had not mentioned anything about the significance of the day to anyone, least of all to Khin. As far as she knew, only Jak and Sabine knew the date.

"How did you—" She stopped, realizing the answer was obvious. "Of course... you were here when I was born."

"Correct. Now, please. Open your gift."

Kenders dropped her gaze to the package in her hands, brought the cloth-wrapped parcel to her face, and took a deep breath. A mouth-watering mixture of a familiar sweet-yet-tart scent swirled with the buttery aroma of fresh-baked crust. The smell transported her back to the Isaac family kitchen, sitting at the table and helping her mother bake them with a portion of the family's harvest. Her eyes widened as her gaze shot back to Khin.

"A grape tart?! How...how could you know?"

"I approached your brothers in the commons the evening before the Sapphire departed. They suggested this."

Kenders gave Khin a grateful smile, instantly feeling terrible for every mean thing she had ever said or thought about him.

"Thank you, Khin. This is very kind of you."

"You are welcome."

Kenders breathed in the wondrous aroma again. Looking back to the aicenai, she asked, "Wherever did you find the grapes?"

"I enlisted the help of Magistrate Ulius yesterday. We opened a port to Hala-wala and found some in season. They might be sweeter than what you are used to."

Kenders could not believe the effort to which Khin had gone to for her. Shaking her head, she said, "They will be perfectly fine, I am sure."

Motioning in the direction of the castle that loomed to the east, Khin said, "I had arranged for people to meet us in the commons. I do hope they are still there. I had not expected today's lesson to take this long."

Kenders cheeks flushed red.

"I am sorry, Khin."

"Do not be," replied the aicenai plainly. "You are learning." Khin shifted his gaze back to the castle. "Let us go. You have a celebration to attend and I must begin my afternoon meditation."

Shaking her head, Kenders said firmly, "Not today, Khin. *You* are coming with *me*." Lifting up the wrapped tart, she added a friendly threat. "You would offend me ever so deeply if you did not try some of your gift."

A small smile stretched over his thin lips as he inclined his head.

"I accept your offered hospitality."

The pair turned and strode through the mist, back toward the castle.

CHAPTER 26: IMPULSE

Kenders and Khin arrived shortly after midday meal was over to find the commons nearly empty. The tables with people at them had only a few souls each, except for the one favored by her and her brothers. That table was almost full.

Sabine and Helene were there, as was Jak, of course. Zecus, Joshmuel, and the other Borderlander, Boah, lined one side of the table, too. Commander Aiden was there when she arrived, but excused himself in short order to attend afternoon drills. Jak and Zecus rose to go with him, but the soldier effectively ordered both to stay and sit with Kenders. He offered her good wishes and left, carrying a slice of grape tart with him.

Lady Vivienne surprised everyone by making an appearance to "convey my desire that you experience a joyful yearday." Once Kenders gracefully accepted the kind words, the baroness gave a curt nod and hastily exited the room, leaving a table full of people with raised eyebrows and hidden smiles. She did not take any of the grape tart.

The tomble White Lion, Tobias, was there as well, apparently at the behest of Khin. He sat at the far end of the table and remained quiet, keeping to himself. He was not overtly rude—if someone asked him a question, he would answer it—but he seemed content to remain in a contemplative silence. More than once, Kenders caught the White Lion's eyes on her, staring. It reminded her of how Broedi watched her and Nikalys the first week or so after he had found them.

Khin spoke fewer words than Tobias even. After a time, she wondered if he had chosen to complete his afternoon meditation during the party.

Despite their shared quiet, the celebration was by no means dull. Jak spoke enough for five souls during the gathering, striving to share every embarrassing story about Kenders he could. She winced with each humiliating revelation, carefully watching Zecus' reaction and hoping the tales were not affecting his opinion of her. Thankfully, the stories seemed to bring a smile to the handsome Borderlander's face, but there was a strange tightness to every grin, a twinge of downheartedness coloring every laugh. Zecus' mind was elsewhere.

They spent the bulk of the afternoon there, and for brief moments, Kenders forgot about the troubles facing them. Unfortunately, as is often the case, the revelry was short-lived.

Joshmuel and Boah excused themselves first, leaving just as the first of the Shadow Mane soldiers began to arrive for eveningmeal. A quick, purposeful look passed between father and son that no one but Kenders seemed to notice. She pretended she did not either, acting as though she was terribly interested in Jak's current embarrassing tale: an account of when she had accidently sewn an apron she was working on to the dress she was wearing.

Soon thereafter, Helene fell asleep in her sister's arms. Sabine explained to the table that the girl had been sleeping poorly since Nikalys' departure, but Kenders knew better. Jak offered to carry Helene back to the sisters' lodgings, an offer which Sabine accepted after a moment's hesitation. Whether or not Jak noticed the pause, Kenders did not know, but she certainly did and it surprised her. To her eye, Jak and Sabine had been getting along exceptionally well as of late.

Khin and Tobias left at the same time as Jak and Sabine, both claiming they had other things that required their attention. Everyone's sudden departure left Kenders alone at the long, wooden table with Zecus across from her. The empty tart dish, filled now with nothing more than pastry crumbs, rested between them.

A few moments of quiet passed. The pair exchanged an uncomfortable smile or two as Kenders glanced around the commons, trying to think of something about which to speak. The large room was close to being half-full now, yet none of the Shadow Manes sat near the same table as her and Zecus. The low din of conversation filled the hall, broken occasionally by an outburst of laughter here and there. The aroma of chicken roasting with Harvest onions and kives filled the room.

Kenders peered at Zecus.

"It would seem we are having chicken this evening."

Zecus nodded.

"Yes, it would."

She smiled again, unsure what to say next.

"Ah. So how is your training going?"

"Well enough. I am still having trouble with the long blade."

Kenders nodded.

"Yes…yes, I heard…"

Another few uncomfortable moments had passed when Zecus leaned forward to rest his arms on the tabletop.

"And your studies? How are they?"

Shrugging her shoulders, she said, "Well enough." She smiled. "I am still having trouble with Khin."

Nodding, Zecus grinned and said, "So I have heard."

They shared a quiet chuckle before both going quiet again. Kenders had been less uncomfortable when she had met the two duchesses than she was now. She was a moment away from claiming the need to work on Khin's meditation exercises so she could escape when Zecus cleared his throat and spoke.

"There is something I must tell you."

It felt as if a lump of lard suddenly appeared in her stomach. Thinking he was about to share his feelings for her, she leaned forward quickly. She should respect his tradition. She should speak first.

"Zecus, I—"

"I am leaving the enclave."

Kenders stared at him with her mouth frozen open, unsure she had heard him correctly.

"You're...you're leaving?"

Zecus nodded once, keeping his deep brown eyes fixed on her.

"Yes. With my father and Boah."

"What—" She cut off and shook her head. "No, why? Wait—no. When?"

After a moment's pause, he murmured, "Tonight."

Her eyes widened a fraction.

"Tonight? You're leaving tonight?"

"Yes," said Zecus, his tone firm. "You heard what happened to Gobas. Chaos' army is marching east, towards Demetus. Towards our families. And when they reach the city, they will do to it what they did to Gobas. *My* family is there, Kenders. Alone. Wondering if father is coming back, if I'm alive or dead." He shook his head. "We will *not* leave our families to die."

Kenders sat in silence, unable to argue with what Zecus was saying. He did not need to explain the primal urge to protect one's family. She admired his bravery and dedication, yet a large part of her wanted him to stay. And before she knew what was happening, that part took over.

"But I don't want you to go."

The moment the words escaped, she wished she could grab them and stuff each one back into her mouth. It was an incredibly selfish thing to say.

Zecus bristled at her comment. She could see his shoulders tense.

"I must."

Shaking her head, Kenders tried to explain.

"I know you do. I'm sorry. I simply meant that...I...ah..."

She trailed off, afraid to give voice to what needed to be said. Steeling herself, she set her jaw and spoke.

"Zecus Alsher, I have feelings for you."

For a moment, he did not move. In fact, he did not react at all. He continued staring at her blankly, his mouth parted slightly. Her heart was pounding so hard, she wondered if he could hear it over the din of the dozens of conversations in the commons.

Worried that she had committed some breach of tradition, she whispered, "Zecus? Did you—"

He reached across the table and touched the back of her hand.

"I am fond of you as well."

Her shoulders slumped and she let out a relieved sigh.

"Oh, thank the Gods."

Hearing Zecus speak the words aloud meant everything to her. Countless assurances from Sabine, Jak, Nikalys, and even Joshmuel did not compare to the quiet declaration.

His touch lingered for a few moments before he withdrew his hand. A slight, almost, bittersweet smile touched his lips.

"However, our feelings change nothing. I still must leave tonight."

Nodding quickly, Kenders said, "I understand. You do not need to tell me how important family is."

His grin turned grateful, his eyes swelling with relief.

"Thank you. Knowing that will make the long journey almost bearable."

Her cheeks flushing, she dropped her head, letting her gaze fall upon the pottery tart plate. As she stared at the crumbs, the impracticality of what Zecus was about to do struck her. Glancing up, she asked, "How do you plan to get there?"

Zecus gave a slight shrug of his shoulders.

"How else? We will walk. At least two of us will while the other rides Simiah. We shall take turns so we do not grow tired."

Kenders' mouth fell open.

"You're going to *walk* all the way there? That's a poor plan! No, pardon me. That's not a poor plan. It's a mad one!"

"What else can we do?" asked Zecus. "We will *not* leave our family to die."

"It will take you at least four turns to reach Demetus! Perhaps five! Chaos' army will have reached the city long before you!"

"I will not sit here and do nothing, knowing they are doomed to die!"

"At least take two of the stable's horses. Surely Lady Vivienne would not mind."

"Perhaps not, but we will not ask her."

"Please don't tell me this is some sort of Borderlands honor thing."

"Not at all," replied Zecus. "We simply wish to slip away without anyone knowing. We do not want to give anyone the chance to say no if we ask to leave. None of us enjoyed being a piece in the nobles' games in Freehaven, despite the results." His eyes grew hard. "My life is my own. *I* will not have another choose my fate."

"Then why are you telling me? Aren't you afraid I might go tell Lady Vivienne myself?"

A sly smile touched Zecus' lips.

"Will you?"

"No. Of course not."

"And that is why I decided to tell you. I trust you. I could not simply disappear without saying goodbye."

Kenders pressed her lips together, grateful for that. She could not imagine waking up tomorrow and discovering Zecus was gone.

Eyeing him carefully, she asked, "Are you going to come back?"

Zecus shrugged his shoulders.

"I cannot answer that question any more than I can answer if it will rain on Thonda's Leisure Day three years from now."

"Do you want to come back?"

Zecus drew in a deep breath, dropped his gaze to the table, and exhaled.

"At the moment? Yes. But I do not know what fate Greya has in line for me."

"So I might never see you again?"

He glanced up, a worried scowl on his face.

"War is coming. Things will get…confused."

Kenders pressed her lips together.

"That sounds like a 'no.'"

Zecus forced a brave smile but remained quiet. Kenders stared at him, wondering at the cruel irony of the situation. For weeks, she had fretted over what to do about Zecus, and now that she had finally told him how she felt, he might be leaving her life forever.

She set her jaw and shook her head. This was not something she was leaving to fate. Or the whim of the Gods and Goddesses. She slapped the table with an open palm, startling Zecus, and stood.

"I do *not* accept this."

Zecus stared up at her and said firmly, "We *are* leaving tonight, Kenders."

"And I will not stop you." She leaned forward, rested her hands on the wooden tabletop, and spoke in a firm, quiet voice, "I want the three of you in the courtyard an hour before third watch begins. Against the southwestern wall."

His eyebrows drew together.

"Pardon?"

"You heard me. An hour before third watch, Zecus. Be there."

Before he had a chance to reply or question her, she turned, stepped over the bench, and quickly strode out of the commons, leaving him gaping after her. As she passed through the commons' entryway, her mind ran through the long list of things she needed to do before tonight. She was about to make a great number of people angry with her, but her mind was made up.

CHAPTER 27: THOUGHTS

Tobias strode across the battlements, his walking stick sending a sharp crack through the courtyard below with each halting step. Using his free hand, he pulled his heavy cloak tighter, trying to stave back the evening's steady breeze from burrowing into his clothes.

"Blasted Winter."

He hurried his pace, staring at the lone wooden door situated in the tower ahead. Beyond, the sky was clear and clean, a mixture of rosy reds and soft oranges filling the western horizon. Mu's orb had only just dropped below the bare treetops and the air was already chillier. Tobias would have never named the days here at Storm Island warm, but he certainly preferred them to the icy nights.

A frown on his face, he murmured, "Why here, Miriel? Why not someplace warm?"

Tobias reached the door in the tower and stopped. An old, weathered statue of an ancient Imperial soldier stood guard. Tobias eyed it briefly before turning his full attention to the door. He lifted his hand to knock but hesitated, wondering if this was his best course of action. Broedi had said the aicenai could be trusted, yet Tobias was still wary. Some things were better left to fate. He was still standing there, wavering, when the door opened.

Khin stood, framed in the doorway, and stared down at Tobias. A single, soft mage light hovered in the air behind him, illuminating the stone room within.

"Good evening."

Skipping all pleasantries, Tobias eyed the aicenai and said, "We need to talk about your student."

Khin said nothing. He simply peered at Tobias, his ice-blue eyes sharp and intense.

Clearing his mind of all thoughts in an instant, Tobias drew forth an image of a fat beeswax candle centered on a silver plate, both of which rested on a table in a darkened, windowless room. Focusing on the flickering flame dancing about the imaginary wick, he glared at the aicenai and waited. After a few moments, a nearly imperceptible twitch rippled over the aicenai's parchment-thin face. Tobias recognized the emotion behind it in an instant.

Surprise.

Giving Khin a slight, lopsided grin, Tobias said softly, "You are *not* the first of your kind I have met."

Khin remained quiet for a time, continuing to stare intently. Eventually, he dropped his gaze, stepped aside, and asked, "Would you like to come in?"

Tobias nodded once.

"Thank you."

As he hobbled into the sparsely appointed room, Khin shut the door behind him. Tobias glanced about Khin's lodgings, eyeing the pair of reed mats on the ground and the plain table set against the wall. The unmistakable scent of Yutian incense hung in the air.

"Not one for decorations, are you?"

When Khin did not answer him, he turned to face the aicenai, keeping the image of the burning candle locked in his head.

After a few moments of quiet, Khin said softly, "This is unexpected."

Tobias let a small chuckle escape.

"It is hard to rattle your kind, is it not?"

"It takes a great deal," admitted Khin. "May I ask whom you have met?"

Tobias let the image of the candle fade away and drew forth his memories of the lush, tree-filled valley in central Cartu. Massive, worn granite rocks jutted from the steep hills. A swollen creek meandered through a clearing populated with a small cabin made of long pine trunks. Patches of white snow lay clumped in the trees' shadows.

Khin stared at him blankly.

"I do not know that place."

"The Yaubno Mountains. Near Glasshollow in central Cartu."

"What is its significance?"

Tobias pictured the primary resident of the cabin stepping from its door, an aicenai, but one with a longer face than Khin and darker eyes.

"Ah," murmured Khin. "Larin Lathruna."

Tobias was mildly surprised.

"You recognize her?"

"I do," said Khin. "How long has it been since you were there?"

Seeing no harm in answering the question, Tobias said, "Close to a century."

"I see," said Khin. "And how did you find her?"

"I was not looking for her if that is your question," said Tobias. "I was looking for the cabin."

Tilting his head slightly, Khin said, "The cabin?"

"For two straight turns, I had the same vision over and over again. Me, marching up that mountainside, through the trees, and to that cabin. Each time, it would end before I ever got to see what—or who—was inside. After perhaps the twelfth time, I set off to find it. It took me years, but I succeeded. And once I did, I stayed a while."

"Why?"

Tobias shrugged.

"Larin was in hiding, I did not want to be found, and we got along. It was a good arrangement."

"How long did you stay? What sorts of things did you discuss during your time there?"

Noticing that the aicenai's eyes were particularly intense again, Tobias quickly reinforced the image of the beeswax candle. Glaring at Khin, he said pointedly, "Stop it. Now. I refuse to let you watch my thoughts."

"I do not observe unless there is ample reason."

"I don't care what your reasons are," said Tobias. "My thoughts are *my* thoughts." He paused and, with a certain significance behind his words, added, "Swear an oath, Khin. Swear that you will stay *out* of my head. I want your word. As an aicenai."

A tiny frown creased Khin's lips.

"Such an oath is not given lightly."

"Swear, Khin. Or I'm leaving and you can be left wondering why I ever came."

Khin's face remained blank as he said, "Larin shared much about my kind, it seems."

Tobias nodded once.

"That she did."

Tobias suspected that he knew more about aicenai than perhaps any living soul not of the ancient race. He was exploiting some of that knowledge now. Honoring a promise made was the pinnacle of an aicenai's moral code. Their word was as strong as the Sea of Kings was deep.

After a long, drawn-out silence, Khin said, "You have my promise."

Tobias let the flickering candle fade from his mind.

"Thank you."

Khin inclined his head and said, "In exchange, I ask that you do not share your knowledge of that which I am capable with anyone."

"Broedi knows, yes?"

"He alone," acknowledged Khin. "It took him twenty years, but he reasoned out my skill. I hold a promise for him as well."

"Yet he told no one?"

"He values the…insight I provide."

A wry chuckle slipped from Tobias.

"That's Broedi. Always wanting to know what others are thinking yet keeping his own thoughts buried beneath five feet of stone."

"Why are you here?" asked Khin, clasping his bony hands before him. "Something about my student, yes?"

Glancing around the room, Tobias nodded in the direction of the table and chairs.

"Mind if we sit down? My leg gets stiff if I stand too long in the cold."

Khin extended an arm toward the chairs.

"Please."

Tobias shuffled to the table, hoisted himself into one of the chairs, and rested his walking stick against the wall. As Khin moved to the other chair and sat opposite him, Tobias asked, "You knew Eliza and Aryn, did you not?"

Khin inclined his head.

"I was here at the enclave while they were, yes."

"Did you know them well?"

Khin shook his head slightly.

"What is the point of your question?"

Leaning forward to rest his elbows on the table, Tobias said, "Whenever Eliza would get it in her mind to do something, something that even the most foolish of all fools would find outlandish, she would get this glint in her eye. It took me years, but I eventually learned that once you saw that, you stopped arguing. You might as well yell at a stone to fly like a hawk."

"I know of what you speak."

Tobias folded his hands, squeezed them tight, and murmured, "I just saw that glint again, Khin." He frowned. "It took two hundred years, but I saw it again."

CHAPTER 28: DECISION

19ᵗʰ of the Turn of Luraana, 4999

Zecus huddled beneath three layers of clothes, shrouded in the shadows of the southwestern wall, a worried frown on his lips. He stood rigid, gripping Simiah's reins in his hand, Boah to his left, his father on his right, the trio of men anxiously staring at the moonlit courtyard. Simiah huffed, sending a misty breath into the night. Zecus reached up and scratched his horse's neck.

Boah whispered, "Are we sure this is wise?"

"You have asked that question a dozen times," murmured Joshmuel.

"And you have yet to give me an answer."

Joshmuel was quiet for a moment before saying, "Be quiet, Boah. Else you will be walking the entire way home." The words were firm, but kind.

Boah hesitated before giving a short grunt in response.

Swiveling his head to his right, Zecus locked eyes with his father. Even in the dim light of the wall's shadow, Zecus could clearly see the worry lining his father's face. Apparently, he shared Boah's reservation. Zecus sighed and stared back to the empty courtyard. That made three of them.

Boah cleared his throat. A few moments later, he coughed again, louder and more insistent this time.

Sighing, his father grudgingly asked, "What is it, Boah?"

"Oh, may I speak now?"

"Will you ask if this is wise again?"

Zecus smothered a smile.

After a short pause, Boah said, "No."

"Then speak," murmured Joshmuel. "But try to do so quietly, please."

"Well," whispered Boah. "I was wondering if either of you had yet to come up with a plausible tale to tell the guards?"

Zecus stared at the open northwestern gate, knowing three men stood outside the keep's entrance.

"We're going for an early hunt in the forest?"

Boah murmured incredulously, "Who in the Nine Hells goes hunting at this time of night? In this blasted cold? Easterners are odd, yes, but they are not mad."

Zecus remained quiet. He did not have answers.

Joshmuel said, "Perhaps they will not ask questions."

Boah grunted, "And if they—" The Borderlander cut off as a horse's low nicker drifted through the courtyard.

Zecus whipped his head around and stared out into the moonlit yard. There was nothing but gravel, stacks of firewood, and benches.

Boah muttered uneasily, "Uh…did anyone else just hear another horse?"

Before either father or son could answer, Zecus heard the crunching of horses' hooves on gravel paired with a quiet chuckling. The sounds seemed as if they were only a dozen feet away, yet Zecus still saw nothing.

Suddenly, a gentle shimmer rippled through the air, like heat rising from the ground on a hot Borderlands day. Within a single breath, four horses and two riders appeared before them. The tomble White Lion sat on Nundle's chestnut, a dark cloak draped over his shoulders—hood flipped back—and his walking stick laying across his lap. Kenders was atop her black and gray horse, Smoke, wearing a pair of tough-spun riding pants and a matching overcoat, her hair pulled back into a single, tight bunch. Their horses—along with the two behind them—were laden with packs and saddlebags.

Zecus' eyes narrowed as he reasoned what Kenders was planning. She had fixed her gaze on him, her eyes hopeful and hard at the same time. She appeared on the verge of saying something, but after a beat, pressed her lips together.

Boah marveled, "Nine Hells, that is an excellent trick."

Tobias grinned as he replied, "It is, isn't it?" He motioned to the empty air around them. "I have extended the Weave around all of us now. To anyone outside it, this particular part of the courtyard will appear quite empty. Be careful, though. This particular Weave does nothing to sound. Keep your voices low."

Zecus barely heard a word the tomble said. He was too busy glowering at Kenders.

Joshmuel took a cautious step towards Tobias and Kenders.

"It would appear you mean to come with us."

Tobias turned to stare at Kenders, waved a hand, and said, "This is your show, dear."

Kenders finally pulled her gaze from Zecus and shifted it to Joshmuel.

"Yes, we will be joining you. For a time, at least."

Zecus ground his teeth. This was foolish.

Joshmuel said carefully, "I am surprised the Manes are letting you go. What say the baroness about this?"

Kenders frowned.

"Nothing. I did not tell her."

Zecus could not believe what he was hearing.

"You are sneaking away?"

She met his gaze but did not answer him.

After a long moment of quiet, Joshmuel asked, "Are you sure that is wise?"

Kenders said firmly, "It is what I'm doing."

Zecus took a quick step forward, protesting in a hushed tone, "You are needed here!" He shifted his gaze to Tobias. "*Both* of you!" Shaking his head, he asked,

"Why are you even here?"

"Because she asked me to come," said Tobias.

"And you *agreed*? How could you permit her to do this?"

"Permit me?" said Kenders, her voice hushed yet firm. "I asked Tobias for his help, not his permission. This decision is mine to make."

"And it is a foolish one! Have you thought this through?"

With a firm nod, Kenders said, "I left a note for Jak explaining my actions. I gave Sabine my mother's necklace should the Manes need to check on me—or Nikalys. Tobias can bring me back here in an instant if necessary. And he can teach me about the Strands as we go."

Zecus gaped at the little brown-haired tomble.

"And you believe this is a good idea?"

Tobias shook his head.

"Gods, no. I think it's short-sighted and selfish. I tried to talk her out of it, but she was going one way or the other. I could agree to come, or let her go on her own. This arrangement is the sweetest of the sour."

Kenders insisted, "We will only stay with you a few weeks. Four at the most. If we have not found your families by then, we will leave you to search on your own." The resolve etched on her face softened. "You are all here because of me, because of what is happening. Let me help you find your families. Please."

Zecus hissed, "This is not your fault! The Gods are driving this! Not you!"

Joshmuel said in a soft, warning tone, "Zecus..."

Shooting a glance in his father's direction, he saw the elder Alsher pointing in the direction of the western gate.

"We do not want to draw attention."

Refusing to be hushed, Zecus said, "But this is madness! She should stay here." He whirled back to face Kenders. "You should stay here!"

Kenders bristled at his near-order.

"As it turns out, you do not get to tell me what to do."

The pair glared at one another, neither willing to back away from their position.

"Son?" murmured Joshmuel. "It is not our place to challenge her. If this is her decision, we will abide by it."

Satisfaction spread across Kenders' face.

"Thank you for your support."

Joshmuel stared up to Kenders and said, "To be clear, I do not support your decision. I, too, find it foolish. However, I am honor-bound to respect your wishes, regardless of their wisdom. You are determined to come. Fine. That is the end of it." Peering back to Zecus, he added, "There will be no argument from us."

Glaring at his father, Zecus protested, "But she—"

"Hush!" said Joshmuel. "This is the way of things. Accept it."

Zecus held his father's steady gaze, wanting to argue further but knowing this was a battle he was not going to win now. Perhaps he could reason with Kenders over the next few days to turn around and return to the enclave. Pressing his lips together, he dropped his chin to his chest.

"Fine."

As Zecus glared at the gravel underneath his boots, Boah spoke up.

"I fail to see how this helps us."

Zecus glanced up to find everyone staring at Boah.

The man stared up at Kenders and said, "You said you are going to stay with us for a few weeks only, yes? We won't be out of the Southlands by the time you mean to come back."

Zecus turned to stare at Kenders. Boah was right. Even with horses, they would barely be over the Fernsford Bridge by then.

"He's right. You'll accomplish nothing other than missing your studies."

Kenders shot Tobias a nervous glance.

The tomble waved a hand and said, "Do not look at me. This was your idea."

She sighed, looked back to the Borderlanders, and said, "I will explain everything once we leave the enclave." Shifting her gaze between Joshmuel and Boah, she added, "Now, if you two would choose a horse, we can be underway." She glanced toward the gate. "Quickly, please. Before the guards change."

Boah stepped forward, gave Zecus a helpless shrug, and moved toward the horses. Joshmuel followed. While they mounted and settled themselves in the saddles, Zecus remained rooted in place, never taking his eyes off Kenders. She avoided his gaze, looking anywhere but at him.

Once situated on one of the horses, Joshmuel said, "Time to go, son."

Zecus' frown deepened. Seething, he faced Simiah, placed his boot in a stirrup, and lifted himself into the saddle. This was not over.

CHAPTER 29: FATHER

Exiting the enclave was simpler than Zecus could have hoped.

The magic used by Tobias to keep them hidden, paired with a Weave by Kenders to muffle their sounds allowed the group to ride past the guards unchallenged. One of the soldiers glanced up as they rode past, a curious expression on his face, but after a few tense moments he shrugged his shoulders and went back to talking with the other guards.

As Zecus and Kenders knew Claw better than the others did, they led the group through the village. Zecus repeatedly peered over at Kenders as they rode, silently urging her to look at him. She refused to meet his gaze. Even if she had, he would not have been able to speak with her. Not only had Tobias ordered them all to remain quiet, Kenders' Weave muted the world. To Zecus, it seemed as if he had a pair of folded, woolen blankets covering his ears.

Upon reaching the western edge of town, Zecus guided them down the dirt road leading west, away from Claw. As they passed beyond the outer limit of the enclave's protective shroud, the town and castle disappeared from sight. Wondering if they should stop yet, Zecus glanced back at Tobias. The White Lion waved his hand, indicating they should continue further into the forest. Zecus complied.

Once the trunks of the winter-bare oaks hid the bluff, Zecus heard the muffled voice of the tomble White Lion call, "Drop the Weaves!"

Moments later, a rush of sound hit Zecus and he started, surprised by how loud the nighttime forest seemed: creaking trees, wind whistling in the branches, an owl hooting in the distance. Moonlight streamed through the leafless branches overhead, turning the ground into a mesh of light and shadow.

Hearing a rustle of movement behind him, he turned to see Tobias urging his horse forward, wedging the chestnut in between Joshmuel and Boah's horse. For the first time, Zecus noted the two tan mounts were actually Nikalys and Jak's horses, Hal and Goshen.

As the White Lion stopped his horse between Kenders and Zecus, he fixed her with a speculative gaze and asked, "Are you sure you want to do this?"

Kenders gave a short, resolute nod.

"Yes."

"My earlier offer still stands."

"No, I want to try."

Zecus peered over the top of the tomble's head and at Kenders' determined profile.

"Try what?"

She ignored him, handed Smoke's reins to Tobias, and began to dismount.

Raising his voice, he asked again, "What are you going to try?"

Hopping to the ground, Kenders strode away from the horses, further down the road.

Worried, Zecus shifted his gaze to Tobias and asked, "What is she doing?"

Tobias turned to look at Zecus, his eyes glinting with more than the reflected light from the two moons.

"Hopefully learning a lesson."

"What does that mean?"

Tobias stared straight ahead.

"You will see."

Turning his head, Zecus called, "Kenders!" He had a bad feeling about this.

She continued to ignore him as she strode through the mottled moonlight. Joshmuel and Boah both directed their horses forward to line up with Zecus and Tobias.

Boah whispered, "What's happening?"

Zecus mumbled, "I do not know." Looking over at Tobias, he added, "And he will not tell me."

The tomble remained silent, his gaze locked on Kenders. She had stopped thirty paces from the horses and was standing motionless in the road.

Joshmuel muttered, "I believe I now understand how she means to help us."

As one, Zecus and Boah asked, "How?"

"It was not that long ago we were all in Freehaven, was it not?" asked Joshmuel. He turned to Zecus. "Yet with but a single step, we were here."

Zecus' eyes opened wide, a jolt of fear stabbing his chest. He whipped his head around to stare at Tobias.

"Have you taught her the Weave for a port?"

Without taking his gaze from Kenders, Tobias gave a small shake of his head. "No, I have not."

Zecus placed his boot on his father's horse and shoved it away, trying to create enough room to dismount.

"Move!"

Joshmuel complied, yet still asked, "What is wrong?"

Zecus did not waste time explaining. He leapt off Simiah in a rush and began to jog to where Kenders stood.

"Stop! Please!"

He had taken but a half-dozen steps when the sound of fabric being ripped in two filled the forest, shredding the night's solitude. Zecus skidded to a stop, gaping at the sight before him. A forty-foot tall black slit had appeared before Kenders, stretching from the ground into the oak branches. On either side of the tear in reality, the forest rippled as though a painting on a slashed canvas.

Movement pulled his attention from the port and back to Kenders as she collapsed to the ground, limp.

"Kenders!"

He sprinted to her side and dropped to his knees. Rocks and stones dug into his shins. She lay on her side, her cord-bound hair draped over her cheek. He rolled her onto her back gently, placed his hand to her chest, and said silent prayer to Khanos, the God of Life.

"Please, please, please…"

Upon feeling the slow thudding of a heartbeat, he closed his eyes and exhaled in relief. Hearing hurried footsteps, he looked up to find his father and Boah running toward him.

Joshmuel called, "Is she alright?"

Nodding, Zecus said, "She's alive."

When they reached where Kenders lay, Joshmuel dropped to his knees and checked for himself, also placing his hand over her heart. Boah stood nearby, alternating between staring at Kenders and the towering port silently looming over them.

Peering back down the dirt road, Zecus observed Tobias still sitting in his saddle, ignoring them entirely. His gaze was locked on the port, an expression of open wonderment on his face.

A hot rage bubbled inside Zecus. Pushing himself from the ground, he shouted, "How could you let her do that?!"

Tobias shifted his gaze to Zecus, then to Kenders. He kicked his horse's sides, snapped the reins, and began to ride forward.

From the ground, his father looked up, his eyes filled with concern.

"I do not understand. What happened to her?"

Zecus stared at his father and growled, "This is what happens to her when she does not know what she is doing."

"Seems like she knows what she's doing," muttered Boah, his eyes fixed on the port.

Frustrated, Zecus said, "There is more to it than that."

Neither of them knew the danger in which she had just placed herself.

He wheeled to face Tobias again, finding the tomble only a few paces away. Forgetting to show any sort of respect for the White Lion, Zecus yelled, "You knew she was going to do this, didn't you?!"

"I did," replied Tobias nonchalantly, his gaze back on the towering blackness.

"And you let her?!"

Tobias dropped his stare to Zecus and nodded.

"Obviously."

"You heard Broedi! He—"

"Is overcautious at times," interjected Tobias firmly. His gaze shifted to Kenders. "Knowing what her mother was capable of doing, I believed she could handle this."

Zecus' eyes went wide.

"You *believed*? You risked her life on a *belief*?!"

Shaking his head, Tobias said, "No. I discussed her talent—and limits—at length with Khin. He agreed that we let her try."

Zecus was about to shout again when Tobias' words registered.

"Hold a moment. Her teacher *knew* she was going to do this?"

A wispy voice wafted from the tree trunks.

"Not precisely, no."

Startled, Zecus spun around, his hand flying to his sword hilt, and peered into the jagged shadows. A few dozen paces away, a thin, hooded figure stepped into a pool of moonlight.

"You need not draw your blade."

The figure reached up and drew back the hood, revealing Khin's skeletal, drawn face. Zecus, his father, and Boah stared in quiet surprise as the aicenai approached and stopped beside Kenders. Bending down, he extended a bony hand, placed two fingers on the side of her neck, and—after a moment or two—removed them.

"She will be fine once she wakes."

Standing tall, he surveyed their group. After a few short moments, Khin said, "There is no need to worry. I have no intention of stopping you."

Quiet surprise registered on Joshmuel's face.

"You do not?"

"None whatsoever. I hope your journey is a successful one."

After the Borderlanders exchanged a series of quick glances, Joshmuel looked back to Khin.

"Are you here to take her back to the enclave?"

"No," replied the aicenai. "She will be traveling with you as she planned."

Surprised, Zecus said, "You're letting her go?" Like his father, he had assumed—and hoped—Khin was here to stop Kenders. "Why?"

Khin stared at Zecus, his icy blue eyes lit bright by the rays of moonlight.

"You can tell a child not to touch a candle's flame a hundred times and, still, they will poke at it. One burnt finger, and they stop."

Baffled, Zecus said, "Pardon?"

"Decisions have consequences," murmured Khin, dropping his gaze to Kenders. "Yet she acts as if they do not. She must learn caution. I could plead, reason, or argue with her for turns upon turns, or I can hope a better teacher than I can convey the lesson."

"Who is that?" asked Joshmuel.

"Not who," murmured Khin. "What."

"Then what?" prompted Boah.

Khin lifted his gaze and spoke a single word.

"Fate."

Before anyone could press him further, Khin shifted his gaze to Boah and asked, "Would you retrieve my horse for me?" He stretched out a hand and pointed into the forest. "She is tied over there."

Surprised yet again, Zecus stared at the aicenai.

"You are coming as well?"

"I am."

As he rose from the ground, Joshmuel asked, "If you wish for fate to teach her about consequences and caution, should you not let her go on her own?"

"Yes," said Khin. "But she needs to learn about other things as well. We do not have time to wait for fate to finish its task. Speaking of time—" he eyed the port "—we should not waste any more of it. I do not know how long this will hold." He tilted his head back to stare at its full forty feet. "Truly, I am surprised it did not close when she fainted."

"I'm not," muttered Tobias. "The pattern she used was similar to the Weave I use for a port, but…different somehow." He sighed and gave a quick shake of his head. "Whatever the reason it's still here, Khin is right. We should not tarry. It could close at any moment. Get his horse and let's go."

Boah glanced at Zecus and Joshmuel, shrugged his shoulders, and said, "I am not one to argue with mages." Turning, he tromped into the dark forest, on his way to find Khin's horse.

Tobias glanced at Zecus and Joshmuel.

"You, too. Get your horses. Quickly."

Zecus gave Kenders one last look-over, and then hurried with his father back to where the four horses stood, munching on patches of grassy weeds not yet taken by Winter's bite. As they grabbed the reins to the horses and began to walk back, Zecus spotted Boah leading a black horse from the trees.

Once everyone gathered, Zecus climbed into Simiah's saddle, after which Boah and his father helped lift an unconscious Kenders to sit in front of him. As he wrapped an arm around her, he stared at the tall void and asked, "Where does it lead?"

Eyeing the port, Tobias answered, "She told me she was trying for a place along the Erona River. The farmhouse of the two sisters with black hair?"

"Sabine and Helene?"

Tobias nodded.

"Yes, It's as close to Demetus as she's been."

Zecus stared at the tomble.

"You have been further."

"I have," acknowledged Tobias. "But it's been ages and I doubt I could picture the destination as is necessary. Short of taking you all to Gobas—inadvisable at the moment, I think—we should take her port."

Zecus protested, "But you ported to the Seat of Nelnora. You remembered that."

Tobias turned his steady gaze to Zecus.

"The city of a God is not easily forgotten. Now, stop asking questions, take the port you have, and be happy she saved you two turns of travel."

Zecus frowned yet kept his concerns to himself.

Nodding, Tobias said, "Good. Now, as I am the only one who can port back should the other side of this thing be atop a mountain in Quan, I'll go first. Once I'm through, count to ten. If I am not back by then, come through."

Without waiting for any sort of acknowledgement, he urged his horse forward and through the blackness. The moment the horse's rear disappeared, Zecus began to count silently. He had only reached seven when Boah announced, "Ten. Let's go," and kicked the sides of Hal. Leading Kenders' mount along behind him, Boah moved through the port.

Joshmuel shook his head and sighed.

"Ever the cautious one."

Smiling, Zecus watched his father follow Boah into the port. As Joshmuel disappeared into blackness, Zecus turned to Khin.

In a soft, airy voice, the aicenai said, "I had yet to reach four." He, too, nudged his horse forward and through the rift in the world, leaving Zecus alone with Kenders in the dark forest.

Zecus hesitated a moment before kicking Simiah's sides and moving forward, into the inky black void. As they crossed the threshold, he instinctively shut his eyes. One moment, he was in the cold and peaceful forest of Storm Island, the next, the thick odor of fresh grass filled his nose, a tepid breeze blew against his face, and dozens of terror-stricken screams assaulted his ears, echoing through the night.

His eyes shot open. He quickly scanned the area while trying to reach for his sword but forgot he was holding onto an unconscious Kenders.

Simiah had emerged atop the crest of a grassy hill. Below him were the remains of a ruined, three-walled cottage. Crop fields flanked the home and a handful of campfires burned in front. Moonlight from a clear, star-littered sky bathed the prairie.

A pair of horses with empty saddles was galloping across the hill, their sharp whinnies joining the screams of men. As Zecus whipped his head around to search for the missing riders, his eyes went wide as his gaze fell upon two enormous creatures marching about the grassy hillside. Shaped like men, the beasts appeared to be made of clumped stone and grassy earth.

The monsters lumbered after a handful of unfamiliar men sprinting toward a wooden cart by the house. Almost a dozen horses were tied to the wagon, tossing their heads, their eyes rolled back in fear. Some men were attempting to mount the spooked horses, while others were fleeing on foot, racing through the grass. One of the mammoth stone creatures reached the cart, bent down, and smacked two of the men with the back of its arm. Both men flew backwards a couple dozen feet, tumbling through the prairie grass like lumps of meat.

Panicked, Zecus looked around frantically for the rest of his companions. Khin was on his horse, two dozen paces to Zecus' right, staring intently at the stone creatures. Spotting movement down the slope, Zecus turned his head to find Boah squatting in the tall grass, crouched between two dark humps on the ground. Based on size alone, one of the forms in the grass was undoubtedly Tobias. Zecus quickly reasoned that the other was his father. Neither was moving.

His heart in his throat, Zecus kicked Simiah's side, urging the horse forward. As he neared the trio, Boah glanced up, his face a mask of shocked sorrow. Zecus' gaze locked on his father. Joshmuel's neck was bent at a very odd angle.

"Oh, Gods...no, no, no..."

Wanting off his horse now, Zecus nearly shoved Kenders to the ground.

"Blast it, Boah! Help me!"

As Boah leapt up and hurried over, Zecus could not take his eyes from his father's head, twisted and fixed in an impossible, perverse position. His stomach clenched, bile rose up, coating the back of this throat.

Boah slid Kenders from the saddle and gently laid her in the grass. Staring back up to Zecus, he said, "I am so sorry."

Free to dismount now, Zecus remained motionless in his saddle, staring blankly at his father. There was no need to rush. Without doubt, Joshmuel Alsher was dead.

After a few tortured moments, he slid off his horse and collapsed to his knees beside his father's body. The screams of the men running away echoed through the night.

"I..."

He trailed off, unsure why he had even opened his mouth in the first place. There was nothing to say now. There was nothing to do now. His father was dead and nothing could change that.

"Hold a moment."

He was in the company of mages.

Zecus lifted his head and shouted, "Khin!"

The aicenai still sat upon his horse, watching the stone creatures chase after the men. At Zecus' shout, his head swiveled to stare at the group. After taking one last look at the fleeing men, he directed his horse to where the group waited. As he approached, his eyes studied each of them, shifting from Tobias to Joshmuel before finally resting on Zecus.

"I am sorry," said Khin softly. "There is nothing I can do for him."

Zecus' eyes flicked to where Boah had laid Kenders.

"But I once saw her—"

Khin interrupted gently, "I am unable to touch Strands of Life. Even if I could, I would not be able to do what you are thinking. No mage could."

The aicenai dismounted his horse and moved to kneel beside Tobias, laying two fingers against the White Lion's neck.

"He is alive. In the midst of a vision, I believe."

"Who cares about him?" shouted Zecus. "Please? Is there nothing that can be done?"

Nodding at Kenders, Khin said, "Not even she could have reversed his fate. Once the soul leaves the body, it belongs to Maeana. Nothing but the most twisted perversion of the Strands can change that." The aicenai stared at Joshmuel. "I am sorry for his passing."

Dropping his head into his hands, Zecus remained motionless, trying to accept the unthinkable and muttered, "What happened?" When neither Boah nor Khin responded, he lifted his head and shouted, "What happened?!"

Boah glanced at Khin before he began to answer, his words halting and unsure.

"When I...when I came through the blackness, the first thing I noticed were the campfires. The great lion's horse was standing on the hillside, his saddle empty. When Joshmuel came through, he pointed here immediately."

He glanced at where Tobias lay.

"We made it here and were about to dismount when a shout rang out. Men started jumping up from the grass, swords drawn. Our...our horses spooked. I managed to control mine, but Joshmuel's tossed him." He stared at the body on the ground, his face blank. "I saw him falling backwards and..." Trailing off, he lifted his gaze and turned it westward, after the fleeing men and the two creatures lumbering after them. "Those...things rose from the ground. And then there was screaming."

"As the men's intentions seemed clear," said Khin "I set Stone fibríaals after them. The brigands' bravery ran before they did." Shifting his gaze back to Zecus, he added, "Then you arrived."

Zecus stared back down at his broken father, wondering what he was going to tell his family—if he ever found them.

"This is not your burden to carry," said Khin in his wispy voice. "Fate is no one's fault."

Surprised and irritated, Zecus peered at the aicenai.

"Pardon?"

Moonlight glinted in Khin's eyes as he nodded at Joshmuel's body.

"I said this is not your burden—"

"I heard you the first time!" growled Zecus. Glaring at Khin, he pushed himself up from the ground. "This isn't fate's fault, Khin!" Pointing at his father, he exclaimed, "This is *my* fault! Mine! He's dead because of me! Had I never left Demetus, I would have never met the Progeny or the Shadow Manes, and today would have never happened!"

Khin stepped forward.

"You believe that one decision alone is responsible for his death?"

"Yes! I do!"

"And what would have happened had I chosen to go first through the port?" queried Khin. "I could have scared away the bandits first, no? Perhaps his death is my fault?"

Zecus shook his head.

"That is different."

"Is it?" asked Khin. He shifted his gaze to Boah. "Perhaps it is his fault."

Boah rose from the ground, instantly tense. His eyes hot, he said, "What are you saying?"

Khin did not flinch from Boah's glare.

"Who chose the horses tonight?"

It was as if Khin's question was a bucket of water tossed on a campfire. The heat in Boah's eyes vanished in an instant.

"I did."

Shifting his gaze back to Zecus, Khin said, "So his choice put your father on that horse. Do you blame him?"

Zecus shook his head and said, "No, of course—"

"What of the White Lion? Is this his fault?

Zecus stared at the tomble lying in the grass, his brow furrowed.

"I don't...I don't think so."

"No?" asked Khin. "Had he not had a vision, he would have been able to stop the bandits. Or what about the bandits themselves? Why are you not blaming them? Surely more fault lies with them than yourself, does it not?"

Zecus did not know what to say. Khin's questions were confusing him.

"What about her?" asked Khin, pointing a bony finger at Kenders. "If you wish to blame someone for what Greya had given you, why not her? She chose to come here tonight. Blame her."

Zecus turned his gaze to Kenders and found himself actually considering the question. Khin had a point. After a few moments, however, he shook his head.

"No. She was trying to help. She did not mean for this to happen."

"Did you?" asked Khin. "Did any of us?"

"Stop twisting words!" exclaimed Zecus. "We are here because of me! Because of choices I made!"

"We are here because of choices we have all made."

Zecus glowered at Khin.

"You are *her* teacher, not mine. Spare me whatever lesson this is."

"This is no lesson," said Khin. "This is fact. The sky is up. Water is wet. Fire is hot. And assigning cause to fate is madness."

Boah whispered softly, "He's right, Zecus. Do not blame yourself for this."

Zecus did not have to listen to any more of this. Staring in the direction the bandits had run, he spotted the hulking silhouettes of the stone creatures lumbering towards the horizon. Screams still carried across the grasslands.

"Do we need to worry about them coming back?"

Keeping his gaze on Zecus, Khin said, "No."

"Good," muttered Zecus, looking back to his father's body. "I wish to bury him. Now."

Nodding, Khin replied, "I respect your custom. Do what you must."

Zecus looked up and scanned the area, truly seeing it for the first time. Without a doubt, they had arrived in the right place. The ruined cottage, the fields of vegetables, and the river sparkling in the moonlight all marked this as Helene and Sabine's former home. He glanced at the field to the right of the house. From the tales Jak and Nikalys had shared with him, he knew the sisters' parents were buried there, beneath the overgrown crops.

Without a word, he bent down, lifted the Alsher patriarch in his arms, and trudged down the slope, heading toward the field on the right. It seemed a fitting place to bury his father. Sabine was a strong soul, Helene an amazingly resilient child. It only reasoned their parents were as worthy as their daughters.

Despite the friendship shared with Joshmuel, Boah did not ask to come. Burials were for families of the deceased only. Boah would need to mourn in his own way.

Walking between the still-burning campfires near the ruined house, Zecus moved into the field, stepping through weeds and un-harvested longpeppers that had fallen to the ground. A number of the yellowing plants still had peppers hanging from them, dry and shriveled. He laid his father gently to the ground and returned to the house.

Finding two shovels along the back wall, he chose one, returned to the field, and began to dig. He focused on each shovelful of dirt, keeping the crushing sadness that hovered on the edge of his soul at bay by holding onto his fury. Anger was easier to handle than sorrow.

Sweat dripped from his brow, falling into the soil. He stopped twice to peel off a layer of clothing. Once the hole was complete, he lowered his father's body into the ground and sat beside the fresh-turned earth. Time seemed to either stop or rush past. Zecus could not tell. Nor did he care.

He stared at the moons and stars, still shining in the night sky. The water in the Erona River continued to flow, the gentle Southlands wind continued to blow. Joshmuel Alsher, a good man, father, and husband, was dead and the world marched on, uncaring.

A rogue tear escaped and ran down his cheek. He wiped it away quickly and bit down hard, trying his best to hold back his grief. Taking a deep breath, he exhaled, shuddering as he let the air out.

In a voice thick with emotion, he said, "I am so sorry, Father."

Reaching down, he undid the cloth band around his father's head and wrapped it around his right arm.

"I swear to you that I will find our family. They *will* be safe."

He could not bring himself to cover his father with dirt, so he sat there in the quiet moonlight, breathing in the sweet, pungent aroma of the rotting longpeppers and musty, fresh-tilled earth. His anger faded away eventually, leaving him numb and empty. Not even the sorrow sought to fill the hole.

After noticing that the eastern sky had lightened, turning a pre-dawn gray, Zecus let a long sigh seep from his lips. It was time. Standing, he turned to retrieve the shovel jammed into the loose earth, glanced up, and stopped abruptly.

Kenders stood at the edge of the field, staring at him, her arms crossed over her chest. Sorrow filled her face, mixed with a heavy dose of guilt.

From somewhere deep within Zecus, a surge of anger rushed forth, unbidden and furious. Perhaps Khin was right. Perhaps Kenders had earned herself a share of the blame. Zecus might be responsible for ultimately bringing Joshmuel to Storm Island, but Kenders brought him to this hillside.

As he stared, Kenders lifted a hand to her face and wiped her cheek. She was crying.

Much of his anger evaporated in an instant, although he sensed a bit remained. A tiny seed of resentment seemed determined to take root. Sighing, he raised a hand and motioned for her to come closer.

After a moment's hesitation, she began to walk through the crops, her eyes locked on his, searching his face. She stopped a few paces from him, her hands clasped before her.

"Boah said I should leave you alone, so I—" She cut off as her gaze flicked to the hole. Taking a sharp, stunned breath, she lifted a hand to her mouth. Her widened eyes glistened, brimming with fresh tears. "Oh, Zecus. I'm so sorry. This is my fault. It's all my fault. If I hadn't come—"

In a quiet but firm tone, Zecus murmured, "Stop."

Kenders started as if he had screamed the word rather than whispered it. She looked as if she wanted to run away and never look back. Part of him wished she would.

Instead, he opened his arms wide.

"Come here."

Relief flooded Kenders' face as she took the few remaining steps closer to him. He wrapped his arms around her and held tightly as she began to sob. He relented and allowed his tears to fall as well.

Chapter 30: Vision

Everywhere Tobias looked, gray-skinned oligurts lumbered past, their tusk-filled faces lit by torches' glow. Tobias dashed about the crowd, dodging the plodding steps of the giants even though it was unnecessary. Within his visions, he could pass through solid objects as if they were not there, although moving through living things gave him the shivers. It seemed wrong, somehow.

The ability to step through things was not the only oddity in his visions. He found that his eyesight was extraordinarily sharp, every sound crisp and clear. Yet while those two senses were heightened, the world was absent any odor. He could smell nothing.

However, the most unusual aspect of his visions was the condition of his right leg. Crippled since he was a young tomble, in this place it was whole and unbent. As far as Tobias was concerned, it was the only redeeming aspect of Nelnora's gift.

As he danced about the vast crowd of oligurts, Tobias searched for the reason he was here. Through the years, he had come to believe every vision important, even though he frequently was unable to discern why. The maddening uncertainty was the primary reason his hatred of the visions had emerged. That and being powerless to stop what he witnessed.

After the scourging of the Carinius coast, he had decided he never wanted to experience another vision again. If they could not help him stop such a tragedy, he did not understand the point in having them.

During the Demonic War and the years following, he had discovered that close proximity to the other White Lions fueled the visions. So he fled the duchies, hoping to halt his 'gift.' The visions slowed in frequency, yet never completely stopped. The ones he did have were potent, powerful events. To this day, one in particular continued to haunt him.

Tobias had been enjoying a nice meal in a mountain village in Cartu one evening when he suddenly found himself standing on a red, wooden bridge. From afar, he watched as a saeljul used the Strands to suffocate an entire village. People fell to the ground, their eyes bulging. The saeljul walked past them all, uncaring, to stand before a stone pedestal at the center of town. The ijul opened the black box atop the stone and withdrew a small, silver stone. It disgusted Tobias that one would kill so many over a simple gemstone. It still grated him.

This vision, like many from his past, was proving to be both enlightening and frustrating at the same time.

He had closed his eyes just before he had passed through the port—a habit of his—and re-opened them a moment later in near complete blackness. He panicked for a moment, thinking that Kenders' Weave had gone awry and taken him to an unintended location. A heartbeat later, however, he realized that he was standing and no longer in Traveler's saddle.

As he spun around, trying to shake the disorientation, he noticed his right leg was whole.

He took a deep breath. No odor.

A quick series of distant flashes briefly illuminated his surroundings. He stood in the middle of a long dirt road with tall, wind-blown, rustling grass on both sides. Hunched balls of dark bushes dotted the prairie as far as he could see. The soft, thudding rumble of far-off thunder tumbled over the plains. Storm clouds covered the night sky, hiding the moons and enshrouding the landscape in near-blackness.

Another lightning flash lit up the wilderness. Moments later, the thunder reached his ears, rising and falling as it rumbled past, going on for longer than it should. It took Tobias only a heartbeat or two to realize that the constant thudding was not thunder. An army was on the march.

Having no idea how long the vision would last, Tobias faced the oncoming army and hurried down the road. Additional flashes of lightning revealed nothing useful about his surroundings. Everywhere he looked, all he saw was grass, bushes, and clumps of short trees. After a time, Tobias spotted specks of light on the horizon that he recognized as torch flames, stretching as far as he could see in both directions.

Eventually, he was able to make out the shifting shapes of bodies trudging toward him, illuminated by torchlight. Razorfiends, oligurts, mongrels, and demonmen moved slowly, methodically through the darkness. Tobias stopped his advance, letting the Sudashians move past him while trying to gauge their numbers. He did not try very long, however. There were simply too many of them. It was like trying to count the grains of sand on a beach.

Oligurts stomped past first, heavy metal-hooked clubs or tall, thick bows slung over their shoulders, talking amongst themselves in their language and leaving Tobias wishing he shared Broedi's knowledge of the oligurt tongue. To him, it sounded like one long series of grunts.

The razorfiends came next, slinking through the grass. Tobias had encountered the small, bladed creatures before, but never so many at once. Unlike the oligurts, they carried no weapons. Razorfiends did not need them. The quills along their arms and legs were sharper than sword blades.

The mongrels he spotted were unarmed as well, which, like the fiends, meant nothing. Their powerful jaws could rip a man to shreds.

The creatures that garnered the bulk of Tobias' attention, however, were the demon-men. The Nine Hells' spawn he saw here were nothing like the ones from the Demonic War. Those monsters had been mindless, raging brutes, dangerous and deadly, but unpredictable. More than once, Tobias had seen them turn on one another during battle.

These demon-men were different. They were calm and in control, an aura of unquestioned command surrounding them. The Sudashians who followed did so with complete obedience.

With each passing moment, the dread inside Tobias' gut swelled. This army was not only massive, but it was organized and focused. A lethal combination.

Now, as the last lines of mongrels moved past him, Tobias watched the army march away, frowning. He still had not learned anything useful other than 'the army is enormous and dangerous.' Deciding to track the army, hoping to discover something else, he sighed and began to walk after them, scurrying to keep up. He had only taken a dozen steps when he noticed the little bit of color gracing the nighttime prairie began to fade.

"No…"

Halting in place, he lifted his hand and stared at it. As expected, he could see straight through it.

"Hells!"

Glancing down, he saw the ground under his foot. His entire body was translucent.

The vision was ending.

Spinning around, he searched frantically for some landmark to tell him where he—and the Sudashian army—might be, but all he could see was dirt, grass, and rocks.

"Blast it, Nelnora! Not yet! I need to know where I am!"

The world faded to black.

* * *

The fresh scent of green filled Tobias' nose. Upon opening his eyes, he found a clear, early-dawn sky overhead. Tall stalks of grass framed his view, wafting back and forth, teased by a light breeze.

He remained motionless, listening carefully to his surroundings, straining to catch anything that might give a clue to where he was. The whistling of the wind was all he heard at first. A horse let out a bored snort of air. It was as if he had awakened from a nice nap in the pastures of Alewold.

Turning his head to the right, he spotted Khin standing nearby, his gaze fixed on something some distance away.

"Did it work?"

Khin swiveled his bald head, peered down, and spoke in his slow, drawn-out manner.

"We are where she intended to take us."

Tobias was both stunned and impressed. He had had his doubts. Even Eliza could not have done what her daughter had.

He pushed himself up, into a sitting position, grimacing in pain throughout the maneuver. The ribs on his left side were sore.

"Did I fall off my horse?"

"We believe so," answered Khin.

Tobias winced, testing his range of movement. Nothing seemed broken. Ketus had been with him, it seemed.

Spotting his walking stick in the grass beside him, he grabbed the white lion knob, braced the point in the dirt, and stood upright to get a better look at his surroundings. He and Khin stood on a grassy slope, alone, save for four of their horses calmly grazing. A ruined stone house rested at the bottom of the hill, flanked by several overgrown crop fields. A wide, expansive river was beyond the house, snaking from the western horizon and disappearing into the southeastern one. Zecus was in one of the fields, shoveling dirt. Kenders stood nearby, arms crossed, watching him. Tobias twisted around, looking for Joshmuel or Boah.

"Where are the others?"

"One took two horses to the river to water them." Nodding to the field with Zecus and Kenders, he added, "The other is being buried by his son."

Tobias's head snapped up.

"What did you say?"

"Joshmuel is dead," replied Khin evenly. "He fell from his horse and broke his neck."

Tobias stared at Khin for a few moments, blinking in stunned quiet before muttering, "Truly?"

Khin nodded silently.

Peering down at the field, Tobias whispered, "Gods…" He had only known Joshmuel for a short time, and not all that well, but he had liked the longleg. Looking back to Khin, he asked, "What happened?"

Absent any sort of emotion, Khin related everything that occurred after Tobias had entered the port. When the aicenai was done—the recounting did not take long—Tobias glanced about at the ruined farm, shaking his head. This was another reason he had hid from the White Lions for all these years. Tragedy hounded them.

"How is Zecus?"

"He is struggling," said Khin, his gaze fixed on the field below. "He is very angry."

"At who?"

"Himself," murmured Khin. "Us. The Gods." He nodded at the field. "Her."

Tobias drew in a long, deep breath and exhaled.

"This is not fair."

"Fate does not care about what is fair and what is not."

"True," admitted Tobias. "But I do. And *this*…this is not fair."

Khin was quiet for a long moment before he responded, his voice barely rising above the rustling of the prairie grass.

"No. It is not."

The pair stood in silence, watching Zecus shovel from afar.

After a time, Khin turned to him and asked, "Was your vision useful?"

"Somewhat."

"Will you share what you saw with me?"

Tobias sighed and nodded, muttering, "Of course."

He then proceeded to tell Khin everything about his visit to the dark plain, relaying every detail he could recall. When he was done, he eyed the aicenai and said, "I wonder if I should return to the enclave and tell them."

"What would you tell them? That a large army of Sudashians marches? That is not new information."

Frowning, Tobias grunted, "No, it is not."

"And if you do return," continued Khin. "The baroness may insist you stay now that you have seen the army. She will want instant notice if you do again." He turned to peer down at Tobias. "Do you wish to remain at the enclave?"

"And what?" asked Tobias "Wait around for everyone to come back?" He shook his head. "No, I'll only return if a vision is more useful than this one was." Nodding to the fields below, he said, "Besides, I can't go now. I have a feeling he's going to want to get as far away from here as he can."

Zecus and Kenders had exited the field and were now striding past the wooden cart before the house. The young man had a determined, cold look to him. On the far side of the cottage, Boah was trudging through the grass, returning from the river with the horses.

Eyeing the approaching three, Tobias muttered, "I think it best if we get moving. Quickly."

Nodding his agreement, Khin stepped past Tobias and walked to where his black steed stood, grazing.

Tobias stayed where he was for a moment, watching Zecus march up the hill, Kenders trailing him, and wondered what words of condolence he could offer. Nothing he could say would help dull the pain and anger. Sighing, Tobias reached up and rubbed his eyes.

"I hate this blasted war already."

CHAPTER 31: PREY

20ᵗʰ of the Turn of Luraana, 4999

Most years, Winter was a time for rejoicing in the Borderlands.

Clouds would come and rain would fall, soaking the brown, dusty country-side and giving it life. Wildflowers sprouted up, dotting the plains and hills with reds, oranges, deep blues and purples, and whites brighter than a lone cloud on a Summer day. For one long and glorious turn, Borderlanders had a nearly unlimited supply of fresh and clean water to drink rather than the brackish muck that bubbled from deep underground wells. A brief growing season was even possible as souls across the duchy planted and harvested hardy, quick-growing grain.

For Rhohn and Tiliah, however, this year's rainy season was more curse than blessing. For over a week, storms came at least once a day, drenching the world—and them—in steady, driving downpours. Rhohn's clothes had not been dry since the day he found Tiliah. His damp skin had been rubbed raw in a half-dozen places, chaffing with each plodding step of their horse. Tiliah had fared better than he had, her thin dress drying quickly once the rains stopped.

For Rhohn, though, the worst part of the daily storms was the fact the rain kept the ground moist, soft, and ripe for tracks. He squirmed with each squish of horse hoof sinking into the mud, confident the slavers were trailing them in an attempt to retrieve the black gem. Rhohn had wanted to be rid of the stone by now, but they had yet to find any place where they could trade it. The two villages they had come across were deserted. If Tiliah were to be believed, their luck might soon change.

Yesterday afternoon, she announced with certainty that they were now in the Marshlands Duchy. As he had never been this far east, Rhohn had no way of refuting her claim. The land certainly looked different. Waist-high brown grass still dominated the landscape, yet strange bushes—some the size of their horse—dotted the area as well, their thick stems sticking straight up like a staff from the bush's center and covered with white flowers the size of his fist.

Mu's orb hung high in the sky behind them, doing its best to dry the land before the next storm arrived. If the past few days' pattern held true, another round of rain would come this evening. The towering, voluminous clouds filling the sky were still white. The heavy gray ones would come later.

Rhohn stared straight ahead, his gaze fixed on the eastern horizon. Neither he nor Tiliah had said much of anything since midday, their weariness muting any conversation. He had set a hard pace, doing his best to keep distance between him and the slavers. They stopped to sleep only when they were in danger of falling off the horse.

His eyelids were drooping closed when Tiliah shifted her weight behind him and broke the afternoon's solitude.

"I'm hungry."

Rhohn sighed. He had known this was coming.

Despite careful rationing, their supply of dried meat had run out last night. The burlap bag was still tucked snuggly into Rhohn's belt, holding only the leather pouch and black stone.

He remained quiet, praying the single mumbled complaint might be the end of it. His silent plea would go unanswered.

"Hey. Did you hear me?"

Leaving her left arm wrapped around his midsection, Tiliah lifted her right and jabbed him sharply in the ribs. He winced, but kept his mouth shut. He did not want to talk. Tiliah proceeded to tap her finger on his sternum.

"Are you asleep?"

"No," grumbled Rhohn. "And stop poking me."

She complied, dropping her hand back to his thigh.

"Did you hear what I said, Mud Man? I'm hungry."

"I heard you just fine. I was ignoring you."

She placed her chin on the back of his right shoulder.

"Surely you're hungry, too?"

Rhohn gave a noncommittal grunt in response. He had been trying hard not to think about his empty stomach.

Tiliah asked, "Does that mean you're hungry or not?"

Rhohn groaned inwardly. Unless he had something important to say, he kept his mouth closed. Tiliah had proven to be the opposite sort of soul. If left to it, she would talk all day. Worse, she expected him to engage and forced him to converse, clawing words from him when he had none to give.

Tiliah asked casually, "What's your favorite dish? Mine is—"

"Hells, Tiliah!" exclaimed Rhohn, his patience cracking. "I don't want to talk about food! Yes, I am hungry. But I am trying to ignore it. So, just this once, keep your blasted tongue to yourself!"

A moment of quiet passed, long enough that he was starting to think she might actually comply. Then she spoke.

"I'm curious, Mud Man. How hot was the fire?"

His brow furrowed, he twisted halfway around in his saddle.

"Pardon?"

"The fire that did this—" She reached up and ran her fingers over the scars on his cheeks, lightly brushing the hole where his ear had once been and causing him to yank away. "Was it so hot that it scarred your heart as well as your skin, searing away your ability to be pleasant?"

Her words were like a punch to the gut, knocking Rhohn's irritation right out of him. This was the first time she had ever acknowledged his deformities. Dropping chin to chest, he stared blankly at the grass as it passed.

"That was harsh."

"Well, you were being boorish. So, I thought I'd give it a try."

He stewed a moment or two longer before realizing Tiliah had a point. Without looking up, he muttered, "I apologize for my outburst."

"Good. You should."

He waited, expecting an apology in response. When none came, he lifted his head.

"Well?"

"Well, what?"

"Will you say you are sorry as well?"

An amused chuckle slipped from Tiliah.

"For what? Teaching you manners? I'm waiting for a thank you."

The corners of his lips curled up a fraction.

"Yes, well...you will be waiting awhile."

Patting him on his back, she said, "That's fine, Mud Man. As it turns out, I have little else to do but wait."

Rhohn turned his head forward and stared east.

"I was starting to think you had not noticed my scars."

"I would have to be blind not to."

Grimacing at her bluntness, he said, "You did not stare when we met. Most people do."

"Most people have not spent weeks treating maimed soldiers in Gobas. Your scars are nothing. Be grateful you have them."

Rhohn's eyes narrowed.

"If that is a jest, it is a poor one."

"It's no jest," said Tiliah. "Thank Greya for your fate, Mud Man. You are alive." A sad, hollow note entered her voice. "Many are not."

Rhohn stared at the eastern horizon, where azure and white met dusty tan. After a few moments, he asked, "You are thinking of your brother again, aren't you?"

A long pause separated question and answer, filled only by the rustle of wind in the grass and squelching of hooves in wet mud.

"Perhaps."

Tiliah had shared how her older brother had journeyed west, planning to help repel the invaders. While Rhohn respected the man's bravery, he found Zecus' action to be a foolish one.

Tiliah was quiet for another dozen steps of their horse. When she spoke again, her tone was wistful, quiet.

"I wish you could have met him, Mud Man."

Rhohn pressed his lips together and, for some reason, he found himself offering encouragement.

"Do not speak of him as though he is passed, Tiliah. He could very well be alive."

The prospect was unlikely, but he did not like hearing Tiliah so despondent. Fully aware that he was spreading false hope, a tiny, bemused grin touched his lips. Were Silas here, his friend would not hesitate to point out his hypocrisy.

A sad, dejected huff slipped from Tiliah. "I saw the army outside of Gobas, Mud Man. If Zecus faced that…" She trailed off and went quiet.

Rhohn did not know what else to say, so he chose to remain silent. Several dozen plodding steps of the horse later, she shifted again, her hair tickling the back of his neck.

"You know, in some ways, you rather remind me of Zecus. My father, too."

The realization almost sounded as if it bothered her. Twisting around, he said, "I shall judge for myself when I meet them." He stared ahead again. "Perhaps your father will have returned from his pilgrimage by the time we reach Demetus?"

"I very much doubt that."

Rhohn frowned. Tiliah was growing more despondent by the moment. He was not helping matters in the slightest, yet he pressed on.

"War has not yet reached the east, Tiliah. The lands there are still safe. Your father will return and find you."

"Sorry, Mud Man. Too many things have gone wrong for me to believe any could go right."

Summoning forth a false sense of confidence, he said, "Tiliah, look at everything you have been through since *you* left Demetus. Through it all, you persevered. You survived. I have to think that the man who sired such a determined soul can manage to ride a horse to Freehaven and back."

He expected a response, but none came. Their horse trod into an extended puddle of muddy slop, splattering their legs with even more of the wet, dirty muck. Rhohn's boots were already covered with the gunk.

As they emerged from the puddle, Tiliah reached up and patted him lightly on his chest.

"You are a good person, Mud Man."

Rhohn smiled.

"I don't know about that, but I will—"

He cut off as their horse suddenly lurched sideways while loosing a low, panicked nicker. Rhohn instinctively gripped their mount's sides with his knees and yanked on the makeshift rope reins. Tiliah squeezed his waist, let out a short, startled cry, followed quickly with a worried question.

"What is it?"

Rhohn ignored her as he labored to bring the horse under control. The mare was strong, however, having had a steady diet of grass and water, and fought Rhohn, breaking into a trot on her own accord. Scanning the ground around them, Rhohn looked for what had spooked her. Nothing stood out. He studied the nearby grass, praying that another razorfiend had not found them. Still nothing.

He was about to attribute the entire experience to a skittish horse in a strange land when a lone, wolf-like howl cut through the air, shredding the afternoon's peace and sending a shiver up Rhohn's spine. He recognized the call in an instant and Tiliah's shouts confirmed it.

"Mongrels! Mongrels are behind us!"

No longer interested in slowing their horse, Rhohn kicked his heels into the beast's sides. The gesture was unnecessary, however, as the mare was already accelerating into a full gallop, her instincts a step ahead of his order.

The howl rose and fell before cutting off. An instant later, a second cry answered the first, coming from a decidedly different direction. Looking over his left shoulder, Rhohn searched the surrounding countryside.

"Do you see them?!"

"Two! To the southwest!"

As he twisted back around to look, he caught a blur of dark brown behind them and to the north. A third mongrel was rushing through the grass, heading straight for them.

"Hells!"

As he stared at it, the third beast opened its jaws and howled. Their horse swerved abruptly to the right, nearly tossing both riders in the process. He gripped the mane of the horse to hold on, eliciting a sharp whinny of pain from the mare. Tiliah squeezed him just as hard. As he righted himself, he spotted a fourth mongrel—this one a shadowy gray—charging them from the northeast. It howled, forcing the horse to change direction again.

A sick, sour taste filled Rhohn's mouth as he realized what was happening: they were being herded. Facing straight ahead, he scanned the grasses and shrubs, studying every large bush, every grass thicket. It only took a moment before his gaze settled on a green and white variegated bush a few hundred paces ahead. His heart climbed into his throat.

A fifth mongrel was waiting patiently, squatting beside the bush, its brown fur peeking through the leaves. Rhohn tried tugging on the ropes, hoping to turn the horse away from the bush, but the mare was not going to take direction from him. Blind fear of the mongrels she knew about was driving her straight to the one she did not.

Tiliah called out from behind, "Gods, they're fast!"

Looking to his right, he saw that the first two were less than a few hundred paces from them, loping on all fours, teeth bared. The ones to the north were even closer, especially the gray one.

Unable to do anything else, Rhohn wrapped the rope around his right hand and gripped the hilt to his Dust Man blade with his left. Somehow, despite the horse's jarring gallop, he managed to draw the sword free from the scabbard without cutting or stabbing himself.

Tiliah screamed, "What are you—" Her cry cut off sharply, only to be followed a moment later by a sickened, "Oh, Hells."

Rhohn guessed she saw the hidden mongrel. Squeezing his sword tight, Rhohn readied himself. To do what, he did not know. Riding at a full gallop toward one mongrel while being chased by four others had never been covered in his Dust Man training.

He kept his gaze on the mongrel straight-ahead while his mind sought a solution to an impossible situation. As he stared, the mongrel behind the bush pulled down a branch and glared back, its yellow eyes peering over a brown and white muzzle.

For a brief moment, it was as if time stopped.

"No…"

Rhohn told himself it was impossible, but the markings were identical. It was Okollu.

Suddenly, the mongrel bolted from the bush and charged them. The terrified horse finally spotted the lurking beast, whinnied sharply, and attempted to stop but ended up sliding through the mud and slick grass. Rhohn toppled forward, lost hold of the rope, and tried to grab the neck of the horse as he flipped over the mare's head. He failed and flew through the air, dropping his sword in the process.

He heard Tiliah scream before he crashed to the softened ground, landing hard on his right side. Air exploded from his lungs, his face smacked hard into a shallow mud puddle.

The horse loosed another frightened squeal, one that came from right above him. Looking up, he saw the mare—its back bare now—towering over him, reared on its hind legs. Just before the front hooves crashed into the earth, he rolled away, tumbling through grass and mud. After a few revolutions, he stopped, ending on his back and staring into the cloud-strewn sky. A blur of brown fur rushed over him and something hard struck him in the chest.

A voice, thick and wet, whispered, "Stand up, smooth-face! Quickly!"

Glancing down, Rhohn saw his Dust Man blade lying across his stomach. Thoroughly confused, he grabbed the hilt and scrambled up as their horse screamed. Looking over, he found Okollu in the midst of clamping his jaws on the animal's neck. Blood rushed from the bite, coloring horse and mongrel crimson.

The muscles in Okollu's neck and back bulged as it ripped backwards, tearing a chunk of flesh from the horse's throat. The beast turned his head and spat the mouthful of meat to the ground.

Spotting Tiliah lying in the grass, dangerously close to the dancing legs of the doomed horse, Rhohn pushed himself from the ground, ran over, and grabbed her arm with his maimed hand. Backpedaling, he dragged her limp body through mud and grass, keeping one eye on the gray mongrel racing ever closer from the northeast. When the beast was only a couple dozen paces away, Rhohn dropped Tiliah's arm, faced the monster, and raised his sword, his heart thudding in his chest.

Moments before the mongrel reached Rhohn, Okollu abruptly sprang back from the horse, reached out, and grabbed the beast's furry, gray scruff along its neck. It stopped almost instantly, its head snapping backward to expose a lone stripe of white running from jaw to chest. Quicker than a lightning flash, Okollu drew a hand across the mongrel's exposed neck, a bone-handle dagger gripped in its hand. A torrent of bright red blood poured down the beast's chest.

Rhohn stared, stunned, as Okollu shoved the wide-eyed mongrel toward him. The beast, its hands clasped over its bloody throat, stumbled toward Rhohn. Recovering from his shock, Rhohn lashed out with his thin blade, jamming the tip into the mongrel's chest. The sword bent slightly, piercing flesh, slipping past thick chest muscles, and bursting through the beast's back. Blood from the neck wound spurted over Rhohn. It was hot and smelled like a freshly sharpened dagger blade.

As the mongrel collapsed to the ground, Rhohn tried to yank his sword free but found it stuck. He stumbled forward, holding onto the hilt as the beast crumpled over to land beside Tiliah. Rhohn stepped on its chest and, with both arms, ripped the sword free.

Whirling around, he watched Okollu take another bite from the horse's neck. The mare—no longer whinnying—took two last, unsteady steps before its legs buckled. Collapsing to the ground, the horse rolled to its side. She was not dead yet, but soon would be.

Okollu turned to face him, standing upright, the dagger from before jammed into a leather harness around the mongrel's waist. The beast's yellow eyes locked onto Rhohn and it spoke in a low, gruff voice.

"I will end the two males. The female is yours."

As Rhohn stared blankly at Okollu, baffled as to what was happening, the mongrel drew back its lips, bared its teeth, and began growling. The ferocious snarl sounded sincere, but the threat in Okollu's voice never reached the mongrel's eyes.

His gaze shot back to the remaining three mongrels. Two approached from the left—one gray and the other brown like Okollu but without the white markings. Rich auburn fur covered the third monster's body, a black patch on its face. Rhohn repeatedly glanced between the three, trying to mark which one was female. They all looked the same to him.

As they neared, the three mongrels joined Okollu's growl. The auburn one stopped by the dying horse—ten paces to Okollu's left—bent down, and sniffed. The other pair halted on Okollu's right, further away. All three stared between Rhohn and the corpse of the dead mongrel, unadulterated hate filling their eyes. It took him a moment to realize that the mare must have blocked Okollu's attack from their view. They blamed Rhohn for the gray mongrel's death.

Okollu, eyes flaring wide, barked, "You have something that does not belong to you!"

Other than his sword and his clothes, the only thing Rhohn had in his possession was the pouch with the stone. Glancing down at the bag tucked into his belt, he pulled the bag free.

"This?"

Okollu sniffed the air twice and tossed his muzzle toward the pair of mongrels to his right, Rhohn's left.

"Toss it there, smooth-face."

Rhohn hesitated, trying to figure out what mongrels would want with a gemstone.

"The bag!" growled Okollu. "Now!"

A light moan drifted from the grass by his feet. Glancing down, he saw Tiliah stir, her hand rubbing the back of her head.

"The bag, smooth-face, or we kill the female."

Rhohn glared at Okollu. He had no doubt the mongrel would follow through on the threat.

"If I give you the—"

"Now!" barked Okollu. Its eyes flashed wide, pleading with Rhohn to comply.

Wondering if he was mad for putting his faith in an animal, Rhohn tossed the bag toward the two mongrels to his left. The sack struck the ground with a solid thud.

Okollu turned to the pair and snapped, "Alege sus si avedea ce nauntru."

The brown mongrel stepped forward and bent down to sniff the pouch.

Feeling a light tapping on his leg, Rhohn glanced down. Tiliah was sitting up now, staring at the four beasts before them. Without looking away from them, she spoke in a hushed whisper.

"What do we do?"

Okollu's gaze snapped back to them.

"Silence!"

Tiliah complied, keeping her hand on Rhohn's leg, her fingers digging into his injured calf. Rhohn squeezed the hilt of his sword just as tightly.

The mongrel inspecting the sack lifted its head, looked to Okollu, and growled, "Ese pitra."

"Bring it here," growled Okollu. The nostrils on its black nose flared. "Lussa, you stay there." Eyeing Rhohn, it gave an almost imperceptible nod in the direction of the auburn mongrel, its hand slipping down to the dagger jammed in the harness.

Rhohn studied the lone beast to his right and guessed it was the female. Which meant the pair to his left were the males. Hoping that he understood Okollu's intent, Rhohn offered a silent prayer to Ketus, the God of Luck.

The brown mongrel grabbed the bag in his hand, stood tall, and strode to Okollu. As he stretched out his arm to hand over the bag, Okollu grabbed his wrist and twisted, spinning the mongrel around and eliciting a sharp, surprised grunt from the creature. The remaining mongrels turned their heads, their ears pointed.

Releasing the male's wrist, Okollu gripped a fistful of fur atop the mongrel's head, yanked the mongrel's head back, and drew the dagger fast and deep across the exposed neck. A plume of crimson squirted to the grass. Okollu shoved him aside, dropped to all fours, and rushed the gray male. A monstrous howl erupted from his throat.

The auburn female answered an instant later with a fury-filled growl of her own and sprinted after Okollu. Rhohn was already running forward and intercepted the female as she leapt over the bloody male. He thrust his blade at her exposed side, hoping to land a quick blow. The mongrel, incredibly agile, dodged the attack, coiling her body around the stab in mid-air. She landed, skidding in the mud, and whirled to face Rhohn, her jaws snapping at him, forcing him to backpedal.

With nostrils flaring and ears pinned back, she stalked closer, her yellow-eyed gaze dancing between his face and his sword. As she approached, she stood upright, her fists clenched at her side, a constant growl rumbling from her throat.

Rhohn lifted his sword, readying himself to fight even though he knew he had no chance to defeat the stronger, more agile mongrel. He was tired, hungry, and nursing an injured calf. This was not going to end well.

Continuing to backpedal, he turned his head to the side and shouted, "Run, Tiliah!"

"No!"

"Blast it, Tiliah! Get up and—"

"Hawk's wing!" shouted Tiliah. "Red, back two!"

Rhohn's step faltered. Her words were so unexpected that he nearly turned his back on the mongrel to stare at her. For the briefest of moments, he was back in the training yards in Gobas, lined up with fellow Dust Men, sword in hand, listening to a sergeant call out orders to teach the new soldiers proper fighting positions. "Hawk's wing" meant to draw back his sword arm, putting his hand at his hip. "Red, back two" told him to place his left foot two paces behind his right. How Tiliah knew any of that was beyond him.

"Blast it, Rhohn!" screamed Tiliah. "Hawk's wing, red, back two!"

The female mongrel was mere paces from him, lowering herself into a crouch, ready to pounce.

Putting his faith in Tiliah, he arranged his body to her shouted orders, sword on hip, one foot before the other. The moment he assumed the correct position, a high-pitched whistle cut the air. The auburn mongrel, ears perked up, stopped her advance and looked past Rhohn to where Tiliah lay on the ground. Taking advantage of the distraction, Rhohn stepped forward, swiveled his hips, and drove his sword forward with all the force he could, piercing the mongrel's body where chest met neck. The blade sunk into flesh, ricocheted off the spine, and exited at the base of her skull.

Loosing a sharp yelp of pain, the mongrel grabbed the sword with her hands as Rhohn drew the blade back, twisting as he did. The edge bit deep into the beast's palms, slicing them open and sending blood down her arms. When the blade stopped, catching on something in the mongrel's throat, Rhohn yanked hard. The mongrel's cries cut off instantly.

Rhohn ripped the sword free and hopped back a few steps, waiting for a counterattack that would never come. The mongrel stumbled backward, her mangled hands clasped around her throat and panic in her eyes. She worked her jaws, perhaps trying to speak, but all that came out was a sickening mix of choking, gasping, and gurgling. She collapsed to all fours, hunched over and gagging, suffocating on her own blood.

Rhohn almost felt sympathy for her. Almost.

Okollu rushed toward the female, a flash of brown and white fur. Upon reaching her, Okollu grabbed her shoulder, flipped her on her back, and plunged the dagger straight into her chest. He—Rhohn had decided Okollu was male—immediately pulled the blade free and jammed it back down again, a few inches to the side of the first thrust. Her body went limp in an instant. The second stab had ended her.

The world was suddenly quiet, filled only by the thudding of his heart and the light rustle of the grass in the breeze.

Okollu was kneeling beside the dead mongrel, his back to Rhohn. The Dust Man stared at him, tense and ready, wondering what to expect next. Chancing a quick look to where Okollu had fought the other male, Rhohn found a scene eerily reminiscent of the one in the house in Ebel. The gray mongrel's throat was gone.

Looking back to Okollu, Rhohn waited for the mongrel to do something. Instead, Okollu remained in place, hunched over the dead female and unmoving. Keeping his eyes on Okollu, Rhohn stepped backwards until he reached where Tiliah was still sitting in the grass.

"Are you hurt?"

"My shoulder's sore, but I'll be fine,"

Nodding once, Rhohn said, "Good."

"Rhohn?"

"Yes?"

"What in the Nine Hells is going on? That thing just saved us." She glanced up at him. "Why?"

Rhohn was unsure how to respond. The truth would take longer to explain than he might have right now. He wondered if he should claim complete ignorance. Perhaps Okollu would let him and Tiliah walk away.

"Rhohn…? What aren't you telling me?"

He stared down at her.

"What do you—?"

"End the show. I can see it on your face."

"Now is not the—"

"Tell me, Rhohn!" demanded Tiliah.

Rhohn hesitated and glanced back to Okollu. The mongrel had yet to move. After hesitating a moment longer, Rhohn let out a long sigh and said, "It…he, I suppose—he and I…we've met before."

The volume of Tiliah's voice increased tenfold.

"You've *met* it?"

Okollu's ears twitched and his head turned to the side ever so slightly.

"I am thinking Okollu is more 'he' than 'it."

Her eyebrows drew together.

"Okollu?"

Rhohn paused a moment.

"That's his name."

"You *know its name*?"

Rhohn pressed his lips together and stared back down to Tiliah.

"It is not how it seems. He and I…made an arrangement of sorts."

Tiliah remained silent for several heartbeats, her deep brown eyes locked on his face and swelling with sudden distrust. Suspicion hung heavy in her voice as she asked, "What kind of arrangement?"

"On my honor, Tiliah, I promise to share everything—*everything*—with you." He paused and glanced at Okollu. "As soon as we're safe."

She looked back to Okollu and asked, "Are you on his side? Or is he on yours?"

Rhohn considered the astute question briefly before answering.

"He's on his, I'm on mine."

"Then what happened here?"

"I just think our sides are overlapping right now."

"Why?"

Rhohn shrugged.

"I said we have an arrangement, not an understanding. Please, I need you to trust me."

A frown on her face, Tiliah eyed the surrounding carnage, turned to peer east a moment, and then looked back up to Rhohn.

"For now, Mud Man."

Rhohn gave her a tiny smile.

"Thank you."

She nodded once and stared back to Okollu, her brow furrowing.

"I think he's going to pass out."

Rhohn shifted his gaze to the mongrel's back and found Okollu listing to the left. A moment later, the mongrel abruptly toppled over, tumbling to the ground.

Tiliah asked, "Is it—is he dead?"

"I don't know," muttered Rhohn. He studied Okollu's prone form for a moment before saying, "I'm going to go check. Stay here."

As he went to step toward the mongrel, Tiliah quickly rose from the ground.

"No. I'm coming."

"Tiliah. It's not safe for—"

Her eyes flaring hot, she interrupted him, saying, "You tell me you are conspiring with a mongrel and then expect me to let you go confer with him? Alone? Unless you stab me with that sword, Mud Man, I am coming with you!"

He held her determined gaze and sighed. There was no point in arguing with her. Turning toward Okollu, he murmured, "Fine. But stay behind me, at least."

They moved through the grass, approaching Okollu slowly. As they neared, Rhohn spotted a gaping, bloody wound on the mongrel's right shoulder. Okollu's breathing was shallow and ragged.

"Well," whispered Tiliah. "He's not dead."

Ending the mongrel now would be easy. Okollu was in no shape to fight back. Mongrels were Rhohn's enemy, the beasts having already killed thousands of men, women, and children. Borderlanders. Rhohn's countrymen. This particular one, lying at his feet, had murdered a friend of his. His heart thudding in his chest, he lifted his sword, readying to plunge it into the beast's chest.

Okollu turned his head, turning his yellow eyes on Rhohn. Man and mongrel locked gazes and Rhohn stayed his hand. This mongrel had saved his life twice now. Rhohn wanted to know why. He needed to know why.

He lowered his sword, pointing the tip to the soft earth.

"Tiliah? Get the rope from the horse. And find the bag. We'll need it for bandages."

"Bandages?" repeated Tiliah. "For who? And don't say him."

Rhohn looked over at her.

"You need to bind his wounds."

Her eyes went round.

"I need to do *what*?!"

He took a deep breath, wiped his blade on his pants leg—both sides—and slid his sword into his scabbard.

"We need him alive. For now, at least."

Clearly agitated, Tiliah exclaimed, "Are you mad? Why?"

"I have some questions for him," said Rhohn, turning his eyes back to Okollu. "The last time we met, there wasn't time to ask them. Now, there is."

"What sort of questions?" prompted Tiliah. "What exactly is this 'arrangement' you two have?"

"Blast it, Tiliah!" snapped Rhohn. "He's bleeding out! Bind him and you can hear the questions when I ask them!"

She glowered at him, her eyes narrowed to mere slits. He was thinking she might refuse to help when she gave a short, decisive nod and spat a single word.

"*Fine.*"

She moved to the body of the dead horse, taking a wide, circuitous path around Okollu. As she bent down to untie the rope from the mare, Rhohn faced the mongrel, praying that he was doing the right thing. Holding the mongrel's steady gaze, he demanded, "Why did you save us?" He waved his hand at the bloody scene around them. "Why did you do this?"

Okollu rolled onto his back and made to sit up, but halted instantly, his black lips curling into a painful snarl. Rhohn saw the shoulder wound actually continued to the middle of Okollu's chest, deep and raw. Giving up, Okollu lay flat, wincing.

"The message you carry is too important, smooth-face."

Rhohn glanced up quickly to find Tiliah glaring at them, having clearly heard what Okollu said. She stood, retrieved the burlap bag from the grass, and moved back to them, rope in hand, her gaze locked on Rhohn's face, a thousand questions dancing in her eyes. Okollu turned his head at the sound of her scuffling steps. She stopped on the opposite side of Okollu, her eyes still skeptical.

"You are sure you want to do this?"

"I am," answered Rhohn.

Tiliah nodded once and turned her full attention to the mongrel's wound.

"If you promise not to bite, I can help you with that."

"No!" growled Okollu. "Leave me."

Tiliah lifted her gaze to Rhohn.

"You heard him, Mud Man. Let's go."

Ignoring her, Rhohn stepped closer to Okollu. Eyeing the meaty gash, he said, "You are losing a lot of blood. You'll die soon if we do not bind it."

"I murdered my pack mates," growled Okollu, his ragged voice thick with disgust. "I deserve to die."

Rhohn could not let that happen. He wanted answers. Drawing his Dust Man blade forth, he stepped forward and pointed the tip at Okollu's neck.

"Let her bind your wound."

Soft, puffing growls slipped from the mongrel's throat. He was laughing.

"Go! Shove your blade into me! I *want* to die!"

Rhohn withdrew the sword tip from Okollu's neck. He had not thought that through. He stared at the mongrel, wondering how to threaten a soul who welcomed death.

In a clear, calm tone, Tiliah said, "If he doesn't want help, he doesn't want help. Leave him to die and let's go."

Staring up into the sky, Okollu said, "Listen to the she-man." His voice sounded weaker than just a moment ago.

Rhohn shook his head.

"No! I need to know about that message! And why you are out here, chasing us for a blasted gemstone?"

Okollu twisted his head to stare at Rhohn again.

"Stone? What stone?"

"The one in the bag," answered Rhohn.

Okollu rolled his head to stare at the burlap bag gripped in Tiliah's hand, hanging freely at her side.

"There is a stone in the bag?"

"Of course, isn't that—?"

"What does it look like?"

Rhohn was confused.

"You were hunting for something yet you did not—"

Okollu whipped his head back around to glare at Rhohn, his eyes intense and burning.

"What does it look like?!"

Rhohn hesitated, sharing a quick look with Tiliah before answering.

"It's black. Smooth and glossy."

"Black?" replied the mongrel. That detail seemed to surprise him. "How big is it?"

Rhohn frowned, wondering at the mongrel's sudden interest in the rock.

"The size of my thumb."

The bloody fur around Okollu's muzzle twitched.

"Does it smell wrong to you?"

"I'm sorry…does it '*smell*' wrong? It doesn't smell like anything. It's a rock."

"Do you squirm when you look upon it?"

Rhohn's face twisted up in confusion.

"What are you—?"

"Yes," answered Tiliah. Rhohn glanced up to find her staring at Okollu, nodding, her eyes just as intense as Okollu's. "It's wicked."

Confused, Rhohn asked, "What do you mean it's 'wicked?' It's a *rock*."

Tiliah shifted her gaze to Rhohn and spoke with complete confidence, "Something is wrong with that stone."

"What?"

"I don't know, Mud Man," said Tiliah, exasperated. "But...I just know that—"

Okollu interrupted her, growling, "I would like your help now, she-man."

Tiliah stared down at the mongrel and snapped, "My name is Tiliah, not 'she-man!'"

"Whatever your name, I would like your help now."

Wondering at the mongrel's sudden shift in attitude, Rhohn asked, "Do you know what the stone is?"

"No."

"Then why—"

"I cannot answer your questions if I am dead, smooth-face! I want your help now, so give it to me!"

Pushing aside his curiosity for the moment, Rhohn pressed his lips together and looked back to Tiliah.

"Do what you can."

Tiliah stared down at the mongrel and asked, "You won't bite me, will you?"

"I will restrain myself," answered Okollu. It almost sounded like he was being wry.

Letting out a tiny sigh, Tiliah moved closer to Okollu, kneeled down, and inspected the wound.

"Without the correct tools, I can only bind it. And it will hurt while I do it. A lot."

Okollu nodded.

"I understand. Do what you must."

She reached out to touch the wound, prodding the edges around the open slice. Blood and clumps of fur quickly coated her hands and arms. Without looking up, she said, "Come here, Mud Man. I need you to hold his flesh together."

Rhohn sheathed his sword and crouched near Okollu's head. Tiliah explained what he was to do as she tore long strips from the empty burlap bag, laying them on Okollu's chest. Throughout their exchange, Okollu lay quietly, eyeing them both.

When everything was in place, Tiliah peered down at Okollu.

"Ready?"

Snapping his jaws shut hard enough that they clacked, Okollu growled, "I am."

Tiliah looked up at Rhohn and nodded.

"Go."

As she had instructed, Rhohn jammed fur and skin together, jumping as Okollu let out an ear-splitting howl. After only a moment, the cry cut off abruptly. The muscles in the mongrel's chest relaxed. Rhohn glanced to Okollu's face and saw that he had passed out.

"Good," grunted Tiliah. "This will be easier." She quickly wrapped the strips of burlap over the wound and bound it with rope, pulling so tight that Rhohn was worried she might be cutting off blood flow. After one last sharp tug, she said, "You can let go now."

Rhohn released the bloody fur and scooted back. As she inspected the binding, he stood upright and turned in a slow, stationary circle, studying every horizon and praying they were far enough from anyone that the mongrels' howls had gone unnoticed. Seeing nothing besides grass, bushes, and sky, he turned his attention back to the bloody scene around them. Tiliah was rubbing her hands through the grass, trying to wipe off as much gore as possible. She glanced up, caught him staring at her, and nodded at Okollu.

"He will probably be unconscious for…" She trailed off, shrugged her shoulders, and said, "Hells, I don't know. He's a blasted mongrel. One day? Two weeks?" Placing her hands on her hips, she peered around at the ground. "And there had better be thornroot nearby else we just saved him today so he can die next week."

"As soon as I get what I want, he is welcome to do just that."

She lifted her gaze and fixed him with a steady stare.

"You have some explaining to do."

"I do," conceded Rhohn. "As do you."

Arching her eyebrows, Tiliah said, "Me?"

"Hawk's wing? Red, back two?"

"Ah…that." A faint smile spread over her lips. "I did not spend every moment of my time tending to the wounded in Gobas. I *might* have wandered by the soldiers' grounds a few times to watch drills."

"A few times?" said Rhohn, incredulous. "You remembered the position calls, Tiliah."

She shrugged and, with the tiniest flicker of embarrassment, admitted, "Some of the Dust Men were rather handsome."

Rhohn could not hold back a smile.

"And the whistle?"

"A footman I tended to taught it to me. Some of the men used it to distract the mongrels. It irritates them for some reason. Took me a while to get it right."

"Well, thank you for taking the time. It saved my life. *You* saved my life."

"No, I saved *my* life. If that mongrel killed you, I was next."

"Regardless, thank you."

Tiliah took one last look at Okollu, stood from the ground, and crossed her arms. She set her gaze on Rhohn, direct and demanding.

"Time to start talking. How is it you know a mongrel? Why are you carrying a message for it? What is the message, who's it for, and why in the Nine Hells didn't you tell me any of this before today?!"

Rhohn nodded through the list, admitting they were all valid questions. When she was done, he let out a long, weary sigh.

"I'll answer them all. But I'll warn you…you might not believe me."

"We won't know until you start sharing, will we?"

"No," muttered Rhohn. "I suppose not."

Standing amidst the grisly scene, a bandaged mongrel on the ground between them, he told the truth of what happened in Ebel. From the final moment that he had seen Silas alive to when he had crawled from the earthen longhouse, covered in his friend's blood. Halfway through his tale, he spotted a tiny ember of fear spark to life in her eyes. By the time he was done, it had grown into a glowing-red coal.

CHAPTER 32: SOUL

21ˢᵗ of the Turn of Luraana, 4999

Tiliah was hungry, tired and—once again—soaked to the skin.

The rain clouds had come shortly after sunset last evening and stayed the night, breaking up at dawn. She had thought the constant downpour would discourage scavenging animals, but it did not. A pack of carrion dogs hounded them throughout the night, fiercely determined to make a meal of the horse and mongrels. Rhohn repeatedly chased them away until the dogs left at daybreak, just as the first blood vultures arrived.

Rhohn was running after them now, waving his sword and shouting at two of the more persistent birds. The vultures snapped at him with their crooked, black beaks, clearly upset that he was interrupting their meal again. Were Tiliah not so miserable, she might be laughing at the display.

Okollu lay a few dozen paces away, still unconscious. The beast had not moved nor made a sound all night. Each time she had checked on him, she half expected to find him not breathing. She looked away from the mongrel, shaking her head in disbelief.

"This must be a dream…"

As Rhohn had shared his tale with her, she—at first—wondered if the Dust Man had struck his head on a rock in the tumble from their horse. Yet the more she heard, the more she believed. The message itself, the one Rhohn was carrying across the Oaken Duchies, convinced her that he was not mad. It explained so much.

Something had managed to bring the full force of the Sudashians—oligurts, razorfiends, and mongrels—together. Tiliah supposed that if any force in Terrene could do so, a God of the Cabal could. It also explained what she had seen the morning she left Gobas with thousands of others.

When word had spread through the city that the Sudashian force was on the horizon, Tiliah rushed to the western wall to see for herself. As she stood, gaping in awe at the army, an advance group of oligurts approached Gobas, riding their bullockboars and managing to stay just out of the catapults' range. What appeared to be a man wearing a horned helmet led the group, only he was running on his own two feet, easily keeping a pace equal to a galloping horse. The whispered rumors were true: this army was led by demons of the Nine Hells.

Approaching footsteps, squishing in mud, whisked her away from the dry and dusty battlements of Gobas and back to the mushy present. Looking up, she found Rhohn trudging back to where she sat, stepping over one of the mongrel corpses. Upon reaching her, he sheathed his sword and collapsed to the ground like a sack of tubers dropped from a wagon cart. He looked as tired as she felt.

Rubbing his eyes, he muttered, "Gods, I truly hope they do not come back."

Tiliah peered up into the gray sky. At least a dozen blood vultures circled high overhead.

"Oh, they'll be back." She glanced in the direction of the corpses and, with a grimace on her face, muttered. "It's a feast for them over there."

"And they are welcome to enjoy it once we leave," said Rhohn. "But I don't want to sit here and watch them eat."

Giving Rhohn a sideways glance, Tiliah suggested, "We could start walking now and leave them to their meal...?"

The Dust Man gave her a sleepy smile and shook his head.

"Nice try. Again. But we are waiting for him to wake up."

Frowning, Tiliah looked back to the mongrel and said, "And when might that be? Today? Tomorrow? Year's End? Hells, he might never wake up. I treated soldiers with lesser injuries than he who went on to Maeana's realm."

Rhohn lay down, apparently not caring about the soaked ground, and let a long sigh slip from his lips.

"I'm not leaving as long as he draws breath. However, if you'd like to go—" he lifted a hand and pointed east "—Demetus is that way."

"Don't think I haven't considered it."

"I would be disappointed if you had not," mumbled Rhohn "Truly? I am surprised you are still here." He lifted his head off the ground and looked at her. "Why are you still here?"

"It's safer."

Rhohn cocked his lone eyebrow.

"With me, you've been attacked by a razorfiend and a pack of mongrels. How is that safer?"

Shrugging her shoulders, Tiliah said, "I'm still alive, aren't I?"

Rhohn dropped his head to the ground with a soft squish.

"You speak true."

Tiliah let out a long, heavy sigh and said, "Well, if we're staying, I suppose I should check his wound."

She made to stand, but stopped when Rhohn muttered, "Hold a moment." He began to sit up. "I'm coming with you."

"I can do this on my own." All night long, he had accompanied her, sword drawn, whenever she went to check on Okollu. "Stay here and try to sleep. I would bet coin he's still passed out."

He stared at her, a battle between fatigue and gallantry playing itself out in his eyes. Fatigue won. Dropping back to the mushy earth, he muttered, "Be careful. Scream if he bites you."

A tiny smile touched her lip as she rose from the grass.

"You don't have to worry about that."

Turning around, she started walking to where Okollu lay, which was the exact place where he had passed out yesterday. Rhohn had thought to move him away from the dead bodies, but Tiliah named it a bad idea. She had seen fevered men attack their caregivers if startled from sleep and wished to avoid such an outburst from a mongrel.

She moved around the corpses, disgusted by the swarms of flies that had already collected on the exposed flesh. The rain had rinsed away the excess blood, leaving each open wound pink and meaty.

She stopped a few steps from Okollu's prone form and eyed the mongrel carefully, wondering if she should perhaps call Rhohn over after all. She considered herself a brave soul, but bravery was not a shield against teeth. As she stood there, staring and reconsidering, Okollu spoke softly.

"I promised not to bite you, did I not?"

Surprised, Tiliah took a quick step back and muttered, "You're awake?"

The mongrel opened his eyes and twisted his head to stare up at Tiliah. For the second time in mere moments, she was caught off guard. Rather than the dull, glassy stare common amongst those who were ill, Okollu's yellow irises were bright and alive.

"Your Dust Man woke me with his shouting."

Tiliah glanced over her shoulder, readying to call out for Rhohn, but saw that he was already scrambling from the ground, his eyes fixed on her. Turning back to Okollu, she found the mongrel sniffing the air, his black nose twitching. His lips curled back to expose yellowed teeth and pink gums.

"You left me to sleep among the dead?"

"I was afraid to move you."

Okollu peered at her and asked gruffly, "Why?"

"I was worried you might awake and rip out our throats before remembering who we were."

The mongrel was quiet a moment before speaking.

"You were wise to leave me, then."

Rhohn arrived to stand beside her, sword drawn and at his side. He no longer appeared tired, his eyes were wide and alert. Hearing mud squish, she looked back to find Okollu pushing himself into a sitting position.

"Please don't move," scolded Tiliah. "You might open the wound."

"I am fine," insisted Okollu, staring at the bandage on his shoulder. Reaching up with his left hand, he immediately began undoing it.

Her voice full of reprimand, Tiliah said, "And if you do that, you *will* open the wound."

When he did not stop, she took a step closer to Okollu and reached out her hand, hoping to stop him from unraveling the bandage. He might be a mongrel, but he was her charge. Okollu lifted his gaze from the rope, stared at her, and let loose a low, rumbling growl. His message was clear.

Taking a quick step back, she threw her hands in the air.

"Fine. Do as you please."

Rhohn said, "Please listen to what—"

"Quiet!" snapped Okollu. "I am fine!"

Rhohn shut his mouth and looked over at Tiliah. She shrugged her shoulders and watched the mongrel in silence. If Okollu bled out now, all the better. They could be on their way east within the hour.

With an irritated huff, Okollu pulled the rope to his mouth and gnawed on it. Tiliah shivered, watching the mongrel's jaws gnash together. He made short work of the binding, ripped the rope and burlap-strip bandages from his shoulder, and tossed the remnants to the ground.

Tiliah's eyes opened wide. Rhohn drew a quick breath of surprise.

The gash that had run from Okollu's shoulder to chest was gone. Only a pink strip of raised skin lined with short, fine hair remained. Okollu rotated his arm in a wide circle, testing his range of movement.

Her mouth agape, Tiliah stammered, "How...how did you...?" She trailed off, too stunned to continue.

Dropping his arm, Okollu peered up at her and asked, "What is wrong?"

She lifted a finger and pointed at the former wound.

"How did that happen?"

Okollu stared back to his shoulder.

"What do you mean?"

She dropped to a knee beside the mongrel, squishing in the mud, and ran her fingers over the leftover scar. The fine hair lining the wound was softer than the fuzzy tuft that topped Winter grain stalks.

"That was two inches deep! It should have taken—"

She cut off as a warm puff of air rushed through her hair. The odor of wet dog filled her nose. Realizing how close she was to Okollu's jaws, she froze and stared into the mongrel's yellow eyes. A low, gruff sound slipped from Okollu's throat. It almost sounded like a chuckle.

"I will not bite you."

Praying the mongrel was telling the truth, she returned her attention to the nearly healed wound. Rhohn stepped closer and leaned down to stare as well.

"That should not be possible."

Okollu glanced between them, asking, "You are...confused, yes? The emotions of your race are difficult to read."

Nodding, Tiliah admitted, "We are quite confused."

"Why?" growled Okollu.

"Why?!" exclaimed Tiliah, her eyebrows raised. "I don't know. Perhaps because this should have taken weeks to heal?"

Okollu stared between them both.

"How long is a 'week'?"

Her brow furrowing, Tiliah answered, "Seven days."

"And a 'day' is one visit of Saule-acu, yes?"

Tiliah stared blankly at the beast.

"A visit of what?"

"Saule-acu," repeated Okollu. He shook his head, a quiet, frustrated growl slipping from his throat. "Argot does not have the right word." He glanced at the sky. "Saule-acu is hidden by the clouds now. She does not like the rain."

Tiliah tilted her head back to stare upwards.

"The sun?" asked Rhohn.

Okollu eyed the soldier, almost with what Tiliah would name a frown on his face.

"That is a name men use. Inadequate though it may be. "

Nodding, Rhohn said, "Then yes—a week is seven visits of…Saule-acu." Tiliah was impressed that he managed to wrap his tongue around the strange word.

Peering back to his scar, Okollu said, "Then it is I who am confused. Why should my mending take so long?"

Rhohn twisted around and pointed to scabbed-over puncture hole on his calf.

"This happened to me just over a week ago. I was shot by an arrow."

Tiliah was happy with how his wound was healing, but it was still weeks from being whole again.

Surprise swelled to fill Okollu's eyes.

"Why are you not mending?"

"I am," said Rhohn "Quite well, in fact, considering what I've endured out here. How is it you are healing so quickly?"

Okollu stared at them both for a few moments before saying plainly, "This is how all kur-surus mend."

Rhohn had warned her last night not to use the word 'mongrel' in Okollu's presence. Apparently, it was an insult of sorts. Kur-surus was the word they used for themselves.

Staring at the scar, she asked, "*All* your kind heal this quickly?"

"It is why we are vicious when we kill," growled Okollu. "You leave an enemy alive, they will heal, find you, and kill you." Tilting his head to the side, he glanced between them both. "This is unknown to you?"

Tiliah nodded, mumbling, "For me, yes."

"Me as well," muttered Rhohn.

A frown resting on her lips, Tiliah mumbled, "Hells, if that's not a brainless way to fight a war." When both Rhohn and Okollu stared at her, she added, "We're fighting an enemy we know almost nothing about."

"*You* are not my enemy," said Okollu quickly. "This conflict is not one of choice."

"Not of choice?" repeated Rhohn, his voice rising in an instant. "You invaded our home! That was a choice! You slaughtered thousands of innocent people! That was a choice!"

"Choices, yes!" barked Okollu. "But not ours!"

"What about Silas?!" exclaimed Rhohn. "*That* was your blasted choice, wasn't it!?"

The mongrel's yellow eyes flashed hot.

"I did what I had to! I'm sorry I killed your pack-mate! But I would do a hundred times more if it would get my pack back to our lands!"

"If you want to go back," shouted Rhohn. "Then go!"

Okollu looked as if he wanted to leap up and rip Rhohn's head from his neck.

"I told you! We *cannot*!"

Tiliah reached out to place a hand on Rhohn's shoulder and, keeping her voice quiet and calm, said, "Rhohn?"

Rhohn whipped around to stare at her, wide-eyed.

"What?!"

"Did you have me save his life just so you could fight him now?"

He was angry and resentful. She understood that. But this behavior was not going to get him the answers he said he sought.

The muscles along Rhohn's jaw twitched as he pressed his lips together.

"No."

"Then you should calm down."

Rhohn remained quiet, silently seething, for a long moment. Finally, he gave a single, silent nod. Content that he was not going to skewer Okollu for the time being, Tiliah looked back to the mongrel.

"You say you can't go back?"

Okollu growled, "That is correct."

"Why not?"

Okollu gave a sharp, furious shake of his head, draped his arms over his legs, and wrung his hands, growling, "Because my pack is bound! We all are! Kur-surus, blade-men, grayskins! We are all bound to the diavoli!" He glared at Rhohn. "It is because of them we are here, smooth-face! This is *their* war, not ours. Not mine!"

Tiliah glanced over to Rhohn, confused by the mongrel's words. The Dust Man seemed equally bewildered. Looking back to Okollu, she asked, "What do you mean you are...'bound?'"

With searing hot resentment burning in his eyes, Okollu said, "Many seasons ago, an outlander entered the lands of the Drept." Before she could ask for an explanation, Okollu glanced up. "My pack. The Drept are *my* pack." A bitter sneer rippled over his black lips. "At least it was my pack."

He shook his muzzle, huffed, and stared to the horizon.

"Understand that amongst kur-surus, to enter a pack's territory without permission is to die. So, as tas-vilku of the Drept, I sent a patrol to slay the interloper. The outlander killed the six I sent and continued toward our den. I ordered twenty more. They died as well."

He shifted his gaze back to them.

"I ordered twenty-six Drept to their deaths and accomplished nothing. *Nothing.* The outlander used nedabiks—magic—to murder my pack mates. I wanted to destroy him, but against such a foe, we were helpless. Kur-surus who can use nedabiks are rare. The Drept had not had one for three generations. We could do nothing to stop him."

He dropped his head and stared at the muddy grass, his voice dropping to a whisper.

"I failed as tas-vilku. I failed to protect my pack."

Tiliah was surprised to feel a flicker of sympathy dance through her.

Okollu lifted his head and continued, saying, "As the outlander neared our den, my mate and I went to meet him, hoping to—" he snarled "—negotiate for the Drept's safety. We found him atop a hill, waiting for us, his white hair twisting in the wind." He paused, glanced at Rhohn, and asked, "Did you share the message with her?"

Rhohn nodded in silence.

Okollu growled, "Then you both can guess who it was."

A deep frown spread over Tiliah's face. She shared a worried glance with Rhohn before looking back to the mongrel.

"Tandyr?"

Okollu nodded once.

"My mate and I smelled the wrongness in him immediately. When I asked what he wanted, he ordered—*ordered*—me to call forth my pack. He said he required our service. When I refused, he..." He trailed off and went quiet. The brown and white fur around his eyes bunched together. "When I refused, he killed my mate. One moment, she was standing by my side, the next, she lay on the rocks, lifeless. Her hearts had stopped."

Tiliah could no longer deny it. She felt sorry for Okollu.

The mongrel growled, "I attacked, but Tandyr held me in place with magic. He threatened to kill *every* Drept if I did not comply with his order." The fur along his muzzle bristled in irritation.. "Had I known what he was planning, I would have let him do just that. Cursed by ignorance, however, I called the Drept. Once we were all there, Tandyr turned to the man with him and—"

"Hold," interrupted Tiliah. "There was a man with him?"

Okollu nodded.

"A small one, cowering behind Tandyr."

"Who was he?" asked Rhohn.

Fury simmered in the mongrel's eyes.

"I do not know who he *was*, smooth-face. But I can tell you who he *is.* "

"What does that mean?" asked Tiliah.

Okollu stared at her and said, "I will explain. The man pulled a black, wooden box from his pack and gave it to Tandyr. Inside, rested a strange silver stone." His eyes went unfocused as his voice dropped to just above a whisper. "It glowed like Saule-acu herself, shimmering and bright." His black lips twitched. "Yet it was… wrong inside. Wrong like Tandyr is wrong."

"What was it?" murmured Tiliah, caught up in the mongrel's tale now.

Okollu shook his head, growling, "I do not know. But it was evil. Wicked and twisted." He paused a moment before adding, "And with it, Tandyr stole a piece of my garthiba."

Rhohn repeated the odd word before Tiliah could.

"Garthiba?"

"Soul, smooth-face," said Okollu. "The closest word in Argot is 'soul.'"

A moment passed, filled only with the buzzing of the corpse flies and a screech from a blood vulture overhead, before Tiliah muttered, "He…took your soul?"

"Yes," growled Okollu. "At least a piece of it. He did it to all Drept. And from that moment, we were bound. We had to obey his wishes."

"Or what?" asked Rhohn. "What if you didn't obey?"

"You do not understand," said Okollu. "We *had* to obey. Not because he threatened or punished. But because of whatever he did with our garthiba." He tilted his head to stare up to them both. "He stole choice itself from us."

Rhohn asked, "So you must do whatever he says?"

A low, angry growl rumbled from Okollu's throat.

"Not him. Another."

"Who, then?" asked Tiliah

"As my garthiba slipped away, the man with Tandyr began to scream." He shook his head. "It sounded as if he was being ripped apart from the inside. As he screamed, he…changed. Bone jutted from his head. His skin turned red and cracked like dried mud." His nostrils flared. "The air smelled of singed hair and burnt flesh."

"A demon-man?" muttered Rhohn.

Nodding, Okollu said, "When the screaming finally stopped, the creature before us announced his name as Baaldòk, diavol of Chaos and the new tas-vilku of the Drept."

"He took your pack?" asked Rhohn.

"No," growled Okollu. "Tandyr took my pack. But he gave it over to Baaldòk."

"And you did nothing to fight back?" asked Tiliah.

"I wanted to!" snapped Okollu. "Blestem argel, I wanted to! I wanted to rip open his pale throat and spit on the rocks." He gave a violent shake of his head. "But I did not. I *could* not. Tandyr's nedabiks compelled us to obey the diavol!"

Tiliah glanced to Rhohn, worried. Okollu's tale grew more disturbing by the moment. The Dust Man did not meet her gaze, his eyes locked on Okollu.

"And the rest of the Sudashians?" asked Rhohn. "Does Tandyr hold the same sway over them?"

"He does," growled Okollu. "My pack was one of the first he subjugated. As word spread of what was happening, other packs joined together to fight him. Blade-men and grayskins did the same. We fought them, killing our own, until Tandyr could steal their garthiba as well. In time, all were defeated and bound to a diavol. Eventually, his great pack turned east, toward your lands." He turned to stare at one of the dead mongrels. "By then, only half of my pack remained."

"Half?" said Rhohn doubtfully. "There were over five hundred of you at Ebel."

"Yes," growled Okollu. "I know."

Tiliah waited a few heartbeats to let the solemn moment pass before saying, "I am confused. If you are bound to do what the demon-man says—" she glanced around at the dead mongrels "—how did you do this? I doubt he ordered you to kill them."

Okollu shook his head.

"No, my orders were to find the stone, kill whoever had it, and return to Tandyr."

"Then how did you manage this?" asked Rhohn.

Okollu shifted his weight and reached up to scratch behind his ear.

"As Tandyr's pack grew, the nedabiks binding some of us faded. Somehow, they regained their garthiba. The moment they did, they rebelled and those of us still bound slaughtered them as ordered." He looked around at the dead mongrels again, adding softly, "This makes twelve Drept I have killed."

After a few quiet moments, the mongrel looked back to them.

"Soon after we crossed into your lands, I felt the binding slip from me. Unlike the others, I did not rebel. I continued to follow Baaldòk as I always had, obeying his every order."

Surprised, Tiliah asked, "Why did you do that? I can hear it in your voice. You hated him."

Okollu glared at her, his eyes simmering.

"More than you know."

Rhohn spoke up, asking, "You did not want to abandon the Drept, did you?"

Okollu shifted his gaze to the soldier and nodded.

"They are my pack. Mine to protect, mine to keep safe. I needed to find a way to free them."

Tiliah's previously harsh opinion of Okollu's race was quickly changing.

"Well," began Rhohn with a heavy sigh. "That explains why Tandyr's army is not tearing itself apart." Dropping into a crouch, he said, "But I still have not heard where the woman who gave you the message fits. Miriel Syncent? Who is she? What role does she play in this?"

The mongrel lifted his head to stare at Rhohn. He appeared confused.

"You do not know of her?"

Rhohn gave a short shake of his head.

"I would not be asking you the question if I did."

Turning to look up at Tiliah, Okollu asked, "And you?"

Tiliah gave a silent shake of her head. While the name sounded familiar, she had yet to place why.

Okollu dropped his head and, sounding perplexed, said, "That is strange. She acted as if she were known in your lands, someone important."

Intrigued, Tiliah asked, "What did she look like?"

"Her skin was fair," answered Okollu. He looked back up to her. "Much fairer than yours. White, like the clouds. Her hair was the color of the red rocks of my homeland. And her eyes matched the blue of a clear sky."

Tiliah looked at Rhohn and concluded, "Not a Borderlander."

Rhohn shook his head, agreeing, "Unlikely, at least." Peering back to Okollu, he asked, "Is there anything else you remember about her?"

Okollu sat up a bit straighter and said, "She is Rodam Upris." Glancing between them, he added, "Which must mean nothing to you."

Rhohn and Tiliah exchanged a look and shrugged their shoulders as one.

Nodding his head, Okollu said, "Rodam Upris is a legend among my kind. The closest words in Argot might be 'untraceable spirit.' Miriel Syncent is Rodam Upris."

Shaking her head, Tiliah said, "I'm in the dark without a torch."

The fur around Okollu's eyes twitched.

"You are where?"

Rhohn said, "It means she does not understand what you are saying. Neither do I. What is Rodam Upris?"

"Kur-surus take great pride in the hunt," said Okollu *"No* prey can evade us." He drew a deep breath, held it a moment, and then exhaled. "One night, shortly after Tandyr's bond had slipped from me, something woke me from my sleep. A figure stood over me in the darkness, blocking the white eye of Zila-acs."

Tiliah supposed he was speaking of White Moon.

"For reasons I cannot name, I did not attack. Nor did I wake my pack-mates. The stranger said that if I helped her, my pack could be free. All kur-surus could be. I merely had to follow her instructions. I did not believe her, of course, and said as much. Then she insulted me."

"She what?" said Tiliah, her eyebrows arching.

"She insulted me," said Okollu. "She said I was a poor example of kur-surus if she were able to sneak up on me like she had. She said that I could not hunt a wounded ralcat on a windless, flat plain. She said I could never catch her, even though she was standing right before me." His black nose twitched in irritation. "I told her to start running, that I prefer my prey to be on the move when I kill it. Before she ran, though, she said that if I could not catch her before Saule-acu arrived, I must do as she asked."

Okollu paused a moment and shrugged his shoulders.

"I agreed, only because I expected to kill her shortly. The moment I said yes, she ran, her red hair flashing in the light of Zila-acs. I leapt up and followed her, sprinting through the sleeping pack. She dashed up a rise and behind a boulder. I was on her heels, yet when I came around the rock, she was gone."

He shook his head in wonderment.

"There was no scent, no sound. I hunted the hills, the trees, I even skirted the camps of the grayskins and blade-men. Still, I found nothing. She was simply *gone*. When Saule-acu came to light the sky, I stood alone on a hill, wondering if I had dreamt the experience. I turned to hurry back to the Drept and stopped before I took a step. There she was, leaning against a tree, staring at me."

Tiliah said, "So, then…you agreed to help her?"

Okollu stared up to her. "Of course. One does not disregard a legend when it stands before you. She gave me her name, the message, and the instructions to tell as many men as I safely could." He turned to Rhohn. "You are the fourth to whom I have given her words."

"There are others?" asked Rhohn.

"I told others," said Okollu. "Although I suspect they are dead. They were weak or old. You, smooth-face, are strong. You are the best chance my pack—all kur-surus—have to regain their freedom."

Tiliah looked over to Rhohn, wondering what he might feel like knowing that he carried the fate of so many on his shoulders. The Dust Man's scarred face was blank, expressionless. After a moment, she looked back to Okollu.

"And these Shadow Manes he's to find? Who are they?"

"I do not know," answered Okollu. "She did not tell me."

"And the prophecy?" asked Tiliah. "What is that about?"

"Again, I do not know."

Tiliah frowned, disappointed that so many questions were left unanswered. She studied Okollu, trying to resolve the feelings churning within her now. As a child in Drysa, she had heard dozens of stories about the fearsome monsters of Sudash. Every playman that passed through the village would share at least one tale of the terrible, vicious, soulless beasts. Okollu was none of that.

The three of them remained quiet for a time, each lost in their own thoughts.

A series of screeches announced the return of some of the blood vultures. Looking over, Tiliah saw three of the birds swoop down and alight on the carcass of the horse. Rhohn stared at them, but made no move to chase them away. Okollu eyed the birds as they tore into the horseflesh and then lifted his gaze to the sky to stare at the ones still overhead. She wondered what he would do if the vultures attempted to make a meal of the mongrels.

She was still staring at the birds when Rhohn mumbled, "The stone..." The words slipped from his lips, barely more than a whisper. Reaching for the purse jammed between his belt and waist, he asked, "That's why you changed your mind, isn't it?" He pulled the sack free. "Why you let us help you?" Opening the leather pouch quickly, he turned it upside down and dumped the black stone into his hand.

The world went dark.

Tiliah teetered on her feet as a wave of icy nothingness surged through her, around her. For a brief moment, she spotted a number of thick, black strings all around her, covering the sky, grass, bushes. She blinked, terrified. As quickly as they came, the black strands were gone, along with the cold, numbing sensation.

She stared at the onyx stone in Rhohn's dirty palm. Something was wrong with that gem.

Rhohn held out his hand and asked, "Is this like the stone Tandyr used on you?"

Okollu rose from the ground to stand on his two pawed feet. He leaned forward, staring at the stone from a few paces away, and said, "It is similar, but black, of course." He sniffed the air once. His lips immediately curled back in a snarl. "It reeks, too. Like a beast cornered in a cave."

Tiliah breathed in the air. All she smelled was muck and the early hints of decay.

Rhohn picked the stone up with his maimed hand and brought it close to his face, staring at it closely. For some reason, he did not seem as bothered by it as she and Okollu were.

"What is it?" asked the Dust Man. "Why does Tandyr want it?"

Tiliah muttered, "I doubt for any worthy purpose."

"Put it away," growled Okollu. "My skin itches."

Rhohn lowered the stone and eyed Okollu for a moment before slipping the stone back into the pouch. Tiliah was glad to see it disappear again. Looking between them, Rhohn asked, "So what now?"

Okollu nodded to the eastern horizon and said, "You go. And deliver my message." He glanced back to the pouch. "And take that with you. That should be as far from Tandyr as possible."

Nodding, Rhohn said, "You're right." He looked to Tiliah. "Let's go."

"What?" said Tiliah, surprised. She glanced at Okollu briefly before staring back to Rhohn. "Now?"

"Yes. Now."

Tiliah looked back to Okollu and asked, "What about him?"

"I got what I wanted," answered Rhohn. "Let's go." He began to turn away, already looking to the east.

Tiliah shifted her gaze back to the mongrel.

"What are you going to do?"

Okollu was quiet for a moment before saying, "I do not know. I cannot return without the stone. Tandyr will kill me."

"Why don't you go home?" suggested Rhohn. "That'll be one less of your kind here."

"Alone?" growled Okollu. "No. I will *not* abandon the Drept."

Tiliah pointed out, "What about yesterday? You were begging us to let you die. That's abandoning your pack, is it not?"

Okollu glanced at the nearby corpses of the other mongrels.

"I was grief-stricken. That is all."

Rhohn said, "Come, Tiliah. We are wasting time." He shifted his gaze to Okollu. "I hope your message does what your mystery woman claims."

"As do I, smooth-face."

Nodding, Rhohn gave a quiet huff of a sigh and started to walk away. He did not even wish a word of farewell. Then again, neither did Okollu.

Tiliah watched him take a half-dozen steps, shaking her head. As it stood, this plan was never going to work. Something drastic needed to be done. Taking a deep breath, she called out, "I think Okollu should come with us."

Rhohn stopped in his tracks and looked back, open shock on his face. Okollu stared at her as well, appearing equally stunned by her suggestion. Rhohn recovered first and quickly strode back to her side.

"You what?"

"I think he should come with us."

Rhohn glanced at Okollu briefly before staring back to her, his eyes wide.

"Are you mad?"

Holding his gaze without flinching, Tiliah spoke, her voice firm and direct.

"You believe he tells the truth, don't you?"

Rhohn glanced at Okollu, a frown resting upon his scarred lips.

"I do."

"As do I," said Tiliah without pause. "Now imagine you make it to this 'Storm Island' and share everything we just heard with these 'Shadow Manes.'" She paused for a moment, letting Rhohn think. As his frown shifted into a deep scowl, she said, "You see the problem, don't you? You would be named madman and tossed from their hall. Assuming they have a hall."

Rhohn gnawed his scarred lip for a moment before saying, "I do not need to tell them everything. Perhaps the message from Miriel Syncent will be enough."

Tiliah crossed her arms gave Rhohn a hard, leveled stare.

"Mud Man, you saved me from slavers in the past week, I have learned that while you can be surly at times, that you're a good soul, a trustworthy man. Yet, last night, as you were telling your tale, I thought you absolutely, unequivocally mad. What do you think these Shadow Manes will say when a strange Borderlander marches in, announces that the God of Chaos is leading the Sudashians, and—oh—you just happen to know this because a *mongrel* gave you the message from a disappearing woman?!"

Okollu growled lowly, "I am kur-surus!"

Keeping her gaze locked on Rhohn, Tiliah corrected herself.

"Fine, then. That a kur-surus gave you the message from a disappearing woman? Every sane soul there would mark you mad!"

Rhohn glared at her, shaking his head.

"You are suggesting I take him to what? Corroborate my story?"

"I am," said Tiliah firmly. "If they hear this from him, they will believe."

Rhohn was shaking his head vigorously.

"Tiliah, it is you who are the mad one."

"Why?"

"Why?" repeated Rhohn, his lone eyebrow arched high. He jabbed a finger in Okollu's direction. "Look at him! If we are spotted, soldiers will surely come! I'll never reach Storm Island with him at my side."

Tiliah shrugged.

"Then avoid towns and cities."

A derisive laugh burst forth from Rhohn.

"What wondrous advice! I had considered marching straight through Demetus with him! Okollu, would you like to visit one of the markets while we're there?"

Tiliah's eyes narrowed to a pair of slits. Yet before she could fire back her own retort, Okollu interjected himself.

"You are wasting your time arguing. I will not go."

Shifting targets, Tiliah stared down at the mongrel and snapped, "Why not? What else are you going to do? Wander the prairie forever? Going east could help free your kind!"

Okollu shook his head.

"The soldier is right. I would put his journey at risk."

"One which I think we must take! Better to face that than the chance no one will believe him when he gets there!"

"I am not going," growled Okollu.

Knowing that she was treading a thin line, Tiliah nodded, lowered her voice, and said, "Ah…I understand. You're afraid, aren't you?"

Bristling at the question, Okollu bared his teeth as a low growl reverberated in his throat.

"I am *not* afraid."

Tiliah glared at him.

"Prove it."

The mongrel glowered at her silently, the white fur along his muzzle trembling, his ears lying flat on his head. After a long stretch of quiet, he turned to Rhohn.

"Will the men in the east not believe you?"

Rhohn pressed his lips together and said, "I would hope, but…" He trailed off and let a long, heavy sigh slip from his lips. "Your tale is rather fantastic."

Okollu gave a disappointed, frustrated huff, shook his head, and stared to the eastern horizon. After another long pause, he growled, "She is right then. I must go with you."

Rhohn shook his head in disbelief, staring between them both.

"I don't see how this can work, Tiliah. He'll be attacked on sight. No—*we'll* be attacked on sight! I'll be marked as traitor!"

"It won't be just you," said Tiliah. "I am coming with you."

Rhohn stared at her, his quiet anger momentarily stifled by surprise.

"You're *what?*"

"This story," began Tiliah. "All of it. His, yours, mine. It is *impossible* to believe. Gods, mystery women dashing about a pack of mon—kur-surus? Demonmen? Slavers? It might take a hundred people swearing it true for anyone to believe. We have three. I'm going with you, Mud Man."

Rhohn's eyes narrowed.

"What about your family?"

"We take a route that skirts Demetus to the south. You and Okollu can hide while I search. It's nothing but hills and swamps. Nobody lives there. I ask for one day, Mud Man. *One* day. Then we continue whether or not I find them."

She spoke decisively, ignoring the hollow, hopeless sensation growing inside her stomach. Even with all the luck of Ketus, she doubted she would find her family in a single day. When she had left a few turns back, the city was terribly overcrowded. She doubted it had gotten better.

Rhohn asked, "You would abandon them?"

She cringed at his word choice, but kept her voice strong and clear as she answered, "If we can deliver this message and it helps defeat—and I cannot believe I am saying this—if it helps to defeat the God of Chaos, then I will be *saving* them, not...not abandoning them." The word tasted worse than it sounded.

Okollu shifted his yellow-eyed gaze to her.

"I do not understand. Your family?"

Tiliah briefly relayed her own harrowing tale to the mongrel and how her mother and younger siblings were still in the city. Hopefully.

When she was done, Okollu inclined his head a fraction and, with respect filling his rough voice, said, "Were you kur-surus, I would ask you to join my pack, Tiliah. You are strong."

The compliment was so unexpected that she had nothing to say in response. Turning from Okollu, she eyed Rhohn and waited for his thoughts. The scowl he wore certainly hinted at them.

"This is madness," mumbled the soldier. "You should go find your family." He stared at Okollu. "And you should stay here."

Frustrated by the man's pigheadedness, Tiliah said, "Fine, then. You go your way. Okollu and I will go to Storm Island on our own."

Rhohn shook his head.

"Your ideas are getting worse, Tiliah, not better."

"Then we go together," growled Okollu. "You know she speaks sense, smooth-face."

Tiliah glanced to the mongrel and gave him a short nod of thanks for the support. Okollu ignored her, his gaze locked on Rhohn, waiting.

The Dust Man crossed his arms, stared into the distance, and remained as motionless as a bulboa tree on a windless day. Tiliah remained quiet. She had said her piece. The decision was in Rhohn's hands now. After an interminably long stretch of quiet, a tiny sigh slipped from Rhohn's lips and he gave a tiny, almost imperceptible nod.

"I think you're right, Tiliah. I wish you were not, but I think you are."

She nodded, saying, "Good, so then it is settled."

"No," said Rhohn quickly, looking back to them both. "It is *not* settled. There is no possible way Okollu can travel to the Southlands without being noticed. A half-blind man could mark him a mile away on a one-moon night."

"He is right," growled Okollu, turning to eye her. "That will be a problem."

The corners of Tiliah's mouth turned up a fraction.

"I have an idea how to make sure it is not."

Rhohn and Okollu both stared at her, clearly dubious. She quickly explained her plan and within minutes, the trio was marching east, leaving the vultures to their meal.

CHAPTER 33: VOYAGE
25th of the Turn of Luraana, 4999

Nikalys ran his forehead side-to-side along the ship's rail, his eyes shut tight, his hands gripping the wood beam. Any chance of receiving a splinter had long passed. Years of use and harsh sea weather had worn the wood smoother than a polished river rock. The sensation of the wood grazing his skin somehow took his mind off the ship's constant, rocking motion.

He could not decide which of the repetitive movements he hated more. The graceful rising up, pausing for a moment, followed by a stomach-twisting drop down. Or the knee-buckling, world-tilting rolls to the left and right.

His insides sloshed about like water in a stable-mucking bucket. His head ached, thumping with each pulsing heartbeat. The snap and crack of the sails assaulted his ears.

"Feeling any better, son?"

Recognizing Sergeant Trell's voice through the roar of the waves, Nikalys squeezed his eyes tighter and mumbled a short reply.

"What does it look like?"

"You really should let Broedi or Nundle help you," said Sergeant Trell, his tone an interesting mix of concern and amusement.

A sharp drop from a wave crest caused Nikalys' stomach to flip. An involuntary, sickness-fueled scowl spread over his face as he muttered, "I'll be fine."

During the first few days of their voyage, most of the Shadow Mane soldiers had dealt with similar seasickness, much to the amusement of the Sapphire's seamen. Broedi offered to perform a short Weave for any of the 'ground-kissers'—as the seamen had called them—to temporarily remove the effects of an ill stomach. Nundle and a handful of longtime Shadow Manes accepted Broedi's proposed solution without hesitation and were moving about the ships' deck within minutes, happy and healthy grins on their faces. Those onboard who were former Red Sentinels forewent the offer initially and continued to suffer. They were Shadow Manes now, but their lifelong prejudices against magic still held.

Even Sergeant Trell had resisted for two days before letting Broedi help him. Moments after granting his consent, the sergeant stood upright, fit, happy, and relieved. After their sergeant's example, every last soldier lined up on deck for Broedi to remove the seasickness.

The Weave only lasted for a day, however. So, each morning, pallid, sickly men arrived on deck and waited for Broedi or Nundle—the tomble had learned the pattern now—to administer to them. After the hillman did whatever it was he did with the Strands, the soldiers would go about their day, lounging about the ship.

Nikalys was the last holdout.

He did not relish having magic used on him, but mostly he wanted to prove that he could conquer something as mundane as seasickness. To himself and to the Shadow Mane soldiers.

Sergeant Trell prompted, "Nikalys?"

Moaning softly as his stomach lurched again, he wished the sergeant would go away. The ship dropped suddenly while lolling to starboard, Nikalys' insides cramped, warning him of what was to come.

"Gods, not again."

Lifting his head from the railing, Nikalys retched. Nothing came out, however, as nothing was left inside him. For a dozen agonizing heartbeats, the dry heaves continued. He peered through watery eyes, squinting at the sea, its dark blue, almost black surface mottled with frothy white wave crests. A cold and wet spray washed over his face and neck. He actually welcomed the mist. The heaving made him hot and sweaty.

When the gagging finally stopped, he dropped his head back to the railing with a soft thud.

"Oh, bless the Gods."

Tiny spasms wracked his midsection from overuse. He took in a deep, shuddering breath and, through half-closed eyes, absentmindedly focused on a square peg jammed in the wood plank upon which he stood. Lifting his head, he tried to spit into the sea, wanting to clear the taste of sick from his tongue. He failed, however. His mouth was as dry as Summer dirt in Yellow Mud.

Behind him, Nundle said, "My goodness, you are being stubborn."

Nikalys groaned. It bothered him that Sergeant Trell had seen his undignified display. Knowing Nundle had as well only added to his humiliation.

"How long have you been standing there, Nundle?"

"Oh, I don't know," said Nundle. "A while, now." Nikalys could hear the smile on his face. "We all came over here with Nathan."

Still leaning on the ship's rail, Nikalys lifted his right arm a few inches, tilted his head forward, and peered behind him. Ten paces back on the deck, Sergeant Trell and Nundle stood with Cero and Wil. Managing a weak smile, he raised his voice and said, "Good days, everyone."

The four of them stared back at him, each displaying various degrees of amusement in their expressions.

Wil wore a small smile along with the blue and gold pants of a Southern Arms uniform, a black coat, and a matching woolen cap pulled down over his ears. Cero grinned wider, his smile poking out from the black Southlands-style beard he had grown. The ex-Tracker had discarded his Constable grays some time ago and now wore brown breeches and a dark blue overcoat pulled tight against the breeze.

Wil tilted his head to the side, mimicking Nikalys' own sideways-leaning head.

"Why won't you let Nundle help? It doesn't hurt."

"If I can do it," said Cero. "Surely you can."

Cero's distrust of magic ran deeper than most. As a Tracker for the Constables, he had hunted mages, despite the fact he was more or less a mage himself. Trackers found outlaw magic users because they could sense the Strands themselves.

Nikalys gave the group a halfhearted shrug.

"I don't need help. I'm fine."

Nundle raised his eyebrows.

"And I'm an oligurt."

As the three men standing with Nundle chuckled at the tomble's remark, the ship suddenly dropped again, sending his stomach cramping anew. Dropping his head back down, Nikalys shut his eyes tight, pleading that his insides remain calm. He counted each thudding heartbeat. By the time he reached nine, it seemed that, this time, mind won out over body.

Sergeant Trell insisted, "Son, you are *not* fine."

Taking a deep breath, Nikalys looked back at the group again. Since arriving at the enclave, the sergeant had taken to wearing a Southern Arms uniform of the same position despite Commander Aiden's insistence he deserved a higher rank. The blue and gold uniform seemed normal now. Nikalys could no longer picture him in the red and black of their home duchy.

Fixing him with a steady gaze, the sergeant said, "I know you are trying to set an example, but you're setting the wrong one."

"Pardon?"

"Stubbornness is not a trait you want the men to emulate, is it?" asked the sergeant. Yet again, the man had displayed the remarkable ability to read a person perfectly.

Shaking his head, Nikalys said, "No, I suppose not."

"Even the best among us needs help at times. And it's not a sign of weakness to ask for it. Rather, it's the opposite."

Nikalys held the soldier's stare as the Sapphire reached the crest of another wave and began its plunge downward. Whether it was the sergeant's wisdom or the new bout of fluttering in his stomach, Nikalys' resistance crumbled. He shifted his gaze to Nundle.

"Do what you can."

Nundle gave a short nod and said, "Good."

The mage was absent his wide-brimmed hat, leaving his wild red hair to the whim of the gusting wind, and wore a set of crimson wool breeches along with a solid black coat lined with silver buttons. Staring into the open air above the ship's deck, Nundle's gaze focused on something only he could see. Nikalys knew the Strands were there and squinted, wishing that—just once—he could see what they looked like.

After a few moments, Nundle shifted his gaze to Nikalys.

First, the dizziness faded. The headache went next, followed quickly by the nausea and cramping stomach. Finally, his feverishness withered away. Within two breaths, he felt fine.

Stunned, he stood tall from his hunched-over position and stared out at the horizon with wide eyes, noticing for the first time the reds and purples of the evening sky.

A moment later, his stomach clenched and, thinking we was about to get sick, he bent over the rail again. He gripped the wooden railing hard, wondering why Nundle's magic had not worked. He waited for the cramping to begin but it never did. It took a moment to realize he was not nauseous at all. The sensation was something different.

Standing tall, he turned around to gape at the four behind him.

"Gods, I'm starving."

Moments ago, the thought of food would have sent him into fits of heaving. Now, he was ravenous.

The three men and tomble smiled wide as Sergeant Trell asked, "When is the last time you ate something?"

Nikalys thought for a moment before shaking his head and mumbling, "I have no idea." His stomach gurgled again. It felt wondrous.

Cero said, "Let me run down to the galley and get you something."

Nikalys nodded his silent thanks, still marveling at his rapid recovery.

As Cero headed toward the foredeck and the stairs leading below, Wil peered after him, a thoughtful expression on his face.

"Wait for me! I'm hungry, too!"

He hurried after Cero, dashing around the foremast and dodging the seamen moving about the deck. Nikalys noticed nearby sailors staring at him with wide, good-natured grins on their faces. He supposed they were mocking him, but Nikalys did not care. He felt too good.

Nikalys took in a long, deep lungful of cold air, wondering at how fresh and clean it felt. Staring back-and-forth between Nundle and Sergeant Trell, Nikalys beamed.

"Gentlemen, you are looking at the biggest fool there ever was."

With a crooked smile, Sergeant Trell kindly offered, "Those are rather strong words."

Raising an eyebrow, Nikalys said good-naturedly, "You didn't dispute my claim."

"No," said Sergeant Trell, his grin widening. "I did not."

Chuckling, Nikalys peered down at Nundle.

"Thank you ever so much. You are a savior."

The already rosy pink hue in Nundle's cheeks deepened to a soft red. The tomble was evidently embarrassed by the compliment. As he stared at Nikalys, his eyes narrowed and he took a step closer. With wonder in his voice, he muttered, "Your recovery is remarkable. The others got better, yes, but you look as if you could swim the rest of the way to Ursus."

Grinning wide, Nikalys boasted, "I feel like I could."

Nundle shrugged, took a step back, and mused aloud, "I wish I had known this Weave when I journeyed to the Arcane Republic. Perhaps I might not have hated sailing as much as I thought I did. The pattern is amazingly simple, you know. Only need a handful of Life Strands and a couple of Soul. That's it. A few loops, a twist, and—it looks sort of like a thistle when you're done. A green and silver thistle. I am quite surprised they don't teach it at the Academies. I wonder if my preceptors ever knew of it. Preceptor Lasavel—he was my teacher at the Academy of—"

"Nundle?" interrupted Sergeant Trell, a tiny smile on his face.

The tomble glanced up at the soldier

"I was going on again, wasn't I?"

Nodding, Sergeant Trell said, "Yes, you were."

"I was actually enjoying it," said Nikalys. "I was going to see how long you could go."

Nundle shrugged and offered them both a smile.

"Tombles in Deepwell always said I was a perfect Babblebrook on account I… well, I babble on like a brook."

After the three of them shared a quiet chuckle at the small jest, the tomble tilted his head back to stare upward at Sergeant Trell.

"Seems Broedi won the bet."

Sergeant Trell eyed Nikalys and nodded.

"That he did."

"Bet?" asked Nikalys. A wave crashed into the starboard side of the Sapphire, coating the ship and its passengers with a thin coating of icy sea spray. Wiping water from his face, Nikalys repeated, "What bet?"

Nundle nodded his head toward the aft of the ship.

"Might be best if you ask him."

Nikalys looked to where the tomble was gesturing, squinting against the orange evening sun. He lifted a hand to shade his eyes and saw Broedi standing tall on the second deck, arms crossed over chest and gaze locked on Nikalys.

"What sort of bet?" asked Nikalys. "With who?" Shifting his gaze to the figure on the White Lion's left, his eyes narrowed. "Never mind."

Captain Scrag, the master of the Sapphire, was scowling at Nikalys, his thick mane of white hair whipping in the wind. Even though he was rail-thin and shorter than Broedi by almost a foot and a half, the captain was one of the most imposing men Nikalys had ever met. His face was tougher than twenty-year old leather, beaten dry by years of salty sea air. His thick, bushy mustache was so large that it covered his entire mouth. He wore a navy blue coat with scarlet stripes running down the sleeves, a pair of matching breeches, and matte leather, calf-high black boots.

Some men conveyed a natural aura of command. Sergeant Trell, for one. Commander Aiden, as well. Whatever it was that those two soldiers had, Captain Scrag had three barrels worth. Like Broedi, his gaze was reserved for Nikalys alone.

"You looked so miserable," said Nundle. "The captain bet Broedi we could not get you to let go of the railing." With a smile in his voice, he said, "Broedi had faith in us."

Nikalys wondered if he should be upset that his misery had been the subject of a bet. After a moment, he shrugged, not caring. If you were not a sailor, there was little else to do at sea but make bets.

Suddenly curious, Nikalys asked, "What was the wager?"

Nundle turned to look up at Sergeant Trell.

"Nathan?"

The sergeant shrugged his shoulders.

"They did not share with me."

Nikalys stared back across the deck. Broedi's expression was stoic as always, but the captain was glowering, appearing rather unhappy he lost. Truth be told, he always looked that way.

"If you will excuse me," said Nikalys.

He strode off without waiting for a response, heading toward the portside stairs that led up to the deck. His course was not a straight one, interrupted both by the rolling deck and by sailors moving about, performing whatever tasks seamen do.

Holding tightly onto the dual railings, Nikalys lurched up the steps and reached the second deck. After waiting for the Sapphire to pause atop a wave, he hurried a dozen paces to stand next to Broedi, grasping the deck railing as soon as he arrived. He turned an eye to the hillman, expecting a greeting of sorts. However, both Broedi and the captain ignored his arrival.

Leaning forward, Nikalys attempted to catch their eyes yet the pair kept their gazes locked on the eastern horizon. With a shrug of his shoulders, he turned forward as well, wondering if something important lay ahead of them. Before he could focus on the distant line of sky and water, the ship itself demanded he pay attention to it. Now that seasickness no longer consumed him, he could appreciate the majesty of the craft.

The Sapphire was a three-masted, full-rigged ship, the mizzenmast a dozen feet behind them, the mainmast rising high at mid-ship, and the foremast further along towards the bow. The soft, warm light cast by the sunset tinted the normally white sails a soft orange.

Days ago, Broedi had tried to convey the exceptional craftsmanship required to build such a ship: the different types of wood necessary, the techniques ship-builders used, the style as well as art that went into a seaworthy vessel. At the time, Nikalys had not listened to a word the hillman had spoken, so consumed was he by seasickness. Now, with his stomach right, he tried to recall Broedi's lesson. He remembered something about oak being used for the keel. He frowned, his gaze traversing the ship as he tried to remember what a keel was.

The sharp crack of skin smacking wood startled him. Swiveling to stare at Captain Scrag, he found the ship's master glaring at Broedi.

"Blast the Nine Hells nine times over!" shouted the man, his already present scowl deepening ever further. His moustache bounced as he ranted, "That's two blasted casks of Starwick I owe you! Do you know the favors I'll need to call in for *two*?!"

Nikalys had yet to get used to the way the captain treated Broedi. Most everyone connected with the Shadow Manes treated the White Lion with respect or reverence. Yet it seemed the ship's commander felt no such compunction to offer any sort of deference to the White Lion.

Leaning forward, the captain said, "Hold a moment—you didn't use any of those blasted strings and cheat me, did you?"

Broedi shook his head, his familiar, slight smile touching his lips.

"Yet again, Captain, they are 'Strands,' not strings. And I did no such thing."

Slapping the railing again, Captain Scrag exclaimed, "Bah! I should have known better than take you twice or naught! Hells, I should never have taken the first bet."

Baffled by their exchange, Nikalys said, "Pardon me…but what is going on?"

Staring at him with eyebrows raised, Captain Scrag said, "Oh, my! So polite. 'Pardon me,' he says!" He leaned toward Nikalys, a teasing grin hiding under his moustache. "It's good to see you have more color in your cheeks than my sails. I nearly had the men run you up the yardarm!"

Since leaving Storm Island, the captain had taken every chance he could to jab at Nikalys. In one sense, Nikalys welcomed the teasing, relieved to be treated like an average soul and not the illustrious Progeny. However, the captain's mocking was relentless and Nikalys had had enough.

Holding the seaman's steady gaze, he said, "Now that I am feeling better, I suppose I should take this opportunity to apologize for the mess I made in your cabin."

The captain's confident smile faltered a bit.

"My cabin?"

With as much false regret as he could muster, Nikalys said, "Thinking I might feel better with something in my stomach, I forced down a large helping of fish stew." He grimaced at the thought. The stew was horrid. "I was wrong. I tried to make it to the deck in time, but I took a wrong turn, ended up in your cabin, and well..." He trailed off and gave a small shrug. "I do apologize."

Not a word he had spoken was truth. He would not touch a spoonful of the wretched stew even if he were starving. The thick, red glop was revolting.

The captain, no longer smiling, stared ahead, eyeing the stairwell that led below deck.

"You got ill in my cabin?"

"I am truly sorry, Captain. I meant to tell you earlier, but I was busy holding up your ship's starboard rails."

Nikalys had managed to keep a straight face to this point, but he doubted he could much longer. The forlorn expression on the captain's face was wholly enjoyable.

Suddenly, a deep, rumbling chuckle rolled forth from Broedi. The rare sound drew both Nikalys' and the captain's attention immediately. As the hillman continued to laugh, Captain Scrag shifted his gaze to Nikalys. A moment later, he began to nod, a knowing smile spreading over his face.

"You give as good as you take, don't you?"

Letting his own smile free, Nikalys nodded and said, "I am a middle child, Captain. I have had plenty of practice doing both." Looking between the pair, he said, "I know about the first bet. Mind if I ask what the second one was about?"

A disgruntled Captain Scrag huffed, "Hells, I bet twice or naught that if we kept silent once you reached the rail here, you would speak before we crested five waves."

"And I believed you would remain quiet," said Broedi.

Tilting his head, Nikalys asked, "How did you know?"

"I did not," rumbled the hillman. "I was trying to return the captain's losses from the first bet." He shrugged his shoulders. "Mark me lucky."

"Last time I bet you on this trip, Broedi," growled the captain.

"Don't say that," said Nikalys with a smile. "We need something to liven things up around here. After all, this voyage has been rather uneventful, hasn't it?"

Captain Scrag's relatively affable mood changed in an instant. Glaring at Nikalys, he slapped the rail with both hands and, with venom in his voice, shouted, "Hells, son! Why would you go and say something like that?! Saewyn curse it all!"

As the captain strung together a long, virulent succession of curses that would sour milk fresh from a cow's udder, Nikalys stared, wholly confused at the explosion of sharp words. Throughout the outburst, Nikalys repeatedly glanced at Broedi, looking for some sort of guidance. A pained expression rest upon the hillman's face.

When the captain finally stopped his shouting, Nikalys said, "I don't understand, Captain. What did I do?"

The captain remained quiet, staring daggers at him. After an uncomfortable moment of silence, Broedi answered instead.

"Men of the sea never mention the ease of a journey, believing Saewyn will hear their words and rectify the situation."

"Rectify the situation? What does that—?"

Captain Scrag interrupted, bellowing, "It means she'll drop a blasted storm on us! We'll be tossed around like apples in a dirgmour's stout keg during the king's high festival!"

Nikalys stared at the captain, his face blank. After a few moments of quiet, filled only by the roar of the sea and the creaking of the ship, he turned to look behind the ship. Mu's orb hovered above the western horizon, peeking through a spattering of clouds in the sky.

"Ah…I don't see a storm in our future, Captain."

"Do not mock what you don't know!" bellowed the old seaman. "I swear, if Saewyn strikes us with a tempest, son, I'm strapping you to the topmast! And you are staying up there until the sun shines bright again!"

The surly captain stomped away, moving further aft to speak to the sailor manning the giant, wooden wheel that guided the ship.

Staring after the captain in a state of minor shock, Nikalys mumbled, "That man is mad."

"Do not judge him harshly," rumbled Broedi. "He is a fair man, steadfast friend, and excellent captain. Ask any of the seamen aboard and they will tell you they would not sail under any other."

As he watched Captain Scrag berate the helmsman for one reason or another, Nikalys muttered, "I sincerely doubt that."

"Truly, Nikalys. Captain Scrag is a good soul."

"I will have to take your word on that."

"Someday, I will tell you about an expedition he and I took to Cartu. Back when the captain's hair was still black. You would enjoy it. It involves a turtle and a merchantman from Quan."

Curious already, Nikalys eyed the hillman.

"How about today? I've nothing else to do."

Broedi shook his head and rumbled, "Not true." With a nod of his chin, he indicated the lower deck. "Your meal has arrived."

Looking at the main weather deck, Nikalys saw Wil and Cero emerging from the stairwell, both carrying wooden platters. From where he stood, it appeared they had brought him dried boar meat and red pears. His stomach grumbling, he was halfway to the stairs when he called over his shoulder, "Tell me your story later!"

Nikalys hurried down the steps two at a time, his mouth already watering.

CHAPTER 34: STORM

26ᵗʰ of the Turn of Luraana, 4999

The rain drops pelting Nikalys' neck and ears felt like a thousand tiny, cold steel daggers stabbing his skin. Jagged lightning cut the blackness around him, providing brief glimpses of the massive black waves coursing about the Sapphire. His feet spread wide, Nikalys held tightly onto the railing on the aft deck, a dozen paces ahead of the helmsmen.

Despite the violent sea and gusting winds, Nikalys refused to believe his comment regarding their uneventful journey had anything to do with the storm raging around them. Captain Scrag, on the other hand, vehemently disagreed.

When the first muffled rumbles of thunder had rolled over the Sea of Kings a few hours past sunset, the captain had shouted below, demanding Nikalys come up to the main deck. Nikalys was reluctant at first, but after Broedi suggested he comply in order to avoid a tongue-lashing, he trudged up to the weather deck. Nervous at what awaited, he emerged from the stairwell and stared around him, stunned by the sea's state. Moonlight lit up waves twice as tall as they were a short time ago.

The sea's growing fury, however, was nothing compared to the captain's already raging storm.

Captain Scrag had grabbed Nikalys by the arm, marched him to the stern, faced him west, and ordered that he watch the approaching storm. A wall of clouds lit by the dual moons slowly marched east, swallowing the stars and burping out little bursts of lighting. When the waning crescent of White Moon disappeared, the ship and sea seemed otherworldly bathed in Blue Moon's light alone.

Once the looming storm covered Blue Moon, plunging the Sapphire into pure black, Nundle and Broedi came up on deck. The pair moved about the ship, creating magical lanterns by binding yellow and amber balls of light to various points of the ship.

The wind picked up, whistling through the ship's rigging and whipping its sails. Just before the full force of the tempest hit, Captain Scrag retrieved Nikalys from the stern and moved him to the aft deck, insisting that he "enjoy the blasted uneventful voyage." He supposed he should be grateful the captain did not strap him to the top mast as threatened.

The storm had been raging for some time now. Shivering in the cold rain, Nikalys squeezed the railing tight as the waves tossed ship and men. He could not have been wetter if he were swimming in the sea itself.

Captain Scrag's booming voice cut through wind and thunder as the old sailor yelled orders to the crew, telling them to tie off one thing, loosen another, or batten down something else.

A sudden, bright flash cast stark, sharp-edged shadows along the length of the ship. The lightning's partner, a deafening crack of thunder, shook the world. The incredibly close strike shocked his eyes, leaving him blind for a moment. He squeezed his eyes tight and waited for his night-sight to return. For a few moments, the world was nothing but roaring wind, creaking wood, and thrashing seas.

Cracking open his eyes, he spotted a sailor scurrying across the deck, lit faintly by the globes of magical light. Broedi stood near the mainmast, staring into the night and using every gift at his disposal to hold back some of the storm's fury and smooth the ship's way. Nundle was below deck with the rest of the Shadow Mane soldiers, riding out the storm. Unlike Broedi, the tomble was unable to 'touch Strands of Water' so he was doing what he could to keep the men from getting ill.

With the sails furled and tied down now, the masts and yardarms looked like three skeletal hands stretching into the black, trying hard to cling to the rigging. The captain had used the strong wind to drive the Sapphire east right up until the storm struck. When the gusts threatened to rip the sails to shreds, he ordered them stowed.

A cry arose from the sailors on the main deck below. Their words were lost to the wind, but the alarm in their voices worried Nikalys. Looking down, he spotted a handful of the men, pointing to the south. Turning his head, he saw the silhouette of a massive wave just off starboard, backlit by another burst of lighting. A black wall of water as tall as the main mast loomed over the Sapphire.

"Oh, Gods…"

The wave closed quickly into the halo of light cast by the magical lanterns on deck. Nikalys shot a panicked glance to Broedi, praying the White Lion could somehow hold back the wave, but found the hillman with his massive arms wrapped around the mainmast and his eyes closed.

Captain Scrag's voice shrieked through the night, "Wave starboard! Hold tight!"

Nikalys crouched low and squeezed the aft deck railing, feeling the wood crack under his grip. He took a deep breath just as the colossal swell rammed into the Sapphire.

As seawater rushed over him, Nikalys' mouth shot open from the shock of the cold and the sea rewarded him by filling it with salt water. Choking, he shut his mouth before swallowing more of the ocean. The ship listed dangerously to port, the creaks and groans it made sounding more wounded animal than wooden ship.

The wave rushed by quickly, leaving Nikalys squeezing the railing and coughing up seawater. The ship righted itself, slowly swinging back to starboard. For two thudding heartbeats, there was nothing but the roar of wind and sea paired with the wooden, groaning protests of the Sapphire.

"Man overboard!"

Nikalys' eyes shot open, burning from the salt of the sea. He stared to the deck below and spotted a number of sailors now pointing north. More men picked up the chilling call, their words clearly cutting through the wind.

Without a moment's hesitation, Nikalys released the railing and rushed portside, stumbling as the ship shifted beneath his feet. Grabbing hold of the port rail, he stared into the murky blackness below. He caught a brief flash of light as a wave rolled, revealing one of the magical lanterns still bound to a piece of the ship. A moment later, another swell obscured it.

"Blast!"

It had only been an instant, but Nikalys had caught Wil's panicked face illuminated by the glow, some thirty feet from the ship. Nikalys wondered what had possessed his friend to come topside.

Captain Scrag unexpectedly yelled into his ear, "Do you see him?"

Turning to find the captain beside him, Nikalys pointed in the direction of the young soldier.

"There somewhere!"

The two men stared into the blackness, searching, scanning. After a few torturous heartbeats, the faint light of the magical lantern emerged again from the swells. Nikalys gasped. Wil was already another twenty to thirty paces away.

"Blast the Hells!" cursed Captain Scrag.

"Turn the ship around!" screamed Nikalys.

Captain Scrag shook his head, his wet, matted, white mane of hair whipping back and forth.

"How?!! I've no sails and the rudder is tied down! I'm not steering this ship! Saewyn is!"

"Then how do we get Wil out of there?!"

The captain did not answer immediately. Fixing Nikalys with a steady gaze, he said, "We don't." A sympathetic frown touched his lips.

Nikalys stared at the captain a moment, initially not comprehending what the sailor meant. Once he did, he exclaimed, "You're going to leave him? He'll drown!"

Captain Scrag nodded.

"I'm sorry, son."

Nikalys whipped his head around to look at the weather deck, searching for Broedi. The hillman was nowhere to be found. A long line of sailors stood at a broken port railing, staring in the direction of Wil. They had stopped shouting, solemn expressions having replaced panicked ones.

Staring back into the black sea, Nikalys caught another flash of light. Wil was farther, still.

"No..."

Refusing to accept his friend's fate, Nikalys glared at the captain and shouted, "Get Nundle up here and tell him to make the biggest light he can!"

"Why?!" screamed Captain Scrag, shielding his eyes against wind and rain.

Ignoring the question, Nikalys stared at the sea, waiting to catch another glimpse of his friend. He reached to his waist, unbuckled his belt, and held the Blade of Horum out to the captain.

"Hold this for me."

Spotting the yellowish-orange ball of light, Nikalys pushed himself up onto the railing, leapt into the open air, and reached inside him, pulling at whatever it was Aryn Atticus had passed to him.

Shift.

Air exploded from his lungs as he splashed into the icy water. The bitterest of nights in his room at Storm Island was a balmy Summer day compared to the bone-chilling cold of the sea. So shocked by the chill, he briefly forgot the need to swim and he dipped beneath the waves. Fighting back to the surface, he burst into the nighttime air and spat out the mouthful of water he had sucked in.

Whipping his head around, he searched for the light he had seen from the ship but saw nothing. The world was black. Waves were nothing but indistinct, dark shapes carrying him up and down.

As he thrashed about in the sea, the heat seeping from his body, he caught a glimpse of light.

"W—"

The word died on his lips as he realized he was staring at the Sapphire, not Wil. Nikalys' could not believe how far away the ship already was.

A shift in the wind brought with it a weak shout, the voice full of despair.

"Don't leave me!"

It was Wil.

Nikalys sought the source, but waves and wind made it impossible to figure out from where it came. As loud as he could, he shouted, "Wil! Wil Eadding!"

Wil responded almost immediately, shouting, "Here! Here! Help! I'm here!"

Nikalys swiveled his head in all directions, spitting out mouthful after mouthful of icy, salty water. Despite the effort he was putting into treading water, much like when he was fighting, he was not tiring or struggling for breath. Horum's gift granted him incredible endurance. Unfortunately, it did nothing to stave back the water's chill.

His teeth chattering, he loosed a scream loud enough that his throat felt like it being ripped raw.

"Louder, Wil! I can't see you!"

He caught a faint reply mixing with the howling wind, but it sounded further away than before. Spotting a soft glow of light a little more than forty feet away, he reached for Horum's gift.

Shift.

Wil was slumped over an impromptu raft of ship's railing. A pole jutting from the wood still had the magic orb of light attached to it, shining light on the deep, dark gash that ran from Wil's nose to his right temple. Nikalys guessed there would be plenty of blood if not for the seawater.

Clapping his friend on the back, Nikalys shouted, "Wil!"

Wil lifted his head to regard Nikalys with glassy eyes and gave an unsteady grin.

"Nice of you to come after me."

"I couldn't let my best teacher drown."

Nikalys hoped the magical light was the reason Wil looked so pale.

Wil's gaze shifted to stare past Nikalys.

"The Sapphire is almost gone."

Holding onto the railing itself, Nikalys looked over his shoulder, and saw Wil was right. The Sapphire was twice as far as before. Swallowing a curse, he turned back to Wil, patted the soldier on the back, and called out valiantly, "No worries, Wil. I was the best swimmer in Yellow Mud."

He looked back to the Sapphire again, a frown on his face. He had no idea how he could get back to the ship. All he knew was that every moment wasted meant the ship was slipping further away.

"Come on, Wil. Time to go."

He helped Wil from the broken railing, looping the young man's arms around his neck. The sea swept away the wooden railing immediately, taking the ball bound to it with it. The pair floated in darkness now with Nikalys treading water for them both. It only took a few moments of doing so before Nikalys realized he could never swim to the Sapphire while dragging Wil along. That left only one thing to try.

Reaching up, he gripped Wil's arms and yelled over the roar of the storm, "Hold on!" Staring in the direction of the ship, he waited until they were atop of another tall wave.

Shift.

Nikalys felt himself falling through the air, having moved from crest to trough. As he plummeted to the sea, he felt sick. He was alone. Apparently, Horum's gift did not extend to others.

He splashed back into the sea, plunging beneath the water. Struggling upward, he broke into the night and screamed, "Wil! Wil!"

He yelled his friend's name repeatedly, hoping to catch a response.

"Wil!"

A series of lightning flashes lit up the ever-shifting seas as Nikalys scanned waves, looking for anything that might be a person.

"Wil!"

He wanted nothing more than to hear Wil's voice call back. It never did.

A deep, dark despair gripped him. His insides turned as numb as his outside.

Suddenly, a dozen feet away, the strangest animal Nikalys had ever seen broke the surface of the turbulent seas. A lightning flash lit up the creature, revealing an elongated nose jutting from a smooth, sloped face and two dark, glassy eyes perched on opposite sides of its head. The beast turned its head to stare at Nikalys with its right eye. As it swiveled, another flash of lightning illuminated a figure on the animal's back, holding onto a curved fin. Nikalys' heart leapt for joy.

"Wil!"

The creature to which Wil clung began to change shape. The nose shrunk, retreating into the face while the eyes shifted forward, rotating around to the front of the head. A chin formed from underneath the mouth and thick, brown hair sprung from the top of its head. The area between head and body thinned out to become a man's neck with wide, muscular shoulders to either side. Within moments, the strange sea animal was gone, replaced with the familiar and very welcome shape of a hillman.

"Broedi!"

The White Lion whipped around to grab Wil before he slipped beneath the surface. Treading water while holding onto the young soldier, Broedi turned to glare at Nikalys.

"What do you think you are doing!? That was utterly, stupidly reckless!"

Nikalys was so happy, he did not care that Broedi had chastised him.

"How did you—"

"Not now!" shouted the hillman. "Take Will and hold onto my fin after I change. We need to catch the ship before it is gone!"

Nikalys reached out and took Wil, ensuring he kept the man's head above water.

Broedi bellowed, "Do you see the ship?"

Nikalys scanned the sea.

"No!"

At this point, he had no idea in which direction the Sapphire lay.

"Then I will have to listen for it!" shouted Broedi.

Nikalys was about to ask how he could hear anything in the storm's rage when a brilliant yellow glow lit up the night. At first, Nikalys thought it was another bolt of lightning, yet when the light did not fade, both Broedi and he turned to find a giant orb of light rising and falling on distant waves.

Nikalys let out a shout of joy.

"Thank you, Nundle!"

Broedi glanced at Nikalys, eyebrows drawn together in confusion.

Smiling wide, Nikalys said, "I told the captain to get Nundle to light up a way back!"

The anger in Broedi's eyes faded slightly, replaced with a hint of admiration. "You were still rash!"

"Yell at me later!" cried Nikalys. He nodded to an unconscious Wil. "We need to get him back to the ship."

Broedi nodded and, almost immediately, his head and shoulders shifted, merging into one. His face elongated, the long snout with a rounded point returning. Within a couple of heartbeats, Broedi was the sea creature again.

The animal dipped below the water and surfaced a second later beside Nikalys. With his left arm holding onto Wil, cradling his body in such a way to ensure his head was free of the sea, Nikalys gripped Broedi's fin.

"Go!"

Broedi began to swim, the muscles along the creature's back rippling with each beat of what felt like a tail smacking Nikalys' legs. It was a struggle to keep Wil's head above the waves as they cut through the water toward the ship. As they neared, Nikalys saw an enormous yellow light bound to the bow's figurehead. Excited shouts of men cut through the storm. They had been spotted.

Sailors tossed a half-dozen ropes into the water. Once Broedi swam to the nearest pair, Nikalys felt the creature's fin slipping from his hand. The White Lion was shifting back to his hillman self. Letting go of Broedi, Nikalys grabbed a rope in one hand while gripping Wil in the other. Glancing at the young soldier's face, he could not tell if he was still breathing.

Once Broedi completed the shift, he shouted, "Tie the rope around him!"

Nikalys did so and then stared up the side of the ship, yelling, "Pull him up!"

The seamen began to heft the injured soldier up to the deck. Holding onto a second rope, Nikalys watched, tense, as the shifting seas caused Wil's body to sway back and forth.

Once Wil disappeared over the side of the ship, Nikalys and Broedi climbed the second rope. Upon reaching the railing, sailors and soldiers alike helped pull the pair over. Nikalys collapsed on the deck, grateful to be on something solid. Nundle's bright light suddenly winked out, briefly plunging the ship into darkness before the smaller amber globes began to pop back into existence.

Lifting his head, Nikalys saw a group gathered around what he assumed was Wil, Nundle and Broedi at the center. Nikalys began to scramble up, intending to go check on his friend, when a firm hand pressed down on his chest. Looking up, Nikalys found Sergeant Trell kneeling beside him.

"Relax, Nikalys." His tone was firm. "You've done what you can. Lie down and let them do what they do." The words, "that's an order" were all but spoken.

Sergeant Trell was right. Nundle and Broedi were both Life Mages. Wil was safe as long as he still drew breath.

Looking to the sergeant, Nikalys asked, "Is he alive?"

Sergeant Trell nodded.

"Judging from the bucketful of water he's coughed up already, I'd say yes."

Nikalys loosed a long sigh and slumped to the deck.

"Thank the Gods…"

The ship rose and fell beneath him, sliding him this way and that. The wind continued to blow, stripping the little heat he still had in his body. He shivered uncontrollably, colder now than he had ever been.

Sergeant Trell called, "Cero! Go get some blankets!"

"Yes, Sergeant!"

As Nikalys listened to the thudding of Cero's boots on deck, the sergeant stared back down at him and shook his head.

"That was an incredibly brave thing you just did."

His teeth chattering, Nikalys said, "I could not leave him—"

"Brave?" shouted a gruff voice.

Nikalys tilted his head back to find Captain Scrag hovering over him, Nikalys' sword gripped in his hand.

"Brave?! Blast the Hells! That was foolish! Brainless! The maddest of the mad would have better sense than do what you did! You are denser than a hunk of white iron! What in the Nine Hells were you thinking?"

"Well, I—"

Eyes widening further, Captain Scrag screamed, "Blast it! I don't want an actual answer!"

Pushing himself up on his elbows, Nikalys began to protest, "But you—"

Captain Scrag bent over, yelling, "The next time you want to do something foolhardy like that, tell me first and I'll throw you in myself!" He shoved the Blade of Horum into Sergeant Trell's hands and turned around, stomping off, back to the aft deck.

Stunned, Nikalys watched the man walk away. Broedi's deep voice cut into his shock.

"Believe it or not, he actually likes you."

Nikalys peered over, finding the hillman standing on his right.

"He has an odd way of showing it."

Broedi bent down, opposite of Sergeant Trell, and fixed Nikalys with a hard stare.

"He is right, though. Your actions were careless."

"But Wil was going to drown," protested Nikalys. "I couldn't let him die."

"You could have and you should have," rumbled Broedi. "Wil is *not* one of the Progeny. You must put the fate of the world before that of a friend."

Nikalys turned to Sergeant Trell, hoping to find support from the soldier. The sergeant's face was sympathetic, but his words were not.

"Broedi's right. A leader must make decisions that are callous by any mark." His expression turned grim as he added, "It is not an easy mantle to carry."

Nikalys wanted to shout at them both, to assail them for their heartlessness. However, he did not. Deep down, he knew they were right.

After a moment, Broedi said, "I must go attend to Wil for a time."

Looking up, Nikalys asked, "Will he be alright?"

"With some sleep, yes," rumbled the hillman. He stood, began to turn away, but stopped and looked back down. "Aryn would be proud of what you did here."

Nikalys blinked in surprise. Broedi's comment had caught him off guard.

Broedi held his gaze a moment longer before turning and walking away, heading to where two men were carrying Wil to the stairs that headed below deck. Nikalys stared after him, shivering against the rain and wind.

Sergeant Trell roused him with a pat on the shoulder.

"Come on. Let's get you some dry clothes. I'm cold just looking at you."

Nikalys nodded and let the sergeant help him up from the wet deck. Cero arrived with two thick, dry blankets and draped them over his shoulders. As the two men helped him to the stairs, Broedi's words echoed in his head, fueling a longing for a father Nikalys had never known.

CHAPTER 35: HURT

8ᵗʰ of the Turn of Maeana, 4999

Jak strode inside from the blustery cold, leaving the courtyard door to crash against the inside wall. Stomping his feet on the stone floor, trying to rid his boots of the slush clinging to them, he left the door open and moved down the hall. One of the other soldiers would close it. Reaching up with his gloved hand, he rubbed the little bits of frozen water stuck to his fledgling beard. Icy drops of water ran down his neck.

"Blasted snow."

Growing up in Yellow Mud, Thaddeus had told stories about snow to Jak and his siblings, but the trio was never sure if they could believe the tales. Father enjoyed telling stories that were not necessarily true.

Yesterday afternoon, Jak had been in his room, lying on his bed sulking, when he spotted the white flakes floating past his window. He leapt from his bed and stood before his window, gaping at the strange sight. Forgetting his bad mood for a time, he rushed down the stairs, through the halls, and burst into the courtyard. A number of former Red Sentinels were already there, gazing around in wonder, watching the fluffy whiteness envelop the enclave. His instinct was to run off, find Nikalys and Kenders, and share the moment with them. Then dismal reality reasserted itself and his foul temper snapped back into place.

Turning around, he had marched back to his room and remained there through the night, skipping eveningmeal. When morning arrived, he awoke, dressed warmly, and headed straight to the courtyard for drills, skipping morningmeal as well. He would have preferred staying in his room, but his new duties precluded him from doing that. A week ago, Commander Aiden had assigned twenty-five men to him and named him a corporal.

Upon reaching the courtyard doors, he opened them and stopped in his tracks. The world had turned white, a thick mantle of snow covering the yard, topping the battlements, and blanketing the woodpiles and benches. As he stepped from the hallway, he sunk into the cold stuff, stunned to find that the snow reached his calves. He trudged toward the other soldiers already in the yard, amazed at how hard it was to walk in the white powder. The typical Storm Island wind blew hard, swirling about the courtyard, whipping up clouds of snow, and blowing it into his eyes.

For the next two hours, the soldiers attempted to go through their progression of drills while slipping and sliding all over the yard. Steady footing was nigh impossible. While most of the men kept a good humor about the situation, Jak had not.

When yet another pair of his men slipped, falling upon one another and then chuckling about it, Jak's temper broke and he unleashed a long tirade of curses on his entire detachment. He only stopped his rant when he realized everyone in the courtyard was staring at him. Catching Commander Aiden's disappointed stare, Jak shut his mouth. He knew he had let his bitterness get the better of him, but did not much care.

For the past three weeks, on the direct orders of Lady Vivienne and Duchess Aleece, he had been acting as though Kenders was still somewhere within the enclave, holed up with Khin and Tobias, focusing on her studies. The sudden absence of Zecus, Joshmuel, and Boah had been explained away with a falsehood that the Borderlanders had requested to return home and the baroness had granted their wish.

At first, people had accepted the lies. Yet when nobody had seen Kenders, Tobias, or Khin for over a week, rumors started. Jak tried to dissuade the gossip, but it was like trying to swim up a waterfall. Rather than face constant questioning, he retreated to his room whenever he was not performing his duties as a soldier and stewed over Kenders' rashness. He had read the letter she had slipped under his door at least a dozen times now and grew angrier each time.

Pulling his gloves from his hands and jamming them in his overcoat's pocket, Jak turned down the hallway leading to the commons. If he hurried, he could grab something to eat before anyone else made it to the kitchens and then retreat to his room.

"Corporal Isaac!"

The shouted words came from behind and echoed in the empty hall. Jak pressed his lips together and let loose a soft curse.

"Hells."

Halting in place, Jak took a deep breath, trying to let the acrimony bubbling within him to drain away. As the commander approached him, his boots clomping against the stone floor, Jak turned to face the head of the Shadow Mane soldiers.

"Yes, Commander?"

With a scowl on his face, the former Knight-Lieutenant of the Southern Arms strode down the long, torch-lit hallway and stopped before Jak. The old soldier stood quiet, hands fixed on his hips, and stared. After a few moments, he spoke in a firm, yet gentle tone.

"You know, I heard the blacksmith is looking for an apprentice."

Jak blinked, confused.

"Pardon, sir?"

"I'd bet you'd make a fine smith. Your father was the best Claw ever had in the years I've been here. Shall I speak to Master Washor about securing you the position?"

This was not the conversation Jak was expecting to have.

"I'm sorry, sir. I don't understand. Smithing?"

Crossing his arms, Commander Aiden said, "Yes. I thought you might want to give it a try as it seems soldiering no longer holds your interest."

"That's not true, sir. I—"

"So you *do* want to be a soldier?"

"Yes, sir. I do."

Commander Aiden leaned forward and, his voice turning colder than the Winter wind, he said, "Then start acting like it! Your behavior this morning was unacceptable! You should be ashamed of yourself!"

Jak flinched and dropped his gaze. The words had an amazing effect on his anger, melting it away much as the warmer air of the hall was thawing the snow now dripping from his clothes and boots.

"Ah," muttered the commander. "So then you do feel bad?"

"Yes, sir."

"Are you embarrassed?"

"Yes, sir."

"Humiliated?"

"Quite a lot, sir."

"Good," said the commander. "I'm glad. Although I suspect your humiliation pales next to my own."

Confused, Jak glanced up.

"Sir?"

"I'm the one who gave you the position allowing you to treat those men like that. Had I given the command to a piglet, I would have seen better leadership."

Letting out a low, heavy sigh, Jak said, "I was wrong, Commander."

"Oh, you were *more* than wrong. I wish I could convey to you just how wrong you were, yet there is no word in Argot for it. Perhaps you should head to the library and research other tongues. I bet you could find a word that describes the breadth of your wrongness. What do you think? Does that sound like something you would like to do?"

Jak shook his head.

"Not particularly, sir."

The commander's gaze bored into him as the old soldier said, "When you are commanding men, Jak, there are times to scream at them, and there are times to laugh with them. Guess which today was?"

"To laugh, sir?"

"Wrong," snapped the commander. "You were initially correct to chastise your charge for not taking their drills seriously. Yet you took it too far, Jak. *Much* too far. You went beyond making your point and moved straight to fostering resentment."

Jak stared at the older soldier and sighed.

"I understand, sir."

"I don't think you do. Because if you did, you would have never pulled that stunt out there!"

By now, every bit of Jak's ill-tempered anger was gone.

"I am sorry, Commander. Truly, I am. I just..." He trailed off and looked away, staring blankly at one of the torches. The reason for his sour mood was not one he could share.

Commander Aiden remained silent for a few moments before letting out a sigh and speaking. The anger was absent from his voice, but an edge of authority remained.

"Look, Jak, I know you miss your brother and sister."

Jak's gaze instantly shifted back to the commander, but he remained quiet. He was not to tell anyone about Kenders' absence.

Commander Aiden looked past Jak, turned around to check the hallway behind him, and then leaned forward, speaking in a low voice.

"I know she's gone, Jak. I confronted Lady Vivienne about it last week."

Jak waited a moment before asking, "How did you know?"

A dry smile spread over Commander Aiden's lips.

"It was not all that hard to figure out. No one has seen her, Khin, or the new White Lion in weeks. And you've been...less than a joy for the same stretch. It only made sense."

Frowning, Jak muttered, "I suppose I have been a bit surly."

"A bit?"

"Fine. More than a bit, sir."

"You are permitted to worry, Jak, but you cannot allow your emotions to affect your duties."

With a firm nod, Jak said, "I understand, sir."

"I hope so. Prove it to me during afternoon drills."

"Yes, sir," said Jak. "I will."

Commander Aiden relaxed, uncrossing his arms and assuming a more informal pose. Eyeing him carefully, the commander said, "I'm going to share something rather important with you. Something I'm supposed to keep to myself."

After this morning, Jak was surprised the man would confide in him.

"You don't need to do that, sir."

"Yes, I do," replied Commander Aiden. "I need you to fully grasp how important it is that you keep focus." He leaned close, his eyes reflecting the flickering of the torchlights. "Once Broedi and Nikalys return, we're leaving, Jak. The army of the White Lions will be moving to the front lines."

A rush of anxiety fluttered in Jak's chest.

"Do we have new information from the west?"

"No, nothing. In fact, it is the lack of information that drives the decision. Things on the First Council have deteriorated. Barons Tilas and Treswell withdrew from the council last week. All of Freehaven is in an uproar."

Considering what he had witnessed in the Council Hall, Jak was not surprised by the turn of events. Nevertheless, it was disturbing to hear.

"Does that mean the Borderlands and Great Lakes are no longer part of the Oaken Duchies?

Commander Aiden shrugged.

"No one seems to know. Apparently, two dozen barristers are arguing the point now. Although, whatever conclusion they arrive at is moot. Old parchments and old men can't shield us from Chaos' army, now can they?"

"No, they cannot," muttered Jak, a deep frown on his face. "This is not good, Commander. Not good at all."

"No, Jak, it's not. But there is some sweet with the sour. The first detachments of Southern Arms have already reached Demetus. More will be arriving over the next few weeks along with the advance groups of the Shore Guard. And the Red Peaks has committed to joining the effort should war break out. Duchess Aleece believes the Foothills are leaning with us as well."

Jak could not believe all of this was happening.

"None of this seems real."

Certain weariness filled the commander's eyes.

"I've been preparing for this for over two decades, Jak, and I feel the same way. We need more time."

"How much time would you need before you felt ready?"

A dry chuckle slipped from the commander.

"A few hundred years ought to do it."

The two men stood silent in the hall for a time, both staring blankly at the walls. Commander Aiden broke the quiet first, speaking in a soft, restrained voice.

"Shorn Rise was the first time any of us had seen an oligurt or razorfiend. The only thing our armies know about our enemy is what they've heard in playmen's sagas. Oligurts, mongrels, razorfiends…"

Jak muttered, "Don't forget demons."

"Oh, I haven't," said the commander. "You know, Jak, the heat of battle tends to draw forth every fear a man already has while instilling a whole set of new ones. Our forces will be terrified by what they face. You and the rest of the men here are going to be the few soldiers in *all* the duchies who are somewhat prepared for what is coming. I'm counting on every one of you to keep our armies focused."

"I hear you, Commander. I will be a better example."

"That's good," said the soldier with a nod of approval. Patting Jak on the shoulder, he stepped past, on his way down the hall. "Be sure and get something to eat, Corporal."

Jak said over his shoulder, "I will, sir."

"And eat in the commons with the men, please. Not in your room."

Smiling faintly, Jak replied, "Yes, sir."

He stood in place a few moments, gathering himself, when he heard Commander Aiden's scuffling steps come to a quick stop.

"Pardon me, my dear—I did not see you there."

A woman's too-familiar voice replied, "No need to apologize, Commander."

Without a moment's hesitation, Jak stepped forward, heading back in the direction from which he had come, away from the commons and the woman. He did not have a destination in mind other than 'not here.'

Sabine's voice rang out from behind him.

"Jak?"

For a brief moment, he considered ducking down a side hallway and pretending he did not hear her. The young woman confounded him. Weeks ago, he had shared a wondrous evening in the commons with her, laughing and jesting. Shortly thereafter, her attitude toward him had shifted. It took him a few days to realize the change coincided with Nikalys' departure on the Sapphire. He was unsure how to feel about that.

"Jak!"

Her voice filled the hallway, echoing off the stone blocks. If he were deaf, he would have still heard her.

Letting out a low sigh, Jak stopped and turned. Sabine hurried toward him, holding the sides of her green dress, keeping the hem a few inches above the ground. The torches lining the hall lit her face, revealing an expression of clear irritation.

Affixing a neutral smile on his face, Jak said, "Oh, hello, Sabine."

Shortly after Kenders had run off, Sabine sought out Jak and revealed that she knew of his sister's absence. Apparently, Kenders had confided in Sabine prior to leaving with Zecus. Jak was furious with Sabine for not telling him before Kenders ran off. Sabine was equally put off by Jak's expectation that she should have come running to him to report. Jak stalked away and had avoided Sabine since. She had come to his room twice in the past week, but he had ignored her knocking both times.

Sabine stopped before him and stared up at him, her silky, raven-black hair hanging loose and free around her face.

"Where are you going?"

"To the armory."

Sabine cocked a disbelieving eyebrow.

"Truly?"

"Yes. I need to get a new scabbard."

He lied. His current scabbard was perfectly fine.

"Odd," muttered Sabine. "Because it sounded like the commander more or less ordered you to go to the commons and get something to eat."

Eyes narrowing, Jak asked, "Were you eavesdropping?"

Sabine shook her head.

"Not at all. I happened to be walking through the halls when I heard the two of you talking. As I did not want to interrupt, I simply stayed in a side hallway until you were done."

"That sounds like eavesdropping."

Sabine shrugged her shoulders.

"To me, it sounds as if I were being polite."

"What did you hear? Exactly?"

"Truly? Not much," admitted Sabine. "You both were talking too quietly for me to hear every word." She sounded disappointed. "Although…I *did* hear Commander Aiden mention that everyone will be leaving when Nikalys and Broedi return."

Jak said firmly, "That's *not* to be shared with anyone, Sabine."

Giving him a level stare, she said, "Gee, thanks, Jak. I was wondering about that." The sarcasm in her voice was as clear as a Summer sky in Yellow Mud.

"You know what I mean," said Jak. "Can you keep that to yourself?"

A tiny huff of a laugh slipped from her lips. "You're asking if I can keep a secret?" Reaching up, she slipped two fingers under the neckline of her dress, and pulled two necklaces free. One was the silver-link chain she always wore given to her by her mother. The other was a simple leather thong with a silver teardrop hanging from it. Jak stared at the pendant with wide eyes.

"That's my mother's necklace."

Sabine nodded once, smiling.

"Yes, Jak. I know that."

"How did you—" He stopped and shifted his gaze back to Sabine's face. "Kenders gave it to you, didn't she? Why in the Nine Hells didn't you tell me you had that?"

Sabine's expression hardened.

"I was going to, Jak, but you ran off before I could. And you've been hiding in your blasted room ever since! Honestly, even Helene does not behave so."

Had this conversation occurred a short while ago, before the one with Commander Aiden, Jak would have reacted with sharp words. Now, however, he bit his lip and drew a deep, steadying breath. She was right. His behavior had been childish.

"I apologize, Sabine."

She shook her head.

"It's no matter."

"No, Sabine," said Jak, his voice firm. "I apologize. For everything. I've acted the lout for weeks."

She regarded him a moment, her brown eyes swallowing him. Eventually, the corners of her lips turned up a fraction.

"Yes, Jak Isaac, you have."

He smiled at the modest agreement and remained quiet. She, too, kept silent, staring at him, the harder edges in her face softening. Yet again, he was struck by her beauty. Before he began gaping like a fool, he glanced back at his mother's necklace.

"So, how are they? Unharmed?"

Even though the pendant had spent fifteen years around Marie Isaac's neck, the magical artifice had originally belonged to Nikalys and Kenders' blood mother. Eliza Kap had knit a Weave into the matte silver teardrop bound specifically to brother and sister. Whoever held the necklace could determine both the wellbeing of the pair and the general direction in which they lay simply by picturing their faces.

A gentle smile spread over Sabine's perfect lips as she said, "If they weren't, Jak, I would have broken down your door last week. Not knocked politely." He was in the midst of letting out a relieved sigh when her brow drew together. "Although…"

A jolt of alarm shot through Jak as he asked, "What does that mean?"

"Don't worry," said Sabine quickly. "They are not harmed. They're…" She trailed off and glanced down at the necklace. "Well, I'm not really sure what they are."

"Are you using it right?"

"There's not much to it, Jak. Hold necklace, think of their faces. Yes. I'm using it right."

"Then what's wrong?"

"Well…for a time, whenever I would check on Nikalys—" her eyes fluttered suspiciously "—I felt ill." She shrugged. "Whatever it was, it stopped over a week ago. He seems fine now. But *every* time I check on Kenders, she…well…" She trailed off, sounding troubled.

Jak stared at her. The uneasy expression on Sabine's face worried him.

"What is it?

Sabine's beautiful eyes locked on his own.

"She's sad, Jak."

Jak blinked. He had not expected that.

"She's…sad?"

As Sabine nodded, he glanced at the necklace.

"May I?"

She held the pendant out to him with the leather cord still looped around her neck.

"Please."

He had expected her to take the necklace off and hand it to him. When it was evident she was not, he took a step closer and gripped the silver teardrop. The faint perfume of rosewater filled his nose.

Closing his eyes, he pictured Nikalys and a sense of calm immediately rushed over him.

"Nik's fine."

He smiled, surprised by how much joy knowing that brought him. A soft, ringing tone—nearly inaudible—tickled his ear. Jak wondered just how far away his brother was by now.

Letting Nikalys slip from his mind, he turned his full attention to Kenders, focusing on her easy smile, Harvest straw hair, and hazel eyes. Instantly, a feeling of intense misery surged through his soul, nearly overwhelming him.

"Bless the Gods…"

The words slipped out in a hushed whisper. She was not physically hurt, but the deep, guilt-ridden sadness he felt was almost as bad. While the soft tone he heard for Kenders was as faint as Nikalys, hers was in the opposite direction. As he opened his eyes, the woeful feeling winked out like a snuffed torch.

Staring at Sabine, he asked, "What could have happened to make her so sad?"

Sabine frowned and shook her head.

"I don't want to know the answer to that."

Dropping his gaze back to the necklace, he asked, "What do we do for her?" He wanted to rush out of the enclave right now.

"Do?" repeated Sabine. "They're too far west for us to *do* anything. Kenders was planning to go to my home in the grasslands. And that was weeks ago."

"But something has happened," protested Jak. "She might need help."

Sabine gave him a gentle smile and said, "She's safe and unhurt, Jak. And Tobias is with her."

Preoccupied, Jak murmured, "Khin, too."

Sabine's eyes rose.

"So he is gone as well, then?"

Jak's heart climbed into his throat. Glancing up and down the hall, he mumbled, "I was not supposed to tell anyone that."

Sabine fixed him with a mock-hurtful look.

"What's the matter, Jak? Don't you trust me?"

Smiling at her, Jak said, "Of course I do."

Her expression shifted, growing playful.

"Good."

Suddenly aware that he was mere inches from Sabine, he released the necklace and took a quick step back. She reached up as if to stop him, stopped short, and dropped her arm to her side. For a few quiet moments, the pair gazed at one another in silence. Then, with a reluctant sigh, Sabine began to speak in a soft, tentative voice.

"Jak, there's something I need to—"

A deep, chest-thudding boom filled the hallway. The floor quivered under Jak's boots, the stone walls rattled, dropping dust and bits of mortar to the ground. A nearby torch fell from its metal jacket, crashing to the floor. Jak shot one arm out to brace against the wall and the other to help steady Sabine.

As the rumble faded, Sabine looked up at him and asked, "What was that?" Her eyes were clear and calm, absent any panic.

Jak shook his head, eyeing the walls around them.

"I don't—"

A second, weaker boom shook the ground and walls again. Another torch fell to the ground. Looking up and down the hall, Jak frowned. The passageway around them suddenly felt like a tomb.

"We should move."

"You're right."

Jak turned, leading them through the halls, heading back to the open courtyard. Cries of alarm echoed through the maze of cold stone ways.

"Jak, I need to get Helene."

Without slowing, Jak glanced back.

"Where is she?"

"In the mages' hall, at her studies."

"We'll cut across the courtyard. It's fastest."

As they turned a corner, Sabine asked, "Do you think the enclave is under attack?" Again, her tone was free of panic.

Doing his best to match her composure, Jak replied evenly, "I don't know." The thought had crossed his mind. "I hope not."

Their defenses were weak presently. Thirty soldiers were on the Sapphire, and with Kenders, Khin, Broedi, Tobias, and Nundle all gone, the enclave's best mages were absent. Over two dozen Shadow Mane mages resided here, but none was as talented as those that were gone.

As they rushed down the hall, Sabine warned, "I sense Strands of Fire."

Surprised, Jak glanced back at Sabine and asked, "Are you sure?" When she nodded, Jak grimaced and faced forward, mumbling, "Oh, Hells."

If Sabine could sense the magic, a very large number were in use.

As they neared the hall leading to the courtyard, Jak smelled smoke. Rounding the corner, he saw the double doors at the end of the hall standing wide-open, flakes of still-falling snow drifting inside with the wind. A handful of people stood at the doors, staring outside into the white courtyard. As Jak and Sabine ran up, one of the men turned around to stare at them, his eyes wide.

Recognizing the man one of the kitchen servants, Jak shouted, "Gregor! What's going on?"

Gregor's gaze flicked to Sabine, worry in his eyes. He opened his mouth to speak, but hesitated.

Nearly at the door, Jak demanded, "Gregor! What is it?"

Pulling his gaze from Sabine, Gregor said, "There was an explosion." He turned, pointing across the courtyard.

They reached the open doorway an instant later and skidded to a stop. Jak stared outside, gaping at the scene before him.

"Bless the Gods…"

On the far side of the yard, a massive plume of black smoke billowed into the air, rising from a section of the northeastern wall. The lower level was missing, chunks of rock dropping from the battlements that still spanned the hole. Dozens of Shadow Mane soldiers were rushing toward the breech.

Shoving him aside, Sabine rushed past him, sprinting into courtyard and toward the ruined wall. Jak stared after her, briefly wondering where she was going. Then it hit him. The smoking hole in the wall was where the mages' hall was, where Helene was.

Bursting from the doorway, Jak dashed across the courtyard, his long strides kicking up snow. He easily passed Sabine—she was struggling with her dress in the drifts—all the while staring at the hole ahead of him. Men and women were stumbling from the smoking breach, helped along by people arriving on the scene.

Upon reaching the wall, he halted and peered up, judging the gap in the wall to be twenty feet tall. The battlements above were still together, but sagging. Staring into the hole and through the smoke, he could see light from the other side shining through. Any wood he saw was on fire, from exposed rafters to the shards of blown-apart furniture littering the ground. He saw at least a half-dozen people with bloody injuries or raw, burnt skin. A man was sitting on the ground, cradling his arm, screaming.

Jak scanned the area, looking for the tiny form of Helene. She was the only child taking lessons. She should be easy to spot, yet he did not see her. As Sabine rushed up beside him and stopped, he asked without looking at her, "You're sure she was here?"

"Yes," answered Sabine, still amazingly calm. "She had a lesson with Marick this morning. I was on my way to get her when I came across you."

Jak felt a sharp pang of guilt. Had he and Sabine not talked, Helene would have been safely gone from here when this had happened.

He took a few steps closer toward the hole, eyeing the drooping battlements.

"That's not going to stay up much—"

"Gamin!"

Sabine sprinted past him, pulling Jak's attention from the wall and to the redheaded mage. Gamin was stumbling about the snow, blood pouring from large gash by his left temple, covering his face and robes. Sabine rushed over, grabbed the man's arms and started talking to him. Jak followed.

Gamin Pargette was a big, strong fellow, but right now, it looked as if a gentle breeze could knock him down. His eyes were glazed over, his jaw slack. A jagged shard of wood stuck out of the cut on his head.

As Jak arrived, Sabine said, "He can't remember where Helene was."

Jak shook his head. In his current state, they would be lucky if Gamin could remember his name.

"Sabine, he needs a healer now, before—"

He stopped suddenly, turned around, and stared into the smoke pouring from the wall. Somehow, he knew with absolute conviction that Helene was inside and that he needed to move now if he was going to save her. Without wasting another moment, he sprinted toward the crumbling opening, unbuckling his belt and dropping it and the attached scabbard to the ground.

Behind him, Sabine cried out, "Jak!"

He ignored her and leapt into the smoke.

The acrid haze clung to his throat like wet mud to boots. Coughing uncontrollably, he stuck his nose into the crook of his arm, trying to filter out the worst of the smoke and pushed through the cloud. Blinking back tears, he climbed up a rubble pile and slid down the other side, moving into what had been the mages' hall.

He stopped in place, marveling at the sheer destruction around him. Anything that could burn was in flames. Shattered ebonwood beams. Broken tables and benches. Shredded tapestries, books, parchments. He wondered how anyone had survived this.

Wood cracked and stone creaked, protesting at the weight of the battlements overhead. He glanced up, praying the broken stone would remain in place a little while longer. Dropping his gaze back down, he spun in a circle.

"Helene!"

Over and over, he shouted the girl's name.

"Helene!"

Stumbling through the ruined room, he noted snowflakes drifting down, mingling with the smoke. Some holes must extend all the way through the battlements.

His foot caught on something, nearly tripping him. Glancing down through tear-soaked eyes, he saw the left side of a man's face, the skin charred black and hair burnt off. The man's eye was open and lifeless.

Knowing what the result would be, Jak nonetheless bent over and pressed his hand to the man's chest, searching for a heartbeat. As he expected, there was none.

"Maeana guide you."

The groan of wood bending drew his attention upward just as a large chunk of stone tumbled down, thudding to the ground but a dozen paces from where he crouched. He needed to hurry.

Suddenly, he knew—somehow—that Helene was behind him. He was certain of it.

Whipping his head around, he stared through the smoke. Near an overturned, smoldering table lay what appeared to be a tan, crumbled-up sack. A sack with raven-black hair.

"Helene!"

Springing up, Jak left the dead man and rushed through the wrecked room, dashing around debris. A fat, wooden beam slipped from above and crashed to the floor, showering him with orange embers. Flicking them from his hair, he reached the tiny form of Helene and dropped to a knee.

"Khanos be with her."

After his quick plea to the God of Life, he stretched out a hand to check her. Gripping her shoulder, he rolled her on her back, revealing her small face. Her eyelids fluttered but remained closed. But at least she was alive.

"Oh, thank the Gods…"

Jak was stunned to discover that she appeared whole and uninjured, miraculously untouched by the blast. He did not understand how that was possible, but now was not the time to question the girl's luck.

Picking her up from the cold stone, he made to move away when something caught his eye. He stopped and stared straight down at the floor. He stood at the center of a perfect ring of gray stone. Starting a couple of paces away, black char radiated outward in every direction. Jak spun in a quick circle, realizing that everything in the room had been thrown back, away from this very spot.

His heart felt as if it stopped. He peered down at the untouched face of Helene. A lost snowflake drifted past, landed on her cheek, and melted.

"Gods, no…"

The deep rumble of stone breaking shook him from his harsh realization.

Turning around, he sprinted back to where he had entered the hall, smoke swirling all around him, chunks of stone falling from above, and fires burning on every side.

The rumbling grew louder. The wall was collapsing.

Spotting the light of day ahead, beckoning him, he rushed forward, leaping over the burning husk of an oak table. Peering outside, through the smoke cloud, he saw people rushing about, screaming and pointing at the wall, at the battlements, at him. Lady Vivienne stood two dozen paces from the breach, her gaze fixed on the wall.

Something hard and heavy struck his head. He fell, losing Helene in the process. Slamming into the ground, his eyelids fluttered shut. Dark tendrils of unconsciousness tugged at him.

He lay there a moment, the stone floor cold against his cheek. Cracking open his eyes, he found little globs of light dancing before him. The world was oddly silent.

Forcing himself on his hands and knees, he spotted Helene several paces away. Crawling over to her, he hefted her tiny body in his arms, and ordered himself to stand. Spotting the bright, snow-covered courtyard less than a dozen paces away, he staggered forward, wobbling and weaving. He could not see out of his left eye. Licking his lips, he tasted blood.

He tottered into the snowy yard, lost his balance, and collapsed again, but managed to not fall atop Helene. He could hear a faint ringing in his ears now, accompanied by distant screams and cracking stone. The ground was vibrating.

Someone grabbed his arm and started dragging him through the snow. The wet, cold stuff plowed its way down the front of his shirt.

"No…I need to get Helene…"

He tried to stop himself, struggling and kicking his legs.

"Helene. I need to—"

A man shouted, "Blast it, Jak! Hold still!"

Opening his right eye—he had not been aware he had shut it—he lifted his head and peered up into the face of Commander Aiden. The soldier looked worried.

Jak mumbled, "Helene is…she's…I dropped…"

He was having trouble getting the words from his mind and past his lips. His tongue felt thick and heavy.

"She's fine, son. Sabine has her."

Relieved, Jak closed his eye, suddenly very tired.

"Jak?"

He wanted nothing more than to fall asleep.

"Jak! Don't you—"

The blackness overtook him.

CHAPTER 36: CONSPIRATOR

Nelnora pulled her gaze from the scene within the shimmering display and glanced at the trio of figures standing on the circular dais with her. She wished, not for the first time, that she had some idea what they were thinking. They at least appeared interested in what they were watching. A good start, she supposed. Pressing her lips together, she stared back to the window.

A handful of people knelt in the snow, surrounding the young man and tending to the large gash on his head. The black-haired woman stood nearby, embracing her sister in her arms, anxiously looking on. Dozens of people wandered about the yard, meandering through the smoke and dust of the collapsed wall.

The figure furthest from Nelnora spoke, his rich, deep voice filling the white marble chamber.

"Will he live?"

Glancing up, Nelnora stared in Ketus' direction but had a difficult time making out the God's face. The cloak covering his head and body shifted and twisted, taking on the shades and pattern of the wall behind him. She frowned, wondering why he felt the need to hide here.

Shoving aside her irritation, she considered his question and determined it a poignant one. Looking back to her window, she eyed the injured man. Making a minor adjustment to her pattern, she shifted the display, moving the view closer to his bloody face.

Ashana murmured worriedly, "That gash looks deep."

"It certainly does," agreed Nelnora. It would be a shame if he died. He had proven useful to this point.

"So," said Ketus. "Will he live or not?"

Looking up, Nelnora turned to stare expectantly at their fourth member, Maeana. The little slivers of sunlight littering the chamber, cut to pieces by the crystalline dome above their heads, danced over the Goddess of Death's brilliant white robes.

Ashana was already staring at her, as was Ketus. At least Nelnora thought Ketus was eyeing Maeana. It was difficult to tell.

Sensing their collective stare, Maeana raised a single, ink-black eyebrow and sighed.

"Are you expecting me to provide an answer?"

"Death is your responsibility," said Ashana, wearing a small smile along with her royal blue silk robes. Yellow, threaded designs of songbirds lined the sleeves. "Can you not answer his question?"

A frown spread over Maeana's lips as she said, "I know as much about when a soul will come to me as any of you. I deal with death's aftermath; I do not predict its coming." She turned her gaze on to Nelnora. "Perhaps you have confused me with your sister."

Shaking her head, Nelnora said, "Your robes alone would prevent such a mistake. Indrida's taste in fashion includes a bit more color."

"And where might she be?" asked Ketus. "I had thought to see her here."

Nelnora turned to Ketus, trying to meet his stare, but could not focus on him. Looking at someone never required so much effort. Irritated, she snapped, "Ketus? Do you mind?"

A moment later, he turned opaque, his cloak morphing into a colorless gray. The God of Shadows and Luck leaned forward, gave Nelnora a thin smile, and said, "Pardon me. It is habit." Cocking an eyebrow, he reissued his question. "So. Indrida. Why is she not here?"

Nelnora steadied herself. She needed to be careful here.

"My sister has absolved herself of this matter."

Ketus and Maeana exchanged a long look. Ashana showed no reaction. Nelnora had already shared this with her.

Turning back to Nelnora, Ketus asked, "She has absolved herself of this matter?"

"We have had…disagreements over this affair. Her ideas of how to proceed are quite different from my own."

"I am disappointed to hear that," said Maeana. "She should be here."

"Why?" asked Ashana.

"Is it not obvious?" replied the Goddess of Death. She stared back to the window, a slight scowl on her face. "This is all her fault."

Nelnora let out a weary sigh. She had expected this from Maeana, but it did not mean she wanted to hear it. Nevertheless, it was best to let the Goddess air her grievances. Maeana so enjoyed doing so.

"Would you mind explaining yourself?"

Maeana turned to stare at Nelnora, her green eyes flashing hot.

"The moment she recited that prophecy, she should have killed the priest who wrote them down, burned the scroll, and scrubbed every syllable from her memory. We would not be where we are if she had kept her mouth shut!"

Ashana muttered, "That seems a touch harsh."

"Harsh?" asked Maeana. "For nearly two centuries, mortals have been altering *everything* they do, trying to shape their future to either meet or thwart her words." She pointed a finger at the window and exclaimed, "Without her prophecy, that castle would house nothing but mice and birds."

With a patient frown upon her lips, Ashana said, "Mice and birds cannot oppose the God of Chaos, Maeana." She nodded to the scene of the snowy courtyard. "They might be the only thing preventing countless souls from perishing."

"Have you ever considered that might be what is *supposed* to happen?"

"Not according to Indrida's words," said Ketus.

Maeana let out a frustrated sigh and turned her head to stare at Ketus, her shoulder-length black hair swishing in the air.

"In the next few moments, you will be thinking of roses climbing a white trellis."

Ketus eyes narrowed.

"Pardon?"

Maeana waited a moment before asking, "What are you thinking of, Ketus?"

A slight frown spread over Ketus face as he muttered, "Roses. On a white trellis."

"So," said Maeana haughtily. "Did I predict the future? Or did I shape it?"

Ketus remained quiet, his scowl deepening.

"Am I wrong, Ketus?" asked Maeana.

Shaking his head, he muttered, "This is pointless."

"Am I wrong?!" demanded Maeana. "Fate is what *should* happen, not what you *make* happen!"

"Says who?" asked Ashana.

Maeana wheeled to stare at the Goddess in blue.

"Says Greya! And as it is her realm to rule, I accept her thoughts without questioning the matter. Do I question you concerning inspiration? Do I question Ketus about luck? Or Nelnora about her precious balance?"

Nelnora closed her eyes and sighed. This was not how she had wanted this to go. Trying to maintain her calm, she opened her eyes and asked, "What would you have us do, then? Nothing? Shall we stand by and watch the Cabal conquer Terrene?"

Maeana fixed her gaze on Nelnora and asked, "Why not? They have yet to succeed in doing so. What makes you think they will now?"

Shaking her head, Nelnora snapped, "You may be willing to throw the world's fate to chance, Maeana, but I am *not!*"

"What a surprise," said Maeana, her tone full of mocking. "Too much good in the world? Nelnora wants to intervene. Too much evil? Nelnora wants to intervene. Too cold and snowy atop a mountain peak? Nelnora wants to intervene."

Letting a bit of heat slip into her tone, Nelnora said, "If you do not care if the Cabal rules all, why did you come today? Why even bother meeting with me?"

"Simple," answered Maeana. "I do not care what the Cabal does with Terrene, but I would like it if they stopped killing indiscriminately. My Seat is overflowing with souls. It is difficult to manage them all."

A dry chuckle slipped from Ketus.

"You are here because you are being inconvenienced?"

"Hold a moment," said Ashana. "Did you not just say that perhaps all of this is supposed to happen? That these deaths are 'fate?'"

Maeana stared back to the shimmering window, a frown on her lips.

"Admittedly, it is a confused situation about which I am conflicted."

Ashana said, "You did not seem all that conflicted—"

"Ashana?" interrupted Nelnora quietly. As the Goddess looked over, Nelnora gave a quick shake of her head. Pressing the issue further would not get her what she wanted. Instead, she asked a question to which she already knew the answer.

"What is the true reason you are here, Maeana?"

The Goddess of Death turned her dark-eyed gaze onto Nelnora, stared silently for a moment, and then shifted it back to the window. A tiny frown creased the corners of her mouth. In quiet, sad voice, she mumbled, "My reasons are my own."

Looking back to the Weave, Nelnora found the raven-haired woman was now crouching in the snow beside the injured man. The younger sister was awake and lying on his chest, crying.

Suppressing a smile, Nelnora murmured, "And to think some say you have no heart."

Maeana ignored her and remained motionless, watching the two sisters in the window.

After an extended moment of silence, Ashana cleared her throat, the sound echoing through the chamber.

"Perhaps we could address the reason for today's summit?"

Nodding, Nelnora said, "I would like nothing better."

"Well, you have my support," said Ashana.

"And just how long has she had it?" huffed Ketus. "From what I have seen and heard, it would seem more than a few of the mortals involved have had some rather opportune moments of inspiration as of late."

Ashana exchanged a long, quiet look with Nelnora before staring back to the window and saying, "Interfering as such is not allowed, Ketus."

"And nobody values the rules as much as you, right, Ashana?"

The Goddess of Inspiration kept her eyes on the scene of the courtyard, wisely choosing to remain silent.

After a few moments, Nelnora turned her attention to Ketus and asked, "Rather than leveling quiet accusations, Ketus, perhaps you would share your thoughts on my proposal?"

The God paused before answering, "Whatever the Cabal is up to, I doubt I would like it if they succeeded."

"Then do something about it," said Nelnora. "Rather than sit in the shadows and watch like always."

Ketus leaned forward, glared at her, and shot back, "Have you forgotten your history? I was part of the last Assembly, if you recall."

"A lone candle does not boil a cauldron," said Nelnora. "Since then, you've ignored every one of my warnings."

"Only because your alarms are like songbirds that won't stop singing. Eventually, I stop listening."

Nelnora shut her eyes tight, drew in a deep breath, and exhaled. At times, Ketus grated her nerves like limestone dragged against granite. Opening her eyes, she managed to keep her voice even as she said, "Will you lend me your support or not?"

Ketus turned a razor-sharp eye on her and snapped, "My promised silence on your activities should be enough! Should the others learn of what you and Ashana have been doing…" He trailed off, leaving the consequences unspoken. "Moreover, without my aid in bypassing Miriel's Weave—" he jabbed a finger toward the window "—we would not have witnessed any of what occurred today!"

Swallowing her pride, Nelnora said politely, "I thank you for your discretion, Ketus. As well as your help with the Weave. Both have been invaluable to my efforts."

Maeana and Ashana turned in unison to stare at her, evidently surprised at her measured response. Judging by Ketus' raised eyebrows and parted mouth, he was taken aback as well.

After a few moments' pause, he said, "Ah, you are welcome." Turning back to stare at the window, he added softly, "And yes, you have my support for Assembly."

With a curt nod and all the grace she could muster, Nelnora said, "Thank you."

Ashana shared a quick, relieved look with Nelnora. With Ketus joining them, their number was at three. Should they gain Maeana's support as well, they would need but five others to form a full Assembly.

The allied trio turned to eye Maeana, waiting for her to give her decision. Maeana said nothing, though, keeping her stare on the window. As the silence drew out, one-by-one, the other three peered back at the window as well. Everyone had stepped back from the injured young man, leaving a single figure crouched over him. Nelnora's eyebrows lifted in surprise.

Ashana asked, "They have aki-mahet in their ranks?" She turned to eye Nelnora. "Did you know that?"

Nelnora frowned and shook her head, muttering, "No, I did not."

Ketus suggested, "Perhaps Thonda's champion brought her into the fold."

Nelnora shrugged, mildly disappointed in herself. Watching the world as she did led to a false sense of omnipotence. .

"Perhaps."

After a few more moments of quiet, Maeana's even, emotionless voice drifted through the chamber.

"Should I agree to support another Assembly, I want to be clear that I will do *nothing* to aid you until a consensus is reached. Do you understand? *Nothing.*"

Nodding, Nelnora said, "I am aware of the laws placed upon us."

Maeana raised a single eyebrow.

"You might be aware of them, but it seems that you do not follow them."

When Nelnora remained quiet, Maeana frowned and turned her gaze to Ashana.

"Nor do you."

Wearing an impish smile, Ashana said, "Pardon me for providing an occasional burst of inspiration to a few mortals. It is my purpose, is it not?"

"It is," agreed Maeana. Looking back to Nelnora, she added, "But I am left wondering who your inspiration is."

Nelnora remained silent, her face a mask of indifference. If Maeana was trying to get an admission of guilt from either of them, she was wasting her time.

Ketus broke their quiet stare down, folding his arms over his chest and saying, "I suppose now I have offered my support, there is something I should share with you."

Intrigued by his words and tone, Nelnora looked away from Maeana and to the God.

"What is it, Ketus?"

"My champion is hiding amongst the Sudashians. She has been traveling east with them for a few turns now."

All three Goddesses turned to stare at him with open surprise. In the same way Nelnora could sense where Tobias was at all times, each of the last Assembly knew exactly where their champion was in the world. The gift given to the mortals saw to that.

After a moment, Ashana shifted her gaze to Nelnora and asked, "You did not know?"

Nelnora shook her head a deep frown spreading over her lips.

"I did not."

Sounding surprised, Maeana asked, "You have been watching Chaos' armies for some time now, have you not?"

"I have," replied Nelnora. "But some things I cannot see."

Maeana's eyebrows drew together.

"I thought only our kind was protected from your prying eye."

"In all but one case, that is true," admitted Nelnora. Turning an eye to Ketus, she said, "His champion avoids me as well."

"How is that possible?" asked Ashana.

A smug chuckle slipped from Ketus as he answered, "If Miriel Syncent wishes to remain hidden, she will do so. The piece of me she carries sees to that."

Glaring at Ketus, Maeana said, "So your champion has been marching with Chaos' army?"

Ketus nodded.

"In secret, yes."

"But why?" asked Ashana.

"I simply know where she is," said Ketus with a shrug. "I do not pretend to know her intentions." He faced the three of them, saying, "I have not seen Miriel since the last Assembly. She came to my Seat over a century ago, but I turned her away." He glanced at Nelnora and added, "As the law requires."

Nelnora forced herself not to react. Recently, she had ignored that particular law, although none but Tenerva knew. She had not even shared the White Lions' visit with Ashana.

"Then your champion is acting on her own?" asked Maeana.

"It would seem so," replied Ketus.

"To what end?"

"Short of asking her, we don't have any way of finding that out, do we?"

Nelnora hoped whatever Miriel Syncent was doing would not interfere with her plans. She let an almost imperceptible sigh slip from her lips. Mortals were like weeds in a well-tended garden, sprouting with impunity, popping up where they were not wanted.

"Have you approached any of the others yet?"

Glancing up to find Ketus eyeing her, Nelnora shook her head, "No. I had hoped that by securing your agreement, gaining additional support would be easier."

Ketus said, "Well, with me and Ashana, you have three to start with." He turned an expectant eye to Maeana. "Do we have four?"

Ashana and Nelnora both gazed at the Goddess as well, waiting for her declaration.

Maeana ignored them for a time, continuing to stare at the scene within the window. Looking back to it, Nelnora saw that the young man and the others were gone. The only two left were the pair of black-haired sisters, the eldest singing softly to the youngest. If anything was going to sway Maeana, it was this image.

Nelnora hid a slight smile. Yet again, Indrida had been right.

Maeana murmured, "I support your call for Assembly."

Nelnora closed her eyes, welcoming the rush of relief that came with Maeana's words. Letting out a short sigh, she opened her eyes and stared at the white-robed Goddess.

"Thank you, Maeana."

In a low, mocking voice, Ketus said, "To be clear, then. You are now *for* interfering, yes?"

Nelnora glared at the God, pleading with him to be quiet.

The skin around Maeana's eyes tightened while most of her face remained blank and emotionless. Speaking in quiet and restrained tone, she said, "No, I am not. But too many souls have already reached my halls before their time. It is wasteful." She pressed her lips together and faced Nelnora. "Once you have nine, I will do as you ask. Until then, I will continue to abide by our laws."

Nodding, Nelnora said, "I understand fully."

As Maeana glanced back to the window, her expression softened.

"Ashana? Thank you for what you did today."

Her tone one of perfect innocence, Ashana asked, "Whatever do you mean?"

Lifting her eyebrows a fraction Maeana said, "You expect us to believe the young man rushed into the building of his own accord?"

Ashana shrugged her shoulders.

"Perhaps he heard the girl cry out?"

Ketus snickered of disbelief and said, "She was unconscious."

"Well, then," said Ashana ponderously. "Truly, it is an enigma."

"Claim ignorance if you like," said Maeana. "I thank you, anyway. Watching the girl perish would have been...difficult for me." The pain that filled her eyes was unlike anything Nelnora had seen in her brethren. It was discomforting to see.

Maeana suddenly pulled her eyes away from the window and, in a voice devoid of emotion, said, "End it please. I do not wish to see any more."

"Of course," muttered Nelnora. As she released the Weave, letting the image fade from sight, she allowed herself a small, content smile.

CHAPTER 37: CHOICE

11ᵗʰ of the Turn of Maeana, 4999

Kenders glared at the swamp before her, shifted in her saddle, and tried not to sigh. This was getting old. Yet another series of interconnected ponds and puddles blocked their path. Evergreens, stunted oaks, and willowy briarbirches lined the opposite side of the marsh, taunting them with the promise of dry, firm land.

Smoke lowered her head to sniff the stagnant water immediately before their stopped party. With a disappointed huff and shake of her head, the horse made her opinion of the mucky water known. Kenders peered down at the pale green film covering the surface and wrinkled her nose. A large belch of swamp air burst from the surface a dozen paces away, startling her.

Kenders turned up her lip. The Marshlands were disgusting.

The air reeked of rotting plants and old eggs, the foul putridness having but one redeeming quality in that it covered her own malodorous scent. Her last proper wash had been week ago at a crossroads inn. Grime and grit covered her from head to toe.

No one had spoken since they had stopped. As the silence stretched out, Kenders realized they were going to make her talk first again.

Three of her companions formed a line beside her, sitting in their saddles and staring across the open marsh. Boah and Tobias both wore expressions of open frustration, while Khin's face was a mask of impassivity. She stared at man, tomble, and aicenai for a few moments, hoping one of them might meet her eye. None did.

Bracing herself, she swiveled to her right and peered over at Zecus. The skin around his eyes was tight, his lips pressed together, deep creases lined his forehead. Unlike the others, Zecus was angry.

"It's not as bad as before," she offered. "At least we can see the other side this time."

Zecus remained perfectly quiet, unmoving.

"Come on, Zecus. We still need to head north anyway, right? So we do it now rather than later, yes? We'll turn west again when we can."

Her optimism was met with a clenched jaw, the muscles in his check twitching beneath his curly, three-week old black beard. Without looking at her, he mumbled a quiet response.

"If we must."

He immediately jerked his reins to the right, turning Simiah north, and kicked the horse's sides. As he rode away, she stared at his back, a quiet, dejected sigh slipping from her lips. Giving Smoke's reins a gentle tug, she followed Zecus. The others did the same with Boah softly cajoling the rider-less Goshen to stop eating and come along.

The group rode in complete silence, heading north along the endless maze of ponds, the third time today they had been forced to alter their path. In the past week, detours such as this were commonplace and with each delay, Zecus' mood grew darker. At times, Kenders barely recognized him. The kind, respectful man she had eyes for was gone, replaced by a sullen, solemn soul.

She shut her eyes, squeezing them tight, screaming inside. This was her fault. All of it.

In the days following Joshmuel's death, Zecus insisted he did not hold her responsible, offering gentle words and smiles. However, as the days passed, Zecus grew increasingly aloof and cold. Any attempt by her—or anyone of their party—to engage him in conversation resulted in terse, clipped responses. Eventually, the others stopped speaking with Zecus altogether. Even Boah, normally boisterous and loud, remained silent around him.

Kenders opened her eyes and stared at Zecus' back. He sat in his saddle, rigid and tense.

She knew he blamed her for Joshmuel's death. She certainly blamed herself.

Dropping her head, she stared at Smoke's black mane without seeing it, wondering at the cruel chain of events that had led to here. Had Broedi not taken them on a path leading to the Moiléne farm all those turns ago, Kenders would have never opened a port there. Yet not going to the farm would mean she and her brothers would not have interrupted the bandits attack on the sisters. Most likely, the pair would be dead now.

Sabine and Helene's lives for Joshmuel's.

It was a dangerous path of thought to follow, nonetheless she found herself weighing their lives, wondering if given the choice, which she would pick.

"I am going to ride with the Borderlanders for a time. You shall ride with Tobias."

Kenders' head snapped up and to the right. She was surprised to find Khin riding beside her, his cool gaze locked on her face. The unprompted words were out of character for Khin. Other than her morning and afternoon lessons, the aicenai rarely spoke.

Before she could form a response, Khin swiveled in his saddle, stared at Boah, and requested, "Come with me, please." Without waiting for Boah's acknowledgment, the aicenai faced forward and urged his horse into a gentle trot.

Kenders watched him ride away for a moment and then turned back to Boah. "What is that about?"

With a shrug of his shoulders, Boah said, "I have no idea. But I'm not going to argue with a mage." He kicked Hal's sides, tugging Goshen along behind him. As he passed Kenders, he added with a wink and a grin, "I bet they'll both talk my ear off."

Kenders smiled at the quip, grateful for Boah's presence. Without him, the somber mood traveling with their group would have crushed her days ago.

As she watched the pair ride to catch Zecus, Tobias trotted up to fall in beside her. Keeping her eyes on the trio ahead, she said, "That is unusual."

"Yes," muttered Tobias. "It certainly is." He sounded curious himself.

Glancing to her right, she asked, "Any idea what prompted it?"

Tobias reached up, smacked an insect that had alighted on his cheek, and pulled his hand back. As he wiped the remains of the squished bug on his leg, he swiveled his head to peer at her, an unusual twinkle in his eyes and a slight smile gracing his lips.

"So, Kenders. What's been on your mind as of late?"

She turned away from the tomble and stared west, out over the swamp. Managing to keep her tone casual, she said, "Nothing in particular. Just that I'm getting tired of these marshes."

"Of course," said the tomble. "The marshes."

She hoped Tobias would do what they had all been doing for weeks: ride in complete silence. He did not.

"Might you still be ruminating on Joshmuel's death?"

Kenders turned to glare at the tomble and lied, "No. Not at all."

Pressing his lips together, he nodded and said, "As I thought." Apparently, he did not accept her claim. "Still carrying the blame on your shoulders, are you?"

Her eyes narrowing, she lied again.

"No."

"You should be careful," said Tobias, his gaze boring into her. "Guilt is like a boulder of granite. The longer you carry it, the heavier it gets."

Annoyed now, Kenders said, "What I am feeling is none of your concern."

His gaze lingered for a half-dozen horse strides before dropping to Traveler's chestnut mane.

"Did Broedi tell you much about me?"

Kenders' irritation dulled a bit at the unexpected question.

"Pardon?"

Looking back to her, Tobias asked, "Broedi. Did he talk about me? About my past? About how I came to be one of the Assembly's champions?"

Bewildered by the shift in conversation, Kenders said, "Well…no."

Tobias appeared trapped between a smile and a frown.

"I see."

"Honestly, besides a few stories about my parents, he never speaks of the White Lions. I've asked before, but he says he does not like to talk of the past."

Tobias nodded slowly, an understanding smile spreading over his face.

"The past grows dull with age, yet some edges stay sharp, eh?"

"Pardon?"

"Sorry," said Tobias, glancing over. "It's an old Boroughs saying. It means…" He paused for a moment. "It means that while most memories fade with time, some do not." He frowned. "Often, those that hurt the most."

Now Kenders nodded her understanding, saying, "I suppose Broedi has plenty of sharp edges in his past, doesn't he?" She eyed the tomble. "You, as well?"

Tobias drew in a deep breath and let it back out.

"More than I would like."

Kenders waited, sensing that the past had trapped the tomble for a moment. She began to face forward when Tobias spoke in a quiet, unassuming voice.

"You should know that I am a murderer."

Wondering if a frog's croak or the muddy squish of a horse's hoof might have mangled his words, she looked back and asked, "Pardon?"

Tobias offered her a slight, remorseful smile. Reading her expression perfectly, he said, "You heard me correctly. I am a murderer."

Assuming he was talking about his actions during the last battle with the God of Chaos, she said, "What a person does during war is not—"

"That is not what I mean," interrupted Tobias with a firm shake of his head. "I had blood on my hands before I was a White Lion."

A quiet moment slipped past before Kenders spoke.

"Pardon?"

Tobias glanced over at her, nibbling on his lip. After a heartbeat or two, he sighed, and stared ahead.

"I am originally from Buttermere Crag, a good-sized town in the Alewold Principal that sits at the base of large cliff. Rock quarries were operated in the bluffs nearby, the stone used to build most of the homes and shops of every town in the region. Half of Buttermere Crag worked at the quarries. My entire family did. I, for much of my early life, however, did not."

"Why not?"

With raised eyebrows, he patted his right leg.

"It's hard to carry rocks and hold a cane at the same time."

Kenders eyes widened a fraction as she said, "Oh. Right. I forgot about your leg." Three weeks of traveling with the tomble and she had grown so used to his crippled limb that she no longer noticed it.

"Good," said Tobias while wearing a tiny smile. "I prefer when people do that." Facing forward, he resumed his story.

"My leg did not keep me from the quarry forever. Despite my limitation, my father wanted me in the rock pit. 'Generations of Donngords have worked the stone, Tobias,' he would say. 'So shall you.'" When a new section of the quarry was opened for mining, he pressed me into service, securing me the position of overseer for the team. I accepted the role, yet within days, I knew I would be poor at the job."

"Because of your leg?"

"Not at all. A bad leg does not hamper one from standing around all day, watching others work. I was bored to no end, dear. I loathed every moment in that dusty pit, watching the sun cross the sky, pleading with Mu that he move his orb faster."

For a few rhythmic strides of their horses squishing through mud and muck, Tobias remained quiet. The expression on his face turned dark, betraying a deep-rooted hurt. When he resumed speaking, his voice was just above a whisper.

"One afternoon, there was an accident. Nine of my team died in a rockslide. My youngest brother, Mallin, was one of them."

"Oh, Tobias," muttered Kenders. "I am so sorry."

He nodded once, mumbling, "Thank you." He remained quiet a few moments before sitting tall in his saddle and taking a deep breath. "An inquiry turned up negligence on the overseer's part. Me. I was supposed to have checked the stakes supporting a load-wall prior to the day's work. I had not. Some of those stakes gave way, letting a pile of stone tumble down onto…" Trailing off, he turned his head away from her, staring eastward.

"That does not make you a murderer."

Facing Kenders, he said, "The families of those who perished disagreed, dear. They demanded the custodian charge me, and he did so. Had I been found guilty, I would have been sent to the stockades."

Her voice full of disbelief, Kenders asked, "Over an accident?"

"Ah, but according to Boroughs' law, it was no accident. I was a criminal. A murderer."

"Nundle claimed the Five Boroughs had almost no crime."

A dry and bitter chuckle burst from Tobias.

"Of course there isn't. Not when punishment is disproportionately ruthless to the offense. Nor restricted to the lawbreaker alone."

"What do you mean?" asked Kenders.

"Had I been deemed guilty, I would have gone to the stockades and the Donngord family name would have been annulled."

Kenders shook her head, saying, "I don't know what that means."

"Simply put, all Donngords—past, present, and future—would be stricken or barred from the Boroughs' namebooks. Until the first child of the fourth generation was born, the entire family would remain nameless. The Donngords would be shunned from 'proper society,' ostracized, cast out."

"All of you?" asked Kenders in disbelief.

"To the last," muttered Tobias bitterly.

"They punish the *entire* family for one person's transgression?"

Shrugging his shoulders, Tobias said, "It is the way things are done."

"But why?"

"Because it's the law."

"It's a brainless law."

With another mirthless chuckle, Tobias said, "Many are, Kenders."

"Where would someone get the idea to do something so awful?"

Tobias stared up at the clear, blue sky, sighed, and said, "An excellent question. Decades after the war, I returned to the Boroughs and spent some time in Gobberdale, researching tomble law. Would you believe it that I could find *nothing* written about annulling a family? Nothing at all? It seems that it was more tradition than anything."

Frowning, Kenders said, "Tradition is an excuse for doing things without a proper reason."

Tobias turned his head to stare at her with raised eyebrows.

"That almost sounds wise, Kenders."

"It is something my father used to say." Wanting to be clear on the point, she added, "Thaddeus, that is, not Aryn." Every time Tobias referred to her 'parents,' he seemed to be speaking of the White Lion pair. Directing the conversation back to Tobias' tale, she asked, "Did you tell anyone what you found? Or didn't find, as it were?"

"Of course. I asked some of the more learned barristers, most never gave me an answer, but the one who did simply said, 'Tradition is law, too.' So, I left and came back to the duchies."

"Does Nundle know about all of this?"

Raising his eyebrows, Tobias asked, "What? About me?" He shook his head. "Gods, no. Right or wrong, the shame of being a law-breaker is branded into you from birth. When I learned Nundle was from the Boroughs, the first thought I had was ensuring he did not find out about my past."

"You don't know Nundle. He would never be so judgmental."

"Perhaps not," admitted Tobias. "But I did not know that when I met him. I assumed he was like every other Boroughs tomble."

"You were so worried about being judged unfairly that you did the same thing to Nundle?"

Tobias' brow drew together, a pair of deep furrows splitting his forehead. After a few moments of quiet introspection, he muttered, "I suppose I did, didn't I?" Glancing over, he said, "Rather blind of me, wasn't it?"

Shrugging her shoulders, Kenders said, "We all make mistakes."

"Very true."

Kenders waited a moment before asking, "You never did say if you were deemed guilty or not. Were you?"

Tobias shook his head, saying, "I never gave them a chance. I fled Buttermere Crag before the hearing."

"Truly?"

Nodding, he said, "I thought I could spare my family the pain of my mistake. I did not even say farewell. One cold, Winter night…I just left."

"Where'd you go?"

"To Marblewater at first, a city on the north coast. I booked passage on the first ship leaving port, not even asking where it was headed, I simply wanted out of the Boroughs. We docked in Keyport in the Northlands Duchy a little over a turn later. Within a day, I found a nice longleg merchant who was looking for a book-keeper. Two weeks later, I was in Tymnasis, learning the intricacies of the iron and copper trade."

A smile—a happy one this time—spread over his lips.

"Despite the strange land, food, and people, I enjoyed my life there. Before the war, Tymnasis was a grand city."

His grin faded, replaced quickly by a grim and dark expression.

"A few years later, stories began to arrive with the caravans from the west telling of a great demon army from the Red Peaks. Soon, war was at our door. Tymnasis was evacuated, the duke at the time seized my employer's metal stores—without payment, mind you—to forge weapons and armor. He was ruined. With no job and a demon army at the gates, I left the city and went south."

"Where were you headed?"

"I told you," said Tobias. "South. It was away from demons and that was good enough for me. I hobbled along, quickly outpaced by everyone else fleeing the city. Late one evening, all alone, I came across a figure standing in the road. A divina, if you can believe it. The first I had ever seen. I stopped in my tracks, terrified. Rumors were the leader of the demon army was a divina."

"Who was it?"

"He announced himself 'Tenerva, first priest of Nelnora,' and asked if I would accompany him to the Celestial Empire." A lopsided grin spread over his face. "I thought he was mad. However, as I was broke, hungry, and trapped in a country being invaded by demons, I went with him, thinking I might be able to swindle a hot meal from the madman. Imagine my surprise when it turned out he was telling the truth."

He took a deep breath and exhaled, saying, "You know the rest: the Assembly of the Nine, a choice offered and taken, abilities granted by the Gods and Goddesses. In short order, we eight strangers were on our way to becoming the 'White Lions,' destined to save the duchies from the God of Chaos."

Smacking another marsh fly and wiping it on his leg, he continued his tale.

"The Assembly opened a port to Bard Island and sent us through. We stood on that blasted beach for hours, staring at one another, wondering if we were all dreaming. It was then that some of us first discovered we could use the Strands.

Me included. Hells, Broedi accidently set your father's backpack on fire with a stray Weave." A wide grin spread over his face. "Twice, actually."

Kenders smiled at the thought of Broedi fumbling with magic.

Tobias shook his head, saying, "We had no idea what we were doing. None. To a soul, we were terrified. Nevertheless, we pushed our fear aside and did what we needed to do. Aided by a few hundred soldiers of the nearby Postia Barony, we marched on a small detachment of Norasim's army. We won handily and earned our name in the process from the baron's pennant: a white lion on a black background. With that victory, the tide of the war began to change."

He went quiet for a few moments, his gaze unfocused. Kenders used the break in the tale to look ahead. Khin and Boah were nominally riding with Zecus, trailing him by a half-dozen horse lengths. She looked back when Tobias began speaking again.

"As the war dragged on, my visions began to reveal moments back in the Boroughs, brief visits of life amongst entire families of shunned tombles. At first, I thought my personal guilt was influencing the visions."

"Were they?"

"Who knows? I didn't understand how the visions worked then, and I still don't. Nelnora never took the time to explain anything. None of the Assembly did. They bestowed us with our abilities, told us to stop Norasim, and sent us on our way."

Kenders wondered why the Gods and Goddesses would do such a thing. It was akin to giving a young child a newly sharpened dagger and asking them not cut themself.

"So what did you do? About your visions?"

"Well, I confided in your mother what I was seeing and she suggested we investigate them. She was the only one of us who had been a mage prior to the Assembly and knew the Weave for a port. She taught me the pattern, I opened a port to the outskirts of Buttermere Crag, and she and I strode into town."

He paused to let loose a heavy, melancholy sigh.

"The town was absent of Donngords. My entire family was gone, our name removed from the namebooks. My running away had not spared them any disgrace. The shame I felt for what I had put my family through…I feel it to this day."

Unsure any words could comfort him, Kenders chose to remain silent.

"There I sat on the green," muttered Tobias. "Feeling very sorry for myself, when your mother suggested something that would not have occurred to me had I thought on the matter for a thousand years." A shrewd smile spread over his lips. "Something to help shunned tombles prove their worthiness while helping us in our fight against Norasim."

Kenders suddenly realized to what Tobias was alluding.

"The tombles who fought in the war? They were the annulled families, weren't they?"

"That they were," said Tobias, pride evident in his tone. "For the next few turns, Eliza and I would port back to the Boroughs whenever we could and go from town to town, offering the option to all outcast families. Most took our offer."

"Was life as an outcast so bad that they would fight against a demon army for a country not their own?"

Tobias fixed her with a steady gaze.

"Families without a name must leave their homes and live outside town limits. They cannot sell any goods they make or food they grow to 'respectable' tombles. They are barred from attending Leisure Day festivals, chantry or chapel, or any learning hall. They can only marry a member of another shunned family. They are not allowed to speak to a 'respectable' tomble unless permission is granted. The family name is not only erased, the tombles are as well."

"I suppose I can see why some took your offer."

"Not some, Kenders. Most."

"What about the Donngords? Did they?"

"Some did. Those who still blamed me for Mallin's death did not."

"I'm sorry."

With a short shake of his head, Tobias insisted, "Don't be. It was their choice to make, not mine. They chose misery over redemption."

"It sounds as if they had every reason to be miserable."

"Absolutely, they did. What happened to them was tragic, unjust, and cruel. Yet they were offered a chance at redemption, and they chose *not* to take it. They let a single, horrible accident shape their life. They let it eat away at them, turning them sour on the inside."

"Perhaps you were better off without them."

"Oh, we were," agreed Tobias. "Much better." He turned to stare at Kenders, his brown eyes intense and bright. "Fate can twist cruel, and it can twist wondrous. Regardless, it is fate. You cannot control it. What you *can* control is your response. It took me a long time to learn that dear. A *long* time. Hopefully, you are a quicker study than I."

Kenders stared at Tobias quietly, her eyes slowly narrowing. Swiveling her head, she stared ahead at Khin's bony figure and bald head.

"Is this one of Khin's blasted lessons?"

The tomble chuckled softly and shrugged.

"I suspected he wanted me to have a talk with you about your constant sulking, and...well, this seemed a good way to convince you not to play 'what if' forever. It solves nothing."

Kenders studied Tobias' face and asked, "Why have you talk to me? Why didn't Khin do it himself?"

"You'd have to ask him that."

She eyed Tobias a few moments longer before muttering, "He sure has a way of getting inside your head, doesn't he?"

Tobias began to chuckle again, louder this time.

Not understanding his sudden mirth, she asked, "What's funny about this?"

"Oh, nothing," replied Tobias, still grinning. "Nothing at all, dear." Facing forward, his gaze locked onto something ahead. "It would seem that our fearless scouts have found a path through the muck."

Looking ahead, Kenders saw that the others had indeed stopped and were facing west. Zecus had dismounted and was testing the ground, gently prodding the marsh with his foot. They had learned the hard way that while some land bridges looked safe, many were like freshly baked bread: firm on the outside, soft and yielding within.

Paying close attention to their surroundings for the first time since she and Tobias had begun their conversation, Kenders peered across the flat, open marsh. The line of trees on the other side was closer now but the strip of soggy land separating them from it was still prominent.

"Does he mean to cross here?"

"Judging by his poking about like that, I would say yes."

Her gaze followed the tree line as it wrapped around to the northwestern horizon.

"There's no reason to do this here. If we go north a little longer, we won't need to cross at all."

"Agreed," said Tobias. "Perhaps you should share your observation with Zecus."

"He's not going to want to hear it."

"Then I suppose we are going swimming," said Tobias. He glanced over, a slight smile on his face. "Mind carrying me?"

As they were near the trio, Kenders did not answer. Stopping beside Khin and Boah—still atop their horses—she stared west, her gaze tracing a thin stretch of grass that wound its way through the ponds and puddles. Zecus was walking onto the strip, poking at the ground with his sword.

Kenders shook her head. This was a bad idea.

She turned and stared at her teacher, hoping he might say something. Surely, he knew this was a poor decision. The aicenai eyed her silently, seemingly more interested in her than the mistake Zecus was moments away from making. Frustrated, she looked to Boah. The older Borderlander was fixated on Zecus, his face lined with worry. He glanced up, met Kenders' stare, and immediately looked to Khin. Kenders' eyes narrowed in an instant. She would bet good coin that Khin had ordered Boah's silence.

She peered down at Zecus, let out a tiny sigh, and asked, "Do you mean to cross here?" She felt like she was the one treading on treacherous soil, about to sink at any moment.

Without looking back at her, Zecus said, "I do."

In as gentle tone as she could manage, she asked, "Are you sure this is wise?"

Zecus stopped prodding the ground, stood tall, and turned around to peer up at her.

"Pardon?"

Pointing northward, she said, "If we go just little farther, the marsh ends. We can turn west then. And not sink."

Zecus stared to the north, the muscles in his jaw rippling beneath his beard. Without even looking back to her, he turned his back to her and strode further onto the strip.

"No. We head west now."

"No," shot back Kenders, glaring at the back of his head. "We will not."

Zecus wheeled around, evidently surprised that someone had challenged his decision. For the past week, no one had.

"*What* did you say?"

She met his stare and held it, refusing to wither under its heat. Without looking away from him, she asked, "Khin? Demetus is still to our northwest, is it not?"

"Yes," replied the aicenai softly. "As far north as it is west."

"See? There is no point in risking this. We can go north, then west. Get on Simiah, and let's go."

He shook his head stubbornly.

"No. We go west *now*."

Deciding that this had gone on long enough, she dropped her eyes and proceeded to dismount Smoke. Letting the reins fall to the ground, she turned to face Zecus and stepped closer, moving carefully across the mushy ground. He continued to glower at her, his eyebrows drawn together.

She glanced at the dirty white strip wrapped around Zecus' upper left arm. Without saying a word, she placed her right hand on what had once been Joshmuel's headband. Zecus flinched at her touch, almost causing her to pull her hand back. Yet she did not. Instead, she wrapped her fingers around his arm and gently squeezed.

"I know you blame me for your father's death."

The skin around his eyes tightened. His lips parted as if to respond, but she spoke before he could.

"Please. I need to say this."

He remained stone-faced for a moment before nodding in silence.

Keeping her voice quiet but strong, she said, "You blame me. You probably don't want to, but you do. I know what you are feeling, because I feel the same. I blame me, too."

She waited for a protest, but none came. Zecus held her gaze briefly before dropping it to his boots. He shifted his weight, squishing in the marshy ground.

Kenders took a moment to swallow the lump that had formed in her throat before saying, "So, then. We both blame me for your father's death. That is the way of things. Perhaps over time, we can both come to terms with that. But what's done is done. We cannot change the past, we can only shape what is to come."

He lifted his gaze to her, the sorrow in his eyes striking her like a slap in the face. She steadied herself before continuing.

"You have a choice before you, Zecus. *We* have a choice. We can both push back against the heartache and the guilt, and try to find a way past it. Or we give up, surrender to the hurt, and let it rule us. What say you?"

Zecus stared at her, his lips pursed together, his eyelids twitching. It took him a while to respond, and when he did, his voice was strained, his tone deliberate.

"I do blame you."

She tried not to wince. Hearing the words hurt more than she thought it might.

He quickly added, "Yet I blame myself thrice as much. I should never have left Demetus. Never!"

"Losing family to Maeana's realm is hard. Trust me, I know. But—and please don't get upset—Joshmuel's life is over. Not yours. You need to move on. It's what he would have wanted you to do."

Even though Khin, Tobias, and Boah were a few feet behind her, to Kenders it felt as if she and Zecus were the only two here.

For a long time, Zecus simply stared at her, his face and eyes revealing a man in conflict. She was done talking and was going to wait for him to respond now. She stood there, peering up into his eyes, listening to the croaking of the frogs and the buzzing of the insects.

Finally, he reached up with his right arm and laid a hand on her shoulder. He took a quick step toward her, bent down, and kissed her lips.

At first, she did not react. A moment later, her heart skipping a beat, she squeezed his arm tighter, pulled him close, and kissed him back. A feeling as bright as the midday sun radiated inside her soul, eradicating every dark and gloomy crevice there was. Time either stopped or rushed ahead, she could not tell.

One of the horses whinnied abruptly, cutting into her perfect moment. Pulling away quickly, she stared up with wide eyes, stunned by what had happened. Her cheeks and neck felt warm and flush.

Wearing a slight smile, his eyes clear and kind again, Zecus whispered, "I choose you."

She stared into his eyes, wondering what to say back when—of all people—Boah spoke up.

"Pardon me for interrupting, but, you two will have to work this out later."

Zecus' eyes reluctantly left hers as he shifted his gaze past her.

"What is it, Boah?"

Kenders turned around and found their three companions staring to the north, Khin with his hood drawn to cover his head. Knowing what that meant, she looked northward and spotted a trio of men dressed in green and white uniforms riding towards them.

"Reed Men," announced Tobias. "Regional patrol."

Boah asked, "What do we do?"

Turning to Khin, Tobias asked, "How far from Demetus are we?"

The aicenai's voice drifted from with the shroud.

"Two days by hawk's wing."

"Good," replied Tobias. He did not sound particularly concerned. Peering at Kenders, he said, "Ride with me up front, dear. The rest of you—follow behind as normal, if you will."

The group used a set riding order whenever they encountered strangers. Boah and Zecus would ride in front, Kenders and Tobias next, with Khin in the rear in an attempt to prevent anyone from marking the aicenai. Tobias had drawn a few stares during their journey, but if anyone were to get a clear look at Khin, there would be no holding back people's questions.

She glanced back to Zecus. All bitterness and anger was gone from his face.

"Are you alright?"

He squeezed her arm gently and said, "I will be." He nodded to the horses. "We should go." He moved past her, she turned to follow, and was in Smoke's saddle moments later. Their kiss already seemed like last turn's dream.

Tobias immediately directed Traveler to the north, towards the soldiers. Kenders urged Smoke ahead and drew alongside the tomble. As she did, he glanced over.

"You handled things well back there. Very well. You showed more wisdom than someone thrice your age."

Kenders cheeks grew warm again.

"Thank you."

Tobias nodded once, stared back to the approaching soldiers, and said, "And as is always the case in trying times, solving one problem only makes room for a new one."

Kenders turned to eye the soldiers as well. She could make out the Marshlands crest on the green and white tabards now.

"What do we say to them?"

"We ask them for the safest, least-populated way to approach Demetus. Then we send them along their way, happy and content that we were just a group of common travelers."

Looking back at the tomble, she said, "It seems unlikely they will consider you or Khin 'common.'"

Tobias stared at her, a twinkle in his eye.

"Broedi shared what you did to the detachment of Southern Arms near the Fernsford Bridge."

An understanding smile spread over Kenders' lips.

"Of course."

Using a certain Weave of pure Will, she would be able to make gentle suggestions to the soldiers that they would accept without questions.

Tobias asked, "Can you keep the Weaves small?"

Nodding, Kenders said, "I can. Nundle helped me a lot with the pattern."

"Good. I don't think we'd need to worry about Constables out here, but the less Strands, the better."

Kenders turned to study the Reed Men, now only a hundred paces away. All three were staring at their group, their expressions wary.

"They look a touch suspicious," muttered Tobias. "Whenever you are ready."

Kenders nodded and began to reach for the golden Strands.

CHAPTER 38: PRIMAL

12ᵗʰ of the Turn of Maeana, 4999

An unending shoreline stretched before Nundle, north to south. A sandy beach strewn with black boulders awaited their shoreboat, along with trees that brushed the sky, taller than even the ebonwoods of Blackbark Forest. Leafy palms drooped from the trees' pinnacles, hanging down to obscure their sheer trunks. Shorter evergreens stood guard at the edge of the forest, a third the size of the behemoths looming over them. Vines draped between the trees' branches, crisscrossing in such a fashion that they reminded Nundle of the Sapphire's rigging.

In a voice just loud enough to be heard over the waves slapping against their shoreboat, he muttered, "Simply amazing."

Nikalys spoke, his voice echoing with wonder as well.

"There's nothing simple about that."

As another rolling wave sloshed under their craft, Broedi rumbled, "I did say the forests here were impressive."

"Oh, I believed you," said Nikalys. "But seeing it myself is…" He trailed off, never finishing his thought.

Nundle and Nikalys sat at the head of the shoreboat, with Broedi behind them both and half the Shadow Mane soldiers behind him. Captain Scrag and Nathan were in a second boat to their right with the remainder of the soldiers.

Glancing back at Broedi, Nikalys asked, "How did they grow so tall?"

Keeping his eyes straight ahead, the hillman said, "Asking such a question is like asking 'why does the sun glow?' I am sure there is an answer, but I do not have it." Pulling his gaze from the shore, he stared at Nikalys. "The trees are tall because they are."

A gentle breeze was blowing off the sea and toward the beach, teasing Nundle's red hair and playing with his wide-brimmed hat. He would not call the weather warm, but as long as he was in direct sun, the day was pleasant.

Moments before the shoreboat's bottom crunched against the sand, Broedi said, "Nikalys, when we reach land, you and I will pull the boat onto the beach. Move quickly, please. And remain ready."

Curious at the hillman's tone and word choice, Nundle turned to peer at Broedi.

"Is something wrong?"

Broedi's expression tightened.

"I do not know. Perhaps."

Nikalys joined Nundle in staring at the hillman.

"You said these parts of the Provinces are unoccupied."

Without taking his eyes from the tress, Broedi answered, "A hundred years ago, they were."

Nikalys exchanged a worried look with Nundle before saying, "A lot can change in a hundred years."

"Which is why I asked that you remain ready," rumbled Broedi.

Nundle twisted around to peer back to the beach. Nothing but sand, black rock, and trees awaited them. He tried to see into the forest, but the thick vegetation obscured the interior.

His voice hopeful, Nundle said, "It looks unoccupied to me."

Broedi rumbled, "Esinty miset merkitse mitan."

Nundle looked back at Broedi, eyebrows raised.

"Pardon?"

"Appearances are merely appearances."

Nundle let out a tiny sigh and faced forward. The excitement he had felt at finally being able to put foot on solid ground again was gone, replaced by trepidation. Suddenly, the decks of the Sapphire seemed appealing.

From the histories he had read, Nundle knew the Primal Provinces to be a loose association of city-states, populated by longlegs and a race of plantlike creatures commonly referred to as 'thorns.' The different races kept to themselves, yet shared a common enemy on the southern half of the continent, a nation centered on the fanatical worship of the High Host.

During their voyage east, Broedi had shared some additional details that were not in any book. According to him, a splintered group of hillmen also lived within the Primal Provinces. Broedi said he had searched for them when last here, but had left having never found them.

Now, a few dozen feet from the beach, Broedi shifted in his seat.

"Be alert."

The bottom of the boat scraped against the sandy shore, throwing Nundle forward and forcing him to throw his hands against the front of the shoreboat to avoid tumbling forward.

Nikalys and Broedi leapt from the boat, splashing into the white-capped surf. Grasping the shoreboat's sides, the pair easily pulled the craft onto the sandy beach while Nundle and the soldiers stayed inside. Glancing to his right, Nundle found the second boat empty, every longleg wallowing through the lapping waves, struggling to lug the boat behind them.

Once Nundle's boat was free from the surf, he and the soldiers exited, his own boots sinking into the sand. He basked in the sun, smiling wide. Solid land felt glorious.

A mist of sea spray washed over Nundle, pulling the tomble's attention to his left. A black boulder loomed over him, standing resolute against the pounding of the sea. The dark color reminded him of the stone that surrounded the Academy of Veduin in the Arcane Republic.

Spotting a smaller sample of the stone sticking from the sand at his feet, Nundle bent down to inspect it and noted countless, tiny holes covering its surface. Running a finger along it, he found its texture matched the lava rock of the academy perfectly. As he pried the specimen from the sand to take a closer look, seawater dripped from the porous stone. Nundle smiled.

"Look at that. Water from a rock."

The Isaac siblings often used the phrase to describe how difficult it was to get Broedi to share information.

"Nundle!" called Broedi.

Looking up, Nundle saw some of the soldiers pulling the shoreboats past the high tide mark while the rest were gathering in a group some distance away. Broedi stood at the center of the group, his back facing the forest and his gaze fixed firmly on Nundle.

The hillman rumbled, "Let us go, please!"

Nundle stood, slipped the black stone in his pocket—he would show Nikalys later—and strode toward the group, finding it difficult to walk in a straight line. Many of the soldiers were also weaving about the beach. Captain Scrag had warned them they might have trouble readjusting to dry land.

Approaching the group of longlegs encircling Broedi, Nundle heard the hillman reviewing the plan. Again. According to Nundle's count, this time made five.

"—together as we move inland. If you see a creature, do not approach it. If you find something you think is edible, do not eat it. If you see a flower with red petals and a purple center, do *not* touch it. If you spot anything that seems unusual to you, bring it to my attention immediately. Is all of that clear?"

As the soldiers nodded slowly, Wil asked, "How far is this 'tree-city' we're going to?" The young longleg had fully recovered after nearly making his way to Maeana's hall.

Broedi rumbled, "Assuming Captain Scrag read the charts correctly—"

"I can read a blasted chart, Broedi," interjected the old captain.

The comment brought a grin to most everyone's face. Wearing his own slight smile, Broedi amended his statement.

"Assuming the charts are accurate, we should have a three or four day march ahead of us. Longer if we get—" He cut off suddenly, his head tilting sideways. A moment later, he spun around and stared at the tree line.

Worried, Nundle peered past the six soldiers tying off the boats above the high tide mark and scanned the underbrush.

"Broedi? What is—?"

A shrill, ear-splitting shriek sliced through the calm afternoon seaside, cutting his question short. The grating sound reminded Nundle of a metal blade scraping across quartz block. Wincing, Nundle threw his hands up to cover his ears.

The longlegs around him did the same, attempting to block out the screech. Broedi dropped to a knee and remained hunched over, grimacing. Nikalys had his left hand clamped over one ear while pressing the other into his shoulder. He held the glowing white Blade of Horum in his right.

Then, as suddenly as it started, the sound cut off.

Broedi immediately rose from the sand and bellowed at the six longlegs securing the boats.

"Get over here! Now!"

The order was unnecessary as the soldiers had already dropped the ropes and were running back to the main group. They had taken but a half-dozen steps when Nundle felt a familiar crackling inside his chest.

Bright green and honey-gold.

"Uh-oh."

Strands of Life and Will popped into existence and hovered over the beach briefly before whipping away, into the dark forest. The strength of the surge was startling. Dropping his hands a few inches, he called, "Broedi! There are—"

"I know!" shouted hillman, staring into the forest where the Strands were flowing.

A few paces away, Nathan asked, "What are we dealing with?" The sergeant had drawn his sword, as had most of the soldiers. Some were unbuckling the small rounded wooden shields strapped to their backs.

Looking back to the tree line, Nundle shook his head.

"I don't know. But it is—"

The shrieking sound returned, a dozen times louder than before. Screaming in pain, Nundle clapped his hands to his ears. It felt as if someone was jabbing a hot knife into his eardrums.

Dropping their swords and shields, soldiers collapsed to the ground, their mouths open wide in screams of agony. Their cries went unheard as the shrieking from the forest drowned them out. The six longlegs who had been tying off the boats stumbled through the sand, running with their hands over their ears. Broedi fell to the sand again, covering his ears and staring at the trees.

Before the shriek rendered him senseless, Nundle reached for Strands of Air and quickly arranged them into a specific pattern. Within moments, a netting of pure white Strands hung in the air. Without pause, Nundle draped the Weave over him and every soldier within ten paces.

The world went quiet. Gloriously, blessedly quiet.

The shrieking was still audible, but muffled drastically. The soldiers' shouting was faint now, the crashing of the waves sounding more like water gently sloshing in a trough.

Every soldier within the protective barrier stared around in open wonderment, clearly no longer in pain. Unfortunately, the longlegs outside continued to writhe in the sand, powerless against the screech. Leaving his Weave in place, Nundle sprinted past the protective boundary, aiming for one of the fallen soldiers. He nearly fell over as the shriek's full force washed over him. Grabbing the arm of the nearest longleg, Nundle tugged as hard as he could, trying to drag him back to the Weave. Through eyes half-shut with pain, he spotted black hair and realized whom he was pulling.

"Let's go, Cero!"

His words were lost to the screech.

In a flurry of sand, Nathan appeared by his side, hauled Cero to his feet and half-carried, half-dragged him back to the Weave. Seeing other Shadow Manes rushing to help their fellow soldiers, Nundle ran back into the Weave. As he passed through the net of white, the muffled quiet enveloped him.

Glancing back toward the forest, he spotted Broedi, Nikalys, and the other six soldiers heading toward them, a Weave identical to Nundle's own draped over the group.

Turning to find Cero standing beside him, Nundle shouted, "Can you hear me?"

Cero looked down, surprise on his face. He nodded and his lips moved, but Nundle could not hear what he said.

Nundle screamed, "You have to yell!"

Cero nodded again and shouted, "I can hear you!" It sounded as if he were a mile away.

When Broedi and the others arrived, the hillman released his Weave and moved straight toward Nundle. Dropping to a knee and motioning to the netting of white around them, he called, "How many of these can you control?"

Calculating his limited ability with Air against the complexity of the Weave, Nundle shouted back, "Three, perhaps four. Why?"

"Three will do! Keep one on Nikalys, one on the men here, and the other on me as long as you can."

"On you?" shouted Nundle. "Why? What are you going to do?"

Broedi shook his head and rose from the sand.

"No time to explain!"

Staring up at the hillman, Nundle yelled, "What is making that sound?!"

Movement near the tree line answered Nundle's question before Broedi could.

A number of the towering palm trees began to sway violently, the thick vines draped between them stretching tight before snapping. What appeared to be an upside-down treetop—bare of leaves—emerged from the dense vegetation and slammed into the beach, sinking into the sand and shaking the ground. Forty feet up, a second four-branched treetop extended from the murky forest, wrapped its long, spindly boughs around the trunk of an evergreen and shoved sideways, snapping the tree near the base. A second woody hand gripped another tree and pushed it aside just as easily, creating a wide hole in the tree line.

Given three lifetimes, Nundle would have never conjured from his imagination the creature that moved onto the beach. The body was mud-brown and gangling, the elongated neck sticking from its shoulders bent forward slightly, supporting a triangular head. Two black-orbed eyes sat above a terrifying maw, frozen open in a perpetual scream. Needlelike teeth the color of tree moss glistened wet in the sunlight. Bark covered the creature instead of skin, streaked with jagged, black ridges along its arms and legs. Four-foot long spines jutted from its torso and upper arms. The fresh scent of tree sap filled the air.

Nundle's eyes opened wide as the creature lumbered toward them, the ground vibrating with each step. The soldiers who had recovered their swords held their weapons slack at their sides, staring in stunned awe.

Broedi yelled in his ear, "Start the Weaves! Now!"

Shaken from his shock, Nundle began to draw together a second pattern identical to the one over them now. Broedi moved to Nikalys and started shouting at him. Nundle tried to listen, but the screeching was getting louder as the creature lumbered closer.

When Nundle finished the second protective Weave, he held it in place, unsure if he should direct it toward Nikalys or Broedi. The hillman turned around, spotted the Weave, and pointed to Nikalys. The moment the Weave was draped over Nikalys, Broedi patted the young longleg on the back and Nikalys bolted toward the creature, the glowing Blade of Horum at his side. The monstrous forest creature halted its advance, turning its full attention to the solitary figure rushing towards it.

A collection of Life and Will Strands exploded around Nundle, drawing together in an instant and disappearing inside of Broedi. A moment later, his body began to shift, his hands and feet morphing into padded paws, his limbs bending into feline legs. Thick, golden-brown fur sprouted his skin. As the White Lion quickly completed the transformation into the lynx, Nundle quietly cursed. He had yet to start the third Weave of Air meant for Broedi.

Reaching for the Strands of Air a third time, he knit the pattern, slower than the last as he had to constantly shift his attention from one Weave to the next. If he let his concentration slip too far from one, it would fall apart.

Before Nundle could finish the Weave, Broedi leapt from the protective bubble, running toward the giant creature. He dropped his head, shaking it in pain, his black-tufted ears lying flat. Completing the Weave a moment later, Nundle whipped it over the lynx, twenty paces away. The massive cat stood tall and began to sprint, kicking up sand with its giant paws. Nundle moved the pattern with him.

Switching his attention back to the Weave over Nikalys, Nundle found that the young longleg had halted two dozen paces from the wood-beast. Nikalys was staring up at the creature, his white sword angled before him, its tip pointed at the creature. The monster, at least fifty-feet-tall, towered over him.

As Nundle wondered exactly what Nikalys hoped to do against the beast, the piercing shriek started to grow louder. Soldiers clasped hands to ears again. Shifting his attention back to the Weave around himself and the soldiers, Nundle tightened the pattern. As he did so, he noticed Captain Scrag waving at him and silently screaming, repeatedly jabbing a finger toward the forest.

Looking back to the tree line, Nundle found that the lynx had outrun his Weave. Broedi was slinking along the sand, suffering the effects of the shriek again.

"Blast!"

The moment Nundle shifted the Air Weave back over the lynx, Broedi lifted his head and resumed his charge towards the creature, rushing straight through the monster's spindly legs. For some odd reason, the beast paid him no attention.

Nundle suddenly realized that Nikalys was no longer on the beach. The Weave meant for him still hovered in place, but the young longleg was gone. Peering upward, Nundle was stunned to see Nikalys perched on the creature's left shoulder, the Blade of Horum sticking from the forest beast's neck. Nikalys was gripping the hilt with both hands, his mouth open as he screamed in pain.

As soon was Nundle whipped the Weave back over Nikalys, the young longleg opened his eyes and yanked his sword from the monster's neck. Nundle expected blood to flow from the wound, but none did. The wood-beast reached to grab Nikalys, but he vanished, only to reappear on the back of the monster's neck, holding onto one of the woody spines.

The shrieking around Nundle grew louder again.

Nundle shifted Nikalys' Weave before returning his attention to the pattern around himself and the soldiers. As the world went quiet, he looked up to find that Broedi was almost to the tree line, unprotected and crawling in the sand again. Once the Weave was back in place, Broedi leapt up and rushed into the forest. Nundle kept the pattern moving with him until he was out of sight then released the Weave. Broedi was on his own now.

Turning his attention back to the monster, Nundle labored to keep the Weave centered on Nikalys as the longleg dashed around and on the forest creature, stabbing and slashing. Wherever the Blade of Horum cut, it revealed white, pithy flesh beneath the bark skin. Despite the number of gashes inflicted, the creature did not slow. It appeared as if the wounds were sealing shut. The beast thrashed about the beach, kicking up sand as it spun in circles, trying to strike Nikalys.

Sensing a unique Weave radiating from within the beast, Nundle tried to get a feel for it, hoping he might be able to unravel it. However, as it was inside the monster and Nundle's concentration focused on keeping his own Weaves intact, he had no hope in pulling it apart.

Suddenly, Wil broke from the protective Weave, his sword at the ready, and rushed toward the creature. He made it a dozen paces before the shriek overwhelmed him. He collapsed to the ground and continued toward the beast, crawling through the sand. Nundle considered crafting another Weave to protect the soldier, but dismissed the idea. He could not control a third one again. He was beginning to have a difficult enough time maintaining the two that were left.

Nathan and Captain Scrag rushed forward, running to the fallen swordsman's side. As they each grabbed an arm and started pulling Wil back, someone slapped Nundle's back. Looking up, he found Cero pointing to the beast.

Looking up, Nundle spotted Nikalys kneeling in the sand behind the creature and clasping his ears. His Weave was hovering on the creature's left shoulder.

As Nundle started to adjust the Weave's placement, the screeching stopped. The beast's mouth snapped shut, its teeth disappearing inside its mouth. The world went silent although a tinny ringing continued in Nundle's ears.

His head snapping up, Nikalys lifted his sword to attack but froze and turned to stare back to the tree line. Looking to the forest, Nundle watched two people step from the forest, walking side-by-side. In his hillman form again, Broedi was accompanied by an equally tall and powerfully built figure dressed in a loose-fitting robe of stitched animal hides. It took Nundle a moment to realize he was staring at another hillman, a member of the Titaani Kotiv-aki, the Titan Tribe.

Broedi was waving his arms and appeared to be shouting. Nikalys stood tall and took a few scuffling steps back from the creature without ever taking his eyes from it.

A moment later, Nundle felt the Weave within the creature start to unravel. The beast began to shrink rapidly, losing a few feet with every breath, as if it were a tree growing in reverse. The tough, wooden exterior softened and turned less ridged yet still kept its bark-like appearance. Gangly arms and legs retreated, the needle-sharp spikes on its chest and back shrinking to mere inches. Fine, dusty green hair sprung from the top of its triangular head, growing like early-Spring grass. In a matter of moments, the fifty-foot tall monster shrank to a five-foot tall creature, six if its hair—waving in the breeze—was included.

Hoping he would not regret doing so, Nundle dropped his Weaves letting a rush of sound to wash over him.

Waves crashing on the rocks.

The sea breeze whistling in his ears.

Soldiers' startled mumbling.

He reached up and rubbed his eyes, trying to clear his head. A moment later, he dropped his hand, suddenly realizing what stood before them. Staring back to the creature, a single word of surprise slipped from his lips.

"Huh."

This might be the first he had ever seen one, but he had read enough books to know what it was.

"Nundle?" muttered Cero. "What is that?"

Looking up, Nundle found Cero staring wide-eyed at the creature. "I believe it's a buhanik." Peering back to the creature, he added, "Actually, I'm certain of it."

"I'm sorry. A what?"

"Thorn," said Nundle, using a more common name. "It's a thorn."

Cero was quiet for a moment.

"Truly?"

Nodding slowly, Nundle said, "Truly."

Another quiet moment passed before Cero asked warily, "Can they all do that?"

"Gods, I hope not."

The thorn and Nikalys remained locked in a steady stare while Broedi and the strange hillman—whom Nundle noted was completely bald—continued their approach from the trees. Nikalys remained taut and tense, his sword held at the ready while the thorn appeared perfectly tranquil and at ease.

Curious, Nundle began to move forward, toward the creature. Upon reaching where Nathan, Wil, and Captain Scrag stood, he glanced at the trio. All three were covered head to foot in sand.

"Careful," muttered Captain Scrag. "Those blasted teeth went somewhere."

Nundle halted his approach immediately. The captain's warning was a prudent one.

Broedi looked to them and called out, "Do not be afraid! It was a misunderstanding!"

"A misunderstanding?" muttered Captain Scrag amidst a skeptical snort. "A misunderstanding is, 'You brought me two flagons, I ordered three.'"

Turning to face the three longlegs, Nundle said, "If Broedi says it's safe…"

After a quick glance at Nathan and Wil, Captain Scrag shrugged his shoulders.

"Fine. But if it turns back into that thing, I'm letting him eat you first, bucket-man."

Nundle winced. The first time Captain Scrag had laid eyes on him, he had exclaimed, "Hah! I could carry you in a bucket!" The name had stuck.

Nathan turned to Wil and said, "Go make sure no one is hurt." Lowering his voice, he added, "And tell everyone to keep hands on hilts."

Nodding, Wil said, "Yes, Sergeant." After one last quick glance at the thorn, he turned and hurried back to the group of soldiers.

Facing the captain and Nundle, Nathan extended a hand, palm upward, toward the thorn and Nikalys, looking as if he was asking them to have a seat at eveningmeal.

"Shall we?"

As they approached, Nikalys spoke without looking at them.

"Is everyone alright?"

"Thanks to you and Nundle, yes," answered Nathan.

The thorn swiveled its head in their direction, its bark-like skin crunching like crispy, dried-out Harvest leaves. Its shiny black-orbed eyes studied them each, pausing briefly on Nathan and the captain before settling on Nundle last. Tilting its head to the side, it leaned forward a few inches as if to get a closer look at him. The thorn's eyes were like a puddle of water on a one-moon night: black with flickers of light dancing here and there.

Without taking his eyes from the creature, Nikalys said, "Thank you for your help, Nundle. I swore my head was going to burst."

The thorn shifted his gaze back to Nikalys and spoke in precise, unaccented Argot, its voice reminiscent of a gentle breeze whistling through the leaves of an oak.

"I am sorry for that."

"You're *sorry*?" asked Nikalys, his eyebrows arching high. "You try to kill us… and then apologize?"

"Remain calm, please," rumbled Broedi as he and the bald hillman arrived to stand with the group. "They mistook us for the Chosen."

"Who are the Chosen?" asked Nundle.

"Our enemy," replied the thorn. "We have fought off their aggression for many seasons."

"Over five centuries," rumbled the tattooed hillman.

Broedi said, "They thought we were invading their shores."

"With only thirty soldiers?" asked Nathan.

"It did seem unusual," whistled the thorn.

"Did it?" growled Captain Scrag. "Did it not occur to you that you might *ask* who we were before howling at us?!"

Broedi held up his hands and spoke in a quiet, firm tone.

"Captain, please. Try to see things from their point of view—a ship full of strange, armed men arrive—unannounced—and set to shore. In a land where war with the Chosen is never-ending, to what conclusion would you arrive?"

The captain of the Sapphire stared at Broedi for a few heartbeats, his white moustache twitching. After a moment, he nodded and said, "I suppose I can understand that."

"Good," said Broedi. "I hope so. Now, I would like it if everyone remained calm. Can we do that?"

As the assembled group nodded their agreement, Nundle got his first close look at the strange hillman and noticed that a web of intricate, green designs covered his cheeks and forehead, forming a mask of leaves and vines around his eyes. The markings resembled the tattoos worn by the seaman of the ship Nundle had taken from Yut to the Arcane Republic, although their designs were limited to arms and chest only. Staring at the hillman's face, Nundle shuddered, imagining how painful it must have been to get the markings.

As odd as the tattooed hillman was, he was nothing compared to the thorn. Nundle turned his attention back to the creature and marveled. Up close, the thorn's skin was not a single, drab color as it appeared from afar, but rather a myriad of nutty browns, soft tans, and charcoal grays. He noted the thorn was not wearing any clothes, although that seemed entirely appropriate.

"Can all thorns do what you did?" asked Nundle. "And by that, I mean turn into that awful beast?"

The question had tumbled from his mouth before he realized it. And rather than wait for an answer, Nundle began to do what he sometimes did.

"And how exactly did you make that screeching sound? Gods! It was horrible! Is the shriek part of the Weave that was inside you? Or was it just you? Oh! About the pattern you used: I sensed Life and Will, but there had to have been something else. What was it? Soul perhaps? Air? No—not Air. I would have felt that. I wonder if…it might…have been…"

He trailed off once he noticed that everyone—including the thorn—was staring at him. Glancing around at his companions, Nundle muttered, "Sorry about that." Turning to the thorn, he added, "I apologize for my rudeness. My curiosity sometimes gets the better of me."

The thorn tilted its head to the side, regarding Nundle as its grassy-hair rustled in the wind.

"Firstly, I am not a 'thorn.' Others have given us that name. We are buhanik."

"I actually knew that," said Nundle, disappointed in himself. "Sorry. Again."

"It is forgiven," whistled the thorn. "I, in turn, am sorry that Fingard and I tried to kill all of you."

Nundle glanced at the tattooed hillman, assuming he was Fingard. If so, Fingard did not appear the least bit remorseful about his role in the attack. Now that he thought about it, Nundle wondered exactly what the hillman's role had been.

As Nikalys sheathed the Blade of Horum, he said with a hint of sarcasm, "Well, then. If you're sorry, I suppose all is forgiven."

Turning its black-eyed stare on Nikalys, the thorn said, "You are gracious to accept our apology. May the sun shine on you." It would seem the creature did not grasp the mocking in Nikalys' tone.

"Broedi?" began Nathan. "Could you explain exactly what happened here?

How is this—" he nodded at the thorn "—the same thing that emerged from the forest?"

Crossing his arms, Broedi rumbled, "The moment I saw the creature, I figured it was a buhanik that had been adapted with a Weave. How, I was not sure. A similar pattern I know that is capable of doing something similar only works on plants." He turned an eye to Fingard. "I would be interested in knowing where you learned such a complex Weave."

Nundle stared at the bald hillman in surprise.

"*You* are the mage?"

He had assumed that the thorn had been behind the Weave.

Fingard's eyebrows drew together as he growled, "I will *not* answer your questions." While the deep timbre of his voice was similar to Broedi's, the sharp tone was foreign. "You might not be of the Chosen, but you are still strangers to our land."

The thorn whistled, "They are strangers only because we have allowed them to be, Fingard." Turning to Broedi, it said, "I am Talulot. I protect these shores with Fingard's aid. May the sun shine upon you." It shifted its black-eyed gaze to the tattooed hillman. "Fingard?"

After a reluctant pause, the hillman rumbled, "I am Fingard Veratrir. Long life to you." He bowed slightly, revealing even more green tattoos atop his head that looked like a wreath of laurels.

Broedi introduced himself as an explorer, giving his first name only before turning to the rest of the group. As instructed before leaving the ship, each of them gave their first name only as well, along with a courteous greeting. Even Captain Scrag managed a civil "Good days ahead." With each introduction, Talulot repeated the same salutation, "May the sun shine upon you."

Nundle went last, taking off his wide-brimmed hat and freeing his bright red hair to blow in the breeze.

"I am Nundle, a merchant out of Deepwell in the Thimbletoe Principal of the Five Boroughs. May your tables bring full bellies and joyful hearts."

For Nundle's introduction, Talulot said nothing in response. It simply stared at him with its dark and oddly reflective eyes. Nundle wondered if he had somehow offended the thorn. Perhaps full bellies were not desirable to a thorn.

Finally, Talulot whistled, "I sense you are not young, yet your growth is stunted. Why is that?"

The question took Nundle by surprise. For a moment, all he could do was stare at Talulot. Every other member of his group, however, enjoyed a quiet chuckle, even Broedi. The thorn looked around at the display, evidently confused by their response.

"I do not understand your mirth,"

After a moment or two, Nundle recovered, smiled politely, and said, "I am a tomble, Talulot. This is as tall as we get."

The thorn tilted its head to its left and whistled, "Noteworthy. Aembyr-The-Ageless had told stories of your kind, but you are the first I have seen with my eyes."

Nundle's heart skipped a beat.

"Pardon," rumbled Broedi. "Did you say Aembyr-The-Ageless?" His tone was intense yet polite.

"I did," said the thorn.

Those from the Sapphire exchanged a series of quick glances with one another, everyone with the same excited glint in his eyes.

Keeping his voice even and calm, Broedi asked, "Is Aembyr-The-Ageless known by another name? Wren, perhaps?"

Talulot tilted his head back to the right.

"He uses that name for himself."

"And where is he?" rumbled Broedi.

"In Buhaylunsod," replied the thorn. "Four days journey towards sunrise."

Broedi glanced to the east, into the forest.

"We would be honored if you would take us there, Talulot. I would like to speak with… 'Aembyr-The-Ageless.'"

Rather than answer, the thorn studied Broedi for a long stretch in complete silence, the breeze tickling its grassy hair. Just when Nundle was wondering if it might ever speak again, Talulot shifted its head in the other direction.

"You are like him, are you not?"

A moment skipped past before Broedi responded, asking, "What do you mean?"

Rather than answer the question, Talulot extended its right branch-hand toward Broedi, spreading its woody fingers wide. Closing its black-orbed eyes, the thorn began to sway back and forth as a bush caught in a gentle Spring breeze. A moment later, it spoke.

"I sense the same great life inside of you that flows inside Aembyr. You shine bright."

As one, everyone turned to stare at Broedi. Their arrival in the Primal Provinces grew stranger by the moment. Broedi crossed his arms over his chest and studied the thorn, a slight frown on his lips.

Tilting its head slightly, Talulot whistled, "Yet you are not alone."

The thorn's hand drifted from Broedi, moving to point in Nikalys' direction. The young longleg stared at the outstretched arm, a nervous frown upon his face. After a few quiet sways, the thorn's eyes snapped open.

"It flows within you, as well. Yet, it is brighter. *Much* brighter. Noteworthy."

Nikalys shot a quick, questioning glance to Broedi. The White Lion's gaze remained fixed on Talulot, his stoic expression revealing nothing.

Keeping his gaze on Nikalys, Talulot whistled, "Gather your followers, Light-From-The-West. We will take you to Buhaylunsod."

As Nikalys shot a curious glance to Broedi, Nundle noticed Fingard's hands were balled into fists, his knuckles white. Glancing up, he found the hillman glaring at the thorn.

Fingard rumbled, "Is that wise?"

The thorn turned to face Fingard and asked inquisitively, "You disagree?"

The hillman bowed his head.

"You know the Mataan do not allow strangers in Buhaylunsod."

While Nundle wondered who or what the Mataan were, Talulot gazed at the sun, seemingly basking in its glow before saying, "The wind carries a shadow on its breath, Fingard. A dark and grim shadow." Dropping its gaze to Broedi and Nikalys, the thorn added, "These two shine bright enough to cast light into the blackest of holes. The Mataan will understand that when they see them." Facing Nundle's group, Talulot whistled, "The time to leave is now. We shall wait for you in the trees."

The thorn turned abruptly and shuffled toward the tree line, dragging its wooden limbs through the sand, barely lifting them off the ground. Fingard shot one last, hard look at the group and turned to follow Talulot.

When the pair was a dozen paces away, Broedi turned and, in a quiet voice, rumbled, "Sergeant? Captain? Gather the men and supplies. We are following them."

The longlegs strode away without question, heading toward the huddled group of Shadow Mane soldiers, shouting orders as they went.

Left alone with Broedi and Nikalys, Nundle asked, "Am I right in assuming Buhaylunsod is a place?"

With a slight nod, Broedi answered, "In Argot, it might mean 'Living City'. Or 'The City Has Arisen.'"

Nikalys asked quietly, "Did you know Wren Aembyr was there?"

Broedi shook his head, rumbling, "I did not. While Nelnora showed me Wren amongst a tree city of the buhanik, she did not name which one."

"Then Nelnora lied," said Nikalys. His words were spoken with complete conviction.

"How so?" asked Nundle.

"All the luck in Terrene could not have brought us here at a more perfect moment," said Nikalys. "To find a thorn who wishes to take us straight to Wren Aembyr? The Gods *are* meddling, I have no doubt."

"I agree," said Nundle. "Which leads me to wonder what else she lied about." He eyed Broedi carefully as he added, "Or kept from us. At the moment, I feel as if I am reading a book with missing pages."

The skin around Broedi's eyes tightened slightly, confirming Nundle's suspicion that the hillman was hiding something. Still, the White Lion remained quiet. Whether it was wise or not, Nundle decided to push a little further.

"You know, I've been thinking perhaps I should go back to the Seat of Nelnora and ask her some more questions. And now that we have arrived on dry land, I could easily port—"

"No!" interrupted Broedi. "We do *not* go back."

"Why not?" asked Nikalys with a frown.

Broedi stared out at the sea and let a soft sigh slip past his lips.

"There are reasons."

"I see," said Nikalys. "And those reasons are…?"

"Not ones I can share with you now."

His frown deepening, Nikalys asked, "Truly, Broedi? More secrets? Here? *Now*?"

The hillman continued to stare at the ocean, perfectly silent.

"Broedi?" muttered Nundle. "We know you are withholding something."

"Of course you do," said Broedi. "I did not expect to hide the obvious from you. I am surprised, however, that it took you so long to mention it." Pulling his gaze from the sea and resting it on them, he rumbled, "Yet you should know I will not share more than that. It is not yet time."

Nikalys crossed his arms and sighed.

"So, what then? We just nod our heads and follow you?"

"If you will," rumbled the hillman. "For a while longer, please."

Nikalys glanced to Nundle, a thin frown on his face, and lifted an eyebrow, apparently asking for Nundle's opinion. Holding the young longleg's gaze, Nundle asked the obvious.

"What else are we going to do?"

After a moment, Nikalys looked back to Broedi, nodded his head, and said, "Lead on."

"Thank you," said Broedi. "I appreciate your—" He cut off as a loud shout rang out over the beach.

"Turn around, you blasted fools!"

Jumping at the cry, Nundle spun around to find Captain Scrag standing in the surf, water up to his calves, waving his arms and screaming.

"Go back to the blasted ship!"

Looking out to where the Sapphire was anchored, Nundle spotted two other shoreboats rowing toward the beach, filled with sailors.

Nikalys mused, "Probably coming to come help us when they saw Talulot." He paused, then added, "The large and scary version, that is."

Turning back around, Nundle stared up at Broedi and asked, "How is it they did that? I've never heard of a Weave capable of doing what we saw."

"It is a variation of one that Wren discovered. One he used on plants, shaping them as they grow. I expect he has refined the pattern and taught it to the Titaani Kotiv-aki."

Nikalys asked, "And how did you get them to stop the attack?"

"I told Fingard that if he did not release the Weave that I would kill him."

Nundle stared at Broedi, surprised at the response.

"You threatened his life?"

Broedi fixed his brown-eyed gaze squarely on Nundle.

"Would you prefer I had reasoned with him? It would have taken longer, I think."

With the shriek of the massive thorn echoing in his mind, Nundle shook his head.

"No. I suppose your method was just fine."

Hearing voices approaching, Nundle turned to find Nathan and Captain Scrag walking back toward them, the soldiers trailing and laden with packs of supplies. Out on the sea, the other shoreboats were in the midst of turning back to the Sapphire.

Nikalys said, "It seems we're ready."

"Then let us go," rumbled Broedi. "We have a long walk ahead of us." He turned and began to stride to where Talulot and Fingard waited by the forest's edge.

As Nundle hurried to follow, he said a silent prayer that he would be able keep pace with everyone over the next few days. Scurrying across the sand, he mumbled, "I wish I had my horse."

CHAPTER 39: AWAKEN

13ᵗʰ of the Turn of Maeana, 4999

Jak awoke, the scent of charred oak smoke filling his first conscious breath.

As he drew in a second breath to confirm, he noticed the persistent popping and cracking of logs aflame. Without a doubt, there was a fire burning. A detail he found odd as his room did not have a hearth. Through the fog of leftover sleep and pain, he noted that he was lying down, but not in his own bed. His mattress was a straw one, scratchy and cold. This bed was soft and warm. He lifted his right hand and grazed lightweight blankets that would be much too thin to hold back the chill of his room.

Apparently, he was not in his room. He considered opening his eyes to inspect his surroundings, but the pounding in his head warned against additional sensation. He wondered if there had been a festival last night. Perhaps he had too much wine. Like a barrelful too much.

To his right, he heard the clink of pottery followed by a soft sigh. He was not alone.

Through dry and crusty lips, he groaned, "Where am I?" His tongue felt it was stuck in mud.

He heard a sharp intake of breath, followed by the quiet rustling of clothes as someone hurried to his side. Now he smelled rosewater.

A woman whispered, "Jak?"

Her voice sounded familiar, but the fuzziness coating his thoughts prevented him from placing it.

"Gods, my head hurts," he mumbled.

"Don't move," ordered the woman.

"Wasn't planning on it," croaked Jak.

The woman moved away immediately, her light footsteps hurrying past the foot of his bed. A door creaked open.

"Go get Chandrid, please. He's awake."

A man replied, murmuring, "Thank the Gods." The relief in his voice was clear.

Heavy footsteps hastened away, echoing as if they were in a long, stone hallway. The sound of boot heels striking stone was loud enough that Jak winced with each one. It felt as if someone was tapping his temples with a small hammer. When the door shut with a soft thud, muffling the retreating steps, Jak relaxed, grateful for the quiet. Footsteps approached him again, different from the first set, softer and somewhat hesitant. Stopping beside his bed, a little girl spoke, her voice full of worry.

"Are you all better, Jak?"

This time, Jak instantly recognized to whom the voice belonged. "Not at the moment, Helene." Hoping to put the little girl at ease, he added, "But I will be."

The woman by the door moved to his side as well, stopping beside Helene and bringing with her a second waft of rosewater. The scent, along with Helene's presence, helped Jak place who she was.

"Sabine?"

"Yes," replied Sabine, her voice soft and reassuring. A hand rested atop his, through the blanket. "And you're right, Jak. You're going to be fine. Absolutely fine." It sounded as if she were trying to convince herself, not him.

"Why wouldn't I be?" he mumbled. Keeping his eyes closed, he turned his head to face them. The pounding in his head swelled. "It's only a headache. A very bad headache."

A quiet moment passed before Sabine asked, "Do you remember what happened to you?" She sounded concerned.

"Did a festival happen to me?" asked Jak, his dry lips turning up into a slight smile. "Too much wine?"

Sabine paused again before answering, "No, Jak. There was no festival." The concern in her voice had grown, which in turn, worried him.

He tried to crack open his eyelids to look up at her, but only succeeded in opening his right eye. Something was keeping his left shut. The Moiléne sisters were by his side, staring at him. Wooden rafters lined the ceiling above them.

"What's wrong with my eye?"

With panic swelling in his chest, he tried to extract his right hand from the blankets but Sabine gripped it, stopping him.

"Wait for Chandrid."

He attempted to pull away, but Sabine clamped down harder.

"Please, Jak. Wait."

Tossing back the covers from his other arm, he reached up to find a thick, soft cloth wrapped over his left eye, ear, and forehead. His heart rate increased, which only made the pounding in his head worse.

Running his hand along the path of the bandages, he asked, "What happened?"

"You *will* be fine, Jak," insisted Sabine. "Chandrid says they are only temporary." Her words were encouraging, but worry still colored her tone.

Looking back to Sabine, Jak demanded, "Tell me what—" His voice cracked and gave out. He choked softly, sending his head pounding anew. "Gods, I'm so thirsty."

Helene spun around immediately and scurried from the bed to a small, round-topped table. She returned a moment later, carrying a small pottery cup.

"You can have my tea, Jak. It's still hot. Sabine just made it."

She lifted the cup to the edge of the bed and steadied it there, waiting for him to take it.

Jak smiled and murmured, "Thank you, dear. That's very kind of you." He went to move his right hand to take it, but Sabine was still holding it, her grip surprisingly tight. He tugged, but she would not let go. Glancing up, he asked, "Can I have my hand, please?"

Releasing him, she said, "Sorry."

Extracting his arm from the blanket, Jak reached for the cup, but stopped short, grimacing as his entire right side began to throb. It felt as if had been punched in the ribs a few dozen times. Lying flat again, he whispered, "Yeah. So that hurts."

"Here," said Sabine. "Let me help you."

She scooted around Helene, moved to the head of the bed, and assisted him in sitting up. With his back resting against the cold stone wall, he looked around the room, still not recognizing where he was.

A fire burned in a recessed hearth on his left. Straight across from him, past the foot of his bed, was an oak door. The dim gray light shining through the lone, small window in the room told Jak that it was either dusk or dawn. Two blue cushioned chairs sat next to the table a half-dozen paces to the right of the bed. A glass lamp, two pots, and an open book rested on the tabletop.

While he wanted to know what had happened to him, his parched throat demanded satisfaction first. Accepting the cup from Helene, Jak lifted it to his lips, took two quick sips, and swallowed. The hot and gloriously wet tea coated his scratchy throat.

Helene said, "I put a lot of honey in it."

Jak could tell. It was thrice as sweet as he liked it, but he was not about to complain. Smiling at the little girl, he said, "It is very good. Perfect, in fact."

Helene held his gaze but did not smile back. Jak found that odd. He rarely saw Helene without a grin on her face. Before he could spend more than a moment wondering at the cause for Helene's melancholy mood, the door opened and Lady Vivienne swept inside, bringing a cold draft of air in with her from the hallway. The baroness moved straight to the foot of the bed and stopped, her gaze dancing over Sabine and Helene before settling on Jak. A courtly blue dress hung from her shoulders and a more-than-determined expression rested on her face.

Jak stared at the noblewoman, surprised and confused as to her presence. Sabine had sent for Chandrid, the hillwoman mage and resident healer of the enclave. Again, his wondering was cut short as the seven-foot-tall hillwoman entered next wearing plain brown robes, cinched at the waist with a turquoise belt. A leather bag hung from her shoulder, much like the one Broedi often carried, although the beads adorning her satchel were both greater in number and more colorful.

Gamin marched in behind Chandrid, also with a bandage wrapped around his head, although his looked smaller than Jak's felt. The mage fixed Jak with a steady stare as he moved to stand beside the baroness.

Chandrid strode to Jak's left, stopped beside the bed, and rumbled, "What do you think you are doing? You should be lying down." She shifted her gaze to Sabine. "I told you not to let him move if he awoke. At least three times, if I recall."

"I know," said Sabine. "But he was thirsty."

"I gave him my tea," added Helene.

Eyeing the cup in Jak's hand, Chandrid frowned and asked, "Only tea?"

"With honey," replied Sabine and Helene simultaneously.

"Honey?" asked Chandrid, her frown deepening. "How much did he drink?" She did not sound pleased.

"Just a few sips," answered Jak. "That's all."

"Fine," rumbled the hillwoman. "But *no* more. Drink only water for now." She reached out, took the cup from Jak's hand, and handed it to Sabine. "Put that down and then help me get him lying down again."

Sabine did as Chandrid asked without protest. As they helped lower him back to the bed, Jak's head began to swim. Within moments, it felt as if the room was spinning. His stomach felt queasy.

"I do not feel good."

"Let me guess," said Chandrid. "The room is moving?"

"Quite a lot," muttered Jak.

"I can help that, but first I must ask your consent to treat you now that you are awake."

Jak tried to focus on her face, but could not.

"Pardon?"

"It is the way of the aki-mahet. I must ask for permission."

"Fine. You have my permission."

"I have not asked properly."

Jak muttered in exasperation, "Then ask. I'm going to get ill in a moment."

The hillwoman placed her palms together, bowed slightly, and said, "I, Chandridkerit Mortanggard, former lakari of the Laksoo, ask your permission to tend to your wounds and ease your pain."

"Please," mumbled Jak. "Ease my pain." He was sweating now.

Chandrid peered into the open air above the bed and, a few moments later, dropped her gaze to Jak. The room went blessedly still.

"Better?" asked Chandrid.

"Ever so much," said Jak. "Thank you." His head still pounded and his side still ached, but at least he was not going to get ill.

Chandrid nodded, lifted the satchel's strap over her head, and placed the leather sack on the bed. As she opened the flap and began to rummage inside, Helene half-climbed onto the bed in an attempt to peer inside the satchel.

Looking up to Chandrid, Jak said, "Broedi never asked permission to help me when I got shot by an arrow."

"He is not lakari."

"And what is lakari?"

Chandrid halted her rummaging, paused a moment, and then said, "'Caretaker' is as close a word as there is in Argot." She resumed rooting through her satchel.

Reaching up to poke at his bandages, he asked, "And I suppose you are taking care of this?"

Chandrid looked up, gently grasped his hand, and placed it back on the bed. "Do not do that."

"I won't as long as someone tells me what happened," said Jak. Glancing at Gamin, he asked, "Did you and I have a disagreement?"

The redheaded mage smiled slightly and shook his head.

"No, we did not."

"Jak?" prompted Chandrid. "Tell me the last thing you remember before today. It will help me evaluate your injury."

Jak studied the faces of the people standing around him. Lady Vivienne, who had yet to say a single word, was staring at him with bright and intensely curious eyes. Sabine's blank gaze was directed to the bed, the lines in her forehead and around her eyes betraying a sense of worry. Helene had finished climbing atop the bed and now was lying next to his legs, her head turned toward Sabine alone. Gamin was peering at her, concern in his eyes. A strange sort of tension filled the room and Jak did not understand why.

Shaking his head, Jak said, "I don't know. My memories are a bit muddied at the moment."

"Please, Jak," said Gamin. "Try. You might remember more than you think."

Jak shrugged his shoulders and sighed.

"Alright. I'll try."

He closed his right eye and tried to draw forth the most recent memory he had before waking up here. Remembering the cold and the snow, he began to think aloud.

"Morning drills. I remember finishing morning drills, coming inside, and speaking with Commander Aiden in the hall afterwards." He halted as most of that conversation came rushing back.

"What did you talk about?" asked Lady Vivienne.

Jak lied.

"I don't remember."

There was no need to share the contents of that exchange with everyone.

"What happened next?" prompted Chandrid.

"Well, the commander left and..." His brow—or at least half of it—drew together. "Ah! Sabine found me in the hall and we talked—" He stopped suddenly, remembering that they had spoken extensively of his siblings' locations and wellbeing. He did not know if Gamin and Chandrid were aware of Kenders' absence.

Misinterpreting his pause, Chandrid said, "Keep going. You are doing well. What did you and Sabine talk about?"

Sabine answered for him, saying, "Nothing of any importance."

Opening his eye, Jak added, "Mostly we talked about the snow. Oh, and about heading into Claw for eveningmeal." The story was plausible enough.

After a quiet moment, Lady Vivienne directed, "Please continue."

Wondering why she even bothered with the 'please,' Jak shut his eye again and tried to remember past the meeting with Sabine. It was a struggle, though. Drawing forth his memories was like trying to snatch a leaf from midair during a raging thunderstorm.

"There was a boom. A large one. Large enough that the hall shook. Then... a second one. We rushed off..." Things were becoming clearer now. He pictured himself and Sabine running through the hall together. "We got to the courtyard door and—" He cut off as a quick series of images flashed though his mind.

Smoke billowing from a gaping hole in the walls.

Snow drifting down as he sprinted across the icy courtyard.

Blood pouring down Gamin's face.

"We couldn't find Helene...so I ran into the hall. The smoke was so thick..." He went quiet again, mentally tracing his path through the burning room as it collapsed around him.

Lady Vivienne urged, "Go on, please."

Her tone prompted Jak to open his eye and lift his head. The baroness' gaze was locked on him, cool and calculating. She was after something. What, he did not know. He shook off her penetrating gaze and dropped his head to the pillow, cautioning himself to be careful.

Bringing back to mind the burning room, he muttered, "There was a man on the ground." Jak turned up his nose, remembering the stench of singed and smoking hair. "He was dead."

Beside him, Helene shifted, reached out to slip an arm around his leg, and hugged him tight. Curious, Jak opened his eyes and stared down at her tiny form. The moment he laid eyes on her, another quick sequence of images flashed through his head, one right after another.

Helene's crumbled body on the floor.

Her, cradled in his arms.

The perfect, untouched circle of stone on the ground.

He sat up a little more. Helene turned her head to look at him, her brown eyes as round as eveningmeal platters.

She knew.

"Jak?" asked Sabine quietly.

Turning his head, he found the raven-haired beauty staring at him, her eyes brimming with worry. He wondered if she knew. His heart thudded in his chest making his headache swell.

"Go on," prompted Lady Vivienne. "What do you remember?"

Jak looked back to the baroness. Her anxious expression betrayed her. She had no idea what had happened in the mages hall. None. Gamin either, from the looks of it. Jak wavered a moment, wondering if he should share what he had seen. In less than a heartbeat, he decided to keep things to himself for now. He should talk with Sabine about this first. Alone.

"I…I turned around and saw Helene by a table. I rushed over and picked her up as the ceiling started to collapse. I started to run out and…and…" He trailed off and did his best to appear as if he was trying to think. After what he hoped was a good show, he shook head. "I'm sorry, but that's all I can remember."

"You can tell us nothing else?" asked Lady Vivienne. "Nothing about what you saw in the room?"

Jak lifted his head. The baroness stared at him expectantly.

"No, my Lady. I cannot."

The lines on the baroness' face lengthened as her expression grew even more suspicious.

"You are *sure?*"

In as even tone he could manage, he said, "Perhaps you might not have noticed, my Lady, but I seem to have had an accident." He pointed back to the bandages on his head. "A rather significant bump on the head it would seem. So you will forgive me if I cannot seem to remember every detail." He offered an apologetic smile that was absent any true regret. "I wish I could be of more help."

The baroness pressed her lips together and gave a tiny huff of a sigh. "Of course you do. I am grateful you are alive and recovering." Her words contained as much warmth as his smile had conveyed remorse. "You were fortunate, young Jak. The Manes were fortunate. Things could have been much worse. The man you found? Marick? Somehow, he was the lone casualty."

Jak instantly recognized the name as belonging to Helene's teacher. He glanced down to the little girl by his side. She squeezed his leg a little tighter.

After a moment, Lady Vivienne sighed again and said, "If you happen to recall anything else, please let Gamin know immediately. He is leading the investigation." She turned to eye the mage. "Which is proving to be a rather unsuccessful one. Five days have passed and it seems we still have little idea what truly happened."

Jak's eye widened.

"*Five* days?"

He started to sit up but was stopped as Chandrid laid a strong hand on his chest.

"Lay down, please."

Struggling against her restraint, he exclaimed, "I've been asleep for *five* days?"

Adding her own appeal, Sabine pleaded, "Please, Jak. Lie still."

Jak relaxed and dropped his head into his pillow, staring at the rafters overhead.

"Five days? How?"

When Chandrid seemed satisfied that he would not rise again, she released him and said, "To continue your tale where you cannot, you ran from the room as the wall came down. The Stone mages who were able attempted to hold back the rocks as they fell." Her gaze shifted to his bandages. "One slipped past and struck your head."

Jak shook his head, muttering, "I don't remember that." His claim was legitimate this time.

"That is not unusual," rumbled Chandrid. "Some souls lose entire days or weeks after such a blow to the head. You are lucky. Ketus was with you, Jak."

"Lucky?" huffed Jak. "Part of a castle fell on me."

"Exactly," said Gamin, his tone somber. "The castle fell on you and you are still alive. I'd consider that lucky, too."

Sabine murmured, "We thought you might not ever wake up, Jak."

As Jak turned to stare at her, Helene clambered further up the bed to snuggle beside him, resting her head on his chest. Jak draped his arm over her and hugged her tight, stroking her hair.

Silence stretched out, filling the room. Throughout the extended quiet, Lady Vivienne kept her eyes on Jak and a frown on her lips. Jak pretended as if he did not feel the weight of her gaze, but he did.

Eventually, the noblewoman let out a quick sigh, breaking the silence, and said, "I must be going. Things must be attended to. Quick recovery, young man."

Inclining his head, he said, "Thank you, my Lady."

The baroness gave a curt nod, spun around—her blue dress swishing as it swirled—and exited the room, leaving the door open behind her. As she strode down the dark hall, disappearing into its gloom, Jak's gaze naturally shifted to Gamin. The head mage stood motionless, his arms crossed across his wide chest, and his stare resting on Helene.

Jak eyed his mother and father's old friend and, keeping his voice neutral, asked, "So you're investigating the accident?"

Gamin's gaze shifted ever so slightly to rest on Jak's face.

"I am."

"And do you have any theories on what happened?"

Gamin hesitated a moment before taking a quick glance over his shoulder to stare into the hall. Lady Vivienne's distant footsteps could be heard, but she was out of sight. Turning back to Jak, Gamin said quietly, "I have told the baroness I do not."

"You did not answer my question."

Gamin let a long, heavy sigh slip from his lips and murmured, "No, I did not." His gaze shifted back to Helene and a tiny frown graced his lips. He knew.

Wearing a slight frown of his own, Jak asked, "Why is Lady Vivienne so intent on getting an answer?"

"Because she fears for the safety of the enclave," answered Gamin. "And she is worried that further incidents might expose us."

"And what will she do if she finds the cause?" asked Jak.

Gamin's frown deepened as he muttered, "Whatever she must to protect the Manes."

Jak stared up at Sabine and found a cold, determined expression on her face. Looking back to Gamin, Jak asked, "Do you have any indications as to what happened in the mages' hall?"

The head mage eyed Jak and said, "Even if I did, I need some time to verify things before I would bring anything to the baroness. And that should take me a while."

"How long?" asked Jak.

Gamin raised an eyebrow and gave Jak a tiny lopsided smile.

"Oh, at least until after Broedi returns. Perhaps longer after I speak with him."

Jak shut his eyes, welcoming the sense of relief that washed over him. Gamin's message was clear. He was going to hold his tongue.

Opening his eyes, he said gratefully, "Thank you, Gamin. I will owe you."

"You owe me nothing, Jak. Consider it a partial repayment for the debt I owed your parents. A very partial payment. Without them, I would not be alive today." He shifted his gaze to Sabine and added, "Please keep a close eye on her, though. And for the time being, no more lessons."

Sabine nodded.

"Of course. And thank you, Gamin."

"You are welcome," said the mage. He took a deep breath, drew himself up, and looked back to Jak. "Quick recovery. Please don't run into any more burning, collapsing buildings anytime soon."

"Oh, no," said Jak with a smile. "At least not for a day or two."

Gamin grinned, held his stare, and nodded slowly.

"I think you should know that Thad and Marie would have been blasted proud of what you did, Jak. I sure as the Nine Hells am."

Jak's smile faded as a sudden swell of emotion surged within him. Gamin's words were unexpected.

"That's...that's a nice thing to say, Gamin. Thank you."

The room went quiet. An air pocket within a log suddenly burst.

Turning his gaze to Chandrid, Gamin asked, "You will keep this conversation to yourself?"

As difficult as it was to forget a seven-foot tall hillwoman looming over him, Jak had done just that. Swiveling his head to stare up at Chandrid, he found her eyeing him, a small frown on her face. He did not know Chandrid well, but she would have to be a simpleton not to have followed that conversation.

"Please?" asked Jak. "At least until Broedi gets back."

Chandrid glanced at Helene, took a deep breath, and sighed, "As you desire."

"Then it is settled," announced Gamin. "The events in the mages' hall remain an enigma. Which means I must go and continue to 'investigate' them now. If you will excuse me?" He gave them all one last nod, turned, and strode from the room.

As his steps echoed down the empty hall, Jak looked back up to Chandrid.

"Thank you."

"I do not require your gratitude," replied Chandrid. "I trust Broedi to make the right decision more than I do the baroness." Handing him what looked like a dried, green pinecone no bigger than the tip of her thumb, she said, "Now, this is a bit of—"

"Meadowsweet," interrupted Jak

Nodding, Chandrid said, "That is a name some use. It will help your headache."

"Broedi had a healthy supply of this on the way here," noted Jak. "I think Kenders used most of it."

"So then you know what to do with it."

Jak nodded and said, "I do." He rolled the balled herb between his thumb and forefinger, preparing to stick it between his cheek and gums.

"Good," said Chandrid. She lifted her head to stare at the air above him, her gaze fixed on something only she could see.

"What are you doing?" asked Jak. "You're using the Strands, aren't you?"

His answer did not come in the form of words. Within moments, the skin beneath his bandages began to tingle. It felt as if someone were pouring warm water filled with thousands of tiny bubbles over his head. Instinctively, he reached up to touch the cloth.

"Hold still, please," instructed Chandrid.

Jak dropped his hand back to the bed and focused on the strange, oddly pleasant phenomenon. The moment passed and the warming sensation faded, taking most of his aches and pains with it.

Chandrid stared down at him.

"I am not as talented with Life as some are. There are others from the accident for whom I must save my strength. I am sorry, but that is all I can do for you."

"Gods, don't apologize," said Jak. "I feel better already."

Nodding once, Chandrid shifted her gaze to Sabine.

"You may talk for a little while, but then he must sleep. Agreed?"

Her gaze never leaving Jak's face, Sabine said, "Of course."

Looking back to Jak, Chandrid said, "I will return later to change the bandage. I will bring you water and broth, then."

"Thank you, Chandrid."

"Please stop thanking me. I require your improved health, not your gratitude."

Jak gave her a thin smile and said, "I require my health, too."

The hillwoman smiled slightly, picked up her satchel, and moved to leave the room. Without another word, she slipped into the hallway and pulled the door shut behind her.

For a few heartbeats, the only sound in the room was that of the crackling fire. Jak placed the small, green pinecone in his mouth. Grimacing at the bitter taste, he peered up at Sabine to find the young beauty staring squarely at Helene, her face lined with worry.

Keeping his voice calm and even, he said, "Just to be clear, then. You know, yes?" He glanced down at Helene.

Her shoulders slumping, she collapsed to sit on the edge of the bed.

"I do."

Quiet for a moment, Jak asked, "How?"

Sabine reached out to brush the hair from Helene's face and murmured, "You came running out with her, Jak, and…Gods, there was *so* much blood! I thought she was…that she was—" She cut off, sat a little taller, and took in a short, fortifying breath. "All of it was yours, though. That gash on your head was deep. *Very* deep."

Jak was glad he could not remember that part.

"I suppose I'll have to take your word for it. I don't remember anything beyond running from the hall."

"Well, when you came out, you collapsed to the ground and dropped Helene."

"I dropped her?"

When Sabine nodded, Jak glanced down at Helene and patted her arm.

"Sorry about that, dear."

While Helene did not lift her head, she at least responded, saying, "It didn't hurt, Jak. Snow is soft."

"Lucky for us both, then, isn't it?"

He looked back to Sabine and was caught off guard by the warm gaze that met him. For a moment, her face was free of anxiety and filled with what was clearly affection. As much as Jak loved the way she was staring at him, he found that it also made him uneasy.

"So what happened next?"

Sabine dropped her gaze and said, "Well, let's see. Commander Aiden dragged you away from the wall. I grabbed Helene and ran. You passed out and the battlements collapsed. Chandrid rushed over, did whatever a healer does, and then had you brought here where you've been asleep for five days. She checks on you quite often. Even through the night."

Jak lifted an eyebrow and said, "Seems I owe her more than a simple 'thank you,' then."

"You certainly do," agreed Sabine. "Lady Vivienne, as well, believe it or not."

"Pardon?"

"Twice over, actually. You know she has some minor talent with the Strands?"

"Yes…?" muttered Jak.

"Well, she was one of the Stone mages trying to hold up the wall so you could get out."

"Truly?" asked Jak.

"I would not lie," said Sabine.

Frowning, Jak said, "You said 'twice over.' Why else do I owe her my gratitude?"

"Well, Jak, She gave over her quarters to you."

"I'm sorry…she what?"

A tiny smile spread over Sabine's lips.

"You are lying in Lady Vivienne's bed right now. At least the one she uses here."

For a long moment, Jak stared at Sabine, stunned.

"She gave me her room?"

Sabine nodded, saying, "Chandrid said it was important for you to stay warm. Lady Vivienne offered up her room immediately. She's been sleeping in the tower—Nik's empty room—when she's not in Freehaven."

"Someone should have told me that. I should have at least thanked her."

Sabine gave a weak smile.

"You will have another opportunity to do so," said Sabine. "She will be back. I am sure of it."

"Why do you say that?"

"Because she sure as the Nine—" She cut off, glanced at Helene, and said, "Because she did not seem content with the answers you gave today."

He drew in a long, deep breath and exhaled slowly.

"No. No she did not."

"There wasn't a scratch on Helene, Jak. She was the only soul from the mages' hall not hurt. And Lady Vivienne noticed. She noticed immediately. She made a comment to that effect as they were carrying you away. And it was not an offhand, 'the sky is blue today, is it not' sort of comment."

Jak frowned, but did not respond. He did not know what to say.

For a long while, they both remained quiet. Jak spent the time staring at the ceiling, trying to decide what this meant. After a while, he looked to Sabine, then glanced at Helene, and then back to Sabine, trying to ask 'does she know' with his eyes alone.

Nodding, Sabine whispered, "Yes. Later that night, she told me everything."

Helene suddenly shifted by his side. Lifting her head, she twisted around to stare up at him with sad, sorrowful eyes that no four-year old should have.

"I'm sorry, Jak. I didn't mean to hurt Marick."

With a gentle smile and firm squeeze, Jak said, "I know, Helene. I—"

"I tried to fix it," murmured the little girl. "I tried to help him. But...he wouldn't come back."

Curious at Helene's words, Jak stared down at her and asked, "What do you mean you tried to 'fix it?'"

Helene held his gaze, her face absent any expression. After a few moments, she laid her head back down on his chest having never answered his question. Jak considered pressing her, but now was not the time. Prying his eyes from Helene, he turned back to Sabine.

"And nobody else knows?"

"If so, I haven't heard. And I believe I would have. It's all the enclave has been talking about."

"I don't see how it's possible that nobody knows. How many mages were in the hall? None of them saw what happened?"

"You aren't the only one with half-remembered memories, Jak."

Jak nodded and let out a quiet sigh. "So Gamin and Chandrid, then. Let's hope that is as far as it goes. Not that I don't trust everyone here, but..." He glanced down at Helene. "I want to talk with Broedi first."

"Thank you," murmured Sabine.

Looking back up, he asked, "For what?"

"For lying for us, Jak. You didn't have to do that."

Without hesitation, he said, "Yes, I did."

"No, you didn't. But you did anyway." Summoning forth a brave smile, she added, "So accept my thanks and say 'you're welcome.'"

Returning her smile, Jak said, "You're welcome, then."

Sabine's gaze shifted back to Helene and the slight smile faded. She reached down to pat Helene's shoulder. The little girl lifted her hand and gripped Sabine's. Watching the sisters reminded Jak how much he missed his own siblings.

"I don't suppose Kenders is back?"

Sabine shook her head once.

"No. I'm sorry."

"She said she'd be back by now," muttered Jak.

"If it helps, I checked on them a little while ago. They're fine." Her expression brightened a touch. "And actually, Kenders no longer seems so sad."

"I suppose that's…that's…" A yawn suddenly overtook him. He tried to fight it off, but lost. Once it passed, he finished his original thought. "I suppose that's a bit of sweet, then."

Sabine rose from the bed and said, "Come, Helene. Jak needs his sleep." When Helene did not move, Sabine bent over, patted the little girl's back, and whispered, "Please, dear. We'll come back later. I promise."

Helene sat up and looked at Jak for a moment before starting to scoot from the bed. She stopped though, turned around, and draped her arms over his chest, hugging him. He got a mouthful of her hair in the process, wincing a bit as her knees dug into his bruised side. He did his best to return the embrace when Helene whispered softly in his ear.

"Thank you for coming back."

He pulled back a bit to stare at the top of her head, curious at her word choice. She glanced up at him, meeting his stare, and then stretched up to give him a quick kiss on his cheek. A flicker of a smile danced over her lips before she pulled away and slipped from the bed.

Glancing up to Sabine, he smiled and said, "That was sweet of her."

Instead of responding, Sabine stepped closer, leaned over, and placed her soft lips on his cracked and dry ones. The sweet aroma of rosewater swallowed him and after a pair of too-quick heartbeats, she pulled back a few inches. Staring into his eyes, she murmured, "Thank you for saving my sister, Jak."

He barely managed a nod in response before Sabine stood, scooped up Helene, and carried the little girl to the door. As she grabbed the rope handle and swung open the door, Helene whispered loudly, "I saw you kiss Jak, Sabine."

"Hush, dear," murmured Sabine, quietly shutting door without having ever looked back and leaving Jak alone and very confused.

Letting his head fall to the pillow, he stared at the ceiling as his mind raced, trying to make sense of what had just happened. Sabine's kiss had been so sudden and unexpected, that he had not even kissed her back. Chastising himself for laying here like a sack of onions, he shut his eyes and muttered, "Way to go, Jak."

Chandrid wanted him to sleep, but he severely doubted he would be doing that anytime soon. Not after what had just happened. Within minutes, however, he was snoring softly.

He dreamed.

CHAPTER 40: UNDERSTANDING

15ᵗʰ of the Turn of Maeana, 4999

A light fog hung in the air, a translucent, gray veil shrouding the world. Mu's orb was just starting to peek over the eastern horizon, lending its soft and warm glow to the fine mist. Countless needled trees covered the hills, their pointed tops lit by the new day's first rays. In the valleys of the slopes, golden-tan grass and swamp plants stuck up from the thicker blanket of haze drifting through the marshes.

Rhohn stood on one of the hills, staring at the scene before him in quiet awe. This was a strange land.

A pair of early-morning birds was peppering the treetops with their incessant chirping, greeting the new day. Leaning against a rough-barked tree trunk, Rhohn stared upward into the boughs to search for the culprits. As all he could see was a thick mesh of branches and needles, he dropped his gaze back to the hazy morning and spoke in a whisper.

"Once the fog burns off, we go."

"I agree," growled Okollu in a low, gruff voice. The mongrel stood on the opposite side of Rhohn's tree. "If we are where Tiliah insists, it is wise to be cautious."

Tiliah whispered, "We are *exactly* where I say we are." She leaned forward to peer past Rhohn, around the tree, and at Okollu. "You said you smelled the city last night."

"I still do," said Okollu. He sniffed the air twice and seemed to grimace. "And it reeks. I worry we are too close."

"Relax," murmured Tiliah "We are at least two or three miles away."

Okollu turned and looked past Rhohn, his eyes peering from deep within the large hood draped over his head.

"I am right to be cautious. This is as far east as any kur-surus has been."

"Is it, now?" asked Tiliah. A sarcastic note entered her voice. "Well, I'll be sure to note that in the saga I'm writing about you."

Her comment triggered a grin to sprout over Rhohn's face. He tried to smother it, but failed.

A low growl emanated from Okollu.

"Are you laughing at me, smooth-face?"

Rhohn continued staring straight ahead. Supposing there was no use in denying it, he said, "Yes. I am."

The mongrel either muttered something in his native tongue or snarled—Rhohn could not tell which—before facing north again. Ignoring the response, Rhohn stared into the misty hills, his gaze tracing a stream that meandered through the slopes and emptied into the marshes. He could not stop marveling at how much water surrounded him. Much of it was mucky and undrinkable, but it was water nonetheless.

The trio had been quiet for a few moments, the constant song of the birds overhead filling the grove, when Tiliah interrupted the morning's solitude.

"You know, if we leave now, we could—"

Rhohn and Okollu interrupted her as one.

"No."

She turned to stare at them, a frown upon her lips.

"Why not?"

"We wait until the fog lifts," replied Rhohn. "It is safer then."

Tiliah's frown deepened.

"I should just go now. By myself."

Again, Rhohn and Okollu spoke in unison.

"No."

"And why not?"

Rhohn shook his head and sighed.

"Must I truly explain why you going into Demetus alone is a bad idea?"

"Yes, Mud Man. Please enlighten me."

"Smooth-face is right," growled Okollu. "It is too dangerous for you to go alone."

Grateful for the support, Rhohn looked over to stare into the dark gloom of Okollu's hood. The mongrel's yellow irises flashed in the early morning light. Rhohn gave a quick nod of thanks.

Tiliah, however, was not to be dissuaded.

"Need I remind you both that I made it all the way to Gobas *alone*?"

Rhohn swiveled his head and glared at Tiliah.

"And need I remind you what happened to you *after* you left Gobas alone?"

Her lips tightened and with a short, irritated huff, she spun around and marched back into the grove, kicking up bunches of the dead brown needles as she went. Moving to the fallen log where their gear rested, she sat down, her back to them.

Rhohn shared a look of mute exasperation with Okollu before they both turned to the north again. Tiliah was upset, but that did not matter. Having her safe and angry here was better than happy and tromping through the countryside alone.

Mongrel and man scanned the hillsides together. An ever-so-slight breeze blew from the northwest and Okollu took in a few short breaths through his nose, examining each the way a hunting dog would when tracking.

"Anything?" asked Rhohn quietly.

The cloth of Okollu's hood rippled as he shook his head.

"Only the rank of the city."

Rhohn nodded.

"Good."

Okollu's sense of smell had proven exceedingly useful in their travels east, allowing them to adjust their route to avoid most settlements or towns long before they came to them.

"I still cannot believe we made it here," muttered Rhohn.

"Nurla inante de sate sunt gercer."

Rhohn glanced over.

"You're going to have to repeat that. In Argot, please."

The mongrel swiveled his head to look over and said, "It means 'Do not howl before the moons are in the sky.'" He stared back to the north. "We have a long way to go, smooth-face."

Rhohn nodded, admitting to the wisdom in the mongrel's words, and said, "That we do." He would not say he liked Okollu, but after the past few weeks, he respected him.

Days after Okollu had joined them in their journey east, the unlikely trio came across a still-populated village. Okollu hid in a shallow ravine some distance away while Rhohn and Tiliah entered the town. Following Tiliah's plan, they sold Nimar's bone-handle dagger and used the coin they received to purchase food, a waterskin, a traveling sack, and a simple hunting sling. Tiliah used some of the ducats—paired with a significant amount of flirtatious charm—to buy a large robe and hooded cloak off a young tailor for a third of what they were worth.

After leaving the village, they hurried back to the gorge, placing bets on whether Okollu would be awaiting them or not. Not only was the mongrel there, but he presented them with a tusked piglet he had killed. That night, they ate better than they had in weeks.

The newly purchased clothes were for Okollu, who, when he put them on, almost looked like a man. The gray cloak and brown robes were long, dragging on the ground as he walked, but they covered his fur and face. As long as he remained upright and walked on two limbs, no one would look twice unless standing within a few dozen paces. Still, to be safe, they traveled from evenings to early mornings, hoping to avoid encounters with strangers.

Early conversations between the three had been short and strained, but after a few days, an unusual, communal spirit emerged to overcome the instinctual acrimony borne by both races. Rhohn would never forgive Okollu for Silas' death, but he was able to see the mongrel's past actions for what they were: a desperate attempt to save his own kind. Were he in Okollu's place, he would have done the same.

Their journey had not been without problems. While they were able to avoid most of the larger settlements without detection, they inadvertently stumbled across a few family farmsteads when the wind was blowing in the wrong direction. Occasionally, Marshlanders would approach, drawn forth by rumors of the west. Rhohn and Tiliah extracted the group as quickly as possible from these unwanted situations while Okollu hovered far back, his hood drawn low over his face. All but one such encounter had ended without incident.

A week prior, a farmer had stopped the trio to talk one sun-soaked morning. The man's dog rushed Okollu's shrouded form immediately, barking nonstop. Rhohn and Tiliah held their breath as Okollu bent over, leaning near the dog's snapping jaws. The animal ceased its yapping, turned, and sprinted away into the marshes, its tail tucked between its legs. The farmer apologized profusely for the dog's behavior and excused himself. Hurrying from the farm, Rhohn asked Okollu what he had done. The mongrel gave a wolfish grin and said, "We came to an understanding."

Thinking on the moment now, Rhohn chuckled quietly.

"What is it?" asked Okollu, sounding alarmed. "What do you see?"

Peering over, Rhohn spotted the tip of Okollu's white muzzle poking free from his hood.

"It's nothing. I just thought of something amusing."

Okollu swiveled his head to look at Rhohn.

"That was laughter?"

"It was."

Okollu stared at him a moment longer before asking, "Are you sure?"

"Quite sure," answered Rhohn. "If it makes you feel any better, I still have trouble marking your sounds as well.

"Why would that make me feel better? I am not ill."

Shaking his head, Rhohn sighed and faced north again. Sometimes understanding one another was difficult.

"No matter."

"Perhaps you require more rest," suggested Okollu. "You are not making sense." With a toss of his muzzle, he added, "Go and sit. I will watch."

Rhohn looked over at Okollu, took a breath in preparation of explaining what he had meant, but stopped before uttering a word. It was not worth it. Pushing himself away from the tree, he began to walk away.

"Call us once the fog burns off."

He retreated into the grove, heading to where Tiliah sat on the log. He glanced around at the trees as he walked, wondering at the strange contrast of forest and marsh. Lower elevations were swarthy, dank, and dismal places, yet the hills were full of vibrant pine trees. A heavy, fetid stench filled the lower marshes while a crisp, clean scent drifted amongst the trees. Even the fallen tree-needles upon which he trod were a contradiction, pointy and sharp on the end, yet a bed of them provided a soft and restful place to sleep. The region was at odds with itself.

He stopped a few paces behind Tiliah and remained standing, a frown upon his lips. The young woman sat rigid, her back as straight as a new staff. Her anxiety was understandable. Today was the lone day she was going to spend looking for her family.

Keeping his voice quiet, he said, "It won't be much longer. We can leave soon."

Tiliah nodded, her wiry black hair bouncing, and spoke in quiet tone.

"I know."

Her soft response gave Rhohn pause. He had thought she was pouting, but perhaps that was not the case. Stepping over the log to stand before her, he dropped to a knee.

"What's wrong?"

Keeping her head tilted down, she asked, "We're not going to find them, are we?"

He pressed his lips together and sighed. Rhohn was confident they would not. One day would not be enough. Without the grace of Ketus, ten days might not be enough. He had seen the sea of humanity moving east. If only a third of them were in Demetus, there would still be too many souls to sort through. Yet, for some reason, he did not want to be that blunt with Tiliah. Not now. She would discover the truth soon enough.

Reaching out with his good hand, he patted her leg and said, "We will do our best to find them." He tried to sound hopeful, but did not think he succeeded. Optimism was as foreign to him as boots were to a horse.

Tiliah extended her arm, took his hand in hers, and squeezed tight, never saying a word.

After a few moments, he said, "We could stay for a few days if need—"

She interrupted him with a firm and decisive, "No." Lifting her head, she stared into his eyes. "*One* day, Mud Man. One day is all I get. Then we go east."

"But—"

"But nothing," said Tiliah. "I'm being selfish in taking today, I won't take more. My family is important, yes, but no more so than everyone—" She cut off as the sound of a stick snapping shot through the grove.

Spotting a flash of movement behind her, Rhohn stared back to the grove's edge and saw Okollu on all fours, facing them. With his robe and cloak still covering him, he appeared to be a man who had tripped and fallen to the ground.

Rhohn stood, drawing his sword from his scabbard as he did, and turned to face the direction Okollu was staring. Other than trees, fallen logs, and an infinite number of pine needles coating the ground, the grove was empty.

Keeping his voice calm and quiet, he whispered, "Get up."

Without a word, Tiliah scrambled to her feet. He reached out with his maimed hand, grabbed one of her wrists, and guided her back over the log, leaving their traveling gear where it was. With his gaze darting about the trees non-stop, they backpedaled the forty paces to where Okollu remained hunched and alert, a steady, subtle growl rumbling from deep within the mongrel's throat.

As they settled beside Okollu, Rhohn muttered, "What is it?"

Okollu's low growl cut off before he answered.

"I heard something."

"Me too," whispered Tiliah. "A stick or twig."

The mongrel's black lips drew back.

"No. That was me. I heard something before that."

Squeezing his sword's hilt tight, Rhohn asked, "What?"

"Voices," growled Okollu.

"I didn't hear anything," muttered Rhohn.

"You would not have," growled Okollu. "They were very quiet voices."

"How close were they?" whispered Tiliah.

"I do not know," said Okollu. "You two were making more noise than a wounded boar in a gravel pit. Hold still and stop asking questions! And do not breathe so loudly!"

After exchanging a quick, worried look, Rhohn and Tiliah followed Okollu's direction and remained silent.

The grove was deathly quiet. The birds in the trees above had gone silent. Rhohn strained to listen, taking in tiny breaths and holding them as long as he could before letting them out as noiselessly as possible.

With two quick sniffs, followed immediately by a fierce growl, Okollu suddenly sprang forward and sprinted across the clearing, running on all fours while, kicking up needles.

A muffled voice of alarm—a woman's, Rhohn thought—came from the middle of the still empty grove. Something was not right here. He squeezed the hilt of his sword tight, his palm moist against the leather.

Okollu was thirty paces away when he halted with an unnatural suddenness, stopping in mid-stride. The mongrel stood inexplicably perched on his back right paw while the rest of his limbs remained off in the ground, hanging as if from invisible twine. It reminded Rhohn of a doll he had seen used in a playman's show when he was a boy in Dashti.

Alarmed and alert, Rhohn stared about, searching for what or whom had caused Okollu's predicament while instinctively raising his sword. Tapping Tiliah's arm, he whispered, "Get behind me."

The young woman did not move.

"I said, get behind—"

"Put your sword down, Rhohn."

Without looking over at her, he whispered, "Are you mad?"

"Just do it."

"Why?"

Pointing to Okollu's arrested form, Tiliah said, "Because whoever is doing that will have no problem in stopping you."

A deep frown spread over Rhohn's lips as he realized Tiliah must be right.

"Wait…whoever? Who's doing that?"

"Isn't it obvious?" asked Tiliah, her gaze dancing around the empty grove. "There's a mage here somewhere."

A second voice, deeper than the first, came from elsewhere in the clearing. It sounded as if the owner was talking with a pile of rags covering his or her face.

Rhohn was trying to distinguish what was being said when Tiliah started to march past him. Reaching out with his bad hand, he grabbed her arm, and hissed, "What are you doing?"

Tiliah whipped her head around to glare at him, her eyes burning. "I did *not* come this far to be stopped now!" She tried to yank free, but he managed to hold tight with only two fingers and a thumb. Glaring at him, she demanded, "Let go!"

"No! We don't know what we're dealing with!"

Raising her eyebrows, Tiliah said, "We don't?" Using her free arm, she jabbed a finger in the air toward the suspended Okollu. "If the mage that did *that* to Okollu wanted us dead, we would already be introducing ourselves to Maeana. So as we are still here, alive and drawing breath, I am going to find out what the Nine Hells is going on." She tugged her arm again, harder this time. "Now, let me go, blast it!"

Rhohn was staring at her, considering whether or not to grant her request, when a raspy voice filled the grove, startling them both.

"That was rather well thought out."

As one, they turned back to the grove and found it was no longer empty.

Four horses—three with riders, one without—stood a dozen feet past where Okollu hung in the air. On Rhohn's far right, a stunning woman—an easterner judging from her blonde hair and pale skin—sat on a tan horse with smoky black legs. An oddly short brown-haired man sat atop a small chestnut beside her. A third figure and horse were a few feet behind the others, shrouded in a hooded cloak. A bony hand gripped a pair of reins that led to a fourth, rider-less horse.

At first, nobody said anything. The three strangers stared at them with as much interest as Rhohn had for them. After a few moments, the young woman lifted a hand and pointed to Rhohn.

"There. It's coming from him."

The diminutive man on the chestnut horse nodded and muttered, "I can feel it, too." He glanced at the woman. "Be prepared."

She nodded once as the little man began to dismount, grabbing his right leg with his hand and guiding it up and over the neck of his horse. He rolled on his stomach, grabbed a pair of black metal rings strapped to the saddle's side, and slid to the ground. Once situated, he reached up to retrieve a stick hanging from a brass hook, turned to the young woman, and handed her the reins to his horse.

"Hold tightly, please." He took a step away from her, stopped, and turned back. "To the weave *and* the horse."

The woman nodded.

"Understood."

A light, airy voice—barely audible—wafted from the figure in the back.

"Be careful. The kur-surus would very much like to be free."

Rhohn was surprised. They knew the true name of the mongrel race.

The short man stared up at the young woman.

"Kenders?"

The girl—Kenders, apparently—said, "Don't worry. I have him. He will not move."

Looking back to Okollu, the little man nodded.

"Good."

Using the stick as a cane, the small man hobbled forward, all the while staring at Okollu, still shrouded in his robe and cloak. He shook his head in quiet amazement as he neared the mongrel. "It hardly seems possible." He stopped, turned around, and peered back to the other two strangers. "Could they be this far east already?"

Rhohn cocked his head, curious at the comment. He glanced over to Tiliah and found her staring at the man, her eyes slightly rounded.

Whispering in quiet wonder, she said, "I think that's a tomble."

Rhohn looked back to the small man hobbling closer to Okollu and muttered, "You must be jesting." The description certainly fit, but a tomble's place was in playmen's tales.

The tomble stopped before Okollu, steadied himself, and then raised his walking stick to Okollu's hood. With a flick of his wrist, he flipped back the covering to reveal Okollu's teeth bared and frozen in a vicious sneer.

"Huh," mumbled the tomble. "It *is* a mongrel."

A deep growl abruptly rumbled forth from the Okollu statue, sending the tomble scurrying back a few quick steps. The strangers' horses nickered, prancing in place as the young woman and skinny, shrouded figure worked to calm them.

Tiliah called out, "He doesn't like to be called that!"

Everyone in the grove—save Okollu—turned to stare at her.

Keeping his voice low, Rhohn hissed, "Quiet!"

"*Don't* tell me what to do," said Tiliah. Digging her fingers from her free hand between his and her wrist, she pried herself free. "And don't *ever* grab me like that again."

Footsteps shuffling through the bed of needles drew their attention back to the strangers. The tomble was limping toward them now, taking a wide berth around Okollu.

Eyeing the little figure's bent leg, Rhohn wondered if he could manage to grab the tomble when he got near, before the others could react. A sword to the throat was a wondrous bargaining position. The infant plan had barely danced through his mind when the hilt of his sword grew impossibly hot, feeling as if the metal under the leather grip had just emerged from a forge.

With a sharp yelp, he released the blade and watched it drop to the ground. Curls of white smoke rose from where the sword lay on the dry tree-needles. Rhohn shook his hand involuntarily a few times before lifting it to stare at lined, red welts matching the pattern on the hilt.

He turned an accusing glare toward the tomble and found the little man standing still and staring at the Dust Man blade smoldering on the ground. After a moment, the tomble turned around and looked back to his companions.

"Was that necessary?"

The hooded figure in the back replied, "I believe he was considering attacking you."

As Rhohn stared at the shrouded man, wondering how he could possibly have deemed that, the blonde woman swiveled in her saddle to peer at the thin figure as well.

"I see," said the tomble. Looking back to Rhohn, he added, "Don't do that." He resumed his approach, keeping his gaze on Rhohn the entire time. Stopping ten paces away, he leaned on his cane and asked, "So, who are you?" He gestured over his shoulder at Okollu. "And why are you with him?"

Rhohn was still considering how to respond when Tiliah spoke.

"You tell us who you are, first."

The little man turned his attention to Tiliah, opened his mouth to respond, and froze. His eyes narrowed.

Tiliah demanded impatiently, "You're mages, yes?"

The tomble shut his mouth and took two more shuffling steps forward, peering closely at Tiliah the entire time.

"I'm sure the Constables are on their way right now," continued Tiliah. "If you were smart, you would get on your horses and ride away now!"

Rhohn admired her attempt at bluffing, yet sensed it would be a futile effort. The tomble seemed as rooted to the ground now as the pine trees around them.

Keeping his eyes focused on Tiliah's face, the tomble twisted slightly and called over his shoulder, "Kenders? Come here, please."

The blonde woman, presently staring at Okollu, pulled her attention from the mongrel.

"Why?"

The tomble shut his eyes and let out a long, weighty sigh.

"Please. I think you should come here."

"What about the horses?"

"Forget the horses," replied the tomble, opening his eyes to stare at Tiliah. "And just come here." Sighing, he half-turned to look at the pair. "Khin, can you hold the mon—ah, the kur-surus for the time being?"

"If you would like," answered the shrouded figure.

Kenders shrugged, glanced at Khin, and asked, "Ready?"

"I am."

Okollu took half a stride before freezing in position again.

"Good," muttered the tomble. "Now, come here, please. Quickly." He looked back to Rhohn and Tiliah, focusing all of his attention on her.

The young woman dismounted and began to walk toward them. The cut of her riding clothes was foreign, unlike anything the citizens of the Borderlands or Marshlands wore. Whoever these strange mages were, they were far from home.

"You are either a Dust Man or you stole that from one," said the tomble.

Rhohn looked back to find the little man staring at the sword lying in the needles.

"I am a—was a soldier before the Borderlands fell."

The tomble raised an eyebrow, asking, "You are a Dust Man yet you travel with him?" He nodded back in the direction of Okollu.

Rhohn frowned.

"It is a long story."

The crunching of needles drew his attention back to the young woman. Sunlight had crept into the grove, setting her unbound golden hair alight. Rhohn could not help but stare. He had never seen hair that color.

Kenders' head remained twisted, her gaze firmly locked on Okollu until she stopped beside the tomble. Glancing down to him, she said, "First oligurts and razorfiends, and now an honest—" She looked up, cutting off the moment her gaze rested on Tiliah. An astonished gasp slipped from her lips and her eyes went round.

Curious, Rhohn turned to stare at his companion. The outlanders' reactions appeared to confuse Tiliah as much as they confused him. A pair of deep furrows split her forehead.

A quiet, uncomfortable moment passed before the strange young woman spoke in a quiet whisper.

"Tiliah?"

As Rhohn turned to gape at the easterner, the young woman took a hesitant step closer. The shock on her face faded quickly, only to be replaced by an unusual combination of joy and sadness.

"Are you Tiliah Alsher?"

Rhohn's eyes narrowed as he glared at the woman.

"Who are you people?"

Kenders glanced at him briefly, her gaze lingering on his scarred face a moment, before staring back to Tiliah.

"Is your name Tiliah Alsher? Sister to Zecus? Daughter of Joshmuel?"

Tiliah remained silent for a long moment before finally asking in a soft, uneasy tone, "How do you know me?" All of her earlier defiance was gone.

The tomble's face fell. Closing his eyes, he dropped his head.

"Blast."

Kenders' shoulders slumped. A moment later, she stared to the north, peering out into the foggy morning.

"If I leave now, I might be able to catch him."

The tomble shook his head.

"Too dangerous. There will be Constables in Demetus."

"I don't much care if there are, Tobias," said Kenders. "I can handle them if need be."

Shaking his head vigorously, the tomble—Tobias, apparently—said, "I know you can 'handle them.' That's not the point. It is not a smart thing to do and you know it. Broedi might very well strangle me if I let you wander in there."

The girl set her jaw.

"Broedi isn't here."

Tobias tilted his head back to glare up at her.

"Your heart has made some poor decisions to this point. I suggest letting your head guide you for a while. What say you?"

The young woman pressed her lips together and looked north again, her eyes bright and alive. Rhohn half expected her to go marching down the hill despite the tomble's evident desire she remain. After a long moment, she glanced back down to the tomble and muttered, "They're going to waste an entire day wandering around, Tobias."

The tomble—Tobias, apparently—nodded.

"Most likely."

He turned his gaze back to Tiliah.

"Although the day itself will not be a waste."

Looking back to Tiliah as well, Kenders said, "But she can tell us where everyone else is."

The shrouded figure on the black horse spoke, his light and airy voice drifting through the grove like a forgotten breeze.

"I doubt she will be able to do that."

Kenders turned to stare back at Khin and asked, "How would you know?"

The figure moved slightly, his hood nodding in the direction of last night's camp by the log.

"They have been traveling. I would assume she has not been to Demetus for some time."

Kenders glanced at the gear resting beside the fallen log before looking back to Tiliah.

"Is that true?"

Tiliah remained stone-faced and quiet. Rhohn frowned. Seeing her silent and emotionless was like seeing the sun at night. It was unnatural.

When it was apparent Tiliah was not going to answer, Kenders glanced back to Tobias.

"So what do we do?"

"We wait until they return."

"That won't be until after sundown."

Tobias peered up at her and asked, "Are you *so* absent of patience that you cannot wait one day?"

Kenders' scowl deepened, yet she relented with a quiet, "Fine." She looked back to Tiliah. "But do we tell her—"

"No!" interrupted Tobias quickly, glancing askance at Tiliah. "It is not your place to share."

Kenders' eyes widened a fraction.

"You want me to sit here all day and *not* tell her?"

Finding her voice, Tiliah asked worriedly, "Tell me what?"

Kenders faced them and said, "Tiliah, my name—"

Tobias held up a hand and said, "Hold a moment! You forget why we came up this hill in the first place. Before anything else, we find out what it is he—" he jabbed a finger at Rhohn "—is carrying and then…" He shifted his gaze to Tiliah. "…then you can tell her *some* things if you wish. Agreed?"

Kenders reluctantly pulled her gaze from Tiliah to stare at the pouch Rhohn had tucked in his belt. She nodded once.

"Agreed."

"No!" protested Tiliah. "Not agreed!" The fierce determination with which Rhohn was familiar had returned. "Tell me who you are. And how in the Nine Hells you know my name!"

Pointing to Rhohn, Tobias said, "If you would first hand over—"

"No!" exclaimed Tiliah again, marching toward the pair. "What do you have to tell me?!"

Kenders stepped forward, reaching out with her hands as if she intended to comfort her.

"Tiliah, we are—"

"Stop that!" snapped Tiliah, glaring at the woman. "Stop using my name like you know me!"

Kenders pressed her lips together, a sorrow-laden smile touching the corners of her mouth.

"But I do know you. In a manner of speaking. I know about you, your mother, Jezra and Jerem."

"How is it you know my family?"

"Zecus," answered the woman quietly. "He's told me all about them."

Tiliah shook her head.

"Impossible. Zecus went west turns ago. And you are obviously an easterner."

Kenders nodded along with Tiliah's words, her eyes glistening with the early hints of tears.

Rhohn sighed, bracing himself. Today was not going to be a good day.

"All true," murmured Kenders softly. "Gods, there is so much we need to share with you."

Resting both hands on his walking stick, Tobias gently insisted, "This should wait, Kenders."

Tiliah demanded, "When did you see him last? Zecus?"

"This morning," answered Kenders. She nodded to the north. "He and Boah are in Demetus right now, looking for you."

Rhohn's eyes narrowed. He recognized the other man's name from Tiliah's tale about her father. Today was going to be a very bad day.

Disbelief coloring every word, Tiliah asked, "Zecus is with Boah? Boah Rasus?"

Kenders nodded once.

"Yes."

"What…how is that—" She cut off. "No matter how." Visibly buoyed by the information, she asked, "My father? Is he with them?"

Kenders' expression was a turbulent mixture of despair, sorrow, and what appeared to be guilt. A person carrying good tidings would not appear so tortured. She shook her head, muttering, "No." Her voice caught. "No, he's not."

Tiliah's brief moment of joy fled thrice as fast as it had come. With her gaze darting between Tobias and Kenders, she asked, "Why not? Where is he?"

Kenders opened and closed her mouth twice before keeping it shut. She reached up to wipe tears from both cheeks. Tobias stood motionless, a melancholy scowl fixed on his face.

Tiliah shouted, "Tell me what has happened! Now!"

Tobias sighed, stared up at a horrified Kenders, and muttered, "You should have waited." He turned his gaze to Rhohn and said, "Come with me, please."

With a firm shake of his head, Rhohn said, "No. I'm staying with her."

Tobias glowered at him and said, "I am entirely capable of moving you wherever I like without your permission, Dust Man. Yet, I asked nicely. Something I will not do again." His gaze shifted to the pouch hanging from Rhohn's belt. "We need to talk about whatever is in there." He eyed Tiliah and Kenders. "And they will require some privacy for a time."

Rhohn was about to protest further when Tiliah spoke.

"Go, Rhohn."

She turned to stare at him, her rich brown eyes pleading.

"Just go."

He had never seen her be anything but strong and resilient since meeting her. She acted years beyond her age. Yet now, standing before him was a young girl, raw and exposed. Rhohn remembered how he had felt all those years ago, waking up after the fire in Dashti and learning his mother was gone. He had only wanted two things: his mother back and to be left utterly, completely alone.

Nodding once, he whispered, "If you need me..."

Tiliah shook her head.

"I won't."

Rhohn reached out and gave her shoulder a gentle squeeze. After a moment, he released her arm, looked back to the tomble, and indicated his readiness to follow. Tobias gestured toward Okollu and hobbled away, leaning on his walking stick as he went. He looked over his shoulder and said, "Pick up your sword if you would like. But keep it sheathed."

Rhohn followed the tomble's instructions, retreating a few steps to retrieve his blade from the ground. The metal underneath the leather grip was still warm, but he could safely hold it without burning his hand now. He slid it back into his scabbard and looked at Tiliah again.

"Are you—"

"Go away, Rhohn."

He hesitated briefly before striding after the tomble. Looking across the clearing, he saw that the third man had dismounted and was now standing before Okollu. Tobias stopped next to the hooded figure and stared up at the mongrel's face. Rhohn glanced over his shoulder to find Kenders already speaking quietly to Tiliah.

As he neared the trio, Rhohn was able to get a good look at Okollu's face for the first time. While the mongrel's muzzle was a visage of permanent, vicious ferocity—his black lips drawn back in a violent sneer—his eyes did not match the fierce snarl. He appeared as confused by things as Rhohn. As Rhohn stopped beside Tobias, he leaned forward and tried to stare into Khin's hood, but the man kept his head tilted away.

Wearing a frown on his face, Tobias glanced up to Khin, and asked, "And you have no doubt?"

"You know I do not," replied the man slowly.

"Well, then," mumbled Tobias, turning to look back up to Okollu. "If you agree to remain calm, Khin will release you."

Unable to hide his surprise, Rhohn asked, "Truly?" He had not begun to consider how to explain away Okollu's presence this far into the Marshlands.

Khin's wispy voice wafted from his hood.

"He is not our enemy. Nor are we his."

Rhohn glanced at Okollu, wondering if he and Khin had spoken, yet the mongrel appeared to be only capable of short, growling breaths.

Tobias said, "Your confusion is understandable. And I promise we will explain. But first..." He pointed at the pouch Rhohn had tucked in his belt. "I must know what it is you carry in there."

Rhohn glanced down at the leather sack containing the black gem.

"In the pouch?"

Tobias nodded.

"Yes, please."

Rhohn locked eyes with Okollu, actually wishing he could confer with the mongrel about what to do or say about the stone.

With a certain intensity in his voice that was not there a moment ago, the robed man asked, "Do you know what you carry?"

Rhohn glared at the side of the man's head, still trying to peer inside the folds of the cloak.

"Why do you hide under your hood, stranger?"

"For the same reason your companion does," murmured Khin. He reached up with a bony hand, hooked a finger under the cloth of his hood, and slipped the wool back, revealing a pale white, bald scalp. "I tend to draw unwanted attention."

Rhohn gaped. A myth stood before him.

Khin's skin, so thin that it was nearly translucent, stretched taut over his skull, little blue veins like spider webs were everywhere. Two small slits rested where there should be a nose and a pair of incredibly sharp, bright blue eyes peered at Rhohn.

A few moments later, Rhohn managed to mumble, "You...you are an aicenai."

The skin around Khin's eyes stretched even tighter. If he had eyebrows, they would have raised a fraction.

"I know."

Rhohn went silent, staring with open awe. If tombles belonged in playman's fables, an aicenai's home was within the whispered myths of the ancients. As he gaped at Khin, he became aware of a soft, restrained sobbing behind him. Looking away, he stared back over his shoulder. Kenders and Tiliah were locked in tight embrace, Tiliah's face buried in the easterner's blonde hair. Both women were crying, but the louder sobs were undoubtedly coming from Tiliah.

Dropping his head, Rhohn turned back to the strangers.

"Her father is dead, isn't he?"

Tobias nodded once.

"Nearly a turn ago."

Rhohn closed his eyes and sighed. This was why he hated hope. The pain it brought when it did not come through was thrice as strong at the joy when it did.

Without opening his eyes, he asked, "What happened?"

"An accident," replied the tomble. "He fell from a spooked horse."

Rhohn squeezed his eyes tighter. The randomness of it made it worse somehow. Sighing, he opened his eyes and stared back to the girls.

"She does not deserve such sadness. She has come so far. Been through so much."

"It would seem you all have," said Khin.

Rhohn turned back and found the aicenai staring at Okollu.

Khin stepped closer to the mongrel and said, "I will release you now. Please remain still."

Shaking his head, Rhohn muttered, "How is it you are so trusting?"

Khin turned his icy, blue-eyed gaze to Rhohn and said, "Trust has nothing to do with it."

Without warning, Okollu collapsed to the ground. He instantly leapt up— pine needles stuck in his fur—and advanced on Khin, a low growl rumbling from his throat.

"Name yourselves before I rip your skinny throats from your necks."

Seeming wholly unconcerned by the mongrel's threat, the aicenai said, "I am called Khin Khastnargad and he—" he turned to the tomble "—is Tobias Donngord." He looked back to Rhohn, adding with purpose, "Tobias is one of the White Lions."

Rhohn stared down at the tomble, blinking in surprise. The tale of the heroes turned outlaws was one he had not heard told in over a decade.

"That's impossible. They are a myth."

Khin said quietly, "I stand before you, and you quibble about what is myth?"

His brow drawing together, Rhohn shook his head and said, "But their tale was from ages ago, back when—"

He stopped in midsentence, his eyes opening wide. The message he carried suddenly made sense. Two words slipped breathlessly from his lips.

"Miriel Syncent."

Shooting a sharp stare at Rhohn, Tobias asked, "*What* did you say?"

Rhohn finally realized why the name had sounded so familiar. His gaze locked onto Tobias.

"You truly are one of the great lions?"

Tobias nodded slowly, eyeing Rhohn cautiously.

"I am."

Taking a chance, Rhohn asked, "Do you know who the Shadow Manes are?"

Tobias' eyebrows nearly lifted to his hairline.

"Pardon?"

Okollu let a snort of wet air escape from his nose.

"What are you doing, smooth-face?"

Rhohn lifted a hand to hold off Okollu's question, stared at Tobias, and asked again, "Do you know who the Shadow Manes are?"

Khin answered instead of Tobias, saying, "We are a part of the organization."

Nodding, Rhohn said, "In that case, we have a message for you."

"A message?" asked Tobias. His eyes bored into Rhohn. "What sort of message?"

Rhohn cleared his throat and began reciting the passage.

"Indrida's prophecy is upon us. The Eternal Anarchist is a saeljul who goes by the name Tandyr. The Borderlands have fallen, the Marshlands are next. Vanson and Everett are in his palm for reasons I still do not understand. Time grows short. The Shadow Manes must rise."

As Tobias and Khin remained quiet for a long moment, Okollu turned to regard Rhohn. No longer tense and agitated, the mongrel now appeared confused.

After a few heartbeats, Tobias took a deep breath, stared at Rhohn and Okollu, and said, "We apparently have much to talk about, but first—" he pointed to the leather sack "—I need you to give me whatever is inside there. I am more interested than ever to learn what you are carrying."

Rhohn pulled the pouch free and quickly undid the drawstring, planning to dump the onyx gemstone into his hand. As he tipped the pouch upside down, Khin lifted a hand.

"Wait!"

The stone tumbled from the nobleman's pouch to land in Rhohn's palm.

The moment the glossy stone touched skin, an icy numbness swelled in Rhohn's chest. He felt hollow and cold, as if his insides had been scraped out and replaced with chilled water. Unsteady and dizzy, he swayed in place, forced to widen his stance so he did not topple over. Horses nickered and pawed at the ground. A pitiful whimper escaped from Okollu as he shied away from the stone like a stray village dog beaten once too often.

Tobias uttered a soft, stunned, "Bless the Gods."

Looking up, Rhohn found the tomble staring at the air surrounding them.

Behind Rhohn, Kenders called, "Tobias!" Her voice was full of alarm.

The tomble shouted, "Don't do anything!"

Khin stepped forward, ordering, "Put that away. Now." The urgency in his voice was unsettling.

Rhohn looked at the lump of obsidian and quickly complied, sliding the stone back into the golden-thread interior of the pouch and drawing the string. He frowned at the pouch, wondering what had just happened.

Khin asked, ""What did you sense?" Looking up, Rhohn found the aicenai staring at Tobias.

The tomble's gaze remained fixed on the nobleman's pouch as he shook his head slowly, mumbling, "Pure, complete Void. Thousands upon thousands of black Strands, all around us." He glanced up at the aicenai. "Hells, Khin. The blasted world went dark."

"I saw nothing," huffed Okollu.

"You would not unless you were a Void mage," said Tobias.

"A what?" growled the mongrel.

"Never mind," muttered the tomble, his gaze returning to the pouch.

Khin stared at Okollu and asked, "You sensed something, did you not?"

Okollu eyed the pouch warily and growled, "A wrongness. It is like what I feel—" He stopped and turned his gaze to Khin. "Tandyr has another one like this. Wrong inside, too. It is silver."

The thin skin on the aicenai's face flinched.

"You are sure?"

A low, guttural growl rumbled from Okollu's throat.

"There is no doubt, old one."

Khin's already thin lips grew thinner as they stretched into a frown. He dropped his chin to his chest to stare at the ground.

"That is disturbing to learn."

Tobias shifted his gaze upward to Khin, his expression one of open curiosity.

"Do you know what this is?"

The aicenai stared at the White Lion for a long moment. Without ever answering the question, he peered back to Okollu and Rhohn.

"Please tell me of your journeys. Do not pass over any moment."

As one, man and mongrel turned back to stare at Tiliah. She and the easterner were talking quietly again. After sharing a quick look with Okollu, Rhohn faced the aicenai and said, "We would prefer to wait for Tiliah."

"You will do no such thing," said Tobias. "Do you have any idea—"

"*We wait*, little man," growled Okollu. The mongrel's eyes were as hard as the edge in his voice.

The tomble stared between the pair. "Well. Aren't you two determined?" With a scowl and a sigh, he said, "Fine. We have the day, anyway." Glancing up to Khin, he said, "We should return back to our camp, though. If any Trackers attuned to Void are in Demetus, they will surely be headed here. That stone is a blasted beacon."

Khin nodded.

"Agreed."

Tobias eyed Rhohn and said, "Gather your things. As soon as they—" he nodded to Tiliah and Kenders "—are ready to go, we move, understand?"

Rhohn nodded silently. Okollu did, as well.

Appearing satisfied, the tomble stared up to the aicenai and said, "Khin? A word, if you please." His eyes narrowed. "*Now.*" He turned around and began hobbling back to their horses.

Rhohn watched the tomble shuffle away for a moment before looking back to the aicenai. Khin was still staring at the leather pouch.

"Never remove that again," said the aicenai. His blue eyes flicked up to peer straight into Rhohn. "*Never.*"

Rhohn had already come to a similar decision on his own. Nevertheless, he nodded, glanced down at the pouch, and pulled the strings to ensure they were tight.

The aicenai remained a moment longer before following Tobias towards the horses. Once they were far enough away, Okollu spoke, growling in a low voice.

"They are a strange pair."

Were it not for the somber mood dominating the tree grove for the moment, Rhohn might have smiled at the irony in Okollu's statement. Instead, he simply nodded and agreed, "Yes, they are."

Tomble and aicenai stopped by the horses and fell into a quiet conversation. Khin appeared to be doing most of the talking while Tobias seemed surprised—and worried—by what he was hearing.

Okollu's thick and wet voice interrupted Rhohn's careful study of the pair.

"Smooth-face?"

"Yes?"

"What is a white lion?"

"Remember what you told us of Rodam Upris?"

"Yes."

Rhohn nodded in Tobias' direction and said, "Well, it seems your legends are not the only ones that have come to life."

CHAPTER 41: CITY

16ᵗʰ of the Turn of Maeana, 4999

Sunlight sifted through the canopy overhead, covering the forest floor with a lattice of light. The pattern was ever shifting as a gentle breeze teased the upper-most boughs, the towering trees groaning and creaking as they swayed. The pines once dwarfed by the palm trees near the beach had steadily increased in both height and number as Nikalys and the expedition had moved inland. Now, the evergreens dominated the forest, the pungent fragrance of their sap filling the air. After weeks on the salty sea, Nikalys welcomed the fresh scent.

Since leaving the beach four days past, the group from the Sapphire had climbed a gradual upward slope through the forest. Talulot and Fingard led them, setting a steady pace and never seeming to tire. Nikalys and Broedi managed to keep up without issue, but the rest of their group labored through the constant uphill slog.

Nundle had the worst of it by far. Midway through day two of their journey, Nikalys offered to carry the tomble on his shoulders for a time. An unusually testy Nundle warned him that should he attempt to do so, he could expect a nice jolt of Charge in exchange. Nikalys—and everyone else—left him alone after that.

Talulot and Fingard wove a meandering path through the trunks, following an invisible path only they knew. Nikalys wondered how they knew where they were going. To him, every tree, bush, and hill looked the same as the last and the next.

He was walking past yet another one of the bushes now—a monstrous, twisted exaggeration of the fingerprick bushes like near home—when, a shorter, less lethal-looking bush on his left shuddered, its leaves rustling quietly. An instant later, a creature crashed forth from the undergrowth, dashing straight toward Nikalys.

Shift.

Standing ten paces back from where he was an instant before, Nikalys was at the ready, the shining, white-metal Blade of Horum drawn and ready to strike. An animal no bigger than an oversized barn cat stood before him, staring, seemingly shocked by his sudden movement. A dark brown fur covered the creature's face and front half of the body while long, soft quills draped over its back, their ends striped with thin white bands. Whiskers sagged from its wide, squished nose, twitching anxiously beneath a pair of black and beady eyes.

A gruff voice overflowing with amusement muttered, "Careful there. He looks ferocious."

Nikalys looked up to find Captain Scrag standing behind him, grinning ear-to-ear. Broedi stood next to the sailor, his gaze on the creature.

The captain nodded at the animal and said, "Don't get too close, it might nuzzle you to death."

Nikalys protested, "It startled me." His ears felt warm.

"Did it now?" mused the captain. "Well that was terribly rude." The man's sarcasm was thicker than the skin atop a cookpot of unstirred stew.

Broedi turned to eye the captain with a single, raised eyebrow.

"I seem to recall a time when you were likewise startled by a hive of briar-wasps. You moved as fast as Nikalys did. Faster, perhaps."

While the white-haired captain lost his grin, Nikalys gained one.

"Those blasted wasps hurt something fierce when they sting!"

"How would you know?" rumbled Broedi. "You ran so swiftly, they had no hope of catching you."

Captain Scrag's scowl deepened. Looking back to the animal still staring at them, he protested, "Briar-wasps are thrice a thousand times more dangerous than that lovesome creature."

"Are they?" replied Broedi, a sly smile on his lips.

The hillman approached Nikalys, stopped beside him, and dropped into a low crouch. Staring at the woodland creature, Broedi let out a low, lupine growl. The white-banded quills on the animal's back sprang to attention, jutting out in all directions. The creature let out a low hiss, spun around, and crashed off through the bushes, its quills catching on leaves and stems as it ran away.

Standing, Broedi stared back at Captain Scrag and said, "Quillhogs can hurt, too. Trust me, I once got a number of their needles stuck in my nose when I was sniffing where I should not have been." With a friendly wink at Nikalys, he turned and resumed his march forward, heading up the hill to where Talulot and Fingard had stopped to wait.

Captain Scrag stared at Nikalys for a moment, shrugged his shoulders, and said with a smile, "Good job staying alert." With that, the old man tromped off after Broedi, patting Nikalys on the back as he passed.

Nikalys watched the captain march away and shook his head. He had spent almost five weeks with the man and Nikalys had yet to figure him out.

"He's just having a bit of fun with you, son."

Nikalys glanced over his shoulder to find Sergeant Trell approaching, his steps heavy and slow. Nundle was at his side looking worse than a horse that had been ridden at full gallop for a week.

Eyeing the sergeant, Nikalys said, "I've yet to decide if he likes me or hates me."

Smiling, Sergeant Trell said, "I stopped trying to figure him out weeks ago." Soldier and tomble stopped beside Nikalys. Nundle was breathing heavily. The sergeant nodded up to the captain, adding, "He's the most unreadable soul I've ever met."

Nundle cocked an eyebrow and asked, "You have met Broedi, haven't you?"

Broedi rumbled, "I heard that, little one." His voice bounded through the forest.

Turning back around, Nikalys spotted the hillman tromping through the trees, his back to them.

Nundle muttered, "Him and his blasted hearing." The tomble's surly tone was so atypical that it was akin to hearing a duck oink.

Sheathing his blood father's sword, Nikalys studied Nundle. The tomble appeared he might collapse at any moment. Nundle glanced up and caught his gaze. The tomble's eyes narrowed in an instant.

"I know what you're thinking and stop it. I will not be lugged about like some playman's journeybag. When I made my way to the Academies, I walked up *and* down the mountains of Jularrn, through the deserts of Yut, for turns upon turns. I can manage a four-day hike through a—" He cut off when a loud gurgling sound rumbled from his midsection. His stern expression fled, replaced by one of embarrassment. Glancing between Nikalys and Sergeant Trell, he muttered, "What? I'm hungry."

Nikalys sympathized. Broedi had forbidden them to hunt here, which meant more of the same dried, salted boar they had eaten the last half of their voyage. The pears had run out two weeks ago. Nikalys had almost resorted to the fish stew.

With a huffy, "Move, please," Nundle pushed past Nikalys and resumed his march up the slope.

Sergeant Trell watched the tomble for a few moments before calling out, "How much of a head start shall I give you this time, Nundle?"

Without turning back, the tomble raised an arm in disgust and waved it.

"Go chew a boot!"

Looking to Sergeant Trell, Nikalys asked quietly, "Why upset him? He's already miserable."

"If he's angry at me, he won't dwell on how tired he is. And, it might make him move a little quicker."

Raising his eyebrows, Nikalys asked, "And you think that will work?"

Nodding toward Nundle, Sergeant Trell said, "See for yourself."

Nikalys stared up the slope and noticed the tomble's pace appeared a bit quicker than it had been.

"Huh. Look at that."

"Something every good leader must learn is how to get people to do what they must. By any means necessary. Call it an old soldier's wisdom."

Smiling, Nikalys turned back to the sergeant.

"You're not *that* old."

"I'm old enough," sighed the sergeant as he rubbed his eyes.

Sergeant Trell was putting on a brave face, but Nikalys could see the muddled exhaustion underneath the mask. Glancing past him, Nikalys watched the other Shadow Mane soldiers trudging up the hill and said, "It's been a long journey hasn't it?"

Letting his weariness slip into his voice, the sergeant agreed, "That it has."

Broedi's deep voice boomed through the forest, "Please do not stop now!"

Turning around, Nikalys saw Talulot and both hillmen waiting for them atop the rise. Captain Scrag and Nundle were still several dozen paces away from the trio.

Sergeant Trell nodded up the hill.

"Get going. I'll be right behind you."

Turning, Nikalys sprinted effortlessly up the hill, rushing to where Broedi and the others waited. Slowing his pace when he reached Nundle, he walked the few remaining steps with the tomble.

Nundle glanced up, frowned, and said, "Must you flaunt your—" He cut off and halted in place, his eyes staring straight ahead, his brow furrowed. "Where are the trees?"

Nikalys looked up to where the thorn, the hillmen, and now Captain Scrag stood and noticed that just beyond them, the forest appeared to stop.

"I don't know."

Nundle reacted first, finding a hidden reserve of energy and scurrying up the rest of the slope. Nikalys was but a step behind him, scrambling through bushes and around one last massive tree trunk before skidding to a stop. His mouth fell open.

They stood atop a cliff, nothing like the gentle grade they had been climbing for days. A great depression lay before him, as if the land was a hunk of bread dough and a thumb the size of Fernsford had pressed deep into it. The trees had not disappeared, as it had seemed, they were simply not as tall as the hole was deep. Great, sweeping wood and rope bridges stretched between the thick trunks, connecting the hundreds of circular, wooden buildings built amongst the branches of the pines.

Looking to his left, Nikalys' gaze followed the ridge and found that it fully encompassed the valley. Three-quarters of the way around—on the southernmost side of the ridge—a river rushed from the trees, launching itself into the chasm below. The waterfall drifted down to the valley floor where the river continued, curling through the tree city's floor before disappearing into a yawning, black cave.

Talulot whistled, "Welcome to Buhaylunsod."

For a few moments, no one said anything. They all simply stared.

Eventually, Nikalys said quietly, "Your words never did it justice, Broedi."

The hillman stepped perilously close to the edge of the cliff and stared down.

"Had I ever been *here*, I would have been clearer with my description. This buhanik city is the most striking I have seen."

Their small group went quiet again. The scene even held the typically vociferous captain in check. The old sailor was gaping with open wonderment, his white moustache twitching in the swirling wind. Nikalys heard the soldiers behind them call out to one another to hurry, apparently realizing that something awaited them atop the ridge.

Nundle asked, "Talulot, why did you not mention that we were getting close?"

Nikalys stared at the thorn. It was a good question.

Talulot tilted its head, its grassy hair swishing softly, and whistled, "Should I have done so?"

In a somewhat testy tone, Nundle said, "Well, it would have made this morning's hike slightly more bearable."

Talulot tilted its head in the opposite direction and paused a moment before saying, "Noteworthy." Its glassy black eyes locked onto Nundle. "If the distance of traveling remained constant, how does knowing if we are near our destination affect the energy necessary to reach it?"

A deep frown spread over Nundle's face. Looking back to the city, he muttered, "Never mind."

Sergeant Trell and the Shadow Mane soldiers ran up, reached the ridgeline, and joined the rest of the expedition in staring. One quiet exclamation of surprise after another drifted from the men.

Sergeant Trell let out a low whistle before murmuring, "Now, *that* is impressive." He shot a glance at Broedi and added, "And if you tell me there are places more striking than this, Broedi, I *will* call you a liar."

Nikalys smiled, the sergeant's comment reminding him of the moment when they had first beheld the towering Blackbark Forest. At the time, Broedi had insisted the trees of the Primal Provinces were even more stunning, as were the cities built amongst their branches. As was most often the case, he was right.

With a slight smile on his lips, Broedi rumbled, "Well, then. As I have no desire to be named a teller of tales, I suppose I will say nothing of the underground cities in the Mourlok caverns. How buildings are carved from the stone walls rather than built from it. How the lamps that line the streets glow green from light cast by a unique moss. How the tiny windows, filled with firelight, flicker like a thousand stars in the nighttime sky."

Leather armor creaked as twenty soldiers leaned forward to gaze at the hillman.

Cero asked, "Are you mocking us?"

Broedi shook his head.

"I do not mock."

"An underground city?" asked Talulot, its voice whistling with an agitated edge. "Where there is no sun?" The thorn began to sway side-to-side, its grassy hair fluttering so fast, it was almost vibrating. It was obviously upset and Nikalys believed he understood why.

During their journey inland, Talulot never took a bite of food nor drank a sip of water, the path it chose seemed wholly dependent on where the most sunlight shone on the forest floor, and whenever the group stopped at a creek or stream to refill their waterskins, Talulot stood in the water itself. It seemed thorns had more in common with plants than just their appearance.

Eyeing Talulot, Broedi said in a calm and gentle tone, "Do not worry. Such places are very far from here."

The thorn's frenzied swaying quickly faded. Turning toward Broedi, it said, "Your words give me comfort. Now, if you are ready to go, we—"

"Talulot?" interjected Fingard. "May I speak?"

Curious, Nikalys glanced at the hillman. Fingard might have said two dozen words since leaving the beach.

The thorn swiveled his torso and head to face the tattooed hillman.

"Say what you will."

With a scowl on his face, Fingard muttered, "I would be remiss in my duties if I do not say—for a final time—that we should not bring them into the city. The Mataan will not be pleased."

Talulot whistled, "Are you of the Mataan?"

The muscles in Fingard's jaw and neck rippled as he ground his teeth.

"No."

"Then you do not know if they will be pleased or not, do you?"

The hillman glared at the thorn, a quiet anger simmering in his eyes.

"No. I do not."

Nikalys' gaze danced between thorn and hillman. The relationship between the pair was puzzling. Talulot was the leader and Fingard the follower. That much was apparent. Whatever Talulot asked of Fingard, the hillman would do. As there was no sense of solidarity or friendship between the two, Nikalys reasoned that Fingard was more servant than companion. Yet, that conclusion did not feel correct, either.

Turning away from Fingard, Talulot shifted its black-eyed gaze to Nikalys and said, "I will now lead you into Buhaylunsod. Light-From-The-West, you and Shining-Cat-From-The-Sea shall trail me." Talulot refused to call either Nikalys or Broedi by their names and used the odd titles instead. "While we see the Mataan, your followers shall remain here with Fingard."

Nikalys' eyes narrowed. Such an arrangement was unexpected. A glance at Broedi revealed the White Lion was surprised, as well.

In an attempt to be tactful, Nikalys said, "We would prefer to remain together."

"So you mean to stay here, then?"

"No," answered Nikalys. "That is not what I meant."

The thorn's glassy eyes remained blank.

"What did you mean, then?"

Realizing he would need to be explicit, Nikalys said, "We would all like to travel into the city. Together."

Tilting its head to the side, Talulot said, "Fingard has been correct with his persistent reminders. The Mataan do not permit strangers within Buhaylunsod." It looked between Nikalys and Broedi. "You two are unique while your followers are not. The reaction to their presence would be severe." It peered about the assembled Shadow Manes, adding, "You look too much like the men of the Chosen to expect anything but hostilities."

Nikalys was about to protest further, when Broedi rumbled, "We accept your terms, Talulot."

Nikalys stared at the hillman, surprised at the quick agreement.

"We do?"

Nodding, Broedi said, "We do." He looked back to the thorn. "As long as Talulot assures the safety of our companions while we are in the city."

Talulot tilted its head to one side, turned to Fingard, and said, "Protect those that remain here. With your life if necessary."

Glaring at the thorn, Fingard replied, "Your request is beyond unusual." His tone was terse, his words clipped short.

"Obey, Fingard," whistled Talulot. "It is your place."

The thorn's word choice prompted Nikalys to share a quick glance with Nundle and Sergeant Trell. Both appeared to have also noticed the odd phrasing, as did Broedi. The White Lion was peering intently at the thorn, a troubled expression on his face.

Talulot stared at the tattooed hillman, seemingly waiting for a response. Fingard held the thorn's gaze for a moment before dropping his head. When the hillman had remained silent for a few moments, Talulot spoke again.

"Fingard? You must obey. I am buhanik. You are aliipin."

A moment had skipped past where Nikalys was wondering at the strange word when a low and angry growl rolled forth from Broedi. Nikalys, along with everyone atop the ridge, jumped at the feral snarl and swiveled to stare at the hillman. Broedi's normal stoicism was gone, chased away by intense rage.

Nikalys reached for his sword while scanning the ridge top, searching for an enemy. All he saw were trees, bushes, and rocks. Looking back to Broedi, Nikalys found the hillman glaring at Fingard. Most of his typical impassivity had returned, yet his eyes remained angry.

Nundle asked warily, "Broedi, is there something—"

Interrupting the tomble, Sergeant Trell stepped forward and asked quickly, "Nundle, would you come help us set up camp?"

Nundle looked up and stared at the sergeant.

"Pardon?"

"I would like your help on finding a suitable place for camp." His eyes flared. "Now, please.

Puzzled, Nundle said, "But what was—"

Captain Scrag stepped bent over, put a firm hand on Nundle's shoulder, and muttered, "Time to go, bucket-man."

Nundle eyed Broedi carefully, his brow furrowed. Nodding his head, he mumbled, "Of course. I'd be happy to help." He did not move, however.

Talulot had watched the entire exchange, its black, lidless eyes wide as always. It seemed oblivious to the burst of emotion.

"Things are satisfactory, then?"

Unsure of how to answer the question, Nikalys peered at Broedi, deferring to him.

"Are they?"

The White Lion was like a statue, still and quiet, his gaze locked on Fingard. The native hillman had dropped his stare and was peering at a nearby bush. He almost looked ashamed. Broedi pressed his lips together, turned his glare on Talulot, and rumbled, "Take us to Wren Aembyr." His eyes narrowed. "*Now*." The word reverberated over the ridge top.

"Then we shall begin our descent," whistled Talulot. "Follow me." The thorn turned and began to tread down a small path cut into the cliff's edge.

Keeping his voice low, Nikalys asked, "Is everything—" He cut his question short as Broedi moved past him, taking three long strides toward Fingard. Stopping before the tattooed giant, the White Lion stared eye to eye with Fingard and asked a short, clipped question.

"How long?"

Fingard met Broedi's gaze but remained silent. Broedi spoke again, his tone more insistent this time.

"*How long*, Fingard?!" demanded Broedi.

The tattooed hillman spoke in a quiet, almost sad voice.

"For Titaani Kotiv-aki? Over a century."

"A *century*?!"

Nodding, Fingard rumbled, "For the tribe, yes. For me, however, my entire life."

Broedi tilted his head back and stared into the sky. After a moment, he turned his back to Fingard and walked toward the path, his jaw clenched and his face rippling like a pond during a breezy day. Without looking over, he rumbled, "Let us go."

Nikalys looked to the others, hoping someone might have some insight as to what had just happened. To a man—and tomble—almost everyone seemed equally perplexed by Broedi's behavior.

The moment Broedi slipped from sight down the path, Sergeant Trell hurried to Nikalys' side, grabbed his arm, and whispered in his ear, "You need to keep an eye on him."

Pulling back to gawk at the sergeant, Nikalys whispered, "*Me* keep an eye on *him?*" The statement was absurd. "Do you know what that was about?"

"Not at all," muttered the sergeant. "Just watch him, please."

Stepping closer to them, Captain Scrag leaned in and whispered, "He's right. I've known Broedi for thirty years." His gaze shifted to the ridge's edge. "And that's as angry as I've ever seen him."

From below, Broedi's deep voice boomed, "Now, Nikalys!"

Glancing back to Sergeant Trell, Nikalys nodded.

"I'll do what I can."

The sergeant patted him on the back and Captain Scrag gave him an encouraging smile as he hurried to the path. He shot a questioning look at Fingard as he passed, but the tattooed hillman did not meet his gaze.

Nikalys started down the path, careful to watch his footing as he went. One wrong step and he was going to reach the bottom quicker than he would like.

Staring at the hillman's broad back, he muttered, "Keep an eye on him, huh?" A frown spread over his lips. "Wondrous. Just wondrous."

CHAPTER 42: NOBLES

Everett tilted his head back, resting it on his chair, and stared at the criss-crossed, oaken rafters overhead. The hunting hall's roof was tall and rose to a peak thirty-five feet above him. Banners hung from the ceiling, long and colorful, although the limited light provided by the floor-level torches lining the room blanched some of the hues.

With his hands folded in his lap, the Great Lakes' duke closed his eyes and let out a long and weary sigh. This gathering had started as an inconvenient necessity, quickly evolved to being irritating, and was now utterly tedious. At this point, Everett would have enjoyed having a glowing fire poker jammed into his eye over this.

"My Lord? Are you going to answer my question or not?"

Everett bit down so hard that he nearly cracked a tooth. The questions had started the moment he entered the room and had not stopped. He had put the nobles off as long as he could, but they were getting antsy. If he did not start providing answers, they might leave.

The soft and sultry tone of a woman's voice drifted from his right.

"Oh, Everett, just give the wolves something to gnaw on. It should not be much longer now."

After taking a moment to steady himself, Everett dropped his head, opened his eyes, and stared at the purveyor of the question. Halfway down the banquet table on Everett's left, Baron Yarrow was leaning forward, his elbows on the table-top. The noble was glaring at him from beneath thick, overgrown brown eyebrows.

Everett muttered, "You want an answer, do you?"

Baron Yarrow nodded firmly, his bushy eyebrows bouncing.

"Yes, my Lord. Yes, I do."

With a sigh, Everett straightened in his chair and leaned forward, matching the baron's posture. Reaching out to grip his wine goblet, he said, "Fine. I suppose you deserve one on this matter."

"Wondrous," said Baroness Monnard, her voice dripping with sarcasm. "And might you provide that answer today?" Her eyes, along with every one of the lords and ladies here, were firmly locked on Everett. "Or shall I leave a man behind to bring it to me when you are done?"

Everett shifted his gaze toward the woman. He did not like the baroness. Then again, he did not much like any of the nobles sitting at the table. But he definitely disliked her the most. Since he had taken the Sovereign's Chair from his father, every interaction with her involved her complaining about one thing or another.

Leveling a steady glare at the woman, Everett said, "Ask a few more impertinent questions such as that and see how long I keep you waiting."

The skin around the noblewoman's eyes and lips tightened noticeably.

"As the civil questions were not working, I thought you might better understand the impolite ones—" she hesitated briefly, her upper lip twitching "—my Lord."

The minute pause before his deserved honorific irritated Everett even further. He opened his mouth, ready to retort when the woman to his right spoke again, murmuring, "It's not worth it, Everett."

Looking over, he found Raela lounging comfortably in her chair, absentmindedly rolling a white grape between her thumb and finger, a bored expression draped over her perfect face. Yet again, Everett wondered how she could remain so calm. This experience was excruciating for him.

He shut his mouth. Raela was right again. Arguing now would be a waste of time and breath.

Every one of the Great Lakes' baronies was represented today, nine ruling lords and ladies sitting at the table in Deartfield's great hunting hall. Knight-General Ober of the Red Sentinels was the lone non-noble here other than Raela. The soldier was a compliant soul who had never questioned a single order, but Everett felt it best he attend today's meeting. It would make things easier.

Eyeing the assembled, Everett said, "Now, while I am under no compulsion to explain why I have withdrawn the Great Lakes from the Oaken Duchies, I will nonetheless share my reasons."

He paused, enjoying the fact that everyone was staring at him.

"When I ascended to the Sovereign's Chair, eight dukes and duchesses sent missives full of flowery platitudes and sweetly worded well-wishes. They were nice, yes, yet they rang hollow to me the moment Duke Vanson strode into my hall to offer congratulations in person. Since then, I have counted Duke Vanson a true friend. To me and to the Great Lakes. And if the First Council is going to make wild, unfounded accusations against my friend—*our* friend—we will stand with him."

"And what of our history, my Lord?" asked Baroness Heraa. "Our tradition? The Oaken Duchies have been united for centuries."

Everett shrugged.

"Things change."

"Things change?!" exclaimed Baron Yarrow. "Do you understand the difficulties your action has placed on our citizens? On *trade*?" He reached out, grabbed a parchment from the table, and held it up. "This is a letter from the Southern Porters saying they plan to charge Great Lakes' merchants double their previous rate to carry goods. *Double*, my Lord!"

"People will manage."

The baron gaped at him.

"How can you be so blasted cavalier about this?"

His eyes narrowing, Everett said, "If I were you, I would adjust my tone. I am the—"

"Hold a moment," interrupted Baron Hed, a portly man with a thick red moustache. "I am still stunned by your earlier statement. Am I understanding you correctly here? You are withdrawing from the Oaken Duchies because Duke Vanson was *nicer* to you than the other sovereigns? Are you mad?"

Everett turned to glare at the man.

"*What* did you say?"

"What? Must I speak louder?" asked the baron. "Perhaps you did not hear me over—" he jabbed a finger to indicate Raela "—her soft whisperings filling your ears!"

If Raela cared about the baron's harsh words, she did not show it. She yawned wide, slowly placed the grape in her open mouth, and chewed. After a moment, she began to stretch, reaching her arms high over her head, appearing as though she were awakening from a nap. Completely ignoring the others in the room, she glanced over at Everett.

"They are here."

Everett felt a wash of relief rush over him. Had this gone on much longer, he would have had a revolt on his hands. Turning to the baron sitting on his left—the man to whom this hall belonged—he asked, "Your servants will not cause any problems, will they?"

Baron Treswell, former representative to the First Council, shook his head and replied in a soft, meek voice.

"No, my Lord. Your instructions were clear."

Everett gave a quick nod.

"Good."

Turning back to the rest of the assembled nobles, Everett said, "If you will all remain patient for a few more moments, everything will be made—"

A thud and a rattle filled the stone hall as the arched oaken door at the room's far end opened. As one, everyone swiveled to stare. From the darkened hallway beyond the threshold, a man emerged and stepped into the room. The screech of ten chairs scraping on flagstone filled the hall as nine nobles and the Knight-General leapt to their feet.

Duke Vanson strolled into the hall, prompting polite, mumbled greetings from the barons and baronesses. He ignored them all, making eye contact only with Everett and Raela before striding along the left side of the table.

Behind the Borderlands' sovereign, a line of men and women marched into the torch-lit room, their dark skin and manner of dress marking them as Borderlanders. As they entered, the Great Lakes nobles went quiet.

Vanson stopped halfway up the table, turned to the Borderlanders, and pointed to both sides of the table.

"Half of you on one side, half on the other."

The Borderlanders quietly complied, separating as ordered and lining up behind those still standing at the table. The nobles twisted around, staring in open confusion at the strangers.

Still relaxing in her chair, Raela said, "You were supposed to be here by eveningmeal."

The duke glanced at Raela and shrugged.

"We have been busy. There is a war going on, in case you were not aware."

"And how goes that?" asked Raela.

"Little resistance as of yet," answered Vanson. "We're into the western Marshlands now. Should be at Demetus within the week."

An anxious murmuring arose from the Great Lakes' rulers as they shared worried glances with one another. Baroness Monnard spoke up almost immediately.

"Excuse me, Lord Vanson? What exactly do you mean by that?"

Vanson glanced at the baroness, a distasteful look spreading over his face. He looked as if he had gulped down a mouthful of sour milk. Turning his attention to Raela, he asked, "Why is she asking me that?"

"Because she wants an answer," replied Raela, a sly smile creeping over her pretty face. "The questions have been coming all afternoon." She eyed Everett, adding, "Everett nearly murdered a few, I think."

Frowning, Everett muttered, "It had crossed my mind."

His comment sent the nobles into a series of fitful gasps and stammering protests. Everett watched them with a dispassionate eye. He did not care what they thought or said now. It no longer mattered.

Vanson raised his voice over the clamor, asking, "Raela, can you please do something about this?"

A weary sigh slipped from Raela.

"If I must."

The Goddess of Deception stared into the air for several heartbeats before glancing around the table, her gaze briefly resting on every noble and the lone soldier. The only two people spared her magic were Everett and Baron Treswell. The baron of Deartfield had been enthralled by the Cabal years ago and did not need further controlling.

As the lords and ladies continued talking, shouting, and demanding answers, Raela stood, her thin, gauzy dress clinging to her diminutive form. In a clear, calm tone, she shouted, "Everyone will be quiet!"

The room went silent.

Everett stared around the quiet hall, shaking his head in wonder. Ruling would be so much easier if he could do that. He had quietly inquired about the duchy for a mage who could do what Raela could, but his search had been fruitless. Perhaps that was for the better, though. Had he managed to find one, the Constables in Redstone would have made life difficult. There was a reason this meeting was occurring on the sparsely populated shores of Lake Hawthorne. No Trackers were within two day's ride.

Raela looked back to Vanson, lifted her eyebrows, and asked, "Better?"

Vanson inclined his bald head.

"Much."

A new voice emanated from the dark hallway.

"I agree. I had no desire to talk over everyone."

A moment later, the owner of the voice stepped into the hunting hall. The nobles turned to stare, their eyes going wide in an instant. Everett rose from his chair, wondering if this was the first time that any of them had ever seen a saeljul.

Tandyr moved into the room with unusual grace, his elongated limbs sending ripples along his midnight black robes. His pale skin and whitish-blonde hair took on a soft, warm glow from the room's torches. Stopping a half-dozen paces into the hall, he peered around the table once, before his gaze settled on Everett.

"And this is all of them?"

Nodding once, Everett said, "Yes. Every barony of the Great Lakes is here. And the head of the Sentinels, as well."

Tandyr's gaze rested on the red and black uniform of the knight-general briefly before the God of Chaos said, "Good. Well done, Everett."

The duke of the Great Lakes bowed.

"You are gracious with your praise."

"Yes," said Tandyr, looking back to Everett. "I am. Especially after your previous mistakes."

Everett would have liked to point out that earlier failings were not actually his fault, but it was best to keep his mouth shut, so that is what he did.

One of the barons, a squat man from Bamson stepped away from his chair and began to hurry toward the door. He had taken but two steps when Raela called out, "Stop!"

The man's exodus was abruptly halted.

Raela said, "Now, Baron..." She trailed off and paused a moment in thought before giving a careless wave of her hand. "Bah, whatever your name is, return to your chair and stay there. And to be perfectly clear, everyone is to remain in place until I say so, is that understood?"

To a man and woman, those assembled nodded, the fear shining in their eyes as clear as Mu's orb in an empty, blue sky at midday. As the stray baron returned to his chair, Tandyr looked to a nearby Borderlander.

"Close the door and bar it."

The dark-skinned man hurried to the door and shut it, sending a solid thud echoing through the hall. After grabbing a thick board of oak leaning against the wall, he dropped it into two braces on either side of the entryway. The only other door into the room was already likewise barred.

Tandyr strode forward to stand opposite Everett at the table's end, unslung a small leather sack that was draped over his shoulder, and placed it on the tabletop. Reaching inside, he withdrew a black, wooden box and held it before him. For the first time in a long while, Everett felt the feathery finger of nervousness tickle his insides.

Eyeing the box warily, he asked, "Pardon me, Tandyr?"

The God of Chaos turned an icy gaze to him.

"What is it?"

"Must I be here for this?"

Earlier today, Raela had described in explicit detail as to what happened next. By no means did Everett have a weak stomach, but now that the moment was at hand, he was unsure he wanted to go through with it.

A slight frown spread over the saeljul's too-wide lips.

"Yes. For this to work, you need to be here."

"And there is no other—"

Tandyr's eyes flashed as hot as a Year's End bonfire, chasing the calm away.

"I *will* have your cooperation today, Everett! The next words from your lips will determine whether or not it will be voluntary!"

The flare-up of anger took Everett by surprise. Most of the time, Tandyr had been nothing but cordial in previous meetings.

As a quiet chuckle slipped forth from Vanson, Tandyr shifted his burning glare to the God.

"What is so humorous?!"

"Now *there* is the old you," said Vanson, a smug expression on his face. "I was wondering how long this might take."

Over the next few breaths, Everett watched Tandyr struggle to purge himself of his quick surge of fury. Soon, the previously calm and cool expression to which Everett was accustomed returned.

"Pardon my outburst. We have had a minor setback as of late."

"Minor?" grumbled Raela. "What is 'minor' about Vanson's foul-up?"

Tandyr's fury flared hot again. Standing tall, he spoke, his voice filling the hall. "Not here! Not now!" The words throbbed with a strange, terrifying power. A few of the nobles appeared ready to bolt for the door, despite Raela's explicit instructions not to. Glaring between Raela and Vanson, he growled, "Let us do what we are here for so I can get back to the Marshlands!"

With a careless shrug of her shoulders, Raela said, "I'm not stopping you, am I? Do what you must."

Struggling to regain his tranquility yet again, Tandyr set the black box he still held on the table, quickly gripped the lid, and flipped it open. The room grew brighter in an instant, as if the number of torches in the room tripled. All but the blackest of shadows died. With the light came a deep, soul-scraping fear clawing at Everett's insides. He winced, almost in physical pain from the sensation. Others around the table fared worse against the malicious surge as some of the nobles began to whimper. Knight-General Oper, mere paces from Tandyr, threw his hands up to cover his face and cowered like a frightened child.

Tandyr reached into the black lacquered box and withdrew a small, silver stone, no bigger than the tip of a man's thumb. Everett stared at the rock through squinted eyes as the last, stubborn shadows perished.

Without looking from the stone, Tandyr said, "Take your places."

Without hesitation, the dark-skinned men and women moved forward, one Borderlander to a baron or baroness. The Great Lakes' nobles swiveled their heads back and forth, staring wide-eyed between the advancing Borderlanders and the stone in Tandyr's hand.

Shooting a quick look at Vanson and Raela, Tandyr ordered, "If any of them run, hold them."

As both of the Gods nodded, Everett closed his eyes and waited, his heart thudding in his throat.

Moments later, the screaming started.

CHAPTER 43: ORACLE

The journey into Buhaylunsod was a quiet one. When Nikalys caught up to Broedi, he remained silent, all the while keeping a careful eye on the hillman. Speaking now seemed a sour idea.

The path into the valley was a gentle descent, a dirt trail cut into the black-rock cliff side encircling Buhaylunsod. Shrubs, vines, and a handful of small trees grew from cracks in the sheer wall.

The deeper they went into the crater, the cooler the air became, reminding Nikalys of his and Jak's journey into Fallsbottom all those turns back. When the path led them from the sun and into the ridge's shade, Nikalys shivered, pulled his cloak from his pack, and draped it over his shoulders.

Upon reaching the opposite side of the crater, he looked back to where they had started atop the cliff. He could make out a few figures standing at the path's start, but he could not tell who was who aside from Captain Scrag with his bright white hair and Nundle from the tomble's short stature. Nikalys kept looking back to the group until the tops of the evergreens hid the expedition from his view. After saying a silent prayer to Lamoth to keep them safe, Nikalys turned his full attention to the city and—with an involuntary gasp of surprise—muttered, "Bless the Gods."

The city of the thorn was stunning.

Each thick-trunked tree supported numerous levels of circular buildings topped by sloping, gently curved roofs. A network of interconnected wood-planked walkways hung between the different buildings, suspended by tough, woody vines. Hundreds of thorn moved through the city, shuffling along platforms and walkways alike. A handful of hillmen and hillwomen—all bald and tattooed—moved with them.

A glance to his right revealed Broedi staring hard into the city. Most of his typical stoicism had returned, yet fury still simmered just below the surface. Nikalys studied the throngs moving through the city, wondering what was fueling Broedi's intensity. After a moment, he realized that none of the hillmen moved independently. Each trailed a particular thorn. His step slowed a fraction as a disturbing possibility flashed through his head.

Glancing back to Broedi's stern profile, he muttered, "Broedi?"

Without meeting his eye, the hillman answered, "Yes?"

"Are they all sla—"

Wide eyes and a quick, warning shake of Broedi's head cut his question short. The White Lion stole a quick look at Talulot—the thorn did not seem to be paying attention—and as quietly as he could manage, Broedi whispered, "It would seem so." His gaze returned to the city. "Every one of them."

Nikalys shook his head, disgusted.

Slaves.

Shocked, Nikalys muttered, "But why?"

Broedi glanced back at him, snapping, "How am I to know?"

Unnerved by Broedi's flash of irritation, Nikalys kept his own tone neutral as he said, "I suppose you wouldn't, but—"

"Remain quiet," rumbled Broedi, cutting Nikalys off again. "No more questions. I must think." He stared back to the platforms with anger in his eyes.

Not wanting to press further, Nikalys simply nodded and followed.

Ahead of them, Nikalys spotted a long vine and wood bridge stretching from the cliff's path to one of the platforms wrapped around an evergreen's trunk. Three thorn were shuffling across the bridge and toward the trail, their black-eyed gazes fixed on Nikalys' approaching group. A single, bald hillman in brown robes followed them, gaping at the group.

Upon reaching the end of the bridge, the group from the city stopped in the pathway and waited, the thorn swaying side-to-side while glaring at Talulot. One stood at the point, apart from the other two, the trio effectively barring entrance to city. While their triangular faces looked nearly identical to Talulot's, Nikalys noticed slight variations in height, the color of their bark-skin, and different shades of green in their grassy hair. The hillman with them moved to stand a half-dozen paces behind them, his curious gaze reserved solely for Broedi. When Talulot was twenty paces away, the lead thorn of the trio held up a six-fingered, wooden hand and spoke.

"Sino ang madala sa aman?"

Talulot stopped in place, forcing Broedi and Nikalys to halt behind him. Nikalys glanced over at Broedi and raised an eyebrow, hoping the White Lion could translate. Broedi ignored him.

Talulot whistled, "In Argot, Puno."

The lead thorn—Nikalys assumed 'Puno' was its name—angled its head and asked, "Why must I use—" Puno halted suddenly and tilted its head, turning its glassy stare to Nikalys and Broedi. After peering at them both for a moment, it whistled, "They are unique." Its voice was slightly higher than Talulot's, as if wind was rustling through an ash grove rather than oak.

Talulot whistled, "See into them."

As Nikalys' eyebrows drew together, Puno lifted its branch of an arm and extended it outward. Closing its black eyes, the thorn began to sway in the same manner as Talulot had on the beach. A glance into the city revealed every thorn and hillmen in view staring at him and Broedi. Nikalys offered an awkward smile but none of Buhaylunsod's residents smiled back. Turning back to Puno, Nikalys did the only thing he could do: he waited.

After a time, the thorn stopped oscillating and opened its eyes. Staring at Nikalys, it whistled, "Noteworthy." The grassy hair on its head shivered in the cool, valley breeze. "Who are you?"

With a soft creak of wood, Talulot twisted head and torso around to stare at them, evidently expecting an answer. Nikalys glanced at Broedi, intending to defer to him. Upon seeing the muscles twitching in the hillman's thick neck, Nikalys decided it might be better if he answered.

Stepping forward, he announced, "My name is Nikalys Isaac."

Puno tilted its head and asked, "Where are you from?"

Following another fruitless glance at Broedi, Nikalys said, "I grew up in Yellow Mud."

The thorn stared at him in silence, its eyes blank.

After a moment Nikalys added, "It's a village. In the Great Lakes Duchy." When there was still no recognition in the thorn's expression, he added hopefully, "In the Oaken Duchies?"

A few heartbeats passed in complete silence before Puno turned its gaze to Talulot.

"How is it they are here?"

"A ship arrived where the sun enters the sea and they came ashore," whistled Talulot. "Believing they were of the Chosen, my aliipin—" Nikalys sensed Broedi tense "—and I defended our lands." Talulot turned to stare at Nikalys and Broedi. "It was only after the battle was halted that I was able to see inside them."

"They defeated you?" asked Puno. It sounded vaguely surprised.

Returning its gaze to Puno, Talulot swayed as it answered, "In a manner, yes."

The two thorn behind Puno shared a long stare while open surprise washed over the robed hillman's face. The tattoos atop his head twisted as his eyebrows raised high.

"Noteworthy," whistled Puno. Turning its gaze back to Nikalys, it tilted his head—again—and asked, "Why have you come here?"

Before Nikalys could answer, Talulot spoke, saying, "They wish to speak with Aembyr-The-Ageless."

"Do they?" asked Puno. "And are there more like them?"

"They have followers, yes, but they are not like these two," answered Talulot. "My aliipin is with them, outside of the center. I promised safety for them until we speak with the Mataan."

Puno began swaying again, its movements more vigorous than before.

"Strangers are not permitted this close to Buhaylunsod. Their lives must be ended."

Nikalys shot an anxious glance to Broedi.

Talulot matched Puno's oscillation with his own, whistling, "Fingard will defend them, Puno. I ordered him to do so." His voice carried a hint of the ear-piercing shriek from days past.

"Then he would die as well," replied Puno, the tone of his voice turning shriller as well.

"You are not permitted to do so," protested Talulot. "He is my aliipin."

A deep, throaty growl rumbled from Broedi, sounding more like hill lynx than hillman. Nikalys glanced up at the White Lion and frowned.

The thorn ignored the growl entirely while continuing their non-stop swaying. Puno spoke.

"Should your aliipin die, we would find another for you."

Broedi took a sudden step forward and barked, "If you harm Fingard, I will kill you all." The sharp words and tone caused the four thorn and the lone, enslaved hillman to turn and stare.

Placing a firm but gentle hand on Broedi's arm, Nikalys moved forward and placed himself between Broedi and the thorn. Keeping his own tone calm yet firm, Nikalys said, "What he means to say is that should you attack our companions, we will defend them."

"There are many more of us than you," whistled Puno. "You will lose."

"Will we?" asked Nikalys, his gaze locking on Puno. Drawing himself up to his full height, he kept his voice steady as he bluffed, "You have seen inside us. You know what we are capable of. Leave our companions alone and take us to Aembyr-The-Ageless now, else we will destroy your city and all within it." He placed his right hand on his sword hilt, readying to draw it both to emphasize his point and to be prepared should his ruse not work.

The thorn stopped swaying and, for a few moments, no one moved. Nikalys kept his eyes on Puno, waiting for a response, one way or the other. Behind him, a low growl continued to emanate from Broedi.

Fortunately, when Puno finally moved, it was to drop its gaze and turn toward the bridge.

"You will follow us."

Relief flooded through Nikalys as he let out a tiny sigh. Dropping his hand from his hilt, he said softly, "Lead on." As Broedi seemed incapable of being Broedi now, Nikalys would do his best to imitate the hillman.

As Puno began to shuffle over the bridge, the other two thorn followed. The tattooed hillman trailed the trio, his gaze repeatedly returning to Nikalys and Broedi as he stepped onto the wooden planks.

Nikalys was about to move to the bridge when Talulot whistled, "How?"

Turning to stare at the thorn, Nikalys said, "Pardon?"

"You said you would destroy our city. How?"

Nikalys peered at the thorn, his face blank. He had already forgotten his empty threat.

"Uh…"

Broedi stepped forward abruptly, glared at Talulot, and growled, "Be thankful we did not show you." Without another word, the White Lion strode past the thorn, marched to the edge of the bridge, and began to cross. Nikalys followed quickly before the thorn could ask any more questions.

Stepping onto the wooden planks, he moved across, trailing Broedi. The vines holding the bridge—already stretched tight—sagged under his added weight. He offered a quick prayer to Duryn, the God of Industry and Crafters, silently pleading that thorn were decent bridge builders. Halfway across, he emerged from the cool shade back into the sun's warm glow. Looking down, Nikalys caught a glimpse of the river snaking through the tree trunks and judged the forest floor some two hundred feet below them. He said another prayer.

Countless stares awaited them as they neared the platform. Each thorn stood motionless, tilting its head side-to-side, observing the strangers with unnerving silence. The sound of Nikalys' boots resounding off the wooden platforms were like thunderclaps on a cloudless day.

Stepping from the exposed bridge and onto the terrace, Nikalys gave up the fleeting warmth of Mu's orb for the shade of the great pine boughs. Rays of sunlight penetrated the canopy's thinner sections, spreading patches of light throughout the city. Red birds with yellow tipped wings darted about the trees, warbling as they flittered.

The pair of thorn that had accompanied Puno to the rocky trail melted into the crowd once across the bridge. Puno—followed by the still-silent, tattooed hillman—and Talulot continued forward, leading them through the city, moving from balcony to platform to terrace. Nikalys swiveled his head in all directions, gaping in wonder at the city's tranquil beauty. Vibrant paintings of leaves, flowers, and trees decorated every building they passed, giving color to a treescape dominated by dusty tans, rich browns, and faded greens. Nikalys wished Jak and Kenders could share this moment with him.

Peering through the triangular holes cut into some of the walls, Nikalys glimpsed simple interiors: tall tables laden with wooden bowls, unnamable trinkets, and square planks of thin wood covered with elegant markings. Assuming he was staring into the homes of the thorn, Nikalys wondered why the race needed structures in which to live. Certainly, it was not to sleep. In addition to never eating or drinking, Talulot had never seemed to sleep. Each evening when they had made camp, the thorn would remain upright, standing in the same position in the morning that it had assumed at night.

He wanted to ask Broedi the reason for the buildings, but one glance at the hillman told Nikalys that any explanation would have to wait. The White Lion was a tightly woven bundle of anger, keeping his gaze mostly straight ahead despite the wonder around him, his glances reserved only for the tattooed hillmen and hillwomen they passed.

Puno led them ever deeper into the city, weaving from one bridge to another. Left to his own devices, Nikalys would have been lost a long time past. The interconnected walkways were a maze. Finally, the thorn turned onto a thick-planked bridge that led to the largest building Nikalys had yet seen in Buhaylunsod.

The wooden structure was majestic, nestled among the boughs of multiple pines. Unlike every other building in the city, this edifice was absent walls. Its sloping roof hung over the platform, suspended by hundreds of braided-vine ropes. Triangular sections were cut into the ceiling to allow sunlight to shine through.

As they reached the end of the bridge and moved onto the platform, Nikalys was surprised to find the pine-board dais utterly bare save for nine figures, all of them standing but one who rested in a single chair to the right. Straight ahead, four thorn stood in a line, each one basking in a pool of sunlight. They were taller and thicker of limb than other thorn, less spindly than the rest of their race. The grassy hair atop their heads was tan and dried out, much as Nikalys imagined the Borderlands' prairies to be. Four robed and tattooed hillmen stood ten paces behind them, one to each thorn.

The ninth and final soul lounged in a wooden chair that was polished to a glossy sheen. The elongated limbs and facial features marked the individual as an ijul. The darker skin—the color of black tea and four thimblefuls of milk—named him a tijul, rather than the fairer saeljul. Glossy, rich brown hair hung to his shoulders, framing a sharp, angular face filled with the wide ijulan eyes and lips. He wore a simple leaf-green tunic that cut off at his thighs, revealing black breeches and leather, calf-high boots. His head was tilted against the chair back and his eyes closed. Were it not for the fact he was lazily running his fingers through his hair, Nikalys would have thought him asleep. An ornate, thick-handled spear rested against the chair's tall back.

Nikalys allowed himself a moment of quiet relief. As this was the only tijul he had seen in Buhaylunsod, he assumed he beheld Wren Aembyr, the Leafwalker and champion of Lamoth.

The scraping of Puno and Talulot's feet against the wooden floor, along with the heavy thuds of Nikalys and Broedi's boots prompted Wren to crack open his eyes and stare lazily in their direction. His hand froze in mid-stroke and he sat tall, his relaxed posture gone in an instant. His gaze tracked Broedi as they moved across the platform. Broedi held Wren's stare, glowering.

Stopping fifteen paces from the four thorn, Puno whistled, "Maring ang araw tumang sa iyo, Mataan."

Frowning, Nikalys turned to his left, hoping Broedi might translate the almost melodic words this time. Broedi ignored him again, his angry gaze remaining locked on Wren. He began to lift the strap to his leather satchel over his head.

Keeping his voice low, Nikalys muttered, "Uh...Broedi? What are—"

Dropping his bag to the platform, Broedi stepped in front of Nikalys and, in two long strides, was already in a full sprint toward Wren's chair, a wrathful growl rumbling from his throat.

For a moment, nobody moved. Nikalys, along with everyone else, watched as Broedi rushed towards Wren, his heavy frame shaking the wooden planks.

Wren moved next, shoving himself from his chair to stand, spin around, and grab his spear.

Broedi's growl grew into an enraged, bear-like roar as his body started to shift, changing as he thudded across the platform.

Wren hefted his spear, clearly readying to throw it at the charging hillman, and shouted, "Don't do this, Broedi!"

When the half-Broedi, half-animal figure did not comply, Wren pulled his arm back.

With his eyes going wide, Nikalys stared at the open platform behind Wren and reached inside of him, grasping at the gift he had inherited from his blood father.

Shift.

Now standing behind Wren, he reached out, wrenched the spear from the ijul's spindly fingers, and launched the weapon as hard as he could straight up, aiming for the sloped roof forty feet overhead. Wheeling around, he spotted Broedi in mid-step, moments from completing his transformation into the golden-coated Cartusian bear.

Shift.

On Broedi's left side now, he swept a foot across the shin of the part-hillman, part-bear, upsetting the White Lion's balance. As Broedi tumbled forward, Nikalys glanced up to find Wren reaching for a dagger's hilt protruding from a sheath on his belt.

Shift.

Reaching out with his right hand, Nikalys grabbed Wren's dagger before the ijul could. Pulling it free from the sheath, he flung it up after the spear that was still wobbling through the air. Using his left hand, he gripped Wren's tunic and yanked backwards, gently kicking in the back of the tijul's knees at the same time. As Wren began his topple backwards, Nikalys looked back to Broedi. The hillman—nearly all bear now—had been unable to halt his fall and was moments from crashing, face-first, into the platform.

Nikalys stared at an open space between the two White Lions—

Shift.

—and waited for the pair to complete their falls, releasing his grasp on Horum's gift.

Overhead, a loud thud, followed immediately by a softer clang, filled the platform as spear and dagger embedded themselves in the roof. Glancing up, Nikalys saw the spearhead fully entrenched in the wood and the dagger buried to the hilt. Broedi the bear struck the wood floor with heavy thump, shaking the terrace. Wren finished his collapse, as well, a surprised "oomph" slipping from the tijul.

Glaring at the sprawled-out Cartusian bear, Nikalys demanded, "What in the Nine Hells are you doing?!"

The bear lifted his head to stare at Nikalys, Broedi's deep brown eyes angry and intense, peering over a golden muzzle. Its gaze shifted back to Wren and the low growl rumbling from its throat resumed.

Nikalys glanced at Wren to find the tijul sitting up, openly gawking at him.

"As Broedi can't answer me at the moment, mind telling me what is going on here?"

Shifting his gaze to Broedi, Wren said, "I will if he promises not to maul me."

The bear glared at Wren and growled even louder, prompting Nikalys to step closer to the hillman and say, "Remember why we came here. He's not much use to us if he's dead."

Broedi turned his gaze back to Nikalys and, a moment or two later, the growl slowly, reluctantly faded away. Nikalys eyed the bear, waiting to see if he would make another move. Content he would not, Nikalys looked back to Wren.

The tijul's wide, elongated eyes were locked on him again, studying every detail. When Wren's gaze flicked to the scabbard at Nikalys' side and the golden hilt sticking from it, the already present confusion in his eyes deepened. After a moment, he looked back to Nikalys' face and muttered, "Aryn?"

Nikalys blinked, shook his head, and said, "No—"

"Ever the fool, Wren" interjected Broedi, his voice terse and sharp. A quick look back to Broedi revealed the White Lion was back to being a hillman and glaring at Wren. "How could that be Aryn? Unless time went back upon itself."

His eyes narrowing, Wren muttered, "Then how is—"

"He is Aryn's son. Aryn and Eliza's son."

Wren gaped at Broedi, his eyes going round.

"Their *son*?"

As Broedi stood from the platform's floor, Nikalys raised his left hand, palm out, and said, "Stay where you are, Broedi. I don't want to knock you down again."

Without taking his eyes from Wren, Broedi muttered, "With one Weave, I could hold you where you stand and do as I pleased."

Nikalys frowned. He had forgotten about that. Apparently, so had Broedi in his anger.

"Are you going to attack again, then?"

After a long pause, Broedi rumbled, "For the moment? No." The hillman's anger was still simmering, yet he seemed to have control over it now.

Turning to Wren, Nikalys asked, "What about you? Will you behave?"

Wren continued to stare at Nikalys in silence, evidently stunned by Broedi's revelation. After a moment, he managed a short nod.

"If Broedi will, so will I."

Peering over to where the thorn stood, staring at them, Nikalys wondered what they thought of this display. From outward appearances, they seemed wholly unconcerned by Broedi's outburst and Wren's response. Feeling an apology was in order—and with Broedi in no condition to give it—Nikalys strode toward the center of the wooden platform.

As he moved past Broedi, he muttered, "Try to remain calm."

The hillman nodded once, his heated gaze still fixed on Wren.

Moving to stand before Puno and what he assumed were the Mataan, Nikalys glanced from one triangular face to another. The four enslaved hillmen—two of which were actually hillwomen now that he looked closely—behind the thorn gazed at him with inquisitive eyes.

Clearing his throat, he repeated the greeting Talulot had offered him on the beach and said, "May the sun shine upon you."

His words had no effect. The four Mataan did not move or speak.

He glanced over at Broedi, hoping for some guidance, but the hillman was still staring down Wren. Sighing, he peered back to the Mataan offered a small smile, and said, "Ah...good days ahead?"

As one, the four thorn raised their left arms, extended their six-fingered hands, and closed their eyes. Just as Talulot had done at the beach and Puno again on the cliff's path, they swayed side to side as mature oaks do in a steady breeze. The platform went as quiet as the Yellow Mud olive groves on a Seventhday afternoon. Taking the opportunity to check on Wren and Broedi, Nikalys found the White Lions no longer glaring at one another. Rather, both were watching the Mataan, Wren with a bewildered expression on his face.

Nikalys turned back to the Mataan and waited. Eventually, the rightmost thorn opened its eyes and dropped its arm. After several moments, it whistled, "You shine bright. Brighter than friend Aembyr, even." Tilting its head slightly, it added, "Noteworthy."

Nikalys glanced back to Wren. The tijul was staring at him again, his eyes cautious and curious.

"I am called Alumon," whistled the thorn. "Who are you?"

Looking back, Nikalys said, "My name is Nikalys Isaac."

"That is your name. I want to know who you are."

A tiny furrow appeared in Nikalys' brow as he considered his answer. After a moment, he took a deep breath and said, "I am the son of Thaddeus and Marie Isaac of Yellow Mud. And I am the son of Aryn Atticus, the champion of Horum, and Eliza Kap, the champion of Gaena. I am farmer, brother, friend, soldier, and child of the White Lions."

With a soft creak of wood, Alumon swiveled its head and torso to stare at the other Mataan. The three opened their eyes, dropped their arms, and stared back at Alumon. For several moments, the four Mataan looked between one another, the crackling of their rough, bark-skin the only sound they made. Eventually, all four turned their gaze back to Nikalys. With a tilt of its head, Alumon spoke.

"Tell us what you would have us do."

A moment skipped past as Nikalys stared at the thorn, his expression blank.

"Pardon?"

"We await your guidance," whistled Alumon. "Share with us our fate."

Perplexed, Nikalys turned to Broedi. Every bit of the hillman's anger had evaporated and had been replaced by muted bafflement. Wren, too, appeared bewildered. Concluding that neither of the White Lions would offer any clarification, Nikalys looked back to Alumon.

"I do not understand. What do you mean, you await my guidance?"

Alumon whistled, "We—and all buhanik—shall do whatever you ask of us."

After a long pause, Nikalys asked the obvious.

"Why?"

"Because we promised to do so."

Nikalys cocked a single eyebrow.

"You…promised?"

Alumon tilted his head in the opposite direction.

"We did."

Nikalys glanced over to find Broedi—a frown resting upon his lips—striding to where Nikalys stood. Stopping on his right, the hillman stared at Alumon and rumbled, "Who did you promise?"

Alumon shifted its glass black eyes to Broedi.

"The savior of the buhanik: the Enlightened Oracle."

Nikalys stared in stunned silence. The title was reserved for the Goddess Indrida.

"Indrida?" rumbled Broedi, his voice a mixture of surprise and doubt. "You promised *Indrida* to do what—" he glanced at Nikalys "—he says?"

"In a sense, yes," whistled Alumon.

"What does that mean?" asked Broedi.

"While we four did not promise, Mataan of Buhaylunsod before us did."

Finding his voice, Nikalys asked, "Before you? How long before you?"

Alumon turned head and torso to eye Wren.

"Seven generations past."

"Seven?" repeated Wren, his eyes narrowing sharply. "That was before I arrived." The tijul began to walk toward the center of the platform, making nary a sound as he did. Nikalys supposed the name Leafwalker was well earned.

"Yes," whistled Alumon. "It was. She visited a cycle before you walked into the city."

"Hold a moment," rumbled Broedi. "That would mean Indrida foretold our arrival over a century ago."

"Yes it would," said the thorn.

"But that is impossible."

"Why is it?" whistled Alumon.

Broedi did not respond. He simply stared at the thorn, a skeptical frown resting upon his lips. After only a breath, Alumon tilted its head and spoke.

"You are the 'champion of Thonda,' yes?"

Broedi was quiet for a long moment before nodding slowly.

"I am."

"She said that you would doubt us," said Alumon, his hair rustling in the wind.

"Did she?" rumbled the hillman. "You will forgive me, but your claim is a grand one."

Alumon adjusted its head again, paused a moment, and then whistled, "The four will hold the names of three."

The odd turn of phrase had a strange effect on the White Lion, washing away all visible disbelief in an instant. The hillman's new expression was blank and impossible to read. Evidently, the words meant something to him.

"Broedi?" muttered Nikalys.

The giant was quiet another moment while gnawing on his lower lip. Letting a small sigh slip from his lips, he rumbled softly, "They speak true. Indrida was here."

Nikalys asked, "Those words. What do they mean, Broedi? What aren't—?"

Wren interrupted him, stepping forward while demanding, "Explain yourself, Alumon!" The tijul was clearly perturbed. "Why is this the first I've heard of a *Goddess* visiting you? And what sort of promise did you make?"

"Her visit was not for you to know," whistled Alumon. "She instructed the Mataan not to share anything with you. The secret was to remain so until 'one who shines brighter than the sun arrives and claims heritage of Horum and Gaena.'" Turning to look at Nikalys, the thorn added, "In exchange for the aid she lent us, we promised to do as you say. Share with us our fate, Light-From-The-West."

"Hold a moment," interjected Wren. "Before Aryn's son shares anything with anyone, I have more questions. What sort of aid did she lend?"

Returning its black-eyed gaze to Wren, Alumon whistled, "She warned us."

"Of what?" demanded Wren.

"That the Chosen were planning a great invasion."

Wren's brow furrowed.

"I warned you of that."

"So the stories go," whistled Alumon. "But you were not the first, friend Aembyr. The Enlightened Oracle appeared on this platform, shining in her resplendence, and told the Mataan that the Chosen were coming, revealing exactly when and where the enemy would venture into our wilds. Our defenses were lax as peace had reigned our lands for six generations. Buhanik believed the Chosen had grown weary of warmongering. Without Indrida's foresight and your aid, we would have been quickly overwhelmed." Eyeing Wren, Alumon added, "She told us of your arrival. And how you would bring the aliipin to aid us."

At the mention of the hillmen slaves, Broedi began to growl.

Wren took a step back from the giant and, in a defiant tone, said, "Before you turn bear on me again, know that a mutual *agreement* exists between the Titaani Kotiv-aki and the buhanik. An arrangement entered into with open eyes!"

"What sort of 'arrangement?'" asked Nikalys.

The tijul glared at him.

"One that does not concern you, son of Aryn. Go 'shine bright' elsewhere and let your elders sort this out."

Broedi growled, "Is it so hard for you to be pleasant!?"

"Spare me, Broedi!" spat Wren. "What? Because he's Aryn and Eliza's son, I'm supposed to be kind?"

Broedi advanced on Wren, rumbling, "If you cannot manage a kind word, I will rip one from your throat!"

"Enough!" bellowed Nikalys. The authority that echoed in his voice surprised him. Both White Lions stopped and turned to stare. Glaring at the pair, Nikalys asked, "What is wrong with you?"

"With me?" huffed Wren. "Nothing." He glanced at Broedi. "If you recall, the overgrown animal attacked me."

Broedi glared at Wren for a moment, fuming, before he rumbled, "I would like it if you answered his question."

"What question was that?"

Before Broedi could respond, Nikalys did.

"What sort of 'arrangement' did you make with the hillmen?"

A frown slipped across the tijul's lips. Looking back to Broedi, he said, "You should thank me for what I did."

Broedi crossed his arms and squeezed his biceps with opposite hands. Nikalys guessed it was taking every bit of self-restraint Broedi had not to leap at Wren and pummel him.

"Thank you?" growled Broedi. "Why should I thank you for enslaving aki-mahet?"

His eyes flashing hot, Wren exclaimed, "Because without me, your kind here would be dead, Broedi! Dead! The bones of your precious aki-mahet would be sticking up from the dirt or used in some Chosen's candelabra! I did what was needed to save them!"

Nikalys reached inside himself for Horum's gift, waiting for Broedi to react violently. Yet the hillman managed to hold still, glaring hard at the tijul. After a number of excruciatingly tense moments, he spoke.

"Explain," rumbled Broedi. "*Now.*"

Nikalys released his hold on the gift inside him as Wren moved to stand on his left, positioning himself so that Nikalys stood between the White Lion pair.

Peering around Nikalys at Broedi, Wren said, "After the First Council's over-reaction to Carinius, Jart and I left the duchies and came to the Provinces. He stayed for less than a year before moving on." Cocking a long eyebrow at Broedi, he added, "You know how he can be."

Glancing at Broedi, Nikalys said, "Jart?"

"Jarthidil Mellark," rumbled Broedi. "Greya's champion."

"'The Nomad'?" asked Nikalys.

"The same," replied Broedi. "It was a name well earned. Jarthidil would… wander. One day he was here…" He trailed off and shrugged his shoulders.

Wren finished the thought, saying, "The next, he was gone. A true pain to keep track of."

"He wandered?" asked Nikalys, confused. "Why?"

"Before the Assembly," rumbled Broedi. "Jarthidil named his occupation a 'traveler of roads.'"

"What does that mean?" asked Nikalys.

"He never explained," said Wren. "And trust me, I asked. Hundreds of times at least."

Nodding in agreement, Broedi said, "I, as well. Jarthidil's past was his own. And whatever wandering tendencies he had before the Assembly were exacerbated once Greya touched him. He went where the winds of fate blew. Should you ever ask where he was going—or why—he would say 'I go where I go because I am go-ing there.'"

"And that is exactly what he did," said Wren. "He would go somewhere on a whim. Without notice. While I found the Provinces a perfectly nice place to live, Jart grew restless with each passing moment. One morning, when I awoke in our camp, Jart was gone. No note. No 'farewell Wren.' Nothing. He was just gone." He shook his head and sighed. "Alone now, I kept to myself for a time, ventur-ing into cities should I crave a bit of company. Although, as there are *no* ijuli here, my presence was often cause for excitement. At first, they called me The-Radiant-Long-Lived, but I did not care for that. Therefore, I became 'Aembyr-The-Ageless.'

Smiling, he ran his fingers through his luxurious brown hair. "I am something of a legend here."

"What is there to be proud of?" muttered Broedi. "Living a long time?"

With a bored sigh, Wren asked, "Would you like me to continue my tale? Or shall I pause a moment or two and give you leave to insult me?"

Broedi pressed his lips together tightly.

"Speak."

With a wide, ingratiating smile, Wren said, "Thank you, Broedi. Ever so much." Running his fingers through his hair, he muttered, "Now...where was I? Ah, yes! So, I was south of here when rumors reached me about the Chosen advancing north. Being the wondrous, kind soul I am, I decided to offer my assistance to the Provinces. Buhaylunsod was the nearest city of any size, so, I came here and showed how one buhanik could become a singular force against the self-righteous Chosen. Yet as few buhanik can touch the Strands, I enlisted the aid of the nearby aki-mahet. *I*, Broedi, *I* am the reason this—" he gestured at the city "—is still here! Were it not for me, the Chosen would have marched north, unchecked! So, as I said earlier—you should thank me for what I did!"

Nikalys noticed the White Lion used the word 'I' quite often.

Broedi remained quiet, staring at Wren. When he spoke, he was surprisingly calm. "Suppose I accept your tale as truth," rumbled the hillman. His tone indicated he did not. "What is the complete nature of this agreement between buhanik and Titaani Kotiv-aki?"

Wren's brazenness faltered as he dropped his glare and muttered, "Well..."

Alumon interjected, whistling, "After showing us of what we were capable with the right aid, friend Aembyr approached the aliipin and negotiated terms such that any who could work the flows of the 'Strands' became ours. In exchange, we guard the remainder of their tribe against the Chosen."

Nikalys stared at the tijul in disbelief.

"You *bargained* them into slavery?"

"Slavery is a rather harsh word," said Wren with a slight grimace. "I like to think that I gave a handful of Titaani Kotiv-aki the choice to protect their entire tribe."

"Accept servitude or perish is *not* a choice!" exclaimed Nikalys.

"I considered reasoning with them," said Wren. "But that would have taken too long. So I told them they could accept my terms or die."

Nikalys could not believe what he was hearing. Glaring at Wren, he demanded, "How in the Nine Hells are you a White Lion?"

Rolling his eyes, Wren muttered, "Oh, please. There is *no* doubt you are Aryn's son." Turning his full attention to Broedi, he asked, "How is what I did *any* different than the things we did to defeat Norasim? 'There are no sweet choices in war.' Sound familiar, Broedi?"

Tensing, the hillman rumbled, "This is different, Wren."

"How?!"

"These are of my blood!"

"So?! Presented with a sour situation, I made the sweetest choice available. I had hillmen who could touch the Strands and buhanik that were perfectly suited for the Weave I had developed. The Chosen were on the horizon, ready to trounce us all. Because of what *I* did, when they attacked, we had hundreds of massive buhanik marching through the forests, shrieking like the banshees of Enstra. Battles ended before they began."

Broedi glared at Wren, shaking his head.

"Justify it all you want, Wren. It was still wrong."

"Should I have let everyone here die, then? Just to satisfy someone's sense of idealistic morality?"

"Broedi's right," said Nikalys. "You stole their ability to choose their destiny."

Wren glared at him and spat, "Yes, I did!" His eyes were bright and unrepentant. "Freedom for security and life. A *more* than worthy exchange from where I stand."

Huffing, Nikalys shook his head, disgusted by the tijul's defense.

Wren scoffed, "Well, then. I see that besides looks, abilities, and that blasted white sword, Aryn has passed along his self-righteousness."

Nikalys glared at Wren, starting to wish he had not interrupted Broedi's attack.

"Broedi? Are you sure we need him?"

"No," rumbled the hillman. A moment later, he added begrudgingly, "However, I would rather have him with us than not."

"Perhaps the prophecy is wrong?"

"Indrida's words are rarely wrong," said Broedi. "Muddled and confused, yes, but rarely wrong."

"Prophecy?" repeated Wren, glancing between them both. "What prophecy?"

Neither Nikalys nor Broedi answered the tijul. Nikalys did not know Broedi's reason for remaining silent, but he simply did not want to give Wren the satisfaction of a response. As he stood there, staring at the tijul and mulling over the recent revelation of Indrida's visit to the buhanik, a tiny frown spread over his face.

Not only were the Gods meddling again, now they were doing it from across centuries. He was tiring of being manipulated. If his entire life were already laid out for him, he wondered what the point was of living it. Nevertheless, it was clear what needed to be done.

Indrida had known he was going to be here, today, at this very moment. And she had arranged for him to direct the buhanik as he saw fit. With war against the horizon, he could only assume what the Goddess wanted him to do.

Glancing at Alumon, he asked, "How many buhanik and aliipin pairs are here? Ones who can do what Talulot and Fingard did at the beach?"

Without hesitation, the thorn answered, "There are but ten in Buhaylunsod. More are patrolling our lands. And still more in other cities."

Broedi turned a hard eye on him and growled softly, "Do not consider it, *uori*!"

Ignoring Broedi entirely, he kept his gaze locked on Alumon.

"And, to be clear, you *must* do as I say?"

The thorn whistled, "We will uphold our promise."

As he eyed the thorn and the slaves standing atop the platform, a tiny, confident smile pushed the frown off his lips. He wondered if Indrida foresaw what he was about to do. Standing tall, he spoke in a clear, loud voice.

"The buhanik agreement with the Titaani Kotiv-aki is over. The aliipin are free and can leave at once."

The announcement had a different effect on everyone gathered on the platform. While Alumon remained still and silent, the other thorn on the platform began to sway side-to-side, Puno and Talulot included. The four bald hillmen behind the Mataan gaped at Nikalys. Even Broedi seemed taken aback, staring at him with slightly widened eyes. Wren was the first to break the silence.

"But the Chosen will—"

Nikalys held up a hand toward the tijul, cutting him off, glared at him and said, "I *don't* want your opinion on the matter. It is my decision, and nothing—*nothing*—you or anyone else can say will change it."

Wren pressed his lips together and—surprisingly—remained quiet. Once Nikalys was content the tijul would stay silent, he turned his gaze to the tall hillman behind Alumon.

"You. What is your name?"

The hillman's eyes widened and he shot a questioning look at Alumon. The thorn swiveled around slowly, its bark-like skin creaking. Upon meeting the hillman's gaze, the thorn whistled, "You no longer need my permission to speak. Your actions are your own. Light-From-The-West has chosen our fate."

Nikalys breathed a small sigh of relief, grateful and a little surprised the thorn had accepted his order.

The hillmen and hillwomen stared at one another in quiet shock. The one Nikalys had addressed said with wonder, "Truly?"

Alumon whistled, "The Mataan are bound by our promise to Indrida. Without her aid, we would not be here." It turned to stare back at Nikalys. "We accept his guidance."

The tattooed hillman shifted his wide-eyed gaze to Nikalys. All of the Titan Tribe members atop the platform did. They stared in silence, their expressions a combination of stunned disbelief and restrained joy. A few moments passed, filled only with the sound of the wind drifting through the treetops and the soft warbling of songbirds.

Breaking the quiet, Nikalys asked in a soft voice, "Your name?"

The hillman muttered, "Evaldersla Reigarja." Then, raising his voice, he repeated with confidence, "My name is Evaldersla Reigarja."

Knowing he would never get the name correct, Nikalys asked, "May I call you Evald?"

The hillman nodded once.

"Many already do."

"Good," said Nikalys. "Evald, you are free to go."

"Truly?"

Nodding, Nikalys said, "Truly. You can go where you like." He paused briefly before adding, "However, before you do, I have a story I would like to share with you." He glanced at a sullen Wren. "One you must all hear."

Broedi said softly, "Nikalys?"

Looking over, Nikalys found Broedi regarding him carefully. The hillman's expression was a stoic one, but caution drifted through his eyes.

"What do you intend to share?"

"Everything."

With a slight frown on his lips, Broedi rumbled, "Is that wise?"

Holding the hillman's stare as he spoke, Nikalys said, "You once told me that knowledge is a weapon, did you not?"

Broedi paused, the skin around his eyes tightening a bit, before answering, "That I did."

"While you like secrets, Broedi, I do not. And while you choose to keep your weapon sheathed, I am choosing to wield it. Now. If you wish to stop me, you had best use the Strands to do so."

The hillman regarded him carefully for a moment before the familiar slight smile spread over his lips. He nodded once and, with a hint of pride in his voice, rumbled, "As you desire."

Looking back to the Mataan and freed hillmen, Nikalys took a deep breath and began to share his story, starting from the beginning: the blazingly hot Summer day when Jhaell Myrr destroyed Yellow Mud. He withheld nothing.

After a time, Broedi joined in and helped tell the tale, sharing his role, the saga of the White Lions, the Demonic War, and the outlawing of magic in the Oaken Duchies. He told of Indrida's prophecy, his recent journey to the Seat of Nelnora—finding Tobias in the process—and of the Sudashian army led by the God of Chaos. Occasionally, Nikalys glanced at Wren and was pleased to see a modicum of concern on the tijul's face.

When their storytelling was nearly complete, Nikalys said, "So, that is why we are here." He turned his gaze to Wren alone. "According to Nelnora, we were supposed to find you."

Wren was quiet a moment before asking, "But why, exactly?"

"Because our task is not yet complete," rumbled Broedi. "The Demonic War was the beginning, not the end."

The tijul shifted his gaze to Broedi, but said nothing. He gnawed on his lip, remaining motionless and perfectly quiet. Nikalys liked him much better this way.

Alumon whistled, "Why have you told us this?"

Rather than answer the thorn, Nikalys turned to face Talulot and said, "On the beach, you said you sensed that the wind 'carries a grim shadow.'"

"It does," whistled Talulot. "A dark one."

Turning back to Alumon and the other Mataan, Nikalys asked, "And do you sense that as well?"

With its grassy hair swishing in the wind, Alumon whistled, "It grows darker by the cycle."

"The Gods of Chaos, Strife, Pain, and Deception march together," said Nikalys. "They have destroyed hundreds of villages, toppled at least one great city, and murdered countless souls. *They* are your grim shadow, Alumon. And if we do not stop them, it will eventually reach your shores."

Tilting its head, Alumon asked, "What do you require of us?"

"I *require* nothing," answered Nikalys. "I will, however, *ask* for your aid. The buhanik—" he glanced at Evald "—and the Titaani Kotiv-aki."

"There is no need to ask," whistled Alumon. "We will do as you see fit. Our promise—"

"No!" interjected Nikalys with a firm shake of his head. "Consider that promise fulfilled. From this point forward, *you* choose your fate. If you aid us, it will be your choice to do so." He shot a hard glare at Wren. "Every soul deserves free will."

With a roll of his eyes, Wren shook his head and huffed, "You are choosing the rocky path for morality's sake? Oh, you are Aryn's son indeed."

Nikalys ignored the tijul's barb. No good could come from engaging him at the moment.

Evald rumbled, "What sort of aid do you require?"

Turning back to the Mataan and hillmen, Nikalys said, "We have no idea how many oligurts, razorfiends, mongrels, or demon-men the Cabal have in their ranks. Thousands, at least. Tens of thousands, perhaps. I pray no more than that. Yet even if we could manage to match them one-for-one with soldiers, they will no doubt have ten, fifty, a hundred times more mages than we will. And if that is the case, we *will* lose."

He paused and looked around the platform, ensuring that he made eye contact with everyone.

"I *ask* you all to join us in our fight. I want you to come to the duchies and go to war."

CHAPTER 44: REUNION

17ᵗʰ of the Turn of Maeana, 4999

After spending the past turn in the open air of sea and forest, the stone-block walls surrounding Broedi felt oppressive and heavy, as though he stood in a Yutian tomb. He stared into the hearth, doing his best to maintain a sense of outward calm, but the heat radiating from his gaze outshone the roaring fire's blaze.

From one of the chairs before Lady Vivienne's desk, Nikalys muttered, "I can't believe she would do this." The young man's hands were balled into fists. "Kenders is impulsive, yes. But to just leave? Now?!"

Broedi shook his head and let out a steadying sigh.

"If it is not one thing, it is another."

Duchess Aleece reached over from her chair, patted Nikalys' arm gently, and said. "I am sure she is fine. She has proven that she can handle herself, yes?"

"Only by Ketus' providence is that the case," rumbled Broedi. "Whenever skill and wisdom are absent with her, luck has filled the holes. That cannot continue forever."

Shooting him a sharp look, the duchess said, "Nevertheless, she will be fine. Do you not agree, Broedi?"

Nikalys turned his gaze to Broedi's face, waiting for a response. After a moment, Broedi gave one, rumbling, "Yes. I do." Hope colored his words more than honest belief.

From her chair behind the desk, Lady Vivienne said, "It is not as if she is alone. Both Khin and Tobias are with her."

Nikalys did not react, his gaze now locked on a torch along the office's back wall.

Standing beside the baroness' desk, Broedi peered down at the noblewoman. "And this was Khin's idea?"

Lady Vivienne stared up at him and shook her head.

"Not at all. It was her idea. But the aicenai viewed it as a teaching opportunity."

Wren—leaning against the wall beside the hearth and sipping a goblet of wine—began choking, drawing the gaze of those in the room. Clearing his throat, he looked up and repeated, "Aicenai?" He shot a questioning stare at Broedi. "Surely she is jesting." A few drops of red wine had dripped on Wren's neatly trimmed tunic.

Broedi shook his head.

"Surely, she is not."

The tijul's eyes narrowed.

"You never mentioned anything about an aicenai."

Glaring at Wren, Broedi rumbled, "I did my best squeezing two hundred years of history into one afternoon in the treetops. Pardon me for leaving a few things out."

Noticing the splatters of wine, Wren frowned and set the cup of wine on the hearth's mantle. Inspecting the droplets, he said, "You might have wanted to include that an *aicenai* was a part of your little group here. That novelty alone would have brought me here."

Broedi reached up and rubbed his eyes, almost wishing Wren had decided to stay in Buhaylunsod.

Following the discussions with the Mataan, the remainder of the Sapphire's expedition was escorted into the tree city. There were quick introductions and immediate farewells as Broedi had Nundle open a port to the beach for the party—Wren included—to go through. Captain Scrag and the ship's crew were returning to Storm Island via the Sapphire while they took a much quicker route.

On Broedi's request, Nundle opened a second port directly to Lady Vivienne's office. Broedi stepped through first and stumbled upon a meeting between a pair of very surprised noblewomen. The others quickly followed him with the twenty Shadow Mane soldiers leaving immediately, all the while bowing and gawking at the duchess. Her presence seemed to rattle even the normally composed Sergeant Trell.

After the room had mostly emptied, Broedi introduced Wren and relayed what had happened in the Primal Provinces. Lady Vivienne and the duchess in return revealed that half of the allotted Southern Arms along with the first units of the Long Coast's Shore Guard were amassing in Demetus. Reports from Duke Rholeb stated that Sudashian scouts had been spotted a week west of the capital.

When the conversation turned to the dysfunctional politics of the First Council, Nikalys asked if he could leave to see his siblings. After a quick glance at Lady Vivienne, Duchess Aleece shared that Kenders had left Storm Island only days after the Sapphire had set sail. She had been gone for four weeks.

Broedi was still rubbing his eyes when Nikalys asked, "Well, can I at least go see Jak?"

The long, silent pause that followed Nikalys' question caused Broedi to drop his hand. The two noblewomen were staring at one another again, frowns on their faces.

On Nikalys' left, Nundle—his ever-present, wide-brimmed hat in his lap—asked, "Oh, Gods. Did he go somewhere, too?"

Lady Vivienne shook her head once. "No. He's here." Looking to Nikalys, she added, "Although, you should know that about a week ago—"

The double doors to the room opened suddenly, interrupting the baroness and ushering in a rush of cold air from the hall. Jak wobbled through the entryway, helped along by Chandrid. Broedi stared at the dressings wrapped around the boy's head and sighed. He could not let any of them out of his sight.

Nikalys leapt up from his chair and exclaimed, "Gods! What happened to you?" He rushed over and wrapped an arm around his brother to help support him. "Are you alright?"

"I'm fine," answered Jak, a weak smile on his face. "And please don't shout."

Chandrid looked around the room and said, "I am sorry for the intrusion. He insisted in coming the moment he heard you had returned." Turning an eye to Jak as Nikalys helped him to the open chair, she added pointedly, "He is a stubborn patient."

Jak collapsed in the chair with a great sigh, peered back, and waved a dismissive hand in the air.

"I am fine, Chandrid. You worry too much."

Nikalys hovered beside him, staring at the thick bandages.

Eyeing the injured young man, Broedi asked, "And what sort of trouble did you get yourself into?"

Jak swiveled around in his chair, looked at Broedi a moment before shifting his gaze to Lady Vivienne.

"You didn't tell them?"

Lady Vivienne shook her head.

"I was about to when you burst in."

"Oh well, then. I suppose—wait." Jak peered around the room while asking, "Is everyone back and safe? Sergeant Trell came—" He cut off as he faced Duchess Aleece in the chair beside him. "Pardon me, my Lady. I did not see you there. I would stand and give you a proper bow but there's an excellent chance I might fall over."

The duchess smiled, inclined her head, and said, "Please stay seated, then. No need to risk an accident. It is good to see you up and about, though."

"Thank you, my Lady," replied Jak, resuming his perusal of the room. "It is good to be up—" He halted again upon spotting Wren standing by the hearth. The tijul was running his fingers through his long, brown hair—an interminably annoying habit of his. "Hey! You found him. I was wondering—"

"Jak!" interjected Nikalys. "Will you tell me what happened to you?"

After taking one last look at Wren, Jak turned around, stared up at his brother, and said, "Part of the castle fell on me."

Leaning forward, Nundle peered around Nikalys and asked, "I'm sorry. Could you repeat that?"

Lady Vivienne said, "We had an incident in the mages' hall. There were two large explosions, a terrible fire, and, ultimately, a section of the northeastern wall collapsed." She stared at Broedi and said with an edge in her voice. "Had you chosen to arrive in the courtyard as is protocol, you would have certainly seen it."

Ignoring her tone, Broedi asked, "Was anyone hurt?"

Jak lifted a hand.

"Me."

"Other than you."

Jak nodded once, winced, and stopped immediately.

"Gamin had a nice gash, too. Ask Chandrid, though. She's been taking care of us all."

As Broedi turned to the hillwoman, she was already answering his unasked question.

"Twelve injured. Jak and Gamin were the most serious by far."

"Then everyone survived?"

The skin around Chandrid's eyes crinkled as her gaze shifted to the oak desk. Broedi stared back to the baroness and found Lady Vivienne shaking her head.

"Unfortunately, no. A young mage perished. Marick."

A cold shiver ran up Broedi's spine. Marick had been assigned to work with Helene.

Turning her gaze to Jak, the baroness added, "And had this brave fool not rushed in and saved her, the young girl from the farm would have died as well."

"Helene?" asked Nikalys in alarm. "Is she hurt?"

Jak stared up at his brother and said soothingly, "Hey, she's fine, Nik. Don't worry." His gaze shifted to Broedi and a shadow passed over his face. "In fact, there wasn't a scratch on her."

Broedi frowned slightly. There was more to this story.

Looking back to his brother an instant later, Jak gave a lopsided grin and said, "So, feel free to save all your sympathy for me. I'm the one who got knocked in the head."

"What about Sabine?" asked Nikalys. "Was she with her? She wasn't hurt, was she?" There was more than simple concern in his tone.

"No," replied Jak. "She's fine. She was…uh…well, she was with me when the explosions happened."

A moment skipped past before Nikalys asked in an overly neutral tone, "She was with you?"

Jak paused ever so briefly before saying, "We stumbled across one another in the hall. We were talking when…boom."

Nikalys eyed Jak evenly as an uncomfortable silence drew out between the pair. One of the burning logs in the hearth cracked, piercing the quiet. Wren was staring between the siblings, an amused smirk on his face. Broedi gave a disappointed sigh and shook his head. There was no time for whatever this was. He stared back down to Lady Vivienne.

"What caused the accident?"

"We still do not know. Gamin recalls a sudden rush of Fire Strands before the first explosion. Nobody else seems to remember much at all." She turned her gaze to Jak. "Including him. His memories remain somewhat 'hazy.'"

Jak's face went still. Pointing to his bandage, he said, "I have a good excuse if you recall."

A tiny frown teased the corners of the baroness' mouth.

"Yes, you do."

Their tones alone told Broedi that Jak was keeping something from Lady Vivienne and the noblewoman knew it. Trusting Jak had a good reason why, Broedi noted the need to corner the young man later. Turning to Chandrid, he asked, "How serious was his injury?"

The hillwoman looked to Jak and hesitated before saying, "Well, as he is on his way to recovery, I suppose it is safe to share this now: he nearly died."

As Jak spun around in his chair, his face turning the color of days-old ash, Nikalys repeated Chandrid's words, his concern pure.

"He nearly died?"

Chandrid nodded, her gaze still on Jak.

"Truthfully, I thought he had. When I reached him, he was not breathing. Nor could I feel a heartbeat. I had nearly moved on to help another when Sabine said she saw your foot move."

Jak looked as if he might get ill. Nikalys did not look much better.

Chandrid folded her hands together, saying, "I was surprised, to say the least. Nevertheless, I stopped his bleeding and have been watching him closely ever since." She turned her gaze to Broedi. "I, however, am not as skilled as you with the Strands of Life. Perhaps you might speed his recovery?"

"Of course," rumbled Broedi. Touching his right palm to his chest, he nodded his head and said, "Kitan teita palvelua, lakari."

Chandrid repeated the gesture and replied, "Se on minun velosuuteni ja ilo." Turning to the noblewomen, she bowed and said, "My Ladies, if you will excuse me, I have others I must attend to."

"Of course," said Duchess Aleece. "Thank you for all you have done."

Chandrid nodded, turned, and strode from the warm offices, closing the doors behind her and cutting off the cold draft.

The door was still rattling in its frame when Nundle said, "I'm not sure whose time was more eventful while we were gone—yours or ours. Sure, we had storms at sea and giant tree-monsters attacking us, but you lost one of the Progeny and then nearly let their brother get killed."

His words carried no malice or criticism, but that did not stop Lady Vivienne from glaring at the tomble. Nundle slouched in his chair, trying to make himself even smaller than he already was.

"Perhaps I should stop talking now."

Duchess Aleece smothered a small grin at the exchange. A quick glance around the room revealed a variety of other reactions. Jak still appeared consumed with the revelation about his brush with visiting Maeana's hall, Wren seemed mostly concerned with the wine stain on his tunic, and Nikalys stood taut and anxious, his empty gaze having returned to the torch on the back wall. Add twenty-five years to the boy's face, and it could be Aryn standing there. Broedi frowned. He knew what was coming next.

A moment later, Nikalys looked straight at Broedi and spoke with quiet determination.

"I want to go after Kenders."

Broedi drew in a slow, deep breath, let it back out again, and said with resignation, "Of course you do."

"Four weeks, Broedi! She's been gone four weeks! Jak almost died here at the enclave. Imagine what could happen to her! Now, I've thought through this. Nundle could take me to the Southlands and—"

"Stop, Nik," interrupted Jak. Looking up to his brother, he said, "You're not going anywhere."

"Why not?"

"Because there's no need to. She's not hurt," said Jak, reaching into his shirt and pulling free the silver teardrop necklace. "As far as I can tell, she's perfectly fine."

Wren glanced at Broedi and raised a single, inquisitive eyebrow. Apparently, the tijul recognized Eliza's pendant. Broedi's return nod was quick and slight, confirming the silent question.

Jak continued, saying, "Her emotions are a bit jumbled, but physically, she's fine." Lifting the necklace over his head, he handed it to Nikalys. "See for yourself."

Without a moment's hesitation, Nikalys grasped the necklace and closed his eyes. A heartbeat later, Broedi spotted faint, silver Strands of Soul dancing away from the necklace and straight through the wall opposite the hearth. He noticed Wren staring at them as well, a deep frown on his face as he sipped his wine again.

Nikalys turned his head side-to-side, searching for the ringing only he could hear, and ended up facing the same direction the Strands of Soul led. A moment later, the Strands faded and Nikalys opened his eyes.

"Jak's right. She's fine."

"What a fabulous artifice," muttered the duchess, staring with open awe at the necklace. "How does it work?"

As Nikalys held it up, the pendant swayed back and forth.

"Simple. You hold it and picture me or Kenders in your mind."

"That is all that is required?" asked the duchess with a raised eyebrow. "No magic? Simply imagine you or your sister?"

Nodding, Jak said, "That is all, my Lady. Anyone can do it."

Duchess Aleece shook her head slowly, murmuring, "Truly wondrous." Her expression darkened an instant later. "It should be destroyed immediately."

Nikalys and Jak turned as one to stare at her.

Jak, his eyebrows raised high, asked, "Pardon me?"

Nikalys shook his head quickly, saying, "Why would we ever do such a thing?"

From beside the hearth, Wren muttered, "Oh, please. Think about it, son of Aryn. You and your sister are this 'Progeny' of Indrida's prophecy, yes? The two of you are destined to save us all from the God of Chaos?"

Nikalys stared at the tijul and nodded.

"So it seems."

Wren put his cup on the mantle of the hearth and glared at Nikalys.

"Tell me then. What would happen if the Cabal got their hands on that necklace?"

Broedi frowned, disappointed with himself. He had never considered such a possibility.

Jak said, "We would never let something like that happen."

Wren rolled his eyes as a sudden rush of bright white Strands of Air whipped about the room. Nundle sat up straight and glanced at Broedi, looking for guidance. As a pair of white Weaves—both of them pure Air—came together into two very different patterns, Broedi held up a hand to Nundle, indicating he should relax. Broedi recognized both designs and prayed Wren was making a point.

The first Weave flew towards Nikalys, wrapping around the necklace before ripping it from his hand. The pendant flew through the air to land in Wren's waiting hands as the second Weave draped over him.

The tijul disappeared in an instant. Broedi—along with Nundle—could clearly see the white Weave hovering around Wren, who was still standing by the hearth. Yet to anyone incapable of sensing or seeing Strands of Air, the tijul was simply gone.

A moment passed before Wren spoke, saying, "And now that I have the necklace and know what you look like, son of Aryn, I can find you whenever I like." A heartbeat later, he dismissed the Weave and reappeared. Tossing the necklace back to a miffed Nikalys, he said, "The duchess is right. That should be destroyed immediately. I'm surprised Eliza ever made it. Motherhood must have robbed her of good sense." Shifting his gaze to Jak, he added, "And you. Work on your secret-keeping skills. You just met me and you shared something as delicate as that? Carelessness like that gets people killed, John."

Jak's eyes narrowed.

"My name is Jak."

Wren shrugged.

"John, Jak, Josephina…whatever. What your name is won't matter when you're dead."

As was often the case in the past, Broedi disagreed with Wren's methods, but the lesson itself was a valuable one.

The brothers glared at the tijul for a long moment before Jak spoke, his tone as dry as a desert wind.

"I'm ever so glad they found you."

"You have no idea, Jak," mumbled Nikalys. "A Soulwraith is more likable."

Wren turned the full wrath of his stare on Nikalys.

"Bless the Gods! It took Aryn at least a turn to grate my nerves, but I am weary of you in less than a day. How is it possible you inherited *all* of his sanctimony yet none of his charm?"

Broedi shut his eyes and growled, "Can you *for once* show a bit of respect?"

Wren snapped, "Respect?!" His eyes were burning. "War is coming, Broedi! Hells, it's here! Do you plan to hold their hands and whisper gentle words of encouragement throughout it?! You can be their blasted wet-nurse! I'm going to ensure they are ready for what is coming!"

Broedi began to stride toward Wren—wholly unsure what he meant to do—when Duchess Aleece stood up swiftly, her deep blue dress rustling.

"Enough!"

Her voice filled the room, bouncing off the walls and arresting Broedi's ill-advised approach. Everyone—including Wren and Broedi—stared at the noblewoman.

Spinning around, the duchess glared hard at the tijul and said, "I have read every word of every history that I can find on the White Lions, Wren Aembyr. And may I say the stories do not do you justice."

Visibly disarmed by what he must have assumed was a compliment, Wren said, "Why, thank—"

"I am *not* done speaking!" exclaimed the duchess, advancing on him. "The histories noted your tendency to be direct and a tad rude, but they apparently were much too kind. Your behavior here is boorish and wholly disrespectful. And what you did in the Provinces was despicable." As the tijul lifted a hand as if to protest, Duchess Aleece raised her voice and said, "Oh, please. Spare me your justifications. I am quite familiar with the 'greater good' argument and I find it is often used by those too lazy to find a sweeter option."

Wren dropped his hand to his side and remained—wisely—quiet as the duchess continued.

"Here you are among people who neither deserve nor will accept your pompousness. You *will* show respect to everyone in this room! In fact, I expect you to show respect to everyone associated with the Shadow Manes! For while you were hiding in the trees, playing god with others' lives and freedom, we have been here, preparing to stop the Cabal from doing whatever in the Nine Hells they are doing."

Wren was without a doubt angry, but to Broedi's great surprise, he also appeared a touch embarrassed. Unable to help himself, a slight smile spread over Broedi's lips. He was enjoying Wren's tongue-lashing. As though she could sense his mirth, the duchess whirled to face him.

"And you! Temper your emotions! I cannot have you acting like this! It is abundantly clear you do not like Wren. And after we have dealt with the Cabal, you are more than welcome to challenge him. I certainly would not begrudge you for doing so. In fact, I believe I would even encourage it. But for the time being, please remember that the God of Chaos is out there, marching this way with a horde of oligurts, razorfiends, and mongrels—all led by demon-men! *That* should be your focus now! Everything else can wait!"

Broedi remained quiet, holding Duchess Aleece's burning gaze and waiting to see if she was done. He certainly hoped so.

Jak, Nikalys, and Nundle were all staring at the duchess with awe in their eyes. A tiny, content smile rested upon Lady Vivienne's face.

After letting a sigh seep out, Broedi turned his gaze to Wren.

"She is correct."

With his eyes still fixed on the duchess, Wren nodded slowly.

"As water is wet."

Duchess Aleece stared back and forth between them, eyes still ablaze.

"So we have an understanding then?"

The tijul gave a miniscule nod.

"We do, my Lady."

"Agreed," rumbled Broedi.

"Wondrous," muttered the duchess. Moving back to her chair, she sat and spent a moment arranging her dress around her. Sounding utterly calm, she said, "Now. As I have just noted, our knowledge of the Cabal's plans or motives is negligible. Perhaps we could discuss that?" Her anger was gone like last Winter's snow.

It took a moment before anyone could manage a response. Surprisingly, Wren spoke first.

"Perhaps he or she does not necessarily need a point? During the Demonic War, Norasim's only motivation appeared to be causing as much chaos as possible. Why would this time be any different?"

Broedi eyed Wren and sighed. Considering the tijul's understanding of the situation, his conclusion was a perfectly logical one. Yet Wren did not know everything. Broedi glanced around the room, studying each face carefully. Nobody here did.

His gaze inadvertently fell on Nikalys. Since finding the Progeny, Broedi had viewed himself as their teacher and they, his students. Yet while in Buhaylunsod, it had been Nikalys teaching him the lesson. The young man had shown more wisdom than a boy his age should.

Contrary to what most thought, Broedi did not enjoy keeping secrets. Mistakes in his past had scarred him, turning him into a soul that held things close. Too close, at times.

Noticing his contemplative stare, Nikalys asked, "What is it, Broedi?"

He eyed them, weighing the trustworthiness of each.

Nikalys had proven himself a dozen times in the short time since Broedi had found him backed up against those fingerprick bushes. He did not know it yet, but he was every bit the leader and tactician Aryn had been.

Jak was as steadfast as any soul Broedi had ever known and, by all accounts, his soldiering skills were coming along well. Broedi did not doubt he would do whatever he could for his brother and sister, blood or not. He had no worries about Jak. Nor did he have any about Nundle. The tomble could be a handful at times, but he had risked so much to be here, and had done so selflessly.

The two noblewomen stared at him, waiting. Duchess Aleece was sitting patiently while Lady Vivienne glared at him, her hands folded atop the desk and a scowl on her face. Despite his differences with the baroness, her dedication to the Shadow Manes was unquestioned, as was the sovereign of the Southlands herself.

That left one soul.

Broedi turned his gaze to Wren. Throughout his life, Broedi had worked with many he did not like. Wren was near the top of the list. Yet the duchess was right. Personal feelings needed to be set aside. Once he did that, the decision was easy. With a sigh and a nod, he made his decision. After taking a deep breath, he spoke.

"My time with Nelnora was…different than I previously conveyed," rumbled Broedi. He noticed Nikalys and Nundle exchange a quick glance but ignored it. He was grateful neither said anything.

With her gaze fixed firmly on him, the duchess leaned forward in her chair and said, "I trust you have good reason for keeping this from us." Her eyes narrowed ever so slightly. "From me, in particular."

"I did what I believed was best, my Lady."

Nodding once, Duchess Aleece said, "I would hope so." He could tell she was miffed by his withholding information, but she managed to conceal most of her irritation. "Do you plan to tell us what truly happened, then?"

"I do."

Her chair creaked as she leaned back in it.

"Please proceed, then. I want it all this time."

A sigh slipped from Broedi's lips as he dropped his head to gather his thoughts. What he was about to share could not be unsaid once spoken.

"Everything I told you truly happened," he rumbled, lifting his gaze to those in the room. "Only there was more. As the window showing Wren faded from view, I readied my list of questions for Nelnora. Yet, before I gave voice to the first, she held up a hand, halting me before I began. She reached inside her robes, withdrew a very old scroll, and handed it to me. As I accepted it, she said, 'Read this, please.' Curious, I moved to one of the magical lanterns lighting the chamber, carefully unrolled the scroll, afraid it might crumble if I handled it too roughly."

Closing his eyes, he could still picture the black-ink scrawled on the time-worn, yellow parchment.

"The very instant I could, I read the first line."

"What did it say?" asked Nikalys.

Broedi opened his eyes, looked to the young man, and said, "The roar of the Lions will drive back the spawn."

Confusion flashed over Nikalys' face. He was not the only one who was bewildered.

"Hold a moment," said Jak. "That's the beginning of the prophecy. Why show you that?"

Nodding slowly, Broedi rumbled, "I asked the same thing. She pointed to the scroll and said, 'Read it all, please.' So, I did. You can imagine my surprise when I reached the third stanza…and saw that a fourth awaited me."

At first, nobody reacted. The room was as quiet as a windless night in the Shakti Desert. It took a moment before Nundle muttered, "But there are only three."

"No," rumbled Broedi, shaking his head slowly. "Indrida's prophecy—as you know it—is incomplete. I assure you, there is a fourth, very important stanza. One that I read three times before I looked back to Nelnora." He paused a moment, remembering the numb, stomach-clenching sensation that had filled his gut. "The moment I did, she began to speak, sharing with me a story that—for a time—I refused to accept as truth."

"What did she say?" asked Wren.

Duchess Aleece lifted a hand and said, "I would like to hear the fourth stanza first if you do not mind."

Meeting the duchess' gaze, Broedi nodded, took a deep breath, and then re-cited the words that had been running through his head nearly every moment of every day since reading them.

> *"In the first year when the fifth eon is done,*
> *In the nation where ignorance and fear has won,*
> *By the third night with two eyes shining bright,*
> *When the tide flows east, rolling with unchecked might,*
> *The four will hold the names of three,*
> *And the start of the end will come to be."*

As the final word faded from the air, Lady Vivienne leaned forward, opened a desk drawer, and pulled free a fresh parchment sheet. Placing it on the desktop, she reached for one of the quill pens sitting in an ornate silver inkwell.

"Could you repeat that, please?"

Broedi took a step closer to the desk and gently placed his hand around her wrist, preventing her from fully withdrawing the quill pen.

"I will be happy to. Yet you should know, that other than Indrida and Nelnora, we seven are the only souls—mortal or immortal—who know those words exist. Should they be written down, we risk them falling into the wrong hands."

At first, the Baroness of Argolles stared up at him, a sharp edge to her glare, but her expression quickly softened. She nodded once and dropped the quill back into the inkwell with a soft clink.

"You are quite correct."

Releasing her wrist, Broedi peered around the room.

"We do not speak of the fourth stanza to *anyone*. Anyone at all? Agreed?"

As everyone nodded slowly, Nikalys muttered, "What about Kenders? She should know."

"Tobias, as well, I should think" added Nundle.

Broedi glanced at them both, saying, "I *alone* will share this—and anything we speak of today—with them. Is that acceptable to all?"

Again, everyone nodded their agreement. Broedi prayed they would keep their word.

His high-pitched voice soft and restrained, Nundle asked, "What does it mean, though?" He eyed Broedi warily. "Please tell me Nelnora at least shared that? I am tired of riddles."

With a short shake of his head, Broedi rumbled, "I am sorry. Riddles are all we have. I asked for an explanation, but Nelnora claimed not to fully understand their significance." A slight frown graced his lips. "I did not believe her, and told her as much. But that did not help matters. She appeared unconcerned with what I thought. Then, I demanded she tell me what it meant." His frown deepened beyond the point he liked to display. "But ordering one of the Celystiela to tell the truth is like trying to climb a waterfall."

"So we are left puzzling," muttered Nundle, his face scrunched up in thought. "That being the cut of it…my first thought would be that 'In the first year when the fifth eon is done' refers the coming year, yes? This is the four-thousandth, nine-hundred, and ninety-ninth year after the Locking. The first night of the fifth eon is…" He trailed off, his brow furrowing even deeper. "Huh. I don't know what the day is. I lost track during our trip to the Provinces."

In a soft and quiet voice, Duchess Aleece said, "Today is the seventeenth day of the Turn of Maeana. There are thirteen days until Year's End."

Nikalys mumbled, "Gods. I forgot all about that."

With a wan grin, Jak said, "You've been busy."

"Many have been," said Duchess Aleece. "Only a few are doing anything useful, though." She glanced around the room, a disappointed frown on her face. "The grandest celebration in generations is being planned in Freehaven. Duke Kyle is holding a city-wide gala to usher in the next eon, putting out a call for every playman and merrymaker within the Freelands, Southlands, and Long Coast to come and perform. Two weeks away, and the city is near bursting already. My carriage to Vivienne's residence took three times as long to make the journey this morning."

Lady Vivienne gave an angry shake of her head.

"He is like a child hiding beneath the bedcoverings."

"You have no idea," said the duchess, frustration coating her every word. "I yet again attempted to bend Kyle's ear a few days ago and all he wanted to do was talk about the festival. I swear the man will not lift a finger until oligurts are knocking on his door."

Jak looked up at Broedi and asked, "So does something happen in thirteen days, then? Besides the celebrations in Freehaven?"

Broedi shrugged his shoulders.

"Truthfully? I do not know."

"That is not the day that concerns me," said Nundle with worry, "The twenty-first day of Sormina's Turn does."

"Why then?" asked Nikalys.

Wren answered, "Because it's the Third Night of Two Moons." Looking to Nundle, he asked, "You are thinking of the 'By the third night with two eyes shining bright' line?"

"I am," answered Nundle.

With a nod, Wren conceded, "It would fit."

Broedi said, "The next line drew most of my attention."

Tilting his head back, Nundle stared up at Broedi.

"I admit that one has me puzzled quite a bit."

Lifting a hand, Jak said, "For those of us who have sustained a recent knock to the head, could we go over what that line is again?"

Broedi, Duchess Aleece, Nundle, and Lady Vivienne answered at once.

"The four will hold the names of three."

Looking around him, Jak muttered, "Bless the Gods, you have good memories." Turning to Broedi, he asked, "Any chance you know what it means?"

Every pair of eyes turned to him. Taking a step forward, he sat on the corner of Lady Vivienne's desk, fully aware that the baroness was glaring at his back. Shifting his satchel around to his front, he laid the leather pouch on his lap and rested his arms on top. He was itching to retrieve his pipe and light it, but knew doing so would set Lady Vivienne off, so he pushed the longing aside.

"Recall that I told you that Nelnora shared a fantastic story with me." He paused a moment and looked around the room before asking, "What do we know of the Locking?"

The question prompted raised eyebrows from nearly everyone.

Duchess Aleece said, "That is an odd question."

"Indulge me," rumbled Broedi. "And answer the question. Please."

Nundle, the ever-flowing fount of information, spoke up almost instantly, saying, "The High Host and those that were Neither battled the Cabal atop a mountaintop. The Cabal were defeated, banished to exist without their bodies or names, and destined to walk the world in mortal bodies. The name to the divine realm was lost forever, trapping the Gods and Goddesses on Terrene."

Broedi nodded along with the tomble's answer and said, "All true." He paused a moment before asking, "What else?"

The group stared at one another, blank expressions ruling them all.

Nikalys spoke first, saying, "I know nothing else. Then again, the Locking was more myth than anything in Yellow Mud. Before meeting you, I thought it merely a way to mark the passage of the years."

"The same goes in the Boroughs," said Nundle. "It was a nice story to tell at Leisure Day festivals."

Both noblewomen nodded quietly, confirming the same was true for them as well. Wren had the sole, unique response.

"I need only go back a handful of generations to find an ancestor who was alive when the Locking happened. I assure you all, it is no myth."

"Wren is correct," rumbled Broedi. "It happened. And Nelnora shared with me details of the battle that day. Events that never made it into the legends. One of which is at the heart of our current fight."

He paused a moment, and stared at the double doors and listened carefully, ensuring the hall was empty. Once he was confident that it was, he continued.

"According to Nelnora, after the battle was over and the Cabal were gone from the mountaintop, nine stones rested upon a chunk of white quartz. Each one made of a single type of pure, concentrated Strands. Fire, Water, Air, Stone, Charge, Life, Soul, Will, and Void. To hear Nelnora tell it, the stones' power staggered more than a few of the Celystiela there."

With an appropriate amount of unease, Lady Vivienne asked, "And what were they?"

Twisting around to eye the baroness, Broedi shrugged his shoulders.

"Nelnora claimed that, at the time, none of them knew."

"And did you believe her?" asked Duchess Aleece.

"I am unsure," rumbled Broedi. "Judging a Celystiela is like reading a book with your eyes closed."

Nundle muttered, "One would think she would be open with us. Half-answers and more questions don't help us."

"Help us?" repeated Wren. With a dry chuckle, he leaned back against the wall again. "She is not helping us. The Gods and Goddesses help themselves alone. Nelnora—and the rest of them—have but one interest in mind: their own. They do and say whatever they think will get you to do their bidding. We are the means to their ends." A deep, dark frown spread over his lips. "They are a rotten, twisted bunch. You'd be better served trusting a thief to return a dropped purse than expect an honest word from them. Veracity and the Gods are wax and water."

Jak swiveled around to face the tijul.

"That seems a bit cynical."

Broedi rumbled, "I agree with Wren. On the point, not the sentiment. Trusting Nelnora is dangerous, trusting *any* of the Celystiela is. Which is why I do not. However, much of what I share with you today I believe, but only because I have been able to verify her account elsewhere."

Nikalys asked, "How could you verify anything from five thousand years past?"

Eyeing the young man, Broedi asked with a slight smile, "You wish me to glaze the sweet cakes before baking them?"

Nikalys dipped his chin to his chest and let out a sigh of resignation.

"Continue your story, then."

Nodding once, Broedi rumbled, "The Celystiela stood upon the mountaintop, staring at the nine stones and discussing what had happened. A number of disagreements broke out, most of which centered on what to do with them. Those of the High Host attempted to claim the stones as their own, promising to use them for the good of all of Terrene. Nelnora—and others—strenuously objected."

"Why?" asked Jak. "Seems like a decent enough idea."

"Live long enough, John," began Wren. "And you'll find that a lot of evil is done in the name of good."

Jak glared at Wren again.

"It's *Jak*."

After Wren gave a careless shrug of his shoulders, Broedi rumbled, "Wren is correct. Fortunately, the Neither also knew that to be true and agreed with Nelnora that the High Host could not be trusted with the stones. When a consensus could not be reached, they readied to return to their divine realm in order to continue their discussions there."

A slight furrow appeared in Duchess Aleece's brow as she said, "But they were trapped here."

Broedi nodded, saying, "And that was when they realized that fact. Two dozen Celystiela stood on that mountaintop, and not one of them could recall the name. Another disagreement arose. Some of the Neither believed the stones were the cause of their predicament and wanted to destroy them. Others, thinking it all another plot by the Cabal, were afraid to touch them. And, yet again, the High Host made a case to take them for themselves."

"I don't understand," said Nikalys. "How could they be of use to the High Host?"

Glancing over, Nundle said, "Much of the effort in crafting a Weave is both pulling forth the Strands and then maintaining control over them. Now, imagine having an unlimited supply of Strands that you could carry in your pocket. In the wrong hands, such power would be…bad."

"And Nelnora recognized that," rumbled Broedi. "When the arguments grew heated, she stepped in and crafted an accord concerning the stones. One that seemed wise at the time, even though it was not. Years later, they discovered their error but, by then, it was too late to undo their decision."

A low, impatient groan drifted from Wren.

"You and your blasted storytelling. Get to the point."

Broedi glanced over at the tijul but did not engage him. It was not worth it. Shaking his head, he continued, saying, "In the end, Nelnora managed to craft an agreement acceptable to all the Celystiela. They would hide the stones, and do so in such a manner than none could know of their location. The potential for misuse was too great. But before they did that, they would use the stones' powers once in order to create a race to serve them while they remained on Terrene."

"They used the stones to craft the divina?" asked Lady Vivienne. "Considering they did not know the stones' nature, that seems rather reckless."

"I said the same thing to Nelnora," rumbled Broedi. "She said it was a concession she was forced to make to get agreement on how they would go about hiding the stones."

"How did they do that?" asked Nundle. "From what you've said, it sounds like none of them would trust another with that task."

"You are correct," said Broedi. "Which is why the Celystiela gave the stones to a group of mortals to do so."

Jak huffed, "That sounds like an even worse idea than the Gods holding onto them."

Broedi shook his head.

"Not if the stones were given to a race of beings who would never be tempted by their power."

"Power corrupts all," scoffed Wren. "No such beings exist."

"I assure you they do," rumbled Broedi.

Pushing himself away from the wall, Wren stood tall and said, "I am as well traveled as you, Broedi, and thrice your age. I have *never* met any such race incapable of falling prey to the lure of power."

"Correct," said Broedi. "*You* have not met them. I, however, have." He paused a moment, looked around the room, and added, "As have the rest of you."

For a long moment, the room was silent before Lady Vivienne broke the quiet, her voice carrying a note of disbelief.

"They gave they stones to the aicenai?"

Broedi nodded once.

"They did."

"Hold a moment," said Jak. "You said a group. Aicenai are rarer than a fish in a tree."

"Not five thousand years ago. The race was dying, yes, but at the time, there were many times more aicenai alive than today. Being the Watcher of the World, Nelnora was aware of one group in particular who could be trusted with the stones: a monastic order in the peaks of what is now northern Yut. A sect based on the belief that knowledge itself was supreme, not what could be done with it. Believing them to be the answer to their problem, the remaining Celystiela—all twenty-four of them—took the stones to the aicenai order and charged them with two tasks. One, to protect the stones from those who would use them selfishly. And, two, attempt to discover their true nature."

Duchess Aleece asked, "What prevented the High Host from returning later and taking the stones for themselves?"

"Because they were not there anymore," rumbled Broedi.

A quiet moment passed before Nundle said, "I'm afraid you've lost me."

Jak raised a hand.

"Me, too."

A slight smile spread over Broedi's lips.

"Eighty-one aicenai where chosen from the order, divided into nine groups of nine, and called the Daputa Devet. In the aicenai tongue, it means 'the Twice Nine.' One stone was given to each group to study and protect. Once they understood their stone's nature and origin, they were to return to the Celystiela."

"Return?" asked Nikalys. "Where did they go?"

"Nelnora had Gaena open nine ports throughout Terrene, one for each group and their stone. Gaena alone knew their original destinations."

"And they trusted her with that knowledge?" asked Nikalys.

"According to Nelnora, she had been the strongest advocate for separating and hiding the stones."

"Makes sense," mumbled Nundle.

"How so?" asked Duchess Aleece.

The tomble shimmied about in his chair to peer around Jak and answered, "The Goddess of Magic would probably want to do whatever she could to keep the stones away from any who might abuse them."

Nodding, the duchess said, "That does make sense." She looked back to Broedi and asked, "So what happened to the stones?"

Broedi rose from the desk corner with a sigh and said, "They disappeared. The Daputa Devet performed their task well, remaining hidden as they studied."

"For how long?" asked Nikalys.

"Eons," rumbled Broedi.

Skeptical, Lady Vivienne asked, "They remained hidden for thousands of years?"

"Again—according to Nelnora—they did. Civilizations rose and fell. Nations made war and peace. All the while, the Daputa Devet remained out of sight."

"Khin," muttered Nikalys.

Surprised, Broedi looked to the young man and found him staring at nothing, deep in thought.

"What did you say?"

Looking up, Nikalys said, "Your conversation with Khin before we left for the Provinces had nothing to do with Kenders' lessons did it?"

Impressed with Nikalys' intuition, Broedi shook his head once.

"No, it did not. As I said, I had a difficult time accepting Nelnora's tale. When I told her as much, she directed me to speak with Khin."

With raised eyebrows, Duchess Aleece asked, "And why did she do that?"

Broedi looked around the room, saying, "None of us were here when Khin arrived at the enclave. Most of you were not yet born. When Aryn, Eliza, and I joined the Manes, he was already a fixture here." He turned his gaze to the duchess. "Yet from what your great-grandfather told me, the leadership of the Manes at the time was very concerned about his arrival. According to him, Khin simply walked into Claw one day—straight through the protective Weave—and professed his desire to aid the Manes. Yet he refused to give any explanation as to why or how he knew of the enclave."

Lady Vivienne said, "Khin has proven his trustworthiness and loyalty many times over. No one here doubts his allegiance."

"Not now, my Lady," replied Broedi. "But at the time, his appearance was cause for great concern. Time might have dulled the urgency of the questions surrounding his arrival, but they did remain unanswered for a very long time." He paused briefly before adding, "Until recently."

A moment or two passed while he waited for someone to come to the logical conclusion. He did not have to wait long.

Crossing his arms, Nikalys said, "Khin was one of The Twice Nine, wasn't he?" His words were more statement than question.

"Yes," rumbled Broedi. "He was. He and eight of his brethren were given what he calls the 'Suštinata na Kamen.' The Essence of Stone. For nearly five thousand years, they meticulously studied the stone, trying to discover its purpose, its origin, its unique properties. As the centuries passed, his companions perished. For the last five hundred years, Khin has continued his task alone."

"Gods," mumbled Jak. "Here I was feeling lonely after just a few weeks."

"So, he figured it out, then," said Nikalys. "He discovered the nature of the stone, didn't he?"

Surprised again, Broedi eyed the young man.

"You are proving to be quite insightful."

Ignoring the compliment, Nikalys raised an eyebrow and asked, "Am I right?"

Nodding, Broedi replied, "Nelnora had given up hope that any of the Daputa Devet would ever return. Their lives may be extraordinarily long, but aicenai are mortal. Then, on a cold Winter day just over a century ago, Khin climbs Nelnora's temple steps and announces he has discovered the stones' purpose."

"And, finally," mumbled Wren. "We arrive at the point of your tale."

Choosing to ignore the tijul yet again, Broedi said, "Once in private with her, Khin shared with her what he believed happened during the Locking, that at the height of the battle, the Cabal recognized their defeat was imminent. Rather than be obliterated, they abandoned their bodies. Whatever comprises the soul of a Celystiela fled into the mortal world. Yet their escape was incomplete, as someone atop that mountain crafted an incredibly powerful Weave, attempting to trap the Cabal for eternity. But they were only partially successful, grasping but a piece of each and binding it within one of nine stones of pure Strands."

"That sounds…impossible," muttered Nundle in disbelief.

Looking around the room and seeing one dubious expression after another, a slight smile slipped over Broedi's lips.

"I shared your skepticism. Yet Nelnora spoke with complete confidence that such a thing was plausible. Interestingly, when I spoke with Khin afterwards, he shared that she was as unconvinced as all of you are right now. She insisted no one could do such a thing and refused to believe him. Until he spoke a single word: the God of Fear's true name."

Sitting tall in his chair, Nundle said, "But their true names were burned from existence."

Broedi shook his head slightly.

"Apparently not. Even though that is what people have believed for five thousand years. The Celystiela, as well. The truth is that their names have been trapped along with their essence, wrapped inside the nine Suštinata."

"Which God or Goddess could—or would—do such a thing?" asked Duchess Aleece.

Crossing his arms, Broedi said, "Nelnora would not answer that question. For me or for Khin. And after speaking with him, he and I agree the reason she would not is simple: she does not know herself. She claimed—"

He cut off as a crackling pulse of white surged through him. Shooting a quick look towards Wren, he found the tijul tense, spear already in hand. Judging Wren not responsible for the magic, he looked to Nundle next. The tomble, like him, was staring about the room, concern in his eyes.

Catching Broedi staring at him, Nundle asked, "You feel that, yes?"

Broedi nodded once.

"Air."

"And Void," added Nundle. "No Charge, Will, or Life."

With his gaze shifting about, Wren said, "No Soul or Water, either." Looking to Broedi, he mumbled, "Then again, you know that."

"No Fire, either," rumbled Broedi. He shot a quick look at Lady Vivienne, the only Stone mage in the room. "My Lady?"

Lady Vivienne shook her head.

"No Stone."

"Void and Air alone, then," said Nundle.

Wren muttered, "A port?"

Broedi turned to Nundle, hoping the tomble could recognize the feel of the pattern, and found him with his eyes closed. A moment later, he opened them and nodded.

"I think so. In the courtyard, I believe."

Those not standing rose from their chairs and the group rushed from the room. Broedi and Nikalys led them through the dark and chilly halls with Wren a step behind. Nundle, despite his short legs, managed to keep pace with them. Glancing back, Broedi found the noblewomen lagging behind a bit as the duchess was helping the still-unsteady Jak along.

Lady Vivienne caught his eye and called out, "Avoid the mages' hall. It is impassable!"

Noting her instruction, they cut through the armory, passing long lines of weapons racks as they did. Hearing a pair of clangs, Broedi looked back and spotted Jak with a sword in his hand. Duchess Aleece gripped a short blade as well.

Nikalys reached the door to the courtyard first, shoved it open—flooding the room with light and bitter cold—and rushed outside. Broedi emerged next, his boot crunching on the crust of old snow. The cloud-splotched sky was clear enough to allow a few stray rays of sun to filter through, temporarily blinding him. Slowing to a stop, he squinted against the dazzling whiteness that filled the yard.

Wren rushed past him, his ijulan eyes adjusting to the light change quicker than the rest of them. Through half-shut eyes, Broedi saw Wren running towards a group of soldiers standing around a dark slit in the courtyard's center. Commander Aiden's voice rang out, shouting orders.

"Full circle, arms drawn!"

"What is going on?" asked Nikalys, a hand shielding his eyes. "Why is it so blasted bright?!" He attempted to draw the Blade of Horum with his free hand, but faltered when he slipped on a patch of ice and nearly fell down.

"Relax," rumbled Broedi. "It is only sunlight on snow." Tapping the young man on the shoulder, he pointed in the direction of the port. "The port is there."

Nikalys moved his hand from his eyes and, still squinting, began to move toward it. Broedi broke into a sprint, careful not to slip on the icy snow.

Wren reached the circle of soldiers forming around the slit and pushed past the men, cursing at them to get out of the way. The men parted and stared, wide-eyed, as the tijul slipped by. Nikalys suddenly appeared next to Wren, his sword held in a ready position. Broedi arrived a moment later and issued a warning.

"Be ready for anything,"

Everyone around the port nodded, their eyes locked on the midnight-black slit in the air. As they waited, Jak, Nundle, and the noblewomen rushed up and moved through the ring of soldiers, stopping to stand a few paces behind Nikalys and the White Lions.

A few anxious moments later, a small figure emerged from the black of the port, hobbling through while leaning on a walking stick. Tobias took two steps in the days-old snow and stopped, staring around the courtyard with half-closed eyes and a frown on his face, completely ignoring his armed reception. A set of horse's reins led back into the blackness.

"Oh, wondrous. Snow."

Broedi rumbled, "Good days ahead, Tobias."

The tomble glanced up at Broedi, nodded a silent greeting, and immediately shifted his gaze to Wren. His frown deepened into a full scowl.

"So, you're here."

"It's a pleasure to see you, too," said Wren.

"Your hair looks nice. Long and shiny as always."

"Thank you, Tobias. How's the leg?"

Tobias sighed and gave a slight shake of his head.

"Haven't changed, have you, Wren?"

Turning to eye the port, Wren shrugged and asked, "Why would I?"

Shaking his head, Tobias eyed the group around him, asking, "Is all this for me?"

"Better to be prepared than to be surprised," answered Broedi.

A lopsided grin crept up one side of Tobias' face. "Bet you a ducat I can still surprise you." Stepping to the side of the slit, he tugged the reins, and said, "No matter what steps through that port, try to remain calm."

Worried, Broedi rumbled, "Why?"

"Because I asked, that's why," answered Tobias. Glancing at Nikalys' sword and Wren's spear, he added, "And lower your weapons. There is no need for them." He eyed the soldiers at the ready. "All of you, please."

Nikalys glanced over to Broedi, looking for guidance. After a moment, Broedi gave a short nod, indicating he should follow Tobias' request. As the young man let the tip of his white blade drop, brushing the snow, Commander Aiden shouted an order that the Shadow Manes were to follow suit.

A moment later, Nundle's chestnut horse began to emerge from the port.

"You stole my horse," muttered Nundle.

Tobias glanced over and said, "Ah, yes. Sorry. But you weren't using him, and he was a good size for me, so…" He trailed off and shrugged. Seeing Wren still holding his longspear at the ready, he snapped, "Hells, Wren. Put your blasted spear down."

"I'll put it down when I'm sure it's safe."

"It's safe," said Tobias.

"So you say."

"Wren," rumbled Broedi. "Listen, please."

The tijul glared at them both before jamming the butt end of the spear into the snow.

"Fine. By chance, are these more lawbreakers from the Boroughs? If so, just tell me now so I can go inside. I do not wish to stand in the cold and greet every one of them."

Broedi shot a quick glance at Nundle and found the redheaded tomble—hat on his head again—staring at Tobias with narrowed eyes. Nundle was sharp. If he had not yet figured out the implication of Wren's statement, he would shortly.

Tobias gave Wren a murderous glare and, with thick venom lacing each word, said, "*No*, Wren. I am—"

Tobias cut his response short as a strange Borderlander emerged from the port and stopped but a pace from the slit, immediately shutting his eyes against the combined brilliance of sun and snow.

Old burn scars covered the right side of the man's face and neck, he was missing an eyebrow, and his black hair grew on only one side of his head. As he lifted his right hand to shade his eyes from the sun, Broedi noticed it was also burned and missing two fingers. The clothes that hung from his body were little more than tattered rags. A beat-up scabbard of Dust Man design was at his side, a sword's hilt poking from the top.

The Borderlander hissed, "Blast the Gods, it's cold!"

Tobias stared up at the man and said, "I warned you, Rhohn. Now, like I told you. Step to the side."

Cracking open his eyes a fraction, the man nodded and scooted a few paces to his right. Behind Broedi, Jak ordered a soldier to get some blankets. Commander Aiden did not object.

Khin stepped from the port next, leading a midnight black horse behind him. He drew in a long, cold breath of air and visibly relaxed, letting out an almost imperceptible sigh of relief. Broedi glanced over at Wren, wondering what his reaction would be. The tijul was gaping like a fish seeing a bird fly for the first time.

Khin's gaze darted about, scanning the crowd before him. Ultimately, his stare settled on Broedi and, in his wispy, slow voice, said, "Remain calm."

Confused, Broedi asked, "Why must—"

Two dozen Strands of Air popped into existence and came together quickly, forming what Broedi judged to be a partially complete Weave. A moment later, an invisible barrier slammed down, creating a perfect ring of crushed snow that separated the new arrivals from everyone else.

"Khin?" asked Broedi. "What is going on?"

As the aicenai stepped aside, he turned his blue-eyed gaze towards Broedi.

"It is for the best."

His eyes locked on the port, Nikalys asked, "Where's Kenders?" The young man's voice was steady, but Broedi could hear the undercurrent of worry in the question.

Tobias glanced up and met Nikalys' stare, but remained quiet.

A moment later, a creature whose type Broedi had not seen in ages stepped from the blackness of the port. Broedi blinked in surprise as he realized a kur-surus stood before him. Covered in thick, brown and white fur, he—Broedi recognize the male scent in an instant—stood tense and taut, his gaze darting about the yard. His breathing was quick, his nostrils flaring. A concerned murmur arose from the soldiers. Some began to raise their swords again.

"Keep them down!" ordered Tobias. Lowering his voice, he spoke in a calm and soothing tone, adding, "Relax, Okollu. You are safe." The kur-surus appeared doubtful.

Broedi shot a number of questioning looks at Tobias and Khin. He hoped the pair had an incredibly good reason for what they were doing.

"Where is my sister, Tobias?" asked Nikalys, his tone insistent. Despite the fact that a kur-surus stood before him, his focus was elsewhere.

The tomble held up a hand and said, "Against my advice, she has gone into—"

Wren interrupted, exclaiming, "There's a mongrel standing here and the first thing you ask is 'Where is my sister?!'"

Okollu's black lips drew back, the fur on the back of his neck stood on end, and a low, threatening growl reverberated in his throat.

"Mongrel is a derogatory term," rumbled Broedi softly. "Please do not call him that."

The growl cut off as Okollu shifted his gaze to Broedi, curiosity shining bright in his eyes.

"Why?" asked Wren.

"Because things will go so much sweeter if you do not," answered Tobias.

Wren glared at the kur-surus, yet had the grace to remain silent.

Stepping forward, Khin said, "You may dismiss the soldiers. There is no need for them."

On the opposite side of the group, Commander Aiden stood, staring at Broedi, silently asking with eyes alone whether or not to give the order to stand down. Broedi hesitated.

After a moment, Okollu smiled, his sharp canine teeth poking from his lips, and growled softly, "If you are the hope of my kind, then my sacrifices have been in vain. I am but one kur-surus yet the air reeks of fear."

He was right. Broedi could smell the soldiers' sweat.

Looking to Tobias, Broedi asked, "Are you sure about this?"

"I am," replied the tomble.

Broedi eyed the kur-surus for a moment longer before rumbling, "Commander, you and your men may withdraw."

The soldier's questioning gaze shifted to behind Broedi. A moment later, Duchess Aleece spoke.

"Do as he says, Commander."

Nodding once, the soldier shouted, "Put your blades to sleep and back away!"

The ring of soldiers sheathed their swords—slowly—and began to retreat to the courtyard's walls. Once they were an acceptable distance away, the partially complete Weave surrounding the new arrivals faded. With a soft pop, the port disappeared as well.

A moment later, Nundle muttered, "Broedi?"

The tomble's bewildered tone was enough to pull Broedi's attention away from the kur-surus.

"Yes?"

Nundle was staring around him, his face twisted up in confusion. "The port is gone, but I still sense Strands of Void." His gaze locked on Tobias and he lifted a hand to point at a leather sack clenched in Tobias' walking stick hand. "They're coming from there."

Eyeing Nundle, Tobias said, "You *are* strong with Void, aren't you?" Releasing Traveler's reins, he took the pouch in his free hand and said, "Here, Broedi. We found one."

With an underhand toss, he lobbed the small sack to Broedi. Lifting a hand, Broedi easily caught the pouch and was immediately struck by how heavy it seemed.

Tobias warned, "I'd highly advise not opening it right now. It's a thousand times worse if it's not in the pouch."

Broedi's eyes widened a fraction as he realized what he held. Quickly shifting his gaze to Khin, he said, "Your oath? I release you from it. For now."

The aicenai nodded, his face utterly impassive, and said, "Understood."

Ignoring the curious stares of those around him, Broedi concentrated on the conversation he had just had in Lady Vivienne's offices, effectively telling Khin that those who stood here now knew of the Suštinata.

Khin's only reaction was a slight crinkling of skin around his eyes.

Broedi wondered if the pouch he held contained the Suštinata of Void.

Khin nodded once.

Broedi glanced at the Borderlander and kur-surus, wondering at the reason behind their presence.

Khin turned to Rhohn and Okollu.

"It is time to share your message."

Shivering from the cold, the scarred Borderlander glanced to the kur-surus.

"Your turn."

Okollu shook muzzle and huffed, "It would be better if it came from you, I think."

Rhohn shrugged, faced the group, and in a clear, crisp voice, said, "Indrida's prophecy is upon us. The Eternal Anarchist is a saeljul who goes by the name Tandyr. The Borderlands have fallen, the Marshlands are next. Vanson and Everett are in his palm for reasons I still do not understand. Time grows short. The Shadow Manes must rise."

A surprised murmur drifted through the snowy courtyard.

Hearing a rustle of cloth behind him, Broedi glanced over his shoulder to find Duchess Aleece marching forward. She stopped on Broedi's right and demanded, "Who gave you that message?" She glanced around the courtyard, eyeing the gathered soldiers, and added, "And answer softer this time."

Rhohn turned to stare at the kur-surus.

"He did."

As one, the group peered at Okollu. Little breath clouds rose from the kur-surus' muzzle as he stared back at them.

Almost without pause, Duchess Aleece asked, "And who gave it to you?"

The kur-surus growled softly, "Miriel Syncent."

For a moment, the only sound in the yard was the gentle whistling of the Winter wind. Broedi stared at the kur-surus, his face blank, as he tried to make sense of what he was hearing.

Recovering quicker than them all, Duchess Aleece asked, "Your name is Okollu?"

The kur-surus nodded in silence.

"Then listen to me carefully, Okollu. Tobias and Khin appear to trust you, so—for the time being—I will treat you with the respect and courtesy I would offer any guest. Do not give me reason to change my mind. Am I clear?"

Okollu growled quietly, "Yes."

"Good," said the duchess with a decisive nod. "Now, everyone inside, please. Whatever else needs to be said should be done in private. And out of this blasted chill." Without waiting for a response, she spun around and began to move toward a pair of doors in the walls, her hair streaming behind her in the wind.

Lady Vivienne and Nundle turned to follow almost immediately. Broedi was about to as well, when Jak came closer, advancing to stand beside his brother.

Tobias stared up at Jak and his bandages and asked, "What in the Nine Hells happened to you?"

Brushing aside the question, Jak repeated Nikalys' earlier query.

"Where's Kenders?"

"She is with Tiliah in Demetus."

The Isaac brothers were stunned silent, and rightly so.

Broedi rumbled, "Then you found Zecus' family?"

Tobias shook his head, saying, "Only her and only because they were carrying that." He nodded at the leather pouch in Broedi's hand.

"Hold a moment," muttered Jak. "Tiliah was—" he glanced at Rhohn and Okollu "—with *them*?"

Rhohn answered, "It is a long, almost impossible tale. One I will be happy to share once I am inside."

"But she is safe?" asked Nikalys. "Unhurt?"

"When she left this morning, she was fine," said Tobias with a frown. "And assuming she does nothing to alert the Constables in Demetus, she should remain so."

Something inside of Broedi twitched. Thonda's sixth sense.

A worried scowl spread over his face.

CHAPTER 45: REFUGEES

The overpowering stench of unwashed filth climbed inside of Kenders' nose, seemingly determined to take up permanent residence. With each reluctant breath she drew, the grimace on her face deepened. The rotten stench in the marshes was better than this.

A sea of grimy, dirt-streaked faces surrounded her. Families huddled together like clumps of muddy leaves on a creek bank after a flood. Using pine branches, rags, and ripped canvas, some had attempted to erect shelters, but the structures were pitiful looking. Most people simply sat or lay in the open, exposed to nature's whim, so beaten down by misery that few lifted their gazes as she rode past.

With her lips pressed together and a scowl on her face, Kenders shook her head in disgust. Fate had been overtly cruel to these people. Their homes were gone, their lands invaded, their lives ruined. Three mumbled words slipped from her mouth unbidden.

"This is wrong."

Sitting tall in Goshen's saddle, Tiliah glanced over and whispered, "'Wrong' is much too sweet a word." Her tone was bitter and harsh, understandably so.

"Where are all of these people going to go?" asked Kenders. She was sure to keep her voice low so only Tiliah could hear her. "What are they going to do?"

With a slow shake of her head, the Borderlander said, "I was hoping you might have an answer."

At least two thousand people were in this area alone, the third encampment Tiliah and Kenders had visited today and the smallest by far. The marshes surrounding Demetus provided only so many scattered chunks of dry land where people could rest. Strips of well-trodden land meandered between islands of refugees.

"How many camps like this are there?" asked Kenders.

Tiliah shrugged.

"Hard to say. More than when I left, though. Many more."

Kenders sighed and returned to scanning the crowd, doing her best to find a trio of faces she had never seen. She prayed the familial resemblance of mother and the two younger siblings was as clear as Tiliah's was to Zecus.

"Have you seen anyone you recognize? Anyone from Drysa?"

"No," muttered Tiliah. "Nobody."

Kenders glanced to her left, eyeing Tiliah. Considering everything that had happened to her, the young woman, only a year older than Kenders, was holding up extremely well. After the first bout of tears in the pine grove yesterday, Tiliah pulled herself together and immediately began interrogating Kenders, asking all the questions one would expect. Kenders was honest with Tiliah and shared everything. To her great surprise, Tiliah accepted every word of her tale without challenge.

Tobias and Khin led their combined group of six back to their original camp atop another Marshland hill. There, they waited for Zecus and Boah to return while taking turns exchanging stories. Only then did Kenders understand Tiliah's easy acceptance of her tale earlier on.

The sun had been absent from the sky for a long time when Boah and Zecus eventually rode into camp. As Zecus moved into the ring of light cast from the campfire, Tiliah leapt from the ground and ran towards his horse. Zecus jumped from his saddle, rushing forward to hug his sister. The pair embraced for a long time, standing to the one side. Everyone—Kenders included—left them alone. Even the mongrel had been exceedingly respectful.

Once they rejoined the group—and after repeated assurances that Okollu was friend, not foe—Zecus, with Boah's help, shared their day's experiences in Demetus. The refugee count had tripled since Zecus had left. Great encampments of soldiers dotted the western and northern areas around the city, the gold and blue of the Southern Arms mixing with the green and white of the Reed Men. There were even a few detachments of the Long Coast's Shore Guard. Forces were amassing, evidently expecting an attack on Demetus.

Following a meager dinner of hard goat cheese and water, the group had set to determining their next step. Khin, who had remained typically silent throughout the day and evening, announced that he and Tobias must return to Storm Island in the morning. Kenders assumed it had something to do with the strange stone of Void, but any attempt to inquire as to the nature of the black gem was met with utter silence.

Rhohn and Okollu were to accompany Tobias and Khin to the enclave in order to share their message and tale. Boah, Tiliah, and Zecus were going to go back to Demetus and continue to search for their families.

Assuming that Khin would ask her to return to the enclave, Kenders was stunned when the aicenai instead asked her what she wanted to do. After only a moment's hesitation, she announced her intention to remain in the Marshlands and help Zecus. Khin accepted her decision without question, but Tobias and Zecus had spent quite some time trying to talk her out of it. She had not listened to either.

Early this morning, as one group of four left via port for Storm Island, the other four rode north toward Demetus. This evening, Kenders and the others were to return to the same camp to wait for Tobias and directions of what to do next. Kenders expected she might see Jak emerge from the port tonight and attempt to drag her back to Storm Island with him.

Before the group bound for Demetus reached the city's outskirts, they divided into two pairs—Zecus and Boah in one, Kenders and Tiliah in the other—and rode into the camps. Unfortunately, midday was nearing and Kenders and Tiliah's search had turned up no one. She hoped the others were having more success.

Kenders sighed and shook her head, fighting back the feeling of hopelessness that was steadily encroaching on her. Finding anyone in this crowd would be nigh impossible.

She was reaching up to rub her tired eyes when her gaze fell on a woman sitting some hundred paces away. She was all alone, her clothes torn, impossibly dirty, and draped over a frame almost as thin as Khin's. Her stare was in Kenders' direction, but the distant, blank look to her eyes told Kenders she was not truly seeing anything. A flicker of hope danced inside Kenders' chest. The woman's face was drawn, but her features were undeniably familiar.

Kenders pulled Smoke's reins, halting the horse. She glanced over at Tiliah and found the young woman riding on, looking in the opposite direction. Before saying anything, Kenders looked back to the woman on the ground and stared hard, wanting to ensure the resemblance was close enough to warrant saying anything. She did not want to get Tiliah's hopes up.

The fact that the woman sat alone among the muck and weeds was not a good sign. If this were Debrah Alsher, Jerem and Jezra should be with her. Nevertheless, the longer Kenders stared, the more convinced she became. After offering a silent prayer to Ceruna, the Goddess of Hope, she took a deep breath, exhaled, and stared at Tiliah's back.

"Tiliah?"

By now, Goshen was a few horse-strides ahead of Smoke. Pulling on the horse's reins to stop her mount, Tiliah looked back. Kenders lifted an arm and pointed in the direction of the woman.

"Might that be...?"

Tiliah turned her head, her gaze following Kenders' outstretched arm, flying over dozens of refugees' heads, and settling on the disheveled woman. Her eyes widening, she leapt from Goshen's saddle.

"Mother!"

Kenders' shoulders slumped as she breathed a sigh of relief.

Tiliah dashed through the crowd, dodging the people sprawled on the ground. She repeatedly called out for her mother, but Debrah did not seem to hear her. The empty expression on her face never changed.

At the edge of Kenders' vision, she spotted movement by the now rider-less Goshen. Swiveling her head forward, she spotted two Borderlands men quickly approaching the horse, one watching Tiliah's hurried path through the crowd while the other had his gaze fixed on Kenders. Both were dressed in rags and looked as if they had not eaten in some time.

"Uh oh."

Once, when Kenders was a little girl, her mother had caught her sneaking from the house one evening after eveningmeal. Earlier in the day, nine-year-old Kenders had seen a stray, starving dog wandering Yellow Mud and she was intent on sneaking it some table scraps. Marie Isaac sternly ordered her back inside the house and kept a watchful eye on her the rest of the evening. The next morning, they learned that the dog had bitten a neighbor boy several times. Her mother's words from that morning leapt to her mind now: the most dangerous creatures in this world are often the most desperate.

Kenders could not imagine any beings more forlorn than these refugees were. Duke Rholeb's soldiers and the orders of the temples within Demetus were distributing food and water, but demand far outweighed supply.

The intent of the two men striding toward Goshen was clear. They were going to take the horse for themselves. Quickly slipping from Smoke's saddle, Kenders hurried forward to Goshen's side, grabbed the reins, and glared at the approaching Borderlanders. With eyes alone, she pleaded for them to walk away.

The lead man's step faltered as he caught her stare, a battle between needy desperation and shame playing out on his dark-skinned face. In their condition, honor had little chance of victory. After a moment, he took a few slow steps closer, bowed, and said, "My pleasure is to meet you in peace today."

The polite introduction threw Kenders. She recovered quickly, however, when he followed the greeting with a whispered order.

"Give us the horse, miss."

Shaking her head, she said, "No." She glanced over to where Tiliah was now crouched beside a very surprised Debrah. "We will need him to get my friend's mother away from here."

The second man arrived to stand beside the first. The pair's beards were unkempt and wild, as was their hair. Both wore bands—white at one time, but now brown with dirt and grime—around their foreheads. Kenders' heart sunk. The strips of cloth meant they were married. They at least had wives, perhaps children as well.

The second man leaned towards the first and murmured, "Bemsiah, I do not believe I can do this."

Bemsiah shook his head and said quietly, "If you and yours would like to starve, you may leave."

For a brief moment, Kenders considered handing over Goshen, letting the men take him and sell him.

The second man hissed, "But this is *wrong*!"

"If you feel so strongly, Hanoch, you can go!"

Glancing around, Kenders noticed that a number of refugees were staring at them. She had no doubt that if these men succeeded in taking Goshen from her, someone would try to take Smoke within moments. The image of a pack of wild dogs fighting over a single hunk of meat flashed through her head. She could not let this happen.

Knowing that reason had no chance to prevail today, she peered to the east and eyed the mud-brown walls of Demetus proper over a mile away. The capital sat atop a sloped hill, clearly visible from the lowlands. A tiny frown spread across her lips. Constables were inside those walls.

Looking back to Bemsiah and Hanoch, her frown deepened. Even though Constables were in Demetus, these men were a bigger threat now. Taking a grand risk, she reached out for the honey-gold Strands of Will, quickly wove two patterns, and directed them at the pair of men. She only used a handful of Strands, hoping she might avoid detection if there were Trackers in the city.

As the Weaves melted into the men, she said, "I understand you want to do whatever you can for your families, but this?" She gave a disapproving shake of her head. "You both look like honorable, respectable men. Perhaps you ought to return to your families now. Quietly, please."

Hanoch bowed immediately while apologizing, "Please grant us your forgiveness, miss. You are right, this is wrong." He reached out and grabbed Bemsiah's arm. "Come, we should go."

Ripping his arm free, Bemsiah snapped, "No! My family must eat!" He glared at Kenders. "I *am* taking this horse. It will be the first decent meal we've had in weeks."

A reflexive grimace spread over Kenders' face. She had thought the men were going to take and sell the horse. Recovering quickly, she drew in a breath and crafted a third Weave, using twice the number of Strands of Will this time. She directed the pattern toward Bemsiah and said, "Leave and go back to your families. *Now*. And not another word."

As one, Bemsiah and Hanoch nodded, turned around, and walked away in perfect silence.

Watching them stride back into the throng of refugees, Kenders muttered, "Oh, bless the Gods." Her relief was short lived as she noticed a number of people staring at her, suspicion filling their eyes. It was time to go.

Spinning around, she saw Tiliah approaching, helping her mother through the crowd. Debrah was thinner than her daughter was and her hair a tangled mess, but there was no doubt she was the Alsher matriarch. Her gaze remained locked on Tiliah as they stumbled along, an expression of disbelieving wonderment on her face. Kenders caught Tiliah's eye and, with a swift jerk of her head, urged them to hurry.

As the pair reached the horses, Kenders offered a quick and friendly smile to Debrah before looking at Tiliah and saying, "We need to move. Now. I had to use…ah, I had to use my talent." She had almost said 'magic.'

Tiliah did not immediately respond. For the first time, Kenders noticed the young woman's brow lined with worry.

"What's wrong?"

It took Tiliah a moment or two to answer. When she did, her voice was quiet.

"I felt it."

Kenders froze.

"You what?"

Tiliah hesitated again.

"I felt it. Your 'talent.'"

Shock shoved aside the urgency to move. Staring hard at Tiliah, Kenders muttered, "What exactly did you feel?"

Tiliah shot a quick look at her mother before whispering, "Sort of like the wind rustling through the grass." She hesitated. "Only the wind…felt gold? Does that make sense?"

Kenders frowned. It made perfect sense. Before she could say anything, though, Tiliah spoke again in an even softer voice.

"Although, it was not as strong as the black from yesterday."

Kenders' eyes widened.

"Why didn't you say anything about this?"

"I was truly hoping that I was imagining it all."

Debrah was looking back and forth between them, clearly confused by the conversation.

Ignoring the woman's bewildered stares, Kenders asked, "Was that the first time?"

Tiliah shook her head once.

"For the black, no. The gold? Yes."

Kenders sighed. If it was not one thing, it was another.

With a wary eye on the refugees collecting around them, murmuring and staring, Kenders muttered, "We'll discuss this later." Shifting her gaze to Debrah, she said, "My name is Kenders—"

Tiliah interrupted, saying, "I already told her who you are."

Kenders stared at Tiliah carefully.

"What did you tell her exactly?"

"That you're a friend of Zecus and here to help."

She glanced back to Debrah. The woman did not look as upset as Kenders would have expected if she had known about Joshmuel.

"Nothing else?"

Tiliah shook her head and said, "Only that Zecus is well and here, looking for them." Her tone shifted, becoming more direct. "That is all, though."

With a quick nod, Kenders glanced at Debrah. The woman's gaze was fixed on Kenders' blonde hair.

"How are you friends with Zecus?"

"It's a long story," murmured Kenders, glancing around at the gathering crowd. "And one to be told another time." Looking back to Debrah, she asked, "Where are Jerem and Jezra?"

A wave of sorrow washed over Debrah's face. In a dry, raspy voice, she answered, "In the stockade."

Kenders' eyebrows lifted in surprise.

"The stockade? Why?"

"For stealing a loaf of bread. They've been locked away for three weeks."

Kenders blinked in surprise.

"Surely you are jesting."

Debrah shook her head slowly.

"I wish I were."

Kenders glanced at Tiliah. Fury burned in the young woman's eyes.

"An army is marching on the city, and they are arresting children for *stealing bread*?!"

"The Reed Men have been harsh in their justice," said Debrah.

"The Dust Men did the same in Gobas in the final days," hissed Tiliah. "Keeping order ruled every action."

"It has been the same here," said Debrah.

Kenders believed she had reached her capacity for grief during her journey to Demetus. Yet as she stared at Debrah's gaunt face, a new sorrow surged forth, flooding her soul. Over the last several turns, this poor woman had endured more misery than anyone should in a lifetime.

Her home abandoned and most likely destroyed.

An arduous journey to Gobas, then Demetus.

Joshmuel headed east to Freehaven to seek aid, Zecus west to defend their lands.

Then Tiliah rushes off after Zecus, leaving Debrah alone with the two youngest Alsher children, wallowing in conditions no one should suffer.

Now, with Jerem and Jezra in the stockades, she had been all alone for three weeks. If it was possible to die from misery alone, Debrah Alsher should be well on her way to Maeana's hall. Kenders worried that learning of Joshmuel's tragic passing might do just that.

This woman—this family—deserved some bit of happiness and it was within Kenders' ability to give it. A determined frown spread over Kenders' lips. Lifting her gaze over Debrah's head, she stared at Demetus and its bastion towers jutting out and up from the long, straight line of walls.

Nudging her chin towards Goshen, she muttered, "Both of you. On the horse. Now."

Tiliah nodded and turned, pulling her mother's arm gently.

"Come, Mother."

Debrah shot a quick, bewildered look at Kenders but went along with Tiliah without protest.

After Tiliah mounted Goshen, Kenders helped Debrah up to sit behind her daughter, moved to Smoke and, once in her saddle, directed the horse ahead of the Alshers, leaving the crowd of gawking refugees behind. A few began to shout out questions, but Kenders ignored them, riding away quickly while choosing a path that brought them closer to Demetus' walls.

It did not take Tiliah long to notice where they were headed.

"Kenders? Where are we going?"

Without looking back, Kenders called over her shoulder, "To Demetus."

There was a moment's pause before Tiliah replied.

"We are supposed to return to camp if we found anything."

Keeping her voice steady, Kenders replied, "I know."

Tiliah was quiet for a few more horse strides.

"Tobias seemed rather insistent about not going into the city."

Kenders pressed her lips together.

"Yes, he was."

"Perhaps we should—"

Kenders swiveled around, stared back at Tiliah, and said, "Jerem and Jezra are in the stockades. They have been for *three* weeks. Do you want to leave them there?"

Tiliah's eyes tightened.

"No."

"So let's go get them out."

While cautious hope flashed over Debrah's face, Tiliah's expression shifted to one of open concern.

"Do you have a plan, Kenders?"

With a confident smile and nod, Kenders answered, "Would I be riding into the city without one?"

Tiliah's eyes narrowed and her frown deepened.

"I would certainly hope not."

"Just follow me, do as I say, and things will be fine."

When Tiliah did not protest further, Kenders nodded and quickly turned around. Upon facing the city, her self-assured grin fled in an instant.

She needed to come up with a plan.

Quickly.

CHAPTER 46: HORDE

Tandyr swiveled his head to the right and eyed Raela. The erijul was leaning against one of the pine trunks, her delicate arms crossed over her breasts.

"Impressive, is it not?"

Raela nodded slowly, her gaze remaining locked on the teeming mass of Sudashians in the valley below.

"Are there any left in Sudash? Or did you collect every soul there?"

A slight smile touched Tandyr's wide lips as he turned back to stare at his army.

"I might have missed one or two."

Sudashians filled the vale, their ranks stretching north and south, horizon to horizon. The southernmost three-quarters were alert and ready to march while the remaining force was still encamped. They were not leaving until tomorrow morning. Great, orange bonfires burned in the oligurts' area, short and muddy burrows rose from the ground were the nascepel slept, while the packs of kur-surus simply lay on the ground, waiting. The demon captains wandered throughout the assembled forces, doing whatever necessary to keep order. So far, only fourteen Sudashians had had to be killed today.

Raela said quietly, "I will admit, Tandyr..." She turned to eye him, reaching up to tuck her hair behind her ear "...I doubted you could do this."

Tandyr's smile widened a fraction.

"I know you did."

The erijul studied him for a long moment before asking, "What about you?"

Tandyr glanced over.

"What do you mean?"

Raela nodded at the amassed force in the valley.

"Did you think you would come this far?"

He lifted his gaze to a pine bough, pondering the question. With a sigh and small shake of his head, he admitted, "No. I did not."

Now it was Raela's turn to smile slightly. Turning back to stare at the army, she said, "I appreciate your honesty."

Considering he was eyeing the God of Deception incarnate, Tandyr chuckled softly before saying, "Hearing the word 'honesty' coming from you is strange."

Raela's smile widened a bit.

"Catch that, did you?"

A comfortable quiet fell over their vantage point, a clump of pines atop one of the many hills that began to rise from the swampy landscape a day ago. Advance oligurt scouts reported the hills increased in both number and height further east, most likely slowing the army's progress. Tandyr did not mind much. A delay of a day or two should not make any difference in his plans.

"He should have already been here," murmured Raela.

Tandyr sighed.

"I know."

"I bet he is torturing the man just for fun."

Tandyr shrugged his shoulders.

"Most likely."

Raela shook her head slowly, quiet for a long moment before asking, "Do we still need him?"

"A little while longer, yes," answered Tandyr.

"He causes more problems than he solves."

Tandyr nodded, agreeing, "True."

"It is a risk to keep him around."

"Risks are necessary at times."

Raela turned to stare at him, a scowl marring her pretty features.

"Tandyr. He *lost* one of the Suštinata."

The glowing ember of anger in Tandyr's chest flared hot in an instant, but he managed to suppress it quickly.

"Do not worry. We will find it again."

Raela cocked a single, thin eyebrow.

"I would have thought your mongrels should have been back by now."

Tandyr frowned. She was right. After a long moment, he spoke in a low, measured tone.

"One way or another, we *will* find it again."

"How can you be so sure?" pressed Raela.

"I am sure because I am sure."

"Is there something you are not telling me?"

He turned his head to regard the erijul, the corners of his mouth curling up a fraction.

"I am sure, Raela. That will have to be enough for you now."

A coy smile spread over Raela's lips.

"What's the matter, Tandyr? Don't you trust me?"

A dry chuckle slipped from him.

"Do you trust me?"

Raela held his gaze for a long, quiet moment before turning away. As she stared back down the hill, her eyes focused on something below.

"Here he comes."

At the base of the bush-covered slope, Vanson emerged from the camp atop the back of a fine-looking roan. Tandyr briefly wondered where the God had found a horse able to tolerate the monstrous races.

He and Raela waited in silence as Vanson made his way up the hillside, weaving between clumps of grass and short trees. Smoke and the scent of charred flesh hung heavy in the air, yet could do nothing to mask the swamp's rottenness. Tandyr would be glad when the Marshlands were behind him. The air reeked.

When Vanson reached them, pulling up his horse a dozen paces short of where they stood, Tandyr did not waste any time.

"Did you bring it?"

Raela glanced over, her brow furrowed.

"Bring what?"

Tandyr ignored her as Vanson slid from the saddle, boots thudding onto some of the only dry land within miles. The former duke unhooked a cloth sack hanging from the saddle and marched the remaining few paces up the hill, his gaze locked on Tandyr.

"No worries."

He extended his arm, holding the bag out. The bottom of the sack, stretched around its contents, was shaped like a cube.

Raela's eyes went wide as she exclaimed, "Are you mad?" She stood tall, glaring at Vanson and Tandyr both. "You trusted him with *another* one? After what he did with the last?!"

Tandyr accepted the sack, glanced over to Raela, and said, "I did. And the way you are reacting right now is precisely why I did not tell you."

Vanson eyed Raela, saying, "No need to worry. It's safe."

Glaring at him, she stepped to Tandyr's side and ripped the bag from his hand. Tandyr let her have it. Resisting would have taken more time than letting her see for herself. Reaching into the bag, she withdrew a redwood box, gripped the lid, and flipped it open.

The world glittered gold as thousands of Strands of Will surged from the Suštinata, flooding the air. With a sharp crack, Raela shut the lid and the strings disappeared. She shoved the box back into the sack and handed both back to Tandyr, eyeing Vanson with a frown throughout.

The dark-skinned man smiled wide.

"Told you it was safe."

As Raela glared at him, Tandyr placed the bag on the ground and looked back to the duke.

"Did you learn anything useful?"

Vanson shook his head, saying, "Nothing new. More and more Southern Arms and Shore Guard soldiers arrive every day. Reed Men reinforcements from the south, as well."

"Numbers?" asked Tandyr.

Vanson gave a careless shrug.

"I did not ask."

"Why not?" asked Raela.

Vanson shifted his gaze to her.

"Why does it matter how many they have? We have more."

Her eyes narrowing sharply, Raela snapped, "It would be nice to know what we face."

Vanson rolled his eyes and turned back to Tandyr.

"The man was only a footman. Utterly bereft of useful information."

"Then what took you so long?" asked Tandyr.

A wicked smile twisted its way over Vanson's lips.

"Once I learned that he has a mother and sister living within Demetus' walls, I spent some time sharing our plans for the city and its citizens. I included as many details as I could."

Raela gave a quiet huff of disgust.

"You have an army waiting to march and you piddled around just to make one man miserable?"

Vanson's eyes widened as he glared at her, snapping, "I held myself in check! Were it up to me, I'd still be down there!"

Shaking her head, Raela said, "Sometimes I wonder if you have any idea what's at stake here."

"Of course I do!" snapped Vanson.

"Yet you *lost* one of the Suštinata."

Throwing up his arms, Vanson exclaimed, "When will you move on to the next act?! This is—"

"Enough!" hissed Tandyr, eyes wide. Both Gods went silent and turned to stare at him. "We must focus on what is to come! Nothing else! Agreed?" Without giving either a chance to respond, he shifted his full attention to Vanson. "Are things ready?"

Vanson shot one last glare at Raela before nodding.

"Yes. The captains have their orders and are waiting."

With a tiny nod, Tandyr said, "Go, then. We will see you in a week."

Vanson nodded and began to turn away, skipping any sort of farewell to either of them. After moving to his horse, he put a boot in a stirrup and pulled himself into the saddle. Laying the reins against his horse's neck, he gave a firm kick to the roan's sides and cantered down the hill, heading back to the horde in the valley.

The moment he was out of earshot, Raela asked, "Are you sure he will not foul this up?"

Tandyr said, "I do not see how he could."

The erijul huffed quietly.

"Then my imagination is better than yours."

Tandyr did not respond. He did not much care what Raela thought. Like Vanson, she was a means to an end.

When Vanson neared the bottom of the hill, he shouted, his words unintelligible to the Gods standing atop the hill. Moments later, a discordant chorus of horns reverberated through the valley. The low, thudding of the oligurt war chant joined the signal, followed quickly by the haunting howls of the mongrel packs. The front ranks of the great host started moving.

After watching in silence for a time, Raela turned to Tandyr.

"Any further word on Nelnora's attempt to form an Assembly?"

Tandyr nodded while keeping his gaze fixed on the army.

"Five in total, now. Saewyn has pledged her support."

Raela frowned.

"She only needs four more."

Tandyr muttered, "I can count, Raela."

Letting his snide remark slide past, she said, "I don't suppose you will tell me how you remain so well informed about her actions?"

Tandyr finally pulled his attention from below, stared into Raela's eyes, and said, "We're not the only ones who want to be free of this blasted realm." A sly smile graced his wide lips. "It's amazing what some are willing to do if the right prize is dangled before them." His grin grew. "Whatever the cost may be."

CHAPTER 47: CHEST

Khin reached the top of the stairwell and stepped onto the battlements, striding toward his tower. The cold Storm Island wind immediately began whipping at his robes. He almost smiled, relishing the chill. He enjoyed the Winters here.

Behind him, a light scuffling of Broedi's surprisingly quiet steps reached the stairs' pinnacle as well, followed a moment later by one last clack of Tobias' walking stick against the stone. Broedi had asked one question during their journey up here, Tobias two. Khin had deflected all three. At this point, showing was better than telling.

As the trio ambled along the battlements in silence, Khin felt the quiet buzz of thoughts of the people rushing about the courtyard below. The images that flashed through their heads were predictable ones, mostly visions of fighting against horrible, yet-unseen foes. Khin blocked it all out for now and focused on the task at hand.

When they reached the door to Khin's room, he stopped and turned to face Broedi and Tobias. The pair stared at him, curiosity in their eyes. He must have been quiet for too long because Tobias and Broedi shared a look between one another, after which Broedi looked to him and spoke in his deep baritone.

"Why did you ask us here?"

Khin did not answer immediately, noting the irony of the situation. The two souls whose minds he wished to view were the two he had given his word to never do so. Turning his attention to Broedi alone, he asked, "Have you now shared everything about your time with Nelnora? There is nothing else you left out?"

"A pair of excellent questions," said Tobias, looking up at Broedi expectantly. "Well?"

Broedi was quiet for a moment before rumbling, "On my family's name, I swear I have shared everything."

Tobias eyes widened a fraction in surprise.

"Good enough for me."

It was for Khin as well. Before Broedi had deduced his ability to see thoughts, Khin had witnessed a few disturbing memories from Broedi's past. The hillman's words were not spoken with flippancy.

Nodding slowly, Khin asked, "Then Nelnora did not mention what became of the Suštinata na Kamen I studied for so long?"

"No, she did not," replied Broedi. "My questions on the subject were met with silence."

Khin frowned.

"Her silence on the issue is intriguing."

Broedi's eyes narrowed.

"Khin, I asked you about this when we first returned from her temple. Perhaps I should be asking you the same questions you put to me. Have *you* left something out of your tale?"

Rather than answer, Khin turned to face the timeworn soldier statue that stood guard by his door. The stone figure had been here when he arrived, its facial features mostly gone, chipped away by the years. Enough of the carved armor remained to mark him an army general from when L'antico Impero had ruled these lands. Khin had watched the nation's rise and fall from afar, just as he had dozens of others through the years. Each time, the reasons behind a civilization's collapse could be traced to two things: greed and lack of compassion. The short-lived races rarely learned from their mistakes.

Staring into the empty air, he reached for a few Strands of Stone, wove them into a quick pattern, and then directed the brown Weave toward the statue's gut. As the Strands melted into the figure, the stone shifted and shimmered, looking like rippling water in a bucket. Extending both arms, he reached into the statue, grasped the box hidden inside, and withdrew it, releasing the Weave when he was free. The stone turned solid once again.

Turning to face Broedi and Tobias, he waited. One of them was bound to come to the correct conclusion. Both White Lions stared at the black wooden box he held in silence, the sea wind whipping through their hair.

"Hold a moment," murmured Tobias. With disbelief coating every word, he asked, "The Suštinata of Stone is in *there*?"

Khin nodded.

"It is."

Broedi's gaze snapped to Khin's face.

"How long have you had it here?"

"Fifty-eight years."

The hillman's eyes flared wide.

"And you never told me?"

"You, too, kept it from others you trust, did you not? If I recall, your exact words were, 'The fewer who know, the better.'"

Broedi's expression softened.

"You have a point."

Tobias stepped forward, his gaze fixed on the black lacquered box.

"But why do you have it? Did Nelnora not want it?"

"I did not give her the choice," answered Khin. "When I went to visit her, I did so without the Suštinata. I hid it before returning to the Seat of Nelnora and retrieved it afterwards."

The tomble's gaze shifted to Khin's face.

"Didn't trust her, did you?"

"No," answered Khin. "I do not trust any of them, the High Host, the Neither, or the Cabal."

Broedi rumbled, "Did she not ask for it back?"

"It was the first thing she asked when I arrived," answered Khin. "And the same question posed to me every day for the next fourteen years."

"Fourteen years?" asked Tobias. "You stayed in the Seat of Nelnora for fourteen years?"

"Not by choice."

"Hold a moment," rumbled Broedi, a hint of surprise slipping into his voice. "Are you saying she held you prisoner?"

Khin nodded slowly.

"She named me her 'guest,' but, 'prisoner' is a more fitting description, yes."

"How did she manage that?" asked Tobias. "I have seen what you can do, Khin. You are one of the most talented mages I have seen."

"For a mortal, my skills are good, yes. But I am no match for a Goddess and a host of divina priests watching me from sunset to sunset."

"So you never gave the stone up?" asked Broedi.

"No."

"Why?" asked Tobias.

"Both because of what it was and because of how much she wanted it. The Nelnora from five thousand years ago was right: no God or Goddess should have that sort of power. Including the Nelnora of today."

Crossing his arms, Broedi asked, "Why did she free you?"

Answering honestly, Khin said, "I do not know. One day, she stepped into my accommodations and rather than ask for the Suštinata, she told me about Indrida's prophecy, the existence of the enclave, and then had me escorted from her temple."

"So she told you to come here?"

"No. But I am sure she expected me to do so. Which is why, after I retrieved the Suštinata, I remained hidden for a short time, a decade or so. Then, I came."

"If you expected you were being manipulated, why did you still come?" asked Tobias.

"I was curious."

The tomble's eyebrows lifted high.

"You...were curious?"

"My order values knowledge above all else. I needed to know what was to happen next. So, I hid the Suštinata again, and came to Storm Island. Only many years later, when I was confident of your mission here, did I smuggle the box into the enclave."

The White Lions went silent and returned to staring at the box.

In a quiet, somewhat skeptical voice, Tobias asked, "And the Suštinata of Stone is inside?" He glanced around the battlements. "Does that mean there are Strands of Stone all over right now?"

"Not yet," answered Khin, bending to a knee to place the small chest on the battlements. Looking up to the pair, he added, "But that is the reason I asked you here."

Unlatching the lid's hook, he opened the box for the first time in fifty-eight years. Inside the box's hammered gold interior rested a speckled stone, its surface flecked with every shade of brown and tan imaginable. All around him, countless thick, robust Strands filled the air, their color matching those of the specks on the Suštinata. There were so many of them hovering about the battlements that the wind seemed to stop as if blocked by the magic strings' presence. Khin had experienced this countless times before, yet still the power within the Suštinata staggered him.

Somewhere to the northeast, he felt a mind consumed by sudden panic. It was like a beacon of light on a dark night, a beacon with which Khin was familiar. Lady Vivienne was alarmed, visions of the enclave under attack dancing through her mind. In moments, she was up and rushing closer, thinking through protocols for responses to assaults.

"We should hurry," said Khin, lifting his gaze to Broedi. "Remove the stone for me, please. It is much heavier than it looks." As Broedi knelt to the ground and reached toward the box, Khin added, "And remember: a portion of the God of Fear is contained within. Contact can be unpleasant."

Broedi paused a moment, glanced between Khin's face and the stone, and then resumed reaching for the Suštinata. His finger barely grazed its surface when an expression of pure terror washed over his face. With a sharp, un-Broedi-like curse, he withdrew his hand and glared at the brown rock.

Khin had expected some unease from the typically stoic hillman, but nothing as intense as this. The Sustinata's aura was growing stronger, then. And that worried Khin.

"Do you think you can try again?"

Broedi stared at him, reluctance in his eyes, and rumbled, "I will try." With a determined grunt, he attempted the maneuver again and wrapped his large fingers around the stone. Gripping the Suštinata, he—with great effort—managed to lift the small stone and place it on the battlements. The moment he released it, he let out a relieved sigh.

Holding out his hand, Khin asked, "Give me the other Suštinata."

Broedi reached into his pocket, withdrew the rich leather pouch containing the stone, and handed it to Khin.

Tobias said, "You said to never open that again."

"I will be brief."

Positioning the pouch over the box, Khin turned it upside down and—being careful not to touch the stone—shook the Suštinata free. The glossy black stone slipped from the sack and tumbled into the box, rattling around the gold plating inside.

A small gasp slipped from Tobias. Somewhere to the north, still within the bounds of the enclave, Khin felt another burst of panic as another mind reeled in shock. Khin assumed it was Nundle, also surprised by the surge of Void.

He waited a moment before continuing, keeping a careful eye on the Strands of Stone, wondering if there would be some reaction now that the second Suštinata was nearby and free. There was not. He hoped that was a good thing and, looking up to Tobias to catch the tomble's reaction, he snapped the lid shut with a sharp crack.

Tobias asked, "Where'd they go?" The tomble was staring around him. "I don't understand, I can't even feel a hint—" He cut off, his gaze locking on the wooden box. "What is that thing?"

Khin breathed a small sigh of relief. Perhaps it worked for them all.

"This," began Khin, "Is a chest my nine had crafted ages ago." Opening the lid—again eliciting a sharp gasp from Tobias—he pointed to the hammered gold lining the chest's interior. "Very early in our studies, we learned that gold masked the Strands emitted by the Suštinata na Kamen. Why that was, we never could determine. But it did not matter. It silenced not only the Strands of Stone, but the other properties of the Suštinata as well. Without this box, I am incapable of carrying the stone with me."

Holding up the nobleman's pouch, he said, "When I saw this in the Marshlands, I wondered how it partially concealed the Suštinata na Ulos." Turning it inside out, he revealed an interior lined with gold-laced thread. "An imperfect carrier, but certainly better than leaving it exposed."

Lady Vivienne's voice shot through the air.

"What in the Nine Hells are you doing?!"

Looking below, Khin saw the baroness glaring up at them. The images rushing through her mind were expectedly unpleasant.

Tobias said, "I'll go talk to her."

"That might be best," rumbled Broedi. As Tobias began to hobble across the battlements, the hillman looked back to Khin and asked, "You know what this means, yes?"

Khin nodded slowly.

"We need another chest."

CHAPTER 48: TIRNU

Demetus was a city on the edge of a precipice, its citizenry ready to tumble into the abyss of panic at any moment. People milled all about Kenders, wandering the flagstone streets, their shoulders taut and fists clenched. Anxious eyes darted about beneath brows covered with more furrows than a freshly tilled garden. Every face—man, woman, and child—was drawn taut. Whether from worry or hunger, Kenders could not tell.

The beds of the horse carts that rattled past her and the Alsher women were either a quarter-full or entirely empty. The few wagons with goods carried more armed men than crates or sacks, the hired guards eyeing the crowd warily with hands on hilts. A close examination of the crowd revealed nearly everyone carrying some type of weapon. A few had swords and scabbards hanging from their waist while others at least had a sheathed dagger on their belt or boot. Most people, however, lugged about any simple, blunt object, grasped in a white-knuckled hand or jammed in the crook of their arm. One thin Marshlander woman walked past Kenders while wielding a wooden candlestick as if it were a club.

A steady, apprehensive hum of voices droned through the streets. The snippets of conversation she caught provided her a spotty, broken view of what was happening in and around the city. Rumors of the Sudashian invasion dominated the chatter. Twice, she heard someone mention recent sightings of oligurt scouts in the marshy forests west of the city. Both times, the information brought a frown to her face. If there were already scouts near, the bulk of the force could not be far away.

The sprawling Marshlands' capital dwarfed the only other cities Kenders had visited in her life, Fallsbottom and Fernsford. Unlike those two mazes, the streets here were long and straight, allowing Kenders to look left and right at every intersection. The mass of people in both directions amazed her.

Demetus' buildings—made of mud-bricks and evergreen logs—were shorter than she had expected. Most were three or four stories with flat roofs sitting well below the tops of the outer walls. Skinny, wood-railed bridges connected the rooftops, spanning the streets. The heavy odor of filth and waste filled the air, coating her tongue and throat with each breath.

They had only just made it into the city, having tried to pass through three different gates. At each one, the green-and-white-clad Reed Men refused them entry. It seemed that Duke Rholeb had declared no one be permitted into the overcrowded city. After being turned away the third time, Kenders reluctantly used another few, small Weaves of Will to get past. Ever since, she had kept an anxious eye on the crowd, praying that she would not spot Constable gray.

By any measure, what she was doing was foolish. She knew she should turn around, return to the camp, and wait for the others. If her brothers were here, they most likely would be dragging her from the city, chastising her all the way back to Storm Island.

However, they were not here. She was. And she was not leaving until what remained of Zecus' family was with her.

Kenders peered to her left where Tiliah and Debrah were riding Goshen. Tiliah's worried expression matched that of the crowds, but Debrah looked happy, newly buoyed by a little cheese, some fresh water, and a lot of hope.

Catching their eye, Kenders asked, "So, where are the stockades exactly?"

Debrah lifted her arm and pointed to the southwest.

"That way. In Tirnu's District."

Kenders looked in the direction indicated. Rising over the nearby buildings was a skinny, sienna-red tower, thrice as tall as any other structure.

"Tirnu's District? Why is it called that?"

"Each of the eight districts is named after a God or Goddess," said Debrah. "Duryn's District has the tradesmen and crafters. Chalchalu's District has the great markets and wealthy merchants. At least it did when we arrived. Most of the markets are closed now."

Kenders' eyebrows drew together in sudden concern. Duryn was the Great Artisan, the God of Industry and Crafters. Chalchalu was the Filler of Purses, the God of Commerce and wealth. She hoped that was coincidence.

Turning to Debrah, she asked, "What else might be in Tirnu's District? Besides the stockades?"

Tiliah answered, giving her a level stare while saying, "Exactly what you would expect for something named after Tirnu."

Kenders heart sunk.

"Such as?"

"The Marshal House," answered Debrah.

"And the Reed Steeple," added Tiliah.

"Reed Steeple?"

Tiliah nodded to the southwest and said, "The giant tower there?"

Kenders turned to eye the spire, a frown upon her face. She recognized what a Marshal house was, a place where criminals were tried before a panel of three marshals. Without a doubt, the building would be surrounded with guards and soldiers. The Reed Steeple was a mystery to her, even though she had a good guess what it was.

"And what exactly is at the Reed Steeple?"

Tiliah answered, "The Reed Men's command post and training grounds."

Kenders shut her eyes tight and drew in a long, deep breath. Apparently, anything to do with law and order was there, in the district named after Tirnu, the

Ruler of Rules. Exhaling, she opened her eyes and kept staring to the southwest. She did not want to make eye contact with the Alshers.

"Tiliah, might Tirnu's District also be where the people Tobias was concerned about have their office?"

She did not want to say 'Constables' aloud. Tiliah, however, knew exactly what she meant.

"Two streets east of the stockades, next to the Marshal House."

Sighing, Kenders turned to stare back at Tiliah.

"Truly?"

Tiliah nodded once, her springy black hair bouncing.

"Will that be a problem?"

Kenders shook her head, muttering, "No. Not at all." Her voice lacked conviction and she knew it.

Debrah, who had been following their conversation closely with an ever increasing confused expression on her face, asked, "Who is Tobias?"

Kenders glanced at Tiliah and shook her head. Now was not the time. Instead of giving an answer, Kenders said, "This way," and directed Smoke down a less crowded alley, heading toward the Reed Steeple. Smoke's hooves stopped clopping as they moved from flagstone to dirt.

As Tiliah turned Goshen to follow, Kenders heard her say, "Don't worry, Mother. We'll explain everything later."

Kenders stared down the alleyway, a frown on her face. She had leapt without looking again. Reaching up, she rubbed her eyes, wondering if she should turn around and wait for Tobias this evening. Dropping her hand back to the reins, she looked ahead and saw a wide street awaiting them. The Reed Steeple loomed over them, ahead and to the left. If she was going to turn around, now was the time.

From behind, Debrah asked, "What exactly is your plan?"

Kenders winced and remained quiet. She could not share her plan because she did not have one.

Tiliah suggested quietly, "Perhaps we should just wait for everyone to come back later?"

Kenders started to turn around and was about to agree with Tiliah when she caught Debrah's hopeful stare. In an instant, Kenders made a complete reversal and said, "No. We are too close to turn back. We are getting Jerem and Jezra out of the stockades."

Tiliah gave her a look that reminded her of Zecus.

"If you aren't careful, Kenders, you might be joining them in there."

Kenders eyes narrowed.

"That is one thing that will *not* happen."

The three women rode beneath the final wooden bridge and exited the alleyway onto another main street. The horses' hooves clacked on flagstone briefly before Kenders pulled Smoke's reins to halt the horse.

Tiliah stopped Goshen beside her, lifted an arm, and pointed across the crowded street to their left.

"There."

A twenty-five-foot-tall fence of pine tree trunks lined the street for two-hundred paces. Bored-looking soldiers stood along it, one every twenty steps or so. A three-story, mud-brick building rested at the midpoint of the fence, cattycorner from her. The Reed Steeple was further down the street, the pyramid-topped sienna tower reaching high into the late afternoon sky. A large, rectangular building, filled with sweeping arched windows and doors, sat beside it. Many dozens more Reed Men stood outside.

"Move, outlanders!"

Looking down, Kenders found an impatient-looking woman glaring up at her and the Alshers. An empty reed basket sat atop her head, held in place with one arm. Using the other, the woman pointed at the alley behind them.

"You and your horses are blocking the way," said the woman. "Move!"

Kenders looked over her shoulder and realized that they were indeed blocking the alleyway. Facing forward, she laid the reins against Smoke's neck to direct the horse to the left.

"I'm sorry. I did not…realize…"

She trailed off, her apology left unfinished as the woman strode past while shooting Kenders and the Alshers a look of open disgust as she disappeared down the way. Kenders shared a glance with Tiliah and Debrah, both of whom shrugged their shoulders at the woman's rudeness.

Moving Smoke completely clear of the entranceway, she stopped again, and ran her gaze over the building beside them. A faded red sign with white script letters proclaimed the location to be Thanon's Arms for Let. The door was shut and wide-planked boards covered the windows. Looking up and down the street, she noted that most of the building here were in similar condition.

As Tiliah directed Goshen to stand between her and the mercenaries' office, Kenders turned back to eye the stockades office and offered a quick prayer to Ashana, looking for a bit of inspiration. She was still absent a plan.

Debrah asked, "How exactly is this going to work?"

Kenders looked over and found the Alsher matriarch staring across the crowded street at the stockade walls. The hope in her eyes was fading fast, the leftover void filling quickly with doubt and worry. Tiliah, too, eyed the stockades, although more with anger than anything else.

"Three weeks," muttered Tiliah. "For three blasted weeks they've been in there, housed with murderers and thieves."

Kenders did not want to leave the children in there a moment longer, plan or not. Swinging her leg over Smoke's rear, she dismounted, moved to the front of her horse, and reached up, handing the reins to Tiliah.

"Hold these. I'll be back shortly."

Tiliah stared down at her but did not take the reins.

"You are going alone?"

Kenders paused a moment before saying, "Yes. I am. Now, hold these."

Still, Tiliah did not take the leather straps.

"What are you going to do?"

"First, I'm going to ask them nicely to let Jerem and Jezra out."

Debrah stared at her as if she was mad.

With a deep frown etched on her face, Tiliah asked pointedly, "Are you going to *ask* them like you *asked* the guards to let us into the city?"

"Let's hope I don't have to," answered Kenders. "But I will if I must." Shoving the reins against Tiliah's leg, she added, "Will you please take the reins?"

Ignoring them still, Tiliah's tone turned even sharper as she asked, "I appreciate what you are trying to do, but you are risking much. Much more than you should."

Debrah leaned to the side to stare at her daughter.

"What does that mean?"

Both young women ignored her question.

"We can still go back, Kenders," said Tiliah quietly.

Kenders shook her head and said, "No. Someone once told me that I have good instincts. That if I follow them, trust myself, and do what comes natural, things will work out. I think I'll do that."

Both Tiliah and Debrah's expressions changed in an instant. Apparently, they both recognized Joshmuel's words of wisdom. Before either of them could protest, she took Tiliah's hand, placed Smoke's reins in them and said, "Hold my horse, please."

She started to turn toward the street but stopped short. With a short sigh, she looked back.

"Should things…not work out, though. Head back to camp and wait for Zecus and the others. Tell him what I did and where I am."

Tiliah nodded slowly.

"Be careful. Think before doing *anything* in there."

With a single nod, Kenders turned away and stepped into the crowd. Two steps in, she mumbled to herself, "Don't I always?"

Chapter 49: Cloak

Kenders stepped inside the stockades office and skidded to a stop. The cramped room smelled like a horse stall that should have been mucked out two turns back. Saying a silent farewell to the relatively cleaner air outside, she closed the door behind her. The room darkened considerably, lit now only by the diffused light coming through four small, square windows along the front wall.

On the other side of the room, two light-skinned Reed Men stood behind a wooden counter, slouched over a parchment and ogling her, the lopsided grins on their faces owning a certain leering quality that she did not appreciate.

She suppressed a grimace and approached the counter, studying the room as she walked. Two rickety wooden tables and seven chairs were jammed against the wall to her left, while, to her right, eight rusty metal shackles were bolted into the wood, four up high, four down low. It was easy to imagine two souls clamped within.

As she looked back to the men, the overweight soldier on her right elbowed his companion, a short a man with thinning brown hair and jagged scar across his forehead. The scarred man smiled wide.

"Good days ahead, my lovely."

Stopping at the counter and seeing no special markings on the soldier's uniform, she said, "And good days behind, Footman…?" She trailed off, hoping he would offer his name. He did.

"Rias," replied the man quickly. "Footman Ethan Rias." He stood a bit taller before boasting, "Although, in short order, I'll be a corporal."

Sensing an opportunity, Kenders steeled herself, gave Footman Rias a sweet, syrupy smile, and swooned, "A corporal? Oh, my."

The overweight soldier stared at Ethan, a gap-toothed grin covering most of his face, and laughed, "Corporal Rias? Hah! When the marshes turn to sand!" He shifted his gaze to Kenders, letting it drift from her face, to her waist, and back up again. "My name is Mitus. How can *I* help you?"

Suppressing another shudder, she said, "Well, I was hoping you could do something for me." Glancing at the parchment on the counter, she saw a long list of what appeared to be names. Taking a chance, she asked, "Might that be a list of the prisoners?"

Short and bald Ethan leaned in front of Mitus and said, "Yes, my lovely, it is." Mitus glared at him from behind.

"Wondrous!" said Kenders. "Could you tell me if you are housing a young boy and girl here? Two young Borderlanders named Alsher?"

The guards looked at one another briefly before Mitus turned back to her, a touch of suspicion in his eyes.

"That's an odd thing to ask. Might I ask why you want to know?"

Kenders hesitated, trying to think of a plausible reason, before saying, "Yesterday, I spotted two young refugees stealing from my father's cooling window. When Father reported it to a Reed Man today, the soldier told us to check here. He recalled you having already hooked a pair of bread thieves."

Mitus' eyes narrowed.

"Why did he send you here and not the Marshal House?"

Kenders stared at the man, a blank expression on her face.

"I don't know why. He just said to come here."

Ethan folded his arms over his chest and frowned.

"When did you see this crime occur again?"

"Yesterday?" offered Kenders. She did not know if the room was hot or not, but she was suddenly sweating.

"How did you know their names?" asked Mitus.

"And what did they take?" followed Ethan.

Kenders' gaze danced between the pair as she wondered which question to answer. She chose the easier of the two.

"Two loaves of rye-grain bread."

"Are you sure?" asked Ethan.

Kenders nodded.

"Yes."

Mitus tilted his head to the side.

"Tell me, miss, has your family managed to craft a recipe for rye-grain bread that does not require rye-grain?"

A pair of deep furrows split Kenders' brow.

"Pardon?"

"All rye-grain comes up from Nebekah," said Ethan. "The fields here are too wet to grow it. And considering the road to Nebekah has been more or less free of caravans for three weeks now, there has been no rye-grain in the city for some time now. Hells, there's no flour, at all. *Nobody* is baking *anything*. Even the duke's table is without bread."

Kenders glanced quickly between the two men.

"Ah…we had some in our stores."

"Did you?" asked Mitus. "Where is your family's bakery? Which district?"

"It's in the…ah…"

As she stumbled with her answer, Mitus began to move down the length of the counter, heading to an opening. Kenders frowned. So far, trusting her instincts was not going well at all.

"Oh…Hells."

If she wanted Jerem and Jezra free, she was going to need to use the Strands to do it. Eyeing the soldiers, she decided she only needed one of them to retrieve the children for her. The other one merely needed to be quiet.

Mitus was on her side of the counter now, only paces away from her, his hand on his hilt.

"What mischief are you up to, girl?"

Had she more time, she could have subdued Mitus using any number of Weaves. At the moment, however, she needed to stop him.

Now.

And quickly.

She stared at the advancing Reed Man, wanting nothing more than for him to fall into a deep, restful sleep. With a suddenness that startled her, a Weave popped into existence before her, fully complete and whole. Mostly silver with a bit of gold and white flickering at the center of the pattern, the Weave whipped toward Mitus. A wave of tiredness washed over her, but it was not as bad as she had expected.

The Weave touched Mitus, his legs gave out and he crashed to the floor like a sack of potatoes. As Ethan leaned over the counter, peering wide-eyed at Mitus, Kenders reached for the golden Strands of Will, knit together a quick Weave, and directed it over him.

Keeping her tone firm and direct, Kenders said, "There's no need to worry, Ethan. None at all. Remain calm and quiet."

The man shifted his gaze to her and, without a moment's hesitation, nodded.

"Of course, my lovely."

"I said, remain quiet. And stop calling me 'my lovely.'"

The man nodded once.

"Of course."

Satisfied that the Weave seemed to be mostly working, Kenders said, "There are two Borderlands children here by the name of Jerem and Jezra Alsher. Bring them to me as quickly as you can."

"Right away," replied the man, already staring at the parchment on the counter while dragging a calloused, dirty finger along the sheet. Halfway down, he stopped, tapped it twice, and turned around, moving to a closed door on the back wall.

As he grabbed the handle, Kenders said, "Do not tell *anyone* why you are retrieving them. In fact, say nothing at all until you are back in this room."

"Of course, miss. I'll be just a moment."

He turned and disappeared into a hallway, closing the door behind him. Kenders eyed the doorway, happy that the man had the manners to call her 'miss' now.

Looking down at Mitus, she wondered if she should move him from the middle of the office floor. Should someone walk into the stockades now, questions would surely fly.

She grabbed the man's right boot with the intention of pulling him back behind the counter and began tugging as hard as she could, eyeing the door the entire time, expecting a Tracker to burst inside any moment. After straining for a short while, she managed to move Mitus only a pace or two. The man might only be as tall as Nikalys, but he weighed as much as Broedi. With a disappointed huff, she dropped his leg back to the floor with a thud.

"You're staying there."

She could move him with magic, but did not want to cause any more of an alert than she already had. A muted, metal jingling drew her attention to the back door. With a rattle and a creak, the door opened. A girl and boy, both dark-skinned with coarse, black hair, emerged from the darkened hall and stepped into the room. Confused yet hopeful expressions rested on their faces.

Jezra was twelve years old and not near the beauty her older sister was, but the resemblance to Tiliah and Debrah was still evident. Jerem was a nine year old, smooth-faced version of Zecus. Both were dressed in rags, their torn shirts and breeches shredded and filthy. Ethan marched behind them, his hands on their shoulders, directing the children.

Kenders allowed herself a small smile. She had found them.

Her smile fled.

Now to get them out of the office.

"Stop there, Ethan." ordered Kenders. "They can come forward on their own."

The soldier halted and removed his hands from the pair's shoulders. Though free of his grasp now, the children did not move. Jerem was staring at the snoring Reed Man splayed out before the break in the counter while Jezra was glaring at Kenders, suspicion in her eyes.

Her tone firm and demanding, the girl asked, "Who are you?" If Jezra was afraid, she did not show it.

Offering a kind, reassuring smile, Kenders said, "My name is Kenders. I am a…friend of your brother's."

The children glanced at one another, their brows wrinkling in confusion. Kenders certainly understood why. They had not seen Zecus in a long time. And when they last had, he was marching west, back to the Borderlands. Her light skin and hair clearly marked her from the east.

Jerem looked back to her and asked, "What's his name?"

"Zecus," replied Kenders. "Zecus Alsher."

"And how do you know him?" asked Jezra.

"We met a few turns past." She paused a moment before adding, "In the Southlands of all places." The truth might be hard for them to believe, but Kenders was done trying to make up stories after failing miserably with the Ethan and Mitus.

"Impossible," said Jezra with a firm shake of her head. "Zecus left us. He went home to fight."

Nodding slowly, Kenders said, "True. But something happened that brought him east. When we met, he helped my family, so now I'm helping his."

Both children continued to stare at her, the skepticism on their faces as easy to spot as a full White Moon in a cloudless night sky.

"He's here, you know," added Kenders. "Out in the camps, searching for you."

That revelation brought some light to Jerem's eyes. Jezra remained dubious, however. Both remained silent.

"Tiliah and I were out—"

"Tiliah's back, too?" asked Jerem, hopeful excitement in his voice.

Nodding, Kenders said, "Yes. She and I found your mother earlier. They're outside, waiting for us right now." She held out a hand. "Come with me and we can go see them."

Jezra glanced over her shoulder, back to Ethan, and asked, "And he's letting us go?"

Kenders shifted her gaze to the bald soldier.

"That's exactly what he's doing. Right, Ethan?"

The Reed Man nodded quickly.

"Of course, miss."

Jezra looked back and forth between Kenders and the soldier, her eyes narrowing.

"Why?"

Kenders doubted saying "I used magic" would earn her the trust she needed right now.

"I reasoned with him, pointing out that for a crime so small, your punishment was unjust. And he agreed with me. Don't you, Ethan?"

Ethan nodded emphatically.

"I do, miss. Terribly unfair, it was."

Looking back to the young girl, Kenders said, "See? Now, come on. We should go."

Kenders was getting anxious. She imagined a half-dozen Trackers pushing through the crowd outside, rushing toward the office. Jezra still did not move, however, and continued to stare at Kenders with a wary eye.

"And Tiliah and Mother are outside?"

With a touch of impatience slipping into her tone, Kenders said, "Yes. Let's go, please."

Jezra's eyes narrowed further. They were almost slits now.

"I don't believe you."

"Well, I do," said Jerem, stepping forward. "And even if I didn't, she's getting us out of here at least."

A soft, metallic jingling filled the room as he moved through the break in the counter. As he emerged, Kenders saw why. Rusty metal shackles bound the boy's wrist, a thick iron chain hanging between them. Moving to the counter, Kenders looked over and found Jezra wearing a matching pair.

Glowering at Ethan, Kenders asked, "Were those truly necessary?"

"All lawbreakers are required—"

Cutting him off, Kenders snapped, "They took a loaf of bread!"

Ethan stared at her, his face blank.

"Yes. And that makes them thieves."

"They only wanted something to eat! They were starving!"

"That doesn't give them the right to steal."

Ethan had a point, but his response nonetheless infuriated her. She glared at the manacles around both children's wrists. She wanted them gone.

Now.

An intricate, crisscrossing Weave of matte brown, gleaming silver, and lustrous white Strands appeared around the shackles. An instant later, the metal turned translucent. The manacles passed through the children's wrists and fell through the air, solidifying just before striking the wooden floorboards with a resonant clang. A wave of fatigue washed over Kenders, one that was much stronger than before.

Everyone in the room—save the sleeping Mitus—stared at the shackles and chains, mouths open, Kenders included. She had no idea that was possible.

A few moments passed before Ethan mumbled the obvious.

"You're a mage."

Kenders looked up and found the Reed Man staring at her, wide-eyed. The soldier took two steps backwards, dropping his hand to his hilt. His eyes shot to the front door, then to the back.

"I...I must warn...I need to—"

Kenders interjected, pointing to the tables and chairs while finishing his sentence for him.

"Sit right there and wait until we're gone. Quickly and quietly, please."

The soldier clamped his mouth shut, practically sprinted to the nearest chair, and sat down, all the while staring at her, fear pouring from his eyes. Kenders almost wished he was ogling her again. Now, she felt like a monster.

Discounting the soldier, Kenders looked back to the children.

"Come. Now we truly must go."

Instead of complying with her order, Jezra reached out, grabbed Jerem by his shoulders, and pulled him close.

"We're not going *anywhere* with you. He's right. You're a mage!"

"Who cares if she's a mage?" asked Jerem. "She's freeing us!" He tried to pull away from Jezra's grip, but the girl held tight and shook her head.

"I'd rather stay in the stockades than go with her."

"We don't have time for this," said Kenders. "We need to go!"

Any Tracker within a mile capable of sensing Stone, Soul, or Air would have felt the pair of Weaves she had inadvertently used.

"No!" exclaimed Jezra, shaking her head. "You are trying to trick us!"

"Why would I do that?"

"I don't know, but you are! Zecus and Tiliah can't be here! They're gone!"

Exasperated, Kenders began walking toward one of the windows, saying, "Come here if you don't believe me. Tiliah and your mother are right across—" She cut off the moment she looked through the window's dirty glass. Her stomach clenched tight and her heart began to race.

The street was completely empty. When she had entered the stockades office, the flagstone way had been full. Now, there was not a single person, cart, or horse to be seen. It looked as if the city was abandoned.

"Hells."

"What is it?" asked Jerem.

Ignoring him, Kenders took a quick step back from the window, moving out of the light. The boy managed to break free of his sister's grasp, hurried to Kenders' side, and peered out the window.

"Where is everybody?"

Kenders stepped into the shadows, pressed herself against the wall, and looked out the window again, trying to see up the street.

"I don't know."

"What are you going to do?"

Looking down, Kenders met Jerem's inquisitive stare yet remained silent.

She briefly considered opening a port to anywhere not in the city. However, as she still did not know the Weave very well, she would need to rely on her ability to will it into existence. And if she did that, she might faint as she had in the forest outside Claw. She thought about using a Weave of Air to hide them, but if a Tracker could sense Air, they would be, as easy to spot as a lone duck on a still pond. One idea after another flashed through her head and as she discounted them all, Kenders realized that fleeing was not an option.

Taking in a quick breath, she stepped back from the window, looked between both children and said, "I want you both to stay here, stay back, and stay quiet. Understand?"

Jezra and Jerem both nodded their silent agreement, although she suspected for different reasons. Jerem seemed to trust her, but Jezra certainly did not.

Shooting a quick glance at Ethan, she said, "You, don't move or speak." As the soldier nodded, she moved to the door, placed her hand on the wood handle, and paused. Taking a deep breath, she muttered, "Broedi's going to kill me."

Lifting the handle, she gently pushed the door. The moment light slipped into the room, she felt a sudden crackling of brown and white.

Alarmed, she shoved the handle, throwing the door open, and stepped from the office into the open air. As she brought a hand up to shade her eyes against the sudden brightness, the pine-paneled door banged hard against the wall, sending forth a sharp crack that echoed throughout the empty street. She looked left and right, searching for the mage responsible for the Strands. Down the way to her right, she spotted a line of Reed Men stretching across the street. To the left, there was nothing but empty flagstone. No mage. No Weave.

Confused, she focused on the feeling of the crackling colors.

Up.

Throwing her head back, she stared into the bright blue sky and spotted a Weave hovering high overhead. She recognized the pattern in an instant, said a silent thank you for Khin's lessons, and reached out to pluck a few Strands from the Weave's center. The entire thing fell apart in an instant.

Hearing a soft, angry curse behind her, Kenders whirled around and spotted a man dressed in Constables' gray peeking around the left corner of the stockade's office. Taller than most Marshlander men, his dark black hair and olive complexion reminded her of Cero, the ex-Tracker, and marked the mage as a Northlander. Yet his clothes—gray breeches, gray shirt, even a gray cape—were Constable's garb.

Her heart—already beating fast—thudded even harder. This man was no Tracker.

"Oh, Hells."

Weeks after arriving at the enclave, Kenders and Jak had been at a table in the commons one evening, playing radigan. Cero wandered up and asked if he could play the winner. They invited the man to sit with them and wait, talking as they played. At some point, the conversation turned to the Constables. Curious, Kenders asked Cero a question that had been bothering her for some time. After seeing the talent of the Storm Island mages and knowing of what she herself was capable, she did not understand how the Constables were able to enforce the ban on magic. A single proficient mage could handle two dozen heavily armed men with ease.

With a rueful grin, Cero revealed that the few mages the Constables actually found were often raw and untrained. In most cases, a rag doused with harot's oil and placed over the mage's face as they slept was sufficient to subdue them. Sometimes, however, when the rare individual was able to thwart such methods, the Constables sent a Gray Cloak, a small, somewhat secretive sect within the organization rumored to be fully trained mages themselves.

Apparently, it was no rumor.

Staring at the man hiding behind the corner, Kenders asked, "You're a Gray Cloak, aren't you?"

Stepping from the shadows and into the sunlight, the man ignored her questions and ordered, "Stand down, mage."

Kenders shot a quick look up and down the street, checking all the corners and alleyways, wondering if he was the only one here.

Misinterpreting her intent, the Gray Cloak called, "There is no way out. Every alley and street is blocked." He began to advance on her slowly, his eyes never leaving hers. In a crisp, clear tone, he called, "In accordance with the law of the First Council, you are hereby placed under arrest!"

Kenders struggled to keep her face expressionless while she tried to think of something to do. The man continued his advance.

"Will you submit to the Constable's authority?"

With a firm shake of her head, Kenders said, "No." She might not know what to do, but she was certainly not surrendering.

"I am permitted to do whatever is required to subdue you," retorted the man. While his voice was even and steady, a clear, threatening undertone was present. "I will give you one last chance to submit."

Remaining quiet, pretending as if she were considering the offer, Kenders instead reached for a few dozen Strands of Will and quickly knit them together, hoping to use the same Weave she had on Ethan. Perhaps she could simply tell the Gray Cloak to let her go. She was only halfway finished when she both felt and watched the Weave suddenly fall apart. Looking back to the man, she found him staring at her, a tiny smile resting on his lips.

"I am quite proficient in Will, mage."

Kenders considered simply willing the Gray Cloak away, perhaps sending him off to a tavern in Fernsford, but knew better than to do so. Such an effort would cause her to pass out. Wondering if she could reason with him, she spoke in a soft, subdued voice.

"Would you believe that I'm not a threat to you?"

The Gray Cloak shook his head once.

"Not for a moment."

"I'm actually here to help."

"Help?" chuckled the man. "Help with what?"

"When the Sudashians get here, you will need—"

"The Sudashians!?" repeated the Gray Cloak. An abrupt bark of a laugh escaped from him. "Don't tell me you've bought some rumormonger's babbling?"

"They aren't rumors."

"Duke Rholeb would like you, girl. He's been insisting for weeks that Sudash filth is coming."

"He's right," said Kenders somberly.

"And how would you know?"

Kenders opened her mouth to answer but shut it a moment later. Even if she could tell him the truth, she doubted he would believe her.

The Gray Cloak's gaze broke from her, briefly shifting to focus on something behind her. Looking over her shoulder, Kenders spotted three Reed Men but a hundred feet away, creeping toward her along the empty street, swords drawn. Without hesitation, she reached for some Strands of Fire, wove a simple but large orange pattern, and stretched it across the street, halfway between her and the soldiers. A wall of fire leapt from the flagstones and stretched high into the air, the tips of the sudden flames reaching the pinnacle of the stockades' fence. A blast of hot air flew past her, whipping her hair and ruffling her dress. The Reed Men not only stopped their advance, but also scrambled back several dozen paces, their eyes wide.

Turning on her heel, she faced the Gray Cloak. He was staring at the wall of flames, his mouth hanging open.

"Please," said Kenders. "All I want to do is leave."

The Gray Cloak continued gaping at the fire for a few moments before shifting his gaze back to her. There was a strange twinkle in his eyes.

"Perhaps you and I could come to an understanding?"

Hoping that he might be considering letting her go, she said, "Explain."

Taking a few, halting steps closer, he said, "The Constables are always looking for upstanding citizens capable of helping us in our duties. You have more control than most lawbreakers I find. Tell me, my dear, do you like the color gray?"

Kenders could not believe what she was hearing.

"You want me to *join* the Constables?"

The man's gaze ran over her travel-worn clothes, mussed hair, and dirt-streaked face.

"You never need worry about food again. Or a place to sleep."

"You must be jesting."

"Now, for bringing someone as talented as you into the fold, I would get a hefty reward. Perhaps I could even share a portion with you? How does ten gold ducats sound?"

Kenders glared at the man. This was preposterous.

"You're mad."

Frowning, the man said, "Fine. Twenty. But not a single—"

"No!" shouted Kenders. "Bless the Gods! I'm not negotiating with you, you fool! Don't you understand? There is an army of oligurts, razorfiends, mongrels, and *demon-men* marching on Demetus!"

A dark, angry shadow crossed the Gray Cloak's face as he hissed, "I *won't* make the offer again."

"Good! That way I won't waste breath refusing it again!"

A sneer darted across his lips.

"So you'd rather sit in a cell for the rest of your life?"

Glaring at the man, Kenders asked, "And will you be the one putting me there? Because I would very much like to see you try."

The man's gaze flicked to the fire still roaring behind her, his eyes showing evident concern. She could almost hear him thinking. Hoping to make his answer easy, Kenders—on feel alone—reached behind her and twisted the Weave within the fire. The flames roared even higher, sending enough heat outward that it was almost too warm for Kenders to remain where she was. Nevertheless, she held her ground. The Gray Cloak did not. His eyes widened as he took three quick steps backward.

After a moment, she reverted the Weave back to its original pattern. She did not want to set Demetus aflame.

The Constable looked back to her, threw back his shoulders, and announced, "Your talents are great, girl. But mine are greater." Less than two dozen paces separated them and he began to close the distance, taking slow, measured steps. "Don't be foolish! I have the authority to kill you if I deem necessary."

Kenders shook her head in disbelief.

"And you'd do that?"

"Of course," said the Gray Cloak. "Mages must be dealt with."

"You're a blasted mage!"

"I'm a Gray Cloak. There is a difference."

"No there's not!"

The Constable shrugged his shoulders.

"According to the law, there is."

Kenders had never been more disgusted than she was right now. This man, a mage himself, willingly oppressed others just like him and saw nothing wrong with it. The hypocrisy incensed her. A hot, bubbling fury ignited deep within her soul and quickly boiled over.

"Blast the law!"

Without thought or hesitation, she reached for a number of Water, Air, and Soul Strands and quickly arranged the rippling blue, white, and silver strings. The Gray Cloak's eyes went wide.

She directed the completed Weave toward two horse troughs beside the stockades office. The water within poured over the sides, splashing to the ground and rushing toward the Gray Cloak, rising from the flagstone, taking shape as it moved. Within two quick breaths, a fifteen-foot tall water fibríaal, frothy and dirty, was sloshing across the flagstone. When the creature was nearly on top of the man, Kenders spoke a single word.

"Hold."

The fibríaal halted mere paces from the Gray Cloak, the water within swirling and twisting. Any spare drop that fell to the ground rolled back into the creature's base. While the Gray Cloak gaped at the fibríaal, Kenders reached for Strands of Life, knitted a dozen Weaves one after another, tossing each at the wooden poles that made up the stockades' fence. Despite having been hewn years ago, the dead and dry pine trunks swelled, and began to sprout new branches. The newly alive trees groaned and creaked, swiftly growing upward and outward, straining against one another as green needles sprang from fresh boughs.

Reaching for Charge and Air next, Kenders wrangled sizzling yellow and airy white together into a large pattern and directed the completed Weave to the empty street, halfway between the Gray Cloak and the long line of Reed Men far to the north. A brilliant flash and a bone-rattling boom filled the abandoned way. Kenders winced against the light and sound. She had not thought that demonstration through.

She shook her head, blinking, as the thunder rumbled through Demetus, echoing about the surrounding hills.

Her eyes adjusted quickly and she peered back to the Gray Cloak. The man was bent over, his hands pressed to his ears. Taking a chance, Kenders willed a small port into existence, wanting one side right before her, the other, immediately behind the Gray Cloak. The black and white Weave popped into being, bringing with it a manageable wave of fatigue. The sound of fabric being rend in two was muted as her ears were still suffering from the thunder's thud. Reaching out, she grabbed a curtain of reality—a tingling sensation ran up her arm—flipped it aside, and stepped through.

She stood behind the Gray Cloak, silent, and watched the man lift his head to stare where she had been a moment ago. His head twisted side to side as he searched the street for her. She savored the man's confusion for a moment before reaching out and tapping him on the shoulder.

He spun around and stared at her, abject fear and wonder filling his face. Backpedaling away, he tripped over his draping cloak and fell hard to the flagstone.

Content that she had made her point, Kenders released every Weave.

With two soft pops, both sides of the port disappeared. The wall of fire winked out, leaving a black, charred line spanning the street. The water fibríaal fell apart and dropped to the ground, lightly splashing her but soaking the Gray Cloak. The pine trunks stopped creaking as their unnatural growth spurt halted. Kenders glanced up at the new trees and decided they were a much-needed improvement to the dirty city.

As she lowered her gaze from the treetops, she spotted Jezra and Jerem on the street, standing a couple paces from the stockades' office, staring at her with equal parts awe and fear. Jezra stood behind Jerem, her arms draped protectively around his shoulders. At least they were not running away. Yet.

Turning her attention to the Gray Cloak sitting a large puddle of water, she said, "Now, I am going to leave and you will sit there until I am gone. No, you'll sit there until the sun sets. Do you understand?"

The man's head bobbed up and down quickly and in perfect silence.

"Good," said Kenders. She gave him a grim, tight-lipped smile. "Farewell, Constable. Good memories behind."

She swept past the Gray Cloak, stepped around the trough water puddle, and marched to Jerem and Jezra, hoping they would not turn and run from her. They did not.

She stopped before the pair and crouched down, placing one knee on stone. Giving them as gentle a smile as she could, she said, "I am sorry if I scared you."

Neither child moved.

Kenders asked, "Would you like to go see your family?"

When there was still no movement from either, Kenders sighed and said, "Please. I truly am a friend of Zecus. And your mother and sister are nearby." She held out her right hand. "I can take you to them if you would like." She glanced to the alleyway where she had left Tiliah and Debrah, hoping the pair was still close.

Jerem began to reach out, but Jezra grabbed his arm, and pulled it back.

Dropping her hand to her side, Kenders peered at the sister.

"I am truly sorry if I scared you."

The girl showed no response.

Jerem muttered, "Jezzy, you're hurting my arm." His plea did not loosen her grip.

Kenders had gone too far. While she had succeeded in intimidating the Gray Cloak, she had also petrified Zecus' sister. She might need to bring Tiliah to them rather than the other way around. Nodding toward the alley, she said, "I'm going to go get your sister. I want you both to stay here while I do that. Will you do that for me?"

Jerem nodded immediately, but before Jezra could give her answer, a strident hawk's cry pierced the unnatural tranquility of the city street.

Confused, Kenders tilted her head back and stared into the sky, shielding her eyes from the bright sun. Two weeks in the Marshlands and she had yet to see a hawk. Nevertheless, swooping down from the northern sky was a massive one, its wingspan fifty feet from tip to tip. Enormous black talons hung beneath its dirty-white breast. Golden-brown feathers covered the rest of the bird, head to tail.

A happy, joyous relief surged in her chest and a quick smile spread over her lips.

"Thank the Gods."

However, as the hawk circled lower, its destination evidently the street, her grin quickly faded. Her relief fled and was replaced with a worried, tight sensation gripping heart and stomach. She felt as if her mother had just caught her sneaking twenty grape tarts.

With a great flapping of wings, the hawk landed two dozen paces from Kenders, directly between her and the Gray Cloak. The colossal bird regarded her silently, its deep brown eyes locked on her alone.

Kenders forced a smile and said, "Good days ahead, Broedi."

The bird's gaze shifted to Jerem and Jezra briefly before it swiveled its head to regard the Gray Cloak. A moment later, she felt a crackling surge of green, gold, and silver. The hawk's shape began to change, prompting surprised gasps from both Alsher children.

The yellow, hooked beak retreated inward, melting into the bird's face. Both wings bent at the midpoint, becoming elbows to a pair of thick, muscular arms. The feathers disappeared, replaced with smooth, tan skin. Its talons morphed into booted feet.

Once Broedi completed his shift, he stood tall, glanced at the Gray Cloak once again—the man looked as if he might become ill—and then approached where Kenders was kneeling before Jerem and Jezra. Stopping beside the trio, he crossed his arms and stared down at her.

"Why am I not surprised to find you here?"

Kenders held the hillman's stoic glare and did not flinch.

"Go ahead. Yell at me if you like."

The hillman shook his head.

"There will be no yelling. You are safe and unharmed. That is all that is important."

Kenders blinked in quiet surprise, taken aback.

"Truly? After all this? Hells, Broedi, even I know this was a mistake. A very large mistake."

A slight smile graced Broedi's lips as he glanced at the fence of pine trees, the smoking flagstone, and the puddle of water.

"A mistake, yes. But not as large as you might think."

Kenders stared at the hillman in silence for a moment or two. Her public display of magic would have only been more public if she had stood in the Grand Square in Freehaven during a Year's End festival.

"I'm very confused right now."

"And I will leave you as such for the time being. Consider it your punishment for forgetting that you have responsibilities to people other than yourself and those close to you."

She winced, but kept quiet. She deserved that.

Broedi turned his gaze to Jerem and Jezra, smiled at the pair, and rumbled, "My pleasure is to meet you in peace today, uori and uora. I am Broedi."

The Alsher children, their heads tilted upward, stared at the giant for a few heartbeats before Jerem replied, his voice small and quiet.

"And may peace bless our parting, great hawk-man."

Broedi's normally small smile widened a fraction. "No titles, please. Just Broedi." Glancing back to Kenders, he added, "It is good you found them. Zecus will be relieved."

Rising from the ground, Kenders asked, "You've seen Zecus?"

"I found him and Boah some time ago. It is you whom I have been searching for most of the afternoon."

Jezra asked, "Zecus is here?" For the first time, Kenders heard true hope in her voice. "He is truly here?"

Looking back down, Broedi rumbled, "Yes, uora. He is sitting at the Duke's Hall now, waiting for me to return." He shifted his gaze to Kenders. "Along with your kaveli."

"Hold a moment," said Kenders, shaking her head. "Jak and Nikalys are here, too?"

"They are."

"And…they're at…they're at the *Duke's Hall*?"

Her confusion was deepening by the moment.

"They wanted to search for you, but—"

A shout cut off Broedi as a familiar voice echoed along the empty street.

"I found them!"

Looking across the way, Kenders saw Tobias by the alleyway, pushing past a group of Constables while smacking them with his walking stick. Two Reed Men appeared to be assisting him in pushing the Constables to the side, causing Kenders further bewilderment. Tiliah and Debrah followed the tomble, leading the horses behind them. Another figure in a green tunic walked with them, carrying a thick-handled longspear. His elongated limbs, darker complexion and hair, and the graceful manner in which he moved marked him a tijul.

Without taking her gaze from the stranger, Kenders asked, "Is that Wren Aembyr?"

"It is," rumbled Broedi.

Jerem and Jezra turned to face the commotion and immediately sprinted down the street toward their mother, shouting for joy. Tiliah and Debrah dropped to their knees and embraced the pair, smiles filling their faces.

Despite the happy moment, Kenders frowned. An impossibly dark sadness awaited three of them. Feeling Broedi's gaze upon her, she looked up. With sympathy in his eyes, he extended an arm and gently squeezed her shoulder in silence. Kenders was grateful both for the gesture and that he remained quiet.

After a moment, she asked, "So Nikalys is safe, then?"

Broedi dropped his hand and nodded.

"He is well."

"And Jak?"

"The same," rumbled the hillman. A slight smile touched his lips. "Mostly."

Kenders was about to ask what he meant by that, but stopped as Tobias hobbled up, Wren and Alsher family in tow. Meeting the tomble's expectant stare, she said, "I can explain."

Tobias leaned on his walking stick, tilted his head to the side, and said to no one in particular, "Try not to do anything rash while I'm gone. And whatever you do, don't go into the city." He made a face as if trying to recall something. "Yes…I am quite sure those were my exact words this morning."

"I'm sorry," said Kenders. She glanced at Jerem and Jezra. "But when I heard they were in the stockades…" She trailed off, paused a moment, and said, "Actually, I'm not sorry. I'm glad I did what I did."

The White Lion regarded her with a tiny frown before looking at the wet flagstone and the line charred street.

"You certainly put on a display, didn't you? Let's see…I felt Void, Air, and Soul. And from the looks of things, you used Water and Fire as well."

"And Life," mumbled Wren, nodding at the new pine trees lining the street. "Unless Marshlanders grow their fences."

"Did you use *every* type of Strand?" asked Tobias. "Seems a bit much."

Unable to take it any longer, Kenders looked between Broedi and Tobias, asking, "Why aren't either of you upset?" She fixed her gaze on Broedi alone. "And why did you change in the middle of the street?" She waved a hand at the dozen or so alleyways up and down the street, now lined with citizens pushing forward and staring. "Everyone saw you. And what about him?" She whirled around and pointed at the man still lying in the puddle of water. "He's a Gray Cloak!"

Broedi shrugged his shoulders.

"It does not matter."

"It doesn't matter?" repeated Kenders. "Unless you plan on silencing him somehow—" fear flashed over the Gray Cloak's face "—the Constables will know all about you now!"

"As I said, it does not matter."

Kenders shut her eyes tight, shook her head once, and reopened them.

"Pardon?!"

"We no longer need to hide because a short while ago, Duke Rholeb suspended enforcement on the ban on magic after a long chat with Duchess Aleece and I in his hall. While what you did here was unwise—for a very long list of reasons—it was no longer against the law."

Kenders stared at Broedi, her mouth slack. She did not know what to say. The Gray Cloak did however.

"He cannot do that!" shouted the man as he scrambled to stand. His clothes wet and streaked with mud, he exclaimed, "The law is the law! One sovereign cannot abolish it on a whim!"

Lifting an eyebrow, Wren said, "Oh, but he already did. And—you are truly going to enjoy this—the Southlands and Long Coast have done the same. Sorry to inform you, but the Constables' services are no longer required there."

The Gray Cloak's eyes opened even wider.

"But we are outside their authority! The law says as much!"

"Perhaps so," conceded Wren. "You know, you might want to take it up with the First Council." Lifting an arm, he pointed east. "Freehaven is that way. I suggest you buy a horse before going. It's a long walk."

The Gray Cloak glared at Wren, his face a deep reddish hue.

"They have no right!"

Shaking his head, Wren muttered, "Gods, I forgot how much I despised your kind." He stepped past the group, striding toward the stockades fence. "You all deal with him." He wandered away, towards the new trees.

Broedi eyed the Gray Cloak and rumbled, "What Strands can you touch?"

"I will not answer the questions of a mage!"

Kenders answered for him.

"Stone, Air, and Will at least. Considering he did not stop me with any of the other Weaves, I'm guessing that is all.

As the Constable shifted his spiteful glare to her, Broedi said, "Good." The hillman nodded at the Gray Cloak and added, "You will come with us, then. You can help when the Sudashians arrive."

"I will do nothing of the sort!" shouted the man. "You are lawbreakers! All of you! No matter what the duke has decreed!"

Beyond the Gray Cloak, Kenders saw Wren suddenly spin around and begin advancing on the man as he continued his rant.

"I do not care what conspiracy Duke Rholeb has entered into, I maintain my authority here! I *will* do what I must to apprehend the lot of—"

The butt end of Wren's spear cracked into the back of the man's head. The Gray Cloak stumbled forward a step, reaching up to clasp his skull. He turned to face his attacker just as Wren brought the spear's thick handle back in the other direction, catching the man in the right temple. The Gray Cloak went limp and collapsed to the ground.

Kenders stared at the man's crumpled form for a moment before looking up to gape at the ijul.

"What'd you do that for?"

Ignoring her entirely, Wren glanced at Broedi and said, "You get to carry him. He looks heavy." The tijul turned and strode down the street, toward the Duke's Hall. "Let's go. We're wasting time."

Kenders watched him walk a dozen paces before staring back to Broedi.

"*He's* a White Lion?"

A slight frown rested on Broedi's lips.

"He is."

Stepping forward, Tobias added, "And as much as I hate to admit it, he's right. We have a lot to do."

"Why?" asked Kenders, glancing between tomble and hillman. "What's happening?"

Turning his stoic gaze on her, Broedi rumbled, "The Shadow Manes are coming to Demetus as we speak, through a port in the Duke's Hall. We are no longer in hiding."

Kenders' eyes widened a fraction.

"Now? But, why?"

Broedi rumbled, "Much has happened in the turn since you left." He bent over, lifted the unconscious Gray Cloak from the ground with ease, and said, "Come. I will explain on the way." Without another word, he began to move off after Wren.

Kenders gaped after him briefly before looking down to Tobias.

"The Manes are coming here? Truly?"

The tomble nodded, an amused smile on his face.

"Truly."

With that, he moved off, hobbling after Broedi, his walking stick clacking against the stone street. After a few steps, he looked over his shoulder.

"And so you know, the lightning was my favorite part! Quite impressive!"

Kenders stared after the trio of White Lions a moment before turning back to the Alshers. All four were staring at her and the others with expressions of open wonder, the pair of horses beside them drinking water from the puddles in the street.

With a tiny shrug of her shoulders, Kenders said, "Let's go meet the duke, I suppose." A bittersweet smile graced her lips as she added, "Better yet, let's go see Zecus."

CHAPTER 50: PARTING

19ᵗʰ of the Turn of Maeana, 4999

A frown rested upon Tiliah's lips as she neared the Reed Men grounds. She eyed the five soldiers guarding the grand archway and shook her head.

"They are *not* going to let me in. Not now."

Zecus glanced at her and asked, "Why do you say that?"

"With all of this?" She waved a hand all around, indicating the crowded street and the city in general. Shaking her head, she added, "They are *not* going to bother with me."

Zecus offered an encouraging smile.

"We will see about that."

His confident tone gave her a touch more hope than a moment ago. Then again, a moment ago, she had none. She sighed and gave a resigned shrug of her shoulders.

"If you say so."

They stepped from the crowded street and moved down the wide flagstone walkway leading to the courtyard gate. Massive columns lined the way, each one thirty feet tall and topped with statues of one ancient noble or another. Tiliah eyed the carvings, wondering how many people actually knew the names of each.

She took a deep breath, relieved to be free of the crowd. The journey from the eastern gate had been slow going as she and Zecus had moved against the flow. The city's evacuation was well underway. Borderlands refugees and Demetus citizens alike were heading east to the safety of the Southlands. Tiliah had been with one of the first groups through the magical ports, escorting her mother and younger siblings from this wretched place and to a world that astounded them all.

Lush, green prairies running to every horizon.

More fresh water than one could imagine rippling down the Erona River.

Strange animals bounding through the grass.

It was almost too much for her to take in.

For Borderlanders, the exodus was a joyous one. Tiliah remained even-tempered, however. Life might be easier than in the camps of Demetus, but by no means would it be without hardship. There would be no homes, no livelihoods awaiting them, only a bit more safety than here.

The Marshland citizens who were forced to go, however, fought the duke's order like whiney children told they could not have another hunk of bread. They still did not grasp—or fully believe—the danger facing the city.

Boah Rasus and his wife were helping organize things in the east. Her father's friend had not wanted the task, but the story of his and Joshmuel's journey to Free-haven had spread quickly amongst the refugees. Much to Boah's chagrin, he was now seen as something of a hero. Overwhelmed by his new responsibilities, Boah had come to Debrah and Tiliah, asking for aid in any manner they could offer it. Tiliah initially volunteered to organize the treatment of the sick and injured, but quickly ended up supporting Boah at every turn.

Two days into the evacuation and things were moving much slower than everyone would have liked. Three mages—Tobias, another redheaded tomble, and an overweight man rumored to be from a nation of mages—were capable of keeping the magical doors open for only so long before needing to stop and rest. At last count, only thirty-five hundred people were through and getting situated in the grasslands. Rumors were that the duke was considering sending only those healthy enough to make the journey on foot overland.

When Zecus had visited the Southlands this morning, he had confirmed the rumors were true. In fact, Duke Rholeb's wife, Duchess Beluna, had volunteered to lead the expedition. Soon, the ports were going to be reserved for the injured, the ill, and the too young or old. Tiliah had pulled Zecus aside and asked that she be allowed to return to Demetus briefly. To her surprise, he agreed without protest.

Now, as the Alshers neared the archway, Tiliah steeled herself, convinced the guards would bar her entry. After this, she was going to the Southlands for good. Zecus, the stubborn soul that he was, was staying behind, insisting that he was going to fight the Sudashians when they came. Tiliah glanced over and eyed his new uniform, a tiny frown on her face. In her mind, Zecus would never be a soldier, but she was forced to admit that he certainly looked the part.

A tough-spun black tabard trimmed with silver thread and emblazoned with a large, stylized head of a white lion hung from his shoulders. His pants were black as was his tunic. Black leather greaves and boots completed the uniform, along with a silver scabbard that held a newly forged longsword.

As they neared the gate, the Reed Man standing in the center of the line of five soldiers, made eye contact with Zecus, turned his head, and called, "Step aside!"

The other four soldiers, all dressed in Marshlands' green and white, moved to let Zecus and Tiliah pass through the arched gateway unimpeded. All five Reed Men eyed Zecus as he strode by, respect and a bit of awe in their stares.

Ten steps into the crowded courtyard, Zecus said, "I told you I could get you in."

Tiliah turned to her brother and spotted a slight, almost smug smile resting on his lips.

"Oh, please. An oligurt could have walked right in if he was wearing that fancy uniform of yours."

Zecus' grin grew again. Nodding across the yard, he said, "Come, they should be that way." He shifted direction, heading for a large, stone archway. Tiliah followed.

Soldiers of all sorts moved about, some in groups, others alone, but all moved with purpose. While most were clad in green and white, other uniforms were visible as well.

They passed a group of three light-skinned men standing together, studying a parchment, and speaking in low tones. Two were dressed in Southland's blue and gold and the third in silver and maroon. Tiliah glimpsed the parchment's surface and saw what appeared to be a map of Demetus. Once past them, Tiliah looked at Zecus.

"Who are they?"

Zecus peered over his shoulder before answering. "Two Southern Arms captains and a knight-general of the Shore Guard." He looked back to Tiliah and added, "The officers are here to meet with Commander Aiden and coordinate Demetus' defense."

Nodding slowly, Tiliah scanned the other groups. She did not spot any brown and tan uniforms.

"And the Dust Men? Where are they?"

Zecus glanced over, smiled slightly, and pointed to the archway to which they were headed.

"Most likely drilling in that yard."

Tiliah offered her brother a grateful smile.

"I am sure you have other things you should be doing instead of this."

He eyed her, the Marshlands sun beating down on his brow, and said, "I do. But this is important."

Tiliah reached up patted her brother's shoulder.

"Thank you, Zecus."

Moving through the archway, the pair stepped into another open yard. Two long buildings lined the area to Tiliah's right, each with several dozen horses standing outside and hitched to wooden posts. The roof of each building extended far over its walls, providing plenty of shade for the animals.

Pointing to the unusual structures, she asked, "What are those?"

Zecus glanced over.

"They are called 'barns.' Easterners keep their horses inside them."

Tiliah eyed him, wondering if he was mocking her.

"They build…houses for horses?"

Zecus shrugged his shoulders and said with a smile, "The forests east of here are grand, Tiliah. There is enough wood to build every animal their own home."

Tiliah waited for his grin to widen, indicating that he was indeed jesting. It did not.

"You are telling the truth?"

"I am."

With a slow, wondering shake of her head, she said, "When this is over, Zecus, I want your stories."

"And you shall have them. Although I expect you will not believe most. I barely do and they happened to me."

Turning a corner, they moved into the shadow cast by the Duke's Hall and passed a large stonework trough. Men stood around the fountain, drinking from long, wooden ladles. Fresh water streamed from a pipe jutting from the wall, replenishing the supply. Tiliah was eyeing the pipe, wondering how such a thing was possible when Zecus pointed to the east.

"There they are."

Staring ahead, Tiliah spotted a small contingent of Borderlanders two hundred paces away, dressed in a collection of mismatched clothes and armor, their weapons as disparate as their garb.

Keeping her voice low, Tiliah whispered, "Those are Dust Men?"

"Yes."

There were at most forty, perhaps fifty men ahead. She had expected more.

"Why so few?"

"These are the only ones willing—and able—to fight. Twice as many came from the camps and volunteered, but Commander Aiden sent them east with the others."

Tiliah glared at her brother.

"They wanted to fight and were turned away?"

Nodding, Zecus said, "That is what I said."

"Why?"

"Would you want someone who has not seen a decent meal for three turns guarding my back? A man who can barely lift a sword, let alone swing it?"

Tiliah was quiet a moment before saying, "I suppose you have a point."

As they neared the remnant Dust Men, some noticed their approach and gently elbowed the others. In short order, most of the soldiers had turned to face them, their gazes resting on Zecus. Like Boah, he had become something of a legend among the refugees, the sole Borderlander amongst the Shadow Manes. He had even earned a title of sorts: Zecus Alsher, the Guardian of the Borderlands.

When it was apparent that Tiliah and Zecus were striding toward them, the Dust Men fanned out and revealed Tiliah's reason for coming back to Demetus.

Rhohn stood at the group's center, no longer dressed in the rags she had become accustomed to seeing him wear. Rather, his new garb made him look like a true soldier: brown breeches, a tan shirt, and an actual Dust Man tabard draped over his shoulders. His sword and scabbard hung from his belt.

As their eyes met, a smile spread over her lips, accompanied by an unexpected flutter in her stomach. Rhohn glanced to the man on his left, said something, and then strode from the group. The man immediately turned to the Dust Men, shouted an order, and the soldiers began to arrange themselves into rows. On their way here, Zecus had shared that Rhohn had been given command over the Dust Men unit. Tiliah thought it a wise choice, whoever had made it.

Rhohn met Zecus and Tiliah two dozen paces from the soldiers, stopped, and gave a slight bow.

"My pleasure is to meet you in peace today."

Returning the bow, Zecus replied, "And may peace bless our parting."

Both men eyed Tiliah, apparently waiting for her to offer her portion of the traditional greeting. A sly smile spread over her face.

"I like your new clothes, Mud Man."

While Zecus frowned at her casual dismissal of custom, Rhohn actually chuckled and said with a smile, "There's a war going on. Who has time for customs?"

Grinning in return, she said, "That's what I say."

Nodding at the group of Dust Men, Zecus asked, "How goes it with them?"

"As well as can be expected," said Rhohn with a shrug of his shoulders. "It's a mixed stew, for sure. A few are veterans of Gobas who somehow escaped, but most are from eastern posts who have never seen a Sudashian. I have two corporals, a lieutenant, and the rest are footmen."

"And how does the lieutenant enjoy taking orders from a corporal?" asked Zecus.

"I don't know," said Rhohn with a slight grin. He lowered his voice. "Commander Aiden told them I was a captain. He said there'd be less arguing that way."

They shared a small chuckle at the falsehood, but their quiet laughter quickly faded. When none of them elected to fill the silence that followed, Zecus cleared his throat and announced, "It seems my throat is rather dry. Perhaps I shall go get a ladle of water." He turned to Tiliah and said with purpose, "I'll only be a moment. Stay here if you like."

With a grateful nod, she said, "I think I will."

Zecus glanced at Rhohn briefly before turning to walk away, his boots crunching on dry gravel. Tiliah watched him slowly amble back to the water trough by the Duke's Hall.

"I am surprised to see you here," said Rhohn. She turned to face him as he added, "I had heard you were in the Southlands already."

"I was," said Tiliah. "But I came back."

"Why, then?" asked Rhohn. The left corner of his mouth turned up a fraction. "Did you miss the marsh and its wondrous smell?"

"No," answered Tiliah with a shake of her head. "I came to say thank you."

His eyes widened a bit.

"Pardon?"

"I never did say it to you. Not once. And I wanted to come back and tell you before…well, before whatever in the Nine Hells is going to happen here."

"A massive, horrible, bloody fight, most likely."

Tiliah nodded.

"Right. I needed to tell you before *that*."

Stepping away from her, Rhohn moved to the mud-brick wall of the Duke's Hall and leaned against it.

"There is no need to thank me, Tiliah. You helped me as much as I helped you. Without you, I would still have an arrow in my leg. Or be dead from wound rot."

"True, but were it not for me, you would have never gotten shot."

Rhohn cocked his eyebrow.

"True."

Tiliah moved closer to him, saying, "And *that* is why I am thanking you. Without you, I'd still be with Nimar and his awful family." She paused a moment. "Or not. Truthfully, I don't know where I would be. But it certainly would not be here, with Zecus, with my family."

A shadow passed over Rhohn's face.

"I am only sorry your father could—"

Interrupting him, she said, "Don't want to talk about it, Mud Man." After sharing her father's fate with her mother, Tiliah refused to speak of it. It was easier that way.

Closing his mouth, Rhohn nodded.

"I understand."

Tiliah shook her head and, in a sharper tone than he deserved, said, "I doubt it."

Dropping his chin to his chest, he said, "The pain digs at your insides, yes? Like someone is trying to scoop out your heart with a rusty, jagged shovel."

She remained quiet, struggling to keep her anguish at bay. She had not shed a tear in days and was not going to do so now.

Rhohn glanced up, took one look at her face, and said, "I was eight when my mother died and—" he pointed to his scars "—this happened. Losing her hurt thrice as much as the burns. Then my father passed to Maeana and…I…" He trailed off, his eyes narrowing, his scarred lips twitching. He drew in a deep breath, held it a moment, and then exhaled. "The pain never goes away, Tiliah. Just hope that it grows a bit duller with time." He offered a tiny, sad smile. "A strong soul accepts that and lives with it. And you, Tiliah Alsher, are a strong soul."

She felt the tears swelling and tried to hold them back.

Rhohn muttered, "I am sorry this was your family's fate. For you, of course, but for me as well. I wanted to meet the man who raised such a remarkable young woman."

Reaching up to wipe the wetness from her eyes, she murmured, "Blast you, Rhohn."

"So I'm Rhohn now?" asked the soldier, a teasing note in his voice. "What happened to 'Mud Man?'"

A quiet huff of a chuckle pushed past her tears as she stared at him. All of him. His mismatched and burnt skin, his scarred lips, the missing eyebrow and ear, his patchy hair. Most women would be repulsed by his disfigured face. Tiliah was not one of them.

Stepping forward, she stood on her toes and leaned close to Rhohn, brushing her soft, full lips against his cracked and maimed ones, reaching up with her hand to caress his scarred cheek. She held the kiss for a few heartbeats, breathing in his scent, before pulling away just far enough to meet his wide-eyed stare.

"Thank you, Rhohn Lurus of the village Dashti. Thank you for everything."

He stared at her and blinked twice, remaining completely silent.

Smiling, she leaned in again, gave him a second kiss, a quicker one this time, and then pulled back, dropping her heels to the ground. She patted his chest twice and said, "Take care of yourself here, Mud Man. We're going to need help in the Southlands when this is all over. I was hoping you might be interested."

A slight smile started to spread over his lips but arrested as his gaze flicked past her. The happy glint in his eye fled in an instant. Turning around, Tiliah spotted Zecus several dozen paces away, marching straight toward therm. She would not say he looked angry, but he certainly was not smiling.

Glancing back to a visibly worried Rhohn, she smiled.

"What? You'll stand face to face with a kur-surus, yet you are afraid of my brother?"

Rhohn, his gaze remaining locked on Zecus, muttered, "I did not just kiss a kur-surus' sister."

"To be clear, I kissed you."

He glanced down at her and smiled.

"I suppose you did."

Arriving a moment later, Zecus immediately announced, "Tiliah, time to go back to the port."

While the protective tone in his voice was predictable, it nonetheless prompted a quiet chuckle to slip from Tiliah. Turning to face Zecus, she gave him a dazzling smile.

"Whatever you say. I said what needed to be said."

As she strode toward him, she was amused to see him keep his gaze locked on Rhohn. Tiliah glanced over her shoulder to find Rhohn staring at her alone. She gave him one last smile and turned to Zecus, hooking her arm in his and gently tugging him back to the yard's entrance.

"Time to go, brother."

Zecus went with her reluctantly, backpedalling a few paces before turning and walking at her side. After a dozen steps, he looked over and murmured, "You said you just wanted to talk with him."

Tiliah nodded.

"I did talk with him."

"I would think it easier to talk when your lips are not pressed against his."

"Oh, please," murmured Tiliah. "I'm older than Kenders is and you kissed her."

Zecus was quiet a moment before responding in a quiet, reserved voice.

"I was unaware you knew that."

Shrugging her shoulders, Tiliah faced forward and said, "We sat around for a day, waiting for you. It was bound to come out."

As they neared the stonework water trough, Zecus glanced over.

"Is he a good man?"

"A very good one."

Nodding once, Zecus announced, "Then I approve."

Tiliah eyed her brother, a wide grin spreading over her face.

"That's sweet. You think you have a say in the matter."

"I thought I did. But then I saw you kiss him." He glanced over, an amused smile of his own on his lips and asked, "The poor soul had no chance, did he?"

Tiliah extended her left arm, reached around her brother, and hugged him tight as they walked.

"No, Zecus. He did not."

She glanced over her shoulder and found Rhohn still beside the wall, staring at her. She smiled wide, very glad that she had come.

CHAPTER 51: EVENINGMEAL

21ˢᵗ of the Turn of Maeana, 4999

A steady breeze drifted over the barren mountainside, tickling the short stalks of dead thistlegrass and whistling through crevices in the gray rocks and boulders. Heavy, dark clouds cluttered the sky, hugging the mountaintops, the air so thick with moisture that a wet sheen covered every bit of exposed stone. Patches of weeks-old snow and dirty ice spotted the rocky ground.

Tobias drew in a long, deep breath and upon finding it devoid of scent, looked down to his right leg. Straight and healthy. He let a tiny sigh escape.

"And where am I now?"

The clouds completely obscured the peak of the mountain upon which he stood. The crags of some other mountains were visible, however, spread out below him and stretching clear to the horizon. Staring up at the sky, he searched for some hint of the sun, but the clouds were too thick. He had no idea the time of day or which direction was north, east, south, or west.

"Wondrous."

Spinning in a slow circle, he studied the empty, rocky landscape around him, looking for the reason he was here. There had to be a reason. There always was.

Spotting a tall, narrow cave opening a few hundred feet away in the side of the mountain, he stopped turning and stared. A thin stream of gray smoke curled out, quickly whisked away by the wind.

"Where there's smoke…"

Tobias scrambled over the mountainside, reaching the cave's mouth in short order, and hurried straight into its dark, jagged fissure. Once inside, the cave narrowed and the floor sloped downward. A smoky haze filled the passageway, but Tobias could not smell it.

Following the path into the dark, he turned a corner and stepped into a large cavern. A tiny campfire burned against the far wall, its paltry light providing just enough illumination for Tobias to make out the cave's interior. A number of squat, bulbous pottery jars were arranged neatly about the cave along with stacks of parchments. Sitting amongst them was an incredibly thin figure, resting cross-legged on a simple mat. As Tobias stared, the individual turned her head ever so slightly, the right side of her face moving from shadow to light. Her eyes were closed.

Tobias gasped, "Bless the Gods." He immediately stepped further into the cave to get a closer look. "Gods, Larin, is that truly you?"

A moment later, he frowned at his foolishness. Larin could not hear him. Nobody could within his visions. Nevertheless, the aicenai's thin eyelids shot open and Larin's gaze darted about the room, her blue eyes glinting with reflected firelight.

"How is it you found me?"

Tobias was stunned silent. This had never happened in any of his visions. Ever.

Before he could overcome his surprise and respond, the aicenai dipped her chin to her chest and sighed.

"And now I must move again."

Finding his voice, Tobias asked, "Larin, what are—"

"I am growing ever weary of this chase," whispered Larin as she stood, her robes draping over her thin frame. "Come if you like, but I will be gone by the time you find this cave." She moved to the stacks of parchments and began leafing through them.

Tobias stared at the aicenai, befuddled.

Larin selected some large sheets, set them aside, and then began feeding the rest to the fire. Dry and crisp with age, they caught immediately, sending large plumes of smoke to the roof and out the entryway. Without pausing in her task, Larin stared about the empty cave.

"One of these days I will learn how it is you can track it. From what I can tell, it should not be possible."

"What are you talking about?" asked the tomble. "It's me. Tobias."

She ignored him entirely now. Her behavior made no sense until Tobias realized the aicenai must think he was someone else. Such a revelation was cause for concern. Someone was pursuing Larin and Tobias had a good idea why.

When Khin had shared the true story of the Locking with him after finding the Suštinata of Void, Tobias had been stunned twice over. The first when he learned of the existence of the stones, and a second time when he discovered that Larin, the aicenai with whom he had spent years in Cartu, had been among The Twice Nine tasked to study them.

Frowning, Tobias stared about the cave, wishing there was some way to communicate with the aicenai but knowing from experience there was not. Larin moved through the cave, gathering various items, rolling and binding some parchments but burning most of them. Tobias tried to read what they said, but they were all written in ancient aicenai. He considered going back outside to get an idea where they were, but that would not help if Larin was planning to leave. Dejected and frustrated, he sat on the cave floor and simply watched the aicenai pack.

"Blast it."

Larin padded softly across the rock floor, heading to a ledge where a black cube rested, alone from everything else. She lifted the box, turned, and held motionless, tilting her head side to side as if straining to hear the faintest of sounds.

"You are still here, are you not?" whispered the aicenai. "I can sense you."

"I am," muttered Tobias, standing from the floor. "Not that it matters." He advanced on her, eyeing the box she held near her waist. As he neared, Larin opened the lid, swinging it back on a pair of hinges to reveal a gold-inlayed interior. An impossibly bright yellowish-white light flooded the cave, forcing Tobias to squint against its brilliance. An intense sizzling sound filled the cavern.

A moment later, a dazzling yellow stone rose from the box and hung in the air where it hissed and spit. Tiny arcs of lightning leapt from the stone's surface, into the air, and back again, popping and cracking. Tobias tried to get a closer look at the stone, but could only glance at its brilliance for a second before needing to look away. It was as if he was trying to stare at the sun.

Tobias finally understood the reason for the burns along the back of Larin's hands and wrists. When he had asked Larin about the scars, the aicenai had simply said that she was a careless cook.

Larin's thin and airy voice managed to rise above the crackling. "Savor this moment." The Suštinata fell back into the box and Larin snapped the lid shut with a crack, plunging the cave into darkness again. "As long as I live, you will never find me or the stone."

Tobias stared up to Larin and realized that the cavern seemed much dimmer than before she had shown him the Suštinata. At first, he thought it was because the stone had temporarily blinded him, but then he realized he could see through the box and Larin both.

The vision was ending.

"Blast you, Nelnora."

* * *

The scent of cloves, melted beeswax, and burning smoking-leaf filled his nose. He was still sitting in his chair, but was slumped over to his right with some-one's arm draped around his shoulders. Considering the seating arrangement at the duke's table, Tobias guessed he had fallen into Kenders.

The young woman confirmed his suspicions, asking, "Perhaps we should lay him down somewhere?"

"That won't be necessary," muttered Tobias with a touch of embarrassment. "I'm back."

Opening his eyes, he found everyone staring at him. Directly across from him, Broedi and Nikalys sat, peering over the candles' flickering flames. Broedi held his long, white bone pipe in his hand, a wispy curl of smoke drifting from its bowl while Nikalys clasped a wine goblet. Both wore expressions of curious concern. A few paces behind them stood the kur-surus, Okollu. The Sudashian refused to sit at the table.

Turning to his to right, Tobias found Duchess Aleece watching him, an inquisitive glint in her eye. At the other end of the table to his left, Duke Rholeb was peering at him, a wary, almost suspicious expression upon his face.

Kenders said, "You sort of fell over into me a little while ago."

"That happens sometimes. Thank you for not letting me fall."

Sitting tall, Tobias stretched out a hand, grabbed his cup of sweet redbush tea, and took a long drink.

Broedi rumbled, "You were not gone very long."

After taking a moment to gather his thoughts, Tobias placed the pottery cup back on the tabletop, looked through the numerous candles at Broedi, and said, "It was a short trip, wasn't it?"

Duchess Aleece asked, "By chance, did you see the Sudashians?"

"Unfortunately, no."

Duke Rholeb cursed quietly, "Blast it." He reached up and ran his hand over his silver beard. Eyeing Tobias with caution, he asked, "And there is nothing you can do to…ah…control that…ability?" His unease talking about magic was clear.

Tobias stared at the longleg and, with years of exasperation twisting his voice, answered, "Trust me, my Lord, I've tried."

Duke Rholeb held up a hand.

"I did not mean to offend."

"And you did not," said Tobias. "My frustration is my own. I've been trying to control it for centuries. Your question is entirely appropriate. This is all quite new to you."

The Duke of the Marshlands glanced around the table at the assembled group, his eyes lingering on Okollu.

"Yes…yes, it is."

Tobias was impressed by how well the duke had assimilated to the drastic changes in his reality. When they had arrived at his hall two days past after riding into the city under heavy cloak and Duchess Aleece gave a cursory explanation of things, the longleg had the keen foresight to recognize that she and the Shadow Manes were his one chance to protect his lands and people. On the spot, in the middle of the reception yard, Duke Rholeb suspended the decree outlawing magic and granted permission for the Manes to enter Demetus.

"So, Tobias," rumbled Broedi. "What did you see, then? Anything relevant?"

Tobias cocked an eyebrow.

"You could say that."

Turning in his seat, he peeked around his high-backed chair and looked at Khin. The aicenai stood before the middle of three tall, arched windows, staring at the city below. The last vestiges of daylight sparkled through panes of colored glass, casting green, blue, and red light on Khin and the room. The lower half of the window was propped open, allowing a nice breeze to drift through the hall.

"Khin? You might want to come over here for this."

The aicenai turned and stared, his face as impassive as always.

"Why?"

"Because I saw Larin."

Moving quickly for an aicenai, Khin strode toward the table, stopping to stand between Kenders and the duchess.

"And is she well?"

"It seemed so." Facing the others at the table, he added, "She still has the Suštinata of Charge."

His announcement prompted a number of soft, surprised gasps.

Broedi pulled his pipe from his lips and asked, "Is it too much to hope that you know where she is?"

"In the mountains."

"Where?" asked Duchess Aleece. "Which range?"

Sighing, Tobias shrugged his shoulders.

"I have no idea. Nor does it matter."

"How does knowing the location of another stone not matter?" asked Nikalys.

"Because in short order, it won't be there any longer."

Tobias went on to share the full details of his vision, stressing the fact that while Larin had unexpectedly sensed his presence, she had thought Tobias to be someone else. When finished, he turned to Khin.

"Did anything like that ever happen to you in all your years studying your Suštinata?"

"It is not 'my Suštinata,'" replied Khin. Before Tobias could clarify, the aicenai held up a bony hand. "I understand your question and the answer is no, I never sensed another's presence." His gaze drifted to where Okollu stood beside a table with two small chests sitting atop of it. "Knowing that Larin does is curious."

Tobias peered across the dining table to eye the wooden chests. Before leaving Storm Island, Duchess Aleece ordered the blacksmith and woodworker in Claw to collaborate and craft a second box made to the aicenai's specifications. After some spirited debate, the stones were brought to Demetus in their respective chests. The eventual consensus was that the sweeter of two sour choices was to have them here rather than unguarded at the enclave.

With his gaze still locked on the chests, Tobias muttered, "In all the years I spent with her, not once did I see her study it."

"You cannot touch Charge," noted Broedi. "Just because you did not see her studying it does not mean she did not."

"I suppose," said Tobias. He tried to think if he had ever even seen the black box Larin held in his vision. "Well, her group also appears to have discovered the effect gold has on the Suštinata. The chest she held was lined with it, too."

Mostly to herself, Kenders murmured, "I wonder if…"

Tobias glanced over and found the young woman staring blankly at a piece of untouched cheese on her wooden platter.

"You wonder what?"

Looking up, Kenders said, "The person—or thing—she's protecting the stone from. Do you think it could be Nelnora?"

Khin said, "If she discovered the full nature of the stone, perhaps. Larin was wise."

Shifting in his chair, Duke Rholeb said in a gruff voice, "Unless this 'Larin' walks through my gates with another one of those blasted stones, I don't care where she is or what she knows." Leaning forward, he placed his elbows on the table and folded his hands together. "All I care about now are the new reports of oligurt sightings. I've had a half dozen come in today alone. And two more of my scouts are missing!"

"I agree, my Lord," rumbled Broedi. "Knowing Tandyr does not possess the Suštinata of Charge is sufficient for now."

"Yet he has Soul," warned Tobias, glancing at Okollu. "And he had Void. He might have more still." Turning his gaze to Broedi, he added with purpose, "*Three*, perhaps?"

Frowning slightly, Broedi said, "And they could have only the one."

"You are guessing that is the case," muttered Nikalys.

"As much as you are guessing they have more," noted Khin.

A quiet sigh of exasperation slipped from Tobias. This had been an ongoing debate between everyone since arriving in Demetus. Two very different opinions had evolved on the issue.

"You cannot deny the prophecy's line," said the duchess quietly. "The four will hold the names of three. There are four Gods of the Cabal working together, yes? And the stones hold their names?"

"I will not deny the line," rumbled Broedi. "But be wary. Indrida's words are *often* misinterpreted." He paused, looked around the table, and added, "We know *nothing* for certain."

Nikalys glanced over and said, "We could at least discuss plans on what to do if they have the others."

As Tobias nodded his silent agreement, Broedi said, "Let us say we all agreed the Cabal hold three stones. What then? They have Soul, we have Stone and Void, and—thankfully—it would seem another of the Daputa Devet has Charge. That leaves five other Suštinata. Five. We could sit around for days, postulating what to do if they have Fire and Water. Or Will and Air. Or Life and Water. Or any of the possible combinations."

"There are ten," added Khin.

"Yes," rumbled Broedi. "Ten. Ten ways to pair two Suštinata they *might* have with the one we know they have. Whatever that trio of stones is—assuming that is what Indrida's words mean—there are countless Weaves that are possible. Shall we prepare for them all?"

A quiet, heavy silence filled the room. Tobias had to concede Broedi's point. Good plans could suffer a bit of guessing while bad ones often involved too much.

Kenders let out a long, weary sigh. She sounded tired. Then again, they all were. Sleep was a luxury few had time for now.

A creak of hinges needing a few oil drops announced a new arrival to the gathering. The door at the far end of the dining room opened and in strode Jak, dressed in the new black and silver uniform every Shadow Mane soldier was wearing. Lady Vivienne had the uniforms distributed prior to leaving Storm Island.

As Jak approached the table, Tobias noticed baggy, dark circles under his eyes. Everyone here was tired, but Jak looked exhausted. Tobias wondered if the longleg had slept at all since arriving here.

Glancing between the nobles, Jak said, "My Lady, my Lord, I apologize for my tardiness. I was—"

Duchess Aleece interrupted him by lifting a hand and saying, "You were busy, Jak. No need to apologize."

Upon reaching the table, Jak faced the noblewoman, and gave a quick yet respectful bow.

"Thank you, my Lady."

Duchess Aleece smiled up at him, saying, "No bowing necessary. Not here."

As Jak stood tall, his gaze darted to the table covered with what passed for tonight's eveningmeal: two silver bowls of nuts—almonds in one, bitternuts in the other—a slab of pungent white cheese, and a bowl of red plums. The fare was light for a sovereign's table, but if one considered the shortage of food in Demetus, this was a feast.

"May I have something to eat, my Lady?"

Duchess Aleece raised an eyebrow.

"This is not my table. It is Duke Rholeb who must give you leave to partake."

Tobias smothered a slight grin, knowing that she was having a bit of fun with him.

Turning to face Duke Rholeb, Jak said, "Pardon me, my—"

In a booming voice, Duke Rholeb exclaimed, "Gods, son! Eat, already! You're politer than a Borderlands' baron at court!"

With a grateful nod, Jak leaned over to grab a handful of shelled almonds. Stepping back, he tossed few nuts into his mouth and began to chew. "Thank you, my Lord. I haven't eaten since…" He trailed off and dipped his head to think. "… yesterday, perhaps?"

Nikalys peered up at his brother, a smile on his face.

"Having a difficult time remembering things, are you? My offer stands."

Appearing somewhat irritated, Jak shook his head, "And it will continue to stand."

Curious, Tobias asked, "What offer?"

With quick and quiet sigh of exasperation, Kenders said, "Nikalys has repeatedly offered to smack Jak in the head to see if he can get things working again."

"Quite kind of him, isn't it?" asked Jak. He reached up to touch his head where the bandage had been. With the help of Broedi's Weave of Life the wound was mostly healed now. A large red welt was all that remained. "I nearly die, and my brother pokes fun."

Nikalys' grin widened.

"I'm only trying to help."

Jak smiled at his brother and tossed a few more almonds in his mouth.

Leaning forward in her chair, Duchess Aleece looked up to Jak and asked, "Will the commander and Sergeant Trell be joining us?"

Jak shook his head, saying, "No, my Lady. Both are waist deep into planning with the officers. They send their regrets."

"I understand," replied the duchess, a tiny frown on her lips. "A shame, though."

Over the past few days, Tobias had noticed the duchess tossing a few extra smiles in the former Great Lakes sergeant's direction during strategy meetings. The soldier had been especially gracious to the noblewoman in return.

Pushing aside her displeasure, Duchess Aleece turned to Broedi.

"And what of Wren? Shall we wait for him?"

Over the past two days, Wren had made abundant use of his primary talent: irritating everyone with whom he came into contact. During one particularly testy exchange with Duke Rholeb over the wisdom of catapults atop the towers, the duke of the Marshlands threatened to toss Wren into a cell for the night if he could not argue respectfully. Wren snapped back that a cell would be an improvement over his current accommodations. Following that meeting, Tobias strenuously suggested to Wren that he find something else to do with his time. Thankfully, the tijul had listened.

Shaking his head, Broedi said, "I do not know, my Lady. He left this morning, intent on investigating the western reaches of the forest."

"Alone?" asked Kenders. "Is that wise?"

Tobias muttered, "Things are best for everyone when Wren is alone."

"He will be fine," rumbled Broedi. "His title of 'Leafwalker' is well deserved. Wren moves through a forest like a gentle breeze, quiet and unseen."

"That's not entirely accurate," said Tobias. "A breeze rustles leaves. Wren does not. It pains me to say, but he is the best blasted scout I have ever seen."

From the still-open door, a too-familiar voice said, "It is ever so nice to hear how much I'm appreciated."

Tobias pressed his lips tight while wishing he had kept his mouth shut a moment longer. He, along with everyone in the room, turned to find Wren leaning against the frame of the open doorway, his longspear clasped before him, its butt end resting on the floor. The tijul glanced at them all, a slight smirk on his lips.

"Pardon the interruption. Please go on. Say something else nice about me."

When it was apparent his only response was going to be joint silence, he gave a careless shrug, pushed away from the doorframe, and sauntered into the room.

"I suppose I should have stayed quiet a bit longer, then."

"How about you try being quiet now?" mumbled Nikalys.

Wren strode by the duchess and Nikalys, patting the young man on the head as he passed.

"So now you're a playman, son of Aryn?"

Nikalys pulled away from the tijul's touch.

Completely ignoring Jak and Okollu, Wren moved to the table and grabbed a Marshlands plum. He took a bite, stared at the fleshy pink inside, and made a disgusted face.

"Gods, this tastes like worms."

Duke Rholeb said, "Those are from one of the best orchards in the duchies."

Wren eyed the duke and said, "You must be jesting." Swallowing, he took another juicy bite, chewed a moment, and then reached for Nikalys' platter. Retrieving it, he spat out the fruit and dropped the remainder of the unfinished plum onto the wooden plate. He put the platter back before Nikalys, looked to Duke Rholeb, and said, "You should do something about the fare you serve your guests. Perhaps you could try to remedy—"

Duke Rholeb slammed his hand on the table, the crack of open palm slapping wood ricocheting through the room.

"That's it!" bellowed the duke. Looking down the table to the duchess, he said, "Blast it, Aleece! I don't care that he's a blasted White Lion! He rubs me rawer than a saddle made of scale bark. Can't you do something?"

A faint smile spread over Wren's wide lips as he reached for the bitternut bowl.

Duchess Aleece raised her hands, saying, "You speak as if they are my pets to control, Rholeb. Trust me, I find him as distasteful as anyone here, but I will suffer him. Broedi assures me his skills are useful."

"How exactly?" exclaimed the duke. "I've yet to see him do anything." He nodded at Wren. "Look at him. I would bet coin he does nothing but lounge about his room all day."

The tijul's appearance was indeed pristine, but that was typical for Wren. He could spend a week in the wilderness and emerge without a speck of dirt on him.

Entirely nonplussed by the duke's reaction, Wren nodded, saying, "If my help is not required, then perhaps I shall retire to my princely accommodations and 'lounge about' some more? Although one can hardly lounge in the closet you assigned me."

Duke Rholeb's face began turning an interesting, deep pink hue.

Shaking his head, Tobias muttered, "Gods, Wren. Try to be pleasant."

Wren looked to Tobias.

"I cannot help if the duke has thinner skin than Khin."

"Perhaps you should go," rumbled Broedi.

Tobias waited for the tijul to slowly march from the room now that he had stirred the hornets' nest. However, he remained in place, chewing slowly, a wide smile fixed on his face.

"I would rather stay."

Despite their many years apart, the mannerisms of Tobias' fellow White Lions were easily recognizable. Wren knew something and was relishing in the fact no one else did. After sharing a quick look with Broedi—the hillman saw it, too—Tobias glared at Wren.

"Out with it, Wren. Now."

Dipping his hand into the bowl for more bitternuts, Wren asked, "Was I that obvious?"

The longlegs around the table—and the interminably silent Okollu—all wore confused expressions. Wren tossed a few bitternuts into his mouth and chewed, staring at their bewilderment with mild amusement.

"These are much better, my Lord. Edible, at least."

Sitting forward, Kenders asked, "What am I missing here?"

"I'm lost, too," muttered Jak.

Wren munched the nuts in silence, enjoying making them wait. Tobias shot a look to Khin, hoping the aicenai might be able to scrape the smirk from the tijul's face. Khin's blue-eyed gaze was locked on Wren's face. Another moment passed before Khin spoke, his voice light and airy.

"He has information about the Sudashians' movements."

Wren's smugness evaporated like a drop of water on an iron bar pulled from the forge as the tijul turned a sharp stare on Khin.

"How could you possibly know that?"

Khin was quiet a moment before saying slowly, "You went to scout, the Sudashians are nearing, it seemed a logical conclusion. Your reaction confirmed my suspicion." He paused briefly before adding, "You are less clever than you think."

More than a few satisfied smiles joined the table at the aicenai's soft rebuke. Jak and Nikalys especially appeared to enjoy Khin's words. Kenders, however, was staring at her teacher with suspicious eyes. It was not going to take the girl much longer to learn the truth. Tobias thought Khin should tell her before she accidently blurted out the realization the moment it struck her. He agreed with Broedi. Having an ally who could hear the thoughts of others was incredibly useful.

"So, Wren," rumbled Broedi. "What did you find?"

The tijul turned from Khin to face the hillman, a frown on his face.

"The forest tells me there is a great force nearby. Two days away. Three at the most."

Tobias bit down hard. That was not much time.

"The forest tells you?" asked Duke Rholeb. "What in the Nine Hells does that mean?"

Before Wren could snap at the duke—which he appeared ready to do—Tobias interjected, "It is part of Lamoth's gift, my Lord. He can, ah…" He trailed off, knowing the truth might be difficult for the longleg to accept.

"I speak with elyrakiil," finished Wren.

The duke shook his head.

"That means nothing to me. You speak with what?"

With an exasperated shake of his head, Wren said, "The best word in Argot is 'nature.'"

"Pardon?" muttered the duke, peering at the tijul as though he had announced the sky was green. "You do what?"

"You heard me," snapped Wren. "I speak with nature. Why is that—" Cutting off, he looked down at Broedi. "We were once heroes! Our guidance sought by all! Now, they stare at us as if we have five heads!"

"This is new to most," growled Broedi quietly. "A simple, *polite* explanation will do. Can you manage that?"

Wren began to circle the table, moving back around the duchess and Khin, heading toward the open window.

"I will do better than explain."

Upon reaching the stained glass, Wren tossed the remainder of his nuts out the open window. Tobias hoped no one was in the courtyard below.

Moments later, a quick rush of silver filled him and the room as a dozen Strands of Soul popped into existence and began to respond to Wren's wishes. Despite not having seen it in centuries, it only took Tobias a moment to recognize the pattern, or at least the portion of it he was able to see.

Kenders murmured, "That's a new one."

Glancing over, Tobias asked, "Life and Soul?"

Kenders nodded, her eyes fixed on the pattern that hovered outside the window.

Grabbing his walking stick leaning up against his chair, Tobias hopped down and began to hobble toward the window.

"Come along, everyone. You should all see this."

Wood scraped on stone as many of those around the table pushed their chairs back, stood, and followed. Stopping near the window, Tobias glanced back to find that most everyone was coming. Okollu remained in place, however. He appeared interested, but the kur-surus would not move from the stones' side, having more or less assigned himself the task of guarding the Suštinata chests night and day. Broedi and Khin were the only others who had remained in place. Both appeared deep in thought.

As Wren's audience assembled, the tijul completed the Weave and, as Tobias expected, the pattern swirled and disappeared, swept along by the wind as a creek might pull a lone drop of tailor's dye placed on its surface.

Tobias glanced up at Kenders and asked, "You can still feel the Weave, yes?"

She nodded, her brow knitted up in confusion.

"I can. But…but it's gone."

"No," muttered Wren, his focused gaze still on the open air outside. "It most definitely is not." The tijul remained motionless, framed by the evening sky and the stained glass window.

After a number of heartbeats passed with nothing happening, Jak whispered, "What are we—"

"Hush, John," ordered Wren.

Tobias glanced up at the young longleg and found him glaring hard at the back of Wren's head.

"This will take a few moments. Relax."

The gathered group remained quiet. Taking the time to look around, Tobias turned his attention to the city below. He had already spent hours going over maps of Demetus with Broedi, the duke, the commander, and the officers of the duchy armies, studying things with the critical eye of a tactician. For the first time since arriving, Tobias took a moment to observe the city itself and was surprised to find it quite beautiful.

Mu's orb, orange and bright, had swelled and dropped below the horizon, only half its globe still visible above the distant line of treetops. A rainstorm had whisked through the region hours ago, rinsing the air, structures, and flagstone streets clean. The buildings and their rooftop bridges were in the process of drying out, their wood and brick walls a wet and dry patchwork of tans and browns.

Other than the holy city of Nebekah in the south and Bluemoss, the former capital, to the east, Demetus was the only city of notable size in the Marshlands. After the Demonic War, the Marshlands duchess ordered a new capital built, one as grand as any eastern city. However, she had wanted her new city to have something those ancient, meandering hubs of civilization did not have: organization.

Four wide thoroughfares ran through Demetus, leading to two great gates on each of the four long and straight walls. The crisscrossing of ways cut the city into nine distinct districts, the Duke's Hall and government buildings resting in the center square. Tobias found the arranged symmetry a touch disturbing.

Feeling a gentle tap on his shoulder, Tobias looked up and found Jak staring down, a quizzical expression on his face. The young longleg bent over to whisper in Tobias' ear.

"I enjoy a nice sunset as much as anyone, but I have things I need to do. Will this be much longer?"

Tobias cracked a grin and shook his head.

"Shouldn't be."

Jak nodded, muttering, "Good. I was thinking—" He cut off, his gaze focusing on the western sky. Standing tall, he lifted an arm, pointed out the window, and asked, "What in the Nine Hells is that?"

Peering to the horizon, Tobias squinted against the orange sun and spotted a small, dark, and oddly shaped cloud shifting about the sky. When Wren did not immediately answer Jak's question, Tobias glanced at the tijul. Wren's face was knotted in deep concentration as he worked to maintain control over the Weave. Wild and free, nature fought any attempt to control it.

As the swirling cloud came closer, the distant clattering of chirps and tweets was audible now.

Nikalys leaned forward, hovering over Tobias other shoulder, and asked, "Are those…birds?"

Through tight lips, Wren muttered, "Bluetail sparrows. I found a flock nearby."

"You…*found* a flock?" asked Duke Rholeb uneasily.

When Wren did not answer, Tobias looked up to find the tijul deep in concentration again. Taking it upon himself to respond, Tobias eyed the duke and said, "Yes, my Lord. Lamoth's gift grants Wren the ability to call nature's creatures to him."

A quiet moment skipped past. Jak broke the silence.

"Well, *that* would make hunting awfully easy."

Kenders muttered, "I doubt that's the point."

From the dining table, Broedi rumbled, "He can speak with them, as well. If he wishes." With a scrape of his chair, the hillman pushed himself up and began to move around to the window. "Plants and trees as well."

Her gaze on Wren, Duchess Aleece said, "So that's how you know what is coming."

Wren did not respond, transfixed by the birds. Individual sparrows were distinguishable now within the flock, their little wings flapping furiously. Wren took a slow step closer to the window, peering into the onrushing flock, deep lines of worry covering his face and forehead.

Tobias frowned. A worried Wren was a bad sign.

The cloud of sparrows got ever closer, seemingly intent on flying straight into the dining hall window. Yet, at the last moment, they broke off, spreading out in all directions before swooping back upon themselves. Over and over, hundreds of birds and flew in great circles outside the window, like the same ocean wave repeatedly crashing against shore rocks. Their constant, shrill chirping was deafening.

Suddenly, the birds' high-pitched cacophony changed, and with a quick staccato of panicked screeches, they darted from the Duke's Hall, breaking into small groups and flying off in a dozen different directions. Wren's shoulders slumped and he reached out to grasp the stone ledge of the window.

As the cloud of sparrows dissipated, Tobias stepped forward, moving to Wren's side, and stared up.

"So?"

Wren spun around and, in voice utterly clear of his typical, smug arrogance, said, "The walls must be manned. *Tonight*."

As everyone exchanged worried looks with one another, Broedi rumbled, "You said they were two to three days away."

"This morning, they were," answered Wren, his brow furrowed with unconcealed confusion. "Yet they are much closer now. *Much* closer." He stared back out the window. "I don't understand how that's possible."

Duchess Aleece asked, "And how confident are you of this?"

Wren turned to face the duchess, held her stare, and said, "They will be here tomorrow, my Lady. I have no doubt."

The noblewoman sighed, pressed her lips together, and eyed the duke.

"Thoughts, Rholeb?"

A deep frown rest upon the longleg's face.

"It's better to have sword in hand than in sheathe. I say we man the walls."

"Agreed," said the duchess. Eyeing Jak, she added, "Inform Commander Aiden we want full details at the western wall as soon as he can manage. North and south soon after. The moment—the *absolute moment*—anyone sees something, I want to know."

Wholly serious now, Jak said, "Of course, my Lady." He nodded to his brother and sister and turned to walk away when Nikalys spoke up.

"My Lady? May I have your leave? There is something I must see to."

Duchess Aleece glanced at Broedi, received a nod from the hillman, then looked back to Nikalys.

"Go."

Nikalys stepped closer to Kenders, gave her a quick kiss atop her forehead, and said, "Be safe." He shifted his gaze to Wren. "Meet me in the stable yards as soon as you can."

Oddly enough, Wren nodded without making any sort of comment.

Nikalys turned and strode toward the door where Jak stood, waiting. As the pair exited the room together, Duchess Aleece turned to Wren.

"Is there anything else you can tell us? Anything at all?"

Wren shook his head once.

"I honestly wish I could."

After taking a deep breath and exhaling, Duchess Aleece said, "In that case, I must return to the enclave to share this development with Lady Vivienne. Rholeb, may I suggest one last patrol to ensure the lands around Demetus are clear of citizenry? It is about to become very dangerous for anyone outside the walls."

"It won't be much better for those inside them," mumbled the duke.

"No," agreed Duchess Aleece. "But most of us will have weapons."

Nodding, Duke Rholeb said, "No worries, Aleece. The lands will be clear."

"The last of the sick and injured will be through the ports tonight," said Tobias. "Nundle is seeing to that now."

"Good," said the duchess with a nod. Turning to Broedi, she asked, "You will see to the mages, yes? Ensure they are ready?"

"Gamin will have to do so, my Lady," rumbled Broedi. "I am returning to the enclave with you."

A flicker of surprise dashed over the duchess' face.

"Why?"

"There is something important I have not yet had the time to address."

"More important than getting the defenses in place?" asked the duchess.

"Perhaps," rumbled Broedi.

Tobias peered at the hillman, curious.

"It must be quite important, then."

Broedi nodded, saying softly, "It could be."

Her tone turning pointed, Duchess Aleece asked, "Is there something I should know? Something I should have been made aware of a long time past?"

Broedi shook his head.

"If you are asking if I am keeping more secrets, the answer is no. I simply have some questions I need answered."

"And you need them answered now?" asked Kenders.

"Yes," rumbled Broedi. "Now."

Nodding, the duchess said, "I must take you at your word, then." Turning to Kenders, she said, "Find Gamin. Tell him what is happening. Do what you must to get the mages ready."

"Yes, my Lady."

Looking to Tobias next, the duchess said, "Can you open a port, please? I would like to be back here as soon as possible."

With a firm nod, Tobias said, "If you are ready, we can leave at once."

"Please."

Tobias stepped away from the window, instructed everyone to stand back, and reached for the Strands of Void and Air. As he crafted the Weave, he kept one eye on Broedi, wondering exactly what his friend was up to now.

CHAPTER 52: STARS

22nd of the Turn of Maeana, 4999

Sabine stood in the cold, all alone, staring into the nighttime sky.

Thin, barely-there clouds streaked the areas of the sky, softly glowing in the light of both moons. Blue Moon was waning yet still dominated the sky. White Moon was a mere sliver of a crescent. A new layer of fresh snow from this morning covered the courtyard, its tiny crystals glistening and sparkling in the soft, azure moonlight.

An involuntary shiver rippled through her and she pulled the blanket draped around her shoulders tighter. She sighed, sending a puff of warm vapor into the chilly air, and moved her feet a bit, shifting her weight. The layer of old snow beneath the new crunched, the sound filling the empty courtyard. It felt as if she were the only person in the world.

The past few days had been lonesome ones. After the rush of activity as the soldiers and mages left for Demetus, the enclave had been maddeningly quiet. She did her best to keep herself—and Helene—occupied, but the days dragged, leaving Sabine too much time to ruminate on Helene and what had happened in the mages' hall.

Sabine had longed to speak with Broedi, but he was here and gone before she had a chance. When Jak had stopped to say goodbye before heading west, he promised to speak with the hillman as soon as he had the opportunity. Five days had passed since that promise and Sabine was beginning to wonder if he had kept his word.

A tiny smile touched her lips. Of course, Jak would. He was a good and trustworthy man.

Moments later, Nikalys' face popped into her head and her smile faded. Sabine dropped her head, stared at the snow, and sighed, sending another small cloud of breath into the night.

"What am I doing?"

Nikalys had also sought her out before leaving. She had been sitting with Helene in their room, keeping her sister calm and sheltered from the heightened activity about the enclave. Following a knock at their door, Sabine opened it and found Nikalys waiting in the hallway. The moment he saw them both, a wide, happy grin split his face. Helene leapt from the bed, ran across the room, and jumped into his arms, squeezing him tight.

Nikalys had sat with the little girl for a long time, patiently listening to every story Helene shared with him. She talked about everything but the explosion. Helene's exuberance prevented Sabine from getting in more than a few words at time, relegating her to offering repeated, slightly uncomfortable smiles to Nikalys. Before she got her own chance to speak with him, Nundle fetched him. It was time to leave.

Both brothers had left Storm Island with neither knowing she had kissed the other.

Shutting her eyes, she muttered, "Blast it, Sabine."

She did not want to have feelings for both, but she did. Something drew her to Nikalys, and him to her, if she read him right. Yet Jak—an admirable and honorable man in his own right—was a better match. She simply had more in common with him. Like her, Jak was the child of simple farmers. Nikalys, on the other hand, was the son of two legendary heroes granted incredible gifts by the Gods.

Logic alone dictated a clear choice. Yet her heart continually rebelled against her head.

Two men.

Two options. Both sweet. Both sour.

One choice to make.

Sabine gave a tiny, frustrated shake of her head. Fate had dealt her a difficult hand.

"Blast you, Greya."

Opening her eyes, she returned her attention to the heavens, trying to clear her head. Her personal issue was insignificant in the scheme of things.

The star-littered sky sparkled, countless specks of light filling the black wherever clouds and moons did not obscure them. She ran her gaze over the different constellations, seeking out a handful of familiar shapes.

Prairie Rabbit in the east.

Rheoc's Pick straight above.

The Nine Brothers to the south.

In the years before Helene, Sabine and her mother would sit on the hill outside their cottage, staring at the night sky, her mother pointing out the different star groupings and sharing the names bestowed upon them by nameless souls of the past.

Swiveling around to face west, Sabine sought out her mother's favorite constellation. A wistful smile crept over her lips as she spotted the familiar clump of stars, a long, sparkling line curling out from a clustered center.

"Hello, Green Dragon."

The memory of sitting with her mother on the hillside, her father leaning in the lit-up cottage doorway, watching them with a content smile pushed Sabine's reflective mood over a cliff into a chasm of melancholy. A tiny breeze swirled about the courtyard, stirring up small whirlwinds of loose snowflakes. As one rushed past her, she felt an icy wetness on her cheek.

Suddenly, the sound of fabric being rend in two filled the yard, echoing on the tall, stone walls. Spinning in a slow circle, Sabine scanned the snow, seeking the sound's source, knowing exactly for what to look. On the northeastern side of the yard, she spotted a flickering ripple where ground met wall. She recognized the telltale tear of a port instantly.

"Hells."

Her gaze flicked to the open gate. With every Shadow Mane soldier in Demetus, men from Claw were left to 'guard' the entrance. Tonight's pair was made up of a fisherman and a wheelwright, neither with a weapon. Nevertheless, Sabine was about to shout an alarm when a short figure stepped through, crunching on the snow. Sabine let a relieved, misty breath slip from her lips, as she recognized the tomble White Lion.

Tobias' gaze settled on her and he gave a short, surprised nod of greeting before stepping aside. Sabine did not know the tomble well, but anxious for details on what was happening in Demetus, she began to stride briskly toward the port. As she approached, Duchess Aleece emerged next and moved to the side, wrapping her arms around herself. The noblewoman wore a straight-cut, blue dress not meant to hold up to Storm Island's wintry weather.

Upon reaching the pair, Sabine gave a short bow.

"Good days ahead, my Lady. Welcome back."

"And good memories behind," replied the duchess. "And, please, Sabine. Stand up. I have no use for formality now."

Sabine stood straight, surprised by the duchess' friendly tone as this was only the second time she had spoken to the noblewoman.

Shivering against the night's chill, Duchess Aleece turned to Tobias.

"Perhaps I should have retrieved a cloak before we came?"

"I loathe Southlands' Winters, my Lady," said Tobias. "Always have, always will." He glanced up at the duchess. "No offense meant."

"And none heard," replied Duchess Aleece. "I much prefer the northern reaches of my duchy as well." She shivered again.

Sabine stepped forward, unwrapped one of the two blankets she had brought with her, and held it out to the duchess.

"Here, I have two. And an overcoat on underneath."

Duchess Aleece accepted the blanket with a grateful nod, wrapped it around her shoulders, and said, "Thank you. How very kind of you." A quizzical glint entered her eyes. "Might I ask what you are doing out here?"

Catching a curious stare from Tobias, Sabine hesitated before saying, "Just thinking, my Lady."

Duchess Aleece nodded, keeping her eyes locked on Sabine.

"You could think while sitting before a fire."

"If you can get past the cold, it's actually nice. Very peaceful."

The noblewoman continued to stare at Sabine, her gaze similar to the way Sergeant Trell sometimes stared at people, judging them, evaluating. Without warning, she approached Sabine, leaned in close—wholly taking Sabine off guard—and whispered, "Both are good men. You cannot go wrong with either."

Pulling away, Sabine peered at the duchess, baffled.

"How could you...?"

A slight, bemused grin spread over the duchess' face as she said, "Men in love are easier to read than fresh ink on new parchment. Women, too."

Sabine continued to stare, unsure what to say.

Tilting her head to the side, Duchess Aleece said, "Have faith. Fate has a way of working these things out."

Before Sabine could think of a response, the duchess' kind, almost sisterly expression faded, quickly replaced by cool interest.

"How is Helene doing?"

There was more than simple inquisitiveness in her tone.

Sabine's own mood shifted as quickly as the duchess' had. In a much cooler tone than she had expected or intended, she said, "She is fine."

Duchess Aleece nodded slowly, studying her.

"Good to hear."

Sabine held the sovereign's gaze without flinching. A steady, calm resoluteness swelled inside her, preparing her to do whatever necessary to protect Helene. The crunch of snow and ice announced another's arrival through the port. A familiar baritone voice spoke a moment later.

"How fortuitous."

Sabine glanced over to find Broedi staring at her, his eyes unusually intense. A small pop announced the farewell of the port as it winked from the courtyard.

Tobias asked, "What in the Nine Hells took you so long?"

Without ever taking his eyes from her, Broedi said, "I was leaving directions for Khin and Kenders. Sabine, do you have a few moments? I would like to speak to you." Duchess Aleece and Tobias both turned to stare at the hillman with keen, interested expressions.

Sabine's heart thudded hard in her chest. Jak must have spoken with him.

Nodding, she said, "Of course."

"Good," rumbled the White Lion. Turning to the duchess, he said, "I will be along to the offices shortly, my Lady."

The duchess glanced between Broedi and Sabine a few times, a tiny frown on her face, before saying, "Try to hurry. I do not want to tarry long here."

"Agreed," said the hillman. Shifting his gaze to the tomble, he asked, "Tobias, will you come along as well? I will need your help."

"My help?" asked Tobias with surprise. "For what?"

"You will see."

Tobias glanced at Sabine, shrugged his shoulders, and said, "Fine."

Broedi looked back to Sabine.

"You look cold. We should return to your room and speak there."

"Can we go to the commons?"

"No," rumbled the hillman.

"But Helene is asleep."

"Then we will speak quietly."

Without waiting for a response, he turned and began to stride toward a set of doors on the far wall.

Sabine stared at the giant's back and frowned. She had spent weeks wishing to talk with him about Helene, yet now that the conversation was about to happen, she would not mind if it were postponed a little longer. Steeling herself, she looked back to the openly curious duchess and excused herself.

"Pardon me, my Lady."

Duchess Aleece nodded once.

"Of course."

When the noblewoman did not move, Sabine glanced at Tobias. The tomble waved a hand in the direction of the retreating Broedi.

"After you."

Sabine turned to follow the hillman, listening to Tobias's uneven steps behind her. She sighed, sending another tiny cloud drifting into the night.

CHAPTER 53: MOTHER

Sabine cracked the door and peeked inside her room. Thankfully, Helene was still asleep, bundled up under the blankets on the bed they shared and softly snoring. Breathing a quiet sigh of relief, she pushed the door open the rest of the way. The dreams most often came later at night, but Sabine had been worried nonetheless.

The hearth's fire had burned low since Sabine had left, letting the room grow dim and cold. Tossing her blanket on the lone chair in the corner, she headed for the stack of wood beside the hearth, grabbed an oak log, and placed it gently on the glowing embers. She heard Broedi step into the room behind her, the sharp crack of Tobias' walking stick striking stone echoing in the hallway. She glanced at Helene, wishing the tomble would be quieter.

Lifting the metal poker hanging from the pin on the wall, she stoked the fire, sending forth a shower of sparks that danced up and out the flue. The new log— kept outside until this afternoon and, therefore, still damp from melted snow— smoldered and smoked rather than catch as dry wood should. Using one of the few tricks she knew, Sabine reached for the Strands of Fire, and on feel alone, caused the flames to surge, forcing the moisture from the log and setting it alight.

In a soft, gentle tone, Broedi chided, "And you said you could not learn magic."

Replacing the poker, Sabine turned to face the hillman. He looked massive in her small room.

"That? No, I've known how to do that since I was a girl. Mother taught me."

Nodding slowly, Broedi rumbled, "Did she, now?"

He remained by the door, his arms crossed over his chest, his steady gaze fixed on her. The pair continued staring at one another in silence, the only sound in the room Helene's gentle snores, the crack of the fire, and Tobias' walking stick smacking the stone floor in the hall. Broedi's intense stare never left her. It was as if he were trying to see inside her.

Oddly uncomfortable, she used Tobias' entrance into the room as an opportunity to look away. Staring at Helene, she asked, "How go things in Demetus?"

"Well enough," replied Broedi.

Glancing up at the hillman with raised eyebrows, Tobias said, "I suppose that's true enough. For now." He reached behind him and gently closed the door. "Ask the question again this time tomorrow, however, and I'll have a better answer for you."

Sabine looked between the pair.

"What's that mean?"

The White Lions briefly reviewed the events of the past few days, sharing the telling of the tale. As she listened, she grew increasingly restless. Things did not sound promising. As they finished with the story about Wren's flock of birds, Sabine shook her head.

"If he's right, tomorrow will be a dark day."

"Most likely," conceded Broedi. "Hope that bright ones follow."

Tobias muttered, "You know as well as I, Broedi, many won't get the chance to see if they do."

A shadow passed over the hillman's face.

"I know."

Sabine frowned. Everyone was in Demetus, preparing to fight the horde of Sudashians. And here she was, hiding hundreds of miles away in the safety of a stone castle hidden by a magical Weave. A large part of her wanted to be in the Marshlands with her friends, doing whatever she could to help. However, Helene's gentle snoring tempered her desire to rush off.

She was staring blankly into the fire when Broedi's deep yet soft, baritone filled the room.

"Jak told me what happened, Sabine."

She froze. While focused on the situation in the Marshlands, she had momentarily forgotten about her and Helene's own plight. She glanced to the hillman, worried.

"Did he?"

"Yes," replied Broedi. "He did."

She studied the stoic hillman's eyes, hoping to glean some idea of what he was thinking.

"And?"

"And there are things we must discuss."

Sabine pressed her lips together and nodded.

"Such as?"

He regarded her in perfect silence, studying her. Again, she felt as if he was trying to see inside her. At least he did not appear angry, and for that, she was grateful.

Glancing between the pair, a deep furrow splitting his brow, Tobias asked, "Would someone mind telling the baffled tomble what in the Nine Hells this is about?"

Sabine looked to Tobias, surprised.

"You do not know?"

"Would I have asked the question if I did?"

Still never taking his gaze from Sabine, Broedi rumbled, "Helene is responsible for the explosions in the mages' hall."

Tobias stared up at the hillman, surprise quickly replacing confusion.

"Truly?"

Broedi nodded slowly and remained silent.

Tobias shook his head, saying, "That's not possible." He glanced at Helene on the bed. "I saw the damage myself. A powerful Weave did that. A *very* powerful Weave." His gaze shifted to Sabine, the question in his eyes plain.

"It's true," whispered Sabine. "I wish it were not, but it is."

Tobias blinked once and stared back to the bed.

"But how?"

"She says she doesn't know," said Sabine. "And I don't press her much. It upsets her."

Broedi moved from the door and took a step toward the bed. Sabine reflexively slid herself in his path, halting his approach. An icy calmness filled her.

"What are you going to do?"

Staring down at her with gentle eyes, he rumbled, "I would like to take a closer look at her if that is alright with you."

"Why?" asked Sabine. "What are you going to do with her?"

"Do with her?" repeated the hillman. "I am not going to do anything with her. I will do whatever I can to help keep her safe, Sabine. I promise."

The cool calm within faded a bit. Curious and a bit confused, Sabine tilted her head to the side slightly.

"I had thought you might be angry."

"And why would I be angry over an accident?"

A flicker of relief tickled her insides, but she held it at bay. Things could still go wrong.

Broedi was quiet several moments longer—staring hard at her all the while—before finally speaking.

"I would like to learn more about your mother and father, if you do not mind."

His request disarmed her. She blinked once before asking, "Why?"

"I hope to learn something that could help us understand what happened in the mages' hall."

Sabine shook her head slowly.

"I don't see how."

"Please," rumbled Broedi. "Indulge me."

Sabine eyed the hillman, considering his request. After a few moments, she decided there was no harm in granting it.

"What do you want to know?"

Standing tall, Broedi crossed his arms over his chest and asked, "About your life by the Erona River. Tell me about the Moiléne farm."

"There's not much to tell. We lived there my entire life. Before Helene, Mother and Father worked the fields together—Spring, Summer, and Harvest. I helped when I was old enough. In Winter, we stayed inside and played games. It was a quiet, rather mundane existence."

"And you never went anywhere?" asked Broedi.

"Me? No. Nor Mother. Only Father. After every Harvest, he'd take the left-over yield to Stooert to sell while Mother and I waited at the farm." The corners of her mouth turned up into a fond, wistful smile. "He would always bring us gifts, too. Trinkets or ribbons for me, but for Mother…he always brought some glass figurine or metal bauble in the shape of an everbloom flower. He called her that. 'My Everbloom.'"

"An unusual name," rumbled the hillman. "Do you know why?"

Sabine thought for a moment before answering, "No. No, I don't. There was patch of them on the riverbanks. Beautiful flowers. Crimson petals with a black center. They bloom year-round, even in Winter."

Broedi nodded, a tiny, knowing smile creeping over his lips. Sabine stared at the hillman curiously.

"What?"

"It is no matter," rumbled Broedi with a shake of his head. "How old was your father when he passed?"

The question took her by surprise. Shaking her head, she said, "We had celebrated his forty-fifth yearday only two weeks before you found us."

"And your mother's age?" asked Broedi. "When she passed, that is?"

Sabine shrugged.

"Forty-one, I suppose. She and Father were the same age."

"How do you know?"

Sabine's eyes narrowed.

"Because they said so."

Nodding slowly, Broedi asked, "And do you and Helene take more after your father or mother?"

"Oh, Gods. Father, most definitely. He had gone gray in recent years, but when I was little, his hair was as dark as ours. Mother used to say it was 'blacker than a one moon night.'"

"And your mother?" prompted Broedi, a strange glint in his eye. "What did she look like?"

"Fair skin, bright auburn hair, and eyes the color of the Southlands plains at dawn," answered Sabine. She turned to look at her sleeping sister, a bittersweet smile spreading over her lips. "You know…when Mother was pregnant with Helene, she would tease Father mercilessly, saying the baby had better look like her as he already had his lookalike."

The happy smiles on her parents' faces flashed before her even now. Not wanting to relive the pain of their loss, however, Sabine shoved the memories aside and looked back to Broedi. As she did, she caught Tobias staring at her, his eyes wide and mouth slightly parted. She stopped and held the tomble's stare.

"What?"

Tobias blinked a few times before running his gaze over Sabine's face, studying her just as Broedi had been earlier. A single, whispered word slipped from his lips.

"Impossible."

His voice filled with an undeniable sadness, Broedi rumbled, "I am afraid not."

Tobias stared hard at her and said quickly, "Your parents' names. What were they?"

Sabine hesitated. Their mannerisms, moods, and line of questioning were all combining to make her very uneasy.

"Why do you want to know?"

"Please," urged Tobias. "Their names?"

Glancing between the two White Lions, she muttered, "Ebrien and Jeanelle. Why?"

Tobias looked back to Broedi.

"That is too close to be a coincidence."

The hillman nodded slowly.

"I would agree."

Tobias' face fell, overtaken by sudden sorrow.

"And if that's the case, it means…"

Nodding, Broedi sighed, "I believe so."

The pair could be speaking a foreign tongue and she would have a better chance of following them. Her gaze shifted quickly from one to the other.

"What are you talking about?"

Looking at her, but speaking to Tobias, Broedi said, "Sabine can barely touch Fire and Water." His gaze shifted to the bed. "Helene, however, is quite gifted with Fire, Water, Stone, and Soul."

"That's four of five," said Tobias. "What about Void?"

Broedi shook his head, rumbling, "She has never been tested." Glancing back to Sabine, he asked, "Has she ever mentioned sensing Strands of Void?"

"No," answered Sabine, growing more anxious by the moment. "What is this about?!"

Broedi glanced to the bed.

"May we wake Helene?"

"Why?"

"I would like to see if she is sensitive to Void. Nothing more. I promise."

Sabine looked over at her sleeping sister.

"Must you do it now? She has not been sleeping well."

"She is still having the dreams, then?"

Staring back to the hillman, she asked, "Kenders told you?"

"Only after hearing about the accident. She was concerned for you both."

Sabine was a little upset Kenders had betrayed her confidence, but could understand why her friend had done so. She remained quiet a moment before answering.

"They seem to have grown less frequent since the accident, but, yes, she still has them."

"I understand you not wanting to wake her," rumbled Broedi. "But we must."

Tobias hobbled closer, his gaze fixed on her.

"One quick Weave and then she can go back to sleep."

Looking between them, she said, "Tell me what this is about."

"After the Weave," rumbled Broedi, his tone gentle yet firm.

She hesitated, gnawing on her lip. It took her a few moments to make her decision. With a short sigh and a nod, she said, "Fine. But I should be the one to wake her."

"Of course," rumbled Broedi.

Turning from the pair, she moved to the bed and sat atop the blankets, sinking into the cushioned top. Lightly placing her hand on her sister's shoulder, she gently rocked Helene's arm.

"Helene? Helene, dear? I need you to wake up."

It took a few more pats and whispered words to wake her, but eventually Helene began to stir, stretching and yawning. Rolling over to peer up at Sabine through bleary eyes, she spoke, her voice small and sleepy.

"You woke me up."

Reaching down, Sabine brushed a lock of black hair from Helene's forehead, smiled, and said, "I know, dear. I'm sorry. But Broedi and Tobias are here." She looked over at the White Lions. "And they need to ask you something."

Twisting her head, Helene peered around Sabine to stare at the pair hovering a few paces away and gave them a small, tired smile.

"Hello, Broedi."

"Good evening, uora," rumbled Broedi. "I am sorry for waking you." He approached them, stopping bedside. "Would you please sit up for me?"

Helene nodded and began to shimmy around under the covers. Sabine helped while also situating herself in order to drape her left arm around Helene's shoulders. When they were ready, she gave Helene a gentle squeeze, turned toward Broedi, and nodded.

The hillman looked to Tobias immediately.

"Something small."

Tobias nodded and stared into the empty air.

A half a heartbeat later, Helene stiffened. Worried, Sabine looked down to her sister and found Helene staring, wide-eyed, at the same empty space as Tobias. Moments later, the room began to grow dim. It was as though the light was being drained from the air. Helene buried her head into Sabine's shoulder and whimpered softly.

Broedi rumbled, "That's enough."

The room's brightness returned to normal in an instant. Sabine stared down at Helene, equal parts concerned and surprised. As Broedi crouched beside them, she shifted her gaze to the hillman. He was focused on Helene alone.

"What did you see, uora?"

Sabine wondered why he even asked the question. Helene's reaction was confirmation enough.

Helene spoke without lifting her head, her voice muffled by Sabine's shoulder and dress.

"The black ribbons."

Nodding slowly, Broedi asked, "Have you seen them before?"

Helene turned her head enough to peer at him and nodded once.

"I don't like them."

"Why is that?" asked Broedi.

"They scare me."

Sabine kissed the top of Helene's head, squeezed her tight, and asked, "Why didn't you tell me?"

When Helene did not answer her, Broedi rumbled softly, "There is nothing to fear, uora. The black ribbons are like the others, but have a different purpose. You still like the other ribbons, yes?"

Helene shook her head vigorously.

"Not anymore."

Broedi nodded, an understanding smile on his lips, and said, "Perhaps you will again someday." He hesitated a moment before asking in the softest, gentlest tone possible, "Do you think you can tell me what happened during your lesson with Marick? With the orange ribbons?"

Sabine shut her eyes tight, knowing the question needed to be asked, but wishing it were not so.

For a long moment, Helene remained quiet, the fire's soft crackling the only sound in the room. When she finally spoke, her voice was so soft that Sabine had to strain to hear it.

"I got mad."

"Why did you get mad?" asked Broedi quietly.

"Because Marick said I wasn't trying hard and I was."

Sabine opened her eyes and stared down. This was more than she had ever gotten out of her.

"I am sure you were trying very hard," rumbled Broedi. "Can you tell me what happened next?"

A long, quiet moment passed before Helene answered in a whisper. "I hurt him." She looked to the hillman quickly, adding, "I didn't mean to, Broedi. It was an accident! I promise!" The anguish in her voice was heartbreaking. She buried her face back into Sabine's shoulder and said, "I tried to make him come back! But he wouldn't listen to me. He kept going."

Sabine's deep concern for her sister stepped aside a moment, making room for confusion. Staring down at the top of Helene's head, she asked, "What was that, dear?"

Broedi lifted a hand and shook his head once, halting any further questions. Reaching out to pat Helene's leg, he rumbled, "You can go back to sleep now, uora. You were very brave tonight. Thank you." He gave her one last pat, rose from his crouch, and eyed Sabine, a thoughtful expression on his face. "Once she is sleeping, we must talk." With that, he turned around and moved back to Tobias.

"Sing to me, Sabine," murmured Helene. Looking down, Sabine found Helene staring up, tears in her eyes. "Sing me my song, please."

Somehow, Sabine managed to summon a smile.

"Of course, dear. Lie down, now."

Once Helene was snuggled back under the blankets, Sabine began to stroke Helene's raven-black hair while softly singing *Happy Times at the Fair*. As she sang, she repeatedly looked back to the White Lions. The pair had retreated to the room's far corner, near the chair and table, and was speaking in low whispers.

It took four passes through the lullaby before Helene fell back to sleep. The moment Sabine was sure the girl would not wake up, she slid from the bed and headed straight for the corner. Tobias, in the midst of speaking as she approached, glanced up and shut his mouth immediately. Stopping before them, Sabine put her hands on her hips and spoke in an urgent, hushed tone.

"Tell me what this means. *Now*."

Broedi gestured to the chair.

"Please sit."

She shot back quietly, "I don't want to sit."

Tobias urged gently, "I think you should."

"I don't *want* to sit," hissed Sabine. "I want to talk."

"That is your choice," rumbled the hillman. He hesitated a moment before nodding back to the bed. "When you were young, did your mother sing to you like that?"

Apparently, the series of odd questions were to continue.

Momentarily caught off guard, Sabine recovered quickly and nodded. "Yes, why?"

"Your voice is quite soothing," rumbled Broedi.

"Very pleasant," agreed Tobias, a wistful smile on his face. "When you sing, you sound just like her."

Not following, Sabine asked, "Like who?"

"Your mother," answered Broedi.

"How could you possibly know what she—" She stopped short as the unusual line of questions suddenly made sense. She remained quiet a moment, looking between hillman and tomble. "Are you saying...no, wait. What are you saying?"

The pair exchanged a look, Tobias nodded once, and Broedi turned back to her.

"Your mother was a White Lion."

Sabine shut her eyes tight. Her mind raced as countless bits and pieces about her life and family took on an entirely new meaning. Feeling a bit woozy, she opened her eyes, moved to the lone chair in the room and collapsed into it. Her dress bunched up beneath her, but she left it alone.

She sat in silence for a time, shaking her head nonstop. It seemed impossible, yet it explained so much.

Why they lived in the middle of the grasslands.

Why Mother never went to town.

Why she was so talented with the Strands.

Why she looked years younger than Father did, even though they were supposedly the same age.

She was about to accept the impossible as fact when something occurred to her.

"Hold a moment..."

Since arriving at Storm Island, she had made frequent visits to the keep's small library, finding—unsurprisingly so—that many of the texts and books focused on the White Lions. By now, she knew quite a lot about the heroes.

Looking up to Broedi and Tobias, she said, "None of the White Lions were named Jeanelle."

"That is true," acknowledged Broedi as he moved closer to her. Standing before her chair, he added, "Most likely, she adapted it to help remain hidden. At times, I went by 'Brady.'"

Tobias raised a hand.

"Toby, here."

Dropping to a knee, Broedi stared at her and said, "You might have known her as Jeanelle Moiléne, mother and wife. But to us, she was Jeanne Palielle, friend and fellow White Lion."

Sabine shook her head, her mind rebelling against what they were suggesting. "No. This is not possible."

"Why?" asked Tobias. Hobbling closer, he stood beside Broedi and leaned on his walking stick. "From what you've told us, it is more than possible. It is truth. Jeanne had auburn hair, green eyes, and a voice that put every morning dove to shame."

Broedi, who had been nodding along with Tobias, added, "And she could touch Fire, Water, Stone, Soul, and Void. The same as Helene."

"If what you say is true, why can Helene touch them but I can't?"

"Perhaps you will one day," rumbled Broedi. "It comes to some later in their lives."

Tobias added, "I knew a longleg who was in his seventieth year when he suddenly discovered he could touch Air and Life. The poor soul was terrified."

Sabine shifted her gaze to the tomble.

"Will that happen to me?"

Tobias shrugged.

"It might. It might not. Who knows? And as you are as much your father's child as Jeanne's, it might be—"

"Stop!" hissed Sabine as another surge of denial washed through her. "This is madness! My mother was not Jeanne Palielle! She was *not* a White Lion!"

With sympathy in his eyes, Broedi said, "Yes, she—"

"No!" snapped Sabine, shaking her head vigorously and sending her long black hair whipping back and forth. "She's dead! White Lions can't die!"

Broedi shared a quick look with Tobias before turning back to her.

"That is the one thing that has us puzzled. Tell us about the day Helene was born."

"Must I?"

This was a memory she avoided.

Broedi nodded.

"Please."

Sabine dropped her eyes and thought back to that day four—almost five—years ago. Shutting her eyes tight, she spoke, keeping her voice as steady as she could.

"It was early Spring, the Turn of Duryn. Father was turning over the fields, getting them ready for planting. I was inside with Mother, sitting at the table and reading. She was cleaning, getting things ready for the founding-wife to arrive from Stooert the following week. Suddenly, she gasped, grabbed her stomach, and told me to get Father. I ran outside, screaming for him. He dropped the shovel and he came running. I was gone for only a moment, but when I got back—"

She stopped, her throat catching as she remembered the scene awaiting her.

"Mother was lying on their mattress. Her dress was soaked red. It took me a moment to realize it was blood. Gods, there was so much blood…"

She felt tears threatening to come and tried to hold them back.

"Father panicked. He had no idea what to do. Mother, like always, remained perfectly calm and talked him through everything. I did what I could to help, but mostly I just held Mother's hand."

Sabine glanced down to her hands in her lap, remembering her mother's tight grip.

"Helene came fast. At least, that's what Mother said. All I remember is thinking how tiny she was, her little body in Father's hands, still covered with dirt. I knew nothing about babies, but I could tell something was wrong right away. Helene's skin was a pale gray color, her arms and legs hung limp. Oddly enough, it reminded me of a doll Father had brought me from Stooert one time. And she was quiet. Absolutely quiet. I thought she was dead. Father did, too. I could see it in his eyes."

"And your mother?" rumbled Broedi softly. "What did she do?"

"She begged. Over and over, she asked to hold Helene. 'Give her to me! I can get her back! I can get her back!' At first, Father refused, but he eventually relented and handed Helene's little body over. Mother pulled me to her, gave me a kiss and hug, and told me to be strong for Father and Helene. She held tight. Gods, did she hold tight…"

For some reason, her arms hurt. Looking down, she found that she was hugging herself, squeezing her upper arms, digging her fingers into the muscles. Releasing her grip, she placed her hands in her lap just as a tear fell to land on her wrist. She did not bother to wipe it. Or the ones that followed.

"She kissed Father, told us she loved us both, and closed her eyes. A few moments later, Helene started to cry, her face turned pink, and she began to wiggle in Mother's arms. I was so happy, but Father started to cry, the first and only time I ever saw him do so. I didn't understand why he was so sad until I looked up to Mother's face."

Sabine paused, looked up to Broedi through tear-blurred eyes, and muttered, "She'd never open her eyes again…"

Broedi looked away and stared into the fire, the tan skin around his eyes twitching. Tobias dropped his head to his chest and remained that way, as motionless as a statue. No one said a word.

After a few moments, Broedi looked back to her.

"What happened next?"

Sabine drew in a long, shuddering breath and let it back out slowly before answering.

"I bundled up Helene while Father buried Mother in the longpepper field."

"Your loss is my own," rumbled the hillman. "Your mother will be missed. She was a good friend."

Without looking up, Tobias murmured, "And a better person." His voice was thick with emotion.

Sabine shook her head—less stridently than before—and said, "My mother was Jeanelle Moiléne, a farmer. She was *not* a White lion. White Lions can't die."

"If the wound is severe enough, we can," said Broedi. He rose from his crouch and took a step back. "Do you know the Celystiela who chose Jeanne to be her champion?"

Sabine's stomach clenched. She did.

"Maeana. The Goddess of Death."

Nodding, Broedi asked, "Did you know that many called her the Soul Speaker?"

"I read that in one of the books here."

Tobias lifted his head and asked, "Did the book say why she was called that?"

Sabine shook her head.

"No, it didn't."

Crossing his arms over his chest, Broedi rumbled, "When a mortal dies, the soul begins its journey to Maeana's hall. Until it reached its destination, Jeanne alone could speak with it. Ask it questions, learn what it knew in life. Sometimes, she would wonder aloud whether it was possible to keep a soul from completing its journey." He paused a moment before adding. "And perhaps even convince it to return."

Sabine's eyes narrowed in confusion.

"What are you saying?"

Broedi said, "That Helene was stillborn. Lifeless at birth. And that Jeanne used her gift to follow Helene's soul and…" He trailed off and shook his head. "To be honest, I do not know what happened then." He shifted his gaze over to Helene. "Something did, though. Something brought Helene back."

Sabine peered over at her little sister, a small lump beneath the blankets. The last stone in her wall of denial fell away. Too much fit.

Turning back to Broedi and Tobias, Sabine muttered, "My mother was a White Lion."

The pair nodded slowly.

Sabine took a deep breath and let out a long, heavy sigh.

"So what does this mean?"

With a shake of his head, Broedi said, "I am not sure. This is unexpected."

"Not exactly," muttered Tobias. "Her death was foretold in Indrida's prophecy, yes? 'One will perish?'"

"That is true," rumbled Broedi.

Staring into the hearth's fire, Tobias said, "Something bothers me about all this, though." He tilted his head back to look at the hillman. "Why would Nelnora not tell you?" His eyes narrowed. "Unless she did?"

Broedi shook his head.

"For the final time, I am no longer carrying secrets about my meeting with Nelnora. If she knew of Jeanne's passing, she did not speak of it to me."

"So she either knows less than she purports," muttered the tomble. "Or she knew and did not tell you on purpose. I would bet a thousand gold ducats on the latter." He returned to staring into the fire, a bitter scowl on his face.

Broedi dropped his chin to his chest and rumbled, "I grow weary of her games." Both White Lions remained quiet. Sabine was about to say something when Broedi lifted his head, stared at Sabine, and said, "I need you to come with us. Back to Demetus."

Sabine's eyebrows rose in surprise.

"Pardon?"

"He's right," said Tobias. "'The Progeny must rise to lead the fight' and all."

"I'm sorry, but what does that have to do with—"

She stopped short as she realized what it meant to be the child of a White Lion.

"I'm one of—"

She cut off again and turned to stare at Helene.

"We're both..."

She trailed off, unable to say the word aloud. Broedi did for her.

"The Progeny?" rumbled the hillman. "Yes, you are. 'Hidden, then found, Willingly come around.' Indrida's words fit you as well."

Sabine dropped her head to stare at the floor, as her mind grappled with the revelation. After a few moments, she looked back up and asked, "But what can I do? Nikalys and Kenders have their parents' gifts. Apparently, Helene has Mother's. But me? I have none of their talents. I can make a fire flare or a pitcher of water cold, but...that's all. What can I contribute?"

"Do not underestimate yourself, Sabine. You proved yourself many times over during our journey here."

A disturbing thought occurred to her. Holding Broedi's gaze, she asked, "Do you intend to bring Helene as well? Because that will *not* be happening."

"No," said Broedi. "Prophecy or not, she remains here. I will not put one so young so close to danger."

"So you are asking me to not only go, but to leave my sister behind? Alone?"

"She will not be alone. I will ask Lady Vivienne to provide a caretaker. Any number of people in Claw would be happy to volunteer."

"But you want me to leave her?"

"Yes," rumbled Broedi. "That is the way of things. I would like you in Demetus."

"Why? So I can 'lead the fight?' I'm the daughter of a *farmer*, Broedi."

"And a White Lion."

"Do you truly believe I am that necessary?"

"Indrida does."

"I don't understand. From what Jak and Nikalys shared, you all have a serious deficit of trust when it comes to the Gods and Goddesses. Why are you are putting so much faith in the mutterings of one?"

"Because she has been right so far," rumbled Broedi.

"According to who? You? Yesterday, you thought Nikalys and Kenders alone were the Progeny."

"Then don't come," said Tobias with a touch of exasperation. "If you want to stay, then do so. I know this is all a shock to you, but we do not have time to stand here and wait for you to grow accustomed to things. There's an army on its way to Demetus and Broedi and I need to be there to meet it." He glanced up at Broedi. "Let's go." He turned and began to hobble to the door.

He had only taken two steps when she said, "Wait."

Tobias halted and looked back.

"What?"

"I didn't say I wasn't coming."

"So you are, then?"

Sabine hesitated.

"I don't know."

Tobias sighed and leveled a steady, direct stare at her.

"Make your choice, Sabine. Quickly, please. Fate is waiting."

Sabine looked back and forth between the pair, the urgency of the moment so tangible that it felt as if a weight were hanging around her neck. This was not fair. Nikalys and Kenders had weeks to become acclimated to their new reality. She had the next few heartbeats.

They were asking her to make an impossible choice. Stay with her sister, remain safe, and leave everyone one else she cared about to face the Cabal alone. Or chase a prophecy and go to Demetus, knowing there was a good chance she might die there and leave Helene without family.

She sat there, wavering, when the levelheaded calmness upon which she prided herself surged from deep within her soul, sweeping through her in an instant and washing away her doubts as quickly as a jump in the cool Erona River chased away the Summer heat.

Rising from her chair, she announced her decision, her voice firm and steady.

"I will come, but on one condition."

Tobias appeared surprised. Whether by her decision or her tone, she did not know.

"What is it?"

"I go wherever you or Nundle do. If things go poorly, I want a port back here *immediately*. No questions asked. No speeches. A port back to this room, right away. I will fight the Cabal—somehow—but Helene comes first. I will not leave her alone in this world."

"An entirely reasonable request," said Tobias, looking about the room, studying it closely. "And if you're half the shot with a bow as Kenders says, I'll be lucky to have you as my shadow."

"You are sure of this?" rumbled Broedi.

"I am," declared Sabine, turning to face the oaken dresser. "Just give me a moment to get a few things together." She began to hurry across the room, wondering what exactly one packed for a battle, when her gaze fell on Helene. The little girl's mouth hung half open, a few stray hair strands draped haphazardly over her face.

"I need to tell her I'm leaving."

Behind her, she heard Broedi and Tobias move to the door.

"Tell her what you will," rumbled Broedi. "But do not take too long. We will be in Lady Vivienne's offices."

Sabine nodded.

"I'll be there shortly."

The pair exited the room quickly and quietly, shutting the door behind them. Sabine stood in place, listening to the sharp clack of Tobias' walking stick retreat down the hall. Before the sound completely faded, she took a deep breath and moved bedside.

This was not going to be easy.

CHAPTER 54: BROTHERS

23rd of the Turn of Maeana, 4999

The western sky was a colorless gray, yet undisturbed by Mu's orb.

Most of the lesser stars had faded, leaving only the brightest to hold to the night. Hundreds of torches lined Demetus' walls, obliterating the dark but powerless against the fog. The low-lying mist swirling below swallowed the torchlight a mere dozen feet below the battlements. Jak peered into the murkiness, his hands cupped to the sides of his face to shield his eyes from the torches' flames so as not to be blinded by them.

"I can't see a blasted thing down there."

Sergeant Trell said quietly, "If anything is down there, Broedi will see it." The soldier stood on Jak's right, staring into the fog as well.

"Unless he can see through walls, he's as useless as I am. That fog is thick."

Zecus muttered, "Then perhaps he is listening instead?"

"Now that's more likely," conceded Jak, looking to his left.

Zecus was leaning on a stout, four-foot wooden staff, having wisely foregone the longsword. A torch burned brightly just beyond the Borderlander and Jak momentarily glanced at its flame. He turned away quickly, peering back into the night, but he was effectively blind now. With a sigh, he dropped his hands to his sides. There was nothing to see anyway.

As a long, ominous silence stretched out—interrupted by a soldier's quiet cough here and there—Jak muttered, "Armies make a lot of noise when they march, yes?"

Zecus and Sergeant Trell both smiled at his nervous question.

"Do not worry," murmured Zecus. "Even if they were silent, I am sure we would smell them."

Jak and Sergeant Trell chuckled softly at the jest, drawing a few curious looks from the Reed Men nearby. As he dropped his chin to chest so as to hide his smile, Jak's gaze fell upon the one thing that made Zecus' Shadow Mane uniform different from his own. Wrapped tightly around Zecus' right arm, just above his elbow, was Joshmuel's white headband. As his gaze lingered on the cloth strip, his smile faded.

Hearing of Joshmuel's death had been like getting kicked in the gut by a horse, for a number of reasons. The first night in Demetus, the Isaac sibling reunion had been a morose one with Jak and Nikalys spending the evening trying to console their sister. At first, she insisted that she was fine, but soon thereafter, the tears began to fall.

Despite an entire evening spent grieving with his siblings, Jak had actually said very little to Zecus about Joshmuel's passing. He had wanted to, but life was busy now. War was literally at the gates.

Zecus glanced over and caught him eyeing the headband. A shadow darker than the gloom of the Marshland's night fell over his face. He looked up to Jak and, for a long moment, the two held one another's gaze.

"I am sorry, Zecus. Truly."

Zecus gave a lone, solemn nod, and in a voice that barely rose above the pre-dawn quiet, he murmured, "Thank you, Jak." He immediately turned to face the foggy morning, his profile backlit by the flickering light of the torches. "We will honor his memory today."

Jak nodded.

"Yes. We will."

He studied his friend a moment longer before facing the blanket of mist. Out of the corner of his eye, Jak noticed Sergeant Trell staring at him. A glance over earned him a silent nod of approval from the soldier. Looking past the sergeant, Jak's gaze traveled the line of green-and-white-clad soldiers standing on the battlements, all of whom were staring westward, their expressions universally sober. A few quiet, subdued conversations dotted the ranks, but most individuals were silent, lost in their thoughts.

Compared to the castle at Storm Island, the mud-brick ramparts of Demetus were spacious, nearly ten feet wide from outer to inner wall, enough to form three lines of men. One stood at the battlements while the other two waited against the back wall with standing orders to 'fill any gap that occurs.' When Commander Aiden had uttered the words, Jak's insides had gone cold.

While the walls were wide and thick, they were also short, their pinnacles a mere thirty-five feet from the ground. Every two hundred feet, a tower rose from the main parapet. Jak was unsure if the structure deserved the designation 'tower' as it was only ten feet taller than the rest of the wall, but it was what people called them. At eveningmeal two nights past, Jak had asked why the walls were no higher and Duke Rholeb explained the loamy soil prevented them from doing so. Anything bigger or heavier would sink.

When Jak had first arrived in the city, catapults had been atop the towers. Now, bowmen alone crowded the pinnacles. During one evening strategy session, Wren repeatedly pointed out—much to the annoyance of Duke Rholeb—how ineffective the catapults would be against an army with Stone or Air mages. The next morning, the giant war machines had been dismantled and removed.

Nearly every soldier on this section of wall was a Reed Man, each one wearing a pointed metal helm polished to shine. A good distance down the way, before the next tower, Jak spotted a group of Southern Arms, their beards and blue and gold uniforms sticking out amongst the sea of clean-shaven, green-and-white-clad men. Here and there, Shadow Mane black dotted the ranks. Somewhere on these walls was the lone Dust Man unit, led by the corporal who had rescued Zecus' sister from slavers. The Shore Guard was absent from the walls, the entire Long Coast contingent being held in reserve within the city, ready to respond wherever they might be needed.

This was the new Army of the White Lions. Men with backgrounds as varied as the selection of spirits once kept at The Lout and The Witch. Yet despite their many differences, they all had two things in common. The first was obvious: they were all here to fight the Cabal. The second was something most every soldier was trying to hide, some better than others. The men were afraid.

Someone to the north sneezed. Half the men within earshot started, their heads whipping around to face the offender's direction. A few moments later, they began to look back west, sharing a nervous grin with their neighbors. Jak sighed.

Over the past few days, one of his primary duties—and that of every Shadow Mane here—had been to spread calm and confidence among the ranks while still conveying the sincerity of the threat they faced. At first, most doubted the claims that the God of Chaos was driving a massive army of demon-led Sudashians toward them. Yet public speeches by Duke Rholeb and Duchess Aleece paired with the ever-increasing oligurt sightings convinced a large majority of the soldiers while unfortunately replacing everyone's doubt with restrained panic. A few demonstrations by Nikalys, Kenders, and the White Lions eased their worries enough that there was not widespread desertion. The reality was that they were being asked not only to stand against Tandyr's wave of aggression, but also to break it.

Hearing the quiet murmuring of voices behind him, Jak glanced over his shoulder and found the back two lines of soldiers staring into the city. He shot a quick look to Sergeant Trell, but before he could ask leave to go, it was granted.

"Go," said the sergeant. "See what it is."

Zecus asked, "May—"

"Yes, you can go, too. Quickly, please."

Spinning around, Jak strode to the inside wall with Zecus right behind. As he approached, he called out, "Move aside!"

Men turned and, seeing their black and white uniforms, parted to let them through. Upon reaching the wall, Jak placed his hands on the rough rock and leaned forward, peering down at the main thoroughfare. The fog was not as dense within the city, but it still obscured anything much beyond a hundred feet.

The lines of soldiers in the streets below were backpedalling slowly, pressing their backs against buildings in an effort to clear the flagstone way. To a man, they had their heads turned, staring into the center of the city.

Standing on Jak's right, Zecus asked, "Do you think it's Nikalys?"

Jak tried his best to see through the fog, but all he could make out were the glowing auras of the torches lining the street.

"Gods, I hope so."

After leaving the duke's dining hall last night with Nikalys, the pair had hurried through the halls, Jak intent on delivering the duchess' order to Commander Aiden. At an intersection of passageways, when Jak had turned left, Nikalys went right. Jak had called after him, asking where he was going. With a wink and a smile, Nikalys answered, "To wake up Nundle."

Shortly thereafter, a stableman had seen the pair, along with Wren surprisingly, step through a 'rip in the world' near the horse barns. Unfortunately, the stableman had a large mouth, and word of their disappearance spread like a Summer grassfire. Just when the soldiers had accepted the idea of mages and White Lions aiding them, rumors quickly spread that the heroes were abandoning Demetus. Jak had done his best to assuage the fears, but it was no easy task.

Jak had a good guess as to where his brother had run off. Eyeing the mist below, he said a quick prayer to Lamoth that he was right.

"Come on, Nik."

Moments later, Nikalys emerged from the gloom with Nundle and Wren at his side, fog swirling about them as the trio walked down the street. Jak allowed himself a smile, happy to see his brother return.

"Now, let's hope you brought some friends."

Soft exclamations of disbelief slipped from nearby soldiers as a handful of strange figures stepped from the mist as well, trailing Nikalys, shuffling along the flagstone. Their limbs, covered with dark, bark-like skin, were more tree branch than arms or legs. Their hair, both the color and consistency of grass, sprang from the top of triangular-shaped heads, swishing about as the creatures stared at the buildings, their glossy black eyes reflecting the flickering torch light.

"Bless the Gods," muttered Zecus. "Every time I think I have a grasp on my world…"

Jak nodded, silently agreeing with Zecus' unfinished thought. Nikalys' descriptions of the thorn had been thorough, but seeing the strange race for himself, marching through the streets of Demetus, was a surreal experience.

Counting the figures as they emerged from the fog, Jak had only reached ten when the line of thorn stopped. A frown spread over his lips. He had hoped for more.

As the thorn shuffled along, Zecus muttered, "Those are the great monsters?"

Jak had been thinking the same thing. After Nundle's grand tales about the fearsome creature encountered on the beach, he had expected something different.

"They look like tree saplings," murmured Jak. "I wonder if Nundle was… exaggerating…" He trailed off, his eyes opening wide as a number of seven-foot-tall figures stepped from the fog.

Twenty bald and tattooed hillmen and hillwomen marched together, looking around the city, expressions of curious wonder on their faces. They all wore drab robes that cut off at their calves, heavy leather boots, and carried wooden staves on their shoulders that were thicker than Jak's forearm.

"They look intimidating," muttered Zecus.

"They certainly do," agreed Jak.

More hillmen followed the first twenty robed giants, but their dress was much different: simple cloth tunics and breeches with thick strips of leather armor strapped to their arms, legs, and chest. Half carried the largest bows Jak had ever seen, while the rest wielded long poles topped with a sweeping metal blade. The wicked weapons were a full foot taller than the hillmen.

Raising his voice a bit, Jak said, "A gold ducat to the first man who spars one of them and wins." The quip elicited a healthy chuckle from the nearby Reed Men who heard it.

As the procession of hillmen continued, Jak's gaze shifted back to his brother. Nikalys was scanning the walls and stopped the moment his eyes locked onto Jak and Zecus. Jak lifted a hand and waved. Nikalys returned the greeting before turning back to the city center.

Holding up both arms, Nikalys called for the group to halt. As the thorn and Titan Tribe members came to a stop, a subdued cheer arose from the soldiers watching, both in the streets and on the walls. The ten thorn stared about them, their glossy, black eyes opened wide. The sound appeared to baffle them.

As the quiet cheer was fading, Jak spotted Broedi pushing through the throng of soldiers, aiming for where Nikalys, Nundle, and Wren stood. A series of nods and whispers rippled through the assembled hillmen the moment they saw him. Broedi, surely aware of the response, ignored it and upon reaching Nikalys, leaned down to speak quietly with him. After a moment, Nikalys pulled back from Broedi, a curious expression on his face, and turned back to peer up at Jak.

A quiet sigh slipped from Jak. This would not be an easy talk. Without taking his eyes from Nikalys, he murmured, "What do you think he'll say?"

Glancing over, Zecus said, "That you are either mad or a liar. Perhaps both."

"My coin is on a long series of blank stares paired with stuttering."

Zecus smiled slightly.

"Was that your reaction?"

"At first, yes. *Then* came the accusations of madness."

In the streets below, Broedi was speaking with Wren and Nundle now. After a few moments, Broedi called out for the thorn and hillmen to follow him, turned north, and hurried along the base of the walls. Wren and Nundle went with him, leaving Nikalys alone to stare up at Jak again. When Jak pointed to the southern tower, Nikalys nodded and began to make his way there.

With a sigh and a shove, Jak pushed himself away from the inner wall, stood tall, and called out, "To your positions! The show is over!"

The soldiers closest to him turned from the scene below and began relaying his order up and down the line, to the north and south. Jak kept his expression blank despite the wonder he felt watching hundreds of men obey him. Six turns ago, he was trimming olive trees. Now, he was giving orders to soldiers, many of whom were five to ten years his senior. And they were listening.

With Zecus in tow, he strode back across the battlements, returning to his spot beside Sergeant Trell. The sergeant glanced over, his face as calm as a pond on a windless day.

"Nikalys?"

Nodding, Jak said, "Yes."

"Good. And buhanik?"

Jak stared back, confused.

"Pardon?"

"Thorn, Jak," replied the sergeant with a small grin. "Did he bring back thorn?"

"Ah," said Jak. "Yes, he did. Only ten, though."

"Ten?" said Sergeant Trell, his eyes widening a fraction. His smile grew. "Excellent."

Jak shared a quick, doubtful look with Zecus before looking back to the sergeant.

"Sergeant? They look like a stiff breeze could blow them over."

The man chuckled quietly and stared back west, into the gloom and fog.

"Remember you said that, son."

Nikalys' voice rang out over the walls.

"Jak!"

Looking to his left, Jak saw his brother stepping from the darkened doorway of the southern tower. Jak lifted a hand, indicating that he should wait where he was. With a nod, Nikalys halted.

"Sergeant? May I—"

"Go," replied the solider. He leaned back, peered down the bulwark to the waiting Nikalys, and gave a nod of greeting. "And Ketus with you, Jak."

"Thank you."

Patting Zecus on the back as he passed, Jak hurried down the torch-lit wall. Glancing east, he noticed the sky had lightened a shade or two. Dawn was near.

Halfway to his waiting brother, Jak reached up to stifle a yawn. While opportunities for sleep had been few of late, even when he managed to lie down for a bit, he rarely awoke refreshed. Ever since his injury, nightmares plagued his sleep. He would awake, his heart pounding, an overwhelming sense of dread filling his chest.

He would sit there shivering, an icy chill radiating from deep inside his soul, trying to remember the dream and failing every time. The images faded like pipe smoke on the wind the moment he opened his eyes.

Nikalys was leaning against the doorway, his arms crossed and head down. Jak guessed the constant, furtive glances shot at him by the men on the walls were making him uneasy. As Jak reached the tower's entryway, Nikalys glanced up, a flicker of relief dashing over his face.

Nikalys nodded and said in a rather formal tone, "Good days ahead, Corporal Isaac."

Amused by the greeting's propriety, Jak stopped a few paces away, fixed Nikalys with a steady gaze, and gave a deep bow.

"And good memories behind, sir."

Standing tall, he added a wink, prompting a tiny smile from Nikalys, one tinted with a healthy amount of brotherly annoyance. Nikalys shook his head, turned, and slipped into the cover of the tower. Jak followed, chuckling to himself.

The tower's interior was dark, the only light inside coming from the torches outside and through the two open archways. Looking through the southern opening, Jak saw the long line of Reed Men continuing along the wall, all the way to the next tower over. Facing his brother, he found Nikalys slumped against the western wall.

"Hey, Nik."

Glancing up, Nikalys said, "Hey, Jak."

Overly formal just a moment ago, both now spoke as if they were sitting in the Isaac family kitchen after a long day in the groves.

Jak stopped a step or two in the doorway and studied his brother. Even in the low light, he could clearly see the bags under Nikalys' eyes.

"No offense, but you look terrible."

A tired, lopsided grin slipped over Nikalys' mouth.

"Negotiating an acceptable agreement between the buhanik and the Titan Tribe was harder than I thought it was going to be."

"Why?"

"Why?" repeated Nikalys, sounding rather annoyed. "Well, to begin with, one race enslaved the other for a century. So that took some time to overcome."

Any other time and place, Jak would have had a quick retort for Nikalys' overly testy response. However, this time, he kept quiet. He needed Nikalys calm and collected, not upset.

After a moment, Nikalys shook his head and reached to rub his eyes.

"Hells, Jak. Sorry. I'm just tired."

"I understand," replied Jak. "We all are."

Nikalys nodded, his fingers still kneading his eyes.

"That we are."

"At least you got them here. That's what matters."

Nikalys sighed, dropped his hand from his face, and said, "Actually, Wren deserves more credit than me. He understands the way thorn think."

Surprised, Jak said, "So then he behaved himself?"

Nikalys shook his head.

"Gods, no. He was still incredibly rude and obnoxious, but the results speak for themselves. Ten thorn, twenty mages, and almost four hundred warriors."

Jak tried not to show his disappointment at the small number.

"Only four hundred?"

"Word is still spreading through the Provinces about their new-found freedom. The four hundred here are those who had reached Buhaylunsod before we were ready to leave."

"Are more coming?"

Nikalys gave a tiny shake of his head.

"Not today."

With a quick sigh, Jak muttered, "Well, then…"

They still had no idea what sort of numbers they would be facing. The counts brought by scouts varied wildly, estimating the Sudashian force to be between six and seventy thousand. Jak did not understand how there could be such a large discrepancy and prayed the lower numbers were the correct ones. Only twelve thousand soldiers stood on Demetus' walls.

Nikalys asked, "Any movement out there?"

Shaking his head, Jak said, "No, nothing." He paused a moment before clarifying, "Well, we haven't seen anything. That fog is like cheese soup."

"Heard anything?"

"I certainly haven't," answered Jak. "And so far, neither has the mongrel."

Nikalys' eyebrows drew together.

"Okollu?"

Nodding, Jak said, "Rhohn convinced it to leave those blasted stones and help keep watch through the night. Surprisingly, Broedi agreed to let it out." Nodding toward the northern doorway, he added. "It's a few towers that way."

"'He,' Jak," corrected Nikalys. "Okollu is a 'he,' not an 'it.' And they are called kur-surus, not mongrels."

For reasons Jak did not fully understand, Nikalys had treated Okollu with complete respect the moment he met the mongrel.

"Regardless, *he* is to alert us if *he* hears anything."

Nodding his approval, Nikalys said, "A good plan."

"Are you sure about that? Gods, Nik. We're putting our fate in the hands—or is it paws?—of a blasted mongrel!"

Nikalys looked over, his eyebrows arched in disapproval.

Shaking his head, Jak said, "Pardon me. 'Kur-surus.' Whatever name I call him by does not change the fact we're relying on him."

"Do you believe his story?"

Jak hesitated a moment before answering somewhat reluctantly.

"Well…yes."

"As do I," said Nikalys, his voice resolute. "And in this fight, we need any and every ally we can find. Even the ones covered in fur and with jaws like a smith's vice. Try to set aside your prejudice, Jak, and offer a prayer of thanks that Okollu is not only on our side, but that he's up on that wall, listening for our enemy."

Jak blinked twice, stunned by the short speech and suddenly seeing his brother in a new light. Nikalys was no longer the boy he used to chase through the streets of Yellow Mud or dunk in Lake Hawthorne. Jak shook his head in quiet awe, suddenly very proud of his little brother.

"Gods, but you grew up fast."

"What other choice did I have?" asked Nikalys. Standing tall, he crossed his arms over his chest and peered hard at Jak. "Now, out with whatever you have to tell me. Broedi said it was important. Nothing happened to Kenders, did it? She didn't run off to the Northlands while I was gone?"

Wearing a slight smile, Jak gave a quick shake of his head.

"No, she's fine. And still here."

"Good. That's the first thing I think of whenever someone says they need to talk to me now."

A dry chuckle slipped from Jak as he said, "I know what you mean."

"What is it then?" asked Nikalys, glancing out the northern door. "I would like to check on things before sunrise."

Jak had been thinking about what to say to Nikalys ever since Broedi had returned from the enclave last night. Every possible approach he had thought up seemed wrong in one fashion or another. With the moment here and nothing prepared, he took a deep breath, let it out slowly, and spoke.

"Sabine's here."

For a heartbeat or two, Nikalys stood motionless, his face blank, before he managed to get out a single, surprised word.

"Pardon?"

Jak motioned to the stairwell that led to the streets below.

"You might want to sit down."

Nikalys did not move.

"Did something happen to Helene?"

Jak shook his head quickly, saying, "No, she's safely at Storm Island. Apparently, Lady Vivienne is watching her herself." He offered a smile and forced a small chuckle. "Heh. Can you imagine that?"

"Now is not the time to jest."

Jak's fake smile fell away.

"No, I suppose it's not."

"Now, why is Sabine here?" pressed Nikalys. His tone turned suspicious. "Have you spoken with her?"

Even though Jak had never said a word to Nikalys about his feelings for Sabine, he was sure Nikalys knew the truth. Just as Jak knew of Nikalys' feelings. Last night, after the stunning revelation of Sabine and Helene's true heritage, Jak had confided in Kenders his dilemma and was rewarded with a bemused grin and the knowledge that everyone at the enclave apparently knew about the confused situation between the three of them. Kenders called it "the worst-kept secret in the southern duchies."

This conversation was not about that, though. Their personal feelings for Sabine were secondary to what Jak needed to share. Eying his brother carefully, he said, "Tell me everything you know about Sabine's mother."

Nikalys' eyebrows drew together.

"And how is that important now?"

A quick and mirthless laugh slipped from Jak.

"That's funny. That was the same thing I said..."

As quickly as he could, Jak recounted his surprising, late night meeting in the Sovereign's Chamber with Broedi, Kenders, and Sabine, watching Nikalys go through the same series of emotions he had. Confusion at first, followed quickly by disbelief, and then quiet denial. At that point, though, Nikalys broke from Jak's progression. Whereas Jak had felt a hint of melancholy over the revelation, Nikalys' expression revealed something different.

Hope.

To Jak, the reason for his brother's reaction was clear. Sabine and Nikalys shared something only two other souls in all of Terrene had. He tried not to feel disappointment, telling himself he had more important things about which to worry, but he must have failed in keeping the emotion from his face. With sympathy in his eyes, Nikalys stepped forward, reached out to grab Jak's shoulder, and opened his mouth as if to speak. He remained that way a moment before shutting it again. He started and stopped thrice more before closing it for good and letting out a soft chuckle.

"I just helped negotiate an agreement between buhanik and the hillmen they enslaved, I'm about to march into battle against demons and Gods, and yet I cannot talk to my brother about one woman?"

Jak almost did not want to smile, but he could not stop the slight grin from spreading over his face.

"You've never had a way with girls, have you?"

Nikalys shook his head, wearing a lopsided smile of his own.

"And you've always been the flatterer, haven't you?"

With a playful shrug, Jak said, "Mother always said I got my charm from Father."

Nikalys' smile froze in place before fading quickly. Jak's followed. The Isaac brothers stared at one another in silence and, for too brief a moment, were reminded of a time when their lives made sense.

"I miss them, Jak."

Jak nodded slowly, murmuring, "Me, too." He patted his brother's shoulder twice. "They'd be proud of you, Nik. The Gods know I am."

With arched eyebrows, Nikalys said with quiet surprise, "Me? Hells, Jak, look at you." He pointed to the white circle sewn on Jak's right shoulder. "Or should I say, Corporal Isaac?"

"I can't let my little brother outshine me, can I?"

Enjoying the moment, they shared a smile. There had been too few lately. For a moment, Jak almost forgot they were standing on the walls of a city soon to be under siege.

That was when the howling started.

CHAPTER 55: STONE

The baying rose from the fog, cascaded over the walls, and drifted through the city streets. Rhohn managed to suppress the shudder the howls brought, but most of the soldiers nearby did not. Looking back to his command, he saw most of the men with hands on hilt. Some had even begun to draw their blades from their scabbards.

"Hold!" called Rhohn. "Unless they can fly, there's no need for that. Let your blades sleep a little while longer."

His Dust Men complied, albeit slowly. Turning back around, he sighed, wondering how many men on these walls besides him had heard the cry of a kur-surus before now. He doubted he would need more than his two hands—eight fingers—to count them.

Leaning forward, Rhohn looked over the edge of the bastion tower, staring north and south to study the walls in both directions. Half the Reed Men soldiers were peering into the mist, listening to the howls, while the other half were staring upward, glaring in Rhohn's direction, the distrust on their faces so clear that a blind man could see it. The moment Rhohn caught their eyes, they turned their heads back to the west.

Sighing, Rhohn glanced to his left and the subject of the soldiers' wariness. Okollu stood beside him, his eyes bright and alert and his ears twitching in all directions. He was draped in the brand new cloak Duke Rholeb had given him days ago when Okollu's presence had been revealed to the combined armies. Hoping to dampen some of the expected ire of the soldiers, the duke declared Okollu a 'Friend to the Marshlands' and bestowed upon him the dark green linen cloak, the back of which was emblazoned with the stitched white mark of the Marshlands: a four-leafed reed plant encompassed by a circle.

The cloak's hood was down, revealing Okollu's brown and white head for all to see. When Okollu arrived at the walls earlier, accompanied by Commander Aiden himself, the commander had made it abundantly clear that no one was to harm the kur-surus. So far, the men had complied in action if not in spirit of the order. Throughout the night, countless narrowed-eye stares or murmured curses had been directed at the kur-surus. To Okollu's credit, he ignored it all.

The tumultuous howling faded for a moment before shifting into quick, isolated yaps and barks. Facing forward, Rhohn peered into the thick fog below, searching for movement.

"I wish I could see something. Anything at all."

On his right, Kenders murmured, "We will remedy that shortly."

Glancing to his right, he muttered, "You will 'remedy' that?"

The fair easterner wore a simple, drab brown tunic, women's breeches, and a black and white Shadow Mane cloak. She looked over at him and gave him a tiny smile.

"Fog is but water and air, Rhohn."

The Dust Man shook his head.

"That means nothing to me."

Kenders' grin widened a fraction.

"Two types of Strands are Water and Air."

Nodding slowly, he muttered, "Ah, I see." He stared back into the mist, a frown on his face. "Magic." He tried hard to keep the disgust from his voice. Kenders was an important soul, one deserving of his respect. But he could not help himself. She was a mage.

If he offended her, however, she did not show it. With a quiet, bemused chuckle, she said, "Yes, Rhohn. Horrible, evil, rotten magic."

"What are you going to do?"

"You'll see."

Rhohn's frown deepened.

"Why are you waiting?"

"We do not want to show our hand too soon."

Rhohn glanced back to Kenders and said, "How is that showing your hand?"

Khin, standing on the other side of Kenders, spoke in a soft, measured tone.

"Their mages will feel us weave."

Rhohn glanced between Kenders and Khin, opened his mouth to ask another question, but shut it a moment later. Looking back to the west, he said, "Now I understand."

Sabine, the raven-haired woman standing beyond Khin, leaned forward to stare at him.

"Do you? Truly?"

"No," said Rhohn with a shake of his head. "But as I don't much like magic and have no desire to learn about it, let's just say I do."

Beyond Okollu, Tobias said, "I'll be sure to give you a lesson after—"

"Blestem argel!" growled Okollu, soft and low. "If you all do not stop talking, I will miss their calls! Now, quiet!"

The top of the tower went silent as the group standing with Okollu watched the kur-surus listen. With each burst of howls and barks—some from the north, some from the south—Okollu would tilt his head and twitch his ears.

Suddenly, with one last bark, the cries went silent. Okollu spoke immediately, growling, "Three kur-surus packs advance. Two from there—" he lifted a fur-covered arm and pointed northwest "—and one from there." He swung his arm to indicate the southwest. Waving it along the wall, he added, "Four tribes of grayskins march between them." Dropping his arm, he snarled, "Each is led by a diavol."

Sabine leaned forward to stare at Okollu.

"Diavol?"

Okollu did not answer. His eyes were alert and angry, his teeth bared, his nostrils twitching. Something was bothering him. When it was apparent Okollu was not going to clarify, Rhohn did.

"It means demon."

Sabine nodded once.

"Good to know."

Khin turned his blue-eyed gaze to Okollu and asked, "How many in each group?"

Okollu continued staring into the fog, oblivious to the query. After a few moments, Tobias asked the question a second time and with more urgency than the aicenai.

"Okollu! How many?"

The kur-surus whipped his head around to peer down at the tomble.

"I do not know exactly, little smooth-face. More than a thousand, but less than two. All on foot."

"That makes no sense," muttered Kenders. "At most, they have fourteen thousand."

Equally confused, Rhohn wondered aloud, "They're going to assault a walled city on foot? With those numbers?" Looking to Okollu, he asked, "Any siege machines?"

Okollu shook his muzzle.

"They do not use siege machines."

"Blast!" hissed Tobias. His eyes wide, the tomble pivoted about his walking stick to face the four Shadow Mane soldiers standing on the tower with them. "One of you run north along the wall, the other south. Tell *every* Stone Mage we have to do nothing but focus on Strands of Stone. The *moment* they sense it, unravel the Weave. Do you understand?!"

Two of the men nodded firmly and immediately hurried in opposite directions, heading down the exterior stairs of the bastion tower, swords rattling as they rushed.

Tobias called, "Run like you're being chased by a blasted demon!"

As both men disappeared below the tower's sides, Rhohn looked down to the tomble.

"What is that about?"

Tobias ignored him, faced west, and pressed his chest against the wall. In a firm, forceful tone, he said "Khin, Kenders, the same goes for you. If you feel Stone, get rid of it at once!"

Khin replied softly, "Understood."

"Me, too," murmured Kenders.

Baffled, Rhohn eyed the pair. Whereas Khin appeared calm and collected, the pretty easterner looked worried.

"What is going on?"

Without looking over Khin answered, "We are to keep the walls together."

Hoping he had not heard correctly, Rhohn asked, "What does that mean? 'Keep the walls together?!'"

Apparently deeming that question worthy of an answer, Tobias looked up at him and said, "The only reason they might attack with such a small force is if they thought they could breach the walls with ease."

Rhohn scanned into the soupy mist below.

"But they don't have siege machines."

In a voice that rivaled Khin's for its calmness, Sabine said, "Mages do not need siege machines, Rhohn." She was casually rolling the shaft of a red-fletched arrow between her fingers, appearing as though she were waiting for a friend at market, not standing atop a wall about to be assaulted by Sudashians. "Kenders turned a wall of my family's cottage into sand."

Okollu growled, "And I have seen boulders fly through the sky."

Kenders muttered, "I've *sent* boulders flying through the sky."

Rhohn blinked, suddenly understanding. The confidence he had standing atop the sturdy walls of Demetus drained from him like water from an overturned cup.

"Oh."

Okollu sneered, "Nedabiks ir lanums lidzeklis."

Kenders and Sabine turned to Rhohn, apparently expecting him to translate. He held their gaze a moment before shrugging his shoulders.

"I only met him a few turns ago. I recognized 'nedabiks.' Magic, I think."

Khin said slowly, "Magic is the tool of cowards."

Okollu turned to glare at the aicenai and let out a short, gruff puff of air.

"You speak our tongue?"

"I understand it, I do not speak it. I doubt I could."

Okollu huffed and faced forward. Rhohn eyed the kur-surus carefully. Okollu seemed extraordinarily agitated.

"You are partially correct, Okollu," said Tobias. "Magic is a tool. Brave souls can wield it as well as cowardly ones."

"All nedabiks is evil," snapped the kur-surus.

"No absolute is absolute," replied the tomble.

Glaring at Tobias, Okollu barked, "I have yet to see anything good come from a 'mage,' little smooth-face."

In an even, somewhat pointed tone, Tobias said, "Funny. Nearly every man on this wall would say the same thing about your race." As the kur-surus glowered at him, the White Lion twisted around and stared east. "The sun will be up in short order. If they were smart, they would attack soon."

Rhohn glanced backward, peering over the great city to stare at the grayish-pink horizon.

Kenders murmured, "Could we not use the Suština of Stone to help reinforce the walls?"

Rhohn turned to stare at the Easterner, confused.

"Suština?"

"No," replied Khin. "There is no situation imaginable where it would be a good idea to do so."

Shaking her head firmly, Kenders said, "I understand your hesitation to use them, but *nobody* knows—" She stopped in mid-sentence and swiveled her head to stare west. Her face grew taut and strained, as if she were trying to hear the rustle of a single leaf miles away. In a quiet, worried voice, she mumbled, "Do either of you feel that?"

"Soul and Air," said Tobias softly.

Kenders muttered, "Will, too."

Rhohn looked west.

"What are—?"

Kenders lifted a hand, cutting him off, stepped closer to the wall, and peered over.

"We need to see what is down there. Now."

As though responding to her, a deep, guttural voice rose up through the morning fog, its pitch rising and falling as it bellowed, "Hugg saumush maurogh! Glurcull ugrogh urdreg! Yuragh raghlag udok!"

Tobias muttered, "I can tell you what's down there."

Rhohn could as well. Enough stories had drifted about the Borderlands that he had no doubt it was an oligurt. Okollu confirmed it for him with a low, angry growl.

"Grayskins."

The lone voice roared again, the rhythm and intonation of the garbled words reminding Rhohn of a playman's poem, only infinitely more fearsome sounding.

"Hugg saumush maurogh! Glurcull ugrogh urdreg! Yuragh raghlag udok!"

There was another brief pause before the chant resumed, only instead of a single oligurt voice, thousands shouted as one, the thunderous, raucous chorus smacking Rhohn in the face.

"Hugg saumush maurogh! Glurcull ugrogh urdreg! Yuragh raghlag udok!"

Forced to shout, Kenders called out, "We can't wait any longer!" She turned to stare at Khin, her eyes wide. "Khin?!"

The aicenai nodded once and the pair peered into the air, their gazes seemingly fixed on nothing. Moments later, they shifted their stares to the blanket of fog below.

Looking down, Rhohn watched a perfect circle appear in the mist. Only a few feet across at first, the hole provided a clear view of the marshy ground below. Reason told him the cutout should not be there while instinct told him the surrounding vapor should swallow it. Instead, the void grew, expanding outward, the mist coalescing into droplets and falling like a quick, sudden rain. Something was squeezing the fog from the air as one wrings excess water from a rag.

Within a few moments, the hole swelled to the size of a full regiment, gaining speed as it rushed outward in all directions. Light from the torches could now reach the dirt below.

The sudden twang of a nearby bowstring startled him. Looking to his right, he saw Sabine, her recurve bow gripped tightly in her left hand, in the midst of drawing an arrow from the quiver strapped to her leg. Staring west, he spotted a red-feathered arrow arching downward, flying toward the edge of the fog. An oligurt emerged from the mist just as the arrow arrived, striking the monster in the forehead. The gray-skinned beast stumbled forward and collapsed to the ground.

Moments later, to the south, a man's voice shouted over the oligurts' chanting. "Bows! Steady fire!"

Soldiers all along the wall picked up the call, repeating the order even as they followed it. Within a pair of heartbeats, the air was alive with arrows, the shafts soaring toward the host of oligurts marching on Demetus.

Each of the monsters wore simple hide armor and carried a weapon similar to a simple club with giant, metal spikes jutting from the end. They strode forward, heads tilted back and staring into the air with expressions that Rhohn interpreted as confusion. He knew nothing about how an oligurt thought—if the beasts even did—but he would have bet coin they were wondering where the fog was going.

As the oligurts gaped upwards, the avalanche of arrows rained down upon them, turning their unified war chants into disjointed, random roars of pain.

Rhohn wished he had a bow. He and his men had acquired armor and swords from the Reed Men armory, but it had been bare of bows. They—and he—would need to wait their turn to fight.

The hole in the fog continued to grow, revealing even more of the slope leading to the western wall. To the south, Rhohn saw a pack of mongrels appear as the mist dissipated. Within a few breaths, they, too, were subjected to a barrage of arrows from the walls. A few dozen collapsed to the ground, howling in pain, their bodies riddled with arrows.

Rhohn glanced at Okollu, anxious to see how the kur-surus would take to seeing his kind cut down like this. Okollu stood rigid, his nostrils flaring. His fur-covered hands were balled in fists.

Shouting over the chants and screams, Rhohn called, "Okollu?"

The kur-surus whipped his head around to meet Rhohn's gaze, his eyes wide and burning. With teeth bared, he snarled. "That is my pack! Baaldòk is driving the Drept to their deaths!"

Rhohn stared back below.

"Hells."

Greya had a cruel sense of humor.

With the fog pushed back, the men on the walls had a clear view of the advancing horde and fired arrow after arrow into the throng. Only moments old and the battle was already a one-sided massacre.

A single, yapping howl pierced the air, followed immediately by similar calls from within the Drept pack. The mongrels halted their advance, turned around, and began running from the walls. The war chants of the oligurts changed, too, as the hulking gray beasts began a full retreat as well. A loud cheer poured from the duchies' soldiers even while they continued to loose arrows at the backs of the enemy.

The fog west of Demetus continued to dissipate, revealing a mottled landscape of marshes mingling with swaths of pine-tree groves. As the Sudashians slipped beyond bow range and into the cover of the trees, calls ran up and down the walls to halt firing. The soldiers complied and watched the retreat, their cheers growing even louder.

Rhohn shook his head, a frown on his face. It was much too soon to cry victory.

The mist's disappearance accelerated, showering the ground with a quick moment of rain as the edge rushed westward. Early dawn now provided enough illumination to light the world below, but not enough to gift it with color. Everything in the murky dimness below was washed-out and pallid. The land looked dead.

After a time, Rhohn began to spot what appeared to be firelight flickering in the distance. With each moment that passed, more and more far-off lights were revealed, quickly forming a long, unending line on the early-morning horizon. His stomach dropped as he realized what he was seeing.

Tobias let out a soft gasp, Okollu a whimper of surprise. Both Kenders and Sabine let a soft curse slip. The joyful shouts along the walls died within two quick heartbeats.

They were torches. Tens of thousands of torches.

Rhohn muttered, "Impossible." His mouth was as dry as Borderlands dirt on a Summer day. "Is that the…?" He trailed off, unable to finish his question. Khin answered it anyway.

"The army of Chaos."

The men on the walls were silent now.

After a few moments, Kenders—a slight quiver in her voice—muttered, "How many?"

"Impossible to know for sure," answered Khin slowly. "And I do not guess."

"But I do," said Tobias. He let out a long sigh before saying, "Forty-thousand."

Rhohn shook his head, muttering, "Bless the Gods…"

"*Forty-thousand?*" repeated Sabine. "Are you sure?"

"Perhaps more," said Tobias. "But I doubt less. That guess is based on what I can see. More might be hiding in the forests."

Rhohn tilted his head back, stared to the lightening sky, and let out a long sigh. At least the odds were better than they had been back in Ebel.

Shouts from along the wall pulled his attention to the north. Seeing the front line of Reed Men pointing to the hill below, Rhohn swiveled his head and spotted a group of four oligurts step from the pine trees, slosh through the marshy ground, and stop just beyond bow range. Another group emerged a few dozen paces south of the first.

Then another.

And another.

All along the length of the wall, oligurts—always in groups of four—strode from the tree groves, stopped where they were safe, and stared up at the walls. Two of each group were bare-chested, their heads covered in either mud or dark brown paint. The remaining two wore long, patchwork leather skirts and had large red and yellow tattoos etched on their foreheads. While none carried weapons of any sort, the tattooed oligurts all clutched a lit torch in their right hand.

Kenders muttered, "Desert Fire mages."

Rhohn glanced over.

"Pardon?"

Nodding to the oligurts below, she said, "The ones with the tattoos. I've seen their kind before. But the other ones are new to me." She glanced over at Tobias. "What about you?"

The tomble shook his head.

"I have no idea. Broedi is the expert on Sudashians."

"They are Kalnu Edaji," growled Okollu, his black lips drawn back to reveal his teeth. "Mountain Eaters. They call themselves Mountain Eaters."

Before any of them could ask why, Kenders drew in a sharp, hissing breath. "Khin!"

"I know," said the aicenai softly. "Unravel what you can."

Moments later, the walls began to shake.

CHAPTER 56: FOOTHOLD

The ground refused to hold still.

Nundle was in the shadow of the western wall, doing his best to remain upright as the city shook around him. Like him, the Reed Men and Southern Arms lining the street struggled to stay standing, bracing themselves against walls, poles, and one another.

The hillmen from the Primal Provinces looked about, their eyes wide. The group of thorn standing nearby swayed side-to-side, like a grove of trees caught in a stiff wind. Nundle wondered how many were second-guessing their decision to come to Demetus.

A few paces to Nundle's left, Broedi stood, his feet wide apart, staring up at the mud-brick wall with a concerned look on his face. Wren, using his longspear to steady himself, appeared just as worried. Whipping his head around, Nundle eyed the tan wall, watching as it shook and shuttered. Chunks of mortar slipped from the crevices in the walls, tumbling to the streets below. Dust filled the air.

"Oh, this is not good."

The low, deep rumbling was felt as much as heard. It reminded Nundle of his time spent at the Academy of Veduin. The dormitories there had been built into the side of the Ciyriel volcano. Earthquakes were common.

As Nundle looked at the mud-brick buildings and walls surrounding him, a deepening frown on his face, the shaking suddenly tempered. The ground still rocked and shuddered, but much less violently than even a moment ago.

Nundle glanced around anxiously.

"What was that?"

"Stone mages, I'd say," answered Wren.

Broedi rumbled, "It would seem so." His deep baritone was nearly lost among the remnant thudding in the city.

Staring at the White Lions, Nundle asked, "Why'd they stop? Much more of that shaking and—" He jumped as a large, irregular chunk of mortar crashed to the flagstone street two paces away and shattered into dozens of smaller clumps. Staring at it with wide eyes, Nundle muttered, "Lots of *that* would have happened."

Pulling his gaze from the walls, Broedi said, "I doubt they stopped of their own accord. We have Stone mages of our own. Two of whom are very capable."

Nundle tilted his head back to stare at the battlements.

"Let's hope they can keep things quiet."

"We need to eliminate their mages," rumbled Broedi. "Quickly." Swiveling to face Wren, he said, "We do not have time to prepare everyone. Take five buhanik and their partners, go to the northern gate now, and get ready."

Wren, his thick-handled spear gripped tight in his hand, nodded and began to move toward the thorn and hillmen mages.

"And wait for my signal, Wren!"

"I'll wait," said Wren, glancing over his shoulder. "You just make sure I can hear it!"

Turning around, he pointed to five thorn and hillmen—including Fingard and Talulot—calling them each by name, and began striding north along the streets. The thorn and hillmen followed without a word, drawing stares from every longleg soldier as they passed.

Wren's agreeable response surprised Nundle. Looking up to Broedi, he said as much.

"That was easy."

Eyeing the tijul's retreating form, Broedi said, "Wren can be disagreeable, but there are few other I would want by my side when steel is drawn." He shifted his intense gaze to Nundle. "Now, you know what to do, yes?"

Nundle nodded, saying, "Spread the mages among the towers and take the warriors to the commander."

"Good," rumbled Broedi. "You had best get moving. Ketus with you." Before Nundle could respond, the hillman spun around and called out for the remaining thorn to come with him, along with their hillmen mages.

Shouts of alarm erupted from atop the walls, pulling Nundle's attention upward. Craning his neck, he listened carefully, trying to make sense of the cries, but the soldiers' voices trampled one another, making their words unintelligible. Hearing the twangs of countless bowstrings, though, and Nundle guessed the Sudashians were advancing again.

"Nundle!"

He looked back to Broedi quickly. The hillman's eyes were bright.

"Do *not* waste time!" rumbled Broedi. He turned and began to jog south, the thorn and hillmen trailing him. Looking over his shoulder, he bellowed, "Go, Nundle! *Now!*"

Nundle spun around to stare at the hillmen behind, tilting his head back to meet their eyes. He could not see past the first few rows, but he knew four hundred stood before him. All of whom were watching him, waiting for direction.

Swallowing the sudden lump in his throat, in as authoritative tone he could manage, he shouted, "Listen! I need you to follow me!" His voice cracked, an event that might have embarrassed him had his words carried beyond the first dozen hillmen. The battle outside and the remnant thudding drowned out his high-pitched voice.

He was about to try again when one of the bald hillmen standing before him faced the group and boomed, "Kutojataka, otelu jopa olen ryhmisa!" He had red tattoos on his cheeks that reminded Nundle of a deer. As he shouted, it almost looked like the deer was leaping through the air.

In awe of the hillman's thunderous voice, Nundle stared upward.

"What did you say?"

Looking down to him, the hillman rumbled, "That we are to follow the words of the tiny man. Tell me what must be done."

Grateful for the help, Nundle nodded and said, "All of you are to follow me—" he spun around and pointed to the dark entryway at the base of a nearby tower "—through there. The mages first, followed by the warriors. When we get to the top, the mages are to spread out to the towers—one to each—introduce themselves to the people dressed in black, and tell them how to counter the thorn's—ah, the buhanik's attack!"

"Understood, tiny man," rumbled the red-tattooed hillman. He began to turn when Nundle held up a hand, stopping him.

"My name is Nundle."

A slight smile graced the hillman's lips.

"I am Ranoteemu Petrikallio."

"Well met, Rano...tea..." He trailed off, shook his head once, and said, "Rano will have to do." He nodded to the group of hillmen. "Tell them now. Oh, and stay beside me. I might need your voice again."

Rano nodded, turned, and relayed Nundle's orders in his native tongue. In an attempt to get a head start, Nundle began walking to the bastion tower. Halfway there, he glanced over his shoulder to see the hillmen warriors and mages following, their long legs quickly making up ground on him.

Ducking into the darkened doorway, he ran up the stairs as fast as he could but had only made it a half-dozen steps when Rano scooped him up with one arm. Nundle was about to protest being ported like a sack of tubers when the alternative flashed through his mind. Four-hundred, heavy hillmen were rushing up the stairwell, their large, booted feet pounding against the same steps upon which he had just been standing. His objection died on his lips.

As they reached the first landing, Nundle peered up the stairwell and at the two doorways above. The sounds of battle roared louder with each jarring step Rano took. Bouncing along, tucked tightly under Rano's arm, Nundle pointed in the direction of the southernmost door of the bastion. The hillman followed his instructions and burst from the dark tower, rushing straight into organized chaos.

All along the wall, longlegs were shouting, pointing and firing arrows. From below, oligurts chanted, mongrels howled.

Nundle watched a volley of arrows fly from the walls to soar high into the air and froze, his eyes going wide. Dozens of boulders were hurtling toward the walls, one the size of his home in Deepwell. The enormous rock tumbled through the air, heading straight for the stretch of wall where Rano stood. Still clasped under the hillman's arm, Nundle reached out for as many Strands of Air as he could, hoping he might somehow cushion the blow. He had only managed to grasp a handful when the massive stone halted its advance and toppled to the ground, surely crushing a number of Sudashians in the process.

Breathing a sigh of relief, Nundle muttered, "Oh, thank the Gods…" He should be thanking whichever mage knocked the boulder from the sky, but a quiet word of gratitude to the Gods and Goddesses would have to suffice for now.

Staring back to the other rocks careening toward the city, a frustrated frown spread over his face. Weaves of Stone were surely responsible, but Nundle was deaf to the brown Strands.

Rano and Nundle moved further onto the battlements, allowing the trailing hillmen to pour from the tower. A great cheer arose from the back lines of soldiers.

Twisting around, Nundle shouted, "You can put me down now!"

Rano complied, lowering him to the stone.

The moment his feet touched the ramparts Nundle spun around, stared up at the hillman, and screamed, "Half of the mages go south—" he pointed down the wall—"and half to the north!" He pointed behind the crowd of hillmen, back to the doorway from which they had emerged. "They are to focus on undoing the Sudashians' magic. Defend, not attack! And to be ready for Broedi's signal!"

Rano nodded, turned, and bellowed, "Pulet magian kattaja menna pohiseen, poli etelaan! Polustaa! Al rahd!"

Five Titan Tribe mages immediately rushed past Nundle, lumbering south with surprising swiftness. The remaining five began pushing back through the warriors, making their way north. Nundle watched them for a brief moment, wishing them silent luck, and then motioned to Rano.

"Follow me!"

He turned and hurried south, stealing quick glances west as he ran, looking through the gaps in the battlements. Occasionally, he spotted a boulder or two flying toward the wall. He hoped none would breach their defenses. Or already had.

Nundle's detachment passed through another tower, prompting more cheers from duchy soldiers. Apparently the sight of four hundred hillmen warriors wielding massive, bladed weapons provided a boost to morale. Peering down the length of the wall, Nundle spotted Commander Aiden halfway to the next bastion, standing still as a statue, his arms crossed over his Shadow Mane's tunic and his eyes fixed westward.

Sprinting the remaining distance, Nundle scampered to the older longleg, calling out, "Commander! *Commander!*"

It was not until Nundle was a dozen paces away that Commander Aiden heard the cries and swiveled his head toward them, his steely gaze running over

Nundle and the long line of hillmen trailing him. Without batting an eye, the commander turned toward them. If he was surprised to see four-hundred hillmen on Demetus' walls, he did not show it.

"I'll take them from here!" Shifting his gaze to Rano, he barked, "Name?"

"Ranoteemu Petrikallio."

Nodding once, Commander Aiden said, "Right. Rano it is." His gaze shifted to the massive glaive gripped in Rano's hand. "You good with that?"

Rano rumbled, "I can take the head off a karju in one stroke." He nodded to the warriors behind him. "We all can."

As Commander Aiden's gaze flicked to the other hillmen, the soldier said, "I have no idea what a karju is."

"It is like a boar," said Rano. "But four times the size. And with five tusks."

"Sounds ugly," said the commander. "Now, I want your group to stretch out in—" He stopped and glanced down at Nundle. "Why are you still here?" He pointed south. "Nathan is two towers over and a mage short! Go!"

Without a moment's hesitation, Nundle rushed away, leaving the commander and hillmen behind. Staring ahead, he saw two Shadow Mane mages standing atop the next tower, their black uniforms like a pair of silhouettes against the pinkish-gray, dawn sky. One of the Titan Tribe mages was with them already, the trio all facing outward, intent on turning back the flurry of magical attacks.

Too short to see over the western wall, Nundle had yet to glimpse the enemy. Curious, rather than run though the tower, he hurried up its exterior steps. Upon cresting the stairs, he turned around and got his first clear look at the battlefield. His eyes went wide.

"Bless the Gods…"

The marshy slopes below were swarming with thousands of oligurts, all running straight at the walls and bellowing their war chants. To the north and south, other groups like the one below, oligurt and mongrel alike, were charging Demetus. The tactic baffled Nundle.

"What are they going to do?" he muttered to himself. "Climb the walls?"

The only figures not moving were quartets of oligurts staggered up and down the wall. Two of the four were bare-chested, their bald heads covered in brown mud or paint. While they were unfamiliar to him, he recognized the others in an instant. The tattoos, flaming torches, and patched-together skin skirts marked them as Desert Fire mages. During the Battle of Shorn Rise, ten of the sect had battled Nundle, the Progeny, and the Red Sentinels.

As he eyed the oligurt mages, his confusion deepened.

Desert Fire mages were masters of Charge and Fire, yet he did not sense the faintest flicker of yellow. And even though he might be deaf to Fire, there was no evidence of the Strand's use. As he stood there, wondering why they were not attacking, movement on the horizon pulled his gaze west, over the marshes and forests.

His eyes opened wide again, growing as round as the moons.

A long, dark line filled the western horizon. More Sudashians.

"Gods…"

A sudden, wall-shaking boom jarred him from his gaping. Losing his footing, Nundle nearly tumbled down the stairs, but managed to steady himself against the tower's side. Recovering quickly, he scurried across the tower's top, reached the southern stairs, and stared down at the next section of walls. A boulder had made it past the Shadow Mane mages and struck the mud-brick ramparts. The battlements had held against the blow, but large chunks of brick and mortar were tumbling from the face of the wall. A massive boulder lay on the ground below.

Regaining a sense of urgency, Nundle sprinted down the stairs and continued south, leaping over a foot-wide crack in the wall, running as fast as his short legs could carry him while dodging Reed Men and Southern Arms alike. Upon reaching the next tower, he ran through the doorways, emerging on the other side. Immediately, he spotted Nikalys standing a hundred paces away, arms crossed over his chest, much like Commander Aiden had been. Nathan was at his side, pointing to the marshes below and talking with the young long leg. Jak and Zecus were a few paces beyond the pair, bows in hand and firing upon the onrushing horde.

Nundle sprinted down the walls and was only moments away from reaching the four when he heard the sharp screech of a hawk overhead. Staring upward, he saw a massive, golden-brown hawk high in the sky, flying south to north. The hawk screeched again. This time, it was three, quick bursts. A heartbeat later, Nundle felt a tremendous surge of Strands to the south, vibrant green and honey-gold.

Nundle gaped at the hawk, murmuring, "Already?" Broedi had not wasted time. Scrambling the final few paces to Nathan's side, he stopped and stared into the air.

The sergeant glanced down and called, "Nice of you to join us!"

Nundle did not bother with a reply as all his attention was focused on summoning as many Strands of Air as he could. All along the walls, he felt pockets of white pop into existence as Shadow Mane and Titan Tribe mages alike were doing the same. He hoped all the towers had been warned in time, but doubted that to be the case. Broedi had given them too little time to spread the word.

Nundle was aware that Nathan had said something else to him, but he was so intent on his Weave of Air he did not hear the words. He stretched the pattern north and south, trying to get its edges to those of the Weaves being crafted at the two nearest towers. It was impossible to protect the walls fully, even with the aid of the Titan Tribe mages, but they were going to try.

Holding tight to the Weave, Nundle stepped closer to the wall, wanting to ensure he did not accidently shield the Sudashians. He stood on his toes and tried to peer over the break in the battlements, but found he was too short. Swallowing his pride, he tapped Nikalys on the leg. The young longleg glanced down, surprise flashing over his face.

"When'd you get here?"

"Just now," called Nundle. Pointing to the wall, he asked, "Would you mind lifting me up? I need to see down there."

Nikalys nodded and jammed his knee against the edge of the wall, creating a makeshift platform. He reached down, slipped his hands under Nundle's arms, and placed the tomble on his leg, perilously close to the edge of the wall. Leaning forward, he called, "Better?"

Staring wide-eyed at the oligurts and mongrels below, Nundle called out, "As long as you don't let go!" Turning his attention back to the Weave, he made few minor adjustments, pulling the bottom edge of the pattern higher, over the heads of the oligurts.

Nikalys asked, "So they've started?"

Nundle ignored the question, too intent on the Weave. He twisted to stare north and was forced to extend his pattern a little further. It seemed the mages on the tower to his right were even less talented with Air than he.

"Nundle!" called Nikalys. "Have—"

"I'm a bit busy right now!"

"Too busy to say yes or no?!"

"Yes!" shouted Nundle, a touch exasperated. "Yes, they started!"

"How long—"

Nearby shouts of surprise cut Nikalys' question short. Stealing a quick glance south, Nundle spotted five massive, terrifying creatures lumbering from the walls and into the thick of the Sudashian army.

Nikalys shouted, "Everyone! Cover your—"

The thorn's shrill, ear-piercing shriek filled the air, drowning out the rest of Nikalys' warning as it rushed over battlefield and city alike. Wincing, Nundle clapped his hands over his ears in an attempt to shut out the screech, grateful that Nikalys did not do the same. Soldiers up and down the wall covered their ears. Some dropped to their knees, their wide-open mouths screaming shouts of pain nobody could hear. The hail of arrows flying from the walls slowed to a trickle.

Nundle held tightly onto his Weave, knowing that without the magical dampening protection, the shriek would be thrice as bad. Through half-shut eyes, he peered below to see how the Sudashians were faring.

Nearly every mongrel was on the ground, pawing at their ears, dragging their heads through the marsh and mud. Oligurts were bumping into one another, knocking each other down, staggered by the auditory assault. The enemy's vicious charge had slowed to a pitiful crawl.

The five thorn stomped through the incapacitated Sudashians, swinging their woody limbs about, bashing any oligurt within reach. As the thorn marched deeper into the helpless throng, decimating the Sudashians as they went, Nundle's gaze rested on the lead monster. To his great surprise, he recognized the creature as Talulot, their escort to Buhaylunsod.

With its fearsome maw open wide, screeching its terrible cry, Talulot wrapped its long, branch-like fingers around an oligurt, picked the beast up, and tossed it westward. As Nundle watched the oligurt soar through the air with legs and arms flailing, he felt a brief moment of optimism. Perhaps the thorn alone might be capable of repelling this assault.

He should have known better.

Through the crackling hum of white, green, and gold, Nundle felt a sizzling flash of yellow. A ball of pure Charge burst from a Desert Fire mage, flew toward Talulot, and crashed into the thorn's left leg, exploding in a shower of sparks. A half-dozen identical Weaves, along with small globes of fire, followed the first, all hurtling toward Talulot. Nundle was capable of stopping the Weaves of Charge, but to do so, he would need to drop the Weave of Air protecting the wall. As he wavered between helping Talulot or not, he watched in horror as one sphere after another smashed into the thorn's legs and torso. In just a few heartbeats, Talulot burst into flame and began to thrash wildly about.

With Talulot incapacitated, the Desert Fire mages shifted targets, sending their globes of Charge and Fire toward a second thorn. Nundle watched helplessly as that one burst into flame as well. Should this continue, all five thorn would be burning within minutes.

Nundle was about to drop the Weave of Air when streams of water rushed from the marshy ground, climbing the legs of the thorn that were alight and extinguishing the fire. Somewhere along the wall, Shadow Mane Water mages were doing what they could to help the thorn. The Sudashians immediately resumed their assault with fire, and soon, a full out battle between mages was underway.

Nikalys leaned forward and bellowed into Nundle's ear, "I need you to open a port!"

Nundle twisted his head around in surprise and immediately felt his grip on the Air Weave began to slip. Looking forward again, he quickly reinforced the pattern. Perhaps he had misheard the young longleg.

Holding Nundle tight with his right hand, Nikalys let go with his left and pointed to a group of oligurt mages currently loosing globules of fire.

"There! Open it there!"

Knowing what the young longleg intended to do, Nundle shouted over his shoulder, "Are you sure?!"

"Do it, Nundle! Now!"

While the shriek of the thorn had lost some of its intensity as the monsters succumbed to flames, if Nundle dropped the Weave of Air in order to craft a port, the screeching would be unbearable. Nevertheless, Nundle stared at the ground at a spot immediately behind the oligurt mages, fixed the image in his mind, and then turned his head to scream in Nikalys' face.

"Put me down and get ready!"

As Nikalys lowered him to the wall, Nundle took a deep, bracing breath and dropped the protective Air Weave, letting the full force of the thorn's cry wash over them. Throwing his hands over his ears, Nundle reached for the Strands of Void and Air, struggling to arrange them in the correct pattern for a port as the shriek clawed at his ears. Suddenly, the thorn's audible attack cut off. They had other concerns for the moment.

Able to concentrate fully now, Nundle arranged the final few loops while envisioning the spot of ground behind the four mages. The ringing in his ears blocked out the typical ripping sound that accompanied the creation of a port, but he saw the familiar ripple of reality as the slit appeared.

Shifting his gaze to Nikalys, he called, "Hurry back!"

Jak turned his head at Nundle's words, glanced at the port, and called, "What are you doing?" Looking to his brother, his eyes widened. Nikalys had the Blade of Horum drawn and at the ready, the white blade glimmering and glinting as though it were held in a pool of midday sun.

Jak repeated his question with a bit more urgency.

"Nik! What are you doing?!"

Nikalys stepped through the black tear without answering him.

Glaring at Nundle, Jak demanded, "Where'd he go?"

Nundle pointed over the battlements.

"Down there."

Whipping his head around to face west, Jak stepped to the wall. Nathan was a step behind him, as both leaned over to scan the battle scene. Nundle moved beside them to look as well, forgetting he was too short to see over. As he stood there, cursing his stature, a pair of strong hands gripped him beneath his arms and lifted him from the ground. Thinking he was about to be tossed from the wall, he threw out his arms.

"Ah!"

"Hold still, please," instructed Zecus as he propped Nundle on the foot wide ledge.

Relieved that he was not about to plummet to the ground, Nundle turned his attention below. The four mages near the other end of the port already lay dead on the ground. Two appeared to be missing their heads. Nikalys was heading south, cutting a swath through the oligurts on his way to the next group of mages. He dashed from enemy to enemy, slashing and stabbing with incredible speed, the Blade of Horum a blur of bright white.

On Nundle's left, Jak asked, "Ports work both ways, don't they?"

Nodding, Nundle said, "Yes, why do—" He cut off, looked back to the port, and watched in horror as an oligurt demon captain—an awful creature that reminded Nundle of an enraged bull—pointed towards the port and bellowed something unintelligible. Oligurts immediately began to lumber toward the slit.

Nundle felt ill.

He was about to ask if he should close it when Jak spun around to face the back two rows of Reed Men and shouted, "All of you! With me!" Drawing his sword, the young longleg leapt through the tear without waiting to see if anyone was coming with him.

Nathan ripped his sword from his hip scabbard and shouted, "Bows! Steady fire! Keep them away from the port!" Then, the sergeant ran through the port, too. A steady stream of Reed Men followed, pouring through the black slit, only steps behind Nathan and Jak.

Nundle looked below and watched the soldiers emerge on the other side, going wherever Jak and Nathan were pointing. Within moments, a crude ring formed around the port, protecting it from the onrushing oligurts.

"Up or down?" called Zecus.

Glancing back, Nundle asked, "What?"

"I am going down there, too. Do you want me to put you down? Or do you wish to stay on the wall?"

Bracing his arms and feet against the battlements' stonework, Nundle called, "Go!"

Zecus released him, bent down to grab his staff, and leapt through the port.

Nundle stood alone, balanced on the wall's precipice, watching more and more Reed Men rush to join the defense below. Those staying on the wall loosed arrow after arrow, their shafts whistling through the air to land amidst the oligurts. The aerial assault slowed the enemy's advance, but did not stop it. The hulking grayskins reached the ring and began to pummel at the soldiers. The northern edge sagged inwards within moments.

Reaching for Strands of Charge, Nundle began to loose quick, small bursts of lightning at the attackers when he heard a great baying. Looking up, Nundle spotted a large mongrel pack rushing the port from the south. A demon man led them, towering over the pack. He had red, leathery skin, foot-long black horns spiraling from his head, and a massive sword resting on his shoulder.

Pressing his lips together, Nundle muttered, "Wondrous…"

If the soldiers below were overrun, Nundle would have no choice but to close the port, thereby sealing the fate of Jak, Nathan, Zecus, and all the Reed Men below. Glancing south, Nundle spotted Nikalys still cutting his way through the army, the gleaming Blade of Horum flashing bright.

"What in the Nine Hells is he doing?!"

Feeling a sudden rush of Void and Air, Nundle looked down to see a second port pop into existence beside his own. His eyes went wide as Khin stepped from the black flap and began loosing Weaves of Charge and Fire into the enemy, deftly directing the blasts around and over the soldiers. The aicenai's speed and skill with the Strands was astounding. A second figure leapt through the new port, bow up-raised and arrow nocked on the drawn string.

Nundle blinked in surprise.

"Sabine?"

She released the bowstring, sending the red-feathered arrow through the line of longlegs to strike an oligurt in its right eye. Thick, black blood squirted as the shaft sunk deep in its head and the monster dropped to the ground, limp and already dead.

Rhohn rushed through the port next, followed by his ragged collection of Dust Men and their mismatched armor and weapons. He started pointing and shouting, directing the Borderlanders to a pair of gaps in the soldiers' ring.

A quick look to the north and south revealed that this was the only true fighting on the hillside. Most of the Sudashians seemed at a loss as to what to do. The thorn's audible attack had disrupted whatever plan the invaders had for the assault.

A longleg's pain-laden scream cut through the air. Looking over his shoulder, Nundle saw Reed Men emerging back through the port, dragging injured compatriots with them. The scream belonged to a young longleg with blonde hair. Something heavy had crushed the poor soldier's hand into a bloody, mushy pulp. His eyes were wide, staring at what used to be his hand.

Nundle scooted backwards, hopped from the battlement, and took a step toward the poor soldier, intent on helping with the Reed Man's injury. Yet he stopped short and glanced back to the port. He had a choice. He could stay here and help the injured, or go below and keep others from joining their ranks.

Shutting out the man's moans of pain, Nundle sprinted for the inky void. He leapt from the hard stone of the battlements, passed through the port, and landed on the soft, squishy ground of the marshes. For a moment, he stood in place, stunned by the battle's volume. Everything was thrice as loud down here as it had sounded from the walls.

The sharp clangs of metal on metal.

Oligurts roaring.

Mongrels howling and barking.

Soldiers yelling and screaming.

Khin's magic globes hissing and sizzling.

Through it all, two voices—Jak and Nathans'—lifted over the chaos, calmly shouting out orders.

Shaking himself from his stupor, Nundle hurried to stand beside the ever calm and collected Sabine. She did not even acknowledge his presence as she was too intent on the Sudashians, firing arrow after arrow into the enemy.

Nundle shifted some of his concentration from the port and mimicked the Weaves Khin was using, knitting patterns of Charge as quickly as he could and directing them at selected targets.

Soldiers were falling quickly. Some were injured. Some, without doubt, were dead.

Nundle did not know how long they could hold this position.

CHAPTER 57: SACRIFICE

Shift.

Standing behind the oligurt mage, Nikalys drew his white blade across its neck, slicing open a black, bloody wound. Flailing, the monster began to spin around, opening its side to a secondary attack. Nikalys jammed the Blade of Horum through its exposed side, aiming for where he thought the beast's heart might be. He wanted to kill the oligurt quickly both so he could move on and because, enemy or not, he did not want the mage to suffer needlessly.

His strike was true. The oligurt stiffened—its eyes round in shock—before it went limp. As the monster toppled over, Nikalys ripped his blade free, heard an angry roar behind him, and spun around. Three oligurt warriors were rushing him, their spiked clubs raised.

Shift.

He drew the blade over the left hamstring of the first and—

Shift.

—separated its head from its shoulders as it bent over, stumbling from the leg injury. Glancing at the patch of marshy ground beside the second oligurt—

Shift.

—Nikalys lopped off its left arm in a single, effortless stroke. The oligurt roared as its severed limb dropped to the ground, the spiked club absurdly still clasped in its hand.

Sensing something flying toward him from behind, Nikalys looked to his right—

Shift.

—and spun around. A massive spiked club was whipping through the air where his head had been moments ago. Staring to a spot of ground behind the now off-balance monster—

Shift.

—Nikalys jammed the point of his sword through the oligurt's back, driving it forward until it burst free of the beast's chest. After giving the hilt a quick twist, he ripped the weapon free. As always, the Blade of Horum emerged clean and unspoiled. Nikalys, however, was coated with black oligurt blood.

As the oligurt tumbled forward, Nikalys felt a flicker of guilt for taking yet another life. He had killed many today, more than he wished to count. All had been necessary, but he loathed every moment of it. To hear Okollu tell it, these Sudashians were as much victims in this war as any duchy man or woman. They were not the enemy. Tandyr was. And these oligurts were his unwilling weapons.

He twisted around, looking for the next group of mages and froze. Nothing but open marshland, distant hills, and pine trees awaited him. He stood at the southern edge of the battle. Spinning around, he stared back to the north. He might be over a mile from where he had started.

"Blast it!"

Nikalys looked to the mud-brick walls of the city and saw the southern gates were shut. During his progression across the battlefield, he had caught glimpses of green-and-white-clad soldiers rushing out to carry the injured, smoking thorn back into the city. Tandyr's army had made short work of Alumon and his kind.

Suddenly, a very familiar—and unusually angry—voice rumbled beside him.

"Uori! What do you think you are doing?!"

Nikalys jumped and spun around, looking for Broedi, but found that he was still quite alone, his only company the corpses of oligurts, some marsh grass, and muddy puddles.

"I am on the walls!" bellowed Broedi. "Where you should be!"

Nikalys stared back to Demetus, scanning the long line of battlements running north. On the third tower from the southwestern corner of the city, Nikalys spotted the unmistakable form of Broedi standing at its edge, glaring at him.

"Get back to the port!" rumbled the hillman. "Quickly! They are holding it for you!"

Looking north, Nikalys muttered, "They're what?"

He had expected that Nundle would have closed the port long ago. As the entirety of Broedi's message registered, he stared back to the hillman atop the tower.

"They? Who's holding—?"

He cut off and shook his head. Broedi could not hear him. Nikalys did not know much about magic, but he remembered that the Weave Broedi was using only worked one way.

Taking full advantage of his gift, he rushed north, darting across the battlefield, covering short distances in an instant. Within a few heartbeats, he found himself in the thick of the Sudashian ranks again, oligurts mostly. He fought only when he had no other choice. He needed to get back to the port.

After a time, he broke through the oligurts and began to encounter a kur-surus pack. Moving past them without incident, he spotted a ring of soldiers around the port. The men—a mixture of Reed Men, Shadow Manes, and Dust Men—were fighting oligurts to the north, kur-surus to the south. Khin and Nundle stood at the ring's center, lobbing small spheres of lightning and fire at the attackers. Sabine was with them, loosing arrow after arrow toward the oligurts. Her eyes were as cold as a Storm Island Winter morning.

Nikalys caught a brief glimpse of Jak, his face streaked with blood and grime. Wearing a determined sneer, he was backpedaling, locked in single combat with a massive oligurt. Nikalys eyed the open space beside Jak's opponent—

Shift.

—and hacked at the beast's side, slicing through tunic and flesh, sinking his blade's edge inches deep into its gut. A torrent of black blood squirted from the wound. The beast roared at the vicious blow and wheeled around, blindly swinging its club. Nikalys ducked, pulled the Blade of Horum free, and stepped to the side, readying a counterattack.

Jak leapt forward first, though, plunging the point of his longsword into the oligurt's ribcage. The monster whirled in place again and grabbed the longsword with an open hand, the sharp metal edge slicing open its palm. It leaned over and roared into Jak's wide-eyed face, spittle flying from its mouth and dripping from its tusks.

Nikalys reached out, grabbed the oligurt's weapon arm, and yanked as hard as he could, ripping the oligurt free from Jak's sword.

Shift.

Standing before the grayskin, he reached out with his free hand and shoved it in the chest, tossing it backwards and into the mass of Sudashians, knocking over a number of the enemy in the process.

Safe for the moment, Nikalys whirled to face his brother. Jak was staring after the oligurt, his eyes still wide, but with surprise now, not fear. He blinked once, shifted his gaze to Nikalys, and smiled with relief.

"Thanks, Nik."

"You're welcome."

Jak's grin fell away an instant later. He reached up, punched Nikalys in the arm, and shouted, "What in the Nine Hells were you thinking?"

He stepped forward, grabbed Nikalys' blood-soaked Shadow Mane tunic, and began pulling him deeper into the circle. For the first time, Nikalys noticed there were two ports, not just the one.

"Gods, Nik! You can't just go running off—"

A blur of brown and white fur rushed from the second port, knocking the brothers to the ground as it rushed past, growling and snarling. Lifting his head, Nikalys spotted Okollu on all fours, charging south, his green cape flapping as he ran. Back by the ports, a too-familiar voice called out.

"Okollu, stop!"

Looking back, Nikalys spotted Kenders stepping from a port, her gaze locked on the mongrel. Pushing himself from the ground, he glared at his sister and screamed, "Kenders! Get back to the walls!"

Her gaze shifted to him ever so briefly before returning to Okollu. She pointed at the kur-surus and shouted, "He's going after the demon! That's *his* pack you're fighting!"

Nikalys turned to find the former pack leader pushing his way past the duchy soldiers, shoving men to the ground. It was a wonder none of them had attacked him yet.

Nikalys made to go after him, but Jak grabbed his arm.

"Let him go, Nik."

Nikalys looked over at his brother, surprised.

"What? Why?"

"He's one of them. If he wants to get himself killed, let him. Now, let him go!"

Nikalys studied his brother's dirt-streaked face, the wild eyes, the set jaw, tight lips. Jak barely looked like Jak right now. Shaking his head once, he ripped his arm from Jak's grip.

"No!"

"Nik, don't you—"

Nikalys did not hear the rest of the Jak's plea as he was already a half-dozen strides away. He sprinted to the southern edge of the soldiers' ring and leapt into the air, soaring over the heads of men and kur-surus locked in battle.

His boots sunk into the soft earth as he landed amidst the Drept. Dozens of kur-surus immediately dropped to all fours, baring their teeth. Squeezing his sword's golden hilt, Nikalys pivoted in a stationary circle, scanning the mass of furred figures, looking for Okollu's Marshland green cape. All he saw was black, brown, gray, and auburn fur surrounding him. They approached slowly, growling and snapping their jaws, the hair on the back of their neck standing straight up.

Nikalys called out, "I don't want to hurt you!"

The pack's snarling told him the Drept had the exact opposite intentions.

He was in the midst of reaching for Horum's gift, preparing to defend himself, when a great whoosh of air rushed from above, buffeting him, striking the ground, and surging outward in all directions. The gale's force was strong, pushing him to his knees while shoving every kur-surus within two dozen feet backwards. The Drept tumbled along the ground like Harvest leaves in a stiff wind.

He stood tall, knowing he had his sister to thank for the help and hoping he could do so later. Free and clear for the moment, he again scanned the battlefield for either Okollu or the demon captain. From Rhohn's stories, he knew the demon leading Okollu's pack to be a towering giant with red skin and black horns. Baaldòk should stick out in this crowd like a saeljul in Yellow Mud.

Nikalys was not wrong. Forty paces to the west, he spotted the Nine Hells' spawn. His eyes went wide.

"Bless the Gods..."

Baaldòk stood eight feet tall from boot heels to horns' tips, a full foot of that was the spiraled horns themselves. Black metal armor, implausibly shiny and unmarred, encapsulated the demon's chest and upper legs, leaving his blood-red arms and calves bare and bulging. A massive sword few mortal men could even lift rest casually on his shoulder, the hilt gripped tightly in his enormous right hand.

As Nikalys stared at the demon, mouth agape, the hunched, cloaked form of Okollu suddenly appeared on his right, slinking past him on all fours, toward Baaldòk. Were it not for the green cloak still hanging from the kur-surus' neck, Nikalys would have attacked.

"Okollu!" hissed Nikalys. "Hold a moment! We need a plan!"

Ignoring him entirely, Okollu continued his approach, rising to stand on his hind paws. The demon-man, already staring at them with a curious, bemused expression, now shifted his full attention to Okollu. The monster's eyebrows arched in quiet surprise.

To Nikalys' left, a hesitant yet firm voice asked, "So how are we doing this?"

Glancing over, Nikalys found Jak beside him, sword at the ready, gaze fixed on the towering demon.

"We?" repeated Nikalys. "You're not doing anything. Go back—"

"No!" interjected Jak. "Even you shouldn't face that alone. We're helping."

"Who's—"

Hearing a light scuffling of boot on ground, Nikalys looked to his right. Rhohn stood there, glaring at the demon. He pointed his thin bladed Dust Man sword at Baaldòk.

"That thing needs to die."

Wondering how both men had managed to reach him, Nikalys glanced over his shoulder and found a long stretch of open marsh leading back to the ring of soldiers. Dozens of kur-surus lined the pathway, hanging in the air, suspended and unable to move. Kenders was striding down the middle of it, a determined, angry expression on her face. He considered yelling at her to go back, but did not waste the breath. She would not listen.

Turning back to Baaldòk, Nikalys saw that Okollu had unwisely continued his approach. Having recovered from his earlier surprise, the demon stared at the lone kur-surus, a maniacal grin resting on his face. Shaking his head slowly, he lifted the giant sword from his shoulder and held it before him.

"Nik?" called Jak over the battle's din. "If you want to save that mongrel, we had better move now."

"The only place you're moving is back to the ports," hissed Nikalys. "You and Rhohn both. Take Kenders with you. Drag her if you must."

"No one is dragging me anywhere," said Kenders as she stopped on Jak's left. "You need me here."

Nikalys glared at his sister.

"I *need* you to stay safe!"

Hearing a wicked, angry snarl to his right, Nikalys whipped his head around just in time to see the kur-surus lift into the air, its limbs flailing, and go flying back, crashing into two others.

"No, Nik," snapped Kenders. "You need me here! Don't argue, you're wasting time."

Nikalys bit his tongue. He wanted her to be wrong, but knew she was right. "Fine, you stay." He glared at Jak. "But you get back to the ring!"

Jak shook his head.

"You might be the Progeny, but you're still my little brother. Go jump off a cliff, Nik. I'm staying."

"Stop squabbling," barked Rhohn. "Must I say it again?" He took a quick step forward, jabbing his sword at Baaldòk. "That thing needs to die!"

Nikalys pressed his lips together and swallowed any further protests. This was not an argument he would win. Truthfully, this was not even an argument.

With a quick sigh of resignation, he muttered, "Fine." Glancing between Jak and Rhohn, he said, "Flank his sides. Make him think you're engaging, but stay clear of his reach, got that?"

Jak nodded once.

"Right. Stay away from the giant demon with the giant sword."

Rhohn stared at him, his lone eyebrow lifted high.

"That is your plan?"

Hearing another nearby growl, Nikalys glanced up in time to watch another mongrel go flying through the air. Turning back to Rhohn, he nodded once.

"Yes. That's the plan. Keep him distracted. I'll do the rest."

A frown flashed over the Dust Man's scarred face.

"There's a thin line between confidence and arrogance."

"You want that thing to die?!" shot back Nikalys. "Go. Flank. Don't die. Got it?"

Rhohn stared back to the demon man, shrugged his shoulders, and then looked over at Jak.

"Let's go be bait."

Jak nodded and the pair stepped forward, advancing on the demon, fanning out right and left as they approached. Okollu continued stalking Baaldòk straight from the front, hunched over on all fours again, snapping at the demon-man as a wild dog would a cornered rabbit. The kur-surus was absent his cloak now. The green mantle lay clumped on the ground.

Before moving forward himself, Nikalys looked over at Kenders.

"Be careful, sis. Don't pass out."

Kenders, twirling in a slow circle while keeping a close eye on the kur-surus surrounding them, said, "Stop talking and go."

Facing Baaldòk, Nikalys spotted a black and gray kur-surus rushing Rhohn from behind, its jaw open wide. He was about to shout a warning when the beast was lifted into the air, flew twenty paces backwards, and crashed to the ground.

"Blast it, Nik!" exclaimed Kenders. "Go!"

Nikalys stared at the patch of ground a few paces past Baaldòk, said a short prayer to Horum, and reached for the God's gift.

Shift.

He slashed at Baaldòk's upper leg, hoping to hamstring the monster. Yet when the ever-sharp blade struck the black armor plating, it bounced off with a resonant clang and sent a sharp, jarring jolt up Nikalys' arm.

Nikalys blinked once and stared at his sword, stunned. The Blade of Horum had never once failed to pierce its target.

Baaldòk whirled around with inhuman speed, lifted his massive sword overhead, and swung it straight down. With his own speed matching that of the demon-man, Nikalys threw up his blade to block Baaldòk's strike, catching the dark metal sword and halting its vicious descent. The demon's blow would have shattered most swords and arms, but Nikalys' sword and arm were not like most. Nikalys held firm, but was forced to his knees. The demon's strength was astounding. Strangely enough, the overpowering scent of wildflowers filled the air.

Baaldòk glared down at him, his eyes throbbing with a wicked, twisted energy. A vicious sneer spread over his black, cracked lips and, in a voice echoing with a God's power, he asked, "How did you do that?"

A ferocious, angry howl shredded the air. For a moment, Nikalys thought one of the kur-surus had slipped past Kenders before Okollu's wide-open, white-muzzled jaw appeared atop the demon's right shoulder and clamped down on the side of Baaldòk's exposed neck. The kur-surus wrapped both arms around the demon and held tight, the reddish-black blood pouring from the wound running down the kur-surus' muzzle and chest.

Letting loose a thunderous bellow of either pain, anger, or a mixture of both, Baaldòk reached his left arm up and across his body to grab Okollu by the scruff of his neck. Taking advantage of the distraction, Nikalys shoved Baaldòk's blade to the side, leapt to his feet and scurried backwards, readying his next attack.

Okollu tried to hold tight, but the demon was too strong. After ripping Okollu free, Baaldòk lifted him high overhead and slammed the kur-surus to the ground. Bones crunched as Okollu seemingly bounced once before tumbling through grass and muck.

The demon advanced on Okollu's prone form, roaring, "Traitor!"

Nikalys eyed the ground beyond Baaldòk, readying to move, but a flash of auburn to his right demanded his attention. A kur-surus had leapt at him, was in mid-air, and only a half-dozen paces away. Nikalys brought his sword up, readying to skewer it when the beast abruptly changed direction and went flying backward. He briefly tracked the kur-surus through the air before looking back to Baaldòk. Rhohn was running forward, his sword drawn back. The Dust Man was aiming for the demon's unprotected left calf. Jak, too, was rushing forward, crouched low, sword up.

Nikalys' eyes went round.

"Wait!"

His warning was a waste of a breath.

Rhohn attacked, stabbing at the back of the demon's knee, just below the edge of the black armor. It was a glancing blow, painful for sure, but not debilitating. Baaldòk roared and swiveled to his right, whipping his massive sword around to meet his attacker. Rhohn ducked down and threw his blade up in a futile attempt to block the demon's counter attack. Baaldòk's sword chopped through Rhohn's as a woodsman's axe would split a dry twig, knocking the Dust Man to the ground in the process. Rhohn's left arm flailed about like a wet rag. Without a doubt, it was broken.

Jak leapt forward, slashed at Baaldòk's other leg, and sliced open the demon's calf, which only served to enrage the Nine Hells' spawn further. Baaldòk spun round, his left hand balled into a fist, and began to swing it at Jak.

Nikalys took one step, lifted the Blade of Horum high—

Shift.

—and slashed at the demon's neck, using Okollu's bite wound as a guide. The white metal sunk into Baaldòk's flesh, but jammed as the edge got caught on the black armor's collar. The scent of wildflowers washed over him.

Not expecting his blade to stop as it did, Nikalys lost his grip, slipped forward, and tumbled to the ground, leaving the Blade of Horum embedded in the demon's neck. As he landed on his chest and stomach, his breath exploded from his lungs. Gasping for air, he started to push himself from the ground when something struck him in the right temple. Hard. Impossibly hard. It felt like a stone-filled burlap sack swung with the force of a hundred men.

He went tumbling, rolling through mud and grass, the world around him a mix of white flashes and swirling colors. The cold hand of unconsciousness wrapped around him, coaxing him to give in to its call. He shoved it away somehow, knowing that if he passed out, he was dead.

When he stopped moving, he was on his back, his head tilted to his right. Opening his eyes, he tried to focus on something, anything, but it was as if he were swimming underwater in the murky waters of Lake Hawthorne. An odd, metallic taste filled his mouth. A woman was calling his name, her voice echoing as if she were in a stone stairwell.

Rolling his head to the left, he was able to make out something moving toward him. Something blurry. Something big.

His left arm lay splayed out to his side, his right, draped over his chest. Summoning strength from somewhere deep inside him, Nikalys managed to turn onto his left side, draw his arm under his body, and push himself partway up. Blinking his eyes repeatedly, he eyed the massive figure moving toward him.

It was black and red.

Baaldòk.

Nikalys tried to stand, but slipped and fell to his knees. Looking back to the demon, he spotted an out-of-focus, black and white blur charging Baaldòk from behind.

The woman shouted, "Jak! No!" Nikalys realized the voice belonged to Kenders.

Nikalys tried to cry out a warning as well, but a garbled moan was all that came out. His tongue was thick, heavy, and currently useless. He spat out a mouthful of blood.

Baaldòk was nearly on top of him now, the long, dark shape over the demon's head warning Nikalys that the demon's sword was high and ready. Nikalys knew he needed to move. Now.

He stared at a blurry spot behind the demon and reached for Horum's gift.

Nothing happened.

He tried again.

Nothing.

Panic gripped his gut, joining the already-there queasiness. He was weaponless, powerless, weak, and wobbly.

Jak's voice shot out over the battlefield.

"Nooo!"

The blob of black and white did not slow as it reached Baaldòk, and rather than attack with his blade, Jak leapt into the air and grabbed the demon's sword arm. Baaldòk still brought his massive sword crashing down, but Jak disrupted the demon's aim. The dark metal blade slammed into the marsh, splattering mud and water over Nikalys' face. Jak lost his grip on Baaldòk's arm and went tumbling past Nikalys.

Baaldòk roared, ripped his sword from the ground, and lifted it high overhead again. Nikalys' vision had cleared enough that he could see the demon's wide, bloodthirsty eyes.

Glancing to another spot of open marsh grass, Nikalys again tried to move.

Nothing.

The blow to his head must have put his gift out of reach.

Hot air rushed over his head and the world grew suddenly bright. Something struck Baaldòk square in the chest, staggering the demon, knocking him backwards but not down. While the monster recovered, his black armor smoking, Nikalys managed to stand upright and struggled to remain so. The world would not hold still. He felt like he was on the Sapphire's deck again.

Trying not to fall back down, he looked for his sword. It had been jammed into the demon's neck, but was gone now. Blinking, he spotted the white blade a dozen paces away, jutting up at an angle, its tip jammed into the soft earth. Lurching through the Marshlands' muck, he stumbled toward it, praying the demon was not on his heels.

Hearing the unmistakable snarling of kur-surus, he glanced up and spotted two of the beasts rushing toward him. A moment later, both were soaring through the air.

Upon reaching his sword, he bent over to grab the hilt, grazed it instead, and fell over, splashing into a puddle of mud. He rolled over, extended his arm upward, and slipped his right palm around the golden hilt. Freeing the sword from the ground, he stared back in the direction of the demon. Baaldòk was lumbering towards him, eyes locked on Nikalys.

To Nikalys' surprise, he spotted Okollu up and moving. He was twenty paces away, crawling toward Baaldòk, a viscous snarl rippling across his black lips as he growled something at the demon in the kur-surus tongue. Nikalys did not understand the words, but the tone was clear.

Rhohn, too, was up and advancing on Baaldòk, his maimed right hand gripping his shattered sword, the steel blade a third its normal length and ending in a jagged edge. He was behind Baaldòk, jogging toward the demon, his face twisted in pain as his left arm dangled limply at his side.

Beyond them, a black and white lump lay in the grass. It had to be Jak. Kenders was making her way to him while tossing any charging Drept back into the pack.

When Baaldòk was only a dozen paces away, he glared at Nikalys and bellowed, "I *will* kill you."

Using his sword to push himself from the ground, Nikalys steadied himself before bringing the glowing white blade to the center of his body, pommel waist-high. Sergeant Trell called it the 'ready position.' Nikalys was anything but ready.

Baaldòk continued to advance, raising his sword, moments away from spiting Indrida's prophecy.

Again, Nikalys tried to give himself over to his gift, to let the instinct take over, but he could not. He felt it there, but each time he reached for it, the gift slipped away. It was like trying to grab and hold onto a handful of water.

Right now, he was not the Progeny. He was not a child of White Lions. He was not leading any fight. He was nothing more than a farmer holding a glowing sword.

He began to backpedal, trying not to fall again. Behind Baaldòk, Rhohn continued his charge, his left arm flopping about like a fish pulled from the lake. Okollu, too, was half-running, half-limping to the demon. Both were utterly quiet now.

Nikalys opened his mouth, wanting to shout for the pair to back off, not to take the demon on alone. Yet before the first syllable could climb from his throat, he clamped his mouth shut.

The son of Thaddeus and Marie would have screamed a warning so loud that the First Council would have heard him in Freehaven. Yet the son of Aryn Atticus and Eliza Kap swallowed the shout whole. The only chance he had to survive right now was to let Rhohn and Okollu continue. A wretched, sick feeling gripped his insides as he watched the pair run toward their fate. Pressing his lips together, he offered a short, silent prayer for them both.

Rhohn was a half-dozen paces away when Baaldòk noticed the Dust Man's approach. Glancing over his shoulder, the demon roared, spun, and brought his sword around to strike at the Dust Man. He would have easily hacked Rhohn in two, but Okollu snuck under the monster's upraised arm and clamped his powerful jaws onto Baaldòk's leg. The demon bellowed and bent over, kicking his leg and sending Okollu through the air. The kur-surus landed hard, collapsing in a heap of mud and fur.

The distraction gave Rhohn the opportunity to rush in and jam his broken blade into the demon's neck, pressing the hilt deep into red flesh. Baaldòk's roar grew even louder as he twisted around to grab at Rhohn. The Dust Man not only managed to hold onto the hilt with his maimed hand, but he twisted the ruined bladed, driving it even deeper into Baaldòk's neck. His eyes were wide and wild, his face primal and distorted. A primitive, furious scream exploded from the soldier, rivaling the howls of the nearby kur-surus.

Baaldòk was able to grip Rhohn by the back of his tunic, ripped him away from the sword, and—in a wicked mimicry of the earlier assault on Okollu—threw the Dust Man to the ground. Grabbing Rhohn's chest, he slammed him a second time.

With Baaldòk facing away from him, Nikalys ran forward, stumbling, and thrust at the demon's lower back. Whether it was luck, chance, or remnant skill guiding his blow, the blade slipped between the demon's torso armor and the waist of the greaves. Upon realizing he had struck his mark, Nikalys drove the sword forward with all his might. The Blade of Horum passed through the demon like a knife through a chicken's egg. Whatever was affecting his ability to grasp Horum's gift had no effect on his strength.

As the sword sliced deep, it caught on Baaldòk's spine. Nikalys jerked as hard as he could to the left and felt a soft pop ripple along the blade. The demon's legs gave way and Baaldòk collapsed to the ground. Nikalys fell with him, still clasping the golden hilt of his blood father's sword. Crashing to the ground as one, they separated when Nikalys lost the sword's handle. He rolled over Baaldòk's back and horns before tumbling through grass and mud again. Coming to a quick stop, he lifted his head to look to the demon, hoping his blow was as effective as it had seemed.

While Rhohn's Dust Man hilt stuck out from Baaldòk's neck at a haphazard angle, Nikalys' blade rose straight up from the demon's back, preposterously perpendicular to the ground. He tensed, waiting for Baaldòk to move, yet the spawn of the Nine Hells remained motionless as thick, red-black blood pumped from its neck, pooling on the ground. The demon's eyes, while still burning with a hot, evil energy, were already beginning to glaze over. Death was near.

Nikalys risked a look around and spotted Jak several dozen paces away, sitting up in the grass, a dazed expression on his face. Kenders was crouched beside him, her gaze locked on Baaldòk.

Nikalys croaked, "Are you hurt?"

Jak glanced at Nikalys and gave a quick shake of his head. Kenders did the same. Neither said a word.

Looking back to the demon, Nikalys stood, his legs still incredibly unsteady. Once upright, he spotted two crumpled forms on either side of Baaldòk. Rhohn and Okollu. Neither of whom was moving. Stumbling to the nearest one—Okollu—he dropped to his knees and reached out a hesitant hand. He had only grazed the kur-surus' fur when Okollu stirred, a low whimpering snarl emanating from his throat.

Nikalys mumbled, "Are you—"

"Go," growled Okollu. "I will be fine." He twisted his muzzle around, staring at Rhohn. "Attend to him."

Nodding, Nikalys crawled to the Dust Man. Rhohn lay on his left side, his back to Nikalys.

"Rhohn?"

Grabbing the soldier's right shoulder, Nikalys rolled him over on his back. The limp manner in which the soldier moved reminded Nikalys of a stricken, lifeless deer after a hunt. He called the Dust Man's name again, slightly less insistent now.

"Rhohn...?"

One look at the man's face and he knew there was no need to call a third time.

The Dust Man's brown eyes were open and blank, staring sightlessly into the morning sky. Blood trickled from the hole where his right ear had once been. Another crimson line dripped from his right nostril.

To be sure, Nikalys reached a hand and placed it on Rhohn's chest. There was no heartbeat.

Nikalys shut his eyes and ground his teeth. Corporal Rhohn Lurus, a good man and soldier, was dead. A single word slipped from Nikalys' lips, quiet and filled with self-loathing.

"Hells."

Rhohn had sacrificed himself, and Nikalys had allowed him to do so, treating both him and Okollu as if they were inanimate, wooden pegs on a radigan board, the same thing the Gods and Goddesses were doing to them all. He dropped his head to his chest and stared at the muck, angry and disgusted.

Hearing footsteps approach, he opened his eyes and looked up, sending his head swimming from the sudden movement. For the first time, he noticed a slight ringing in his ears. Pushing the dizziness aside as best he could, he focused on the figure walking toward him. It was Jak, walking slowly, his sword at his side with its tip pointed down. He was staring all around them, a confused, wary expression on his face.

Curious, Nikalys lifted his gaze, stared at the surrounding Drept pack, and was surprised to find every kur-surus standing motionless. No longer were they charging him and his siblings. Their aggressiveness was gone. Those closest were glaring at the demon's body, hate burning in their yellow eyes.

Despite the ringing in his ears, he could hear that the sounds of battle had shifted. Oligurts' grunts and men's shouting were still present, but the Marshlands air was free of kur-surus' snarls and growls. To the north, Sergeant Trell was yelling for the men to disengage the kur-surus pack and turn north, to the oligurts.

Hearing another set of hurried footsteps, Nikalys looked up and spotted Kenders rushing toward them, her eyes locked on Rhohn. She reached Nikalys' side, crouched down, and ordered, "Move, Nik."

Nikalys knew she was going to try to heal him. He also knew it was pointless.

"He's already gone, sis."

Her hazel-eyed gaze flicked to his face.

"Are you sure?"

Nikalys nodded. Kenders' face fell and she squeezed her eyes tight.

"Blast it."

A single, sharp howl sliced through the air, startling them both. Brother and sister stood quickly and spun around to find Okollu, amazingly, standing upright. The kur-surus cradled his left side with his right arm.

In his thick, wet voice, he called, "Drept, ascuta la min!"

Every kur-surus turned to stare at him.

Spinning in a quick circle, Okollu barked, "Mes cimes!" Releasing his injured side, he pointed to Baaldok's corpse. "Diavol naret bahir tas-vilku il Drept!" He tapped his white-furred chest. "Tiyale bahir tas-vilku il Drept!" Turning to face Nikalys, Kenders, and Jak, he extended his arm, pointing it at the siblings. "Gludu mus zems il Drept! Kunan hiret!"

A few hundred yellow-eyed gazes shifted to the Isaac siblings.

Jak muttered, "Uh-oh."

Nikalys glanced over at Baaldòk's corpse and the sword sticking from the demon's back, wondering if he should go get it now.

Okollu did not give him much time to consider as he tossed his bloody muzzle northward and barked, "Noga adas! Omaroo peil gril!"

As one, the hundreds of kur-surus turned and ran north, rushing past the startled siblings and straight for the ring of soldiers around the port. Sergeant Trell's voice shouted over the racket.

"Do not strike! Let them through!"

The cry was quickly picked up and repeated by the duchy soldiers.

Nikalys watched in awe as the kur-surus bypassed the soldiers, ran through the protective ring, and charged straight into the oligurt ranks, turning their ferocious jaws and teeth against the gray-skinned beasts. A single, stunned word slipped from Nikalys' lips.

"Huh."

The Army of the White Lions seemed to have gained a new ally. A very unusual ally.

Okollu approached where they stood, clearly wincing in pain, his yellow-eyed gaze fixed on Rhohn's body.

"Is he dead?"

Nikalys nodded, muttering, "He is." He had not been around the kur-surus enough to understand his expressions, but if he had been pressed, he would have said Okollu appeared sorrowful.

Okollu was quiet a moment before growling softly, "Grieving comes later." He looked up to the three siblings. "The battle is not over." He turned and began to jog north, back to the fighting, limping as he went.

"He's right," said Jak. "We're not done yet." He, too, began to hurry back to the fray. Looking over his shoulder, he called, "Let's go!"

After one last glance at Rhohn, Kenders followed Jak without saying a word.

Nikalys looked to Rhohn's scarred, slack face and sighed. Reaching down, he closed the Borderlander's eyelids, murmuring, "Maeana welcome you with open arms."

Making a silent promise to come back to bury the Dust Man himself, Nikalys stood and faced north just as a series of three, quick horn calls cut through the air. Looking back to the south, he spotted a great host of mounted soldiers sallying forth from the southern gate to charge a group of oligurts now cut off from the rest of the Sudashian army.

"Good…"

Turning his back on the dead Dust Man and battle to the south, he strode to Baaldòk's corpse, gripped his sword's hilt, and pulled his white blade clear. He stared at the lifeless monster and spat, "Go back to whatever Hell you came from." He kicked Baaldòk's face with the tip of his boot, hard enough that something cracked.

Facing north, he jogged back to the ports.

The combined force of the duchy soldiers and Okollu's pack were quickly overwhelming the oligurt force to their immediate north. They were not only driving the enemy back, but small groups of men and kur-surus were actually pursuing the grayskins as they ran. The skirmish here was going so well that Khin and Nundle had halted their magical attacks. Sabine stood with her bow lowered, staring intently at the battle raging before her. Her hip quiver was empty, but she held one last arrow at the ready, already nocked on the bowstring. Jak was at the ports, directing fresh men as they came through, and the injured as they were carried back to the walls. Sergeant Trell and Zecus were nowhere to be seen. Nikalys hoped they were among those hunting down the fleeing oligurts and not the injured. Or worse.

Bodies of Reed Men and Southern Arms littered the field, along with countless oligurts and kur-surus. Even a few black tunics lay among the dead, the white lion emblem more often than not covered in blood, gore, and Marshlands muck. Nikalys tried not to let every death here weigh on him, but failed miserably. Had he stayed on the walls, this would not be.

As he approached the group, Kenders fixed him with a steady, almost wrathful glare, and said, "To be clear, you *never* get to chastise me for being rash—" She cut off suddenly, her eyes shooting open wide. Whirling around, she stared north. Khin did the same, albeit at a slower, more measured pace. A moment later, the aicenai spoke.

"We must return. Now."

He had taken two steps toward the ports when one disappeared with a soft pop. Halting, he stared north again, worry in his ice blue eyes.

"They are breaching the walls."

Nikalys looked north and was confused when he found the walls clear of the enemy. All he saw were colors of the duchy forces. Oligurts and kur-surus remained outside the walls.

"What are you…?"

He trailed off as entire sections of the northern walls began to collapse. Solid stone appeared to shift and shimmer before flowing outward like sand, spreading down the hill. The Sudashians were indeed breaching the walls, just not in the manner in which he had thought.

"Oh, Gods," muttered Kenders. "Tobias was on one of those towers…"

Glancing at his sister, Nikalys asked, "Are you sure?"

She nodded silently, her gaze fixed north.

Nikalys eyed the melting walls, searching for any sign of the tomble, panic swelling in his chest. Besides causing the deaths of countless soldiers, Nikalys' decision had led to the death of a White Lion. If he had not come down here, Kenders and Khin certainly would not have. And with them on the towers, the walls might very well still be solid.

He set his jaw and swallowed his guilt. It would do him no good here and now while there was a battle still to be won.

Facing his sister and the aicenai, he ordered, "Kenders and Khin. Get back through Nundle's port and hurry over there." He pointed to the disintegrating walls. "Stop that."

Kenders, already moving back to the fluttering black port with Khin at her side, said, "Good idea."

"Hold a moment!" called Nikalys.

She halted and looked back

"What?"

"Tell every soldier—and I mean *every* soldier—between here and there to come through the port."

Kenders hesitated a moment, but rather than question him as to why he wanted the soldiers, she nodded.

"Just promise me you aren't going to do anything brainless."

"Will you do the same?"

Cocking an eyebrow, she said, "I'll send your men. Be safe." She glanced at Jak and Sabine. "All of you." Without another word, she hurried through the tear with Khin a step behind.

Staring down at Nundle, Nikalys briefly wondered where the tomble's ever-present hat was before saying, "Nundle, get back to the walls, keep that port open, and help the injured. And get those soldiers to hurry."

Nundle nodded, his red hair bouncing.

"Do you want mages, too?"

Nikalys shook his head.

"They stay. If you can't wield a blade, you stay on the wall, understood?"

"Certainly," replied Nundle. "Anything else?"

"Yes," answered Nikalys. "If you see Broedi, tell him I'm heading north. We are going to attack the Sudashians' flank."

Jak, standing a few paces away, looked over his shoulder.

"We're going to do what?"

Ignoring his brother, Nikalys said, "Go, Nundle. Quickly."

Rather than move, Nundle glanced north, a frown spreading over his face.

"You're going to...attack? Is that wise?"

"Probably not, but it's what we are doing. Right now, we have the numbers. We need to clear these fields before Tandyr's western reinforcements arrive."

Nundle glanced west, sighed, and nodded. Eyeing Nikalys and Jak he said, "Ketus with you, then. You'll certainly need him." The tomble turned and hurried through the port, dodging a number of fresh Reed Men and Southern Arms soldiers moving from the walls to the field.

Steeling himself, Nikalys turned to Sabine. The young woman was staring at him carefully, her eyes narrowed.

"Sabine, I need—"

"If that sentence ends with 'go back to the walls,' don't finish it."

Keeping his expression blank, Nikalys exchanged a quick look with Jak. In a way only brothers can, Jak understood what he was thinking in that one glance.

Jak looked back to Sabine and said, "You're going back to the walls."

Sabine shifted her cool, collected gaze to Jak alone.

"Interesting theory. Will you be carrying me there?"

Jak shrugged.

"If I must."

Nikalys said, "And I'll help."

Sabine shifted her stare to him, her eyes full of the same icy determination as when she had sliced open the neck of the unconscious bandit at the Moiléne farm. It made him incredibly uneasy, yet he forced himself to hold the glare.

"I'm one of the Progeny, too, which means you don't—"

Jak interrupted her, asking, "Do you know how to use a sword, Sabine?"

"I don't need one. I have a bow."

Nikalys pointed to her empty quiver.

"You're out of arrows."

Setting her jaw, she said, "I'll go get more."

Jak nodded and waved a hand at the battlements.

"You'll find plenty up there. And as long as you are up there, you should probably stay."

Sabine glared at Jak for a moment before turning her chilly gaze to Nikalys.

"I have just as much right to be here as you." Glancing back to Jak, she added, "And more than you."

Jak flinched at the comment, his eyes narrowing sharply.

"Please," said Nikalys. "You can do just as much good for us on the walls as you can down here." She opened her mouth to protest, but he continued on, raising his voice. "This is not about *you*, Sabine. It's about Helene." Jabbing a finger at the walls, he exclaimed, "You have a sweeter chance of getting back to her up there than you do down here!"

His plea thawed her icy stare a bit, about as much as a candle could warm a block of ice. Nevertheless, she pressed her lips together and nodded once.

"Fine."

She turned on her heels, walked to the port, and stepped through without looking back. Any soldier moving from the walls took one look at her and moved out of her way. Nikalys sighed and shook his head.

Jak leaned over and asked, "That went well, don't you think?"

A slight grin graced Nikalys' lips.

"Could have gone better."

Jak studied his brother, one eyebrow cocked, and asked, "What about me? You sending me back to the walls? Or do I get to come along on your mad charge? And, to be clear, I do think this *is* madness."

"If I order you to the walls, will you go?"

"Oh, Gods, no," huffed Jak. "Remember, you're still my little brother."

"Mad charge it is, then."

Jak nodded once.

"Should be fun."

The stream of men coming through the port had increased already, the soldiers quickly bunching up into disorganized clumps.

Keeping his voice low, Jak muttered, "Have you seen Sergeant Trell?"

Shaking his head, Nikalys said, "No." He glanced at Jak and frowned. "Zecus, either."

"Noticed that, too," said Jak. "I'm glad Kenders didn't." The brothers stared west, into the forest where groups of Reed Men were chasing oligurt stragglers. "Let's hope they're safe."

"Let's do that," said Nikalys. Looking back to the growing force around them, he added, "For now, though, we need to get this assault organized."

"Agreed," said Jak, staring at the confused groupings of soldiers. "Excuse me." Stepping forward, he began to shout orders, getting the men to line up in formation. "Ranks of nine, three and three! Quickly! We have a war to win!"

The soldiers leapt to obey.

As his brother organized the ranks, Nikalys scanned the remnants of the battlefield. Okollu's pack was helping chase down the last of the oligurts here. Okollu lagged at the rear, too injured himself to do much more than limp about the marsh and howl orders. Three, quick horn blasts pulled his attention back south. Some of the mounted Reed Men were riding north now, heading for Nikalys and his growing force. Facing them, he began waving his arms to get the attention of the lead horsemen, saying a silent prayer that he was doing the right thing.

CHAPTER 58: PROPHET

Kenders rushed along the battlements, her boots pounding on stone as she ran, still one tower away from the first of the gaping breaches in the walls.

The persistent buzz of Strands was deafening, the crackling sensation filled her chest and the air around her. Thousands of Strands—sizzling yellows, rippling blues, fiery oranges, glittering silvers, warm golds, and muddy browns—whipped around her, flying through the air, summoned by friend and foe alike. The display's intensity was nearly overwhelming.

As she hurried, she glanced west, ripping apart Sudashian Weaves when she could, picking and choosing the ones with the most Strands to unravel. Even though she did not recognize most of the patterns the enemy was using, she figured it was her best approach.

Sabine ran at her side, having caught up halfway to the gaps. Kenders was surprised her friend had not stayed with her brothers, but was too busy to ask why not. As they sprinted over the walls, Sabine grabbed any free arrow she could find, plucking them from men's quivers and dropping them in her own. They were keeping a quick pace yet Khin was only a few paces behind them, moving swifter than she thought possible.

Two towers back, they had emerged to find the walls empty of men. Whether ordered to or not, the soldiers of the northern ranks were streaming into the streets below, perhaps afraid to be standing atop the ramparts as stone turned to sand beneath their feet. With empty walls and the massive breaches, the advantage had shifted to Tandyr's forces here.

Kenders cursed herself. She should never have left Tobias.

Reaching the tower, she rushed up the outside stairs to gain a better view of what was happening below. Sabine was right behind her, taking the steps two at a time. Upon cresting the tower stairs, Kenders scurried to the side of the northwestern corner and peered over the wall's edge. Her heart stopped.

"Blast the Gods…"

A two hundred foot section of wall between the tower she stood upon and the next had disintegrated. Tens of thousands of once-sturdy mud-bricks were now nothing more than a massive pile of sand filling the hole, the western slope, and the streets of Demetus as well. Some of the soldiers who had been positioned on the wall were now stuck in the sand, struggling to get out. Her gaze locked on a single, booted leg jutting from the sand, not moving. She swallowed the lump that had suddenly appeared in her throat.

Reserve soldiers from within Demetus were clambering up the sand pile to help free those submerged in the walls' remains. A pair of Shadow Mane soldiers was leading a contingent of maroon-clad Shore Guard over the pile to face a group of oligurts attempting to push into the city. Wil Eadding and Cero were at the head of the charge.

Sabine arrived to stand beside her and remained quiet. There was little to say.

"Are you going to do something about those oligurts?" asked a gruff voice. "Or just stand there and gape all day?"

Looking to her right, Kenders eyes grew round when she spotted Tobias standing at the top of the northern stairs. She took a few steps towards the tomble, joyfully exclaiming, "Tobias! How did you—"

He held up his hand. "Not now." Jabbing his walking stick towards the collapsed wall, he instructed, "We need to stop them."

She halted in mid-step. He was right.

Turning her attention below, she studied the scene again, this time with a less frenzied eye. The quick twang of a bowstring and arrow's soft whistle as it whizzed through the air told her Sabine had resumed the assault. She needed to do the same.

Glancing back to the tomble, she asked, "What should I do?"

Tobias was in the midst of pulling together a Weave of pure Air. Without taking his attention away from the bright white Strands, he said, "This is not one of Khin's lessons! Do what needs to be done!"

Turning her head, she sought the thin frame of the aicenai, hoping Khin might be more help. Her teacher stood on the other side of Sabine, his attention focused below as he worked on a Weave of his own. She was on her own.

She stared below, gauging the number of oligurts rushing up the sand to be close to four hundred. Easily ten times that many were rushing from the north and south, up the slight hill and towards the gap. Her gaze flicked to the western horizon. The bulk of the God of Chaos' army still waited in the distance. Her eyes narrowed as she stared west. There was something unusual about the distant Sudashians. A soft, flickering ripple of silver radiated from the western horde.

"Kenders!" shouted Tobias, cutting through her thoughts. "They're breaching the walls!"

Her gaze snapped back to the chaos below, landing squarely on the demon captain leading the assault. At one time, it had been a man, but the grotesque figure below now had a long, piggish snout and curled, brown horns like a ram jutting from the sides of his head. He spun around to bellow something, revealing six giant spurs of jagged white bone running along his spine.

Kenders decided to eliminate the Nine Hells' spawn, hoping the same thing would happen that did when Baaldòk perished. Whatever thrall the demon had over Okollu's pack had dissipated the moment he died.

Pulling together Strands of Air, Fire, and Stone, she knit a large Weave and directed it to a lump of fallen stone near the wall's edge. The chunk of brick and mortar launched through the air, bursting into an unnatural flame as it hurtled toward the demon. The monster saw it coming and, with surprising speed, leapt ten paces backwards just as the burning stone struck the sand, sending a plume of dust and smoke into the air. She had missed.

Smacking the wall, she hissed, "Blast it!"

"You'll need to do better than that!" shouted Tobias. "They're quicker than they look!"

Kenders stared at the tomble White Lion, looking for direction.

"Like what!?"

Tobias was too busy to answer as he sent a Weave into the city proper, arched it back to gap, and directed it to slam into an oligurt who had reached the sand pile's peak. The monster flew backwards to crash into three other gray-skinned beasts.

Kenders considered simply mimicking Tobias' Weave, doing the same thing she had done to keep the kur-surus off her brothers, but that would be only a momentary fix against the thousands rushing the gap.

Determined to think things through before acting, she cleared her head while ignoring her thudding heart, the roar of the oligurts, and the throbbing, persistent hum of magic all around. Her mind went over the dozens of Weaves she had learned, trying to find one that would help now. She discounted one after another, though. Some might slow the enemy, but none would stop them.

Suddenly, the oddest, most out-of-place thought popped into her head: her sitting with Joshmuel in the enclave's courtyard, watching Zecus and Jak spar. She remembered the Alsher patriarch's deep brown eyes looking at her, his words echoing inside her as though he were speaking them to her now.

"You have good instincts. Follow them, trust yourself, and do what comes natural. Things will work out."

The words were so clear, so crisp, that Kenders glanced to her right, half-expecting to see Joshmuel beside her. Only Tobias awaited her quizzical stare, but his attention was held by the scene below.

Shaking her head, Kenders turned to peer at the sand pile. Pressing her lips together, she chose to take Joshmuel's advice. Her instincts screamed that she act now, not think. So, she did just that.

Staring at the long line of oligurts rushing into the breach, Kenders willed that any of the Sudashians near the peak of the sand pile be thrown backwards. Immediately, close to a hundred bright, white Weaves of Air popped into existence along the gap and slammed into the foremost oligurts, tossing the lumbering beasts into the next few rows of the enemy. A wave of exhaustion rushed over her, accompanied by a shouted warning by Tobias.

"What are you doing!? That's not what I meant!"

Ignoring the tomble, she reached out to steady herself against the tower wall. A hand gripped her elbow and helped keep her upright. Glancing over, she found Sabine staring at her, her eyes as cold as old snow.

"Don't do that again."

Kenders shook her head, muttering, "I won't." She doubted she could, even if she wanted to.

The flight of the oligurts had done two things. First, it gave Wil and Cero the opportunity to set up a defense along the sand pile. Shore Guard soldiers rushed to form a thick line of men shouting at the Sudashians. The other benefit to Kenders Weave was that it had distracted the demon captain.

The spawn stood, his back to the city, staring as his oligurts rolled down the sand. Glaring at the demon, Kenders reached for Gaena's gift again, wanting nothing more than the loose earth around the demon's ankles to turn into solid stone. A dark, solid brown Weave appeared, fully complete around the demon-man's feet and instantly morphed the shifting sand into a heap of hard rock. Another, smaller wave of tiredness swelled inside her. The demon stared down at his feet and began to struggle.

A tired smile crept over Kenders' face.

Relying on skill alone this time, Kenders pulled together Air, Fire, and Stone again, repeating the earlier Weave she had first used to strike at the spawn. Lifting another, much larger stone from the ground, she hurled the boulder through the air, aiming for the oligurt legion's leader. As the rock spun toward its target, hot, yellow flames oozed over its surface as though the fire were being squeezed from inside the stone. The demon spotted the flaming boulder and began to struggle harder, bellowing a deep, resounding roar while bashing at the rock around his feet with the massive metal hammer he carried.

With a shuddering, satisfying thud, stone and fire crashed into the demon captain, bending the monster backwards, twisting its body into an impossible pose. Flame, dust, and rock exploded in all directions, ending the spawn's existence. Just as when Baaldòk had perished, Kenders felt a short, intense burst of silver. Strands of Soul exploded outward, blinding her briefly as if she had glanced at the sun.

Kenders brought a hand to her eyes and tried to rub the remnant flash away, intent on wanting to see what the oligurts were doing. Dropping her hand, she stared below, blinking and waiting for the fuzziness to turn sharp. After a moment, she saw that most of oligurts atop the sand pile had stopped their advance. They stood in place, staring at one another.

"Run, blast it…"

A thick, guttural call coursed through the air. A large oligurt stood near the line of Shore Guard, bellowing something unintelligible as it pointed its spiked club to the west. Nearby oligurts turned and began to retreat down the sand, running away from the city. The long oligurt's shout echoed repeatedly as more and more of the grayskins began to retreat.

Kenders watched, relieved, as close to two thousand oligurts lumbered west, colliding with another group still compelled by their demon captain to invade the city. The two groups began to fight amongst themselves.

Sabine asked, "Can you stand?"

Kenders glanced at her friend and nodded once.

"I'll be fine."

"Good"

Sabine released her arm and rushed to the westernmost point of the wall, drawing another arrow, nocking, and releasing it in less time than it took Kenders to blink. Sabine loosed three arrows in such rapid succession, Kenders wondered if she was even aiming.

A great cheer roared forth from Demetus. Glancing down, she saw the soldiers standing on the wall's remnants—as well as those within the city proper—throwing their arms into the air as they belted out a victorious cry. Catching a bit of movement at the edge of her vision, she looked north and spotted five of the monstrous thorn creatures a half-mile away, battering oligurts and kur-surus alike. Soldiers were pouring from the northern gate on horse and on foot to engage an already staggered enemy.

From beside her, a soft, airy voice murmured, "That was a reckless choice."

Turning to her left, she found Khin standing there, his blue eyes locked on her. She wondered how long he had been standing there.

"Pardon?"

"Your strategy to eliminate the demon," said Khin, his gaze calmly traveling over the battle below. "It was reckless." Both his tranquil manner and the steady pace of his speech were entirely out of place in the battle's chaos.

She gaped at him, stunned he would be so dismissive of her effort. She was half a heartbeat away from offering a short retort when Tobias did it for her.

"Blast it, Khin! Give her some credit!"

She glanced over to find the tomble approaching, leaning on his walking stick as he hobbled over to them. He stopped beside her and stood on the tips of his toes, trying to peer over the lip of the tower wall.

"I thought what she did was quite clever."

"Clever, yes," acknowledged Khin. "Yet reckless." He stared hard at Kenders, his eyes alive and bright. "I followed your thoughts. You were diligent at first, you thought through your actions. Yet, you resorted to your gift."

Kenders blinked.

"I did not know what else to—"

She cut off as Khin's words sunk in.

"You followed my…" She trailed off, her eyes narrowing sharply. "I knew it!" she muttered. "All this time, you've been inside my head, haven't you?"

"Most of it, yes," admitted the aicenai, unfazed by her accusatory tone. "It was decided it was the best manner in which to teach you."

Frowning, Kenders asked, "Was it, now? Decided by whom, exactly?"

Khin held her gaze but remained quiet.

Feeling both disappointed and violated, she shook her head and spoke, her tone firm and unyielding.

"My thoughts should be my own."

Tobias said, "They can be." He glanced at the aicenai. "Make him swear to stay out of your head. He will hold true to it." Khin turned his gaze to Tobias, an expression of slight displeasure on his face.

Glaring at Tobias, Kenders asked, "You knew?!"

"Live alone with an aicenai for a few decades, and you eventually figure it out."

"Who else knows?"

Tobias answered, "Broedi."

With a raised eyebrow, she replied, "That's it? You, Broedi, and myself?"

Khin nodded.

"That is all."

Staring at her teacher, Kenders asked, "Is that true? If I ask you to stay out, you'll stay out?"

Nodding once, Khin said, "It is."

"Swear it, then," said Kenders. "Swear to keep away from my thoughts."

"I ask that you keep my ability a secret in return."

"Why?"

"Because," said Khin softly. "The fewer who know the truth, the greater an advantage it is. Both against our enemies and amongst our allies. Would you not like to know if and when Lady Vivienne is lying?" He paused. "Or the duchess?"

Kenders was quiet a moment, wondering at the implication of his question. Now was not the time to press him, though. Not in the middle of a battle.

"Fine," answered Kenders. "Stay out of my thoughts, and your secret is safe with me."

"You can tell no one," clarified Khin. "Your brothers—" he shifted his gaze to Sabine at the western wall "—or your friends."

Kenders considered the condition briefly before giving a short, decisive nod.

"I accept."

"Agreed, then," said Khin. "You have my promise. Although this means we must—"

A great howling filled the air, cutting off Khin while startling Kenders and Tobias. All three turned to stare westward.

"More?" muttered the tomble. "Already?"

Listening to the cry a moment, Kenders noticed a low thudding accompanying it. Shaking her head, she said, "I don't think so." She began to sprint to the tower's western wall. Looking over her shoulder, she urged, "Come on!"

The trio moved west, stopped at the tower's edge, and watched as the Drept pack and Reed Men on horseback rushed from the south, past the tower, and into the flank of the oligurts. Nikalys and his white sword stood out, flashing bright as he dashed through the horde. She searched frantically for Jak and Zecus, but of the few black and white tabards she saw, none resembled her brother or the man who held her heart. She offered a short, silent prayer to Mu, the God of War, that he keep them safe.

She spotted a familiar, giant hill lynx loping beside the lead horses. Broedi pounced on oligurts as they ran, his teeth and claws shredding the enemy. The lynx's viciousness was so unlike the quiet, stoic Broedi that it made her uneasy to watch.

Scanning the northern battlefield, she spotted dozens of miasmic, black masses plaguing the remaining demon captains. Lifting an arm to point, she asked, "What in the Nine Hells is that?"

Tobias stared below and answered, "Probably every flying insect within a few miles radius." He paused before begrudgingly adding, "Wren has his uses."

One of the twisted demons collapsed to a knee, too distracted by the insect swarm to see the contingent of Southern Arms rushing him from behind. The duchy soldiers overwhelmed the distracted demon captain, making relatively short work of him. Anticipating another burst of Strands, Kenders shut her eyes. She felt the explosion of silver this time, but was not blinded by the flash.

This group of the Sudashian army was in full retreat. She sighed and, with a sick feeling in her stomach, gazed westward to stare at Tandyr's distant reinforcements.

"It's not over, is it?"

Tobias muttered, "Not even close."

As she studied the distant line on the horizon. Frowning, she asked, "Why haven't they moved?"

Again, she caught a slight ripple of silver from the west. This time, however, she noted a flash of white and gold mixing with the Soul. The use of Strands by the duchy forces had decreased substantially, making whatever was to the west that much more noticeable.

Her gaze still focused westward, she said with a worried voice, "Khin...?"

"I sense it too."

Kenders was quiet a moment. Something about the combination felt familiar.

"What is it?"

Rather than answer her, Khin turned to Tobias.

"Where is Wren?"

"North somewhere. Why?"

Guessing what the aicenai was thinking, Kenders pointed west.

"Because we need to know what that is."

Tobias stared to the horizon.

"I sense...Air."

"Will and Soul, too," added Kenders.

A deep frown spread over Tobias' lips.

"You're right. We need Wren."

Kenders looked north, to the tower on the other side of the collapsed wall. The three mages—two Shadow Manes and a Titan Tribe hillman—stood atop the tower and appeared to be resting. One of the black-and-white-clad mages was tall, barrel-chested, and had red hair. Pointing to the tower, she asked, "Can you open a port there? By Gamin?"

Glancing at the tower, Tobias said, "I can't see the top. Would the southern stairs work?"

"Good enough."

She felt and saw the black Strands of Void and white of Air pop around them and watched Tobias craft the Weave.

"What are your plans?" asked Khin quietly.

Looking over to the aicenai, Kenders shrugged.

"I don't have one. Unless 'move north until we find Wren' counts."

Khin tilted his head slightly.

"An honest answer, at least."

A tear in the fabric of the world appeared a dozen paces away.

"Let's go," called Tobias, already moving toward the port. Khin was a step behind him.

Kenders looked over and waited until Sabine loosed her next arrow. The moment the shaft was flying, as Sabine was already reaching for the next, Kenders called out, "Sabine!"

Her friend turned to face her. Sabine's gaze remained even and emotionless.

"What?"

Nodding to the port, Kenders said, "Come on, we're going north."

Without question or pause Sabine nodded and strode from the western wall. Turning, Kenders found both Khin and Tobias were gone, already through the port. Looking north to the tower, she spotted the pair climbing the stairs. Gamin and the other mages were turning to face them.

Before Kenders could take a step forward, there was an explosion of Strands to the west.

Bright, burning orange.

Stout, heavy brown.

Sizzling, buzzing yellow.

Gleaming, sparkling silver.

Vibrant, pulsating green.

The surge was so strong that Kenders stumbled, startled by its intensity. She had never felt so many Strands concentrated into a single Weave. She spun around, searching for its source and found a swirling mass of fire, lightning, and rocks hurtling toward the city from the west. Her eyes went wide, her lips parted to draw in a gasp of air.

The ball was twice as wide as the city walls were tall.

"Bless the Gods…"

"Hells!" cursed Sabine. "What is that?"

Kenders did not answer immediately because she did not know. The immense Weave soared through the air, the elements within morphing, taking the shape of a man's malformed torso and head. Only then did she realize at what she was staring.

"It's a fibríaal."

This creature was not unlike the one that had destroyed Yellow Mud, although this was made of Fire, Charge, and Stone and not Water. Her heart sank as she realized its trajectory. Her eyes flashed to where Tobias, Khin, Gamin, and the other mages stood on the next tower, gaping at the fibríaal. She doubted they could stop the attack. The Weave was much too large.

She sprinted toward the port and leapt through, hearing Sabine's startled cry of, "Ken—" cut off as she passed into the inky blackness.

Her boot slapped down on the stone steps of the other tower and, without breaking stride, she bound up the stairs, reached the top, and spun to face west. From here, she had a much better look into the heart of the Weave. The ordering of the Strands appeared to be nothing more than a tangle of countless strings, like five balls of colored wool yarn all rolled into one.

Khin and Tobias were in the midst of working together on some sort of Water and Air Weave. Gamin was staring into the Weave's center, perhaps trying to figure out how to unravel it. The other two mages, one Shadow Mane and one hillman— stood motionless, stunned into inaction.

As Gamin noticed her arrival, his eyes went wide.

"Get out of here! Now!"

She ignored his pleas and peered into fibríaal, searching for a weak spot. The half-ball, half-man globule of fire, stone, and lightning tumbled through the air, rushing ever closer. The Strands were spinning so quickly, she could not grab a hold of a single one.

A scream of utter frustration burst free from deep insider her, tearing at her throat.

They were not going to stop it.

She needed more time.

Now.

A myriad of colors exploded all around her. Thousands of black, silver, gold, green, white, yellow, orange, blue, and brown Strands popped into existence, fully formed in a perfectly complete, impossibly intricate pattern. It covered the sky, the city, the marshes. It covered the world.

A wave of pure, complete, bone-weary exhaustion rolled over her. Her legs buckled and she dropped to the tower's stone floor, banging her knees hard and scraping her hands. She opened her eyes—unaware she had shut them—to find her vision blurry and unfocused. Unconsciousness was trying to claim her, but she fought back with everything she had. If she passed out now, everyone on the tower—and countless others nearby—would perish.

Her heart thudded in her chest as she sat there on all fours, wasting precious time she did not have. Try as she might, however, she could not push herself up. She was too tired.

"No…"

Reaching deep inside, she found a hidden reserve of resolve, drew upon it, and ordered, "Blast it. Get up!"

She managed to lift her head at least and peered west, expecting the fibríaal to be mere paces away, ready to crash into the tower and end it all for her. That was not the fate awaiting her, however.

The fibríaal hung in the sky, motionless, locked in a fixed position. For the briefest of moments, she thought Khin and Tobias had somehow succeeded in halting the incoming boulder, but then she noticed the flames on the fibríaal's surface were not moving. Neither were the jagged bolts of lightning. The entire Weave was frozen in place.

"What in—"

She cut off, stunned by how loud her voice was. She blinked in surprise, realizing it only sounded loud because the world around her had gone totally, completely silent.

Her gaze shifted to the other mages on the tower. All five were as still as statues. Gamin had his arm outstretched, pointing at the incoming Weave, his mouth open, frozen in the midst of a scream. Tobias and Khin were staring at their combined, half-completed Weave. After somehow finding the strength to push herself from the ground, Kenders stumbled forward to the tower's western edge.

It was as if she were looking upon a tapestry from Duke Rholeb's dining hall. Nobody was moving. The entire battle below was halted, frozen in place. Arrows hung in the air, men's swords and oligurts' clubs locked in mid-blow. The group of Titan Tribe warriors was engaged with the second kur-surus pack, their great weapons petrified in mid-swing. She spotted Nikalys, standing behind an oligurt, the Blade of Horum inches from the beast's neck.

Her eyes went wide as it struck her what had happened.

"I…I did this…"

"Of course you did," said the unfamiliar voice of a woman. Her words echoed with a strange, thudding power. "Now, quickly, please. You do not have much time."

Whirling around, Kenders found a remarkable, resplendent woman standing atop the tower. While it was still early morning, the stranger appeared as if she stood in a pool of brilliance, the midday sun shining down upon her. A long, flowing dress hung from her shoulders, covered with dazzling bright colors, all swirling together in an intricately complex pattern that would make all dyemasters envious. Her skin was the color of stained oak, her ring-curled hair a few shades lighter and hanging just past her shoulders.

The woman held Kenders' gaze a moment before looking past her, at the fibríaal.

"What you have done will not last. Do not tarry."

Kenders stared in silence, unable to form a coherent response. She had never conceived of such a being as what stood before her.

With an impatient shake of her head, the woman glared back to Kenders.

"Please hurry. Dally much longer, and the path you must take will be closed forever."

Deep, complete confusion prompted an almost involuntary response.

"Path? What path?"

"Go," ordered the woman. She lifted an arm and pointed to Gamin. "Look, your Weave is failing already."

Looking over to Gamin, Kenders found him unchanged from before.

"What do you—?"

She cut off as she realized he was moving now. It might be at the pace of a snail climbing uphill, but he was moving nonetheless. She turned to stare at the fibríaal and found the jagged bolts of lightning were moving now, slowly crawling over its surface.

Staring into the center of the Weave, she found that she could easily discern its pattern now that it was not tumbling through the sky.

The corners of her mouth turned up a fraction.

"There."

She picked a knot where all five types of Strands looped together and ripped it apart. The Weave began to unravel on its own, but she helped the process along, pulling one Strand from another, quickly turning the Weave into a disorganized clump of magical strings.

As the fibríaal Weave fell apart, so did her own, apparently. The movements of those around her began to accelerate. The sounds of battle began to assault her ears once again, although the clamor was unusually deep. The cries of those fighting were long and drawn out. The entire experience was both surreal and unpleasant.

Suddenly, the fibríaal exploded, bursting outward in a shower of sparks, stones, and fire. A great, chest-thumping boom shook the Marshlands.

Reacting even before she had time to panic, Kenders willed a giant Weave of Air into existence to protect the hundreds of duchy soldiers exposed to the blast. As the first shards began to crash to the ground, she extended the protection to cover any kur-surus she could see, willing to risk saving the enemy if she could guard the Drept.

Her vision went blurry. Sweet, black unconsciousness beckoned to her. Like before, she fought it, refusing to pass out. Her legs buckled, though, and she began to fall backwards to the tower's top. Yet before she smacked into the stone, someone caught her from behind.

"Don't worry," mumbled Gamin. "I have you."

Kenders would have thanked him, but she was exhausted. Letting him help hold her upright, she turned a weary eye to the scene below.

The explosion had brought the battle to a standstill, with its participants either staring up at the rocks and fire raining down upon them or running from the storm. She had managed to protect most of the duchy forces, but not all. A ball of burning stone landed in the midst of a group of Reed Men, killing at least a half-dozen of them. When another boulder crushed two Shadow Mane soldiers, Kenders shut her eyes, unable to watch good people die. The screams carried on, however. She wanted to craft a Weave to block them out, but was too tired.

As the last few rocks tumbled to the earth, the sounds of fighting resumed. Kenders opened her eyes and was greeted by a field littered with debris, dead bodies, and smoke. It looked like what she imagined the Nine Hells to be.

"How did you do that?"

She dropped her gaze to her right and found Tobias staring up at her, his eyes wide and brimming with curiosity.

"I…wished…" She trailed off and took a deep breath, trying to summon a little more strength. "I wished I had more time and I…I don't know what I did."

Moving to stand beside Tobias, Khin peered at her and said, "You halted the world's passage."

Kenders stared into the aicenai's ice-blue eyes for a moment. As preposterous as it sounded, it seemed she had. Nodding slowly, she said, "It was an accident."

Gamin, his arms still helping support her, said, "A fortunate one, at least."

"I fell down when I did it," said Kenders. "I nearly passed out, but the woman—" She cut off quickly.

The woman.

With a surge of newfound energy, she pulled away from Gamin and turned to face the tower's top. Only Sabine and the other two mages were standing behind her. The bronze-skinned woman in the colorful dress was gone.

"Woman?" asked Tobias. "What woman?"

Confused, Kenders spun in a circle, muttering, "There was a woman here." She pointed to the eastern wall of the tower. "She was standing right there, bathed in sunlight that wasn't there, wearing a dress of a hundred colors. She told me I had to hurry. That my Weave was failing. That I had a—" She caught Sabine's doubt-ridden stare and stopped short.

Shaking her head, her friend sounded concerned as she said, "I watched the tower from the moment you stepped through the port until I arrived. There was no woman."

"Yes, there was," insisted Kenders. "She spoke to me!"

"Perhaps you overstrained yourself?" suggested Tobias.

Glaring hard at the tomble, Kenders exclaimed, "I did not 'overstrain' myself! I am telling you, there was a woman here!" She turned to the aicenai. "Khin, I swear it!"

In his soft, drawn-out manner, Khin said, "I believe you."

Relieved, Kenders said, "Thank you." She was about to ask why when Gamin spoke.

"As do I," murmured the mage.

His words alone were cause for surprise, but paired with the oddly pensive tone in which he spoke them and the strange glint in his eyes, they were thrice as curious. While his response intrigued Kenders, it had a much greater effect on Khin. The aicenai turned to peer at Gamin, the parchment-thin skin around his eyes crinkling with honest shock.

Before any questions could be asked, Tobias stepped forward and asked, "Whatever it was that happened can be discussed later. Just be happy we're not dead and let's focus on the fact that this battle is not over yet." He jabbed his walking stick in the air, pointing to the west. "The rest of Tandyr's army still waits."

Nodding, Kenders said, "You're right. If we could find Wren, he might be able to—"

She stopped short as the constant, humming undercurrent of magic to the west went quiet in an instant. It was as if she had been standing beside a massive waterfall that had abruptly stopped, freely flowing one moment and dammed the next.

In a stunned, quiet tone Gamin muttered, "Bless the Gods." The large red-headed mage was staring westward, his eyes wide in surprise. Swiveling her head to stare into the Marshlands, Kenders gaped.

The horizon was empty. Nothing but trees and marshes awaited their stares. Tandyr's army was gone.

For a few moments, nobody said a word. Then, Sabine broke the silence by asking the obvious.

"Where did they go?"

A chorus of surprised cries from the walls told her they were not the only ones to have noticed the army's disappearance.

"Are they hiding?" asked Sabine. "Could they be using magic to conceal themselves?"

"No," said Kenders, shaking her head slowly. "There are fewer Strands now. Before, there...were..." She trailed off, thinking over what she had been feeling.

Silver. White. Gold.

Her eyes went wide. She knew why the pattern had felt familiar. She had felt the combination before, not long after discovering that she was a mage, at the foot of the cliff a few miles south of Fallsbottom.

"Hells," she muttered. "I know what happened."

"You do?" asked Tobias.

Pressing her lips together, she whirled to face Khin.

"If you want to make someone see something that is not there, what Strands are needed?"

The aicenai did not answer with words, but the slight widening in his eyes was enough to tell her he knew what she was getting at.

"Soul, Air, and Will?" pressed Kenders. "Am I right?"

Khin remained silent, staring westward. The worried look in his eyes made her wish she could read his thoughts.

After a moment, Tobias answered her question saying, "Yes, you're correct. But in order to fool this many people—" he waved at the walls "—you would need a nearly infinite number of all three types...of..." He trailed off and stared at nothing, his face blank. A heartbeat later, he shut his eyes tight, shook his head, and sighed, "Oh this is bad. Very, very bad."

Khin spoke aloud what at least a handful of them were thinking.

"The Cabal have three of the Suštinata."

"Or more," added Tobias bitterly. "But at least Will, Soul, and Air."

Sabine asked, "So what does this mean?"

Kenders stared back to the empty horizon. She felt ill.

"It means we have no idea where the rest of Tandyr's army is."

CHAPTER 59: LOSS
25ᵗʰ of the Turn of Maeana, 4999

A gentle, cool breeze blew past Jak as he emerged from the port. He drew in a deep breath, relishing the fresh, clean air, thick with the scent of grass. Coming from the rank odor of Demetus, he more than welcomed the change.

He took a few steps forward, stopped, and scanned the Southlands prairie. Much of the landscape was exactly how he remembered it—endless fields of waist-high grass stretching from horizon to horizon—yet three things were decidedly different. For one, the grass was a dusty green as the land weathered Winter. Secondly, to the south, the profile of a small town rose up from the prairie. During his time in the grasslands, the only structure he had seen had been the Moiléne homestead. The final difference was a bit more prominent.

Shaking his head, Jak marveled, "Gods, that's a lot of people."

Thousands upon thousands of refugees were scattered amongst the plains. Much of the grass within the bounds of the temporary settlement was flattened, trampled by the Borderlanders living here now. Jak spotted a few nearby tents, but most people simply sat on the ground, gathered in small groups. Wagons, carts, and horses were strewn about the area, laden with supplies and, hopefully, food. Bearded, blue-and-gold-clad Southern Arms soldiers were everywhere, ostensibly patrolling the area to keep order.

Several dozen paces away, two soldiers noticed his arrival and stopped. They stared at him, the expressions on their faces a mixture of curiosity, distrust, and a hint of awe. The pair turned to one another and began to speak amongst themselves, repeatedly glancing in Jak's direction. A quiet argument broke out within moments.

Hearing the swoosh-swoosh sound of boots moving through grass, Jak looked down and to his right in time to see Tobias arrive at his side.

The tomble nodded in the direction of the soldiers and asked, "What's with them?"

"Well," sighed Jak. "If I had to guess, they're debating who gets to greet us, and who gets to report that two people just stepped out of thin air." In most situations, Jak would have added a smile with his quiet quip, but today was different. Smiles were not appropriate.

The soldiers apparently reached a decision as one of the men turned and began hurrying through the sea of grass and people, away from them.

"I bet he won," mused Tobias.

Jak was thinking the same thing. Suspending the ban on magic did nothing to erase people's fear and distrust of it.

A worried frown on his face, the remaining soldier began to approach them, his pace slower than one might expect under normal circumstances. While waiting for the reticent soldier, the third and final member of Jak's group arrived, again with the soft rustling of grass.

Jak glanced over and, keeping his voice low, said, "You don't have to be here. Just let me tell them—"

"No, Jak," murmured Kenders. Her voice was quiet yet firm, her face drawn, her eyes red and puffy. "I need to do this." When a quiet sigh slipped from Jak's lips, she turned to glare him. "Don't, Jak. Just don't."

Jak held her stare a moment before saying, "Fine." Both he and Nikalys had tried to encourage Kenders remain in Demetus and let Jak come alone, but she had refused. Looking forward, he said, "We'll do it your way."

The lack of sewn symbols on the soldier's tabard marked the Southern Arms man approaching them a footman. He stopped a half-dozen paces away, made a valiant effort at smiling, and said with a touch of nervousness, "Good days ahead to you all."

Jak waited for his sister to respond. When she did not, Jak moved on to the next most important member of their group and glanced down at Tobias. After a moment, the tomble looked up at him and shook his head.

"Sorry, Jak. I'm just the horse and cart to get you here and back. This is your show."

Nodding, Jak looked back to the soldier.

"What's your name, footman?"

"Gales Bienne."

"Well, then, good memories behind, Footman Bienne," said Jak. Lifting his right hand, he pointed to the single white circle stitched on his black tabard. "I'm Corporal Isaac."

The footman's eyes widened a fraction.

"Yes, Corporal. Sorry, Corporal. I apologize. Your arrival…knocked me off my guard a bit."

"Not every day you see that, is it?" asked Jak, nodding back at the where the port still hovered.

Footman Bienne's gaze shifted past them. With a quick shake of his head, he said, "No, Corporal, it's not. This would be my first." A soft pop filled the air as Tobias let the port close. The soldier's eyes widened further as he took a quick step back.

Ignoring the man's response, Jak said, "Can you take us to the command area, please?"

The man continued staring at the empty space behind them while nodding quickly.

"Of course, Corporal. Follow me."

Footman Bienne faced northeast and began walking. Tobias moved after him immediately with walking stick in hand, leaving Jak alone with Kenders. Turning to his sister, Jak said, "After you."

Without meeting his stare or responding, Kenders stepped after Tobias. Jak stared at her back as she walked through the grass, wishing there was something he could do to help her. Kept awake last night yet again by unremembered dreams, he had tried to come up with a way to ease her misery. By the time dawn came, he was still without answer. Reaching up to rub his tired eyes, he let out another sigh, dropped his hand, and followed the procession.

They garnered stares from nearly everyone they passed. Jak pretended he did not notice the whispers and pointed fingers, but he did. If he moved near enough a group of Borderlanders, he would sometimes get a word of thanks or encouragement. Word of the battle's result had been sent yesterday via a port. Jak expected that while most were happy with the result, they would have preferred a proclamation of complete victory over the Sudashians. Jak had a feeling they would be waiting for that for a long time.

Tobias' measured pace slowed their progress through the camp, but they eventually reached a concentrated group of tents. More soldiers milled about here, more wagons and horses were lined up nearby. Even though nothing marked this place as the camp's hub, Jak suspected that was exactly what it was. His hunch was confirmed when he spotted Boah standing outside one of the larger tents, a wide smile fixed on the stocky Borderlander's face. It began to fade quickly as he looked them over. Each step closer killed more of the grin.

To Boah's right stood a tall soldier, well built with a thick blonde beard and shaggy hair. Jak guessed he was looking at the captain of the Southern Arms detachment here, a Captain Lette. Once he was close enough, Jak noted the markings on the man's shoulders, confirming his suspicions. The soldier watched the trio approach with an indifferent, almost detached expression on his face.

As the footman reached the tent and stopped, the entrance flaps parted and Tiliah stepped from the dark interior.

Jak's step faltered, his heart leaping into his throat. He thought he had prepared himself for this moment. He was wrong.

He shot a worried look at Kenders, but could only see the back of her head, her Harvest-straw blonde hair blowing freely in the breeze. He said a silent prayer that she would be as fine as she kept claiming she would be.

Tiliah's gaze fell on them and a quick smile flashed over her face. Like Boah's grin, though, it slowly slipped away as her eyebrows drew together. Jak wondered just how forlorn they looked.

Tobias and Kenders drew even with the footman first and nodded quiet hellos to Boah and Tiliah. Jak arrived a moment later, offered a forced smile to them both, yet turned to the captain to speak.

"The duchess sends her good wishes, Captain Lette."

The soldier—who had been staring curiously at Tobias—lifted his gaze to Jak's face. In a bland, emotionless voice, he said, "Thank you, Corporal."

Jak waited for the man to say more, but he did not. The duchess had assured Jak that what Captain Lette lacked in charisma, he made up for in efficiency.

Looking to Boah, Jak asked, "Is this your tent, then?"

With a modest shrug, Boah said, "It's where I'm at from before sunrise to past sunset, if that's what you're asking. I sleep under the stars like the rest of us, though."

Nodding to the tent entrance, Jak asked, "May we step inside?"

"Of course," said Boah, stepping aside. "Please."

Jak motioned for Tobias and Kenders to enter first. The tomble deferred to Kenders, and after a moment, she stepped forward. Tiliah stared hard at her as she moved past, but Kenders did not meet her gaze.

Steeling himself, Jak asked, "Tiliah, will you join us as well?"

The furrow in her brow deepened.

Quickly shifting his gaze to Boah, Jak added, "Can you send for Zecus' mother, please?"

Boah flinched as though someone had started to throw a punch at him. He glanced at Tiliah, nodded quickly, and said, "I'll fetch her myself."

"What's wrong?" pressed Tiliah, her voice turning hard. "If something happened, I want to know now."

"I'll tell you everything," said Jak quietly. "I promise." He nodded to the tent. "Inside."

Tiliah stared back in the direction from where they had come.

"Where's Zecus? He promised to come as soon as he could after the battle."

Jak's heart felt as if it was being squeezed by an oligurt's fist.

"Please, Tiliah," he muttered.

Tiliah lingered a moment longer, shot a questioning glance to Tobias, but remained silent as she turned and stepped back into the tent. Tobias let out a heavy sigh and followed, leaving Jak alone with the two soldiers and Boah.

Captain Lette asked, "Am I right in assuming this meeting has little to do with the camp's organization, Corporal?"

Without taking his gaze from the slit of the tent flaps, Jak murmured, "You are, sir."

"Then I'll leave you alone," said the captain. "Footman, you're with me." He moved away, toward one of the other tents. Footman Bienne followed.

Jak looked to Boah.

"Go, Boah. Debrah only, not the children."

The skin around Boah's eyes tightened. He nodded in silence, turned, and jogged away. All alone now, Jak stared at the entrance for a long moment before stepping forward. Slipping a hand between the canvas flaps, he slid one to the side and moved into the darkened interior.

The grass inside had been trampled to the point where Jak could see dirt. The air was warmer in here than outside, laden heavy with both moisture and tension. Two small flaps in the canvas ceiling were pulled back, letting in two sunbeams that lit the square table and three chairs that sat in the middle of the tent. Tiliah and Kenders already occupied two of the seats, the third stood empty. Not seeing Tobias, Jak looked around and found the tomble standing in the corner to his left, his eyes cast downward.

Jak moved to stand beside his sister and placed a hand on her shoulder. Kenders reached up, grabbed it with one of her own, and squeezed so tight that Jak wondered if a bit of Horum's gift of strength had slipped into her blood along with Gaena's.

Tiliah stared at their clasped hands a moment, looked to Kenders face, then lifted to Jak's before speaking, her voice firm and demanding.

"One of you had better start talking. Soon."

Jak muttered, "We should—"

"Talk," ordered Tiliah. "Now."

He was determined to wait for Debrah. He did not want to have to go through this once with Tiliah and then a second time with her mother. Yet the stubborn, demanding glare from Tiliah told him she would not stop asking until he started answering. Therefore, he decided to talk, just not about why they were here.

"What have you heard about the battle so far?"

Tiliah shook her head.

"Nothing much. Only that we won."

A quiet, cynical huff slipped from Tobias. "Won?" repeated the tomble. "We did not win. We were duped."

Tiliah stared back to the corner and asked, "What does that mean?"

Jak took a deep breath and exhaled before saying, "I'll do my best to explain."

He launched into a long tale about the battle, starting with the very first howl of the mongrels. Occasionally, Tobias would interject to add something that Jak left out. Kenders remained silent.

Jak was describing the intense fighting around the two ports when Boah arrived with Debrah. After quiet, subdued hellos were exchanged, Tiliah's mother sat in the remaining open chair, opposite her daughter, while Boah moved to the other side of the table to stand across from Jak and Kenders. Once everyone was settled, Jak resumed his story, telling them of Nikalys' return to the soldiers' ring and Okollu's mad charge from the port. After a long pause and deep breath, he then began to describe the resulting battle with the demon Baaldòk.

"So, there we stood, staring at this blasted horned thing. Nikalys told me and Rhohn to go—"

"Rhohn?" interrupted Tiliah. Her eyes brightened. "Rhohn was with you?"

Looking to Tiliah, he paused before answering. This was not going to be easy.

"Yes. He and the Dust Men had come from Kenders' tower."

Her eyebrows raised a fraction.

"You're saying Rhohn helped you kill a demon?"

When Jak hesitated, Kenders squeezed the hand he still had on her shoulder. In a voice that wavered only slightly, she said, "Let me, Jak."

Jak looked down to his sister. He did not have a clear view of her face, but what he could see revealed a determined woman. Nodding, he said, "All right."

Facing Tiliah, Kenders said, "Rhohn not only helped kill the demon, he saved my brother's life. Nikalys would be dead if it were not for Rhohn's actions." She paused a moment before continuing. "But in—" She stopped again, her voice catching as the words stuck in her throat. As Jak squeezed her shoulder, she tried again. "But in saving Nikalys' life, Rhohn lost his."

Up to now, Jak's experiences with death had been direct. His parents. The soldiers on Shorn Rise. The mage at the enclave. The countless dead in Demetus. While handling it never got easier—rather it seemed to be getting harder—he decided then and there while standing in the stuffy tent and watching Tiliah's face fall as a bit of her withered away forever, that he much preferred it over this. This was infinitely worse.

"He's…dead?"

"Yes," murmured Kenders. "I'm sorry."

Tiliah's gaze shifted to the table's center, her eyes unfocused and distant. Debrah stood from her chair, scooted around Boah, and bent to a knee, throwing her arms around her daughter and murmuring quiet words of consolation. Boah looked on, an expression of sympathy mixing with sorrow on his face.

"I am sorry," said the Borderlander. "From everything you've told us, Rhohn was a good man."

Tiliah did not respond at all. Her face was blank.

A long silence stretched out, filling the tent.

After a time, Debrah looked up to Kenders and said, "You honor us by coming and telling us yourself. You did not have to do so. Surely, Zecus would have told us later."

The knot in Jak's stomach twisted even tighter.

He could not see Kenders' reaction to Debrah's words, but whatever it was prompted an anxious, worried expression to wash over the Alsher matriarch's face.

"What?" muttered Debrah. "What's wrong?"

When Kenders remained silent, Debrah's gaze shot to Jak.

"Where's Zecus? Why isn't he here?"

Tiliah finally pulled her dead-eyed stare from the table and looked up. Jak wondered how much more sorrow the young woman could take. He was about to find out. He took a deep breath, steeled himself, and spoke, trying his best to keep his own voice from wavering.

"Zecus was last seen with Sergeant Trell, chasing after a group of retreating oligurts."

Debrah's eyes grew wide, her lips parted as she took in a quick breath. Jak pressed on.

"Most of their group was found in the woods, dead."

Debrah began shaking her head, muttering, "No, no, no..."

"However," continued Jak quickly. "Neither Zecus nor the sergeant were there."

While reaching out to comfort her mother, Tiliah asked, "Why not?"

"I don't know," answered Jak honestly. "In the past two days, we've managed to recover and account for all of the Manes who lost their lives, and neither of them is among the dead. They are simply missing."

A flicker of hope danced in both women's eyes.

"Then Zecus might be alive?" asked Tiliah.

Jak swallowed his initial response that it seemed unlikely, but before he could summon a brighter answer, Kenders spoke, her voice thick and heavy.

"We can only hope, Tiliah."

She dropped her head to stare at her lap.

"We *have* to hope."

CHAPTER 60: AFTERMATH

The pair of servants exited the great hall, gently shutting the pinewood doors behind them. A low thud echoed through the cavernous hall, a sound everyone clearly heard. Only one individual in the room heard the soft click that followed as the handles engaged, though.

Sighing, Broedi pulled his gaze from the double doors and ran it along the walls and the few dozen torches that now lit the hall. Night was near and the room had grown dim. Broedi had offered to light the torches for the duke, but Rholeb insisted on having his servants do so. The sovereign did so with diplomatic grace, but the uneasy quiver in his voice was noticeable if one was listening for it, which Broedi was doing. It seemed that even though magic had helped save his city, the nobleman's distrust of the Strands remained.

The duke's misgivings did not bother Broedi. Glaciers did not melt overnight.

The room remained quiet long after the doors shut with everyone lost in his or her own thoughts, the battle still much too fresh in their mind. There were plenty of things to discuss, but not yet. Not until everyone who needed to be here was.

Other than a creak of a chair or quiet sigh, the only sound within the hall was the Drept's mournful baying that drifted through the great arched windows lining the northern wall. A number of the colored glass plates sat propped open to allow the cool evening air to wander through the hall.

"Gods, how long are they going to keep that up?"

Broedi looked up, staring at the asker of the question. Duke Rholeb rested in the Sovereign's Chair, his head tilted back against the thin, dark green cushion back, his gaze fixed on the pine-timber ceiling. Dropping his chin a bit, he stared out the windows.

"They've been at it for almost two days."

Broedi rumbled, "If I recall, my Lord, Grif Rol lasts for three."

"That is correct," murmured Khin. The aicenai stood beside one of the open windows, staring into the city.

Duke Rholeb sat a little straighter, a frown quickly spreading over his face.

"You mean that will go on for another day?"

Duchess Aleece, sitting to the duke's left, glanced over and said, "They deserve our patience, Rholeb."

"I know," muttered the duke. "I simply would like some sleep."

Seated in one of the many chairs haphazardly arranged before the two sovereigns, Jak offered, "Perhaps you could ask Okollu if they might howl a little quieter?" The young man's eyes had been closed for so long that Broedi had thought him asleep. "I expect he'd be happy to accommodate your request."

With a flicker of hope on his face and in his voice, Duke Rholeb asked, "Do you think he might?"

A tiny smile tickled the corner of Jak's mouth.

"Gods, no. I already tried. The mon—ah...pardon me, the kur-surus was, shall we say, 'not amiable to my request.' Although he might be more open if the request came from someone more important?"

"So he *will* listen to me then?" asked Duke Rholeb.

"Begging your pardon, my Lord," said Jak. Cracking an eye, he rolled his head over to look at Nikalys. "But I was thinking of someone more important to Okollu's pack."

Nikalys sat in another chair, his right elbow propped on an armrest, holding his chin in hand. He had chosen a seat at the group's edge, furthest away from the windows and the last light of day. Staring at the flagstone floor, his face blank and his mind clearly elsewhere, he muttered, "No, Jak."

Broedi frowned slightly. Nikalys sounded thrice as tired as he looked.

Jak shifted his gaze from Nikalys to the pair of tombles sitting beside one another. Tobias appeared relaxed in his seat, his walking stick leaning against his chair. He had his eyes closed as well. Nundle was on Tobias' right, his mass of red hair glowing in the torchlight. The tomble had lost his hat during the battle and had not yet found a replacement.

The slight, weary smile on Jak's face spread a little wider.

"In that case, I nominate Nundle."

The tomble's head snapped up.

"You what?"

Jak nodded in the direction of the windows.

"I think you should be the one to ask Okollu and his pack to quiet down."

Nundle's green eyes went round.

"Are you mad? How could you possibly think that would be a good idea?"

"Oh, I don't," answered Jak. "I was merely jesting."

Relief quickly spread over Nundle's face, followed a moment later by a good-natured glare in Jak's direction.

"I hope a hundred fire ants crawl into your underbreeches tonight."

A quiet laughter, welcome by most, rippled through the room. Broedi was glad to see smiles again. There had been too few in recent days. He turned his gaze to Kenders. Sabine sat beside her, holding her hand, patting it lightly. Broedi had hoped Nundle's quip might summon even a slight smile to Kenders' face. It did not.

Broedi shook his head, torn. He should chastise her for her reckless actions atop the tower. She still did not grasp how serious it was to give herself over to Gaena's gift. There was a terminal limit to her ability. However, now was not the time for sharp words. She was grieving. And as much as he wanted to comfort her, he had remained distant. She—like Nikalys—needed to learn the harsh truth of war. People died.

He shifted his gaze to Nikalys. The young man had fully recovered from his injuries. Broedi had been wondering if the gift of immortality given to the White Lions by Sarphia had passed to the Progeny, and Nikalys' condition seemed to indicate that was the case.

Nikalys sat in silence, undoubtedly brooding over the lives he had taken, just as Aryn had always done. Unlike after the Battle of Shorn Rise, however, Broedi chose to leave Nikalys alone. Wren was right. Broedi could not hold their hands. The Progeny needed to grow up.

Sensing Broedi's stare, Nikalys lifted his head and held the hillman's gaze. Torchlight glinted in the young man's brown eyes, along with the same sort of agony Broedi had seen far too often in Aryn's stare. Leaving the young man alone for now, Broedi looked away.

Wren, the final member of their small assembly sat in his chair, stroking his hair, a frown on his face. The tijul met Broedi's gaze, gave a quick, disdainful shake of his head, and looked away. Broedi guessed it was taking all of Wren's self-control not to snap at them for enjoying a moment of light levity.

A rattle and gentle creak announced the arrival of another. Looking over his shoulder, Broedi saw a single door along the southern wall open. Gamin strode through the entryway, shut the wooden door softly behind him, and walked toward the assembly. The tall, muscled mage was still dressed in his Shadow Mane robes.

One more, and the meeting could begin.

As Gamin reached the small gathering, all eyes turned to him. They knew Broedi had sent for the mage, but—other than Khin—they did not know why. Broedi glanced at the aicenai and found Khin's cold, blue-eyed gaze already fixed on Gamin.

Twenty paces from the Sovereign's Chair, Gamin halted and gave a short bow. "My Lord." He angled to face Duchess Aleece, sitting in what traditionally was the chair reserved for Rholeb's wife. "My Lady."

After both sovereigns returned the greeting, the duchess turned to the duke and asked, "May I speak first, Rholeb?"

With a dismissive wave of his hand, the duke said, "Speak whenever you like, Aleece. I have little use for formality—" He cut off as the tone of the Drept's howls shifted.

The cries of Grif Rol took on a new harmony, haunting and discordant. Those in the hall stared to the windows and listened quietly. While Broedi thought the strange chorus uniquely beautiful, most in the room wore uneasy frowns.

Seeing their discomfort, Broedi reached for Strands of Air, knitted them into a quick Weave, and directed it toward one of the windows. Before the pattern had settled over an open pane, Khin was duplicating his effort. Realizing what they were doing, Nundle helped seal the openings as well. Wren, while wholly capable of touching Air, sat and watched. Kenders did not aid either. She did not even lift her gaze from the floor.

Within moments, the kur-surus' howls cut off. The gentle evening breeze still wafted through the windows, but the Weaves prevented any sound from passing into the Duke's Hall.

Duke Rholeb stared to the north wall.

"Are they done?"

"No, my Lord," rumbled Broedi. He sat upright, his chair groaning in protest at the shift in weight. "Some of us simply put measures in place to quiet their calls. I hope you do not mind the liberty we took."

"Mind?" asked Duke Rholeb. His eyebrows arched high. "I am wondering why in the Nine Hells you didn't do that earlier."

Broedi started to smile when he heard a soft click at the back of the hall. Turning in his chair, he watched the massive, dual pinewood doors swing open. The evening breeze, now offered a new outlet, picked up, tickling the room's torches. The wind's direction outside must have shifted, for the surge of air rushing through the windows brought with it the funeral pyres' stench. The thousands of oligurt corpses had been stacked in enormous piles west of the city and were now alight. They had been burning for over a day now, their morbid glow lighting up the marshes at night.

Glancing about the room, Broedi spotted a few queasy expressions and considered modifying the Weaves to keep the air out, but he restrained himself. They should get used to the odor.

Looking back to the doors, Broedi was surprised to see two figures moving through the entryway. While he had only requested the presence of one, he saw no harm in both being here.

Alumon, the only member of the four Mataan to come to Demetus' aid, shuffled into the hall, studying the room with its strange, reflective, black eyes, the draft blowing through the door rustling its grassy hair. Accompanying the buhanik was Fingard, Talulot's former aki-mahet slave. While the pair strode through the hall side-by-side as equals, a servant stepped inside and shut the doors.

Halting beside Gamin, Fingard and Alumon faced the two nobles.

"Greetings, friend of Light-From-The-West," whistled the buhanik. "I am called Alumon. May the sun shine on your children."

This was the first time either noble had met with the buhanik. The chaos both during and after the Battle of the Sandwalls—as people were already calling it—had prevented any sort of formal introductions. Both the duke and duchess conducted themselves with appropriate aplomb, yet Broedi detected a hint of child-like awe in their expressions. Duke Rholeb rose from his chair, stepped forward, and offered a formal bow.

"Welcome to my hall, Alumon. I am in your debt for the aid you and your kind lent. Please accept my condolences for your losses."

Four of the ten buhanik—including their guide, Talulot—had perished in the battle, suffering irreparable harm from the Desert Fire mages' flames and lightning.

Alumon gently swayed side to side, its bark-like skin creaking quietly.

"Those who wilted knew the danger of facing the great shadow."

"And their sacrifice will not be forgotten," said Duke Rholeb. He shifted his gaze to Fingard. "Nor will those made by your tribe. Their deeds will live forever in song and word. Thank you."

Fingard raised his hands, clasped them before his chest, and dipped his head.

"Your lordship is most gracious."

Duke Rholeb turned to his left and said, "May I present Duchess Aleece?"

As the duchess rose from her seat also to thank Fingard and Alumon, Broedi looked over to Khin. The aicenai's gaze was quickly shifting between the two new arrivals and Gamin. Broedi would have liked to know what he was seeing.

Duchess Aleece was in the midst of offering her condolences when Alumon abruptly swiveled away from her, turning to stare at Kenders and Sabine. The duchess trailed off as Alumon peered at the pair, its dry grassy hair rustling in the breeze. After a long, drawn out moment, he whistled, "You are like Light-From-The-West, are you not?"

Broedi sat forward. This was one of the reasons he had asked Alumon to come today.

Nodding, Kenders said, "I am his sister."

The buhanik tilted its head, shifting its gaze to Sabine.

"I was speaking of you both."

Sabine held the buhanik's steady, inquisitive gaze and remained quiet.

Alumon studied the pair in complete silence, its glossy black eyes fixed on them both. After several moments, Kenders shifted nervously in her chair. Duke Rholeb cleared his throat as though he was preparing to speak, but Broedi lifted a quick hand, indicating that the duke remain quiet. Finally, as Broedi had hoped, Alumon raised its left, branch-like hand and closed its eyes.

Everyone remained impossibly quiet as Alumon swayed side-to-side, its arm outstretched. Eventually, the buhanik stopped moving, dropped its arm, and opened its eyes. With its stare fixed squarely on Kenders, it whistled, "You shine bright. As bright as Light-From-The-West." It twisted around to face Nikalys. "Yet whereas he glows like a thousand suns—" it turned back to Kenders "—you shine like a thousand rainbows after the storm."

Kenders stared up at the buhanik with a look of deep bewilderment. For his part, Broedi was intrigued.

Turning its gaze to Sabine, Alumon whistled, "Your light is faint. Like a half moon on a foggy night." It paused, tilted its head, and added, "Noteworthy."

Broedi allowed himself a small, satisfied smile. Sabine's heritage was confirmed in his mind.

Kenders glanced at Sabine before leaning forward in her chair.

"I don't understand. I...shine?"

"You do, Colors-From-The-West," whistled Alumon. "Brightly. Our lore only speaks of Light-From-The-West. You and Moon-In-The-Clouds are unexpected. The Enlightened Oracle never spoke of you."

Duchess Aleece spoke up, saying, "And that brings us to why we are here this evening." She moved to her chair, sat down, and turned her gaze upon Broedi. Her eyes alight with curiosity, she said, "The hall is yours, Broedi."

Chairs creaked as everyone shifted to stare at him.

When he had pulled the duchess aside earlier and asked that she arrange this assembly, she had of course inquired as to its purpose. All he had shared was it had something to do with the Goddess Indrida.

With a polite nod, Broedi rumbled, "Thank you, my Lady." Pushing himself from his chair, he looked to those still standing and said, "Those of you who can, please, sit. Make yourselves comfortable."

Duke Rholeb returned to resting in the Sovereign's Chair while both Fingard and Gamin selected an empty seat. Alumon remained standing, as did Khin.

Wanting a clear view of the room, Broedi moved to stand beside Nikalys. Khin was against the opposite wall, watching in more ways than one. Crossing his thick arms over his chest, Broedi fixed his gaze on the youngest Isaac sibling.

"Kenders, share with us what happened when you stopped the fibríaal, please."

Kenders blinked, obviously surprised by the request. She glanced around the room, her gaze lingering on Gamin, the new arrivals, and the duke.

"Are you sure?"

She was wary and rightfully so. Not everyone here knew of Indrida's involvement.

Broedi nodded once, rumbling, "I am."

Kenders hesitated a moment before saying, "If you think it best."

Sitting a little taller in her chair, she began to recount everything that had occurred the moment she set her foot upon the tower stairs. When she reached her encounter with the unusual woman, Broedi looked to Khin and waited. The aicenai's gaze was locked on Gamin and remained so as Kenders described the woman's appearance. A moment after she mentioned the woman's colorful dress, Khin looked to Broedi and shook his head once.

A slight frown spread over Broedi's face. He had hoped for more. Shifting his stare to Gamin, he nibbled on the inside of his lip while waiting for Kenders to complete her story.

"Honestly," said Kenders. "I have started to wonder if I imagined it. Perhaps I passed out for a moment and dreamed her."

"She was not imagined," rumbled Broedi, finally pulling his gaze from Gamin. "Nor did she come from a dream."

Looking to him, Kenders said, "How can you be sure? Broedi, I'm the *only* one who saw her."

"Two days ago, atop that tower, yes," said the hillman. "But others have seen her before then."

"Who?" asked Jak.

Turning to Alumon, Broedi rumbled, "In the lore of the Mataan, how is Indrida described?"

"'A creature, woman and yet not, bathed in the light of a thousand suns, draped in the colors of a thousand flowers.'"

Broedi let the buhanik's words settle, wondering how long it would take before someone made the connection. He did not have to wait long.

"Hold a moment," mumbled Kenders. With a look of complete incredulity, she asked, "Are you saying it was *Indrida* on the tower?"

Broedi nodded.

"I believe so."

A moment of quiet filled the room.

"So…" muttered Jak. "Does that mean the Gods are helping us now?"

"Only if an Assembly has been formed," said Tobias. "And if that had happened, I would have expected they might notify us somehow."

"A note would have been nice," muttered Wren. "Something simple, like 'To those of you trying to stop the God of Chaos from ripping apart the world, we have decided to lend aid.'"

"I agree," rumbled Broedi. "Had an Assembly been formed, we would have known it. The Celystiela involved would not need to meet in secret atop a tower in the midst of a battle. They would be able to aid openly."

"Then, if there's no Assembly," began Jak. "How do you explain Indrida? Both on the tower, and her visit to the thorn all those years ago? Did Nelnora lie to you? Again?"

A long sigh slipped from Broedi's lips.

"It is possible. Likely, even. But I do not know for sure."

Sabine said, "None of that matters. Assembly or not, Indrida was on that tower. Which leads to the only question we should be asking: Why? Indrida has now inserted herself twice to help shape events to her liking. Why?"

Broedi withheld a slight smile. It was an excellent question.

The room remained silent as everyone waited for someone else to offer a prospective answer. Broedi would be surprised if any of them could. He had been trying since leaving Buhaylunsod and had yet to come to a sensible conclusion. What he needed was more information. Turning to the man he hoped could provide it, he rumbled, "Gamin?"

The mage was sitting in his chair, his head tilted down with chin in hand, gazing at the floor.

"Yes?"

"When Kenders shared what she saw on the tower, what did you say to her?"

Gamin dropped his hand into his lap and looked up. His gaze darted to Kenders, back to Broedi, and then—oddly enough—to Jak.

"Ah...I do not remember."

Sitting forward in her chair, Kenders twisted around to face the man.

"I do. You said you believed me."

Gamin stared at the young woman, a slight frown on his face.

"I don't recall saying that."

"Then let me refresh your memory," said Tobias. "Khin said, 'I believe you.' Then you—with a rather strange look in your eye, I might add—said, 'As do I.'"

Gamin's gaze shot to Tobias before returning—again—to Jak.

Sitting forward in her chair, Duchess Aleece spoke, her tone crisp and direct.

"Gamin, is there something you are not sharing with us?"

The mage's posture was rigid, the small muscles in his cheeks twitching as he worked his jaw.

"Perhaps."

"Either there is or there is not," replied the duchess.

Gamin stared at the noblewoman and, after a moment, nodded once, mumbling, "There is." His tense countenance cracked and his shoulders slumped. "I am sorry, but..." He trailed off, shifted his gaze to Jak, and asked, "Your father enjoyed telling some good stories, did he not?"

While the mage's question took them all by surprise, Broedi sensed there was a point to it.

It took Jak a moment or two before he responded with a bewildered, "Pardon?"

"Thad's tales. They were grand, weren't they? I told him a number of times that he should leave Claw and be a playman. He would have made good coin at it. I doubt Marie would have much enjoyed the life, though."

"What are you talking about?" asked Jak.

Gamin paused a moment, glancing between the three Isaac siblings.

"You know your parents met in Fernsford, yes?"

"Of course," said Kenders. "Father was a smith's apprentice. Mother was a tailor."

Nodding, Gamin said, "Yes, and when they married, they lived across the way from my family's bakery, in the smithy with Master Claude."

"Who?" asked Jak.

"The blacksmith who apprenticed Thad," said Gamin. "Your parent's never mentioned him?"

"Not to me," said Jak. He glanced at his siblings for confirmation and received quick shakes of the head from both. Nikalys had finally stopped staring at the floor, his gaze now locked on their parent's friend.

A sorrowful expression took root on Gamin's face as he muttered, "After what happened, I'm not surprised…" He trailed off and went silent, his eyes glazing over.

"Gamin?" prompted Broedi. "What does this have to do with what Kenders saw on the tower?"

"Everything," said the mage. "Absolutely everything." Folding his hands in his lap, he took a deep breath, exhaled slowly, and looked between the three siblings. "Do you remember why your parents left Fernsford?"

Kenders nodded, saying, "A fire destroyed the smithy."

"And half the market district," added Nikalys.

"Both true," replied Gamin. "Did they tell you that we fled the city as Fernsford burned? The very night of the fire?"

"You 'fled?'" asked Jak.

"Absolutely," said Gamin. "As fast as we could, we ran into the night." The skin around his eyes twitched. "You could see the fire's glow from miles away."

"Why were you running?" asked Kenders.

"Because I caused the fire," said Gamin.

Broedi's eyebrows lifted in surprise. This was the first he had heard of this.

"*You* caused the Great Fire of Fernsford?" asked the duchess.

"I could argue the Constables are to blame," sighed Gamin. "But, yes. When they came to take me away, I called the Strands that set the city ablaze. I am sorry, my Lady."

"For what are you apologizing?" asked Duchess Aleece in surprise.

"For firing a quarter of Fernsford. We had no idea of the extent of the damage until word reached us many turns later."

"That was decades ago, Gamin, long before I sat in the Sovereign's Chair. I vaguely remember my father having to deal with the aftermath, but I hold no ill will toward you if it happened as you say it did."

Relief flooded Gamin's face.

"You are very gracious, my Lady."

"Gamin?" rumbled Broedi. "Why are you telling us this now? What exactly happened in Fernsford?"

The mage eyed Broedi and gave a short nod.

"In the Summer of my fourteenth year, I discovered I could touch Strands of Fire. Then Charge a short time later. Air, a couple of years later. I was terrified at first, but then a little curious. Soon, I was taking every chance I could to experiment with them."

"Weren't you afraid of being discovered?" asked Kenders.

"Gods, yes," said Gamin. "But wisdom comes with age and I was quite young. The choices I made were poor ones. Eventually, the Constables became aware there was a mage in the city. About the same time, I noticed that Marie and Thaddeus started to look at me differently. Turns out, they knew my secret and kept it for me. They protected me because I was their friend." His expression darkened. "Even when the Trackers came to take me away."

Again, Gamin went quiet for a few moments. When he resumed his tale, his voice was husky and thick with emotion.

"I do not wish to relive much of that icy night. Suffice it to say your parents attempted to sacrifice themselves for me. The Tracker threatened my family if I did not cooperate. He threatened Thaddeus, Marie, and Master Claude. He…made me angry."

He leaned forward, dropped his head in hands, and pressed his fingers against his temples.

"A short time later, Constables and soldiers were dead in the street, along with…along with Master Claude. He was trying to help me and got struck down by a soldier…"

He stopped a moment, gathering himself.

"My…actions had set alight the thatchers' roof beside our bakery. Straw burns quickly. It was windy…" He trailed off and shrugged. "The fire was spreading fast. Thaddeus and Marie knew we needed to run. So we did. We ran, leaving our old lives behind. Thaddeus, a promising life as a blacksmith. Sevan and I, our parents. Marie, the same."

His eyes glistened in the evening's torchlight.

"*Hundreds* that night died because of me."

"You were right earlier," rumbled Broedi "The blame lies at the threshold of the Constables, not you. If you had not been persecuted, perhaps none of that would have happened."

The mage shook his head slowly while reaching up to wipe away the wetness from his eyes.

"Ifs and perhaps cannot undo what's been done, Broedi. People died because of me."

Seeing little chance of convincing the man otherwise, Broedi rumbled softly, "So you fled, then?"

Gamin glanced up and nodded.

"South. Into the Blackbark Forest. For two turns, we meandered about, never staying in one place more than a day or two. We were afraid the authorities might find us. Soldiers, perhaps Constables. Every morning I awoke thinking that would be the day we were going to be caught. We never were, though."

"One bitterly cold night, I used a minor Weave of Fire to light a campfire. A short time later, a man stepped from the woods into the glow of the fire. He said he was a local trapper, but in actuality, he was a mage. *And* a member of the Manes. He joined our camp for the night and, unbeknownst to us at the time, used a few Weaves of Will to extract our story. The next morning, he invited us to come with him. As he promised protection from the Constables, we went, of course."

"A few weeks later, we arrived at Storm Island and were quickly accepted by the community. Marie was an accomplished tailor. And even as a journeyman, Thaddeus was the best blacksmith Claw had seen in decades. I studied with the mages, learning how to control what I was. And Sevan—" he smiled slightly "—well, Sevan was born with a golden tongue. He could talk his way past a pack of feral wolves if he wanted to."

Feeling a touch impatient with the man's tale, Broedi rumbled, "I still fail to see how any of this pertains to Indrida."

The mage peered over at him.

"For you to understand the destination, I needed to take you on the journey."

"Might the destination be coming soon?" asked Wren.

"We are close," said Gamin, nodding slowly. "Something happened during our last night in Fernsford. Something *I* did not learn of until we had been living at the enclave for a time."

Hopeful, Broedi prompted, "And what might that be?"

"Five years after we arrived, Thaddeus and I were sitting alone in a tavern in Claw. It was Rintira's Leisure Day and the town had celebrated appropriately. Claiming exhaustion, Marie had excused herself early—" he glanced at Jak "—she was carrying you at the time. After one or six cups too many, Sevan had left as well. I don't remember how, but somehow Thad and I got to talking about our escape of Fernsford. I asked him—jovially, mind you—if Marie and he had second thoughts about helping me escape."

A harsh chuckle slipped from the mage.

"His demeanor changed quicker than the weather at Storm Island. One moment, he was smiling and jesting, and the next, he was deadly quiet. He stares at me across the table and says, 'Can you keep a secret?' I claimed I could and he proceeded to tell a story that, until two days ago, I thought was nothing but the ramblings of a wine-addled friend."

"You are talking about our father, yes?" asked Nikalys. "He never drank more than a cup of wine at any festival."

Gamin looked over at the young man.

"Perhaps he learned his lesson. Too much of the stuff loosens the tongue. He certainly would not have shared the tale he did otherwise. He sought me out the next day—bleary-eyed, mind you—and made a point to laugh off his story as a playman's tale."

"What did he share?" asked Broedi.

Looking up to him, Gamin said, "That when he returned to his room in the smithy, he found a strange woman there. A woman 'draped in a dress that had been dipped in a rainbow.' That she 'shimmered in light as though she stood on a mountain's peak at midday."

His subdued announcement was met with stunned silence. Even Broedi was taken aback a bit. He had suspected Gamin was harboring some sort of knowledge of Indrida's involvement, but nothing like this.

Gamin continued, saying, "He said the woman—Hells, I might as well name her for who she was, shouldn't I? He said that Indrida ordered him and Marie to leave Fernsford that night. She told them they were 'important.'" He turned his gaze to Nikalys and Kenders. "We all know why, now, don't we?"

The pair, along with Jak, remained quiet, clearly taken aback by Gamin's revelation.

An amused chuckle slipped from Wren, as unexpected as a seagull's cry in the middle of the Borderlands.

"Based on those faces, might I assume your foster parents never shared this with you?"

Kenders, Jak, and Nikalys all shook their heads slowly, almost in unison.

"No," mumbled Jak. "This was one story Father never told us."

Nundle chimed in quietly, "So Indrida has inserted herself into…whatever is happening three times, then?"

"Three times of which we are aware," rumbled Broedi.

"Oh," muttered the tomble. "Good point."

Everyone in the room went quiet as they tried to sort out this new information. After a few moments, Nikalys sat tall in his chair, cleared his throat and announced, "Well, that settles things, then."

Broedi, along with everyone else, turned to stare at the young man. Nikalys pushed himself from his chair and stood tall, placing his hands on his hips.

"We have two tasks laid before us."

The confidence with which he spoke surprised Broedi. He himself had yet to come to any sort of conclusion as to what their next move should be.

"And what might those be?"

"First, we need to find out where the bulk of Tandyr's army truly is. We all agree now that Demetus was merely a ruse to keep us occupied, yes?"

Heads around the room bobbed up and down.

Turning to face Duke Rholeb, Nikalys said, "My Lord, send messengers to every town and city in the Marshlands, seeking *any* word of the Sudashians' passage. Rumors, whispers, whatever. Also, I would like as many scouts as you can spare to your northern border. Duke Everett has thrown his lot in with the Cabal. Perhaps Tandyr has gone there with intentions to invade the northern duchies."

"What are you basing this on?" asked the duke. "Logic or intuition?"

"Both," said Nikalys. "More of the latter than the former, though."

Duke Rholeb's eyebrows rose high.

"You're asking me to take a lot of definitive action based on a guess, young man."

"Yes, I am," agreed Nikalys. "But we cannot wait around, hoping Miriel Syncent will smuggle us another message about Tandyr's plan. We need information and we won't get it by sitting here. Send the messengers and scouts, my Lord."

Duke Rholeb sat in silence for a moment, rubbing his fingers over his moustache, before nodding once.

"Agreed."

"Good," said Nikalys. Turning to Broedi, he added, "Secondly, we need to know what Nelnora's true intentions are. To my eye, she is putting the outcome of this struggle in jeopardy. Although, to be honest, I am starting to wonder if that might not be her goal."

Broedi frowned slightly. Nikalys had just given voice to one of his own concerns.

Sabine asked, "Why would she do that?"

"Don't forget who we're dealing with," said Tobias. "Nelnora's dominion is balance and order. She strives for equilibrium. Too much good in the world is as abhorrent to her as too much evil."

Jak muttered, "I would say evil's got the better hand at the moment."

"Agreed," conceded Broedi. "Yet Nikalys is correct. We must try to determine what her intentions are."

Reaching up to scratch his chin, Tobias asked, "I suppose that means you think we should go back to the Seat of Nelnora, then?"

"I do," said Nikalys. "I'm tired of the Gods and Goddesses playing with our lives like we're some blasted peg on a radigan board. *My* fate should be decided by one person alone: *me*." Looking around the room, he added, "I'm not the only one who feels that way, am I?"

As most everyone nodded in agreement, Broedi shared a look with Tobias and Wren, silently inquiring what they thought of Nikalys' plan. Both nodded.

"Agreed, then," said Broedi.

"And what if she won't tell us the truth?" asked Jak. "Or worse, what if she does and tells us the Gods aren't going to help. What then?"

As Nikalys turned to his brother, his face moved from a shadow into the light. A set of deep lines spanned his forehead. The muscles in his jaw rippled.

"Then we fight the blasted Cabal ourselves."

The skin around his eyes twitched.

"*Alone.*"

Epilogue

Year's End, 4999

A tiny vibration ran through the cold, damp stone floor.

The lone figure in the darkened cell opened his eyes and looked to the dim rectangle on the far wall. Stubborn bits of light fought their way through the crevices of the door he knew was there. Lying on his side with his bearded cheek pressed on stone, he stared and waited, wondering if he had imagined the sensation, hoping he had.

He could not judge how long it had been since her last visit, whether it had been days or weeks. The gloom of his windowless cell was constant. There was no day here. No night. The only way to mark the passage of time was counting the number of putrid breaths he drew, and he had ceased doing that a long time past. Years ago. Decades perhaps.

As he stared at the dim edges of the doorway, waiting, a broken part of him rose up inside, silently pleading the door to open, yearning for a break to his life's maddening monotony. He shoved that part of him away, knowing what was to follow should she be coming.

A deep thud filled the hall outside, followed by a hollow, echoing clang. Dread—and a bit of relief—washed over him.

He tried to push himself up from the cold stone, determined to meet his visitor on his own two feet, but his first effort was a futile one. His captor fed him enough food to keep him alive, nothing more. The trough in his cell was full of water that was so dirty and rank that he only drank when he had to. The dark, crawly things living in it seemed to like it fine, but he did not.

Grunting, he tried again to rise from the floor. He failed to stand, yet managed to shift into a sitting position. The effort left him panting and exhausted. He reached up to pull back his long hair and smooth his matted beard as best he could. He slowed his breathing, composing himself for what was to come.

In a cracked, dry as dust voice, he whispered, "Stay strong."

Scuffling footsteps approached the other side of the cell door.

"Be resolute."

He lifted his head to face the entryway.

"Live well."

With his gaze fixed on the dim rectangle, he summoned forth an old memory and locked the scene in his mind's eye. It was the only way he could survive these sessions.

"Love fully."

A young boy with sandy brown hair matching his own scrambled into his lap and, using the broken speech of a toddler, demanded to see the baby he held cradled in his arms. Smiling wide, he helped situate the boy on his right knee, careful to ensure the toddler did not inadvertently bump his new sister. The baby cooed softly, drawing the attention of father and son alike. Tiny curls of golden hair the color of Harvest straw poked from under the blanket wrapped tightly around her. Her rich, brown eyes stared up at him, wide and alert. He shifted in his chair, trying to get comfortable, and accidently let the sunlight streaming through the window shine in her face. Her eyes flashed hazel before she quickly shut them against the sudden brightness. A small whimper of discomfort slipped from her, prompting the boy to reach out and grasp his sister's hand.

In the cell, the man smiled, happy and interminably sad at the same time.

A click and a clink announced the door's lock had been undone. Setting his jaw, the man stared at the lines of light. His eyes turned cold.

The heavy iron door opened with a rattle and swung into the cell slowly, letting in a rush of light. Squinting against the sudden brightness, the man lifted a hand to shade his eyes as a waft of sweet, fresh air washed over him. The hallway beyond was lit with torches and magical lanterns alike.

Before the pain began anew, he took a brief moment to play a game with himself. Betting that it was night, he blinked repeatedly, trying to see past the figure looming in the doorway and down the long hallway. At the far end was the only window he had seen in years. It was dark outside. He smiled, right yet again.

His captor spoke, her voice echoing with a dark and worrisome power.

"You are in a good mood today."

The man shifted his gaze to the silhouetted figure. Light from the hallway shone through the edges of her long, lustrous hair, creating a haloed line around her head. It reminded him of the sun shining behind a dark and stormy cloud.

"I had a good rest," rasped the man.

"Did you now?"

Nodding, he turned his head to look about his filthy cell.

"Although I would sleep better if I had that mat I requested. When might I expect that to arrive?"

"And here I was, considering having a bed made for you. With a goose-feather mattress, even. But if you would prefer a mat, I can surely accommodate that."

Her sarcastic tone triggered a flicker of alarm in his chest. His captor did not have a sense of humor.

He hesitated for only a moment before replying, "How kind of you, Cadrin. The bed sounds wondrous. I rescind my request for the mat."

Cadrin tilted her head to the side while remaining ominously silent. He could feel her eyes studying him and was glad he could not see them. They made him uneasy.

The silence between them stretched out.

His gaze flicked down the hallway and, for a brief moment, he considered another attempt at escape. As his gaze locked onto a spot below the window, Cadrin spoke.

"Oh, please try. I would enjoy watching you fail again."

She was right. Any attempt to flee would be futile. The part of him that had once made him special was still there—he could sense it—but his body was incapable of responding to his will. Years of malnutrition had withered him. With a defeated sigh, he dropped his gaze to the floor.

"As I thought," muttered Cadrin. "A pity, though. You were much more fun to play with before you had given up."

The man glared at her and spat, "I have *not* given up." The strength in his voice surprised him.

"No?" inquired Cadrin as she took a few, slow steps into the cell. "Are you sure about that?"

He stared at the robed figure still shrouded by the shadows, drew in a quiet breath, and let it back out again.

"Can we just begin today's session? I have a busy day ahead of me and you are wasting my time."

"There will be no session today."

Unable to keep the surprise from his voice, the man asked, "Why not?"

"There is nothing you can tell us that we do not already know for ourselves now."

A sick, empty feeling gripped the man's chest. Trying to keep his voice even, he asked, "What does that mean?"

Cadrin lowered herself into a crouch, arranging her robes as she knelt. The soft, bluish tint of one of the magical lantern lights illuminated the left side of her face, revealing pale, wrinkled skin. A blood-red pupil surrounded by a cat-like, bright orange iris, peered at him. She spoke, her voice soft and full of wicked anticipation.

"I have a recent development to share with you."

He remained silent, waiting, the pit in his chest yawning wide.

An evil, supremely confident grin crept over her face.

"We found them."

He shook his head, muttering, "You have tried this tact before, Cadrin. Didn't work then, won't work now."

The smile on her face widened.

"Ah, but *this* time I speak the truth."

"Forgive me if I don't believe you."

Cadrin remained motionless, her unnatural eye boring into him, studying, watching. Her smile widened a fraction more as she whispered, "Believe whatever you like, you poor, broken, foolish man. I no longer care."

With a great swish of robes, she stood, spun around, and strode to the door. Reaching out with a pale hand, she gripped the ring handle, stopped, and half-turned to look over her shoulder.

"Apparently, your son looked just like you. At least how you did when you first came to us. He was a strapping lad from all accounts. Good with the blade, too."

Bile rose from his stomach and caught in the back of his throat. He struggled to show no reaction, not wanting to grant her satisfaction or confirmation. She could be guessing.

"And your little girl?" continued Cadrin. "She grew into a true beauty, her hair golden and bright. Just like her mother's."

He bit the inside of his cheek so hard that blood filled his mouth. Any bit of hope that Cadrin was lying went plummeting down a deep, black chasm inside his soul.

With a soft, delighted chuckle, Cadrin said, "You would have been proud of them. They fought valiantly."

Unable to help himself, he asked, "What does that mean?"

"It means what it means. They fought valiantly. Then they lost, dying as Demetus' walls came tumbling down on them both. How sad for you."

"Impossible," muttered the man. "You are lying! The prophecy—"

"Is wrong, apparently," interjected Cadrin. "It would seem Indrida was wrong. Again."

Cadrin, the mortal incarnation of the God of Pain, turned back to the hall, stepped through the entryway, and began pulling the door shut.

"Have a good night, Aryn. Sleep well."

Aryn watched the door shut with a resounding thud, plunging the cell into blackness. Utterly numb inside, he dropped his head into his hands and squeezed his eyes shut tight.

"No...please, no..."

APPENDIX

The Gods

The High Host—the nine good Gods and Goddesses

Name	Other Names/References	Sphere
Ceruna	The Hammer of Innocence	Purity, Hope, and Justice
Khanos	The Vital Soul	Life
Luraana	The Villager	Community
Mu	The Bright Blade	Light, Sun, Honor, War
Rheoc	Delver of the Deep	Earth, Mines, Smiths
Roden	The Rebellious One	Change and Freedom
Sormina	Graceful Guider of Hearts	Beauty and Love
Sutri	Guardian of Eras	Summer and Time
Tirnu	The Ruler of Rules	Law

The Gods and Goddess that are Neither

Name	Other Names/References	Sphere
Ashana	The Inspired One	Ideas and Innovation
Chalchalu	Filler of Purses	Commerce and Wealth
Duryn	The Great Artisan	Industry and Crafters
Gaena	The Master Weaver	Magic
Greya	Cold Twister of Fate	Winter and Fate
Horum	The Strong Arm	Strength and Athletic Skill
Indrida	The Enlightened Oracle	Knowledge and Prophecy
Lamoth	She Who Walks the Woods	Forest and Wild Nature
Maeana	The Final Friend	Death
Nelnora	Watcher of the World	Civilization and Balance
Ketus	The Shrewd Fox	Shadows, Cunning and Luck
Rintira	Dodgy Gatherer	Autumn and Trickery
Saewyn	The Untamed	Spring, Sea, and Storm
Sarphia	Eternal Queen	Immortality
Thonda	The Great Tracker	Beasts and Hunt

The Cabal—the nine evil Gods (None has a name)

	Other Names/References	Sphere
	The Eternal Anarchist	Chaos
	The Great Quarreler	Strife
	The Bringer of Misery	Sorrow
	Agony's Friend	Pain
	Immortal Teller of Lies	Deception
	The Mad One	Madness
	Bearer of Grudges	Vengeance
	Terror's Maiden	Fear
	The Loather of All	Hate

THE CALENDAR

The calendar of Terrene is a symmetrical one. Some scholars suggest the Gods altered the world and the moons to facilitate such a perfectly aligned set of dates. A year on Terrene is exactly 360 days, divided into 12 turns of 28 days per turn. A week is seven days long; four weeks make up a single turn.

Between each turn is a two-day period that belongs to neither the turn before nor the turn that follows. They are commonly referred to as Days of Leisure, and throughout the year are used for feasts and other celebrations.

The turns of the year and the Days of Leisure between are as follows:

Turn of Khanos – named for Khanos, the God of Life (Winter in the southern
    hemisphere, Summer in the northern hemisphere)
Days of Leisure for Khanos and Indrida
Turn of Greya – named for Greya, the Goddess of Winter and Fate
Days of Leisure for Greya and Sarphia
Turn of Duryn – named for Duryn, the God of Industry and Crafters
Days of Leisure for Duryn and Ketus
Turn of Roden – named for Roden, the God of Change and Freedom
Days of Leisure for Roden and Rheoc
Turn of Saewyn – named for Saewyn, the God of Spring, Sea, and
    the Wilderness
Days of Leisure for Saewyn and Nelnora
Turn of Sormina – named for Sormina, the Goddess of Beauty and Love
Days of Leisure for Sormina and Tirnu
Turn of Lamoth – named for Lamoth, the Goddess of the Forest and
    Wild Nature (Winter in the northern hemisphere, Summer in the
    southern hemisphere)
Days of Leisure for Lamoth and Horum
Turn of Sutri – named for Sutri, the Goddess of Summer and Time
Days of Leisure for Sutri and Mu
Turn of Thonda – named for Thonda, the God of Beasts and the Hunt
Days of Leisure for Thonda and Gaena
Turn of Rintira – named for Rintira, the God of Autumn and Trickery
Days of Leisure for Rintira and Chalchalu
Turn of Luraana – named for Luraana, the Goddess of the Community
Days of Leisure for Luraana and Ceruna
Turn of Maeana – named for Maeana, the Goddess of Death
Days of Leisure for Maeana and Ashana

THE MOONS

There are two moons that circle Terrene with two very different cycles. White Moon has a twenty-four day full moon-to-full moon cycle while Blue Moon has a thirty-six day cycle. This creates a very uneven pattern of light/dark cycles at night. One of the moons is always visible in the sky; at no point are both moons at the new stage. Five times every year, though, both moons are at the full stage. These are known as Nights of the Two Moons. Nights of the Two Moons occur every year on these dates:

First Night of Two Moons – 27th of Turn of Khanos
Second Night of Two Moons – 9th of Turn of Roden
Third Night of Two Moons – 21st of Turn of Sormina
Fourth Night of Two Moons – 3rd of Turn of Thonda
Fifth Night of Two Moons – 15th of Turn of Luraana